TSENTURION BRIDES

A SCI FI WARRIOR ROMANCE

LEE SAVINO

GOLDEN ANGEL

ALIEN CAPTIVE

DISCLAIMER:

The authors are not responsible for any actual alien abductions that may result as a consequence of your purchase of this book.

1

D^{awn}

It was a dark and stormy night.

I know, such a cliché, but it is. Dark and rainy with rumbles of thunder in the distance like the sky is growling. I curl up under an old quilt my grandma made and hope the weather quiets soon so I can sleep. The power went out earlier, so the only light is from my e-reader propped up on my knees.

I swipe and read the next page in my current book obsession: *Tsenturion Tales: The Captive Bride.*

The Tribute takes her first step out of the Jabolian capsule onto the Tsenturion deck.

Lines of soldiers in full battle dress line her route to the bridge. They stand at attention to honor their High Commander as he accepts the human female as his Tribute and bride.

As the Tribute approaches the great High Commander, the Bride Trainer around her waist comes to life. Activated in the presence of her new master, the Trainer ensures she bonds to him right away. A low vibration begins between her legs, stimulating her sex. The Trainer continues to brew her pleasure as she comes onto the bridge and kneels to greet the High Commander. It will stimulate her as long as her master desires. Only he holds the key.

The wind howls in the eaves as I reach "The End." *Damn.* I was hoping these books would get me through the night.

Thunder crashes overhead, and I shudder, taking deep, even breaths, the way I instruct my students to do when I'm teaching one of my yoga classes. My e-reader is still at half -power, and though I just finished the Tsenturion Trilogy, I already want to read them again. I press my thighs together against the ache the last book created, my mind drifting back to some of my favorite scenes. What can I say? These books are so hot.

There are three books in this story, all of them about a human woman who gets sucked through a portal to an alien galaxy, where she's married off to a "Tsenturion Master," a huge, muscular warrior who sees to her every—*ahem*—sexual need. The Tsenturions are a space-faring race without a home, without a planet, and without enough females, so women are taken from other planets and given to them as mates. The story's kinda kinky and a little unclear on some things—like who fetches the women to be the Tsenturions' mates and who the Tsenturions are fighting. It's pretty much focused on the mating aspect, which is how I ended up getting sucked into the story. Women are so scarce, they're treated with extra care but also trained to be responsive to their Masters' needs. It's pretty awesome. Most of the training comes through rewards of multiple orgasms.

A flood of light blinds me as my e-reader begins to glow...

Dammit. I shake the device. It better not break. It's the only thing that will get me through this bad weather.

I hate storms. I never met my dad; he was killed in a tornado before I was born. My mom died in a storm when I was four—she ran off the wet road in bad weather. My grandma raised me, until she passed from brain cancer last year—again, during a bad storm.

Storms are bad luck.

Another rumble of thunder shakes the house like deep, evil laughter. The storm is getting louder, and the wind picks up, the rain battering my windows with a loud clatter. I snuggle deeper into my blankets, ignoring the tightness in my chest. Ignoring the little voice inside my head which always gets louder during storms, insisting something terrible is going to happen. I'm safe in my bed. Nothing can happen to me. The worst thing that can happen is my e-reader breaking. Right?

I shake my device, willing it to turn back on. The glow from the stupid thing is growing brighter, the color changing somehow, as if the screen is a crystal reflecting back a hundred million rainbows into my eyes. I can't figure out what's wrong with it, but I can't look away.

The storm grows louder, the thunder roaring in my ears, and the glow from my e-reader has turned into a ball of light in my hands. There's a tugging sensation on my body, as if I'm in a wind tunnel and the wind is so roughly fast that it's tearing the skin from my body.

I open my mouth to scream, but there's no air.

Rings of light and color burst ahead of me, and darkness is all around. I start to panic, but I don't have much time because the pain is excruciating, as if I'm being crushed, flayed, and pulled in twenty different directions all at the same time. Then...nothing.

I DON'T HURT.

Thank God. Not only do I not hurt anymore, but gone is the patter of rain, the howl of the wind, and the loud rumbles of thunder. It's almost blissfully silent. Although...there is a strange hum. Very quiet, very subtle.

Frowning, I open my eyes.

My heart stops.

This is not my bed.

"Greetings, Dawn Cahill."

A face looms over mine, but, like the bed and the salutation, it's wrong. Eyes, nose, mouth, they look *almost* right, the way CGI looks almost human, but there's something wrong enough that the more human a CGI creation looks, the more wrong it feels because it's not quite right. The skin doesn't help either; it's flesh colored but almost translucent looking, shiny in a way no human would ever be.

I scream, trying to jerk back against the bed that's not mine, and the being—whatever it is—flinches, losing its shape so the face and head melt away, the body turning into a large, amorphous blob. The only thing that doesn't change is the color. I scream louder, not only because watching a humanoid-looking thing turn into a non-human thing is freaking terrifying, but because when I try to scuttle away, I find I'm secured to the bed around my waist. I'm also completely naked and completely panicking.

"Dawn Cahill! Dawn Cahill! Stop! Calm down!" It's the same voice, although I can't tell how the creature is speaking without a mouth, but I'm freaking out way too much to listen to it.

Calm down? Seriously?

I'm naked, tied to a bed that's not mine, and there's a *thing* speaking to me. If there was ever a time to panic, it's now.

The thing makes a sound like it's irritated, and the next thing I know, there's a puff of some kind of smelly air in my face and—

Blackness.

"Second attempt at communication with the Hu-man." The voice says 'human' in a weird way, like it's never said 'human' before. "Dawn Cahill?"

"Mmm?" I feel calm. Rested. Maybe a little loopy. I open my eyes. There's...well, it's not a human looking down at me, even if it vaguely looks like one. I remember that now, but the memory and my panic seem very far away. "What *are* you?"

The thing's expression doesn't change. The facial features might be vaguely human, but they apparently only have one setting. Kinda constipated looking, actually.

"I am Frllil, a Jabols Luminary."

I blink. "I know you spoke words, but none of them made sense."

The thing makes a weird trilling noise. "I believe the closest thing to my profession in your vocabulary would be a scientist."

"And you're an alien?"

"I believe that is the correct terminology you would assign me."

"Holy crap. Um...why aren't I freaking out more?" Because I should be, and logically I knew that, but I couldn't quite work up the energy. I was definitely becoming a little agitated, but nothing like how I'd been before.

"After your poor reaction to me earlier, I concluded we would be able to communicate more effectively if you were given a sedative." The complete lack of expression and intonation in the thing's voice was starting to creep me out. Well, sort of. As creeped out as I could be while whatever he'd given me was influencing my reactions. Whatever the sedative was, it was powerful.

"Oh." I did have to admit, in a lot of ways this was much preferable to my earlier freak out. Information was good, panic was bad.

Okay Dawn, you've been hijacked by an alien—that can melt into a blob, I wasn't questioning that at all—and he's a scientist and he has you tied down to a bed in what is, presumably, his spaceship. He's also made it so you can't panic. That's good, right? Because if I was panicking, I wouldn't be able to figure out how to escape, but since I'm calm, I should definitely be able to. So really, he's already started working against himself and for me...right?

"Congratulations, Dawn Cahill, your interest in and completion of the Tsenturion trilogy made you eligible to be a Tsenturion Tribute. You have been chosen from your people as the first Tribute in the Tsenturion's mating program."

I blink. "Um...what? You stopped making sense again."

Or to put it another way, he was making too much sense, but my brain didn't want to believe what he was saying. Because I'm pretty sure that sentence was *directly* from the incredibly exciting, sexy, and *terrifying in reality* books I'd just finished reading on my e-reader right before it had started glowing, and then I'd started to hurt, and then I'd passed out and woken up here...

"Dawn Cahill, you will calm down," Frllil said. He isn't commanding though, he sounds almost nervous and whiny.

"I'm not mating with you!" I squeak, trying to shrink away from him and only then remembering that I was secured to the bed. My heart is starting to beat faster again. My fear feels strangely distant, but it's rising. The thought of mating with freaky Frllil is overriding my artificial calm.

"I am a Jabols," Frllil reminds me impatiently. "Jabols do not have mates. Our procreation is much more sensible and less messy and requires no outside partner. You will be the mate of a Tsenturion, High Commander Gavrill."

Okay, I'm not mating freaky Frllil, I'm mating a Tsenturion warrior. An alien species I'd thought was entirely fictional. An alien species which, according to the trilogy I'd read, was made up of huge, hulking warrior mercenaries with metallic golden skin, huge cocks, and a penchant for spanking their mates.

"Nope. Nope, nope, nope, nope, nope. Whatever trippy drug ride this is, I want off! Do you hear me?! I want *off*! I'm not doing this! This is fucked up! I don't care what you spray me—"

The gas gets me right in the face again.

I BLINK. Yawn. Try to figure out why the lights are so bright.

Oh right. Captured. Alien spaceship.

This is the third time I've woken up on it.

Any hope that I'm on some loopy drug trip or that this is all a terrible dream is fading away. I wait for the rise of inevitable hopelessness, but all I feel is numb.

"Dawn Cahill, you will be calm."

Is it my imagination, or is Frllil starting to sound really petulant?

"Yeah, yeah," I yawn. Not super interested in being knocked out again. "I'm calm. Look, I know I read the books and—okay, they were pretty hot—but I'm not really interested in being an alien bride. I have a life on Earth, you know. I have..." My voice trails off. I was about to say *people who care about me,* but that's not as true as I would like to be. I definitely used to have people who cared about me. Now...well, my yoga students would be upset when I didn't show up to teach the classes. Maybe.

"I have personally examined your life-profile, Dawn Cahill," says Frllil. Either I'm projecting, or I'm getting better at interpreting his emotions, but to me he sounds kind of smug now. "You are what your race defines as a 'loner.' You have no strong emotional attachments or connections. You have no family, your friendships are shallow, and no one in your life will notice that you have gone missing. The only attachment you currently display is to the residence you inhabited. There is no reason you could not easily begin a life elsewhere with little adversity."

Wow.

"Brutal, Frllil," I mutter under my breath.

"I do not understand this comment."

"Don't worry about it," I say dryly, a little louder. Even heavily sedated and mostly numb, it's still not exactly easy to hear how lonely and sad my life sounds. My deepest attachment is to my house? Yeah...that's probably true. But it's my gran's house. That's a real connection. Still...his summation of my friendships is pretty on point, sadly. Lots of acquaintances, no true friends. My truest friend in years had been my e-book reader.

And now it has betrayed me.

With friends like that, who needs enemies?

"Okay, so what now?" I ask tiredly, trying to prod my tired brain into remembering exactly what came next in the Tsenturion books. Something to do with an examination and changing...

HORROR SLIDES THROUGH ME. Distant horror. Like my emotions are on the other side of the glass wall. But I know I should be horrified.

"What have you done to me?" I whisper, looking down my body. It didn't look any different. But would I know? "In the book, the women, they went through...changes."

"Yes," Frllil says. "I have implanted a translator and made other improvements. Your cellular regeneration rate has been increased considerably, resulting in an extended lifespan equivalent to that of a Tsenturion warrior."

"What does that *mean?*" I can't help but feel a little dizzy. Should I be excited? Horrified? Longer life, that's desirable...but the circumstances and quality of life are important to exactly how desirable. "How much longer?"

Frllil sighs. "You will remain calm."

"If you don't tell me how much longer I'm going to live, I can't make any promises," I snap, though I don't want to get zapped again.

"Approximately eleven hundred Earth years." Frllil eyes me as I grab the edges of the bed I'm lying on, my chest tight with shock. Horror definitely seems to be winning out. Approximately eleven hundred years as an alien's mate, his Tribute. And I still don't know what that means, except the descriptions from the book which I'm now hoping were greatly exaggerated. "Breathe, Dawn Cahill."

Frllil makes a trilling sound again and moves closer. I look down and realize he's on some sort of platform that holds his blob-like body off the floor. A floating platform. An alien modifying my body. If I wasn't sedated, I'd be out of my mind with panic.

I let my head fall back and suck in lungfuls of air. Frllil hovers close. If I didn't know any better, I'd say the amorphous blob looks vaguely displeased.

"According to my records, breathing is an innate function your body performs automatically. I should not have to instruct you."

"Oh, so you're the expert?"

Another trilling sound, this one pleased. "I am. I based my studies on the Tsenturion form and finding a compatible race to supply females. I received a commendation. My superiors put me in charge of the Tribute program."

"Okay, Frllil," I try his name out, mimicking the rolling trill that the alien makes. "I'm new to all this. This Tribute thing—walk me through it."

"But you know of the Tribute mating program. You accepted our communication and have read the manual."

"Manual?" Light dawns. "The e-reader and the books, you mean? You sent it?"

"Yes. After basic monitoring, you were selected for further study."

I remember the day the e-reader showed up in my mailbox. I was so pleased, I didn't stop to wonder where it came from. I figured I'd won a contest I'd forgotten I'd entered.

"It was calibrated to unlock only for you. Then it monitored your responses."

"My responses... to the stories?" I blush so hard, I'm afraid my face will catch fire. The Tsenturion stories were so hot; by page three, I was reading them one-handed. "The stories about the Tsenturions —that's the manual?"

"Yes. The manual served a dual purpose: to test you and start your training as Tribute. You'll be pleased to know you are the first to pass the test, Dawn Cahill. Your eagerness to study the manual and responses to it made it clear you were perfect for the mating program."

"Oh," I say weakly.

"You are welcome. I am pleased the process went so well. It was my design." Frllil floats away. It's a good thing I'm strapped to this table, otherwise I would fall off. The e-reader. The stupid e-reader. If only I hadn't read the stories so many times... if only they hadn't turned me on so much... but that isn't exactly knowing consent either.

Before I can start to get angry, Frllil is talking to me again.

"Dawn Cahill, you will give attention," Frllil instructs. He's down at the foot of my bed, beside a floating piece of what looks like glass. As I watch, an image appears on the glass—it's a screen playing a movie. "It is time for you to learn your duties as a Tribute." The image comes into focus, showing the nose of a huge silver spaceship.

"This is a Tsenturion ship. The Tsenturions are a warrior race, sworn to protect the galaxy. They live on a fleet of spacecrafts, as they have no home planet."

"They used to though," I say, reciting what I know from the books. "It was destroyed by an enemy race. Only a few warrior males survived, which is why they needed Earth brides."

"Very good, Dawn Cahill. You remember." Frllil makes a movement, and the image on the screen changes. He reminds me of an adjunct professor I once had, a nerdy guy who barely looked at the class, preferring to simply recite his lessons from a slide deck.

The image on screen changes, and I gasp.

2

———

D^{awn}

"THESE ARE TSENTURIONS," Frllil says. Three huge figures fill the screen. They're huge, with Arnold Schwarzenegger-sized muscles under skin that shimmers like it's made of metal. Their faces are covered by some sort of helmet. At least I hope it's a helmet.

"Are they wearing... armor?"

"Yes. The suits are Jabol-design. The suits are protective and enhance the Tsenturions' physiology. In addition to being strong enough to withstand most weapons, the suits regulate their bodily functions for optimum lifespan."

"Will I get one of them?"

This time, Frllil's trilling sounds amused. "No, Dawn Cahill. You are a Tribute. You have no need to withstand weapons. Your Tsenturion master requires you to be accessible." He turns back to the screen, and the image zooms in on the central figure. "Besides, Jabol technology has advanced. Your body has been modified without need of a suit. You will receive a training belt before the presentation ceremony. During the ceremony, it will imprint to the High Commander. He will use it to modify your responses and prime you for him."

I barely take in all of this. I'm too busy studying the sharp, helmet clad face and massive body of the figure on screen. After a second, parts of the helmet retract, revealing a hard-boned face with a strong jaw and glittering eyes. His facial features are pretty humanoid; two eyes, one mouth, one nose. His nose is broad, and his jaw is squarer than most humans I've seen, but other than the golden sheen of his skin, he could blend in with the human race. The shiny gold of his skin contrasts with the silver-grey of the armor, making him look incredibly exotic.

Unfortunately, the armor doesn't pull back anymore, so I have no idea what he looks like elsewhere. My eyes instinctively drop to his groin, and I can't help but think about the Tsenturion books I was reading and wonder exactly how accurate they were...

Frllil makes a sound to catch my attention, and I pretend I wasn't checking out the Tsenturion's crotch.

"This is High Commander Gavrill. He commands the entire Tsenturion fleet."

I shift in my bonds, feeling both frightened and a little aroused, but I don't look away. I memorize the rest of his body. Forewarned is forearmed after all. A row of short spines protrudes from his forearms, but maybe that's the suit. The 'manual' definitely didn't mention any death-spikes. As I watch, the suit color darkens from silvery-gray to deep copper.

"The suit responds to changes in mood. You will want to pay attention and modify your behavior when the suit darkens. A lighter color means he is pleased. You should feel honored to be chosen as the first Tribute to the Tsenturions, as you have been paired with The High Commander Gavrill."

"Hang on," I begin when something pricks my neck. "Ow!" I

writhe in my bonds. A machine stands beside my bed, a needle extended on one of its mechanical arms. "What the hell was that?"

"A stimulant," Frllil says matter-of-factly. "It encourages the correct response to your Tsenturion master."

"My what?" I'm still jerking as much as the restraints allow. A prick of pain is supposed to encourage my response? I'm not reassured by that or Frllil's use of the word "master." My brain is starting to send all sorts of warning signals to me. Frllil and the picture of the High Commander have distracted me so much that I'd forgotten exactly how, um... demanding the Tsenturions were in the books. That had to be embellishment though... right?

"Your master. Tsenturions have strict protocol when it comes to their Tributes. Do not worry, the High Commander will train you. It is part of the bonding process.

Train me!? I'd scream, but my mouth is too busy hanging open. Then again, I know exactly what Frllil is referring to. The books on the e-reader made it pretty clear—the Tsenturions treated their women like a BDSM-practicing dom would treat a hardcore submissive. Maybe even a sexual slave. In the books, it was super-hot. I loved the thought of an alien dom training his bride, rewarding her with orgasms and punishing her with spankings. Not to put too fine a point on it, the stories... uh... got me off. Big time. Apparently, I'd responded *too* well while an alien life form was watching.

How mortifying.

"In the future, your training belt will prime you. We must use primitive methods for now." Frllil motions to the needle.

"What did you stick me with?"

"Pay attention," Frllil instructs. The screen images change to a long angle view of the ship. Two rows of armored Tsenturions line a path right up to a gangplank. At the top stand four figures. The High Commander is in the front, with two hulking giants on either side. A smaller figure stands behind him. As the image zooms in on Gavrill, I notice my body heating up. Not naturally like it had before when I'd been checking him out and wondering what was behind the groin armor... no, this is more intense. More frightening.

I'd press my legs together if they weren't held down as my lower body comes to life, a tingle starting between my thighs. When Gavrill fills the screen again, arousal blooms like a mushroom cloud, filling my head with screaming pressure, stealing my breath. My nipples pucker, and I can feel my pussy spasm emptily, the tingle turning to a full-on throbbing ache to be filled. It's the horniest I've ever been in my life, and it scares the heck out of me.

"What's happening?"

"You are being primed," Frllil says. "This is the proper response to your master."

"No," I grit out, clenching my fists. It's no use. The ache between my legs intensifies. Wet trickles down my leg. I moan, shuddering and trying to reject the feelings stirring inside of me, the need that's growing... looking at the High Commander again, I whimper as my pussy quivers. I feel like I could orgasm just from looking at him long enough, which is crazy, but... fuck me if I don't want to.

The image zooms out, and the pressure lessens. I come down from the heights, panting.

"*No.*" Despite myself, I moan. I'm not used to being denied.

"Only your master can trigger climax. Until you meet him, you can only be primed."

My pussy throbs, angry at being denied.

"This is messed up," I mutter. My fingers twitch. If I wasn't tied down, I'd show him just how well I can trigger my own damn climax, thank you very much. I glare at Frllil, who completely ignores my reaction. He's way too pleased to let something as *insignificant* as my ire affect him. I'm really starting to hate Frllil.

"That was most excellent, first Tribute. I knew I'd chosen well. The Commander will be pleased."

Something pricks my neck again. Frllil moves away, and the lights start to dim, his voice sounding like it's coming from a distance. I struggle to keep my eyes open, but it's useless. "You will sleep now. In a few cycles, you will be fitted for your training belt. After that, the Tsenturions will arrive for the mating ceremony, and you will meet your new master."

~

GAVRILL

THE BORAL NEBULAE is a thing of beauty, cloudy rings interspersed with patches of glittering dust, like gems in space. Our ship hovers on the edge of the outermost ring. Waiting. Watching.

Preliminary scan complete, the bridge screen flashes. We're all silent as my warriors study the data collected from three days of analysis. Looking for the proof of our enemy. The reason we're here. If we can find them, and if we can get to them once we do.

"There." I tap the screen, and it zooms in on a dark patch behind a particularly thick cloud of dust. "The Vgotha ship."

The ship's shield hid any heat signature but couldn't escape a density scan. Triumph surges.

Anticipation hums through the deck as our armor darkens, a display of our high emotion and readiness for battle. There is not one of us who would not die to see our mission through, though it has already been a long mission and the years stretch endlessly before us before it is complete. The Vgothas destroyed our entire planet, the whole population, in one day. No survivors... except for us. It was their only mistake.

They couldn't have known that our ship was late returning home for the festival. Everyone knew that Tsenturions returned to Tsentur for the Mating Festival. It should have been a complete genocide. Instead, we came home to a planet of rubble, of melted slag... there were no bodies to bury, the surface had been scoured clean. We still didn't know what weapon they had used or how they had done it, but it didn't matter.

We carried the only knowledge we needed with us—their identity.

"Carrion scum," my second, Bogdan, mutters. "They cannot hide, not even behind a cloud of their own mercenary stench. Commander, we must engage." His rage is greater than mine, for he'd not only had a very large family of siblings, all of which were now gone, but he'd been ready to attend the Festival and find a mate.

But our people were dead, and we were alone. The Jabols had promised to find us new mates, but none of us are all that hopeful.

We concentrate on our vengeance instead.

I keep studying the scan readings. I will not rush into battle, as my second wishes. I am the High Commander, and I will not be reckless, even if it is to wipe out our enemies. Not if it means the destruction of my ships, and with them, the last of my race. The Boral Nebulae is dangerous, and we cannot rush in. Somehow the Vgothas made it through the rings, evading the debris and moving belt of rocks and radiation, but I cannot immediately see the path they used, though we have now located them.

As they remain completely stationary, I can only assume they only know one route in and out of the minefield the nebula creates. They will wait for us to leave... unless we can outwait them or outwit them.

"Commander," Arkdhem, commander of our scout ships, appears on a lesser screen. His armor glitters bright, a reflection of his mood. Surprisingly, his usual stoic expression is not in place, he looks almost excited. "I received a hail from Frllil. They have payment ready for us."

"Tell them to leave it at the waystation, as usual." Every twenty semicycles, the Jabols reimburse our people for protecting them. They provide weapons, foodstuffs, ship supplies and technology while we guard their planets from the thieving Vgothas and fulfill our need for justice at the same time. A symbiotic relationship that has lasted over a thousand years.

"It's not the usual payment." Arkdhem's suit shimmers with excitement. Curiosity lightens my armor.

"Then what is it? Make your report," Bogdan snaps, his suit flashing red streaks of annoyance through the black. He is completely focused on our mission, as always. His determination to wipe out the Vgothas nears obsession. I am nearly as eager, but I sometimes think

Bogdan would be willing to throw our lives away if it meant taking out *one* Vgotha ship.

That is why he is second and I am the High Commander. Cool logic rules me, rather than emotion.

"We have found a Vgotha ship," I inform my third, because Bogdan is correct—our priority is the enemy. Whatever the new shipment of supplies is, it can wait. "I am determining if we will engage."

"Apologies, Commander. I would not have interrupted, but you ordered me to report as soon as I heard the Tribute was ready."

My suit flashes from black to bronze to silver, reacting to my surprise. I am not prone to such displays of emotion, but this is a momentous occasion. Hope claws its way up my chest.

"The Jabols have found a suitable match?" I keep my voice even, but I cannot stop my suit from reacting, a shimmering silver that was echoed around the bridge by the listening crew. I am not the only one affected by Arkdhem's announcement. Only Bogdan's armor remains firmly black, and he glances at me, grimacing with annoyance at the interruption.

"Indeed, Commander. A far-off system, accessible only through a *direth* wormhole." Arkdhem uses the Jabol word for 'small and almost unstable.' A journey through such a wormhole is very dangerous, causing immediate ire—not just in myself, but in many of those who look the most hopeful. That was not good news.

"They risked the Tribute?"

"It was the only way. Apparently, this life form is the only one suitable to our race. The Jabols report that the initial training is proceeding nicely, and she will be ready soon."

Bogdan snorts derisively. "No matter how they train her, she still won't be Tsenturion."

Arkdhem says nothing. His glowing skinsuit relays his happiness. The good-natured warrior won't be baited, no matter how much Bogdan tries to pick a fight. The two of them often clash, their natural competition often creating the best ideas for me to use.

"Commander," Bogdan says in a voice that drips both annoyance and disgust. "Surely you are not thinking of abandoning our post just to dally with... the *Tribute*." From the tone of his voice, he might as well have said 'animal.' A mate does not figure into his priorities at all. "The lead Vgotha ship is almost in our hands. We do not have time for distractions."

A thousand tsencycles of need.

No obvious route to the Vgotha ship.

The promise of a future for my crew.

It is an easy choice.

"Preserving the continuance of our race is not a 'distraction,'" I observe. Arkdhem's suit beams, and there are more silver flashes around the bridge. Bogdan's teeth are practically grinding together. "Besides, entering the nebula is too dangerous at this juncture. Rather than sitting and waiting to see whether we or the Vgothas have more supplies, we will see to our future. Third, inform the Jabols that we are on our way to collect the Tribute. She should be made ready for the imprinting ceremony."

Bogdan grimaces but doesn't argue. Once I have made a decision, he knows to fall in line. With a flourish, Arkdhem salutes and flashes off screen.

"Second, set a course for the Jabol's ex-planetary lab. The third moon, I believe, of the eighth planet in the Jabolian System."

"Aye, Commander," Bogdan grunts, even as his suit darkens blacker than the deep space around us.

Dawn

CLAD in the ceremonial mating robes, the Tribute awaits her master. Her quarters are lush, decorated in the pale colors of Earth's sunrise. She lays down on the sleeping platform, letting the robe open to display her body for her master's delight. As she waits, she breathes deeply, letting her body start to prime.

The door opens. The High Commander enters, his armor shimmering gold, growing brighter when he sees her. The Tribute doesn't move but watches him approach. When he steps onto the sleeping platform, the Bride Trainer fitted around her hips and between her legs hums to life...

"Dawn Cahill, you will wake up." Cool air caresses my face. I open my eyes as the travel pod opens, letting in the light. I recognize Frllil's voice.

That fucker.

The Bride Trainer is a device like a chastity belt, wrapping around my pelvis, fitted tightly to my skin around my hips and between my legs. It's made from the same material that makes up the Tsenturion suits—soft as cloth, tough as metal, pliable as rubber. From what I understand, there's some nanotechnology involved that binds the belt to my skin. It's self-cleaning. It's also smart enough to thwart my attempts to pretend I'm going to the bathroom so that I can touch myself. When I need to go, it opens *just enough* for me to do so and not a millimeter more.

According to Frllil, only my new alien master can unlock it, although he might choose to keep it on indefinitely.

I've already been through some 'training.' Every cycle—the alien equivalent of a day—Frllil plays a new movie for me, usually clips of the Tsenturions. Whenever the High Commander walks onscreen, the Trainer buzzes to life. It vibrates in all the right places, stimulating me to the point of orgasm and holding me there. No amount of whining, wailing or begging will push me over the edge.

And, like a chastity belt, it keeps my fingers from my aching pussy.

"Your pleasure is no longer yours," Frllil scolds me as I writhe and beg for release. "It belongs to the Commander."

I don't think I've ever hated anyone as much as I hate Frllil. Life on Earth seems distant. I can't even concentrate on missing it, no matter how much I hate what's happening to me. It's like my brain has been hijacked by the unfulfilled needs of my body. There is no future, there is no past, there is only the ever-aching awful need of the present. The early days, when I'd tried to use my yoga training to calm my body, seem like a distant memory.

Earth is even farther away. According to Frllil, it's not like I have much to miss anyway. Sadly, he seems to be right. Other than my love for my grandmother's house, there was nothing holding me there, nothing to cling to other than my anger at how I've been picked up and what I'm being trained for. Even that's hard to hold onto though, when the demands of my body have become far more urgent than anything else.

I know I'm being brainwashed by Frllil's training, but I can't seem to stop it. Self-awareness will only get you so far.

So as the pod opens and a cool computer voice instructs me to stand and exit, I'm a hot mess. Nervous, distracted and frustrated with the never-ending loop of arousal.

Not to mention excited because, for the first time in days—maybe even weeks, I've kind of lost track—I might finally find completion. According to Frllil, the High Commander is the only one who can give me the climax I'm so desperate for, and that's who I'm here to meet. There's some tiny bit of self-preservation in me telling me to run, to look for an escape...but it's miniscule compared to the part of me practically sobbing for completion.

As I step away from the Jabolian capsule, onto the vast platform in front of the Tsenturion ship, my legs shaking with both nerves and need, I catch sight of my reflection in the silvery pod. The new and improved Dawn Cahill looks stunningly beautiful. In the past few cycles, I've been groomed, plucked and prodded until every inch of me is perfect. My blonde hair is a shining cape that hangs past my shoulders, and my skin looks like it's glowing next to the golden color of the filmy robe I was dressed in. Even my hazel eyes seem larger, brighter.

The door on the side of the Tsenturion ship opens, and out march rows of soldiers in two straight lines. They're intimidating as hell— their suits molded to their powerful forms, shining silver in the sunlight. Their shoulders are as broad as a doorway, and they're all at least half a foot taller than me. As I wait to see Gavrill in the flesh, my body quivers like it's been trained to do. Just seeing his soldiers has my pussy creaming and nipples puckering under the thin robe.

My mouth is dry. Fear? Anticipation? Excitement? An unholy combination of all three?

In a murmur beside me, the Jabolian capsule orders me to walk between the two lines of soldiers and present myself to my master.

My pussy clenches at the word 'master' without any prompting from the damn belt. I'm the kinky version of Pavlov's dog, but knowing that doesn't help me.

My filmy robes dance around my legs as I move forward, feeling almost like I'm sleep-walking. This whole situation is surreal. I don't look left or right but keep my eyes on the dark entrance to the ship. I'm afraid if I look directly at a soldier, I'll faint dead away. I would never have considered myself the fainting type, but I know that looking at them will be too much for me. Make it too real, too soon.

The movies Frllil showed me explained why there were no Tsenturion women. Long ago, a thousand years as Earth would calculate it, an enemy race called the Vgothas were persecuting the Jabols. Decimating them, determined to wipe them from existence. No one knew precisely why. They'd come out of nowhere and begun hunting Jabols like it was sport.

The peaceful scientist race, desperate to survive, created an alliance with the Tsenturions. While the Tsenturions weren't as technologically advanced as the Jabols, they had military might that the Jabols could never hope to achieve. It was a good alliance... but as soon as the Vgothas realized they were outmatched by the Tsenturions, they'd done something no one could have expected. Something so heinous, so brutal, it defied imagination.

They'd targeted Tsentur, the entire planet, and blown it up during a Tsenturion mating festival, a week dedicated to their future as a species. It was utterly horrific, and I hadn't been able to keep from feeling sorry for the Tsenturions. The few hundred remaining soldiers were alone in the universe now—no families, no mates, no home. They were even more alone than I was.

That didn't make any of what was happening to me less anxiety-inducing.

I swallow hard. The commander is waiting for me, his warriors on either side—none of them have even seen a woman compatible with their species in over a thousand years. That's why the Jabols changed their alliance slightly and began looking for Tributes instead of giving the Tsenturions more technology.

That's why Frllil searched for, and found, me.

I might be projecting when I think I see hope in all of their nearly-blank expressions, but it would make sense. The air seems to be hanging heavy with expectation. I've been over this so many times with Frllil that it seems almost like déjà vu to actually be doing it, like I've already done it a million times before... like this is the moment my entire life has been moving towards. It's like the book I was reading when I was taken, although that seems very long ago and very far away.

My present is my overwhelming need to orgasm, and the knowledge that I will finally—*finally*—get satisfaction draws me onwards. To the ship, to my future... to *him*.

The words from my book—*the manual*—flit through my mind.

The Tribute takes her first step out of the Jabolian capsule onto the Tsenturion deck.

Lines of soldiers in full battle dress line her route to the bridge. They stand at attention to honor their High Commander as he accepts the human female as his Tribute and bride.

It's just like the stories on the mysterious e-reader I read over and over in my attic bedroom... and now I'm here, living them in real life, about to meet my new alien 'master.' My legs wobble a little as I step forward and start climbing the ramp to the Tsenturion ship.

I'm halfway up when he appears. Gavrill, Tsenturion High Commander, the leader of an entire alien race. The male I've been trained to respond to, and the sight of him in the flesh takes my breath away in an automatic response. My legs tremble, and my knees go weak. I'm on the verge of orgasm just from seeing him. My breath is coming more shallowly and more rapidly, making me feel almost light-headed. I can feel my clit actually swelling against the unmoving trainer. It would take the lightest touch, the brush of a feather to make me actually come.

His armored suit shimmers in the light, a gun-metal grey. I try to remember what that color means. Not happy, but not sad or angry either. I get close enough to see the set of his jaw under the helmet, the obsidian eyes. He looks stern, expectant. A Commander, through and through.

There are others standing around him, but I barely see them, because my eyes are locked on him. It's like the entire world has narrowed to one small point, and he stands at the center of it. The closer I walk to him, the faster my breathing accelerates, the higher my pleasure rises, yearning for the peak that has been denied me for so long. It's like nothing else in the universe exists except for the two of us.

When I finally reach the top of the ramp, I feel like I can't breathe. He's so close to me, a head taller, larger than life, and it's like my entire body is aflame, pulsing and throbbing. Frllil had told me not to look him in the eyes, but I can't look away. His gaze is almost hypnotic, drawing me closer to him, step by step... and closer to orgasm the same way.

He does not look displeased as his gaze sweeps over me, from the top of my head down to the bottom of my feet and back up.

When he speaks, his voice is deep but strong, ringing out loudly enough for everyone assembled to hear.

"I, High Commander Gavrill, accept my Tribute."

The receiving deck rings with the gathered Tsenturions' shouted salute. Beneath my robes, the trainer comes to life. It turns off almost immediately, as if the nanotech is smart enough to realize I'm already too close... but it's too late.

A faint sense of triumph is threaded through the crashing waves of ecstasy that roll through me. *Fuck you, Jabol technology.* I'm drowning in my orgasm, and nothing can stop it. Nothing except the blackness that rises up over me from the very intensity of my climax, and even as my rapture is rising, I am falling.

The last sensation I feel before everything goes dark is strong arms folding around me, and my utter erotic bliss is complete.

3

———

G avrill

ALARM SURGES through me as my Tribute shakes and begins to collapse, her eyes rolling upwards before they close.

She's beautiful. So different from a Tsenturion female and yet so similar. Her hair is like a galass plant, bright and soft, waving gently in the wind as I catch her up in my arms and hold her against my chest.

"Dismissed!" I bellow to the assembled warriors. Many wear startled expressions on their faces, their suits reflecting worry, but I cannot take the time to address that now. I turn to Medik, feeling helpless.

"What's wrong with her? What happened?"

He's already stepping forward, scanner in hand, and he runs it over her body, ignoring my questions. Impatience seethes, but I relax slightly as he looks at the output of the scan and his tension releases.

He would not have such a reaction if something were seriously wrong.

A small smile plays on his face, something that makes me stare for a moment. He hasn't smiled since our planet, and his mate and family, were lost.

"She is fine. A simple loss of consciousness as a result of overwhelming sensations."

"The Tribute is weak," Bogdan mutters. He's at my back, hovering in the door as if he can't stand to be near her, but I hadn't missed the way he moved when she fell, just as ready to catch her as I had been. His retreat had been just as swift. Which was just as well. After all, she is *my* Tribute.

The amount of possessiveness and protectiveness I feel is a little startling, and definitely unexpected. But I am used to being a protector, and she is very small. Her skin is soft, completely vulnerable, unlike my own. The nanotech of her training belt protects those areas, but its influence is limited.

"She is actually quite resilient," Medik corrects. "Dense bone structure, decent musculature, healthy tissue..."

He holds the scanner over her leg, and her foot twitches. I hold her a little tighter.

My body is primed to her already, my *seela* writhing and my cock pulsing with anxiousness to be buried inside her softness. I stroke her hip as Medik continues to examine the readout. Then he presses the scanner to her knee, releasing a small injection of nanos into her. I recognize the process, which he uses on minor injuries not needing much intervention.

"Some scar tissue," he mutters to himself. "The Jabol made enhancements to her physiology but missed this. An old injury..."

"Is that why she fell?" I ask.

"No, no." Medik doesn't look up from his scanner as he taps the screen, directing the nanos working on her. "She, ah... was overwhelmed with pleasure." His lips twitch, almost smiling. "Her body's responses overrode the trainer... that, or Frllil was overly industrious with using it to prime her for you."

"When will she regain consciousness?"

"Any minute now. I have her in stasis sleep while the nano repairs her knee injury. She will awaken as soon as it is done. When that happens, you should be alone with her." Medik turns to face me, an almost fatherly look on his weathered face. Our nanosuits preserve all of our organs, including our skin, so that we do not age, but by the time Jabols gave Medik nanotechnology, he was already old. In many ways, he has become a kind of patriarchal mentor for the rest of us, as we are without our fathers. "After all, you will need to seal the bond between you in order for this mating to be success-ful. That is done best alone. If you are pleased with her as your Trib-ute, that is."

"I am satisfied," I say carefully. My words match the steady grey of my suit.

The doctor snorts. He is more expressive than the rest of the Tsenturion legion combined. Before the destruction of Tsentur, he had been retired from the fleet for many, many years, and he still retains many of the habits from civilian life. We all rather enjoy it; a taste of the life we never got to lead.

Except, perhaps now we'll have a chance to. I look down at the female in my arms. The *compatible* female. A miracle, even if she is soft, defenseless, and a different species.

"You do not believe me?" I ask. The doctor is the only one who would dare challenge me.

"I think being calm is just a sign you have no idea what you're in for."

Instead of being insulted, I am curious. "How would you be feeling?"

"Excited. Nervous." The doctor rattles off emotions I have not felt —have not allowed myself to feel—for a millennium. "I remember when I met my Sulli." His smile warms his suit to a glittering blush— a color no Tsenturion soldier would ever allow. Not until they had retired and had a family of their own. "She was the most beautiful creature in the Nine Galaxies. In her presence, I could not even speak."

"A rare event," Bogdan says under his breath. Both of us ignore him.

"If you could not speak, how did you win her bond?" I ask curiously. When our world was destroyed, I had not yet felt an interest in attending the mating festival and so had never given the process much thought. I'd assumed that I had years before I needed to consider how to win a mate, and after Tsentur was gone, there had seemed no point, especially as the years had stretched on without the Jabols finding any compatible females.

Now that I had a female of my own, real and in the flesh, I couldn't help but wonder how others had proceeded when they'd bonded. Their experience would be different, because Dawn is a Tribute and not a Tsenturion, but perhaps some of the general ideas would be similar. I had read the books on the courtship rituals of my Tribute's race and found them to be titillating. Certainly, the differences from my own culture had not seemed too great from what I remembered... but it had been a very long time, and my knowledge had never been complete.

Medik's smile grew nostalgic, his gaze unfocusing as if he saw something very far away. The glittering blush of his armor dimmed, the hue deepening. "I gave a lecture at a medical clinic near her home. She was in the audience, in the back. She chose to approach me. That's the thing about bonding. Both partners can choose. They are equal."

Bogdan snorts. "Not anymore. This Tribute is nothing like us. No Tsenturion woman would have been weak enough to faint from mere pleasure."

He was not wrong. But I was not displeased either. We were similar enough. Frllil had started her training, and I would complete it, and then she would be a perfect companion for me. My Tribute.

"You should write a manual," I tell Medik.

"Perhaps I will." His suit dulls further, turning blue-grey as his grief for his lost mate and family return. Sometimes I think he wishes he had been on-planet when it was destroyed, where he should have been—where he would have been if our usual physician had not been killed in action. Medik had agreed to one expedition with us, while a replacement completed training and instead had ended up with us for a lifetime.

He returns his attention to his scanner.

"The repair to her knee is complete, she should wake any moment." He glances at Bogdan, who is staring at my Tribute again. I repress the urge to growl, unsure of why I don't like him looking at her. He does not appear hostile... although perhaps if he was, I would not mind so much. As derogatory as he has been about my Tribute, I cannot help but remember that he had been about to retire and claim his own mate when we lost our people.

But he cannot have her. She is mine.

"I will take her to my quarters," I say, holding her a little tighter. "To complete the bonding. Bogdan, you have the bridge. Get us back to the nebula. We will pick up the Vgotha's trail."

He nods, and I swiftly turn and walk back into the ship as she makes a small noise. I pick up my pace, nodding to my soldiers as I pass by them. They watch me go with varying expressions of worry and hope, although they seem reassured that there is nothing wrong with my Tribute when they see I am focused on my path but uncon-cerned—and since Medik is no longer by my side, they know she is well enough.

She shifts slightly in my arms as I enter my quarters, and I look down to see her eyelashes fluttering. Anticipation rises in me, my cock swelling with interest as my excitement begins to grow again. Bogdan is right, she is not Tsenturion, but my body responds to her regardless.

Opening her robe, I look her over with interest. Her skin is slightly patched, slightly darker on her limbs, face and belly in comparison to the light cream of her breasts. Pink nipples harden on her chest under my gaze. Her coloring is interesting and not unat-tractive.

I stroke my fingers over the trainer belt, and sensing my inten-tions, it retreats into a thin band about her hips, uncovering her lower body completely. There too she is lighter. It is as if her body coloring is arranged to attract the most attention to those parts of her which can bring her the most pleasure. I decide I like it.

Pulling her legs open, I inspect her more closely, intrigued by the pink of her inner folds, which is darker than the pink of her nipples. All the color variation on her body fascinates me. The pink is shiny because she is wet; a sign of arousal according to the texts of her people. There is a small bud at the apex of her folds. I cannot tell if it is swollen or not, it looks very innocuous and unimportant, but according to the texts the Jabol provided, it is one of the keys to her pleasure. I take careful note of all of her parts, including the darker, wrinkled entrance to her body that is below her puffy pink lips. The texts indicate that it can be used for enjoyment or punishment, although she may initially be resistant to the idea, even for pleasure. The area was taboo in their culture, although that apparently contributed to the appeal.

Tsenturion rituals demand that we claim our mates in every way possible, so in that manner it seems we are alike. Although I say we will bond, I do not know if we will be able to complete it fully, the way Tsenturion couples do so that they may completely share their lives and emotions with each other. It seems unlikely. Even knowing this, there is a part of me which yearns to see my claiming mark on her skin, announcing to the universe that she is mine irrevocably.

I am determined to be a good mate, so I will bring her great pleasure and she will pleasure me, and we shall lead the way for the future of the Tsenturions. Although bringing more Tributes through an unstable wormhole is a risk, it may be one we have to take if we are to survive as a race.

Even more so if we are to survive as ourselves. Just the announcement that one Tribute has been retrieved has sent morale surging higher than I can ever remember it being. There are a few males, like Bogdan, who remain unconvinced, but the majority are just as hopeful as I feel now.

As her eyelashes flutter again, she stirs, her arms and legs moving slightly. Feeling strangely nervous, I pull my armor back into my spine, so its pale-yellow hue does not betray my unruly emotions. I cannot remember the last time it was that color and am thankful we are alone and no one can witness my uncertainty.

~

Dawn

I MOAN as I open my eyes and try to jerk back as a golden-hued face fills my vision. I recognize his harsh features immediately, and my pussy flutters… but the trainer doesn't immediately vibrate. My body has been primed to respond all on its own, but it's still odd not to feel the vibrations of the trainer.

Even more odd—I can actually think clearly for the first time in days.

LANDING on this planet and presenting myself to the commander feels like a dream that I just awoke from, and though I feel arousal at the sight of him, the orgasm I had has helped clear my mind. I'm no longer a complete slave to the impulses of my body, because the urgency has subsided, having found recent satisfaction.

Chalk up one for the home team. Take that, alien tech!

I purposefully don't think about how often the alien tech had defeated me prior to that moment. A win is a win, darn it.

"Greetings, my Tribute," he says, that low voice doing all sorts of things to my lower anatomy. I ignore my reaction as best I can.

"Dawn," I say, my voice croaking slightly, the word coming out slightly fuzzy and slurred.

He frowns at me. "What?"

"Dawn," I repeat firmly, getting a better grip on myself. I enunciate carefully, determined not to slur again. "My name is Dawn."

I purposefully leave off my last name, because after so many days of Frllil's insistence on calling me by my full name, I kind of never want to hear it again.

After taking a moment to consider my statement, he nods formally. "Very well. Dawn."

The English word sounds strange when he says it. It's a common word, as well as a name, but somehow the translator knows the difference and leaves my name alone, which is a relief. He meets my eyes.

"I am your Master."

Dammit, that shouldn't be so hot, but the muscles of my pussy flutter again.

"Gavrill," I reply firmly. "High Commander of the Tsenturion fleet. But *not* my master. I don't have a master." No matter what he, Frllil, or my training has told me.

He frowns, which is intimidating as heck, especially when I'm flat on my back in what I can only assume is his bed, but after a moment his expression clears. To my annoyance, he actually looks kind of smug.

"Ah, yes, your courtship rituals," he says seriously. "I will earn my place as your master by dominating and pleasuring you until your resistance is broken and you submit to me fully."

I blink, nonplussed. "Excuse me? What courtship rituals are you talking about exactly? That is definitely not my how-to advice on dating."

The little smile that plays on his lips is both hot and frustrating, like he thinks I'm lying to him or something.

"The Jabol provided me with manuals on your planet's courtship rituals, they are copies from something they called your 'reader.'" Turning his head, he nods at the table next to his bed. I try to wriggle away from him to get some space and look to see where he's looking at the same time.

But as soon as the small pile of books on the little table beside his bed catches my eye, I freeze in horror.

Oh, fuck a duck.

They went through my freaking e-reader and gave those books to this massively large, already dominant, far too eager alien?! I recognize those names. Lee Savino. Golden Angel. Tracy St. John. Renee Rose. Aubrey Cara. Sara Fields.

Oh, this is bad. This is so, so bad.

"Those are *not* manuals," I say, now scooting away from him in earnest. Unfortunately, the bed is big and he's on the edge closest to me, so all I end up doing is scooting into the middle of the bed, which prompts him to follow, his eyes gleaming with interest. Crap! This is a serious Catch-22... I can either resist him, in which case he'll think I'm following the stupid "courting rituals" of my dirty romances, or I can stop resisting him... in which case I'll get fucked sooner rather than later.

My traitorous body votes for the latter, as if it hadn't already had an orgasm not that long ago.

"They were quite descriptive. Very similar to how a Tsenturion conducts himself with his bonded mate," he says, moving after me, which is when I finally catch sight of what he's got going on between his legs.

"Wha- wha- wha-" I can't even get the word out or look away from his groin and the freakiest looking cock I think I've ever seen. Way, way freakier than any I ever imagined.

It's golden, like his body, but it's got *way* too many parts. The tip of it looks almost like a cobra's mane; there's no mushroom head here, instead it flares out slightly and there's a ridge along the top of it that looks like it would feel really freaking interesting. The actual shaft is almost normal looking, long and straight, although it grows incrementally wider from the head down to where the really freaky stuff is going on.

Waving in a fringe around it is not pubic hair, unless pubic hair moves on its own and is flesh rather than hair. Less than half an inch long, the tiny tentacles writhe and my pussy pulses as I can't help but wonder what that would feel like against my vulva... even more intriguing is the extra-large one, the only one that's about an inch long, writhing above his cock. My clit pulses in response, because surely that kind of appendage is there for one reason and one reason only, and no matter how freaky looking it is, I'm still turned on.

I blame the training.

I point, managing to choke out the words. "What... is... that?!"

He looks down to where I'm pointing. "Ah, yes, I saw no mention of *seela* in the descriptions of your courtship. Perhaps Tsenturions are unique. They are to facilitate pleasure and breeding, as well as our bonding process."

Okay, the bonding process I knew about thanks to Frllil. The armor the Tsenturions wore was nanotech that had become so much a part of them that it was nearly biological. By having sex, some of the High Commander's tech would transfer to me and he would be able to fully control my training belt with just a thought after that—definitely not something on my to-do list—and theoretically they would also help me achieve the biological bond that Tsenturions had with their mates. If it did so, a mark would appear somewhere on my body that would actually help me sense and share his emotions as he would be able to sense and share mine.

But no one had mentioned a freaky alien cock. My perverted brain immediately wonders how all those little tendrils would feel moving against my most sensitive parts. Especially the big one that looks like it would line right up with my clit.

I'm so distracted that the High Commander manages to grab my ankle, and I squeak in dismay as I'm quickly dragged across the bed toward him.

4

G avrill

My Tribute's skin is soft against my hand, and the squeaking noise she makes as I pull her towards me is very appealing. There is no need for armor like mine to display her emotions—they are telegraphed across her expressive face. Surprise. Dismay. Arousal.

I can see that her nipples are tightly budded, the cleft between her legs shiny with moisture, and the pupils of her blue eyes dilate, filling the color with black. All signs of her interest.

"Wait! Stop!" She slaps her palms against my chest as I loom over her, planting a hand on either side of her body and caging her in, pushing at me to my amusement. She is much weaker than I am. Having her in this position arouses me further, my *seela* writhing and trying to stretch towards her. But I am unsure whether or not to immediately complete the bonding or if I should assert myself first.

Tsenturion males are naturally dominant when it comes to plea-sure. I have dim memories of my mother smiling as my father swatted her bottom when she passed by. Perhaps there will be similar moments with my Tribute? She certainly is not smiling now, although she is highly aroused.

The ways of our people, once mated and no longer military, have passed on with our planet. But my Tribute would not know them anyway. I studied the rituals and training outlined in her people's manuscripts closely. There were even some on interspecies relations, all with similar instructions. They mostly align with my distant memories of our people, and they certainly appeal to my sense of order.

I will be in charge. She will submit. Thwarting the traditions of my people, I shall continue in command on my ship rather than becoming a civilian after my mating, but it's not as if ours will be a full bonding, so there should be no objections. I will pleasure her often, as a good mate should, and she will ease my physical needs and lonely nights. Eventually, if the Jabols are correct about our compatibility, the Tributes will assure the continuation of our race and we can find a new planet to settle on once the Vgotha threat is eradicated. It all begins with Dawn.

I am also aware of how important this will be to all of my men. Although she is only one Tribute, I am determined she will not be the last, for their sakes. Travel through an unstable wormhole is not ideal, and the Jabol will want reassurances that the energy expenditure is worthwhile before they begin to provide us with Tributes in number.

Staring down at her, I sigh inwardly. Although I yearn to bury myself inside of her immediately and attach my *seela* to her flesh, I realize I have not completed the most basic of her courtship rituals. I nod.

"You are correct," I say, though my body aches with need. "We should not skip steps."

Confusion, relief, and then disappointment flit across her face as I pull away.

When I pull her with me, easily flipping her face down across my lap, she shrieks with surprise. I like the noise. I also find the position to be quite enjoyable. My *seela* begin to explore the side of her body, where they can reach as my hard cock throbs against her soft flesh. Her bottom is tilted upward, vulnerable and pale. I look forward to seeing the change in color her manuals spoke of.

Dawn

WHEN I SAID "WAIT—STOP," this was definitely not what I had in mind.

Talk about out of the frying pan and into the fire. There was no mistaking what his intentions were, and yet the words came spilling out of my mouth anyway.

"What are you doing?" My voice quavers, my brain still trying to deny the obvious... the inevitable. I can feel something writhing against my side, exploring me with soft little touches that caress and pull at my skin. It's incredibly distracting, especially because I can feel a certain area of my body perking up with interest—*what would that feel like there?*

"I am establishing my position as your Master, in the manner of your people," he says sternly.

Part of me wants to laugh hysterically, because his formal pronouncement is so over-the-top... and yet I can't because he is entirely serious. My mind goes frantic, trying to think of a protest that will work, a way to talk him out of his obvious intention, but it's like my brain has gone entirely blank in the face of danger, and then -

Smack!

"Ow!" I kick my legs. That really freaking hurt!

"Ah. That is very nice," he says, sounding pleased.

"No, it's—"

Smack!

I howl, more in outrage than pain as his hand comes down on the other cheek.

I haven't been spanked since I was a young child, and then it was never more than a swat or two. I've read about it. Fantasized about it. Masturbated to the idea.

But nothing could have ever prepared me for the reality.

It fucking *hurts*.

The initial sting is followed by a flaring of pain that burns much deeper than the surface, and then *throbs*. Especially as he lays down more hard swats atop already spanked flesh. There's no chance of squirming away as his left hand holds me firmly in place on his lap and he shifts his legs so that my upper body is tilted forward even more, lifting my bottom higher in the air.

Smack! Smack! Smack!

"Please! Stop," I babble, begging and clinging to his tree trunk of a leg, tears already sliding down my cheeks. It feels like my entire ass is on fire.

To my surprise and relief, the spanking stops and his hand rests on my hot flesh. In my mind, I imagine his golden skin against the flaming red that my skin feels like. "You are ready to acknowledge me as your Master already?"

I hesitate, everything inside of me rebelling at his words even as my pussy clenches. I tell myself that's just from the Pavlov dog training that Frllil put me through, that's not *me*.

Unfortunately, *me* is not what he wants. He wants my submission, he wants a sex toy, he wants a submissive female... but he only wants it from me because I'm the only female here.

"Ah," he says when I don't answer.

"Wait—*no!*" I let out a wail as his hand comes crashing down again, but this time he doesn't stop immediately, apparently determined to make an impression on my poor ass before he gives me another chance.

I writhe, bucking. Maybe it's because he paused and gave me a short break, but it feels like he's spanking even harder now. I kick my legs frantically, trying even harder to get away now, despite how useless it is. It feels like my bottom is swollen and thoroughly roasted, from the crest down to the delicate sit-spots just underneath the curve of my mounds. Every time his hand comes down on that tender area, I howl.

And I know that the next time he asks, I will call him 'Master' just to make this stop...

∼

GAVRILL

MY TRIBUTE'S reactions are very much in line with the manuals, pleasing me greatly. Although Tsenturions might mete out physical discipline to their mates when it was required, I find that I am quite enamored of her people's penchant for using such measures for both pain and pleasure. Despite her pleas and howls, it is apparent she is not ready for this first step to our courtship to be over, as she chose not to end it when I offered. Although my arousal is becoming painful, I find I am not averse to continuing it either.

The pale flesh of her bottom is now a bright pink, her skin hot to the touch. Whenever she kicks, the swollen lips of her sex become even glossier and wetter with her arousal. The musky-sweet scent is pleasing, and I wonder how she will taste.

I am using a harder hand than I will for pleasurable spankings later. The manuals make it clear that there should be a difference. As this is my first time spanking a female, I am not entirely sure I am doing it correctly. Fortunately, it is obvious that her reaction is one of erotic excitement, despite her pained cries. The Jabol had done *very* well, I decide. My Tribute is more than I could have hoped for.

When I stop, she hangs over my lap, crying. I trace patterns on her pink bottom, fascinated by the heat rising from her flesh.

"Will you call me Master, now?" I ask, hoping that she will say yes. As enjoyable as I am finding this interlude, I am eager to move onward and find more personal pleasure for myself. My *seela* that can reach her are rubbing almost frantically against her body, and my *prime seela* is thrashing with the desire to touch her as well.

"Yes..." She gulps. "Yes, Master."

Satisfaction washes through me at the sound of her tearful voice acknowledging me as her Master. Not just because it fulfills the rituals of both of our races, but I feel a sense of personal pleasure as well. It surprises me how much I enjoy hearing her acknowledge me and the possessive gratification that fills me. The emotion is unexpected.

"Good girl," I say, sliding my fingers to the swollen, wet flesh between her legs. She moans as I begin to explore that area with the pads of my fingers, searching for the little bud that was described as the penultimate point of pleasure for her species.

Moving my other hand from the small of her back to her hot bottom, I gently squeeze her punished flesh as I circle the small, swollen bud of pleasure with my fingers. She bucks, shuddering slightly as she cries out. There is some unhappiness in her voice, but as wetness coats my fingertips, I know that she is enjoying this. The texts warned that human females tend to feel a sense of shame at being aroused when they are mastered; it is a sign that I am proceeding correctly.

"Oh no..." She shudders again as I pinch the pleasure bud, rubbing it experimentally between my fingers.

Later I know I will enjoy using the training belt to discover exactly what affects her most, but for now I am too impatient to be inside of her, too eager for my own release. Pulling my fingers from her body, I inspect the glossy sheen she's coated them with before touching the tips to my tongue.

She tastes like sweetness and flowers, and my body immediately hungers for more. I've heard that the bonding process triggers intense physical reactions and an overwhelming need to claim one's mate, but I hadn't expected the force of it. Feeling more bestial than logical, completely unlike myself, I toss her onto her back on the bed. She shrieks, trying to roll off her bottom, but I am already prying her legs apart to reach the source of her nectar.

My vaunted self-control is gone as the taste of her juices on my tongue has sparked a craving that thunders through my body. She looks up at me, dazed, but my focus is on the sweetness calling to me between her thighs.

I fall upon her, my tongue sliding up the sweet center, groaning as my body recognizes its mate. Perhaps we are more compatible than even the Jabol realized. I have no experience that compares to this, nothing to help me control the urges raging through my body.

She cries out, writhing against my hands as I hold her legs spread wide open, making her vulnerable to the lashing of my tongue as I lick every crevice of her sweet folds. The flavor intensifies, growing sweeter as my body chemistry adjusts to hers, beginning to align with hers.

Mine.

All mine. Instinctively, I know that from this point forward no other female will ever taste this sweet, will ever satisfy my craving or bring me as much satisfaction as my Tribute. I suck and lick voraciously, and I can feel my armor buzzing along my spine, the nanotech beginning to respond to the addition of her cells within me.

"Please," she begs, her fingers sliding over my scalp, trying to find purchase. "Oh, please..."

I do not know if she is asking me to stop or if she is asking for more, but for her sake I hope it is the latter... I could not stop if I wanted to.

And I *don't* want to.

~

Dawn

My ASS IS THROBBING from the spanking, but the way he's licking me —like he's starving and I'm the first food he's had in days—is making me throb and pulse in an entirely new way. I don't know if alien tongues are different, but I know it *feels* different. My entire pussy is tingling, burning almost hot and then cold, and instinctively I know that something is happening that is different from anything else I've ever experienced before. It'd be terrifying if I weren't so aroused.

He has no hair for me to grab, and I can't tell if I'm trying to push him away or pull him closer. My body is a maelstrom of sensation, my emotions conflicting with the greedy, needy ache that's burgeoning inside of me. I want to be furious, I want to hate him, but either the Stockholmian training or the fact that he's so focused on giving me pleasure is making it hard for me to feel either emotion right now.

It's like the orgasm I had out on the ramp never happened, and I whimper and sob, writhing for him like I'm in heat... which is exactly how I feel. I'm burning up inside, not just the surface of my ass, but from the inside out. I can feel the heat spreading outward from my pussy, making me shake and gasp at the unusual feeling.

When he sucks on my clit, hard, I cum almost immediately with a high, loud cry that is nearly a scream. I'd always thought that 'screaming in orgasm' was just exaggeration, but it's like the intensity of the ecstasy is too great for my body to contain and the only way to release it is vocally. It pulses through me in waves, filling me, and yet not quite satisfying me, even as I am wracked with hot bliss.

Then he looms over me and I spread my legs further, reaching for him. Maybe it's my training, maybe there's just something in the animal part of my brain that's running on instinct, but I *need* him inside me. Somehow, I know he's the only one that can make this burning cease, the only one who can give me the satisfaction that my body is demanding. Even the long days of training, of being primed for him without ever being allowed to orgasm, hadn't created this kind of desperate compulsion within me.

I honestly feel like I might die if we don't finish this.

Tears rise in my eyes, and I choke on a scream as he thrusts into me, hard and fast, with one purposeful stroke. He's big and oddly shaped, and, even aroused as I am, the hot pleasure is mixed with some pain as my muscles contract around him, adjusting to the stretch that his proportions require. The little fringe of tentacles around his cock stroke my pussy lips, an incredibly odd and yet pleasurable sensation.

My back arches upwards as the long one slides around my clit, stroking and pulling at the tiny nubbin in much the same way his fingers had. His guttural groan as he shudders against me tell me that he's feeling the same inexpressible pleasure at being joined together. My hands cling to his biceps, fingers attempting to dig into the steely flesh, as I pant for breath.

With one hand planted on either side of me, his large body feels like it's caging me in, trapping me, and yet I feel oddly protected. He holds himself still, as if he realizes I need a moment. It's not until I wriggle beneath him, in reaction to the insistent stroking of the little things he called his *seela*, that he begins to move.

The initial thrusts are deep, long strokes as he moves slowly, making me arch and pant at the hot sensation. He leans down and takes one of my nipples in his mouth, sucking and laving the sensitive bud with his tongue. It tingles with the same growing heat that my pussy had when he'd been licking it, and when he switches his attention to the other nipple, the same thing happens.

It isn't until he's trailed his tongue up to my neck before claiming my mouth in a searing kiss that I realize I'm now tingling and burning everywhere that his tongue has touched. When he kisses me, I automatically kiss him back, our tongues rubbing together as my passion intensifies. He tastes like chocolate and fine red wine, igniting a craving that I don't understand, and I become almost wild beneath him.

Strong hands pin my wrists to the bed as he begins to fuck me harder, his kisses swallowing my cries, my nipples rubbing against his hard chest as my sore ass bounces off the sheets. Heat and pain and pleasure clash and mix, and I begin to feel lightheaded as the ache inside of me grows, my rising ecstasy climbing higher and higher. Being held helpless beneath him only increases my passion as he dominates me with nothing more than his weight holding me down.

I can cry out, I can writhe, I can take his cock... and that's it. The kiss ends as his strokes become more wild, leaving my lips burning.

His strange cock rubs along the inside of my walls, and I swear I can feel the head flaring, moving separately from the thrusting, stimulating the sensitive flesh of my pussy. I can feel every bump, every unexpected ridge, as he moves inside of me, his thrusts becoming harder and faster. Every time he fills me, his *seela* make a sweeping stroke through my sensitive folds and around my clit, making me thrash beneath him.

It's too much.

It's not enough.

The burning inside of me intensifies almost painfully even as ecstasy swirls.

He lunges, filling me completely. The *seela* don't stroke this time —it feels like they surround my sensitive flesh and *pull.* Something squeezes my clit.

Everything *pulses.*

His mouth comes down on mine again, swallowing my scream as I writhe for him, shuddering in utter erotic rapture. The *seela* pulse and pull, sending wave after wave of sweet ecstasy through me, massaging my pussy lips and clit and adding an entirely new level of sensation to my orgasm.

I'm drowning, and I don't even care.

GAVRILL

SOMEWHERE IN THE back of my mind, I am aware of my armor sliding around my hips to join with her belt, artificially locking us together the same way my *seela* suction to her skin. From this point on, her belt will only respond to me and I will be able to control it, and her, completely.

What is more unexpected is how my *seela* have fully latched onto her, triggering my bonding sequence. Whether or not it will ever be complete, I have no idea, but the sensations are even more intense than I could have predicted, and my ecstasy is explosive. I can feel her contracting around me, her muscles rippling over my length and practically sucking my seed out of me.

The sensation is more amazing than I could have ever anticipated.

Panting for breath, I let my arms fold so I can rest my weight on my forearms, laying them alongside hers. She is soft and lax beneath me, still moaning softly as my *seela* detach and begin to soothe and caress her now swollen sex. Little shudders wrack her body, and at first I am concerned, but as they are giving her pleasure, I decide they must not be harmful. They seem almost like tiny echoes of her climax, and I am fascinated.

My Tribute is *highly* satisfactory. Bogdan is wrong; the Tributes will be a blessing for all of us.

As if my thoughts have summoned him, my nanotech pulses with an alert from the bridge.

I barely manage to suppress my growl as I hunch around my Tribute, unhappy with the interruption. Logic asserts itself—they would not bother me now if it were not important.

Drakk, I curse in my head.

My armor slides up my spine to extend a communication tendril into my ear.

"I'm sorry for interrupting, Commander," says Bogdan, his voice neutrally crisp and not at all apologetic. "We have a situation that requires your attention on the bridge."

"I am coming," I respond, my voice low and threatening. If the situation is not urgent, I will have Bogdan cleaning out the most foul area of the ship I can locate.

Beneath me, my Tribute blinks. The almost peacefully satisfied expression on her face clears, and I am sorry to see it go. Her lips tip up in amusement.

"I thought you already did that," she says, her voice teasing.

No one has teased me in so long that I almost don't recognize it. Even so, I don't understand her words. I frown down at her in confusion.

She sighs, her small smile slipping away. "Never mind."

When she turns her head away from me, the moment is over. I can feel a strange sense of unhappiness and regret—both foreign to me, and they do not feel like my own. It takes me a moment to realize my tech is transmitting her emotions to me.

Scowling, I pull away. Obviously, the bond is not working as well as it should if those are her current feelings. Still, I can see from the flush of her body, the small round red marks my *seela* have left on her swollen flesh, and the looseness of her muscles that she was been well-pleasured. The language barrier between us is not vast, thanks to the translators.

If I were not needed on the bridge, I would have her explain her words, but the demands of my crew and my ship must come first.

Still...

I find I am loath to let her out of my sight so soon. She will accompany me to the bridge.

Standing, I pull away from her and walk over to the closet, where suitable garments have been stored for her. I had them made in the replicator on the way here, based off the garments Tsenturion females would wear during the Mating Festival and their courtship. The filmy material seems out of place on the ship, but I am already looking forward to seeing my Tribute in them.

"Here," I say, picking up a blue one that will closely match her eyes and turning to hold it out for her. "You will put this on."

5

D^{awn}

I DON'T KNOW what day or hour or cycle or whatever alien time unit these guys use it is. I do know that I feel both drained and very awake. My legs are wobbly as I follow the High Commander—my *Master*—down the hallway. I don't want to call him that, and yet somehow it feels easy and right.

Can Stockholm Syndrome be trained into someone? Because I feel like that's what's happened to me.

It's as if I've been split down the middle into two Dawns; Dawn #1 is appalled and horrified, not to mention seriously pissed off, and Dawn #2 wants nothing more than her Master's attention and approval—and another orgasm. I'm not even sure which one feels more real right now.

I catch my reflection in the shiny metal lining the hall and quickly avert my eyes from the image, gritting my teeth. *Will. Not. Blush.*

Part of me is furious about being dressed in nothing but a filmy, practically see through gown, collar and leash. Another part of me likes the way the fabric swishes around my legs. I peek at my reflection again and see the front and back slit opening and revealing the stupid Trainer, which my *Master* has me wearing like a chastity belt again. I'm actually relieved for the coverage it gives me, as much as I hate it.

I also keep telling myself that as long as I'm sarcastic when I call him 'Master' in my head, then it's okay.

"Where are we going?" I ask as he turns down another hall, my steps slowing as I realize it looks exactly the same as the last one. All the halls look the same. How does he know where to turn? And how am I ever going to find my way around?

"The bridge. There is a situation I must deal with. Come." He tugs the leash, and I pick up my pace again. It's that or fall over, because he's definitely not stopping just for me. The collar and leash make me feel both more submissive and more infuriated. I'd resisted when he'd first attempted to place the collar around my neck. It had taken just two hard swats to my already sore bottom to convince me that wasn't a fight worth having—at least not right now.

Especially since I didn't currently know of a way off this ship. I'm his prisoner, and I can't forget that, no matter that he's currently treating me as some kind of sex toy or exotic pet. We're somewhere in space, and the ship is filled with his crew. If I'm going to escape, I'm going to need to be sneaky about it.

Those "training manuals" he's been reading—they aren't just about sex. They're about women being abducted by alien males intent on dominating them; women who always get into a lot of trouble when they fight. So I'm going to pretend to be the perfect little Tribute that he wants. I'm going to pretend that my training worked completely, and once I learn all about his ship and the best way off it, I'm out of here.

I am also going to ignore the little voice inside my head that says I'm not pretending quite as much as I like to think I am.

I *will* escape.

With as few spankings as possible.

I walk with my eyes downcast, avoiding meeting the eyes of any of the warriors gawking at the sight of their Commander and his Tribute, and also because Frllil told me that I'm not supposed to meet any of the warriors' eyes. At the time I'd thought it was bullshit, but now I'm almost grateful. It's bad enough that I can feel their gazes on me, and I know they can make out the outline of my nipples under the almost see through gown. I don't want to see them actually staring at me.

Especially not if it gets me punished again.

My resolve lasts until we enter the bridge where a few other alien warriors are waiting. It's my first glimpse of space, and I lift my head to look outside of the windows. The glittering stars against the blackness are stunningly beautiful, like something out of a movie. It almost doesn't seem real.

Movement catches my eye, and then a giant Tsenturion with angry dark armor meets my gaze. He scowls fiercely at me. *Shit*. I've broken protocol. Immediately, I return my gaze to the floor like a good little Tribute. Make it look like I'm thoroughly cowed. Although, if I'm being totally honest, the angry warrior is definitely scaring me a little. I shift closer to *my* warrior. Even if he spanked me, fucked me silly, and then put me on a leash, I still feel safe next to him. It seems crazy to me, but I can't deny it.

Just as I think that, he makes an odd clicking noise and pulls me forward by the leash. *Jerk.* I can feel my cheeks heat with embarrassment. Now I *am* blushing. He sits in a large chair at the head of the bridge. When I hesitate, wondering where to sit, he points to a spot next to his chair. There's some sort of cushion on the ground, and I realize I'm supposed to sit on it like a freaking dog or something.

Oh, hell no.

"I can't sit there," I say, pulling back against my collar to show how serious I am. "I have a knee injury, I can't sit on the ground for long periods of time." I'm stretching the truth a little—years of yoga practice made me more resilient, though my knee does get sore after a time.

He gives me a look, every inch the High Commander who is

unhappy to be questioned. Especially in front of his men. My knees feel a little weak, but I refuse to drop down. I'm not lying after all.

"Medik has repaired your knee, you need not worry about it." The calm way he states the impossible has my mouth popping open in surprise. I've been doing physical therapy and yoga for years to keep my knee working properly, because it was the only option. I narrow my eyes at him, crossing my arms over my chest, and jut out my chin, ignoring the stares of the warriors on deck. I don't believe him.

Sighing and shaking his head, he begins to wind the leash around his hand, drawing me closer by my throat. I'm uncomfortably reminded of Jabba and Princess Leia, except that this is actually really freaking sexy, even if I don't want it to be.

"You know what happens when you disobey."

I dig in my heels as I realize his intention, but it's too late. The leash pulls me down and over his lap, ass in the air, and I squeal as I feel the training belt receding, uncovering my already reddened cheeks.

"What?" I kick out, feeling frantic as I try to push myself up. "You can't spank me here. Please! You didn't even give me a chance to sit down!"

"Didn't I?" He sounds amused, and my anger surges. My intention to be sneaky, to be meek, goes flying out the window in the face of his freaking amusement when he's about to spank me with a *freaking audience!*

"No! Not here, dammit," I grit out, kicking my legs as I try to roll off his lap. I'm aware all the warriors are watching. I'm even more aware of the High Commander's cock, growing long and hard under my belly, the *seela* beginning to writhe. The ridges strain the front of his suit.

It gives me an idea.

He pins me down, but I keep wriggling, rocking side to side a little in an effort to... er... stimulate things in my favor.

It has no discernible effect on him. At least not one which is helpful to me in any way.

My wrists are caught in his large hand, my legs weighted by his heavy one. I gyrate like a belly dancer but am caught fast. My ass is still burning from the spanking he gave me in his cabin, and I want to wail in denial.

He pulls aside the flimsy garment I'm wearing and bares my ass to the entire deck. I freeze, my whole body flushing with humiliation. There's no way they can miss the signs of the spanking he already gave me, and now they're going to see me receive another one.

Even worse, I can feel my lower body pulsing in anticipation. My vagina has committed the ultimate betrayal. I'm getting wet. Considering the books I read and the training Frllil put me through, maybe I shouldn't be so surprised. Considering how much my ass already hurts and how embarrassed I am, I am pretty shocked that I'm turned on at all. But there's something about being vulnerable and exposed that is just flat out doing it for me, no matter my other emotions.

"If you did not want to be punished here, you should not have misbehaved here," Gavrill murmurs. Defiantly, I think of him by his name rather than as the High Commander or my Master—even sarcastically. His free hand smooths over my skin, leaving goosebumps rising in its wake. My mortification and arousal grow in equal measure.

"Please don't," I beg, now with a much more proper tone than I'd used before. Large fingers caress my bottom, soothing the sore spots but also readying me for the punishment to come.

"This is mine to do with as I please," he reminds me, sounding way too satisfied with himself. The possessiveness in his voice triggers something inside of me, even though intellectually I know he'd be this way about any woman presented to him. This has nothing to do with *me*, so I can't let myself react too much to it. "Mine to punish, mine to reward. And I must set an example for my men."

I shouldn't have pushed him in front of the others. *Stupid, Dawn.* That was just common sense. Although I hadn't meant to exactly... or had I? Had some part of my brain wanted to see what he would do? How he would react? Had I been trying to find the line?

If I had been, I definitely found it. He's the head honcho, he *has* to be in control of his Tribute in front of the others. Maybe I can talk back a little bit when it's just the two of us, but not when there's an audience.

His palm cracks down once on both cheeks, quick as a whip, reigniting the burn from my previous spanking. I cry out, my legs automatically kicking. The way I'm propped over his leg, my entire backside is on display except for the narrow strip covered by the belt... something he could rescind at any moment. If any warrior on the deck looks closely, they'll be able to see *everything*.

Including how excited this spanking makes me.

Smack!

Smack!

Smack!

I hold still, internally praying that the spanking is already over, as Gavrill cups my right butt cheek, molding it to his palm before smacking it. He repeats the motion with my left, his movements slow and methodical. Thoughtful. As if he's realizing something. I feel the training belt recede, uncovering me completely, and I moan.

He plumps one cheek, and I suck in a breath. I'm practically dripping on the floor. He's got to notice—it's only a matter of time.

His fingers stray lower, and my lower half twitches.

"You're still enjoying this." He sounds a little surprised.

"No!" I crane my neck. He's examining the sticky wetness on his fingers, a satisfied little smile on his face. His armor shimmers— changing colors?

"Commander," one of the warriors pipes up.

"A moment," Gavrill growls and jerks my shimmery robes over my bare skin, covering me up against prying eyes. The training belt slides over my ass and pussy again, cool against the heat of my bottom. Oh, so now he's concerned about privacy?

He swings me upright, propping me between his knees facing him. I can barely meet his eyes. His suit shifts to a more neutral grey, but there are small flashes of gold that nearly match his skin. I know from my training that the gold is arousal.

"We will continue this later." He strokes my hip, and I shiver, trying not to imagine all the punishments he might think up in the meantime. "You will take your place as my Tribute and *keep quiet.*"

I bite my lip and nod. He makes a chiding noise, and I add quickly, "Yes, Master."

I'm in a good position to learn about the ship up here on the bridge, so if I can just keep my mouth shut, then maybe I can take the first steps in escaping from here eventually.

Nodding in satisfaction, Gavrill shifts me off his lap. This time, I obediently kneel on the large cushion—which is surprisingly comfortable. By the time I've lowered myself down, I realize he must have told the truth about my knee, because it didn't even twinge when I put my weight on it.

As Gavrill conducts his business, I review my circumstances. I'm the captive of a large, dominant alien, but he's only going to spank me if I've been bad, and otherwise I think he'll treat me pretty well even if he thinks of me as a pet. Things could definitely be worse, right? Studying the other warriors out of the corner of my eye, I'm not sure I'd be better off with one of them. Certainly not with the big one at the station to the right of Gavrill's chair. When he's not addressing the Commander, he's scowling at me. I recognize him from the presentation ceremony. He was standing behind Gavrill along with another, older Tsenturion.

"Bodgan," Gavrill says, and the glowering warrior snaps his attention from me to the Commander. "You found sign of the Vgothas?"

"Yes, sir. Along the edge of the Boral Nebulae. Likely, they are trying to use its energy as camouflage for their ships. It is effective, the trail is very hard to follow, and it looks as though it's leading towards Outer Rim space, where they are sure to have allies. We will likely not have an opportunity to engage them from such a position of power again." Bogdan lowers his gaze to me again. If looks could kill... I duck my head and scoot closer to Gavrill's chair, using the commander's thickly muscled leg to block some of his warrior's malice. Gavrill reaches down and strokes my hair absently. I should be pissed at him petting me like a cat, but I feel safe and protected instead.

"There will be plenty of opportunities to engage the enemy, especially if we bait them."

Bogdan's suit abruptly lightens to a cloudy silver.

"Send coordinates to Arkdhem. Tell him to send out the scouts. They should cloak their ships and cruise along the meteor belt. They're authorized to use firepower to clear a path."

"The Vgothas will sense the weapons' emissions."

"Yes," Gavrill says, sounding suddenly fierce. I almost lift my eyes up to look at him, feeling just the tiniest bit afraid at this other side to him. "Then we will engage them."

"You propose we use subterfuge?" I can't tell if Bogdan is happy or disgusted.

"The enemy is stealthy. They will not expect it of us." Gavrill settles back in his seat with a satisfied grimness that makes me glad his attention is on the Vgothas and not me. "Then we will destroy them."

~

GAVRILL

MY TRIBUTE'S eyes are downcast when we enter my chambers. She's been quiet since her little outburst on the bridge. While I appreciated her silence there, I find I am growing more uncomfortable with it. She was certainly not quiet when she woke up, so why is she now silent?

I stride to the edge of our resting place, snap my fingers and point to a spot in front of me.

With a wary gaze, she approaches and stands before me, eyeing me warily. She's intelligent enough to be nervous, and yet she still obeys.

"Good girl," I murmur. Her lips press together, and I can tell she's aggravated by the praise for some reason, but I enjoy it almost as much as her reluctant obedience. I like her strong spirit, as long as she obeys. For her, my will is law. Always. Still, disobedience will give me reason to punish her, which I also enjoy thoroughly. I do not wish for it to occur again in front of my men though.

When I'd had her over my lap, I'd nearly forgotten they were all there, gazing upon her... coveting her. Feeling their eyes on us was why I'd cut her punishment short. She is *my* Tribute, I don't have to share any part of her, not even the sight of her, if I don't wish it.

Her very presence has also been a distraction from matters which need my attention. It was easier when she was on the cushion and I hadn't actually had my hands on her.

"You disobeyed me on the bridge, my Tribute. But I am fair. I will give you a chance to explain before finishing your punishment."

Her shoulders lift and fall, slumping a little. She looks like she is trying to appear meek, but she looks more sulky than anything else.

"Speak," I order, goading her. "You are a sentient being. You have language. Use it."

Her mouth knots into a defiant pout. Red stains her cheeks. She might not know her hands have curled into fists, but I notice it— along with her heightened body temperature. Sensations seep into me, conducted from her Trainer to my suit. She's angry... and aroused.

"With all due respect," she says, straightening up and daring to look me directly in the eye. I shouldn't like it, but I do. "You don't treat me like one."

"What?" My suit flashes with surprise.

"A sentient being. You don't treat me like one. You treat me like a pet." She indicates her necklet and lead. "A collar? A leash? I'm not your fucking dog."

"What is a dog?" I ask, frowning at the unfamiliar word as I attempt to approximate her pronunciation. 'Pet' I understand, we had those on Tsentur, but 'dog' does not translate.

"It's... it's a pet." She stammers out the words, caught off-guard. "An animal. A smart one which can be trained but is not equal to a human."

Just as she is not equal to me, but I choose not to point that out. It would be rude and possibly even cruel to highlight the superiority of Tsenturions to humans.

Still, I shrug. I am the master, she is the Tribute. Of course, I treat her differently than I would one of my men. Tsenturion brides were often courted in a similar manner until they are mastered, after which they were allowed more liberties… but she is not a bride.

"You are my Tribute. You belong to me. If I choose to declare my ownership to my men by marking every inch of your skin, it is my right."

Her chest flushes pink, and she looks away, casting her eyes downward. The joining of our nanotech seems to be more complete than anticipated, as I can actually feel her growing ire, though she tries to hide it.

"You might as well. It won't be as embarrassing as walking around practically naked with all your men staring at me." Her shoulders hunch in.

Jealous heat flares through me. I recall every warrior who laid his eyes on her exposed form, and I'm ready to march to the com and order all of them blinded. It pleases me that she obviously prefers to be covered in front of them, that she does not wish for them to look at her.

"Very well. To be clear, in the future you will respect your Master. You will not argue with me in front of my men. In fact, you will not speak to me when I am on duty unless given permission."

"I thought you wanted me to use my language?" There's a slight edge to her voice, a little hint of sarcastic sass, and I have to hide a smile. Why I find her attitude endearing, I cannot say. There are very few of my men who would dare to address me so, but she does it without fear, though her bottom must be burning from the spankings. It was still very pink when she was over my lap on the bridge.

"Not in public. But you are right—I have contradicted myself. But I trust I have made myself clear now. If you think you are unable to follow my orders, then I will procure a gag for you."

Fear flickers across her face and then is gone, but I can still feel it. She is very brave, my Tribute. An admirable quality.

"Wonderful," she mutters. "Thanks for making it clear."

I allow myself to smile. She glances at me and shivers. I smile broader.

"Now that the matter is settled, I owe you a punishment," I say calmly. Inside, I'm quivering with glee as I sit and pat my knee.

She hesitates, then begins to reluctantly move, very slowly. I reach out to take her hand, pulling her forward faster, and she allows me to draw her small body over my legs.

I take my time arranging her, undoing the binding from her hair and spreading the shimmering mass over her shoulders. The blue fabric of her dress slides off her pearly skin, exposing the darker pink between her legs.

Her gown really is not sufficient to hide her from my warrior's scrutiny. I will order the replicator to design more concealing garments for her to wear outside our chambers. It will make her appear more like a bride than a courting Tsenturion female but... she *has* been claimed by me. Even though she is not Tsenturion, in a manner she is now my bride. A fitting argument if anyone dares to speak up.

Inside our quarters, it will be an entirely different matter. Perhaps I will order her to go without clothes. Yes, and command her to disrobe within the first minute of entering or face punishment.

Punishing my Tribute is far too enjoyable. Even now she is squirming in anticipation. The color of her bottom has faded somewhat to a soft pink, but I can tell it is still sensitive to my touch as I caress the soft mound.

When I clear my throat, she ceases moving, going quite still in fact, almost as if she's hoping I will somehow not notice her.

"Your skin still has color from your previous sessions," I announce proudly, thinking she will want to know. The manuals indicated that human females have an interest in knowing what their bottoms look like after punishment. "Because there was some ambiguity to my statement, I will make this brief. Next time you disobey publicly, I will be much harsher."

Little grunts and huffs of air escape as I smack my broad hand over her small, tight cheeks. I pay special attention to the crease between her leg and rounded buttocks, an area I had attended to before but not focused on. Every time my palm lands on that sensitive area, her breath catches and she lets out a little cry. I pause, wondering if I should push this session further. The manuals outlined the benefits of spanking a Tribute until she releases emotion. After all she's been through, she might need a good, hard cry.

Yet I find that, like before, I am eager to move on to the next part of a spanking. My cock, *seela*, and *prime seela* all press against my suit, threatening to burst out, eager to be inside of her once again. And I'm not the only one who notices.

My Tribute wriggles, pressing herself against my cock. I know she is attempting to incite my lust and end her spanking sooner. Amused, and highly aroused myself, I decide to indulge her. Apparently, I am feeling *very* lenient now that we are alone. And her bottom is already a nice, hot pink, thanks to having been attended to earlier. The cream between her legs is a clear indicator of her arousal.

Lifting her up from my lap, I move her to the side so that she is bent over the edge of the bed. My armor sends a message to the bed, and she lets out a little noise of startled surprise as the bed begins to rise until she is at the perfect height to receive my cock. The new placement means she is barely touching the floor with the tips of her toes, leaving the full weight of her body resting on the bed.

Once she's impaled on my cock, she won't be able to move, she will be pinned between the bed and myself. I smile, greatly pleased by her predicament.

"Master... please... wait," she begs. "Let me turn over..."

"No," I say, gripping her hips and shoving my cock into her wet heat.

6

———

Dawn

I CRY out as Gavrill thrusts inside of me, hard and fast. I knew I was going to be sore, both inside and out, but that hadn't been why I'd wanted to turn over. Just as I thought—feared—the long tentacle above his cock immediately probes around the entrance to my ass as he holds himself inside of me. I try to lurch forward and away from the intrusive touch, but in this position there is nowhere for me to go. All I can do is try and wriggle to the side as he holds himself deep inside of me, groaning. His *seela* stroking my pussy lips while the long one circles my anus.

It feels better than I want it to.

Invasive. Perverse. Pleasurable.

I try to clench my cheeks, but my position doesn't allow for it, and I make a high-pitched whining noise as I squirm uncomfortably.

Yeah, I read about this stuff, but I've never actually *done* it. Some fantasies are supposed to remain just that—fantasies.

Yes, I'd been trying to distract him from spanking me again—I would much rather have sex than take any more punishment—but I thought he'd put me on my back again. It hadn't occurred to me what I was risking until he had me bent over the bed and the way everything would line up had flashed into my mind.

When he pulls back, I relax slightly until he's pushing forward again, burying himself inside of me. Every time he does, I can feel his long *seela* probing, exploring... and I don't dare say anything because I don't want to give him any ideas he hasn't already had. Considering the reading material, I don't have a whole lot of hope for keeping my ass virginal, but I'll cling to whatever hope I can.

But, as usual, my fantasies aren't helping me one bit.

The more his tentacle teases my tiny hole, the better it feels, and the more my mind starts racing with all the scenes from my favorite books. The dominant alien master demanding his human slave's submission, probing *all* of her despite her protests, and finally taking her ass... maybe even making her enjoy it, but maybe not.

His hard body slaps against my tender cheeks as he rides me, reigniting the sting in a way that makes my pussy clench around him. Despite how sore I am, both inside from our previous encounter and outside from the spankings, I respond readily to him. The ridges massage the inside of my walls, that odd-shaped head fluttering inside of me and stimulating me in all the right places.

I don't know if it's the training or if I've gone full-on Stockholm syndrome, or if it's just the fulfillment of my fantasies, or some unholy combination of all three, but it's like my entire universe has narrowed down to this one room, to this one moment. I spasm around him, my back arching slightly, my pussy lips plumping under the massage of his *seela*. The embarrassment and trepidation I feel about having my virgin ass probed seeps away as my pleasure rises, the sensations coming from that area contributing to my growing ecstasy.

My sense of helplessness only increases my arousal, and I moan as he takes his time, obviously enjoying riding me. Each thrust brings me a little closer to orgasm, but he's so deliberate, each stroke so measured, that it's starting to drive me a little out of my mind. I'm clawing at the sheets as I strain towards an orgasm I can't quite reach yet.

"Please..." The plea escapes my lips, my pussy clenching around his thick shaft, trying to drag him in deeper, hold him there longer. "Please..."

Gavrill

The sweet sound of my Tribute's begging incites me.

I had been taking my time, testing my control after the wildness of my first time with her, and had been reassured that it had been an aberration. That it allowed me to wallow in the pleasure of her body was an added inducement. But when she begins to beg... I can feel my urges growing again, responding to her submissive plea.

Groaning low, under my breath, I begin to move a little harder and faster, my *seela* writhing and stroking. The small, crinkled hole which so disturbed her when it was touched winks at me from between her pink cheeks as they jiggle against my thrusts. I have many plans for exploring that opening, one that Tsenturions do not possess, but which figures prominently in all the texts of her people.

My *prime seela* probes at its tightness with every thrust, and I can only imagine how pleasurable such a narrow channel would be, especially as my Tribute whimpers and submits beneath me, very much as she is now. Her wetness increases with every thrust, her moans becoming louder as I plow into her from behind, my hands gripping her hips, pinning her to the bed and holding her in place while I take my pleasure.

She is obviously enjoying it as well, and it is as though my need is feeding off hers... my control is slipping from my fingers, and I don't care anymore. My entire focus is on the sweet clasp of her body, her delicious cries of pleasure as she begins to spasm and clench around me, and my own urgent desire.

I rut her harder, faster, groaning with pleasure as she sobs out her own climax. The way her legs kick, I can tell she is becoming overloaded with sensation, and it only spurs me to take her harder. I grip her hips, pinning her down and holding her in place while I fill her, over and over again. The walls of her body tighten, trying to hold me in place, but she is too slick and my thrusts too strong.

Her cries have become incoherent, filling my ears and feeding the dark craving that her presence has created. I growl, low, pumping relentlessly until my own orgasm finally surges. My seed spurts as I bury myself inside of her, letting the spasms of her body milk me of my offering. My *seela* have latched onto her again, pulling at her body and keeping us firmly joined as I empty myself into her. Panting, I shudder, groaning, and she whimpers delightfully beneath me, her breath coming out on a ragged sob.

My own body feels oddly slack, my satisfaction so overwhelming that I would be alarmed if I didn't feel so good. So right.

Bemused, I run my hand down her back and over the soft cheeks of her bottom, which are still slightly warm to the touch. The noises she makes are so quiet, I can barely hear them, just enough to let me know she's still conscious and responsive.

When I lean back slightly so that my fingers can explore the area my *prime seela* was probing, she becomes much more responsive.

Dawn

"Wait!" My voice comes out in a high squeak, making me sound like a cartoon mouse as one of Gavrill's big fingers pokes at my rear entrance. My legs kick, but my muscles are so watery and weak after my orgasm that I might as well have just lain there. Not that it would have made much of a difference even if I wasn't feeling so pathetically limp.

Ignoring me, his finger dips down between our bodies to where he's still embedded inside of me, gathers the cream there and returns to push at my crinkled hole. I'd finally gotten used to the sensation of his tentacle thing circling and teasing me there, and then the way it felt like it had actually been sucking on the tender bundle of nerves that I hadn't known existed, but it hadn't actually gone inside of me.

"No..." My cry of protest is barely a whimper as the tiny hole stretches and his finger slides inside. Embarrassment flushes through me as he probes the virgin entrance to my body, his finger burrowing inside and making me uncomfortably aware that it doesn't feel entirely unpleasant. The slight burn of stretching isn't enough to truly hurt, and being so full feels almost good.

I whimper as he pumps his finger, exploring, and my body clenches down instinctively, trying to push him out. All that means is that I can feel every millimeter of his digit as it moves inside of me.

"You are very tight here," he says, sounding pleased. "I look forward to finishing your subjugation by taking you in this orifice."

The very formal wording he uses for the act only makes it sound even more depraved. I'm also not super happy about him calling it my 'subjugation', but I can't bring myself to argue either, because that's exactly what it feels like. Like he's literally fucking me into submission with his strange, alien cock.

A cock which had been softening inside of me but is now beginning to harden and thicken again. The uber-sensitive walls of my pleasure-soaked pussy can feel the difference easily, and I whimper. I can't possibly take any more pleasure. Humans aren't meant to. I don't care what upgrades Frllil gave to my body to ready me to be a Tsenturion Tribute, if Gavrill fucks me again, I think I might die.

Unfortunately, Tributes don't get a say.

I sob as he begins to thrust again, my sore pussy fluttering in protest and my ass clenching around the finger he is now pushing in and out of my bottom.

~

GAVRILL

. . .

By the time Bogdan calls to ask if I am coming to the bridge for my shift or not, his voice full of disapproval, my Tribute is nearly insensate. I have pleasured her into complete submission. Her nipples are reddened from the attentions of my mouth and fingers, her pussy lips are just as red and swollen and marked with many purple circles from the suction of my *seela*, and she didn't even protest when I used the training belt to fill her bottom, stretching that tight hole for my eventual use. Tsenturions do not have the "plugs" which her manuals mention, but I have used the belt to create what I think is a good approximation.

I have lost count of the number of orgasms I've had; much less how many I've given her. Learning her body, exploring what she does and does not enjoy, how to make her climax hardest, has utterly consumed me. I have also lost count of the hours. Unheard of for me. For the first time in my life, I am late to my shift.

Yet, I still find myself oddly reluctant to leave her, though she is no longer in a position to entertain me. While I feel energized, it is obvious that she requires rest. Probably food as well.

Frowning, I make a fast decision and hail Arkdhem. While I would like to bring my Tribute with me to the bridge, that will not be very restful for her and will be distracting for me. But I do not wish to leave her alone, especially as she may awaken hungry or thirsty after all the rigorous activity. Indeed, I will be ordering someone to bring me some sustenance as soon as I am on the bridge.

Out of all of my men, other than Medik, I trust Arkdhem with her the most. He is the commander of our scout ships and young for the post, but it was well-earned. From the beginning, he was vocal of his support for the Tribute program, but he does not have a covetous personality and looks up to me as an older brother. None of my men would disrespect me or harm my Tribute, but... Arkdhem will be the most respectful and least envious.

"Yes, Commander?" Arkdhem answers my hail immediately.

"Arkdhem, I have a new assignment for you, if you are willing to accept it."

"Yes, Commander," he says without hesitation. "Whatever it is you wish."

"You might want to hear it first," I reply, somewhat amused. "I am on duty on the bridge, but I do not wish to leave my Tribute entirely unattended. She is currently sleeping but will likely require sustenance when she awakens. I would ask you to be her escort on the ship while I am otherwise occupied."

"Commander, it would be an honor." The sincerity in his voice confirms my choice. "I will return to the main ship immediately."

"She is in my quarters. I will give you access before I leave."

It will not take him long to dock his ship and make his way here, and it is unlikely my Tribute will awaken anytime soon. As much as I enjoy the look of her the way she is now, I exert my will on the nanotech, and it spreads downwards from the front of her belt and upwards over her pussy from where it's embedded in her secondary entrance. I leave it inside of her there, to facilitate my eventual breaching. All of the manuals indicated that being filled there would help human females remain in the submissive mindset, reminding them of their helpless vulnerability to their Master.

Once the nanotech is in place, I pick out the most covering of her garments, an opaque pink gown with slits up the side, and dress her. She barely murmurs as I move her about on the bed, other than a small whimper when I caress her breast before covering it. Arkdhem has still not arrived, but I cannot delay any longer.

Shoving down my unanticipated reluctance, I force myself to leave the room. It feels wrong to separate myself from her, which only increases my determination to do so. This swiftly growing attachment makes no sense and is not at all convenient.

Just how much so becomes more apparent when I reach the bridge and face Bogdan's glower. My second is fuming, his armor dark and streaked with simmering red, and he does not even bother to contain his emotion.

"Is this going to be the new way of things now that you have a Tribute?" he asks, his voice full of demand.

Normally I would not allow him to question me in such a manner in front of the crew, but they all deserve an answer.

Calmly, I meet his gaze, my own armor not flickering one iota from its neutral grey. I actually feel quite serene now that I am on the bridge, more focused.

"It will not happen again," I say. "However, I will recommend that in the future, those receiving Tributes also receive some time off. It is unlikely any of us will be able to resist indulging deeply after such a long period of abstinence. Perhaps it is unreasonable to expect that things will continue completely as normal when a Tribute first arrives."

My statement makes quite a few of the crew brighten. Whether they are excited by the idea of their own Tributes or by the idea of additional time with the females once they arrive, I am unsure. Bogdan just looks angrier than ever.

"So you are saying that that human is now your first priority?" He is practically seething, and his accusation makes some of the excitement in the room dampen.

I scowl back at him, my own armor darkening slightly. "My first priority is, and always will be, our people. I came the moment you called earlier, did I not? As I always do and always will. But allowances must also be made for the change in our situation."

His jaw clenches, and he is obviously not entirely appeased by my answer, but I have no other to give him. Having a Tribute is more consuming than I had realized, and I think my men will find it so as well at first. The fascination for something new will fade, even the urge to copulate should grow less as my desires are satiated, and Bogdan will eventually see that.

"You will understand when you have your own Tribute and are able to sate your needs," I tell him.

"I do not *want* a human Tribute," he spits out, his voice full of disgust and derision, before storming off the bridge.

Silence reigns in his absence, and I resist the urge to rub my head. I don't know why Bogdan is behaving like a child, but I will not chase after him either. Obviously, he needs rest.

"I'll take his if he doesn't want her," Vander, my pilot on duty, pipes in. Laughter breaks the tension in the room, and even I chuckle.

"We'll see. Now update me. Where are we on the search for the Vgotha?" I ask.

Still looking, since following the trail through the ion pathways of the outer edges of the cloud is difficult, and so far they have not taken the bait our scout ships have offered. As the bridge reports in, Arkdhem sends me a message that he has arrived at my chambers and my Tribute still slumbers. A small part of me I hadn't even known was tense now relaxes, and I am able to focus entirely on the matters at hand, knowing she is watched over.

~

Dawn

I COME AWAKE WITH A GROWL. Not that I'm growling, my stomach is. I'm *starving*. Not too surprising considering the last time I ate was before I was presented as a Tribute, and... well, I have no idea how long Gavrill had erotically tortured me, but it had been a long time. My pussy feels thoroughly abused, my thighs feel like I'd run a freaking marathon, and though I've been asleep, I still feel really drained.

I am also very... full... in a place that I'm not accustomed to being full.

Reaching down, I groan when my fingers meet the hated training belt, which is covering me underneath the filmy dress I am now wearing. I have a fuzzy memory of Gavrill eagerly watching my expression as he pushed the belt's nanotech up inside my ass, making me squirm even though I had been practically dizzy with exhaustion by that point. The control he had over the belt was more than a little terrifying, since the belt was *on* me.

The dirty pervert had then fucked me while my ass was full, and I'd come so hard, I'd seen stars before practically passing out.

"Tribute? Are you awake?" The deep voice came out of the darkness and makes me shriek and scramble... what exactly I'm scrambling for, I have no idea, but my hands and legs go every which way.

"Who's there?" I ask, my heart pounding. That was *not* Gavrill's voice, and I don't think it's one I had heard before. Although, it's not like I've been memorizing voices. I think I would remember the angry one on the bridge though, Bogdan.

"Cabin, lights." At the order, the lights in the cabin come on, and I blink rapidly as my eyes adjust. Sitting on one of the couches in the main area of the cabin is a Tsenturion warrior, fully armored except for his head. His armor is a light grey, almost a sky blue. It's a very unthreatening color, and I relax again.

"Greetings, Commander's Tribute, I am Arkdhem, and I am here in case you require anything while the High Commander is on the bridge."

I nearly giggled at his eager formality, except...

"Please, call me Dawn, not Commander's Tribute or Tribute." I plead, already anticipating that he'll turn me down, but instead he nods his head and looks like he's concentrating.

"Very well, Dawn," he says, sounding out my name the same way Gavrill did when I made the request of him. A request that he has since ignored. "Is there anything I can do for you right now?"

As if on cue, my stomach growls.

"Food?" I ask hopefully. "And water? Maybe something to brush my teeth?"

For a Tsenturion, Arkdhem turns out to be pretty easygoing. He kind of reminds me of an eager puppy. He shows me how to use both the shower and cleaning facilities in the bathroom, although I only actually use the latter for now. While I definitely need a shower, I need food first. Brushing the sleep out of my mouth felt good though. I feel a little odd just rinsing my mouth out with a flavorless liquid that basically just seems like it's water, but I can feel it tingling, and my mouth does feel cleaner afterwards.

Food is in the cafeteria. Arkdhem offered to order it brought to us, but I wanted out of the cabin. If I'm ever going to escape, I need to explore, right? When I tell him I'd rather see more of the ship, he's completely amenable and escorts me right out of the door. Walking on wobbly legs, I tell myself that this is a good idea. My muscles could do with some movement that doesn't involve my legs being spread or hanging uselessly. Fortunately, the training belt is soft against my pussy, or else I would be a lot more uncomfortable.

Truthfully, I feel way better than I should. My limbs are long and loose, like I've done a satisfying yoga session. I can't help but wonder if it's the tinkering Frllil did to my body to prepare me for being a Tribute.

Gavrill's collar is still around my neck, but Arkdhem didn't attach a leash, to my relief. Apparently, that's a right reserved only for my *master*. I'm definitely not complaining.

Out in the corridors of the ship, I look around at everything, and, since Arkdhem is so accommodating, I ask as many questions as I can think of. Not that any of his answers are very helpful to me.

Where are we in relation to my galaxy? *No idea.*

Does he know how I got here? *Through an unstable wormhole.*

How does someone travel through a wormhole, much less an unstable one? *Through a portal or a pod designed by the Jabols. But as far as he knows, I'm the only being who has ever travelled through one.*

It quickly becomes apparent that he has no problem answering my increasingly unsubtle questions that would help me escape because there *is* no escape. The Tsenturions don't even know the general vicinity of Earth, because they had nothing to do with picking me up. To get back to my home, I need the Jabol. To get back to *them*, I'd need a ship and a navigator.

Hopelessness is swamping me by the time we make it to the cafeteria.

"Don't worry," Arkdhem says gently, patting my shoulder with his huge hand. "You'll be happy here with us. The High Commander is the best of the best, and he will treat you well."

"Right." Bitterness wells. "I just have to accept that I'll never see my home again."

For a long, solemn moment, Arkdhem studies me. "I know you don't think I understand, but I do. We all do."

Shame rushes through me as I realize that he does. They all lost their entire planet and everyone on it. At least I know Earth is still there. My beloved house still stands. My yoga class students are going on about their lives as if everything is totally normal. And I don't have any immediate family, no one who would be significantly hurt by my abduction. My life has completely changed, I've lost everything... but at least I know it's still out there.

"Sorry," I whisper.

He just smiles and pats my shoulder again before leading me to a machine in the wall. There's an opening there with a tray in it. I assume this is how they get food. Frllil used to just bring me trays, so I don't know where he was getting it from, but at least I had some time to learn what I like. Arkdhem also insists on adding a few of his favorites that I haven't tried before—it wasn't like the Jabol ever provided me with a buffet or anything.

It's nice having someone care what I want, even if it's just for a meal. I don't want to admit it, but some little part of me aches, wishing it was Gavrill beside me, helping me try new food and not Arkdhem.

7

———

G avrill

WHEN CORIN ARRIVES on the bridge to take over command for the next shift, Arkdhem and my Tribute are still dining. They have been there for quite some time and I frown in concern as I stride down the hallway. Do humans take an abnormally long time to eat, or has something else detained them?

When I reach the dining hall, the scene that greets my eyes is unexpected and not entirely welcome.

My Tribute sits at the center of a group of my warriors, all of them watching as she bites into what looks like a piece of korrun fruit. Immediately, her eyes widen with delight at the rich flavor, her entire face lighting up.

"It tastes exactly like chocolate!" She shoves the rest of the fruit into her mouth, looking almost blissful and humming with a noise that is far too close to the sounds she made in my bed.

Jealousy rips through me, so hot and fast that my armor actually flickers with the bright orange color, as if it's been shot through with meteors. Seeing the color, I push down my unruly emotions before the color streaks can catch anyone's eye. There is no reason for jealousy, just because they can hear her. No one is touching her, they are just watching her.

Listening to her.

And they seem as enthralled by her as I am.

It is only understandable, I tell myself. They are curious. And she is beautiful. Interesting. Exotic. The first of the Tributes. The hope for the future.

Despite my logic, I can still feel my possessiveness, my jealousy, seething underneath the surface of my forced calm. At least none of it shows on my armor where my warriors can see it. Not that any of them seem to have Bogdan's attitude, but I am the High Commander, and I would not display any weakness by choice.

In control of myself again, I start forward, and the movement catches Arkdhem's eyes. He immediately stands and salutes, thumping his hand against his chest, which causes a chain reaction as the rest of my warriors notice and do the same. My Tribute looks startled at the sudden formality—which is not strictly necessary when in locations like the cafeteria or on the bridge when work is being done. Arkdhem tends to salute when he sees me, regardless of what he's doing, unless it would be dangerous to do so.

"High Commander," he says. "I did not realize how much time had passed. We were introducing Dawn to more of our cuisine than the Jabol had provided."

"So I see," I respond, nodding my head. "She seems to be enjoying the korrun fruit."

My eyes drop to hers, and she smiles hesitantly at me. Hopefully. I do not understand what it is she hopes for, but she appears pleased to see me, and that pleases me, as well as soothing some of my jealousy.

"It tastes just like my favorite dessert back home," she says, almost shyly, as though she is wondering whether or not it is appropriate to speak. I am even more pleased that she is obviously already adjusting to the expectations I have set down for her.

"Then you shall have as much of it as you like," I say, feeling rather magnanimous. "Right now, I'd like to go back to the cabin. If you are still hungered, then we can bring some with us."

There is no sign of disappointment by the males around us, but I can feel it like a palpable thing. But they have had my Tribute's attention for long enough.

My Tribute shakes her head. "I am finished, thank you. Master."

The honorific is tacked on to the end as if she almost forgot, but I will be lenient, as she is still learning, and it does not seem deliberate. My warriors begin to disperse as I move to her side and clip the leash to her collar. As soon as I've done, so I can feel myself relaxing even further, as though having her physically attached to me in some manner has completed something that was missing within me.

I am uncomfortably aware that some of Bogdan's accusations may have been closer to the truth than I want to admit.

～

Dawn

STUPID LEASH. The sound of it clicking into place is heavier than a door slamming shut. The brief illusion of being myself again is gone.

Worse, there's a part of me that felt joy at seeing Gavrill walking up and that now feels a sense of satisfaction at being leashed by him. I had been happy to see him, although slightly wary since I definitely wasn't being quiet and the blank expression on his face hadn't seemed particularly promising. But he didn't seem angry.

For some reason, I get the sense that he's feeling possessive, maybe even jealous, but I can't imagine where I'm getting that from because I can't read that in his expression or body language at all.

"Thank you for taking care of my Tribute," he says to Arkdhem. Again, I'm torn into two Dawns—the one that wants to bristle at being dehumanized back to 'Tribute' and the one that is stupid enough to feel special about being called *his* Tribute.

He would have called any woman that, I remind myself. *If something happened to me, they'd probably just replace me with another woman, and then he'd call* her *his Tribute.*

I'm stupid enough that the thought actually hurts. If Stockholm Syndrome was water, I'd be swimming in the ocean right now.

"It was my pleasure, High Commander," Arkdhem says, absolutely sincere. I smile at him. I like Arkdhem; he seems like a nice guy—a nice Tsenturion.

After relieving Arkdhem of his babysitting duties, because that's pretty much what it feels like right now, Gavrill leads me back to his cabin. He's silent the whole way, and so am I. Talking with the other Tsenturions hadn't been easy exactly, because they'd all been strangers, but somehow it had been easier than talking to this particular Tsenturion. I hadn't cared what they thought of me except in a very general way.

As much as I didn't want to admit it, I definitely cared what Gavrill thought of me.

I was also torn between a sense of relief and peace at being in his presence again and being annoyed as all hell at being on a leash again. I'm also getting tired, and as he leads me into the cabin, I yawn.

His dark, sharp eyes immediately take in the action. "You require more rest?"

"Probably," I say, trying to hold back what feels like another yawn coming on. "I think being hungry kind of woke me up before I was finished sleeping. Master."

The look in his eyes sharpens. I feel my heart rate pick up a little as he steps forward, looming over me slightly. His fingers cup my chin, tilting my head back so he can look me in the eyes.

"It is your first day, and you are tired, so I will be lenient," he murmurs, his voice gentle but firm. "But you will learn to call me Master, or you will be spanked until you remember."

"Yes, Master," I say immediately, the honorific coming very easily now when he's looking at me like that and holding me like this. I am suddenly very aware of my body, the cheeks of my bottom tingling in a kind of anticipation despite still being sore from earlier, my nipples hardening, my pussy lips plumping, and my ass clenching around the nanotech plug the training belt created.

I want to fight the reaction, but how can I fight myself?

"Good girl," he says, and warmth flushes through me. Dammit, I shouldn't like it so much when he says that. I shouldn't care what he thinks, because my complaisance is supposed to just be an act.

But I do care. And I do like it.

Then he's pulling on the leash, drawing me in closer to him using the leash and collar around my neck, as his mouth lowers to mine for a kiss. How I can still be horny after being fucked multiple times, I have no idea, but arousal immediately flares within me, and I can feel myself becoming slick and swollen in the belt.

He groans against my lips, picking me up and carrying me over to the bed, one arm around my waist, the other holding the back of my neck as I wrap my legs around him for balance. His armor is already flowing back and disappearing into his spine, leaving bare skin behind. He practically rips the flimsy dress I'm wearing off my body, the training belt immediately receding from my pussy, but not from my ass.

I moan as it moves inside my rear channel. Not growing, exactly, and not fucking me, but just rippling inside of me and creating an entirely new sensation that is pure pleasure.

GAVRILL

I TRULY HAD MEANT to let her rest without having her again, but when she called me 'Master' so sweetly, especially after my jealousy had been roused, my cock and *seela* had immediately come to life. I wanted—needed—to possess her again. To truly master her.

My Tribute whimpers beneath me as I manipulate the belt's invasion of her rear entrance, approximating the movements of my cockhead inside of her tight ass. Grasping her wrists, I take them both in one hand and hold them down above her head as I cup one of her ample breasts with the other. The soft flesh is pleasing in my grip, and I lower my mouth to her nipple as my cock dips between the lips of her pussy.

"Oh...oh please..." she moans, arching slightly as I begin to push inside of her. "Too full... please, Gavrill... Master... I'm too full..."

I should punish her for calling me by my name, but I find I like to hear it on her lips. Immediately, I make the decision that as long as she addresses me properly in public, I will not punish her for what she calls me privately, in the throes of passion.

Ignoring her plea, knowing she can take it, I feel the wet clasp of her heat and the ripples of the belt through the thin lining between her channels as I push deeper. Laving her nipple with my tongue, I gently nip at the tender bud, making her clench around me as I suck it deeper into my mouth. She writhes, her arms pressing upwards against my hand as though she is trying to break free, but to no avail.

Next time I take her, I will use bindings to secure her to the bed, so I may have my hands free to do what I wish, but right now I am too impatient to be inside of her again. I hold her down with my own weight as I begin to thrust, groaning with pleasure around my mouthful of breast flesh as the muscles of her pussy ripple around me.

My *seela* stroke her pussy lips and clit, my body having already learned the way she likes it the best. Being inside of her again gives me a relief that is almost indescribable; the closest I can come to it is saying that it feels like coming home. She strains beneath me, arching, as I pump in and out of her, manipulating the training belt so that it begins to grow and recede inside of her. While it cannot thrust, it is the closest I can come to approximating fucking her ass with it.

The sensations of it moving alongside my own shaft are incredible. The feel of her beneath me, around me, the scent of her filling my nose... it is everything I want, everything I need, and I become lost in her.

~

Dawn

THIS TIME I'm sure I'm really going to die from an overload of sexual pleasure. I am completely dominated by him, totally overwhelmed by what he's doing to me.

I can't even protest as I sob in growing ecstasy.

I'm so full, so sensitized. Every single one of my nerve endings has turned into a receptacle for pleasure. The movement in my ass matches his thrusts into my pussy, creating perverse and satisfying sensations that drives my rapture higher. My clit is begging for mercy even as it swells under the attentions of his *seela*. Thankfully, whatever soreness I had felt when I first woke up had dissipated while I'd been eating, and my body is ready to receive him again.

Even if it hadn't been, I'm not sure he'd be able to stop.

His thrusts are relentless, his hands and lips possessive, as if he's drinking me in, as if he can't get enough of me. I know how it feels, because I feel the same. My legs spread wider, my hips tilting up to receive his thrusts, my body greedy to feel him as deep inside of me as I can, to be even fuller although I already feel as though I'm about to burst.

When the belt begins to vibrate inside of me, I scream as sheer erotic ecstasy rips through me, untamed and unyielding even as it overloads my entire nervous system. The waves of rapture sweep over me, curling my toes, my legs, and arching my back against Gavrill's rough thrusts, each one sending me higher and higher on planes of pleasure. The vibrations shake the very core of my existence, and my entire universe narrows to just the two of us.

There's a moment where I can feel his pleasure, his need, his loneliness and his possessive joy at having me...

My climax hits another intense wave, and I feel his body latch onto mine, his tentacles sucking at my pussy lips as he swells inside of me, throbbing as his seed spills into me. I'm blinded by the white-hot ecstasy, the sensation of being *one* with him in every way, and even as I writhe in orgasmic euphoria, the dark of unconsciousness begins to drag me under, saving me from the intensity of the physical and emotional frenzy I'm experiencing.

GAVRILL

I AM WRAPPED around my Tribute, her exhausted body tucked against mine, when my com beeps. I have been awake for a while but loathe to move when I am so comfortable with her warm, soft body cuddled so close. Tsenturions seems to require less sleep than humans—or perhaps I am just more used to large amounts of vigorous physical activity.

The message is from Medik, who wishes to speak with me about my Tribute and the Tribute program in general. I am not opposed. Back on Tsentur, warriors transitioning to their civilian phase of life would often have a mentor to help them through the process. Although I am not transitioning, and my Tribute is not a Tsenturion bride, I do have a few questions for a male who has been mated before. I would also like him to examine her and reassure myself that her exhaustion is normal and she remains healthy.

As I am composing my own message back, another one arrives.

Bogdan, with the same desire as Medik. Although I doubt his thoughts on the program align with Medik's.

I respond to both of them—we will dine all together before my next shift. It will be interesting to see Medik and Bogdan's opposing arguments, and I will be able to stay well out of it while sifting through their points and thinking through their merits without having to take either side. When we have the time to plan our military excursions, I have found such tactics to be a useful tool in making my decisions.

Fortunately, there are several hours before I need to meet with them.

Laying here with my Tribute is not the most productive use of my time, but my motivation to do anything else is very low. I cannot think of anything else that *requires* my attention. There is no shame or wrong in focusing on her during these moments when I am not on duty. Perhaps doing so will aid in focusing on my mission when I am on the bridge.

Once I am used to having a Tribute, she will no longer be so distracting.

8

———————

D^{awn}

"FOR OUR NEXT MEAL, we dine with company. I trust you will behave."

As he instructs me, Gavrill runs his large hands over my naked body. I can't keep from shivering with pleasure at his touch. The trainer hums between my legs, and I moan. I can't believe I'm still horny.

I should be sore. Chafing even.

But instead he woke me up with soft caresses and the belt vibrating against my clit and inside me, and I'm squirming on my back. I also woke up with my hands bound to the headboard of the bed, leaving me completely vulnerable to whatever he wants to do. Apparently, what he wants to do is torment me by touching every part of my body but not actually bringing me to satisfaction. The fact that his armor is on, concealing his bare skin, makes me wonder if he's going to fuck me or just drive me mad with need.

"Yes, Master," I answer dutifully. I struggle to think rationally as

Gavrill's hands continue to roam. I force myself to focus. "Who will join us?"

"My second, Bogdan, for one."

Great. The glowering warrior from the bridge. Sounds like fun.

Gavrill must have picked up on my dismay, for he adds smoothly, "Do not worry, Dawn. Obey me, and I won't let any warrior speak against you."

"Thank you, Master. I will be good," I whisper, a very Tribute-like answer. There's a part of me that is insisting I'm just playing the part I need to in order to survive—preferably survive without more spankings—but deep down I know that I also don't want to jeopardize his standing with his men, and I want him to be proud of me, as Stockholm-Syndrome-y as that sounds.

"If you are, then you will be rewarded," he says smoothly, his hands sliding over my stomach. My muscles quiver beneath his palm, making me whimper. It doesn't tickle exactly, but it's close. "Bogdan may try to antagonize you. It is his nature. Follow protocol, and even he won't be able to speak against you."

"Follow protocol." I sigh. For all my determination to play the good little Tribute, even I know I haven't been great at that. Tsenturion protocol, as explained by Frllil, is ridiculously strict. My understanding is that it's not meant to be followed *all* the time, but apparently in my case... "In other words, be quiet and obedient like a good little trophy wife."

His big hands pause. "What is a trophy wife?"

"Similar to a Tribute," I say quickly, not wanting to explain in any detail. They are close enough after all, but as Gavrill and the others seem to revere the idea of Tributes—even if I'm being treated more like a pet than a human being—I don't want him to think I'm disparaging Tributes. I doubt that would go over well.

Accepting my explanation, his hands begin to move again, stroking the sides of my breasts as he explains.

"During our meal, you will be required to be obedient, yes. Silent, no. Our second guest wishes to engage you in conversation. Medik is the most well-versed among us when it comes to mating and bonding. He had a family and a mate before the Great Attack. On his advice, I instructed the Jabol to search the universe for suitable brides."

So I have the doctor to thank for my abduction.

Despite the arousal humming through my body, my anger stirs.

Gavrill places a finger at my lips as if to wipe away my frown. "You will treat him with respect. Medik is my oldest and closest friend, as well as a mentor."

"Is Medik his real name?" I ask. "My translator makes it sound like 'doctor', and it seems like that's the position he fills for you…"

"He is our physician, and his name *is* his title. We all called him that while he was on duty, and his true name was lost with our world. He does not wish to be called by it." His eyes unfocus, as if he's thinking hard about something. "I do not even remember what it was."

I barely keep from shaking my head. The closest thing to a friend Gavrill has in the known universe, and Gavrill doesn't even know his real name. If that doesn't warn a girl off from getting emotionally attached to him, I don't know what would. Unfortunately, I'm not sure it will be that easy.

I don't *want* to like him, but I do.

Not just because he seems intent on pleasuring me into the stratosphere either. Yes, he's spanked me, put me on a leash, and treated me like a pet… but he's also obviously a good leader, he can be exceedingly gentle, he looks at me with something like reverence, and he's incredibly straightforward. I'm not sure Tsenturions even know how to lie. From everything I've seen, they're all completely sincere in everything they say and do.

There is definitely something appealing about all of that.

No guesswork, no games.

Which means it's very clear right now that Gavrill is enjoying tormenting me for his own amusement.

"Mealtime approaches. Soon it will be time to make ready." His hands fit over my hips and the trainer recedes, baring my pussy. My ass, on the other hand, is still full, and I can feel the thin strip of it leading down between my cheeks from the belt part. Instantly my body seizes, my pussy creaming even more than it had for the belt in anticipation of him taking me again.

"Are you primed for me?" Gavrill murmurs. One hand strokes my labia, while the other covers my right breast. Since he's been touching me everywhere *but* those places for what felt like hours, the sensations feel doubly intense and I arch against his fingers. They slip inside my pussy, testing my wetness and probing just inside my lips.

"Yes..."

"Yes, what?"

"Yes... Master." My breath comes in little pants. Sensual need ripples through me, pulsing at my nipples and between my legs.

"I don't know." If I didn't know any better, I'd say he was teasing me right now. But he's too stoic for that... isn't he? "Perhaps I should leave you primed and waiting until tonight."

I whimper as he pinches my nipple, the hot sting of pleasure zinging straight down to my pussy and making me clench around his fingers as they slide deeper inside of me. The idea of him leaving me on edge like this makes me feel manic. I know I've gone through worse, while Frllil was priming me for him, but right now that doesn't matter... I want my orgasm, and I want it *now*.

"If you let me come now, I won't be distracted during the meal," I point out. As aroused as I am, it's amazing that I can form a logical argument.

"Or you'll be focused entirely on me, waiting for the command that allows you to cum."

I flush at the idea of being brought to orgasm in front of an audience, unsure of whether I'm more horrified or just more aroused. I don't really want to find out. "You don't want me to... perform for them, do you?"

His reaction shocks me. At first, I think I must be imagining that I can actually feel what he's feeling, but the darkening of his suit and the way his jaw clenches makes me wonder if I'm right... if I can actually feel the violent possessiveness gripping him. I gasp as my skin prickles almost painfully, as if reacting to the strange surge of outside emotion.

"You will never perform for them." His dark eyes spear me, his hand tightening on my breast, fingers thrusting deeply into me. I gasp, arching, my wrists tugging against the restraints at the pleasurable and painful sensations tingling along my nerves, and it's only getting stronger as he speaks. "Do not speak of it again. Do not even think it."

"Master," I gasp as the buzzing energy along my skin grows. I feel like I've been Tasered or struck by lightning. If every hair on my head isn't standing up, I'd be very surprised. It *hurts.* "I meant nothing wrong. Please—"

The electric current dies away. Gavrill pauses, steadying me as I choke on air. The possessiveness gripping me, making my skin too tight, relaxes, and I slump, gasping for breath. The hand on my breast has relaxed, and his fingers slide out of me, no longer trying to punish me with rough thrusts.

"Forgive me," he says, and I jerk in surprise. An apology was the last thing I'd expect from my stern master. Judging by the dismayed look on his face, his behavior has shocked him, too. "I did not mean to upset you. It has been a long time since I possessed anything so rare and treasured. I do not wish to share."

Jealous. I'd asked if he wanted me to perform sexually for his friends, and his response was a jealousy so intense, it nearly choked me. Although he didn't seem to realize what had been happening to me. Had I felt his emotions? Or had what I thought were his emotions actually just been him manipulating the training belt? Could it do that to me?

He runs his hands over me, stroking what now feels like raw skin.

I whimper again, and he hushes me, his voice and hands soothing.

"You are *my* little Tribute. You belong to *me* and me alone." His armor recedes as he shifts above me, spreading my legs with his palms. The electric current left me both sensitive and wanting more. Being bound before him only makes me wish I could touch him, and yet it arouses me that I literally can't. His cock brushes over my clit, moving toward my entrance, and I moan. "Shhh. I am your master. I will take care of you and give you pleasure, and you will want for nothing."

I cry out as he thrusts inside of me, my hips rising off the bed, silently begging for more.

~

GAVRILL

I AM out of control again, but I do not care.

The idea of my Tribute showing this side of herself to others... of them hearing her soft moans, seeing the way she throws her head back in ecstasy, has inflamed me with passion, possession, and anger. For the first time, I understand the Tsenturion impulse to mark our mates, so that all may see who she belongs to. I almost wish it were possible to do so with a human, even though everyone already knows she is mine.

It is an illogical desire.

But that does not matter to me in this moment.

Growling, I fuck her harder, feeling her hot wetness clasp me tightly as she writhes beneath me. Having her hands bound is just as enjoyable as I'd imagined it would be. While I am not averse to being touched by her, having her so helpless is exhilarating.

I can feel the head of my cock flaring inside of her, stroking her walls, and my *seela* writhe. The lips of her pussy have little marks all over them from how often I've climaxed inside of her, my body attempting to fully bond with hers. Sliding my arms under her legs, I spread her wide so that I may watch my cock sliding in and out of the plump lips of her pussy. All the little marks I have left on her there fill me with a sense of supreme satisfaction, as well as a desire to leave more on the rest of her.

Leaning forward, I practically bend her in half, pounding into her as I bite down on her shoulder. Not hard enough to draw blood, but hard enough to make her gasp. I suck, pulling at her flesh, the same way my *seela* pull at the lips of her pussy when I climax. I can taste her skin on my tongue as I suck. The manuals said that doing so would leave a mark.

It is not the mark of a Tsenturion, but it will be *my* mark on her.

"Please... oh please... Master..." Her body tries to move against mine, despite the restraints on her wrists, and I can feel her muscles beginning to flutter around my cock as her climax approaches.

I release the mouthful of her shoulder, seeing the dark red blotch that I've left on her skin with a sense of keen relish.

"Come for me," I say, demanding more than giving her permission. "Come on my cock, Dawn."

Her name slips out, unintentionally. It sounds odd and feels odd on my tongue but also seems very right. In the manuals, during the penultimate moment, the master would often use his female's name. Especially when ordering her to come for him.

The high cry she utters as her body clamps down around me is everything I want to hear. She is coming apart beneath me as I move harder, faster, my body urging me to fill her, claim her, *own* her.

Mine... she is mine... all mine.

My *seela* latch on to her pussy, my cock swelling against her clenching walls as the head goes rigid. I let loose my own deep groan of intense ecstasy as I begin to throb, my seed spilling into her, filling her. She pulses around me, pulling at my cock, like her body is hungry for whatever I can give her. I hunch over her, panting as each spasm of her body causes me to jerk against her, my *prime seela* pulling at her clit and catching us in a circle of passion which feeds off each other's reactions.

By the time I am spent, my Tribute is drowsy again with pleasure, whimpering slightly as I gently dislodge myself from her body. Her pussy lips are freshly plumped, the marks from my *seela* standing out against the paleness of her thighs, but not as much as the deep red mark my mouth has left on her shoulder. I look at it, both pleased and yet... unsatisfied. Something about it is not enough, though I know more is not possible.

As I am contemplating how to satisfy myself—perhaps by making it larger?—my com beeps and I realize we are late for our meal. Bogdan is hailing me, obviously annoyed at the delay.

Immediately, I instruct the training belt to cover her again, obscuring the delightful sight of her pussy. I wish it had enough tech to cover her body fully, but such a need had not been anticipated.

At least more opaque dresses had been delivered to the room earlier, while she was still slumbering.

"Come, my Tribute," I say, getting up and going to fetch one of them. The red one, I decide, to match the mark on her shoulder even though it will be hidden beneath the fabric of the garment. "We must hurry, we are late for our meal."

Medik will not mind, but Bogdan is liable to be more surly for it.

I am also unsettled. Tardiness is not something I tolerate in myself or in anyone else. What disturbs me the most is my annoyance at being interrupted from being able to cuddle my Tribute. It is not the reaction I would have expected myself to have.

But this is just a meal, not a duty, I remind myself. I would be more upset at becoming so distracted and less annoyed about the interruption if I were tardy to the bridge again.

Then again, before meeting my Tribute, I would have thought that about being tardy to anything.

An unsettled feeling trickles through me as I watch my Tribute pull on the red dress. I am changing, and I am not sure what to think of it.

~

Dawn

· · ·

Gavrill is silent as he swiftly leads me to the room where we'll be eating. It's not the cafeteria, it's a smaller room near the cafeteria. A meeting room? An officer's mess? I'm not sure.

Both of the other Tsenturions are there waiting when we enter, both standing rather than sitting. Actually, it kind of looks like they were arguing, both of them stepping away from each other as we come in.

After what Gavrill told me about Medik, I'm not sure how to greet him. While I want to be angry that he is responsible for the Tsenturions requesting the Jabol find them mates, it's not like it was something that was personally done against me. Plus, Gavrill describing him as his 'oldest and closest' friend instinctively makes me want to make a good impression on him. So when Gavrill leads me to be introduced to him first, I flush and bend my knees in a small curtsey as Gavrill proudly claims me as his Tribute... and then immediately feel stupid as all three of the males look at me with confusion at my genuflection. But the old alien's eyes are kind.

"Tribute," he greets me in a deep, slightly reedy voice. "I have waited a long time to greet you. On behalf of myself and the remnant of the Tsenturion race: welcome." Placing a hand on his chest, he bows his head to me. It's not quite the same as the salute the warriors give to Gavrill, but it still feels ceremonial. Tongue-tied, I jerk my head up and down and half-curtsey again before I realize what I'm doing.

I look helplessly up at Gavrill, who didn't prepare me for anything like this. Neither did Frllil for that matter. Nope, Frllil was all "keep quiet, be submissive, please the Commander", and Gavrill was all "sex, sex, sex." No one told me what good manners for communicating with a Tsenturion who actually wanted to *talk* to me would be. Gavrill just looks back at me, expressionless. I have no idea what he's thinking.

Behind him, Bogdan snorts in derision. Yeah, no guesses as to what *he's* thinking. The dark-suited warrior salutes to Gavrill and completely ignores me, marching past me to his seat at the large table. At least he didn't say anything rude aloud. He's still a jerk though. I bite my tongue to keep from sticking it out at him.

As I look back at Medik, the Tsenturion gives me a slight smile that crinkles the corners of his eyes. He's like the Tsenturion version of a grandfather, and the small moment between us makes me feel better.

"Please, sit, Medik." Gavrill rests his large hands on my shoulders, steering me towards the table; the firm weight of his touch settles me. "You do us honor to join us at our table."

"A celebration is in order, is it not?" The doctor straightens as much as his stooped shoulders will allow. His movements are a tad stiff and slow, compared to the warriors' stride. He must be much older.

The table is shaped like a triangle. Bogdan stands on one side, the doctor takes another. That leaves one side for both me and Gavrill. My face heats as I realize I might be delegated to a cushion on the floor. So much for proving I'm a sentient being. I grind my teeth, determined not to say anything. While Gavrill got pretty possessive about having me do anything sexual in front of his friends, I don't know whether or not that will extend to being spanked as well.

He'd already demonstrated that he's perfectly willing to punish me while there's an audience.

I stumble a little as Gavrill maneuvers me into position. There's no cushion, but there's only one seat. The High Commander sits and pats his knee. Cheeks pulsing hot with embarrassment, I twitch to the side and perch gingerly on his lap. At least I don't have to sit on the floor.

Spots on the table glow, and platters of food appear. A whole smorgasbord of completely weird looking dishes, only a few of which look familiar from what the warriors in the cafeteria had shown me. I want to reach for the delicious korrun fruit, but Gavrill pulls a different dish towards us—several multi-colored mounds with the consistency of ice cream, if ice cream came glowing in jewel tones. The doctor peers at me from around what looks like a stack of green sea crab legs with red thorns.

"I consulted the Jabol for food of your people," Medik says. "The nanos changed your system to accept nutrition from our foods, but food is more than nutrition, wouldn't you agree? "

I nod and gulp. If I'd really thought about it, I should've prepared myself for a feast of strange dishes. I'd already learned in the cafeteria that Frllil hadn't exactly shown me all the things the Tsenturions eat.

The plate in front of Bogdan holds what looks like a hunk of charred meat. A long claw-like razor extends from the warrior's suit, and he uses it to hack into his meal. Purple goo oozes out from the blackened carcass. That is definitely not something I've seen before. I close my eyes for a moment and tell my panicking stomach to calm down. I don't have to eat that.

9

————

G avrill

I CAN FEEL my Tribute's tension as she examines the food in front of us. The memory of seeing her in the dining hall with my warriors rises in my mind, and I immediately want to be the one to introduce her to new things as well. I pick up one of the severill balls, sure that I had not seen one of them when she was trying new foods earlier.

As I move to hold it for her to eat, she begins to reach for it with her hands and I making a chiding noise. I will provide her with what she needs. Catching my eye, she quickly lowers her hands to her lap and obediently opens her lips, pleasing me. Even the act of feeding her arouses me, despite my recent release. Everything she does arouses me.

The expression on her face as she tastes the sweet and sour flavor makes it appear as though she is unsure whether or not she likes it. Certainly, she'd enjoyed the korrun fruit much more, but I want to show her things she didn't taste for the others.

"Perhaps in time we can teach you how to use the replicator," Medik says to her, obviously also watching her eat. I do not mind, as he has a vested interest in her health.

Bogdan mutters something about 'wasting time catering to the weak,' but Medik ignores him. I shoot Bogdan a dark look, which he avoids, although he re-focuses his attention on his own meal, obviously aware that he has sparked my displeasure. It is also unlike him to be so derogatory towards those weaker than us. Tsenturion warriors are built to be protectors, and there is nothing dishonorable in not being a warrior. Perhaps my tardiness for the meal has stoked his ire even more than I thought.

"It will ease her transition if she can surround herself with familiar things. And we will make use of the settings again and again, with each new Tribute." The doctor takes one of the thorny vines and starts to peel it. "That is, if you deem the program a success and decide to continue it."

"Yes," I say immediately, tightening my grip on my own Tribute. I may have just acquired her the previous cycle, but our compatibility has already been demonstrated. Whether or not we will be capable of procreating has not yet been proven, but I trust the Jabol's assessment, and I will not deny my warriors the comforts and relief of Tributes of their own just to wait for it to actually happen.

"Wait!" My own Tribute sits up straight in my lap, interrupting. I frown—not because I am displeased, but because I feel her distress and I don't understand it. "You don't mean you want to bring *more* women here?" She sounds appalled, and I do not know how to answer. Surely, our aim was obvious.

"The survival of our race depends on it," Medik says quietly.

"No." She turns on my lap, her distress growing with every word. I should punish her for being so outspoken—though I had told her she did not need to be quiet, she is verging on disrespect—but the strong swell of her emotion is affecting me, and I do not know how to react. "You can't do this. The women you'll take--they'll have lives, maybe even *families*..."

"Commander, if I may speak," Bogdan puts in, but my Tribute

talks right over him, not even glancing at him. I do not look at him either, I am studying her face. Her blue eyes are filling with tears, her cheeks flushed with the strength of her upset.

"You can't just rip women from their lives and expect them to settle down with a Tsenturion. I don't care how many orgasms you give her, she will never forgive you."

"Did you have a family, Dawn?" the doctor asks in his quiet voice. The question jerks both of our attention to him. I already know the answer, and I know he does as well, but he is trying to make a point. I decide to let him take the lead, although I am not sure where he is going with this yet, but our aims are the same.

"No. I mean, I did, but they died when I was younger." She twists back to me, her blue eyes large and imploring. Strangely, I feel her plea tugging at me, even though I know what my answer must be. "*I didn't have anyone, but the next woman might. You might take her from her children—*"

"What if we take women who do not have ties to Earth?" Medik interrupts. "The program is designed to lure unattached females." It was done so on purpose. Tsenturions do not want females who already have mates or children.

"How is that possible?" She throws up her hands. "If they're from Earth, they'll have ties."

"Did you have ties?" Medik presses. He's not upset or trying to be cruel. His face is patient, even a little sad. I feel the same melancholy. Even Bogdan has become more subdued, unwilling to interrupt. While he might not want more Tributes from Earth either, the subject is bringing up the stark loneliness we endure. He has stopped eating, his gaze turned towards the windows and the emptiness out there.

No Tsenturion has ties to a planet or a family anymore. Those of us who are left are each other's family, but it is not the same. We would never deprive someone not an enemy of the same by choice.

Dawn

"It was different for me," I tell Medik. "I was more alone than most people."

It's true. The revelation had hurt when Frllil pointed it out to me, but it doesn't anymore. If anything, I feel relieved that there's no one on Earth who would miss me. I didn't have regular friends or ties to anyone. Funny how it took being sucked into another galaxy where I'm the only human for me to realize how alone I'd been.

But it's better this way, because while I'm determined to get home eventually, I'm also pragmatic enough to realize that might not actually be possible. I'd rather no one be desperately searching for me, without answers. People go missing all the time, and it leaves devastation in their wake; at least my disappearance won't do that to anyone. I wouldn't call myself resigned to my fate, but I recognize this might be it for me.

At the very least, I have to keep this from happening to anyone else.

"I was alone," I repeat, a little desperately. "But with the next woman, that might not be the case. You can't keep doing this."

"We have no choice, Dawn," the doctor says, his voice tired and heavy. Gavrill's hand suddenly rests on the back of my neck, over the collar, in an almost comforting gesture. I can feel tears welling as I realize they're in earnest. "We have been alone too long. The warriors almost don't remember what it is like to be around a female. Now that you are here, they remember. They have begun to desire a mate, and, for the first time in countless cycles, they have hope. We cannot stop the program now."

A weighty silence fills the room, and I can almost feel the sadness hanging heavy in the air. Even Bogdan is affected, although his gaze cut to the doctor when he said they could not stop the program now. All of their armor shimmers silvery grey, and I swear, I can feel Gavrill's emotions again. That or the nanotech is somehow tuning me in to his feelings.

He's sad, but it goes beyond that. A deep grief that feels old—memories of his lost loved ones? And something fresher, more familiar, a pain that mingles with his own regret. The regret is his, but the pain feels like mine. An echo of my own feelings. I turn to stare at the hard angles of his face without seeing him. Am I feeling what he's feeling? And if I am—is he empathizing with me?

"Commander," Bogdan cuts in as Gavrill and I look at each other. "If I may. I object to the program."

Well. Never thought I'd agree with Tall, Dark, and Moody. Silently, I turn to look at him as Gavrill changes his focus to his second-in-command. The sad grey is gone from his armor already, and it has darkened to a more neutral gray. How I can tell the difference, I don't know, but I feel sure of it.

"I am aware," Gavrill answers him, his voice serious. "But having heard Medik's conclusion, what is your argument?"

"These Tributes are not necessary to our mission." Bogdan waves a hand in my direction. It wouldn't look so menacing if the claw he used to cut his food wasn't still sticking out of his suit arm. Red streaks momentarily through his armor. "They are a distraction. They will not aid us in our objective."

"And what is our objective?" Medik asks, turning to face Bogdan and raising his eyebrows. I'm reminded of a teacher, facing off with an unruly student.

Bogdan's large hands clench into fists, his dark eyes fierce. "To destroy our enemy."

"And then what?" Medik asks. "What do we do once the enemy is gone? Continue on our mission to protect the Jabol? What about our species? The needs of the warriors for life outside of revenge? For deca-cycles we have lived as warriors, protecting the weak and bringing order to the galaxy. But when is it their turn to have a life? A family?"

Bogdan's suit is so black, it seems to suck light into its obsidian depths. "Commander, we do not require—"

"I disagree," Gavrill says, his fingers stroking the back of my neck.

"The warriors are fascinated by my Tribute. Many of them already want their own now that we know it is possible. We've gone too long as warriors focused on one objective. Many of the warriors are tired. Our memories are long, but revenge cannot sustain us forever. We need something to fight *for*, and I believe the Tributes will provide that."

"And when they don't want to fight at all?" Bogdan asks, growling his response as his eyes flash. "We retired our warriors when it was time for them to mate for a reason. One cannot be both a warrior and a mate."

"That has been true in the past," Medik acknowledges. "But our circumstances have changed. We no longer have the luxury of separating our lives the way we did before."

"But—"

"I agree with Medik," Gavrill says, interrupting whatever argument Bogdan was about to make.

Bogdan's boots thump the floor as he rises. Red slashes skitter like lightning across his armor. "If it's already decided, then I see no point to my presence here."

I sit quietly on Gavrill's lap as Bogdan storms out of the room, obviously irate at Gavrill's decision. It sucks because I want the same thing as him, although for a very different reason. On the other hand, I can see what Medik and Gavrill are saying. What was that old *Star Trek* saying? Something about the good of the many coming before the good of the one or something.

They are willing to sacrifice the lives of a few human women for the good of their entire people. It's really more than a few, but Frllil had told me there were only several hundred Tsenturions left now. Compared to the number of women on Earth, that's a drop in the bucket. And without them, the Tsenturions will become extinct.

There is no right answer, and it makes my heart hurt.

"Give him time. He'll come around." The doctor helps himself to a piece of the blackened meat on Bogdan's abandoned plate. The purple goo has hardened and turned... orange. Eww. "He feels things more deeply than most. So he likes to pretend he cannot feel anything at all."

"Perhaps," Gavrill murmurs. He picks up another disc thingy to feed me, but I push it away. Still unsettled about the feelings I'm feeling—my own amplified and mirrored back to me—I shake my head. Nausea rises up in the back of my throat. Even though I know it's hopeless, even though I understand their reasons why, I have to ask again.

At least I know what happened to all of my relatives when they left me. I can't imagine how awful it would be to have someone I love disappear and not know what happened to them... to *never* know. And for that person to be clear across the universe, wondering what their loved ones back home are thinking, what they're doing...

The Jabol got it right with me, but who says they'll get it right every time? Even one mistake would be too many.

"Promise me you won't continue the program." I blink back tears, placing my hands on his chest and looking into his eyes, pleading with my own. "Promise."

Gavrill's eyes turn black as Bogdan's suit, a deep well I could drown in. Endless, empty space. The emotions I've been feeling swell, like our solitude, our loneliness, is feeding off each other the same way our passion does.

Suddenly, I'm gasping, choking on tears, a deep desolation draining me and leaving me empty... a thousand years of heartache, of isolation, of hopelessness, and I'm drowning in it. The darkness of his eyes expands and swallows me whole, and I'm falling, falling.

Two thoughts rush through me, filling my empty body:

I'm all alone.

And... the barest whisper....

I don't want to be alone anymore.

~

GAVRILL

. . .

As my Tribute passes out in my arms for the second time in two cycles, I am nearly undone. Surely, it is not normal or healthy for her to be unconscious so often. There must be something wrong with her. Although I trust the Jabol, I worry that perhaps they did something to her detriment through ignorance. She is the first human either of our species has seen, after all.

"What's wrong with her?" I ask, trying not to sound as frantic as I feel. Medik is already standing, a frown on his face, as he moves around my side of the table. I push back so that he can examine her with the scanner he always carries. Panic is rising in my chest, making it tighten painfully.

"Patience, Gavrill," he mutters as he holds the scanner up against her and begins to run it from her shoulders down to her hips, checking her vital signs. Calling me by my name rather than my title is a sign that he recognizes my distress, although he is not rude enough to comment on it.

My armor is a burgundy red with shimmering violet overtones, displaying my upset and anxiety for him to see. Medik makes an odd humming noise under his breath as he looks at the scanner's readout.

"What?" I ask.

"Nothing."

"It is not nothing, tell me what's wrong with her," I demand.

Medik glances up at me, his eyes kind. Patient. "I am not trying to hide bad news from you, there is literally nothing wrong with her that I can see. Her body is in perfect working order, other than being unconscious."

As I watch, he moves the scanner up beside her head, and that's when his eyebrows lift.

"There is something wrong with her, isn't there?" Fear grips me, the kind I haven't felt in deca-cycles. "Can it be fixed?" Had going through the wormhole harmed her? Or something the Jabol did? Or, worse, something I had done?

"Nothing permanent," Medik says firmly. He gives me a look, lifting his eyebrow. "This is actually very interesting. These are similar to the kinds of readings I would expect from a Tsenturion female in the process of bonding with her male. I think some of the changes to her brain waves may have overwhelmed her."

I am surprised to feel a pang of disappointment at his description of it being 'similar' to rather than the same. Also, a touch of worry that it would cause her to faint. That didn't happen to Tsenturion females, did it? I realize I do not actually know. I was never interested enough in attending the mating festival to learn the specifics, although I had the general knowledge from watching my parents and other bonded pairs before I had begun my military service.

"That... would a Tsenturion female react to the bonding process the same way?" I ask curiously.

Medik dashes my hopes immediately.

"No," he says, shaking his head and tapping at something on the scanner. "They were Tsenturion after all, their brains would go through a maturing during courtship as the bond grew, but biologically we were all designed for it. Not being Tsenturion, it is not surprising that Dawn would have some different reactions. She seems unharmed, although I'd like to take her to the med bay for closer observation. We can learn a lot about what to expect for the future Tributes from her."

"Of course." Immediately I heft her in my arms, feeling slightly calmer as she sighs and nestles against me even in her unconscious state. I hadn't even realized I'd begun to harbor a faint hope for a full Tsenturion bonding, but it seems unlikely now.

Still, perhaps there will be a facsimile of one, as she is going through a 'similar' process. Whatever she manages, and the influence of the nanotech which has already allowed me to sense much of her physical reactions and interpreted her emotions for me, will have to be enough.

We are nearly to the med bay when my comm hails me. I open the line, already feeling impatient with whoever feels the need to speak to me *now*.

"High Commander?" The uncertain voice of Corin, currently

captaining the ship while Bogdan and I are off duty, fills my ear. I frown, because normally Corin is just as confident as myself or Bogdan, otherwise he would not qualify to sit in the Captain's chair.

"Yes, Corin?" I try to keep my impatience out of my voice.

"Ah, High Commander, I ah... well, third shift has started and..." His voice trails off, uncertain and hesitant, because it is difficult to tell the commander of what is left of the entire Tsenturion race that he is late for his shift.

I close my eyes, torn between my duty and the female in my arms. That I feel so is shocking to me... but I am protective of her. Not only is she mine to care for, but she is so helpless and weak. How could I be anything but protective? I cannot allow that to interfere with my duty, and I know it. The impulse to stay with her makes no sense to me, yet I feel it keenly.

"High Commander? I can call Bogdan to the bridge instead, if—"

"No." I cut Corin off immediately, my voice sharp. The last thing I need is for Bogdan to know that I was late for my duty because of my Tribute. He requires no more ammunition for his arguments against the Tribute program. I will have to be better about demonstrating our ability to balance our lives as warriors with our Tributes. "I will be there momentarily. My apologies for my tardiness."

"Yes, High Commander."

I can practically feel Corin's salute through the com.

Medik raises his eyebrows at me as we turn into the med bay. "Is there a problem?"

"No," I say stubbornly. I will not allow it to be a problem. "But I must go; it is my shift on the bridge and the ship requires its High Commander. Do what you must for her. I will send Arkdhem to escort her when you are finished. We will have to continue our conversation about the program at some other time."

"Very well. Please lay her over here," Medik says, gesturing to one of the empty beds.

Gently, I lay my Tribute down. Her pale face tugs at my heart, and the desire to stay by her side until she opens her beautiful blue eyes again is overwhelming. My feet feel heavy as I turn and head for the door, but I force myself to keep moving anyway, already sending a communication to Arkdhem. It grates that I cannot care for my Tribute myself, but at least I can provide her with a suitable escort—one who will immediately report to me when she awakens.

10

———

D^{awn}

Beep. Beep. Beep. A machine chirps in time to my heartbeat. I open my eyes to a grey-beige blur.

"Be at ease, Tribute."

"Dawn," I mumble. "Please. I am so freaking tired of being called Tribute, like that's all that matters about me." Especially when I'm flat on my back, vulnerable, and aching, I want to hear my name. My real name, spoken by someone who pretends to care.

"Dawn, then," the deep voice repeats, gentle and filled with what sounds like sincere care. My vision clears as I blink back the moisture suddenly threatening my eyes. The Tsenturion doctor hovers over me, his lined face soft with concern. "Stay calm. You are well."

"What happened?"

His lips quirk into a smile. "Actually, I was hoping you could tell me that. As an outside observer, it seemed as though you were talking to the Commander before you rather suddenly passed out. The scanner indicated new brainwaves that I have not recorded from you before, closely matching those of a bonded Tsenturion female, but I need more information before I can say anything definitive."

New brainwaves? That sounds vaguely terrifying. Was my brain actually changing?

Strangely, despite the fact that he's a Tsenturion and I don't really know him, I feel just as comfortable with Medik as I did with any of my doctors back home. I instinctively trust him, too, and I just want him to tell me what was wrong and how to fix it... but what he says makes sense.

I blink as I push myself up to a sitting position. Immediately his hand hovers near me, in case I should need assistance, but I manage to sit up on my own.

"I... I just remember looking into Gavrill's eyes, and they were so dark, and then it felt like I was falling into them. I felt so alone, too, though I was sitting on his lap, I felt overwhelming loneliness and sadness and grief... but it didn't feel like those emotions were really mine, if that makes any sense."

To my shock, a smile blooms across Medik's face, wide and joyful and making him look about ten years younger than the seventy-something human years he currently resembles.

"You felt his emotions!" The excitement in his voice takes me aback slightly. "A side effect of bonding. The bond can act as a mirror between partners. If two partners share the strong emotion, the feeling is amplified between them. This most often manifests itself as passion, but... in this case obviously it was otherwise. You must have accessed the Commander's emotions while you already were experiencing your own influx of feelings. Your body was unable to handle it and shut down. A simple loss of consciousness."

I stare at him, with no idea what to say when he's obviously so excited and I am so confused.

Practically chortling, he turns away, and when he turns back he has a glass of water in his hand. "Here, drink. You will need to keep hydrated, well-fed, and rested. Obviously, the bonding process is harder for a Tsenturion-human pairing than for two Tsenturions."

Obediently, I take the glass and drink as I try to remember the moments before I passed out. What was I feeling? Loneliness. Extreme, soul-crushing loneliness. The sort I never let myself dwell on. On Earth it was easy to pretend I was an introvert or super independent, that I was too busy for more than a quick chat with a student while refilling my water bottle at the yoga studio. I'd told myself I was happy that way.

Out here, in deep, alien space, without a human or anyone I know, I can't hide from the feelings anymore. And when they were amplified by Gavrill and his own deep, untreated angst...I literally had all the feels.

"So basically I fainted." Thanks, nanotech. Not enough that I have to deal with my own emotions, now I might have to deal with someone else's? And exactly how deeply permanent is this bond going to be? "Is this going to be a common occurrence?"

The doctor waves a disc-shaped instrument over my body, hovering a moment over my heart until it gives a satisfied beep. He shrugs. "As your brainwaves seem to have adjusted, I do not think it will happen again, although we must make allowances for your biological differences."

"You mean the fact that I'm a human and not made for bonding."

"Not made for it, perhaps, but obviously it is possible," he says, smiling widely again, obviously overjoyed at the prospect. "If you felt his emotions, then the bonding is already progressing further than I would have guessed."

I fidget. I'm not sure I want to get used to the bond, but honestly, I can already feel something tugging at me, demanding to know where my master is. Even if I don't want to necessarily think of him as my master or my mate. "Where's Gavrill?"

I want to know what he thinks of all these sudden revelations.

"He wanted to be here," Medik says, his voice turning sympathetic. "His presence was required on the bridge, as it is his turn for a shift. Arkdhem is already waiting for you in the next room, and he will escort you to wherever you wish while the High Commander is captaining the ship." With a wave of his hand, Medik summons a floating chair so he can perch close to me. "You are certainly well enough to go, but before you leave, I wished to have some time to speak with you."

I eye him warily, and he makes an amused sound, close to a chuckle. "Nothing invasive, I assure you. I merely wish to see how you're settling in."

"Really?" Despite how nice he's been right now, despite his relationship with Gavrill, I can't help but glare at him. This... male who suggested the Tribute program in the first place. Who is just thrilled that I'm successfully bonding to an alien master I never wanted. Who insists that other women should also be abducted and put into my position. I don't want to be nice. I want to rant. "You want to know how I've been treated? Imagine being transported from your home in the middle of the night. Imagine waking up in a strange place millions of light years away and being told you can never go back. Imagine a big, strong, weird but hot alien doing all sorts of things to you that you'd only read about—only it's twenty times more intense in real life—and he's going to do it over and over again no matter how many times you orgasm or beg him to stop—and worse! He makes you like it..."

I stop to catch my breath. I've been shouting, but the doctor doesn't seem to mind. I've also gotten myself worked up in other ways. My body is primed from just thinking about Gavrill's 'bonding' methods. "And then you're expected to be with him forever, with no say so in your future, and have his babies and wear filmy dresses while he parades you around on a leash and... hell, I don't know. This whole thing is a fantasy gone way, way too far. That you want to bring more women here is just... look, I get it, but this whole situation is fucked up. It might be a good solution on paper, but that doesn't make it any less wrong."

There's silence as the doctor waits to make sure I've finished. Then he nods, sighing. Some of the joy has leaked out of his face, which makes me feel a little better.

"I understand, and I do not disagree with you, but being on the other side of the equation, I do not feel we have a choice. And things are not too bad, are they? You appear to be adjusting admirably. The courting rituals of your people are very close to the rituals of ours, so perhaps that accounts for some of it."

I shake my head, rolling my eyes. "Those books are not our courting rituals."

"But they come from your manuals, and the methods outlined in them seem to be working, though, even better than I thought they would. Gavrill requested them, and I suspect he's been following them to the letter, although I encouraged him to use more... intuitive methods. You must realize, he's been a soldier for deca-cycles. He thrives on rules and regulations, especially during times of crisis. And we have been in a crisis for a long, long time."

"Since your planet was destroyed," I blurt and mentally kick myself at the doctor's wince. His face goes blank in a way that makes me suspect he's hiding great pain.

"Yes," he agrees softly. "The greatest catastrophe any species has borne. You cannot be too hard on him."

"Says you. You're not going to be... biologically bonded to a guy who thinks that spanking is required foreplay!" I blush but forge on. "All these years floating around space, and he never found the time to learn about relationships. He doesn't even know your name!" I throw up my hands. Medik looks on patiently and doesn't correct me. "And when it's time to learn about bonding, he reads BDSM novels as his guide—"

"The Jabol informed me those manuals were widely read. They are popular, no?"

I flush. "Well, yes, but—"

"The Commander wished to integrate your courtship rituals into our own. He was pleased they were so well-structured."

"Look, those books aren't talking about relationships manuals. They're fictional, meant to be read for pleasure, not as guides."

"But surely you want your bonding to include pleasure." Medik looks confused.

Argh, why is this so hard to explain? Maybe Tsenturions don't have a concept of fiction?

"Well, yes, but not like that...I mean, I don't want that sort of pleasure all the time." Great, now I'm blushing and talking about my sex life with a guy who looks like a grandfather, but I started it, so it's hard to complain.

Medik makes a sound I translate as disbelief.

"Well, maybe I do. In the bedroom. But I want him to treat me like a person, not a pet."

Now Medik looks even more confused, his head tilting to the side as he waits for me to continue.

"I mean, you want me to be the savior of your race. The one who starts this whole breeding program. Half the time, Gavrill treats me like a... naughty little girl, and the other half like a thing, a trophy on a shelf or a prized pet he can show off and sit on his lap and feed..."

"You dislike this treatment? Your responses say otherwise." Medik gestures to the machine just as it gives a smug beep. He still appears confused. "Our females have always been pampered and protected. They too enjoyed the courtship rituals."

Crap, I'm making a muddle of this.

"I just want him to treat me like a person. I'm not totally opposed to the... structure. The punishment/reward games. But deep down, I need to know he respects me. Wants me—and not just for my body. For my... for who I am. For me."

"Ah," Medik tilts his head. "You are speaking of bonding."

"Bonding... is that like..." I can't quite bring myself to say "love." I take a deep breath and start over. "You were bonded, right?"

Again, the blank face, shielded against showing pain. "Yes."

I swallow my apology. He shouldn't have abducted me if he didn't want a troublesome Tribute on his hands. "How does it work?"

"Bonding happens in stages."

For the first time, he looks away from me. The expression on his face is a little distant, like he's seeing something that's not there.

"How long were you bonded?" I ask curiously.

"Almost twenty deca-cycles."

I calculate quickly in my head.

"Two hundred years," I whisper in shock.

Medik smiles. A sad smile, his eyes still staring at something that I can't see. "We met at a mating festival, but it took several meetings before I was able to begin the courtship. Once we pledged to each other, the bonding was swift. It was the most glorious experience I will have in this lifetime."

I swallow. "Did she...?"

"She was on planet, along with our offspring."

"I'm sorry."

"It was quick, at least." He passes a hand over his face and murmurs so quietly, I wonder if I'm supposed to hear him. "I only regret I that was not with them."

I sag back on the floating table and cover my own face with my hands. Giving myself and Medik some semblance of privacy. As much as I want to be angry with him, it's really hard. If he were a hardened soldier, or as much of an ass as Gavrill can be sometimes, it would be easier. But he's very open and very patient and kind. He's just trying to do what is best for his people, just as I am for mine. And he's doing it while grieving his family and probably dealing with the biggest case of survivor's guilt in the galaxy.

My emotions are running through me too fast to catch or understand.

I try to break things down logically as I catch my breath. There's been a lot of new information in a very short period of time.

Fact 1: I am an alien captive and will probably be one for the rest of my life.

Fact 2: I belong to the High Commander, and he is doing everything he can to bind me to him. But apparently, the bond goes both ways.

"If Gavrill and I fully bond... there won't be any chance of me going back to Earth, will there?" My voice isn't as bleak as I thought it would be. What's happened has happened, and I can't think of anything I can do to change it. If anything, I'm becoming resigned to that fact.

The look Medik gives me is sympathetic. "A broken bond is more than painful. There would always be something missing, a void that could never be filled. That's if it were physically possible for you to even return. The wormhole the Jabols used is unstable. Just one journey is perilous. I doubt the path can be reversed, but even if you could return that way, you probably would not survive a second trip."

I gape slightly at him. Yeah, I remember how much it hurt to be brought through, but I hadn't imagined it was quite that dangerous—just painful.

"But you will keep bringing women through it?" I ask, and—again—I can hear the resignation in my voice, along with a hefty amount of censure.

"We don't have a choice. We need females to bear offspring, or our race will not survive. You have made good points though. I will speak to the Jabols and make sure the screening process selects women who don't have any strong ties to Earth. Who display fortitude as well as an interest in the Tsenturion way of life and indicate a willingness to live the life they read of."

"You're basing all of this off a few stories on an e-reader." I face palm, because seriously, what else is there to do? "It's not a foolproof process."

"The Jabols studied your race from afar. They determined the most effective way of communication is through story. They also experimented with sound waves and frequencies, but felt the messages weren't clearly received."

"Wait, what? Sound waves? What kind of sound waves?"

"A form of entertainment that your species uses. I believe they called the experiment 'electropop'."

"Oh my god." I wrack my brain for everything I know about the 80s music style that involves synthesizers. "You mean the members of Daft Punk are really aliens?"

"They received the first messages, yes. The program was changed when the Jabols found the transmissions were better received when translated by female humans. Two messengers became very popular. One was called 'Madonna', and the other was referred to as 'Lady Gaga'."

"No way. Madonna and Lady Gaga's music was inspired by alien transmissions?" I think about it for all of a second before nodding. "That explains a lot."

We look at each other, and I finish off the water in my glass, trying to think of something else to say. I can't think of anything though. Medik still has something left that he wants to address though.

"I take it your worry about the Tribute program is for future Tributes and their ability to assimilate their duties. But what about you, Dawn? Do you think you could be happy as a Tribute?"

I blink at the kindly old alien. He's basically said out loud what I've been afraid to admit. I'm not totally hating my experience as a captive alien bride. There's been lots of kinky punishments and erotic pain, yes, but Gavrill hasn't really hurt me. The sex is fantastic. The male is... well, if I'd met him on Earth, I might have found him stodgy and bossy, but there's also a lot to like about him. And part of me even likes the stodgy, bossy parts.

Not that I'm actually falling for him. No way. But the reassurance that my alien master will care for me, keep me safe, and treat me well is important. It's simple self-preservation.

Even if it feels like more.

"Tell me this. Do you think he'll ever..." I choke on the word, "c-care for me? Not as a Tribute or for what I represent, but for me, as an equal? The way he would for a Tsenturion woman he bonded with?"

"I think, from what I've learned today, that you two have a chance of completing a full bond, in the Tsenturion manner. Emotionally as well as biologically. And once the bond is complete, yes, he will care for you, although I cannot say that his treatment of you will drastically change." The doctor watches me carefully. "Is this what you wish? That he care for you?"

"Yes." As I say the word, I realize that yes, that's exactly what I want. Not just to make the best of this situation, but also because I actually am coming to care for him. Sure, there's some part of me that cynically thinks my brain chemistry has been all messed up by everything since I barely know him... but at the same time, I feel a stronger attachment to him than I ever have to anyone on Earth.

Maybe that's what the bond is, a way to join two beings together in a much faster manner than we do it on Earth. That's certainly how it sounded to me when Frllil explained it during my training. Like soulmates. I'd been skeptical at the time, but now I can't deny that I feel a physical and emotional yearning for the High Commander. I can't think of another way to explain the depth and strength of that yearning after so short a period of time.

I want the bond. I want him to care for me. Because I want him to feel the same things I am. And maybe once the bond is formed, I'll have more influence on him. Medik already seems open to being more selective about choosing Tribute candidates. Since I'm already stuck here, I just have to do what I can.

I lick my lips. "What can I do to, um, facilitate the bond forming?"

"Exactly what you have been," Medik says, smiling almost like a proud father. "The bond usually manifests physically at first. From the amount of time you've spent in his cabin, I would say you're well on your way there. Our courtship rituals truly are not so different; the more possessive and protective he feels over you, the deeper all of his emotions become. I have read your manuals. Submitting to him in the manner of your people is close enough to Tsenturion courtship rituals, but do not make it too easy on him. Not that I can see that happening."

So there's some hope. We could have a full bond. He might come to care for me, even love me in the Tsenturion way... but it sounds like the courtship has to be more than just hot sex, even if that's where it begins. Somehow, I have to teach a big, dominant alien who is over a thousand years old and has never had a real relationship, to emote. No biggie.

I take a deep breath, clenching my fists together in determination, and I nod. "Okay. I can do this."

Medik looks at me, his eyes filled with so much hope, it's almost painful, because it's not just hope for me—it's hope for the future of his entire people. "If anyone can teach him how to bond, Dawn, it's you."

11

———

G^{avrill}

ARRIVING ON THE BRIDGE, I relieve Corin of duty, extremely thankful that Bogdan is not on duty and hopefully knows nothing of my lateness. If I am truly lucky, he will never learn of it. My second is the only one capable of reprimanding me, and he would be correct to do so.

Fortunately, Corin does not know why I am late and—unlike Bogdan—does not demand an explanation. In many ways, Bogdan is more like a sibling to me than an underling; other than my Tribute, there are none other in our fleet who would challenge me the way he does. I doubt he would appreciate the comparison, although my Tribute might.

Dawn.

Her name echoes through my mind even as I read through Corin's shift log.

Medik used her name. So did Arkdhem. I used it when I was pleasuring her... perhaps I should do so more often. She did ask it of me in the beginning, I remember. While her name does not give me the same visceral satisfaction as calling her *my Tribute*, there is something intimate about it.

My Dawn.

I will think on it.

But for now... I force myself to focus on the readout Corin left behind. It doesn't make any sense.

Frowning, I look up at Corin, who has been standing off to the side waiting for me to read his log, rather than quitting the bridge. Obviously, he anticipated I would want to speak of the strange events he reported. I could feel the crew glancing at us from the corners of their eyes, probably waiting for my reaction. They've been on duty for a while, although not as long as Corin—it would not do to have the entire bridge crew changing shift all at the same time—so they are well aware of the anomalies as well.

"They aren't attacking at all?" I ask, completely baffled by this change in Vgotha tactics.

They have never had compunction in the past about attacking when they know they have a chance of winning. The only reason the ship we'd been pursuing had fled without a fight had been because it was outgunned and engaging with us would have been a suicide mission. What I was seeing here was completely different. One of the scouts reported that he practically ran into one of their advance guard—which meant that he was hopelessly outclassed and should be dead. Instead, he'd been allowed to slip away. The tone of his report sounded as confused as I felt.

"No, High Commander," Corin says, shaking his head. "All the reports are the same. The scouts have become more and more reckless, almost as if they're daring the Vgothas to come after them and yet... nothing other than sightings."

"What are they up to?" I murmur, scrolling through the readout, my disturbance growing.

New tactics that make no sense are far more concerning than even a fully armed armada. Changes that cannot be anticipated, for reasons unknown, can do far more damage than a frontal attack, even by a larger force.

"I thought about hailing you, but I did not know what to say." Corin sounds exasperated. "*High Commander, I need to report that the enemy has been sighted but they have not engaged... we have no casualties...*"

"Well, it would have gotten my attention." My lips quirk. "But none of this is exactly urgent, is it?"

"No, and I did not want to interrupt your time with your Tribute." Now there is a thread of envy in his voice, which I do not begrudge him. Still, as much as I appreciate the sentiment, I know I cannot allow it to continue.

My duty must come first.

"Next time, if something unusual is happening, report in." I closed the readout and meet his gaze. "I may not come to the bridge, but I do want to know." I realize that I would not have appreciated the interruption, but having seen the readout and reports for myself, I am uneasy about what the Vgothas are doing. Besides, before Dawn arrived, Corin would not have hesitated to hail me. I should not allow her presence to change that.

"Yes, High Commander." He nods smartly, his fist coming up to pound against his chest in salute.

"Dismissed. Enjoy your break."

As Corin leaves, I turn my attention to the current situation. The scouts *are* being reckless, but I cannot blame them. Still, we need to know what the Vgothas are up to. I am about to hail Arkdhem when I realize I have re-assigned him to watch over my Tribute rather than command the scout ships. I send my communication to Rorick, second in command of the scout ships, instead.

"Bring up the vid screen, with the information Rorick is about to send," I command. Immediately, the screen on the far-left lights up and a moment later is filled with the patterns the scout ships have been flying and where each Vgotha ship was spotted along the lines... and where they dropped out of sight again.

Examining the display, I feel my jaw clench.

Some of the places the Vgothas have been disappearing from make no sense. There is nothing there that should hide their ships or the trails.

"High Commander?" The hesitant voice of Borodem, one of my communications officers, interrupts my thoughts. His focus is also on the display, his worry writ clear across his face—and he is not the only one. "The Vgotha... they have some kind of new camouflage technology, don't they? That's the only explanation for this." He waves his hand at the display, his question bolstering my own conclusion after examining the data.

"Unfortunately, I think you may be correct," I say grimly.

What I still don't understand is why they're using it to play with our scouts rather than blowing them away.

Still, I contact Rorick again. The scouts need to be extra careful. While the Vgotha are playing with them for now, there must be some endgame coming up that we can't see. They are doing it for a reason, which means we must be extra vigilant and not play into whatever plot they've concocted.

I am surprised that the emotions welling up inside of me as I try to determine the Vgotha's motivations are as much anxiety and protectiveness as they are determination. I have always considered myself protective of my warriors—we are all each other has after all... or, at least, we were. I realize now that I have lost the edge of that worry.

There has been so much death over the years, so much loss, and as we continue our quest for revenge we mourn each life ended as it happens, but it is *acceptable.* Each warrior knows the risks, each gives his life willingly so that we may obtain our ultimate goal—justice and revenge for our people and safety for the rest of the universe from the Vgotha scourge.

Now though...

I have someone to protect who isn't a warrior. A life on board who did not choose to be here. Who did not sign up for revenge or justice. A helpless female life, who has already roused my protective instincts more than once.

I have been so focused on attacking for so long, realizing that I now have something to defend... no wonder my anxieties are sharper. But knowing the reason does not help to allay them.

Silently, I send a non-verbal message to Arkdhem, requesting an update.

I receive a response in a matter of moments.

Dawn is conscious but still in with Medik; they are conversing.

I am relieved to hear that she is awake, but not entirely soothed. My immediate impulse is to return to the med bay, no matter that I am on duty, to look her over for myself. For a moment I am tempted to direct Arkdhem to bring her to the bridge when she is finished in the med bay, but doing so would not be constructive. It would definitely be distracting.

As the leader, I am the one who must set an example for my warriors, especially since I have decided the Tribute program is to continue. They will witness how I handle my own Tribute and follow my example. We cannot have a bridge full of Tributes, so I will not bring her here again.

While we cannot separate the two parts of our lives—warriors into civilians with mates and families—we can at least separate our Tributes from our time on duty. Even if the desire to have her by my side makes me feel as though I am perpetually missing something.

THE FEELING of relief when Bogdan comes to take command of the bridge is overwhelming and unsettling. Normally I am reluctant to take leave of the bridge, now I am practically impatient to hand over command and find my Tribute again. Just the thought of knowing I will soon be able to touch her again has my *seela* beginning to writhe beneath my armor.

The difficulty I have in controlling my emotions is also unsettling, although I manage to keep my armor to a light, neutral gray, letting none of my impatience show as I update Bogdan on the situation.

There were several sightings of Vgotha ships while I was on the bridge, none of them engaged with our ships. Not even the pilot who decided to pretend he was having some kind of shields malfunction, making him the perfect target. Bogdan is as confused as I am, although no less vehement in his passion to eradicate the Vgotha threat.

"Perhaps we should engage in force," he says, studying the map the scouts' explorations have created, as well as the pattern of appearances by Vgotha ships. "They appear to be testing their capabilities rather than engaging, but the size of these ships would not be able to withstand an assault by *this* ship. The scouts' firepower isn't enough, and so far they haven't approached any of the fighters."

"Or perhaps that's exactly what they want," I murmur, frowning at the map. Even as I feel the tug to go and find my Tribute and bury myself inside of her, to feel her presence beside me, I force myself to focus on this threat. It is a threat to her as well. Bogdan has made a good point, which is why he's a good second, but I do not agree with his instincts to rush in. "See if we can get any fighters close to their ships... we will continue to pursue them at a slower pace for now, unless one of their destroyers appears. So far we've only seen the smaller ships, but there must be one that they're reporting back to. Send the scouts further out to see if they can locate any larger ships. I want to see what they do next."

Bogdan grimaces but nods his head in agreement, seeing the wisdom of letting events play out. While we can take on a destroyer—and win—it will not necessarily be easy or without loss of life. Caution may not come naturally to him, but he is smart enough to recognize when it is needed. We will go forward with our eyes peeled.

Done with my duty, I barely recognize myself in the eager warrior who practically races from the bridge. Normally I would linger, although not too long so as not to undermine Bogdan's authority now that he's on duty. Instead, I am walking as quickly as I can without feeling rushed, my tech already reaching out to hail Arkdhem.

As usual, he responds immediately.

We are back in your cabin, High Commander. She asked for any texts on our history and customs and has been reading them for a while now.

I am more than pleased with Arkdhem's response. Both because of her interest in learning more about us, beyond the information Frllil would have imparted during her initial training, and because she is in my cabin. While I would not confine her there unless necessary or if she needs to be punished, the possessive need riding me is soothed a little by knowing she is alone and in my rooms.

Not that my stride slows at all, for I am still eager to join her, but my chest feels a little less tight and my shoulders relax. Although Ardkhem had informed when they'd left the med bay, I had not felt as though I could ask for frequent updates while I was on duty. The rest of the crew would surely have noticed. I must set the example for how Tsenturion warriors with Tributes should act, for I will not require my men to behave differently than I myself do. Once we have more Tributes, the crew on duty cannot be constantly checking in on their Tribute, therefore I cannot do so.

Perhaps it would be wise to designate a room in the ship where Tributes whose warrior is on duty may stay so that the warrior will know where she is and will not be distracted by wondering, the way I have been. The idea has merit.

When I arrive at my cabin, my Tribute is sitting curled up in the corner of the couch, while Arkdhem sits on the other side, both of them reading. The translator the Jabol gave her should allow her to read any of the texts I possess, and she seems engrossed.

As always, Arkdhem jumps up to salute me when I enter. "High Commander."

"Arkdhem," I respond, acknowledging him. "Thank you for escorting my Tribute. You are relieved."

"Thank you, High Commander," he says before turning. "Farewell, Dawn."

"Bye," she says, smiling at him, placing the book she is holding down and rising to her feet. As she turns her blue eyes towards me, I can already feel my body responding to being in her presence. My *seela* begin to move, my cock engorging. I barely take notice of Arkdhem leaving the room.

"Dawn," I say in greeting and am rewarded with her entire face lighting up. She does like being called that. Very well. It does not satisfy me as much as claiming her with her title, but I do enjoy seeing her pleasure.

"Master," she says, smiling up at me. My armor flashes gold before I order it to recede, and the nanotech flows over me to my back, leaving me naked and erect in front of her. Her eyes widen as they drop to my groin, and I can practically taste her arousal as it surges.

"Come here," I command, holding out my hand. She moves to me, but to my surprise she does not take my hand. Instead, she drops to her knees in front of me, her hand reaching out to wrap around the base of my cock, caressing the sensitive bulges located there which hold my seed. I groan at the sensation of her delicate fingers caressing me, and my *seela* immediately reach for her hand, stroking it. When I speak, my voice is strained. "What are you doing, Dawn?"

"Something that we do on Earth, but which I haven't heard or seen mention of here," she says. There is something almost mischievous in her expression, and I am unsure of what to do.

Then she leans forward and licks the flared head of my cock, and the sensation is exquisite. I groan, my hands coming forward so that I can sink my fingers into the pale strands of her hair, holding on for all I'm worth as she begins to explore my cock with her *tongue*. It's an act I had never even considered, and when she opens her lips and takes the tip of my cock into her mouth, my knees buckle.

Hot. Wet. But deliberate. Her tongue moves like a *prime seela*, stroking and exploring, and eliciting the most exquisite pleasure. It was perverse, there is no breeding benefit, and yet... I don't want her to stop. While the manuals had made mention of this activity, it had not particularly appealed to me at the time. Human cocks are different, and I had no interest in a Tsenturion woman's mouth, so I did not think I would have one in hers.

I was wrong.

I groan, thrusting my hips forward, my hands tightening in her hair. It is just like in her texts. The very unusualness of the activity adds a piquancy to it that I find greatly appealing, on top of the physical pleasure running through me. She hums with pleasure, and I shudder, thrusting more deeply and causing her to pull back slightly.

"Enough," I growl, because I do not know how much more I can take without losing my control and I do not wish to harm her. My fingers grip her hair, pulling her mouth off my cock, with much reluctance on my part.

I pull her up against me, taking her parted lips in a fierce kiss as I begin to yank her dress from her body. The fabric falls easily away, and I carry her to the bed, her legs around my waist, and she whimpers as the underside of my cock rubs against her wet heat, my *seela* stimulating her plump lips.

We practically fall onto the bed, her touch and kisses frantic, as if she is as desperate for my touch as I am for hers. I feel as though I have waited another thousand years for her, my need is so great. I do not bother with bindings or tormenting her, having her mouth around me had been enough torment for us both. Instead, I pull back my hips and thrust home, making her cry out as she clamps down around me in happy ecstasy.

Just being joined with her fills me with satisfaction, a sense of rightness, of gratification, that I have never found anywhere else.

Once I am inside of her, some of my need is soothed... just enough to allow me to keep my initial thrusts slow and steady, rather than pounding into her without care. She writhes underneath me, a sob rising in her whimpering cries as I move, stroking her insides with my cock and her outsides with my *seela*. I grunt, fisting my hands beside her head, pumping in and out of her and doing my best to hold onto my control.

"Yes... please... Gavrill... Master... *harder, please!*"

My name on her lips, her desperate plea, and all my careful efforts at holding myself back are undone. I oblige, taking her as hard as I want to, enjoying the high cries of her pleasure filling my ears. My *seela* latch on to her as she clenches around me, and we both tumble into erotic oblivion.

Dawn

Cuddled up against Gavrill's side, I stroke my fingers over his broad chest, enjoying the moment of intimacy. He has me tucked up against him, my head resting on one arm while he strokes my lower back, his other hand caressing my bottom and the leg that he has draped over his hip.

I know that I only have a limited amount of time before the quiet moment turns to ardor again. Is it just his libido, or is it the physical influence of the bonding that Medik referenced? I can only hope it's the latter. As much as I enjoy having tons of orgasms, I want the physical connection to lead to an emotional one. I want the bonding... I want Medik's hope to be realized, because I think that's the most likely path to happiness for me. It might even be the only path, because of the way my own emotions are becoming engaged; if they aren't returned, it's going to hurt. A lot.

"Master, why is there no mention of the Vgothas in any of your books?" I ask.

I knew what Frllil had told me, and so I understood the references the other Tsenturions made toward their enemy, but I'm still curious. I don't know what they look like, how formidable an enemy they are, or how likely the Tsenturions are to be able to get their revenge. I did know that we were currently chasing Vgotha ships, but that was about it.

His muscles tense beneath my fingers but relax again as I continue stroking.

"We did not know anything of them when those books were written," he answers, his voice quiet. Sad. "Before they destroyed our planet, we had never even heard of them. They targeted us because they discovered the Jabol had reached out to us for protection."

That, I knew from Frllil. According to him, the Vgotha had been trying to either enslave or eradicate the Jabols for a long time. The peaceful race was very intelligent, scientifically superior, but they were not warriors. So they'd gone searching for protectors and found the Tsenturions; but the Vgotha were so merciless, so cruel, that they thought nothing of massacring an entire planet to keep the Jabols vulnerable.

"Have you ever seen one?" I ask.

"Why do you want to know?" Gavrill leans back so he can frown at me. There's some suspicion in his expression, although I can't imagine what he thinks he should be suspicious of. I swear I feel a touch of jealousy as well. I almost roll my eyes at the irrational idea that he would feel possessive or jealous because I'm asking about his enemy, but with him looking directly at me, I don't dare.

"I'm just curious," I explain. "This is a whole new idea for me. I've never had an enemy before, and now we're chasing after a whole fleet of them."

"You are not, my warriors and I are," he says, almost fiercely. I might have taken offense at being left out if I couldn't sense his sudden surge of protectiveness. I squeak as I find myself being turned over onto my forearms and knees, his hands coming down on top of mine to pin me in position with my ass high in the air. I can feel his *seela* stroking against my bottom as his cock hardens. "You will be protected and cared for, and the Vgotha will never be close enough for you to worry about them."

I would explain that I wasn't worried, but I don't think it would matter. The moment of intimacy is over; I've riled both his need to protect and his possessiveness.

He thrusts deep, his *prime seela* immediately rimming my anus, and I groan as he ripples inside of me. With his body over and around me, I can't help but feel surrounded and completely protected, as if he's created a haven for me with his muscles.

"My Tribute," he says, and as much as I prefer it when he calls me by my actual name, I can't help but hear the pride, possessiveness, and—dare I hope it's not my imagination—affection in his statement. But his next words make my heart soar. "My Dawn."

12

D^{awn}

AS TIMES PASSES, I go from being resigned to my fate to feeling almost hopeful about it. Medik's hypothesis that physical intimacy will lead to a deepening of the bond and more emotional intimacy seems to be coming true. There are times I worry that I'm imagining things or reading too much into things, because my own emotions are growing, and I don't want to be the only one feeling this deep attachment... but I swear there are times I can feel Gavrill's emotions.

I don't even get annoyed with being called "my Tribute" anymore, because he seems so pleased, so possessive when he does so, but not in a way that makes me feel like an object. I swear I can feel the affection he has for me when he does so, the way calling me that is like an endearment for him. My favorite is when he calls me "my Dawn," but both feel good.

When he is on duty, I have begun to get to know some of the other Tsenturion warriors. Despite how intimidating they are, they're nice guys—pretty desperate for feminine attention, which makes me feel kind of bad about being against the Tribute program. They deserve mates and happiness as much as anyone else... but does it have to come at the cost of a woman's Earth life?

Unfortunately, I can't think of an alternative.

"Why don't you work with Medik on it?" Gavrill asks when I express my continued unhappiness with his plans, his fingers stroking my hair. Our pillow talk often comes between bouts of kinky hot sex and his delight in experimenting with my training belt to see exactly how much it can affect me, so I have to get the conversation in when I can. Every time he returns from the bridge, it's like he's desperate to reforge our physical connection, and my own need matches his.

Being apart from him makes me feel antsy and almost itchy with need to be reunited with him. No matter how short the time period of separation, it spurs a compulsion to be as physically close to him as I possibly can. Honestly, it's a minor miracle I'm not sore and chafing from all the sex, but I can't seem to get enough of it, and neither can he.

"Work with Medik?" I ask, confused. "On the Tribute program?"

"After you spoke with him, he told me he wants to revise some of the parameters to assuage some of the concerns you had. If you work with him, you can address your misgivings with the specifics of the program directly."

Immediately, I am torn by conflicting emotions. Be directly responsible for the women who are chosen? On the other hand... isn't it better that those women at least have someone like them advocating for them if the Tsenturions are going to bring them here regardless? The idea of having a purpose, beyond being fucked to unconsciousness on a regular basis, also appeals, especially since Gavrill spends long hours on the bridge.

I've filled my time with doing yoga, keeping my body strong and supple, even when it's hard to concentrate on the poses when I have the training belt as a constant reminder of my master and his ultimate control of my body. It certainly makes some of the poses *way* more interesting.

I also read more about Tsenturions from their own texts, getting to know the others on the ship, and asking Arkdhem questions about Vgothas, but that's not the same as having something to *do*. Something meaningful. And the moment Gavrill suggests it, I realize that I want that.

In fact, if I think about the consequences of my involvement in such a project with so many repercussions for both Tsenturions and humans, this might be the most meaningful thing I could *ever* do. That Gavrill suggests it, that he would trust me with such a task, means more to me than I can say.

It feels like proof that he really sees me for me. As a person with valuable input, a person who can do something useful, who can make a difference, and more than that, a person whose feelings matter.

"Yes," I say, answering him with so much enthusiasm, it surprises both of us. "Yes, I want to do that."

Pressing my hand against his chest, I lift myself up slightly so that I can give him a kiss. Despite my physical desire for him, I am rarely the aggressor when it comes to sex—I don't need to be. For the first time, I am the one on top. Well, sort of on top. Leaning over him, at least.

One hand comes up, sliding into my hair to cradle the back of my head as our kiss deepens. His other hand, which had been on my hip, moves until he is cupping my ass cheek, squeezing and kneading the soft flesh while his fingers work closer to the small hole he is so fascinated with. Something that I learned through a Tsenturion biology book—they don't have the same digestive system humans do, and so they don't have an anus.

Which explains at least part of why Gavrill is utterly fascinated with mine. His finger presses against the crinkled star, pushing inward and making me squirm. I've gotten used to the sensation and to the belt stretching that hole, and I know it's only a matter of time before he uses his cock there. I don't know whether I'm more aroused or frightened by the idea at this point.

I whimper as his finger pushes deeper, the lack of lubrication making the insertion burn a little more than usual, and my pussy pulses in response to the erotic sting. His finger feels even larger than usual, and I'm practically humping his thigh as he moves it gently, delving a little deeper with each pass. With the way he's holding my head for the kiss, I can't verbally protest even if I wanted to.

GAVRILL

MY SWEET TRIBUTE's alternate entrance grips my finger tightly as I probe deeper, although it opens easily thanks to the training with the belt that I've been doing. She moans against my lips, her arousal wetting my thigh as she moves against me.

Excitement rises as I realize the significance of her kiss, of her rising passion. Not that she has been passive to my advances, but this is the first time she has clearly initiated our joining. I have finally mastered her fully, by giving her a task. The irony is that she will be helping me by completing it, but that does not seem to matter to her.

Her submission is offered up to me, her body ready for the final claiming, and I respond immediately. My grip on her roughens, the way she likes it, and she whimpers in the back of her throat as mutual desire sweeps through us. After a long, deep kiss, I slide my finger from her bottom and switch our respective positions, pushing her arms up above her head so I can bind her to the bed.

"Oh... no, Master, please, I want to touch you," she begs, but I shake my head. When she touches me, I lose control too quickly, and I want to make sure I can go slowly, for her own pleasure, as well as to savor this moment.

"No," I say firmly, running my hands down her bound arms to her breasts and cupping the soft mounds. I run my thumbs over her nipples, making the hard buds swell even more. She makes a whining noise, and I pinch the tender nubbins in response, feeling her shudder beneath me as the erotic pain mixes with her pleasure. Her breath is now coming in soft pants as I manipulate her body, rousing her need along with my own.

She writhes slightly, arching and trying to rub herself against me. I chuckle.

"Naughty Dawn," I say, for I have found that using her name at such times elicits more of a response than calling her Tribute or even 'naughty girl' like the examples in the manuals. "Do not try to manipulate me."

Moving away from her and ignoring her sound of protest as I abandon her breasts, I easily flip her over so that her bottom is high in the air, ready for spanking.

"I wasn't—!" She starts to protest, but my hand is already coming down on her vulnerable bottom.

Smack!

The manuals all made it clear that her bottom should be a nice, hot pink, if not red, before I claim it. The spanking I give her will not be punishing, because I know she was not truly trying to manage me, but by now she also knows I need no excuse to redden her bottom if I wish. Indeed, I have found that turning that particular area nice and pink has a most salutary effect on the level of ecstasy she can reach.

Smack! Smack! Smack!

Realizing that I'm not actually disciplining her, my Tribute drops her head and lifts her bottom higher, inviting more swats, her soft moans encouraging me to swing a tad harder and sting her soft flesh a tad more. Her hips wag up and down, her bottom cheeks clenching slightly, and the tiny hole between them looks more inviting than ever.

Her feminine lips are swollen and marked from my *seela*, the sight filling me with satisfaction. I have come to enjoy leaving marks all over her, especially her neck and breasts, in lieu of the mating mark she is incapable of wearing, but the small circles on her sex are my favorites. My *seela* stamp her in the Tsenturion manner, at least.

Smack!

I deliberately aim for paler patches of skin on her bottom and the crease between that sweet curve and her thighs. Her cries are a little higher every time my hand goes lower, slapping that sensitive area. The cream coating her inner lips is glossy, announcing her growing arousal.

Exerting my influence on the nanotech, I send the belt upwards in thin trickles to her breasts. I cannot see them, but I know they have created a line from the belt to her nipples, where they tighten around the little buds, creating an all-encompassing, painful erotic pinch that even my fingers couldn't duplicate. Another thin tendril slides down to her clit, covering the swollen nub with the nanotech and doing the same thing, giving me total mastery over her pain and pleasure as I prepare to claim her completely.

MY NIPPLES and clit throb in the confines of the nanotech, which squeeze so tightly that I hover on the edge between pain and pleasure. The growing heat in my ass has me squirming and bucking against Gavrill's hard hand. Each swat by itself is not particularly punishing, but the overall effect of stimulation has me gasping for breath as I'm bowed submissively before him.

I can feel my pussy creaming as the erotic stimulation of all my most sensitive parts fuels the need growing inside of me. I cry out as the tech begins to pulse, squeezing and releasing rhythmically and confusing my senses as to whether I'm feeling pain or pleasure. All the while, Gavrill's hand continues to come down in firm, measured swats designed to drive me wild.

"Please..." I beg, my toes curling as my ecstasy rises, but nothing he is doing is quite enough to bring me to orgasm. I swear he's made a science out of figuring out exactly how far he can go before I tip over that sweet edge, and he enjoys keeping me teetering on it for as long as possible. "Please, Master, I want you inside of me."

I can feel his usual sense of satisfaction at the honorific, his nearly savage satisfaction at reducing me to pleading for pleasure at his hand. I don't care; I get my own satisfaction from pleasing him, and my arousal is only enhanced by his domination.

"Good girl," he says, his hand smoothing over the hot curve of my ass, rather than swatting it again. "My sweet Dawn. I am truly your Master now."

"Yes," I agree eagerly, my wrists tugging slightly at the bonds around them as I lift my hips up, knowing how much the sight of my reddened bottom will entice him. The nanotech pulls at my nipples and clit, like tiny mouths sucking on them almost too hard, and I moan, wagging my bottom.

A moment later, his cock presses against my opening—just not the one I was expecting. I gasp, trying to surge forward and away from him as the tapered tip of his cock pushes into my ass. Even though I had half-expected this moment, I can't help but try to flee from it.

His fingers curl around my hips, holding me in place easily as he pushes forward.

"Please, not there, Master," I beg. "Not yet, Gavrill, please!"

"Yes, my Dawn, now," he says, and his cock thrusts in, making me cry out as I'm opened.

It doesn't hurt as much as it might have, because I have become accustomed to the invasion of the nanotech, but the flared head of his cock feels very different. It stretches me, moving inside of me, and pushes deeper as I squirm and moan in ambiguous pleasure. Feeling him filling me, claiming me, in this intimate manner is affecting both of us.

I can feel every ridge, every bulge of his alien cock as the strange shape pushes past the tight ring guarding my channel. My muscles flutter around him, clenching, trying to grip him. He slides backwards, and I cry out again at the strange dragging sensation, only to choke on my cry as he thrusts in even deeper than before.

~

GAVRILL

MY TRIBUTE'S bottom is more exquisite than I could have ever imagined. The crinkled star of her opening has stretched to create a smooth ring around my cock, gripping me so tightly, I know I would not be able to move if it weren't for the additional lubrication I had received from my armor before entering her. Now I understand why the texts had been so adamant on that point.

She is not wet here, but she is hot, and the spasming walls of her body feel incredible. My cock widens as it nears the base, and I can hear the sob rising in her voice as I press deeper, rocking my hips back and forth, thrusting a little deeper each time. While there is some pain in her voice, there is pleasure as well, and by now I know when something is truly hurting her.

This is pain she is taking for me, enduring because she wants to please me, to submit to me. Pain that will eventually turn to pleasure, I believe.

To assist, I instruct the nanotech on her clit to vibrate, and I feel her clench around me in response as she squeals in surprise. Her grip loosens, and I thrust deeper, stretching her to her widest point yet as my groin nestles against her hot bottom. Both of us pant for breath, moaning as her muscles play over the full length of my shaft and my *seela* stroke her spread cheeks. The sight of myself buried in her unusual hole, hearing the strain in her voice as she adjusts to my invasion, is gloriously erotic.

After holding myself still for several long moments, doing my best to memorize exactly how her reddened cheeks look split by my golden cock and stroking *seela*, I begin to thrust.

Her moans are ambiguous, but I can hear her pleasure as well, I can practically feel it as she quivers under my hands. There are no more pleas for me to stop, only willing submission as she slowly loosens, able to take my cock more easily with every thrust.

Now I understood what the manuals had meant. There was an intimacy to this act that I could feel, though it was unknown to Tsenturions. Tsenturions were focused on procreation with our pleasure, but this... this is nothing but pleasure. Her mouth had been similar, but she couldn't take me between her lips as deeply or as fully as she could in her ass. It didn't cause her the same kind of discomfort, which she was now enduring solely for my pleasure.

There is something pure about being offered this gift of her body, of knowing there is no guarantee for her own pleasure and no possibility of breeding. It is an act done completely for me, for my enjoyment and domination over her body... I can feel her submitting to me, giving over to me, and it's an ecstasy that outweighs even the physical rapture.

～

Dawn

THE EROTIC BURN of Gavrill's cock filling my ass while my pussy spasms emptily makes me feel as though I'm splintering apart. I'm wracked with need even as I want to beg him to stop. I can't tell if it hurts or if the sensations are just so overwhelming that my body can barely handle them.

I can feel his cock moving inside of me, his *seela* gently stroking my cheeks each time he slides home. The ridges and bumps on his cock rasp against my delicate insides, my nails dig into the mattress as I cling to it for dear life, feeling like I'm adrift in an ocean of sensation in the middle of a storm. The pain from my pinched nipples is nothing, barely a drop, but when the nanotech around my clit begins to vibrate, I can feel my toes curl as a whole new dollop of pleasure is added to the chaos consuming me.

If it wasn't for Gavrill's firm grip on my hips, I'm sure I would have collapsed beneath his heavy thrusts by now.

Agony.

Ecstasy.

Two sides to the same coin, and I'm caught in the middle.

Not just claimed, *consumed*.

My orgasm slams into me, and I keen with the intensity of it, my ring clamping down tightly around his cock and burning at the sensations as he shoves himself deep inside of me one last time. I can feel the hard suck of his *seela* as they latch onto my skin, the throb of his cock as he begins to come, and his possessive triumph as he fills my ass with liquid heat.

13

G avrill

THE SOFT CURVES of my sweet Tribute are nestled against me, her breathing slow and steady in her slumber. I have worn her out utterly. Her little nipples are soft now but still reddened, as is her clit, and even her bottom hole appears pink and well-used. I am not much better off. I feel drowsily content, as if I could lay here in this bed beside her and never move ever again.

Which is why the furious message from Bogdan, informing me that I am late for my shift, feels like a slap to my face, bringing me back to reality.

Late.

Again.

Cursing under my breath, I pull myself away from Dawn, resentful at having our time together interrupted and yet knowing I am being illogical to feel so. These emotions, this urge to stay by her side is becoming stronger the more time I spend with her.

I had thought by now I would have myself more under control, but to be late again...

Worse, to wish that I didn't have to go to the bridge at all...

I don't need Bogdan to tell me that the situation is getting out of hand. Not that it will stop him from doing so. He is waiting for me outside of the bridge, his armor a dark black that flashes with occasional streaks of red in his fury. Normally I would stand my ground against his temper, but knowing I am in the wrong has me inwardly flinching in a way I haven't done since I was a raw recruit.

That he is waiting for me—and not on the bridge—tells me all I need to know about his intentions.

Worse, I deserve the dressing down.

I still try to bypass it.

"I know," I say, growling out the words the moment I'm within earshot, letting him see my own upset at myself as my armor flashes with emotion. "It won't happen again."

Red streaks across his chest.

"It has already happened multiple times," he says, stepping in front of me to block the door. I hadn't realized he knew, and I mentally curse whoever told him. There is heat flashing in his eyes, contained rage, and the fact that he is actually controlling his temper drives home exactly how angry he is. This is no vent and steam, this is righteous, justified anger. "I know about the last time too, I saw the log. I did not say anything, but now I think that was a mistake. Someone needs to hold you accountable since you are apparently no longer doing so for yourself."

My jaw clenches in anger. Not at him, but at myself.

He faces me, fists clenched, his fury contained but palpable. "The Vgotha are taunting us, engaging in tactics we have never seen from them before, and we still don't know the reason why, and instead of focusing on them, instead of leading our people, you are distracted by that human. You say we must protect our future, but there will be no future if we are all killed in the present. How can you be our leader if you aren't even thinking of us half the time?"

I have no answer for him.

He is right.

I *have* allowed myself to become distracted. I *haven't* been focused on the threat the way I should be. I *haven't* been thinking about the present. Not only have I failed in my duty, but I am putting us all in danger—including my Tribute. I am behaving in a manner that is not only unfit for a Commander, but for a warrior.

Bogdan holds himself stiffly, looking me directly in the eyes. "I do not want your position, High Commander. I do not."

Don't make me step into it.

The words hang unspoken in the air between us. I know Bogdan does not want to be High Commander. He often wants his way, he often wishes I would choose his line of thinking, but he does not want my rank. Nor do I want him to have the position. I know I am the best suited for it... at least I was.

Before I received my Tribute.

Before I became distracted.

Before my attention was torn.

My first duty must be to my Tsenturion warriors, in the present, but my eyes have been entirely to the future as if the Vgotha threat is already eradicated. I have been indulging myself with pleasure while Bogdan and Corin and the others worry over the Vgotha's new antics. I have forgotten what it means to be in command, what it means to be holding all of our lives in my hands.

"It will not happen again," I say softly. My armor shimmers to a bluish-grey, a deliberate show of contriteness for him. "You are right. I have been distracted. I will fix it. There is time for the future when the present Vgotha threat is eradicated."

His expression lightens with relief, as does his armor. Not much, but enough to know that he at least believes my sincerity. I cannot help but feel grim as he steps aside to let me pass. I have neglected my duties too much in favor of my Tribute.

My words to Bogdan echo in my mind as I enter the bridge.

It will not happen again.

～

Dawn

WAKING up alone in bed sucks. On the other hand, I'm just a tiny bit relieved because I'm so freaking sore all over. Thankfully, Gavrill didn't have the belt do more than cover all my lady bits before he left me. I don't know if I could have handled having something inside my ass right now.

I sigh, knowing that he must have had to go to his bridge shift.

As soon as I make the noise, I hear Arkdhem's voice.

"Dawn? Are you awake?"

"Yes, hello, Arkdhem." I try to sound more enthusiastic than I feel. I like Arkdhem, but it would be nice not to have a constant babysitter. I don't know why I feel so irritated right now. Especially since I'd probably feel kind of lonely without him.

Apparently, my emotions are sort of out of whack.

"I will leave the room so you can dress," he says cheerfully.

When I hear the door whoosh shut, I think about what I want to do. I don't know when Gavrill left, but it's unlikely he'll be back quickly. His on-duty shifts are long, which does currently have the benefit of giving my body time to recover. I take a moment to perform a few sun salutations, concentrating on my breathing as my body flows from pose to pose. There's a hollow in my gut, almost like the emptiness I felt when I lost my mom and grandma. I take my vinyasa, seeking the peace in fluid movements. On an alien ship a million light years away from everything I've known, I need the balance between my body and my breath more than ever.

By the time I'm done, the ache in my chest has shrunk to a pea-sized throb. I bow and whisper, *Namaste* to the wall. Away from my master, the pain never truly goes away. Only sex will soothe it completely. I'd chalk it up to the Pavlov-type training, except that I felt the same hollowness on Earth.

Pulling on a deep violet dress, I decide I want to go visit with Medik and talk with him about the Tribute program. Arkdhem has no objections, and after he takes me to eat, we go straight to the Med

Bay. It turns out that Arkdhem also has a lot of good thoughts about the program. I definitely wouldn't call him soft—I wouldn't call any Tsenturion warrior anything close to that—but in a lot of ways he's more empathetic and open than his compatriots. Definitely more so than Bogdan or Gavrill. While he's excited about the Tributes and wants a female for himself, it's obvious he would prefer one who *wants* to be here.

"Why not have them click on something that's an actual agreement?" Arkdhem suggests as Medik and I wrangle over the questionnaire that I think women should have to answer so that we don't end up with anyone who has a significant other or children or other strong ties to Earth. What constitutes strong ties is somewhat up for debate, with Medik having a much looser definition than me.

I sigh. "No one's going to take that seriously. They'll think it's a gimmick. We'll get all sorts of women clicking it just to see what the link takes them to."

"We could do both." Arkdhem tilts his head as he looks over the screen of notes Medik has been taking. "It would narrow the pool..."

Medik gives him a stern look. "Do you want a Tribute or not? The pool can't be too narrow."

"I think you'll be surprised how many swipe right," I mutter under my breath. I'm self-aware enough to know that I would have. Although I don't know that I would have been any happier about showing up on an actual Tsenturion ship and expected to be a warrior's mate. But I would have clicked.

"Swipe right?" Both males are now looking at me with confusion.

"Don't worry about it."

Neither of them lets it go that easily, and I found myself explaining about how humans *actually* hook up, which led to a fair amount of confusion on their part.

"I'm starting to think we're doing Earth females a favor," Arkdhem says, shaking his head after I finish explaining 'ghosting.'

Despite the fact that Earth women would definitely rather choose their own mates, even if sometimes our choices are terrible, I'm having trouble coming up with a good rebuttal. Ask a woman what she wants out of a relationship, and a strong, loyal, kind male who is completely devoted to her and gives her multiple orgasms on a regular basis is going to sound pretty damn good. Granted, some of them might have issues with the collar, leash, and spankings... but maybe not.

Medik strokes his chin thoughtfully, his eyes focusing on me. "Do you think women will 'swipe right?'"

I sigh. "Yes. I think there will be plenty. Even if they don't believe that it's real."

My stomach gurgles, and I realize I'm hungry again. I frown. How long have we been here? If I'm ready to eat again, then surely Gavrill must be off duty by now...

"Arkdhem? Is Gavrill still on the bridge?" I ask. For some reason, now that I'm thinking about *my* Tsenturion mate, I feel strangely bereft. I can't quite pinpoint the emotion, and I definitely don't know why I'm feeling it, but it feels like more than the longing I'm used to experiencing when we've been apart for a while. That's still there, but instead of feeling a return of it, I feel strangely empty. Like something is missing.

Both Medik and Arkdhem frown as they check the device they use as a clock—which I still haven't figured out how to read.

"No, he should be done by now," Arkdhem says. "Would you like to go back to your cabin?"

"Yes, please," I say. Anxiety is rising in my chest as I wonder why Gavrill hasn't already summoned me there.

GAVRILL

BLACK SPACE STRETCHES BEFORE ME, an endless road I have travelled since taking my first orders. I was so young when I joined the Tsenturion forces, pledging to serve and protect. If I had known the chance to settle into a civilian life would be wiped out in a horrible instant of

Annihilation, would I have made a different choice? Would I have embraced a simple life, mated young, produced children, and died in a flash of fire during the Great Loss?

I never would've known the loss of my world. I never would've known the empty years, protecting the Jabol race as I could not protect my own.

I never would have met Dawn. Never held her in my arms, demanded her obedience, commanded her pleasure.

I wouldn't be wishing I was with her now.

But my duty must come first, no matter how it makes me ache inside. I have pushed down my emotions, my desires, because I need to prove that I can, even if it's only to myself. Arkdhem has reported in to me that he has escorted my Tribute back to our cabin. I have stayed away as an exercise in self-control. It is both harder and easier than I expected.

I have neglected my duties, including spending time with my warriors, and there was much I needed to catch up on. They were happy to see me again in my free time and had many questions for me—both about the Tribute program as well as the Vgotha. Morale is not low, but there is palpable concern over the new tactics and what it might mean. Concern that I did not even know about until today, because I have been spending all my free time with my Tribute and not my warriors.

I had meant to find a balance, but now I can see I have done a poor job of it.

That helps motivate me to stay away.

My body yearns for her. My chest pangs with a painful emptiness each moment I am away from her. Yet, I know it's necessary now, for the good of us all. Bogdan is correct. If the Vgotha kill us all because of my distraction, I will have failed not only my people, but her as well.

She did not come all this way just to die at the hands of my enemies. If that is what happens, the guilt and shame will burden me into the afterlife.

Eventually, I do return to the cabin—I must rest after all.

Arkdhem has reported that she seems sad but has fallen asleep. I feel relieved. Surely, she must be less distracting when she is slumbering.

But when I slide into the bed beside her, pulling her against me, my body rouses with a passionate fury, as if suppressing all my emotions has allowed them to build. She comes awake with a whimper as I roll atop her, my hard cock seeking her opening, my hands already rough on her breasts.

"Gavrill—" she starts to say, and I catch her lips in a kiss, silencing her.

Our joining is hard, rough, and she is just as desperate for my touch as I am for hers. Once isn't enough. I take her again… and again… until she is limp beneath me and my seed bulges are emptied. Curling around her, I hold her tightly as the darkness draws me down.

But when I wake, I force myself to leave immediately rather than waking her again or cuddling her close in her sleep.

I am early for my bridge shift, and Bogdan actually smiles with relief. He's not the only one, compounding my guilt. My warriors have missed my presence and leadership.

I vow to do better by them.

Perhaps it had been a mistake to accept my Tribute so early, before the Vgotha threat is eradicated… but now that she is here, I will protect her with my last breath.

Nodding to Bogdan, I look up at the screens, seeing the new patterns of the Vgotha Raider ships as they play hide and seek with our scouts and fighters, putting Dawn from my mind.

14

D awn

I wake up alone.

Again.

This is bullshit.

I want to feel angry, because that would be a hell of a lot better than the sad loneliness creeping through me, but somehow I can't muster the energy.

"Dawn?" Arkdhem is here, sitting in the darkness. My watchdog. "You are awake?"

"Yes," I say heavily as I roll onto my back, staring up at the ceiling that I can't actually see. I don't know exactly how well Tsenturions see in the dark, but I know it's better than humans do. My inner thighs and pussy are sore from Gavrill's visit last night, although at least the ache there is pleasant, not like the empty ache currently residing in my chest. "I am awake."

"You are well?" he asks tentatively, obviously hearing something in my voice that worries him.

Physically? Yes. Emotionally? Not so much.

Rather than answering him, I ask my own question. "Arkdhem, is something going on that I should know about? Something that's keeping Gavrill busy?"

I would have much preferred to ask Gavrill last night, but he hadn't exactly been interested in talking, just fucking me into oblivion. I feel like I had something precious almost in my grasp, only to have it snatched away.

Reaching up, I scratch at a spot on my shoulder while I wait for Arkdhem's answer.

"The Vgotha have changed their tactics," he says immediately. "No one knows for sure what they're doing or why. It is worrisome."

Immediately, I feel terrible. I hadn't even noticed that Arkdhem was worried or anyone else. "What are they doing?"

"Toying with us," he says grimly. "The High Commander believes they may be testing their camouflage capabilities. They do not always show up on our scanners."

Well, that is scary. No wonder Arkdhem is worried. It makes me feel a little better about Gavrill's abandonment except... vague memories from the one time I'd been on the bridge, my very first day on board, prod at me.

"How long has this been going on?" I ask.

"Since you arrived."

Okay, so that doesn't explain Gavrill's absence. Unless...

"Are they attacking now or something?"

"No," he says, almost absent-mindedly, like he's thinking about the Vgotha and what they're up to. "So far there have been no casualties at all. It's actually making us all very anxious, because we can't understand why they aren't engaging."

I feel both relieved that no lives have been lost and even more forlorn, as well as a little pissed, that Gavrill's suddenly changing how he's treating *me*. Does it have anything to do with the Vgothas? Or is it something I've done?

Does he suddenly not respect me since we had anal sex?

Or does he think his 'job' in claiming me is done, so now he's going to stop spending time with me?

The thought makes my entire body chill.

I vow to talk to him about it the next time I see him again, but he doesn't come until after I fall asleep. Again. And again, I awaken to his hands and mouth on me, his cock thrusting inside of me. Again, he uses me until we both pass out.

Again, I wake up alone.

Staying awake the next night doesn't help either. When I angrily try to demand he speak with me, all I do is I earn myself a spanking before his cock is sliding into me again.

Even as I scream in ecstasy, I can feel my heart breaking.

GAVRILL

"COMMANDER, DO YOU HAVE ORDERS?"

I stare at the swirling black matter. Vast and beautiful, and potentially deadly. Emotion bursts in me, as the sight of it seems to echo the gaping hole in my chest, and my fingers curl around the com desk. The pain I feel in my hearts has worsened every time that I tear myself away from my Tribute and focus on my duty. It is the burden I must bear. Loneliness... and something more.

"Commander?"

"Skirt the edges," I say. "We need more information."

Sholtorin nods, peering at the screen the same way I am, as if we might actually be able to see inside the cloud of nothingness.

"Do you think they could be hiding inside?" he asks. "Where would they have gotten the technology?"

"Stole it, probably," Bogdan says, standing at my side. He should have taken over command already, but once the Vgotha ships disappeared right outside the mass of black matter, I hadn't needed anyone to tell me that I needed to stay on the bridge.

We were dealing with the unknown.

"Maybe that's what they keep testing," Sholtorin mutters.

It is possible. If they have new, stolen technology, then that could explain some of the Vgotha's current antics. That doesn't mean anything good for us.

"Send probes," I order tersely. "A few from different points. Bogdan, you have the deck. Hail me if we find anything."

Bogdan nods, already stepping into place and giving orders.

As has become my usual habit, I make rounds of the ship, speaking with my warriors and hearing their concerns and thoughts before making my way to my cabin. Tonight, I move a little faster. There is a strange feeling in my chest, brought on by seeing the black matter and the disappearance of the Vgotha ships.

As I approach my cabin, the strange feeling grows. Something is wrong.

The door slides open, and Arkdhem straightens from his position on the couch. The room is dimly lit, but not darkened the way it is when she is sleeping. He gives me a short salute before retreating from the room, leaving us alone. I frown at the small lump on the bed.

"Dawn?" I ask softly, in case she has fallen asleep. "Dawn?"

The lump moves as I approach, and Dawn sits up. Her hands flutter over her face, wiping at her eyes. Her skin is flushed, and she does not meet my gaze. It almost looks as though she has been crying, but I do not see any actual tears.

"Master? Do you need me?" There is a touch of irony in her voice, almost as though she is mocking me. "You are back early." Now I hear a hint of accusation, and she still won't meet my eyes. She is displeased that I have spent so much time away, but tonight she does not try to chide me. The spanking she received for being waspish corrected that behavior.

My body responds at the sight of her, my cock stirring, but the great weight on my chest does not move. Perhaps my suit is malfunctioning. Well, I shall make things up to her now. I will pleasure her, and she will not feel the lack of my attention.

I move to the bed, my armor already retracting into my spine.

She is so pretty and pleasing, even with her eyes downcast and hiding her emotions.

"I wanted to see you," I say, crawling onto the bed toward her. Everything in my body is yearning to touch her.

Her face starts to lift, then crumples again. She clenches her jaw. "Did you? You've been very busy lately."

"I have," I agree, reaching out to take her by the wrist and pulling her to me. As she seems sad rather than angry tonight, I am gentle as I wrap her in my arms and begin kissing down her neck. There is a red angry spot on her shoulder. "What is this?"

"Just an itchy spot," she mutters, somewhat stiff in my arms.

"Have Medik see to it," I order her, tipping her head back to take her lips in a kiss. She turns her head away, making me frown down at her.

"Do you not wish to spend time with me anymore?"

"It is not about my wishes. I have a duty to my warriors and my people," I tell her, beginning to grow frustrated. I am here with her now, and she wishes to remonstrate with me instead of enjoying ourselves? "Just as your duty is to me. You are my Tribute."

"Yes." Why is there such sadness in her tone? My frustration grows and then ebbs. If she is sad, I will cheer her up. She will writhe and cry out for me, and then she will be happy again. After so much attention and pleasure, the adjustment to my new schedule must be harder on her than I realized.

I stroke her back, breathing in her scent. I feel her arch against me slightly, squirming under my touch. My hand strays to her front to caress her soft curves under the gown. Her breath quickens as her nipples bud against my palms. My rod swells under her sweet bottom as my *seela* begin to writhe.

I touch my lips to her neck. "I am already primed for you, my Dawn."

She shudders against me as my hands slide under her gown and begin to rove, hungry. I want to feel her, all of her.

"I will make you feel better now." I squeeze her breasts, pinching her nipples to arouse her further, and feel her sudden intake of breath. I rock my hips against her, seeing the future I so desire laid out in front of me, as soon as our enemy is eradicated. "When we defeat the Vgotha, then I will be able to attend to you properly and you will bear my children."

She suddenly breaks away, throwing her body backwards, leaving my hands and lap empty.

"I'm sorry," she says, her face knotting in the way that heralded tears. "I can't do that. I don't... I don't want children with you. Not like this. I'm sorry." She rolls away from me, rejecting me, rejecting her future with me.

I should punish her. Tributes should not reject their masters. I could use an enforcer or her training belt to punish her. I could spank her. There are so many things I could do to her for pushing me away.

Instead, I stare at her shaking shoulders as she curls around one of the bed cushions, her back to me, for the sadness is back, a black despair that I can feel all through my chest. The pain of loss.

And Dawn is the source.

If she were not so upset, I would marvel at the wonders of the nanotech, how attuned it has become to her and how well it transmits her emotions to me, mimicking the bond. I do not know what to do now that she has rejected me.

I still do not want to leave her though. Not until I have to again.

"Lights down," I say, and darkness descends on the cabin.

We lay there, side by side but not touching, lonely even as we are together.

GAVRILL

THE SADNESS LINGERS, following me for a tsencycle. My officers fall silent as I take my post on the bridge. Bending over their workstations, they pretend not to study me, perusing my suit for a hint of my emotions. Their entire chance at a mate rests on the success of this Tribute program. I cannot let my emotions dictate the outcome between me and my... Dawn.

I clench my fists on the panels alongside my command chair.

I will train my Tribute. I will breed and bring her to heel. I will do my duty to uphold the breeding program and ensure the survival of our race.

My determination does not quite fill the void inside me. Nothing can replace the warmth of my Tribute's regard. But I cannot allow her moping to derail my duty. She will learn her place, in time. Her needs belong firmly behind those of my mission and my men.

"Commander, we located a warship!"

The screen fills with the space craft we've spent a millennia trying to discover. Their warships are not as big as our destroyers, but they are closely guarded. We still don't know why.

"A warship," I say, half-rising from my seat as if that will give me a closer look. The enemy tech is dull and unassuming, almost blending in with the surrounding space. Small and remarkably fast, the Vgothan ships have a habit of hiding in dust clouds or meteor belts, refusing to stand their ground and face us—even before they had the cloaking technology we're facing now. Despite tsencycles of fighting, we have few visuals of their warships.

Now we've come upon one just sitting here, on the other side of the mass of black matter. There is no sign of the hunter ships and raider ships we were following, although it's possible they've retreated to the bowels of the warship rather than remaining outside of it.

"Scan shows no evidence of hyperdrive or engines." The warrior continues with his report. "And the sensors aren't registering any heat signatures that might mean armed weapons."

"They're scuttled. They've run out of fuel or life-resources. Or both." Bogdan almost sounds gleeful. His suit is the lightest I've ever seen. "Permission to destroy it?"

I stare at the enemy ship, still and silent as if waiting. My senses prickle as if the nanites are trying to tell me something is wrong.

"Keep scanning," I order. "I want to know why they're sitting in open space."

"Yes, High Commander." The science officer bends over his panel, pressing buttons and frowning at the strange readings.

I wait for Bogdan to protest, but the big warrior is also frowning at the exposed enemy ship, much more concerned now that he's had a moment to think about why a warship would just be sitting here. Waiting for us, right where the smaller ships had led us.

My instincts are right, I know it. Something's wrong.

"High alert," I announce. "All warriors to their post."

~

Dawn

I TRACE the outline of the stars on the glass. So small, so infinite. It is hard to look at them and feel that, in this great swirling galaxy, one matters.

Gavrill doesn't care about me. He cares about his precious tribute, but that could've been any woman. I am a trophy, a toy to take down off the shelf and admire. An object to show off. He doesn't care about Dawn. For all I know, he's incapable of caring. Of love.

This is my life now, a toy to a male who will give me great pleasure, but who will never love me in the way I wish he would. The way I love him.

Gathering up my skirts, I stride from the massive viewing deck, unable to bear the sight of the stars anymore. Arkdhem follows at a discreet distance, obviously realizing my wish to be alone. Which is almost funny, because the truth is I don't want to be alone at all.

But I don't want to talk either. Definitely not to any Tsenturions.

I retreat to the cabin, my silent escort shadowing me. I decide to read, because then at least Arkdhem won't try to entertain me or talk to me.

I don't know how much time passes when an alarm blares. A light over the door flashes from green to purple. My head jerks up from the book I've been sitting and reading. Well, pretending to read. I've had some trouble focusing on it, but at least trying to read helped pass the time. When the light came on green a few minicycles ago, Arkdhem didn't seem concerned, but now he's tense.

"What's happening?" I ask him when it doesn't look like he's going to say anything on his own.

With a slight shake, he faces me, trying—and failing—to give me a genuine smile. "What do you mean, Tribute?"

I sigh. Sometimes he can take the protecting me thing way too far. "Something's wrong. That light has been lit for fifteen minutes—uh—minicycles, and it just changed color."

"It is an alert for all warriors to report to their stations."

"Why?" I prompt, sitting up and setting my book down. "What is happening? Are we being attacked?" I'm trying to stay calm, but I can feel anxiety rising up in the back of my throat. Which is probably exactly what he was trying to protect me from by not telling me in the first place, but not knowing would just make me even more fearful in the long run.

"You should ask the High Commander." Arkdhem fidgets with his armor.

I grind my teeth. "I would ask him, but he's not here. He's hardly ever here anymore. He keeps leaving me with you."

"The High Commander has many duties—"

I shoot to my feet, pacing to the end of the room in a savage burst of energy.

"He would be here if he could," Arkdhem calls after me.

"No, he wouldn't," I half-laugh in despair.

"Tribute..." Arkdhem's voice trails off.

"You know it's true. He's avoiding me."

"He is very busy—"

"Then maybe he's too busy for a Tribute," I snap.

"It will be different once you have bonded—"

"It's not going to happen. I've tried. I can't bond with... a robot."

Gavrill has feelings somewhere, deep down. He just refuses to show them.

"The High Commander is not a machine," Arkdhem frowns.

"He certainly acts like one sometimes. The pilot light is on, but there's no one home."

Arkdhem's suit shimmers as he tries to figure out what I'm saying. I'm not sure myself. The doctor seems so sure Gavrill is capable of bonding, but the more I fall for the Commander, the more he pulls away. Maybe the nanites have taken over and he's only a shell of a Tsenturion. A lean, mean, fighting machine, steady and reliable and as emotionally available as a refrigerator. I would've noticed his lack of emotion sooner if he didn't also have the stamina and orgasm-inducing ability of a Sybian.

"The Commander regrets his duties have called him away for so long. He wished for me to tell you." Arkdhem sounds desperate for me to believe him. Poor guy. It's unfair for me to take my anger out on him. He's such a nice guy.

Too bad I'm not his Tribute. I eye Arkdhem's muscular form, perfect and balanced under the bronze suit. I've never seen any other warrior's suit get as light as his; he must always be in a good mood. And with his strong jaw and long lashes, he's pretty, too.

But even if I could get Gavrill to give me up, I know I can never love another. My master might be incapable of loving me, but my stupid heart is lost to him, my body enslaved along with it.

"The Vgotha are executing an attack," Arkdhem keeps explaining. "Until we know what they are up to, the High Commander must remain on the bridge."

"What if we went to him?" I ask, hating myself for even considering seeking the High Commander out. Do I want to go running to him, curl up at his feet on my little cushion and hug his leg as he works? Am I that pathetic?

My pussy tingles and drips a little at the memory of being on the bridge. Apparently, I am.

"Oh no, Tribute, we must stay here. These quarters are at the heart of the ship. Perfectly safe." Arkdhem laughs nervously. "If the enemy breaches them, we are already lost."

"Fine," I say and drop down on the couch in a swirl of floaty silk. I pick at the filmy folds with a perfectly manicured fingernail, feeling useless. Just a pretty little trophy, lounging around in a powder pink dress while the menfolk are off fighting.

"Perhaps we can play a game," Arkdhem offers, and I sigh. He is trying. I don't know what's worse: being left alone like a house bound pet or having a babysitter.

"I can use the replicator now. Would you like something to drink?"

"Yes, thank you, Tribute."

I rise and head to the silvery machine in the corner. I should order some Earth drinks for him. A juice or a soda. A root beer float or a margarita with a tiny paper umbrella. Maybe he'll be impressed.

I could test the limits of the replicator. This dress I'm wearing is soft, but I'd love a pair of yoga pants. If Gavrill likes dresses, he can wear one. I'll even replicate one for him. I don't have his size, but I can use Arkdhem; if I can get my warrior babysitter to drink enough margaritas, I bet he'll agree to it. We can have a party—a luau with grass skirts and flower leis. We can turn the giant tub into a hot tub and make Gavrill jealous.

It's official, I think glumly as I reach the replicator. I'm so bored, I'm designing clothes and mentally throwing elaborate parties. Maybe I'll produce a new reality TV show: *Desperate Housewives of Tsentur.*

I'm so preoccupied, I don't notice the warning lights over the door flashing red a second before the doors explode.

The blast lifts me off my feet. I hit the side of a blush-colored couch and sprawl on the ground.

"Tribute," Arkdhem cries, throwing himself between me and the door. I pick myself up, coughing as smoke billows through the room. My ears are ringing, my vision filled with sparks.

"What—" I cough.

The smoke clears, swirling around a shadowy form just beyond the door. Not human, not Tsenturion, but something strange and massive. In the acrid aftermath of the blast, I shrink back against the couch as the intruder moves through the door, stepping closer on a giant clawed foot.

15

G avrill

"Commander, our weapons are ready," Officer Kalexston reports.

"Hold fire." I tap my earpiece. "Hail Medik. Come to the bridge. High alert." Medik confirms that he received my message, and I end the transmission. I turn back to the science officer. "Sholtorin, have your crew scan all surrounding space for life forms. As soon as you have readings, make a report. I want to know *why*, after a lifetime of hiding, a Vgotha *warship* is sitting in barren space as if waiting for us."

"Commander!" Bogdan's voice is somewhat strangled as he points at the screen in front of us.

The warship is beginning to move.

Away from us.

Lumbering through space like an injured animal.

"Something's wrong with their thrusters," Sholtorin mutters under his breath. "At least... I think there is. The scans are spotty, and there is interference from the black matter cloud."

"What about the hunters and raiders?" I demand, turning towards him. The tension on the bridge is palpable. We all want to attack and bag one of the few warships that the Vgotha have... but we're all aware it could be a trap. "Are they on the warship? Or are they hiding around us?"

"We don't know." Sholtorin's voice is grim.

Beside me, Bogdan mutters a curse.

Medik arrives on the bridge as we all stare at the warship. His steps falter as he takes in the scene.

"A warship," he says, sounding just as awed as I feel.

Turning to him, I nod a greeting. "Medik. You have the most knowledge about the workings of the mind. I would like your opinion on the situation."

~

Dawn

I SHRINK behind the couch as the giant rectangle fills the doorway. Smoke streams around what must be a shield covering all but the clawed feet. Whatever it is, it's taller than Arkdhem.

"Tribute—run!" Arkdhem orders, but where am I supposed to run to? The attacker is blocking the only avenue of retreat. Arkdhem rises, his weapon humming. The laser hits the shield, and the thin red line redirects, cutting into the wall. Smoke and the smell of charred machinery rises.

"Surrender, Tsenturion," a deep voice reverberates through the room. The voice is almost... wooly. It gets in my head, expanding until it fills every corner. I put a hand to my face to relieve the pressure.

"Come closer, and I'll shoot," Arkdhem rasps. A front panel of his helm hangs askew.

"And risk hitting the Tribute?" The amused tone is the voice of reason. "Lay down your weapon." That voice, slipping between my ears. All I want to do is lay down my weapon. I don't even have a weapon.

"You won't take me alive," Arkdhem grits out.

The creature lowers its shield slightly. "Warrior." Its voice is almost a purr. "I do not need you alive."

The intruder pads closer, shield sagging to reveal a behemoth shoulder, muscled and covered with intricate patterns. Its face is a mass of tubes—some sort of helmet that covers everything but a narrow goatee. Above the mask, black antlers rise proudly. The spiny rack is so tall, the thing dips its head to enter the door. Poking out from the coil of tubes are pointed ears, tufted with fur.

I search frantically for a hint of familiarity, a mark or hint that would let me figure out what it is, but the thing looks more like a beast from *Where the Wild Things Are* than any species from Earth.

"You cannot fight me. Embrace oblivion." The voice rolls out, echoing as if at the bottom of a deep well. *Oblivion, oblivion.* My eyelids weight, and I sway a little at my seat on the floor.

Arkdhem's gun wavers. He's succumbing to the voice, too. It reverberates through my head, the wooliness making my thoughts feel as though they are stuffed with cotton.

The creature lowers its shield completely, revealing something out of a nightmare. Tattoos scroll across a broad chest divided into deeply grooved muscle. A dark mane with a greenish tint tumbles down its back between its antlers, reaching a tattered loincloth suspended over enormous thighs. Furred limbs end with clawed hands and feet. More fur tufts from the ridges of its elbows, shoulders, knees. The rest of its body is part-fur, part-green-grey skin, thick and leathery, covered with black markings. As it steps into the light, its tattoos writhe in a hypnotic dance.

Balanced on clawed feet, the monster advances. *Oblivion.* The echo of its last whisper conquers the very air.

Slowly, as if moving through water, Arkdhem's gun tilts down.

The smoke scrapes down my throat, making me choke. A dagger of pain in my lungs is exactly what I need to shake off the intruder's spell.

"Arkdhem," I hiss. "Wake up!"

My Tsenturion protector shakes his head, mouth slack and eyes dazed, even more affected by whatever is happening to us than I am. The creature's face twitches towards me. The gigantic body stops in its tracks. Not a hair moves as it studies me. I recognize the preternatural stillness of a predator waiting to pounce. I cower alongside the couch, my fingers grasping at my silky robes, the only protection I have between my skin and the creature's glowing white eyes.

I marshal my breath, welcome the pain and let it clear my head. Tightening every muscle I have, I open my mouth and let loose the only weapon I have—a scream.

GAVRILL

THE VGOTHA WARSHIP SITS EXPOSED, tempting us. I've never seen one out in the open like this before. Unguarded. Vulnerable. "What are they planning?"

"Maybe they wish to surrender?" Bogdan offers. A thin chuckle ripples through the bridge, breaking some of the tension.

The Vgothas and Tsenturions have been locked in mortal combat for a millennia, ever since the Jabols hired us to protect them from the bully race. We embraced our mission with even more vigor when planet Tsentur was destroyed.

"Why would they be waiting there for us to fire on them?" Medik's voice is a murmur

Bogdan's eyes are fixed on the dun-colored ship on screen. "If we fire, we give away our position," he murmurs, but not as if he's rejecting the notion, just weighing the option.

"What could they do with that intel?" I ask.

My second officer shakes his head, still staring at the enemy ship. "If there are no other ships in the area... nothing."

"The readings report a single life form. One. A large one." Kalexston keeps checking his readings, searching for an explanation.

Medik and I exchange glances. He has long entertained a theory that the Vgothas ships are actually alive, a planet-based symbiot evolved to be useful in space travel. That allows the Vgothas to spread their forces wide, because partnering with the symbiot means it only takes one or two Vgotha to pilot a ship.

"Why would they abandon a warship?" I muse aloud. If the tech was truly a living symbiot, abandoning it would be like cutting off a limb and losing an entire battalion of warriors all at once.

Beside me, Bogdan makes a sound of annoyance. "Does it matter why? They would not have done so unless they had no choice. Our weapons are superior. We must fire on the ship and destroy it."

Beside me, the doctor makes a noise of agreement.

We cannot just leave a warship here. They might come back for it. They might be trying to find a way to repair it. Or it might be a trap, but we won't know until we spring it.

"Lock weapons on the Vgotha ship," I order. "You may send a warning shot. Fire at will."

"Firing," Bogdan says gleefully as the image flares with a sudden bright explosion.

The whole screen lights up for a moment, blinding us. Someone cries out as the floor under my feet vibrate, tossing as our ship is hit by the biggest blast I've ever felt. The entire bridge shakes, tossing warriors to the ground.

Alarms blare. Bogdan's crowing turns into a curse. I reach out and steady the doctor, helping him find his feet.

"Report," I shout.

"Sensors down." Kalexston sounds shaken. "Commander, the ship detonated some sort of energy pulse."

"They have a new weapon," Medik murmurs.

"Whatever they hit us with, it's affecting our sensors. My team needs to recalibrate them," Kalexston says.

"Do it now," I order.

"Commander, we must lock weapons again and destroy them," Bogdan snarls. "This is our chance."

I meet Medik's gaze. We've destroyed Vgotha ships before, but never one that's scuttled. Something doesn't feel right.

"Lock weapons on their coordinates again," I order.

"Die, alien scum," Bogdan says, his armor practically glowing, seething with righteous victory.

The bridge hums with the powering up of our weapons, almost drowning out the science officer, who whirls from his com desk. "Commander! Our shields have been breached!!"

Dawn

THE ROOM SHAKES like something hit the ship.

I kick backwards, scuttling across the floor. My dress rips. The creature reaches for me.

A roar blasts my ears along with the sinister hum of a weapon. Arkdhem is upright, firing.

The creature angles the shield, and the laser reflects back on Arkdhem, slicing into him until he falls.

"No," I scream. I race to Arkdhem's side, whimpering in sympathy at the gash in his suit, peeling away from his burned body.

"Tribute," he rasps. "You must run. You must survive this." His eyes flutter closed. "Tell the High Commander I fought well." His suit dims as if shutting down.

"Arkdhem," I whisper, planting a hand on his chest to feel the slight movement of his breathing. He still alive, I think, but unconscious.

Dammit, where are the other Tsenturion warriors?

Blood rushes from my face as I remember what I was told—*These quarters are at the heart of the ship. Perfectly safe. If the enemy breaches them, we are already lost.*

Oh my God... is everyone else dead? Is Gavrill dead?

The horned creature stalks forward. I've seen sketches of the Horned God, leader of the Wild Hunt according to fae-lore, a giant satyr-type god with a stag's head. This alien looks exactly like that pagan deity come to life. Terrifying and intimidating and...

And it's coming for me.

I hoist the gun and rise, scrabbling for the trigger even as a scream rises behind my clenched teeth. But I'm too late.

The creature rips the weapon out of my hands and wrenches it apart. I throw up my hands to shield myself from the spray of gun pieces, staggering backwards.

If I can run and reach the adjoining room, maybe I can lock myself in and radio for help.

A few steps, and a claw yanks me back, whirling me around. Another claw closes around my throat, and the creature hoists me in the air. I grasp at the rigid arm holding me aloft, my feet kicking wildly, looking for purchase as I choke. Spots swirl before my eyes, and I put all my strength behind one desperate kick to the alien's gut. It drops me, I think more out of surprise than the force. A second later, I'm cuffed and thrown against the couch. My head is numb from the blow, and I can already feel a bruise forming over the side of my face.

"I see. You must be the High Commander's Tribute," the creature murmurs thoughtfully. A purring hum rumbles from its chest, the soft sound at odds with its powerful body.

It reaches for me. I kick again, much more weakly this time, but it's much faster as it grabs me and scoops me up. Not by my throat, in fact it cradles me almost gently, and I don't understand the change in its demeanor. I meet its blazing white eyes in terror.

"Peace, little creature," it growls, and the voice fills my senses again, trying to make me sleep. There's a shushing sound, an exhale, a rush of soporific fog enveloping me. It's a gas, not a spell, and if I can just tear off its mask, the creature won't be immune. I try to hold my breath, but my limbs are already feeling heavier and heavier, like I'm trying to push through Jell-O as I lift them.

As my fingers reach the knotted coils, my head lolls on my neck and darkness rises to swallow me whole.

GAVRILL

THE SHIP on screen flares with light, and the bridge shakes with another pulse. Consoles light up, and the alarms whine louder in protest.

"They can reverse the weapon's path and send an energy pulse back! Disengage!" I order. Suddenly, the scuttled ship before us doesn't seem so harmless.

"Get me readings. I want to know what just hit us."

"The pulse blew our sensors offline for a moment, but they are returning," my operations officer, Miths, reports.

"Weapons are disengaged," Bogdan adds gruffly. "Permission to take a pod to engage the enemy personally." My second looks ready to grab a gun and storm the enemy ship all by himself.

"Denied. We need to know what we're dealing with first."

"No change in the enemy ship," Kalexston says, his eyes on his beeping panel.

"Keep running scans." I turn to my operations officer. "Miths, did we sustain damage?"

"Negative, Commander. All sensors are functioning again." He frowns. "Except for some slight damage to an exterior portal near the lower right quadrant."

"Exterior portal?" Medik asks. "Was there a breach?"

Miths frowns. "I'm trying to gather more data. My crew informs me there's a number of sensors offline in that area. They're headed onsite to repair them now."

An alarm clangs in the back of my mind. "Was the portal damaged with the pulse?"

"Unsure, Commander. My crew should arrive to secure the area soon." He pauses to listen to his crew's report before continuing. "There's a row of damaged sensors extending from the exterior portal down the halls leading towards the core. The aft quadrant."

"The aft quadrant," Medik repeats. "That's near the officer's quarters."

I'm on my feet a second before Miths cries out, "Commander, we've found wounded Tsenturions."

"High alert," I shout. "The enemy breached the hull! Kalexston, report." An enemy on the ship is unthinkable.

"My crew is working to secure the area. We've found six Tsenturions down in the halls. They appear to have been overpowered by their own weapons."

Drakk. The enemy is here, on my ship. And instead of calmly accepting this and sending my crew to kill the intruders, I am seized with fear. The situation below decks requires caution. I have a Tribute, a defenseless female I've sworn to protect. I cannot risk her being caught in the crossfire.

For the first time in a thousand tsencycles, I have something to lose.

We wait in tense silence. Medik looks like he might say something but bites it back at the last minute. Every muscle in my body is rigid. The moment I decide to grab my weapon and run down there to save Dawn myself, Miths stiffens as he receives a piece of news.

I know what he's going to say even before he turns around. "Commander, we've found evidence of a Vgotha intruder. He entered one of the portals, found his way to infiltrate your quarters, wounded Officer Arkdhem, and left via the same exterior portal."

"The Tribute?" Medik asks before I can find my voice. His face holds all the fear I refuse to show.

"Gone," Miths looks at me, his armor flickering sickly, and I feel my hearts sink in my chest. I already know what he's going to say, and it's all I can do to keep from howling at the pain already ripping into me. "The Vgotha took her."

D awn

THERE's something cool plastered on my face. It feels good on my bruised skin, tingling lightly. Healing me? I definitely don't hurt as much as I expected to. Gingerly I pluck the cloth from face, sitting up and tossing it to the side so I can see where I am.

The space is dimly lit and close, the air a mix of humidity and mist, a warm, flower-scented gloom. The walls look like a blend of moss and some sort of fungus, almost... breathing.

I lay on a soft mass that shifts slightly under me. It feels like a cross between a bean bag and a water bed. The supple form has a soft, slippery skin that's bright yellow.

A giant shadow moves out of the corner of my eye, and I stiffen. My tattooed captor paces forward on large, clawed feet. The mass of tubes that were a sort of gas mask are gone from its head, leaving a more humanoid face with a pointed, goatee-tipped chin and wide cheekbones framing large, limpid eyes. Back on the Tsenturion ship they were glowing white, but now they're a comfortable brown. Beneath the tattoos is a gray-green skin that reminds me of stone.

I've been abducted by aliens—again.

He opens his mouth, and sharp teeth flash at me. "Are you awake?"

There's a buzz in my ear as my translator works overtime to interpret what the creature is saying. The voice seems to go directly into my head.

I nod, then realize it might not understand the gesture. "I'm awake."

"Are you hurt?"

I reach up to touch my face where it hit me. The soreness is gone, though a slight numbness lingers. "No. I'm good."

The creature settles on its haunches before me. I flinch as it reaches out, but it—he? I definitely get a male vibe—only lifts the wet cloth I discarded and tucks it into his belt. His gaze meets mine, and he tilts his head, studying me as much as I'm studying him.

As we stare at each other in silence, a door opens and a second creature stalks in. This one is a slightly smaller version of my captor, only with large bat-like wings draping down his back. I'm pretty sure it's a he because of the loincloth hanging between his legs.

"Tor, why did you bring that back here?" he asks, looking down at me in disgust. "We needed a high-ranking captive, not a pet."

"She belongs to the High Commander," the first Vgotha—Tor—answers. In the gloom of the ship, he looks even more like the Horned God, though his antlers look slightly smaller. Maybe they can grow at will. His teeth are long with canine-like incisors, and his ears are pointed. The second Vgotha also has elfin ears, along with the rippling muscles of a beast with fur tufted at the joints.

Of all the alien races who could kidnap me, I'm the captive of ones that look like elf-demons. Great. Just great.

The winged Vgotha cocks his head to the side, studying me in the same manner Tor is, a slight look of disbelief on his face. "She is the Tribute? But she is so small. Is she sentient?"

"I believe so. The Tsenturions have high standards."

The winged one laughs. I scowl at them, using anger to help cover my fear. Obviously, they don't think much of the Tsenturion standards.

"Welcome, Tribute, to the Vgotha ship," the winged Vgotha says mockingly, his leathery wings shifting with a sound like crackling paper.

I don't answer, pressing my lips together to keep my temper at bay. I have no idea what these creatures will do to me, but I don't think a spanking would be their first move. My heart pounds, but my fear feels muted. Maybe I'm getting used to being abducted.

"What now, Tor?" Mr. Demon Wings asks.

Tor studies me thoughtfully. "Let's see just what lengths the High Commander is willing to go to in order to save his little Tribute."

I shrink into my seat on the bed as the giant monster alien rises and stalks away, Mr. Demon giving me an assessing look before following. The door closes behind them, leaving me all alone. Which I should be happy about, but I'm not. I'm even more terrified than before.

I suck in a breath, trying not to panic. There's a little hum in my chest that tells me not to worry. A little voice in my head that says —*My mate is big and strong, and he will save me.* Talk about being brainwashed. I realize I'm stroking my collar, as if for reassurance, and immediately snatch my hand away.

Who am I kidding? Gavrill doesn't want *me.* He can just ring up the Jabol and order another Tribute. Brunette this time, or maybe a redhead. One who won't fight him so much. The Jabol can put together a catalogue, complete with swimsuit photos. Maybe even Bogdan will get on board. And me? I'll be trapped with new aliens whose only use for me is apparently to bargain with the Tsenturions.

So what's going to happen to me when they realize the Tsenturions don't think I'm worth bargaining for?

The yellow blob I'm sitting on quivers and hums a little, as if to reassure me. It sounds like it's alive. In fact, the whole ship feels like I've been swallowed by a living, breathing creature. That would explain the rainforest feel.

I gulp and push myself up. I already know there's going to be no white knight riding to my rescue. I don't mean enough to any of the Tsenturions. Heck, I doubt Bogdan would even think twice before blowing up a ship I'm on if it meant he got rid of all the Vgothas on it, too.

I'm not tied up, I'm not in a cell, I'm not even sure I'm guarded... and it's up to me to get myself out of this.

~

GAVRILL

"COMMANDER, we're picking up a frequency from a Vgotha ship," Sholtorin says, cutting through the panic that has gripped me ever since I knew Dawn was taken. We still don't know where or even how.

The camouflage on the small Vgotha hunter and raider ships is frustratingly sporadic, allowing them to wink in and out of existence on our scanners. Whatever technology they're using to hide is not perfect, but it is enough to keep us from knowing which one managed to board us and take Dawn.

"The warship?" I ask.

"I don't believe so, Commander, but I'm not sure which ship. It's definitely one of the Vgotha though."

"Put them through," I say with a growl.

The main screen flickers, and a Vgotha appears. Sickeningly gray-green skin, puny horns, and brown eyes stare back at me. Beside me, Bogdan growls at the sight of our enemy.

"You are the High Commander?" the Vgotha asks, looking at me.

"I am," I say, my armor flashing dangerously. The entire bridge is full of black armor now, ready for battle. "Who are you?"

"I am Tor, Chief of the Vgotha."

I want to demand to know where Dawn is, what they've done with her, but to do so would be to show weakness. Instead, I pretend that nothing is amiss.

"Why did you hail us?" I ask, keeping my voice level. "To surrender?"

Tor chuckles. "I infiltrated your hold and snatched something of yours right from under your nose. You can't even find our ships. Why should I surrender?"

"Because you're spreading yourself thin and dying in the scramble to find enough food and weapons to live through the next cycle. Surrender, and your deaths will be quick."

"Your pride will be your downfall, Commander. I have someone I'd like you to meet. Or perhaps you know her."

The screen flashes to Dawn, exploring a mossy looking room of wherever they're holding her. A sharp pang rips through my chest as I stare at her. Other than a bruise on the side of her face, she doesn't look as though she's been harmed. As I watch, she brushes her long fall of blonde hair back from her shoulder in a familiar motion, scratching at the tender spot that has been bothering her. Something clenches in my gut.

"Your Tribute has come for a visit." Tor returns to the screen. "As you can see, she has not been damaged."

"You will return her to us. Now." I can feel Bogdan looking at me from the corner of his eye, but I ignore him. I am not thinking, I am acting on my emotions, but I can't seem to help it. Just that small glimpse of my Dawn is enough to tear any logic I have to shreds.

"Or else what, Tsenturion?" Tor mocks. "My ships fly undetected past your sensors. I boarded your ship, infiltrated your personal quarters and took your prize. What's to stop me from disappearing and taking her with me?"

"What do you want?" I ask, clenching my fists. "If you think we will surrender, you are wrong. We will fight."

"With Jabol weapons, I know." Tor stares at me. "The time for fighting has passed. You, Commander, will come to my warship *alone*, within the next cycle, or you will not see your Tribute again."

The screen goes dark.

"Drakk," I shout as the visual of the Vgotha's ship disappears, along with Tor's hard-eyed gaze. Pacing, I smash a fist into a wall panel, and the warriors around me startle. My crew has never seen me like this. I'm a microcycle away from losing control. "Where are they? What do our sensors tell us? Report!"

"We're scanning the area, High Commander," Klaxeston says tightly, head down and eyes on his instruments. "They cannot have gone far."

I curse again, and Miths and Borodem twitch. Shouting at them will not help. Nor will ripping my chair from the floor and throwing it.

"Commander." The low voice at my elbow makes me whirl. Medik's eyes meet mine, full of understanding. "She wasn't hurt. She looked well. We will find her."

No, we won't. Because Tor is right. And even if we did somehow manage to locate the ship that she's on, it might be too late. I won't risk her that way.

"I'm going to the warship," I say grimly, turning toward the door to the bridge. I can see the crew jumping up, protests halfway out of their mouths, as Bogdan steps in front of me, barring my way.

"You cannot abandon your post."

"Do not," I growl, "tell me what to do."

"We need you here, in command," Bogdan barks. "With all due respect, you are not in possession of your senses."

"Is this mutiny?" I roar. "Get out of my way!" I'm taller, but my second has more bulk. He is a mean fighter, but I do not want to fight with him—that will take up precious time. I just want him out of my way. Red flashes from my suit and seems to leap to his. My anger reflects on his face.

"Stop it, both of you," Medik snaps. "We need to talk about this."

"We cannot throw away our chance to capture a Vgotha ship." Bogdan points to the side screen, where the abandoned ship still sits in empty space. "If we can cripple it, can bring it in for testing, we will have a chance to learn of their weapons and defenses. It could turn the tide of war to our favor. *That's* what we should be scanning for, what our goal should be."

"And what of my Tribute?" I grit out. I know what he's going to say, but I want to hear him actually voice it. If he dares.

"They are using her against us."

"You heard the Vgotha. I have a cycle to get to that warship. They will kill her."

"An unfortunate casualty of war," Bogdan says softly. To my surprise, he almost looks sorry, but he does not back down. "But she is not even one of us. There will be other Tributes, you can have whichever one of them you want."

I surge forward, ready to correct my second's arrogant opinion with my fists. Medik steps between us, keeping me from my target, and I shout over the older Tsenturion's shoulder at Bogdan.

"I don't want another Tribute. Dawn is *not* replaceable."

Shock is clear on Bogdan's face at my reaction.

"Commander," Medik murmurs. "I agree that we must retrieve the Tribute immediately. Their population has also been depleted in this war. If we take too long to enter into negotiations, they might decide to breed her."

"That's not possible." Klaxeston's suit flares bright green with horror. Even Bogdan looks ill at the thought.

"From the information the Jabol gave us on them, Vgotha anatomy is close to ours. She might be compatible," Medik says. "We must free her before they decide to find out."

I stare at the blank screen, willing Dawn's image to reappear.

"I will go," I repeat. "Bogdan, you are in command. If you want to find a way to capture the warship, you will have to do it while I am on it. You are correct, I am emotional, and I am no longer fit for duty. I am giving in to the Vgotha's demands, what happens next with them will be up to you."

The bridge is silent with shock.

Bogdan's eyes darken. "This is not what I want, brother."

"I know. But it is necessary." I would do anything to have Dawn back, safe in my arms.

"Commander—"

"Know this," I raise my voice so the entire deck hears, "Dawn is more than just a Tribute. She is my mate. I would give my life a thousand times to spare her any harm."

The men around me stare at the statement. At my side, Medik wears a sad smile. Bogdan slowly shakes his head.

"The bridge is yours," I say, stepping around both Medik and Bogdan as I begin to run towards the bowels of the ship, where the scout ships are docked. The sooner I reach the warship, the sooner Dawn will be safe.

If not, the universe will not contain my rage. I will hunt the Vgotha down and destroy them all.

D awn

I PACE THE SMALL ROOM, trying to figure out how I'm going to get out of here.

It's feels like it's been hours. There's still some wishful part of me that hopes help is coming... but I can't see it happening. Not when I'm so replaceable.

I pause in front of one of the walls of my prison where the Vgothas had exited. Once the door shut, the wall reformed as if the entryway never existed. Creepy, but kinda cool. The whole interior of the ship feels alive—in more than a vegetation sort of way. The air is moist and heavy like a rainforest, and I can't get over the feeling that I'm being watched.

I put my hand on the wall and press. It feels like damp moss, and I'm tempted to rip it off, but if it's living material, the Vgotha might be alerted that I'm trying to escape. The forest has eyes. Instead of yanking at anything, I start patting my hands over it, checking for weak spots. Maybe I can find the crack to the door. There's got to be a way out.

"Please let me out," I whisper, feeling kind of silly, but I can't shake the feeling that the ship can hear me. Understand me. I keep running my hands over the wall, moving to the next one beside where Tor and the other Vgotha left through. "I don't belong here, I don't want to be here... please... my name is Dawn, and I just want to go home... please..."

I keep moving my hands over the wall, pleading the whole time.

To my shock, the moss suddenly melts away, showing a small tunnel, just wide enough to fit a smaller sized being... like a human.

"Thank you." I don't feel so silly now. Maybe a little creeped out, but... I'm not throwing away my shot.

I duck inside and start crawling. Once I'm a few feet in, the wall behind me forms back in place. I take a moment to swallow my panic along with a slight dose of claustrophobia. Only one way to go—forward. I keep crawling. The light at the end of the tunnel seems to get further away—and at one point, the tunnel twists as if to stop my progress. I keep deep breathing and wait for the way to open up again. After a moment it does, as if the tunnel closing down was a test and I passed. At one point, I have to contort myself to twist around a particularly hard right turn. Good thing the Tsenturions healed my knee and that I've kept up with my yoga. I don't know if I could handle this tunnel if I couldn't contort with the best of them.

At last, the tunnel widens and light floods in. I pull myself to the edge and look out into a long, low-ceilinged room. No sign of a Vgotha, but there's a tiny pod, a lot like the one the Jabols used to deliver me to the Tsenturions a lifetime ago.

Not quite believing my luck, I wait a moment in the mouth of the tunnel. The walls around me contract with a slight murmur, pushing me forward, a lot like the bean bag pushing me to my feet. This is unreal, but if the ship is helping me escape, I'm not going to question it.

"Thank you," I whisper, drop to the floor, and rush to the pod. It's long and narrow, just large enough to fit one person. I press my hand to the panel beside it, and it lights up. The pod door opens upward. After a moment's hesitation, I climb in and lie down. The panel beside the pod beeps a few times, and the door closes with a sigh. I practice my deep breathing again, trying not to compare lying in the pod to lying in a coffin. A slight shudder, and the wall in front of the pod grows around a large dark spot, widening like an ink stain on the brown-green wall. Another shudder, a whooshing sound and the pod shoots forward. I scream as points of light rush over me, the air growing close and suffocating for a moment, and then the pod is floating in black space, faraway stars like little bright diamonds twinkling to guide the way.

I did it. I'm free. The Tsenturions won't believe I got away with only the help of a sentient ship. I bet the Vgotha have no idea I'm even gone. I can't imagine why the ship would let me go and then tell them. I guess the only thing I can rely on is the aliens underestimating me. Except for the ship. I frown trying to think through the ramifications of that, which is kind of hard when I'm so jittery.

The pod keeps floating smoothly along, fast enough that the starscape changes every few minutes or so. The panel beside my face has all sorts of buttons, but I'm afraid to touch it. I hope the Tsenturions are out looking for me and that I can figure out destination coordinates, otherwise I'll be lost in space. But one thing at a time.

Shadows crawl over the glass like clouds over a sky, interspersed with rays of light. The pod shoots past a sun—a giant burning ball bright enough that the glass seems to tint, and I still have to shield my eyes. Then we're past it and flying through dark space again, coming out to weave through a field of meteors. I don't know how I'm moving so fast and I'm still able to see the sights close up. Silt hits the pod like a spray of pebbles. A giant rock looms close, and I throw up my hands, afraid we're going to hit it. At the last second, the pod zooms around it. After a few close calls like that, I close my eyes until we hit darkness again. The pod knows what it's doing. I hope.

I don't really have a choice except to trust it.

A soft light warms my face, and I open my eyes to clouds of pinkish interstellar dust. Golden streaks swirl through the cloud. It's so beautiful, I forget to be afraid. A part of me wishes Gavrill were here. If I have eleven hundred years to live with him, we could take some great trips. Explore the universe. A visit to one of these nebulae would make a hell of a honeymoon.

Darkness encloses the pod again, and I realize I'm holding my breath whenever we hit these black patches. This time we're slow coming out. Flashes of light in the distance make me tense. It looks like lightning, a million miles away. My heartbeat picks up as the flashes grow closer. There's a storm in front of us, and we're heading right towards it.

I fucking hate storms.

"No, no, no." I press on the walls of the pod. I even risk hitting a few buttons on the panel. It chirps at me but doesn't alter course. Grey-brown dust billows around us, clouding my view. We hit another meteor belt, and tiny rocks pelt the pod like hail on a windshield. A few larger ones hit with enough force to make me yelp. The lightning in the distance is a lot closer, and the dust is now swirling like a tornado, sucking us forward.

Fuck. We're going right into the storm.

White light splits the mist of greyish particles swirling around the pod. I scream. Lightning racks the pod again and again while I cover my head, whimpering. The storm took everyone I loved—my mom, my grandma, my dad before I even knew him. It sucked me through a vortex into another galaxy, and now it's trying to wipe me out before I return to him.

"No," I scream. "No!" I kick the smooth glass top of the pod and punch the air. I will not go quietly into the night. Wet tracks down my cheeks, and I'm sobbing, my chest cracking into pieces to let the emotion out, but it doesn't feel like dying. It feels good. Few more lightning strikes, and the air around the pod shimmers. The violent clouds are fading in the distance, disappearing into the blissful darkness.

My shaky sniffles turn into a giggle. I've weathered the storm and come out the other side. Alive. As laughter bubbles in my chest, I raise my arms and whoop.

Stars sparkle on a clean velvet backdrop. The pod dives through rings of colored gas, then navigates past a planet, moving at record time. I resist the urge to flatten my face against the glass and study the gorgeous grey and blue orb. The temperature falls slightly, and I shiver. A rummaging study of the pod unearths a thick fur, and I pull it over me. It smells like a Vgotha, earthy and rainforest-y with a slight musk that reminds me of a shaggy dog. It's not unpleasant. I snuggle beneath the fur and resist to urge to laugh.

I was captured by Vgothas, and all I got was this lousy fur robe. I still don't know how I managed it. I completely lucked out with this pod. Not only is the autopilot working like a dream, but the ship is regulated to my body temperature. Frllil told me human anatomy was similar to Tsenturions; that was why we were considered compatible mates. Maybe the Vgothas are the same?

The more I think about it, the less I think luck was involved and that the ship and this pod have to be sentient and decided to let me go for some reason. I mean, what are the chances the tunnel from my prison room would lead straight to an escape pod? That the coordinates would be set to get me as far away from the Vgotha ship as possible? Not that I have any hopes of doing much more than drift in space until someone finds me. I can only hope it's a Tsenturion ship.

Then I see it—shiny black and floating out from behind the frozen planet like a lesser moon. I know the shape from all the videos Frllil made me watch. It's Tsenturion, and not just any ship—the High Commander's.

"Hey," I shout, as if they can hear me hail them. I study the panel buttons, frantically looking for one that will let me open a communication channel, send up a flare, do the Hokey-Pokey... something to get them to notice me. Hell, I'll take off my shirt and wave it if that might help flag the guys down. Gavrill might not like me showing my body off... but Gavrill might have already written me off as lost. God, that hurts more than I want it to—like a knife in my heart. For a second, I struggle to breathe.

But I know it's probably true.

I grip the fur robe and stare at the huge Tsenturion ship, looming larger as it grows closer. Suddenly, I'm not in a rush to be rescued anymore. Homesickness, a longing for Earth, for *humans*, for thinking I have even a chance at love fills me. But that's not what I'm going back to.

Still, at least I'm alive. Think positive and all that. Besides, it's not like I have anywhere else I can go. Drifting off into space and dying alone in the blackness doesn't exactly appeal either.

A microcycle later, the pod jerks and a hum fills my ears. A whitish glow surrounds me, enveloping the whole pod. Beyond it, the stars blur. We're caught in a light beam of some sort, and it's pulling us towards the Tsenturion ship at high speed. I grab the fur with one hand and press the other to the wall for balance. This pod needs some 'oh shit!' handles. A panel on the side of the Tsenturion ship opens, revealing a loading bay. Thank God. I was afraid for a moment I was going to crash into the side of the ship or get blown to bits by the tractor beam like a mosquito caught by a bug zapper.

The approaching side of the ship fills my window, and then my pod is safely inside. The doors close, and Tsenturion soldiers pour onto the deck, weapons in hand to deal with my unidentified pod.

I throw the fur off my shoulders in case the Tsenturions think I'm an undersized Vgotha and blow me to bits. Gavrill has probably trained his men to be more discerning than that, but I bet a lot of them are pretty trigger-happy right now, and I'm in a Vgotha escape pod.

The pod opens, and I suck in air. It's over. I've done it. I'm back—for better or worse. I can't deny the relief I feel at the sight of so many Tsenturions as I look up from my seat. Judging from the light colors of their suits, they're glad to see me too.

"Commander, we found her!" one of the warrior cries. Relieved to be back on the familiar ship, I don't even protest at the mistruth. The Tsenturions didn't find me. I saved myself.

Before I can pull myself out of the pod, the group of soldiers parts and Gavrill emerges, rushing to my side with more urgency than I've ever seen before.

"Dawn. My Dawn. Are you hurt?" His voice is full of anxious

worry, and his hands roam over me, searching my exposed skin, delving under the thick fur on my lap. With a growl, he rips the fur off and tosses it away. The colors on his armor are rippling, like a muddy rainbow, making it impossible to know how he's feeling.

"I'm fine," I say, trying to reassure him.

"Commander, keep your distance, they might have contaminated her in order to poison us—" Bogdan sounds serious and worried.

"They didn't," I say, but before I can finish my sentence, Gavrill is already picking me up, ignoring Bogdan's warning and shouting for the doctor.

"I'm fine, I'm fine," I repeat, even as I mold myself against his firm body, relaxing in his arms.

"Bogdan is right. They could've given you poison. Medik!" He calls out again, turning as he looks for the older Tsenturion. The rippling colors on his armor intensify, flashing so quickly it almost makes me nauseous to look at it, as close to out of control as I've ever seen him. "We need a medkit here, now!"

The crowd of warriors parts to make way for the stooped Tsenturion, who is hurrying forward as fast as he can. Gavrill moves to meet him, holding me out slightly in front of him like I'm an offering. Quick as a wink, Medik runs a scanner up and down my body.

Beside us, the Tsenturions examine the pod I came in.

"What is this technology?" one of the warriors breathes. Another pokes it with his gun.

"Don't hurt it," I snap, then bite my tongue. I need to explain my theory of the ship being alive to Gavrill. Hopefully, he'll be interested enough to believe me and not harm it considering I wouldn't have been able to escape without it.

"Commander, I must protest, she may have been infected with their symbiote—" Bogdan starts again.

"She's clear," Medik says hurriedly as Gavrill's face twists with anger. "Just the rash that she acquired here."

"I'm taking her to my quarters," Gavrill barks at his second.

"We need to debrief her—"

"Stand down," Gavrill roars. The warriors snap to attention, even

Bogdan. Ignoring all of them, Gavrill carries me between the saluting rows with ground-eating strides.

"I'm fine," I reassure him softly, patting his chest. I know he's more upset that his special tribute prize was taken and that this doesn't mean he actually cares about *me*, but it's still nice to pretend. Being held by him again, I feel protected, and I know that's true.

"You could've been killed." He practically growls the words, but I can also feel something else—anguish? Maybe. It's too faint to really know. Or maybe that's just wishful thinking on my part.

"Is Arkdhem okay?" I ask, since I don't see him.

Lips pressed together, Gavrill nods.

"It wasn't his fault. The Vgotha hit him with some sort of trance spell. It didn't seem to work as well on me."

"I know," Gavrill says, although his expression is still implacable. I huff. Hopefully, he isn't holding a grudge against Arkdhem, although I don't know what I can do if he is. It's not like Gavrill will listen to me.

18

G avrill

I CARRY Dawn to my cabin, my hearts pounding inside my chest so noisily that I can barely hear my thoughts. I feel split in two. I was about to board a ship to rescue my Tribute, when the sensors picked up the advance of a Vgotha ship. I was ready to bring it on board and tear it apart myself and torture the occupants until they told me where to find Dawn. When the pod opened and revealed her pale face, I couldn't keep myself from touching her.

I've broken protocol in front of all of my warriors. Possibly even put them in danger. Fortunately, there was nothing wrong with her, but Bogdan's paranoia could have easily proven true.

I know he's also right that we need to debrief her. We need to know what she saw, what she heard, any information she can give us on the Vgothas and their ships. She's the only being we know of who has ever been on one and made it out alive.

But that duty wars with my personal need to check her over, to ensure she is unharmed, and to protect her. I want her safely tucked away from everyone, to have her completely for myself, just for a bit.

"Where are we going?" she asks.

"Our temporary quarters." Our old quarters need repairs after the infiltration. "I need to check you over."

"I'm *fine*," she says again, sounding exasperated. I know she's telling the truth, and yet I also know I won't be satisfied until I've examined every part of her with my own eyes. Possibly my hands too. Just having her in my arms is rousing my need to claim her irrevocably. "They didn't do anything to me except put me in a cell. They seemed to think I was a pet."

If I wasn't so out-of-sorts, I would have chuckled at the disgruntled note in her voice. "You might seem like a pet to them. I doubt they have ever seen a human before."

The cabin door opens before us as she lets out a little snort.

Gently setting her down on the bed, I begin to look her over, frowning when I come to the dark red spot on her neck. Medik had assured both her and me that it was just some kind of rash, but it looks as though it has gotten worse.

"Does this still itch?" I ask, my finger hovering over it.

Dawn shakes her head. "Not really. It just looks bad."

She blushes a little, her eyes slightly downcast as she looks away from me. I do not like that she will not meet my eyes. Before the Vgotha took her, she was sad, but now she doesn't seem so... if anything, the sense of her emotions that I get is determination.

"Anything else?" I ask, running my hands over her arms.

"No, I told you, I'm fine... look, stop, just stop touching me." Suddenly she jerks back, leaving me empty-handed and shocked.

A few semicycles ago, I would have pulled her over my knee and spanked her until she acknowledged my right to touch her however I pleased. Right now, though? Having her just returned to me, only for my touch to be rejected?

"What did they do to you? What did the Vgothas do that you don't want my touch?" I demand, rising and stepping back to give her the space she apparently needs.

"Nothing, I told you, they did nothing!" She stands too, her eyes now meeting mine, wide, blue, and filled with tears. "But I can't stand you touching me like you care, I can't sit here and pretend everything is fine between us when it's not."

"I do care—" I start to say, but she cuts me off.

"You care about *your Tribute*," she says, the sarcasm in her voice mocking the endearment I enjoy so much. "You care about me as your Tribute, but nothing more. Someone came and took your shiny toy, and you're happy to have me back, but you don't really care about me. You made that abundantly clear before I was taken, and I cannot deal with you acting like anything has changed just because I was taken away from you for a while."

I stare at her, my armor dulling to grey as I try to understand what she's saying to me. Of course I care about her, she is my Tribute. My future. My Dawn. I was willing to abandon my post to save her. I don't understand how she can think I wouldn't care about her. Her words don't make sense to me.

"What do you want from me?" My words are a baffled plea for instruction. None of her manuals covered anything quite like this. I thought I had earned my place as her Master, but...

I do not understand what is wrong, so I do not know how to make it right. Whatever it is, I will do it.

Big blue eyes look up at me, filled with tears.

"I want to go home," she whispers. "Back to Earth. I don't want to be your Tribute."

Something inside of me tears, ripping through me with a greater force than any weapon she could have used on me. I would give her anything but that.

But it is what she wants.

Not trusting my voice, I nod and turn away, retreating because I cannot think what else to do. The agony crawling up the inside of my chest is hauntingly familiar. I felt it the last time I lost everything.

Dawn

It's the right decision.

That's what I tell myself, even as the expression on Gavrill's face, the sad grey of his armor, and my own needs make me want to call him back. Or chase after him.

My shoulder twinges, right where the red spot is, and I put my hand over it. It had spiked with pain when I told Gavrill I wanted to go back to Earth, and I'm starting to think that Medik is wrong about it being a harmless rash, but it doesn't really matter right now. I'm not sure anything matters.

Slowly, I sink back down onto the couch and curl up into a little ball.

I'd sworn to myself at the beginning of this that I would escape. That I would find a way back to Earth. That's what I was doing. I can't stay here, in love with an alien that sees me as nothing more than a possession.

Soon enough, he'll have another Tribute.

One who actually signs up for the experience, even if she thinks it's a joke when she does it.

It won't—can't—be me. I can't handle being in love with someone who just sees me as an incubator for his babies. Someone who is happy to fuck me into oblivion but pulls away from me just when it seems like his emotions are becoming involved.

The door swishes open, and I don't even look up. If my friggin' Tsenturion Master wants a little sub to greet him, he can replicate and program a sex robot. Maybe Frllil could make one for him.

"Tribute?" a soft voice calls from near the door. Not Gavrill—the doctor.

"Here," I raise a hand, too tired to ask him to call me Dawn again.

The older Tsenturion approaches me warily. "Are you feeling well?"

"I'm fine," I wrench myself up to prove it. "The Vgothas didn't do anything to me."

"The Commander wishes me to check and debrief you."

"Okay. Fine." I sit and let him scan me, turning my head and offering my wrist when prompted. I'm still thinking about calling Frllil and asking him to make Gavrill a sex doll, maybe one that can incubate Gavrill's sperm until they replicate a female Tsenturion ovum. Or better yet, Frllil could clone him. That's just what the universe needs, twenty million hard-jawed Gavrills, commanding ships and guarding every corner of the known universe.

"Dawn..." I realize that Medik has been calling my name for some time. I blink and focus on his frowning face. "Your vitals are normal, but there seem to be some lingering effects on your conscious state..."

"There was a gas. Or a spell or something—" I explain the way Tor seemed to hypnotize me with his voice.

"I have heard of a drug that can do this. It comes from a mushroom that an ancient civilization cultivated on their planet. If one ingests enough of the fungus, their skin emits a pheromone that makes the people around them susceptible to suggestion."

"That sounds about right."

"The mushroom was destroyed along with the planet. The Vgothas must have gotten a specimen and cultivated it."

"That would make sense," I say. "Their whole ship was like a garden." More like an indoor marijuana farm.

"The High Commander will want a full account of your experience, but he will question you later about it."

I nod. Of course he does. That way, he and Bogdan can get down to the business of destroying the Vgothas. No sense in importing more Tributes if your sworn enemy is just going to break all your pretty, pretty toys.

"I think perhaps it would be good for you to rest," Medik continues.

I shrug. "I can do it now, while the memory is fresh."

"I do not think that is wise. Physically you are healthy, but there seems to be a lingering malaise."

"No, I felt this way before the Vgothas took me. I just didn't have the courage to talk about it." The trip through the storm took care of that. After my family died, I hid in my grandmother's house and never made any close connections, as if by having no relationships I could avoid the pain.

I know better now. Life is brutal and dangerous. And it's beautiful. I can shrink from it, or I can brace myself and enjoy the ride.

It only took a trip to another galaxy to teach me how to live on Earth.

"Is there anything I can do?" Medik asks.

I take a deep breath, ignoring the ache rising in my chest. "Yeah, actually. Can you start by taking this collar off me? Also, since you're so involved in the Tribute program, can you contact Frllil for me?"

He straightens. "The Jabol?"

"Yes." I clench my hands into fists to keep from rubbing my chest. "I just told Gavrill, I want to go back to Earth. I just need to talk to Frllil to see how we can make that happen."

"You wish to leave?" Medik seems shocked, stuck on that one point.

"I don't think there's any reason for me to stay," I say quietly, looking down at my fists where they rest in my lap. The pain in my chest is growing, an empty ache that causes tears to spring up in the back of my eyes. "All he really needs is a womb and a female willing to lend her genes. He doesn't need me... and I can't do this anymore. I just can't."

A pause. I keep my head down, not looking up because I know there will be disappointment on Medik's expression. After a long moment, he speaks again.

"I thought you and the Commander had started to bond."

I wince. Yeah, so had I, but that just shows what we both knew.

"I honestly don't think he's capable of it, and there's no way in hell I'm having kids with a man who treats me like an object. You'd have to strap me down and sedate me." I glower at Medik, just daring him to try. Although my birth control shot would keep that from happening for at least another month. Definitely not mentioning that, though.

He sighs. "That would not lead to healthy children."

"No, it won't." I clear my throat, feeling a bit sorry for the old alien. "I won't do it willingly, but I bet another woman would. I can work with Frllil, see if we can make contact and find someone else for Gavrill."

"You'd do that?" Medik's suit tints in surprise.

Do I want to? Hell no. But will I? Yes. I'm leaving. I... okay, I'm going to be honest, if only to myself—I love him. I want him to have everything I can't give to him. Will it suck the big one, choosing my replacement? Yes. I'll still do it.

"He deserves the life that he wants. A mate and children. I want him to have that." Jealousy nearly chokes me, but I push it away. There's no point in being jealous when this *is* my choice.

"If you really feel that way, I will see what I can do—"

"Thank you."

"—if you tell me why you want to go."

I sigh and rub my shoulder. It still aches, although at least it has dulled since the initial stabbing spike of pain.

"Look, this isn't working. I know you want me to be the Commander's bonded mate and all, but," I shrug to hide my roiling feelings. "I don't think it's possible."

Medik stays silent while I massage the sore patch of skin below my neck and try to think of how to explain it to him. *The sex is great, but he doesn't care about me. I can't go through a thousand years feeling like a casual hookup.*

"I thought about it when I was on the Vgotha ship. No, the Vgothas didn't say anything. To them I was just a bargaining chip— something they kept safe but didn't mess with at all. I might as well have been a piece of furniture." My throat and chest tighten, making my voice rasp a little. "That's how Gavrill thinks of me, too. I'm fun and diverting and pretty to look at, but he doesn't care about me any more than... a prize on a shelf."

Beside me, Medik jolts as if he might say something but doesn't interrupt as I press on.

"I didn't even think he'd rescue me," I tell him, sadness welling all over again, the sense of abandonment stinging the backs of my eyes as tears threaten. "That's why I escaped. I didn't think he'd come for me. Why rescue me when he can just get another Tribute?" I clench and unclench my fists, trying to get some blood moving through them, not meeting Medik's eyes. "So that's what he should do. Replace me. I can't be with someone like that. I won't. Having children with him—forget it."

Would he even care for his children? Or would he see them as little soldiers ready to be trained to carry out the Tsenturion mission?

The silence descends heavily between us.

"He cares," Medik says after a long moment. His voice is soft but sincere. "He was very upset when you were taken."

"That's just because the Vgothas took something he thought belonged to him. It's simple one-up-man-ship. In a few cycles, he won't care about me again. Maybe he'll be grateful that I helped start the Tribute program." My shoulder twitches with a stab of pain, and I rub the marked skin. "There are probably plenty of women on Earth who would be happy to be his Tribute, even though he'll never love them. But not me." Just the thought of it makes me feel nauseous. I've lost too many people in my life. I'm ready to love again. I can't imagine sharing a life with someone who will never love me in return.

Somehow, I have to get my body back to normal and get myself back to Earth. If Medik won't help me get in touch with Frllil, then I'll probably have to ask Gavrill to. Just the thought makes me quail, but I will if I have to.

Medik and I sit in silence a while. I still can't meet his eyes. It feels like I'm bleeding inside, the jagged shards of pain like glass cutting through my chest.

When Medik finally speaks again, it's the last thing I expect him to say.

"If I could prove to you Gavrill cared for you? Then would you stay?"

I start to shake my head. "I don't... how would you prove it?" Stupid heart. Stupid hope blooming in my chest. Stupid me for asking.

"Let's just say I could. Do you care enough about him to stay?"

I blink a few times, but I can't stop a few tears leaking out.

"Yes," I whisper. "I would stay. I want him... but only if he wants me. *Me*. Dawn. Not just a Tribute, but me as myself."

Medik nods with a satisfied smile. "In that case, I have something to show you."

19

G avrill

ON THE BRIDGE, I stare at the picture of empty space where the Vgotha ship once sat and baited us. Around me, the warriors are running scans to try to find it again.

It's no use. The enemy has disappeared again, taking their scuttled ship. Maybe even that had been a ruse, maybe there had been nothing wrong with it in the first place. We've lost this skirmish, just as we failed to protect our flank and the most precious person on board. I should be angry, channeling all my energy into hunting the enemy down. Instead, I can hardly bring myself to focus on anything except Dawn's voice echoing in my head.

My Tribute. The thought is mournful. Wishful. Because she no longer wants to be mine.

She wants to leave. Even if she can't, she never wants to see me again. *I didn't think you'd come for me.* Have I failed so much as her Master?

I rub at an itchy patch on my arm, which feels like it's throbbing in time with my heartbeat. The edges sting as the nanotech tries to heal the strange wound. Every so often, I feel a sharp pain, like needles pricking into it.

Kalexston's panel beeps as it finishes scanning. "No sign of the Vgotha, Commander," he reports.

"I knew it," Bogdan mutters. I barely notice him glancing at me, but I can't think of anything to say. Clearing his throat, he speaks louder. "What about the Vgotha pod the Tribute stole?"

"My crew is still running preliminary tests. It seems to be a living organism," Miths says. My interest is stirred, in a very distant kind of way.

"Sentient?" Kalexston asks, intrigued.

"Undetermined. It does seem to have some shielding capabilities that bypass our scanners," Miths continues. "Commander, permission to modify our scanners to sense this, ah, organism."

I wave a hand. To my left, Bogdan huffs. He's been cheated out of a battle, he's not going to get to destroy the pod, and he's upset. I should feel the same, but it's like I'm numb.

Perhaps I should step down and give command over to him, for the sake of the mission while I'm in this mindset, but... I can't bring myself to do so. Without Dawn, I will have nothing to live for but endless cycles of patrol.

Pain stabs through me like a shot to the chest, and I grimace. If I had known I would gain a Tribute just to lose her, I would never have agreed to the program.

No, that is a lie. Because any amount of pain is worth the few cycles I held Dawn in my arms.

"Commander, have you asked your Tribute about the Vgotha?" Bogdan turns to look at me. He almost looks regretful but also determined. I don't answer, but he can tell from my expression what the answer is. He sighs. "Permission to question her. Or perhaps Miths can, since his crew is working on the pod?"

"No," I order, my need to protect her rousing. "Leave her alone."

"Commander, I must protest, the Tribute—"

"I said no. I will question her myself. Later." Much later. When I can actually face being in her presence again while knowing she is no longer mine. My pain in my chest is growing, and my armor flashes before I can control my emotions.

Bogdan turns away, mumbling something that sounds like "grown too attached to a breeder."

"She is not a breeder. She is leaving the Tribute program and returning to her home planet," I announce to the bridge. I will have to tell them eventually, and I do not think I can feel any more pain than I currently do, so I might as well now.

"What?" Kalexston gasps, ugly streaks of yellow shooting through his grey suit.

"You allowed this?" Miths asks.

"It was her choice," I say above my crew's disturbed muttering.

"But what about—" Kalexston bites off his question, obviously wanting to ask whether the program will continue.

"You can't do that," Bogdan protests, an abrupt reversal of his previous position. I am so numb to emotions that I do not even feel shock, although the rest of the bridge is looking at him as though he's grown a second head. "The continuation of our race..."

A small rushing sound signals the arrival of the lift and the doors opening to allow someone to enter the bridge. I can't even find the energy to look and see if it's Corin, arriving for his shift.

"I thought you wanted us to focus on our duty," I say to him, my bitter words almost taunting. I didn't expect my second to look so shaken at the end of the Tribute program. "You thought Dawn was a distraction. You thought I should spend less time with her. You thought she didn't matter and that any female would be acceptable as my Tribute. You were wrong. Dawn gave me purpose. She made my life better, made me better, she is the only Tribute I want, ever... and I failed her."

My hand is over my arm, where the stinging patch of skin is under my armor, and it feels like the nanotech is finally working, because it is starting to feel warm and tingly rather than painful. I look around to see the warriors are all staring in the direction of the lift. Turning, shock slams into me as Dawn steps on to the bridge, a wide-eyed, intent expression on her face, Medik behind her on the lift.

~

Dawn

"Dawn?" Gavrill rises from his command chair. His face looks like it's carved from granite. If I hadn't heard his words with my own ears, I would have never known he'd just been talking about me. That he'd just been confirming everything I'd heard on the video. His expression flickers to something closer to alarm. "Is something wrong?"

"High Commander, I apologize," Medik calls from the lift, sounding way too happy for anyone to think that he's serious about his apology. "I could not stop her—she demanded to come."

I take a step towards Gavrill, my eyes trained on him. No one else matters.

"You were going to trade yourself for me?" My voice is husky. I already know the answer, but it feels like a dream. I want to hear him say it, to *me*. Purposefully and meaningfully. The words from the video the doctor showed me still ring in my head: *Dawn is more than just a Tribute.*

His suit glitters as he nods.

"Me. And not just any Tribute. You wanted me."

"Yes."

I would give my life a thousand times to spare her harm.

"I didn't think you cared for me," I croak. My face is wet. I swipe at my cheeks as I walk to Gavrill. The rest of the bridge has faded to nothing.

As I near him, Gavrill reaches for me, then checks himself. His hands hover between us, wanting, but not daring to touch.

"Dawn," his voice is husky, "I cannot... I will not live without you.

There is nothing I wouldn't do for you. If I lose you... there will be no other."

She is my mate.

"You love me," I whisper. "Not just your Tribute. Me."

His brow wrinkles in confusion. "You are—were—my Tribute. I don't understand."

That, right there, is the crux of our miscommunication I realize. His voice practically caresses the words 'my Tribute', and he doesn't even realize that being called that makes me feel as though I'm not valued as an individual. To him, it's the most loving endearment he could call me.

I just didn't realize it.

"I love you, too," I choke out the words. "I want to stay and be your Tribute."

His eyes widen, his armor flashing to a pure, brilliant gold.

I gasp as the mark on my shoulder flares—the sensation is so intense that I can't tell if it's painful or pleasurable, and I cry out. I cover the spot with my hand as the pressure turns to heat, shudders wracking me. Facing me, Gavrill mirrors my movement, his large hand covering a spot on his forearm. I stare at him as the sorrow and tension of the past cycle melt away, leaving a warm, liquid pleasure flowing through my body. I lurch towards him, suddenly unwilling to go a second without his hands on me. He reaches out to catch me, my hands falling into his, and his armor slides back, up to his elbows. I stare down at the dark gold symbol on his forearm, darker than the rest of his skin. If he were human, it would be like he had gotten henna done or something.

"Dawn." Awe fills his voice. Awe, shock, and utter delight. I can practically feel it pulsing through me... no, no, I really *can* feel it—his emotions. They are separate from my own, utterly foreign to me, and yet somehow it feels right too. His hand slides to frame the marked spot on my shoulder, and I scrunch my neck to see. The itchy red mark is gone. In its place is a bright gold brand, a circle filled with delicate angles, like the cut of a jewel.

"What—" I let go of his hand to touch the symbol with a hesitant finger. It doesn't hurt or itch or anything anymore. The smooth design feels like it's been there forever, like an old tattoo. And Gavrill's forearm bears an identical one.

Gavrill reaches out to trace the gold circle on my shoulder, his touch raising goosebumps all over my body. Okay, when he touches it, it feels totally different, and a rush of pleasure spreads through my body.

"The bond," he says softly. My eyes widen; his meet mine. Suddenly, an emotion floods through me, a tidal wave stealing my breath. I hang on to Gavrill, shaking a little as I make sense of the feelings inside me. A curious lightness has replaced the stark ache. Instead of a hollow pain, there's a strong glow, pulsing like a heartbeat, leading straight to...

I stare up at Gavrill. He's there on the edge of my senses like a fifth limb, only more—bigger, stronger, and full of a warmth. The pain in my chest is gone, filled with a presence, a second heartbeat, a perfect peace.

"Holy hell." My voice is thick. "Does this mean what I think it does?"

"We share a mark." Gavrill strokes my shoulder with reverent fingers. His face reflects my own awe.

"It's a heli crystal," Medik breathes, "symbolizing eternal union." He and the rest of the officers on deck are all staring at us.

"The bond is complete," Gavrill murmurs and draws me close to him. I feel a thread of concern through his emotions. "You are sure now, you want to stay with me?"

"Yes." I press my fingertips against his chest, looking up at him so he can see the sincerity in my eyes, willing that he'll be able to feel me as easily as I can feel him. "I never wanted to go. I only wanted to be yours."

"You are mine," he says, smiling down at me. No one sighs, but I swear the entire bridge crew is practically humming with satisfaction at the romance of the moment, totally enthralled by the drama playing out between Gavrill and myself. "My captive. As I am yours. The bond binds me to you as much it does you to me."

"What about your duty?"

"You're my Tsenturion mate. We will figure it out. Together." The bond between us hums a little, filling my heart with happy music. I step back a moment, hand on my chest, as warmth rushes over me. Gavrill lets me go, as if he understands I need a moment to catch my breath. To find my footing in this awesome flood of love. The screen stretched over my head shows nothing but black, empty space. My heart beats against my palm as I find myself in the new current that flows between us. I am still me, and he is still himself, but if we give ourselves over, we are also one. It's enough to overcome a lifetime of loneliness.

I turn back to face Gavrill. My eyes meet his, and a new surge of warmth fills me. One prick, and it could pour out from my skin, filling the bridge, the ship, the black velvet expanse to the nearest star and beyond.

I open my mouth to tell him all this, but he already knows. Anything I say would sound maudlin. There aren't words to describe it.

Perhaps I will invent some. I have a thousand cycles to do it.

Around me, golden light flashes from the warriors' suits, making the bridge look as though we're bathed in golden sunlight. Everyone, even Bogdan's. The entire race benefits from knowing our bond is complete.

It's still a little embarrassing that such an intimate thing happened in front of everyone.

"I, uh, interrupted your shift." I blush and start to edge away as everyone's eyes on me starts to make me feel a little shy.

"Yes," Gavrill matches my bland tone. "But the interruption had merit."

"I'm not in trouble for coming onto the bridge without permission?"

Mischief glimmers in his eyes, and he steps towards me. Aw crap. I don't need to be in tune with his emotions to know what his intentions are.

"I didn't say that. After all," he continues in a louder tone, "we warriors cannot allow our Tributes to trample over protocol. When we return to the room, you will be chastised."

I raise my chin, about to say something defiant, when the lift swooshes open behind me. I turn to see if Medik has left, but no, he is standing beside the door. Corin is disembarking from the lift. Uh oh.

"Fortunately," Gavrill says as I whip my head back around to look at him. "I am officially off duty now." The wicked smile he gives me makes me press my thighs together even as my hands move behind me to cover my bottom. Pointing to a spot in front of him, Gavrill commands softly, "Come here."

I hesitate, my head turning back towards the door and the lift...

"Dawn," Gavrill warns. A second before I decide to dash, he strides forward, dipping at the last moment to plant his shoulder in my belly. He lifts me easily in a fireman's hold as I squawk.

"Corin, you have command, as my Tribute requires my attention," he announces. Cheers erupt around the bridge, along with several ribald suggestions that make me blush furiously. One hand grips the cheek of my ass, holding me in place as he points to Bogdan.

"You're next," Garvill tells him, and I get the satisfaction of seeing the surly warrior's suit whiten. Balancing on Gavrill's hard shoulder, I laugh. He claps his hand against my bottom, and I yelp.

"I am not finished with you, naughty one," the High Commander growls as he carries me to the lift, his hard fingers firmly pressing into the soft cheek of my ass. "It is time you learned to respect your Master."

My muscles clench in eager anticipation.

GAVRILL

The door to our quarters barely slides shut before I toss Dawn on the bed. Catching the hem of her dress, I rip it from her body, directly up the middle as I direct the nanotech of her belt to recede, baring her body to me. My cock stands at a stiff angle from my body, my *seela* quivering and waving in the air, reaching for her. Instead of grasping

Dawn's hips and plunging inside her primed body, I stretch out over her, my body atop hers but not inside of her yet.

"You belong to me," I say, bracing myself on my forearms and tracing the golden edge of her mark. A true, full Tsenturion bonding. I can feel her inside of my head—happy, warm, loving... She fills a void that I hadn't even known was there. Sharing my emotions with her is strange, but it also feels right.

"Yes," she breathes, lifting her face for a kiss. I bow my head to claim her lips but stop just short, brushing mine against hers as I reach up to pinch her nipple. She squeals at the little burst of pain, but I can also feel her excitement and arousal despite the noise of protest she makes.

"Yes, what?"

"Yes, Master," she giggles. I roll us both and rise to settle her over my broad thighs, her bottom turned up for my palm.

Smack! Smack! Smack!

The sound reverberates from the walls, interspersed with her breathy cries. I paint her cheeks pink with my hard hand, spanking her quickly but not harshly. The excitement I feel pulsing off her is growing, and my cock is aching to be inside of her. I pause long enough to command her Trainer to trickle down the crease between her cheeks and fill her bottom hole.

Shifting her further forward on her lap, my *seela* brush against her clit and wet folds, teasing her sensitive bits as I begin to spank her again. This time my hand comes down harder, on already pink cheeks.

Smack!

"Gavrill! Please!"

Smack!

She shudders as my *prime seela* circles her clit, even as my hand smacks against her tender bottom. The sight of her trainer bisecting her red cheeks, burrowing into her ass, urges me on to greater heights.

Smack!

❧

Dawn

"Master, *please.... I need you!*"

I feel like I'm about to explode from all the sensations filling me. The pain, the pleasure... my desire, his passion...

Smack!

"*Master!*" A sob rises in my throat. My ass clenches around the trainer as it thickens inside of me, buzzing slightly like a vibrator.

When he suddenly picks me up, putting me back on my back, I cry out as the trainer feels like it's pushing even deeper while my sore bottom flares with the impact of my weight on the bed. Then he's on top of me, his cock thrusting inside of me, his hands pushing mine above my head and pinning them there as his mouth lowers to mine.

Thigh to thigh, hip to hip, chest to chest. Mark to mark. Pleasure pulses from my mark to his.

He thrusts hard, fast. My legs wrap around him as his tongue slides against mine. I can feel him inside of me, stretching me, filling me. The nanotech in my ass buzzes faster, swelling larger as I clench around his cock. My clit pulses against his *prime seela* as it strokes me each time he sheathes himself.

I arch, my breasts rubbing against his chest as his hands tighten around my wrists. As our passion rises, I feel his *seela* latch on to my pussy. The tendrils pull us closer, sealing us together as we both cry out in ecstasy. The rise and fall of our shared orgasm crests and flows between us, pleasure upon pleasure, his and mine together until the intensity amplifies a hundred, a thousand times.

I don't see stars... I see galaxies.

But slowly we return to the ship, to each other. Our breath slows. The ecstasy ebbs. I pant for air, nestling my head against his shoulder. I feel quivery all over.

"Dawn. My Dawn. My Tribute." His lips move over my temples, and I can feel the complete love, the awe, the happiness that infuses each word.

Now I understand that it doesn't matter whether he's calling me by my name or by my title. Both mean the same thing to him—*his love.*

"My Gavrill," I whisper back, tilting my lips up to kiss the underside of his square chin. "My Master."

My love.

Against all the odds, we've found our happily-ever-after... and I no longer feel so bad about the Tribute program. Every woman should have the chance to find the same happiness.

EPILOGUE

P areena

Beep. Beep. Beep. I never thought the hum of hospital machines would become the soundtrack to my life. But the sound, along with the rattle of breath in my chest, tells me I'm alive. The sound is sweet because I won't hear it for much longer.

Hospitals are never quiet. A never-ending stream of doctors, nurses, and food service workers, coming in, checking charts, dropping off food trays and picking them up. The doctors frown. The nurses murmur "how ya doing, honey" and force smiles as they plump my pillows and check my vitals. The food service people don't comment as they pick up the food trays with most of my meal uneaten. I can only manage a few bites a day, another sign that I can measure the rest of my life in minutes and hours versus weeks and years.

I used to be so busy. Used to be one of the white-coat workers hustling past patient's doors. I used to hate being late, hate waiting, hate making small talk. I had so much time, I had the luxury of complaining that I had none.

Now my seconds are measured by the drip, drip, drip of my IV. I have nothing to do but doze or watch silly sitcoms on the tiny TV suspended in the corner of my room. Both early and late to my death, I'm happy to wait. I have nothing left to do but die.

My fingers crawl to the edge of the bed and find the smooth surface of my new best friend—a glossy black e-reader. I don't know who left it on my hospital bed but it's full of stories I'd never let myself read before. The ones I'd avoided at the library—the ones with strong-jawed, shirtless guys on the cover, with bulging muscles, and another bulge straining the front of their tight pants. I was always tempted to read them, but too embarrassed. I was such an elitist coward. I missed so much.

The Tribute rises from the Jabolian pod. Her body is lithe and strong, all the scars from her past are gone. Her skin glows and her hair falls in shining waves past her waist.

Now that's a fantasy. I haven't had hair in a long time. The chemo took everything, including my eyebrows.

Her Tsenturion master stands on the receiving deck to greet her. His suit molds his strong frame, a glittering grey color that reflects his impatience. As his female tribute approaches, the suit glimmers with a silvery sheen. By the time she has walked the long path to stand before him, the silver has turned to gold.

She is a worthy Tribute.

I finish the story and sigh. Becoming a Tsenturion bride sounds great right about now. Fix all my imperfections and heal my disease. Replace the cancer cells with healthy ones. Throw in a pair of eyebrows, and it'd be worth getting abducted.

I click back to the beginning of the story, ready to read it again, but as I swipe to the first chapter, the e-reader blinks a few times. A new screen appears.

Initiate questioning phase.

New words form onscreen: *Are you Doctor Pareena Singh?*

I jolt awake and glance around the empty hospital room. How did the device learn my name?

The e-reader gives a little chirp as if reminding me to answer the question. *Are you Doctor Pareena Singh?*

I click "Affirm identity" and type in my full name and title as prompted. I haven't referred to myself by my title since I stopped working as a psychologist, after the first round of chemo failed. The staff around here don't know I have my doctorate.

It feels good to be recognized. I turn the e-reader over, checking for signs that someone has tampered with it. Whoever sent it to me must have programmed it with my name.

Another question appears on screen. *Do you have children?*

What the hell? That's invasive. I should throw the thing aside in protest. Instead, I hit "No" in a huff. I must be really bored.

Another question pops on the screen. It keeps chirping, so I keep answering.

Over an hour later, I lay back on the pillows, exhausted. I've answered over a hundred questions. They just kept coming—asking about my family, my career, even whether or not I had a cat. It reminded me of a dating site one of my friends got me to join—answer all the questions and they'd match you with your true love. After my diagnosis, I stopped dating. I didn't want to find my true love only to tell him I had a few years to live.

I close my eyes for a moment until the device beeps impatiently. New words swim across the screen.

<Swipe right for abduction>

That's new. The text blinks at me, green.

<Swipe right for abduction>

This has got to be the weirdest computer game ever invented.

<Swipe right for abduction>

Well, what can it hurt? I touch the screen with a finger, pressing lightly to steady it. My hands are bony with veins standing out. They look like they belong to a much older woman.

<Doctor Pareena Singh> My name scrolls across the screen once again. *<Swipe right for abduction>*

What the hell. I'm stuck in this hospital bed, dying of Stage IV cancer. My e-reader wants me to swipe right to play a stupid game?

I have nothing to lose.

I place a trembling finger on the screen. The e-reader gives an encouraging chirp as I slowly slide my finger to the right. The screen starts to glow.

Is something happening to my eyes now? The doctors didn't say anything about my eyes possibly being affected, but I'm not sure that means anything. They don't tell me a lot of things these days if they don't think I need to know.

I can't tear my eyes away to find the call button for the nurse though... it's like the screen is fracturing into rainbows, filling my vision... and it's beautiful. Something tugs at me, pulling at my body.

Am I finally dying? Is this the light that I'm supposed to go toward?

I open my mouth to call for help—I'm not ready!—but there's no air and suddenly it feels like there are tight bands around my chest, pulling me towards the light. Tears slide down my cheeks in despair. I'd hoped to come to accept my death but now I have no choice.

Rings of light burst ahead of me as the darkness closes in. Pain, which thankfully feels distant because of the morphine, swirls as I shatter apart.

My last thought is mournful.

I'm not ready.

AUTHOR'S NOTE

Once upon a time, in a coffeeshop far, far away, two authors met to talk about reading books, writing books, publishing books, cosplay and more books. Naturally the conversation turned to giant alien cocks.

Okay, maybe that's not how it happened, but over soup and salad, we started playing with the seed of a story. The seed took root and now you have this book. If you like it, please let us know —we have plans to continue the series, starting with Bodgan's book. If you nag us, you might get it sooner...

Love to our editor Miranda, our author friends and supportive family, the Goddesses and Angel Legion on Facebook. And to you, who read this book all the way to the end.

XOXO
Golden & Lee

ALIEN TRIBUTE

ALIEN TRIBUTE

<Swipe right for abduction>

Who knew that reading sexy alien romances could lead to abduction?
Or that aliens could cure my cancer? Not me. But here I am, the captive bride-to-be for an alien warrior, just like the heroine in the book I was reading in my hospital bed on Earth.

Except the surly warrior who's supposed to claim me **doesn't want a mate.**

Disclaimer: The authors are not responsible for any actual alien abductions that may result as a consequence of your purchase of this book.

PROLOGUE

P areena

Beep. Beep. Beep. I never thought the hum of hospital machines would become the soundtrack to my life. But the sound, along with the rattle of breath in my chest, tells me I'm alive. The sound is sweet because I won't hear it for much longer.

Hospitals are never quiet. A never-ending stream of doctors, nurses, and food service workers, coming in, checking charts, dropping off food trays and picking them up. The doctors frown. The nurses murmur "how ya doing, honey" and force smiles as they plump my pillows and check my vitals. The food service people don't comment as they pick up the food trays with most of my meal uneaten. I can only manage a few bites a day, another sign that I can measure the rest of my life in minutes and hours versus weeks and years.

I used to be so busy. Used to be one of the white-coat workers hustling past patients' doors. I used to hate being late, hate waiting, hate making small talk. I had so much time, I had the luxury of complaining that I had none.

Now my seconds are measured by the drip, drip, drip of my IV. I have nothing to do but doze or watch silly sitcoms on the tiny TV suspended in the corner of my room. Both early and late to my death, I'm happy to wait. I have nothing left to do but die.

My fingers crawl to the edge of the bed and find the smooth surface of my new best friend—a glossy black e-reader. I don't know who left it on my hospital bed but it's full of stories I'd never let myself read before. The ones I'd avoided at the library—the ones with strong-jawed, shirtless guys on the cover, with bulging muscles, and another bulge straining the front of their tight pants. I was always tempted to read them, but too embarrassed. I was such an elitist coward. I missed so much.

The Tribute rises from the Jabolian pod. Her body is lithe and strong, all the scars from her past are gone. Her skin glows and her hair falls in shining waves past her waist.

Now that's a fantasy. I haven't had hair in a long time. The chemo took everything, including my eyebrows.

Her Tsenturion master stands on the receiving deck to greet her. His suit molds his strong frame, a glittering grey color that reflects his impatience. As his female tribute approaches, the suit glimmers with a silvery sheen. By the time she has walked the long path to stand before him, the silver has turned to gold.

She is a worthy Tribute.

I finish the story and sigh. Becoming a Tsenturion bride sounds great right about now. Fix all my imperfections and heal my disease. Replace the cancer cells with healthy ones. Throw in a pair of eyebrows, and it'd be worth getting abducted.

I click back to the beginning of the story, ready to read it again, but as I swipe to the first chapter, the e-reader blinks a few times. A new screen appears.

Initiate questioning phase.

New words form onscreen: *Are you Doctor Pareena Singh?*

I jolt awake and glance around the empty hospital room. How did the device learn my name?

The e-reader gives a little chirp as if reminding me to answer the question. *Are you Doctor Pareena Singh?*

I tap "Affirm Identity" and type in my full name and title as prompted. I haven't referred to myself by my title since I stopped working as a psychologist, after the first round of chemo failed. The staff around here don't know I have my doctorate.

It feels good to be recognized. I turn the e-reader over, checking for signs that someone has tampered with it. Whoever sent it to me must have programmed it with my name.

Another question appears on screen. *Do you have children?*

What the hell? That's invasive. I should throw the thing aside in protest. Instead, I hit "No" in a huff. I must be really bored.

Another question pops on the screen. It keeps chirping, so I keep answering.

Over an hour later, I lay back on the pillows, exhausted. I've answered over a hundred questions. They just kept coming—asking about my family, my career, even whether or not I had a cat. It reminded me of a dating site one of my friends got me to join— answer all the questions and they'd match you with your true love. After my diagnosis, I stopped dating. I didn't want to find my true love only to tell him I had a few years to live.

I close my eyes for a moment until the device beeps impatiently. New words swim across the screen.

<Swipe right for abduction>

That's new. The text blinks at me, green.

<Swipe right for abduction>

This has got to be the weirdest computer game ever invented.

<Swipe right for abduction>

Well, what can it hurt? I touch the screen with a finger, pressing lightly to steady it. My hands are bony with veins standing out. They look like they belong to a much older woman.

<Doctor Pareena Singh> My name scrolls across the screen once again. *<Swipe right for abduction>*

What the hell. I'm stuck in this hospital bed, dying of Stage IV cancer. My e-reader wants me to swipe right to play a stupid game?

I have nothing to lose.

I place a trembling finger on the screen. The e-reader gives an encouraging chirp as I slowly slide my finger to the right. The screen starts to glow.

Is something happening to my eyes now? The doctors didn't say anything about my eyes possibly being affected, but I'm not sure that means anything. They don't tell me a lot of things these days if they don't think I need to know.

I can't tear my eyes away to find the call button for the nurse though... it's like the screen is fracturing into rainbows, filling my vision... and it's beautiful. Something tugs at me, pulling at my body.

Am I finally dying? Is this the light that I'm supposed to go toward?

I open my mouth to call for help—I'm not ready!—but there's no air and suddenly it feels like there are tight bands around my chest, pulling me towards the light. Tears slide down my cheeks in despair. I'd hoped to come to accept my death but now I have no choice.

Rings of light burst ahead of me as the darkness closes in. Pain, which thankfully feels distant because of the morphine, swirls as I shatter apart.

My last thought is mournful.

I'm not ready.

1

———————

P areena

I DON'T HURT.

That is my first thought. A thought filled with as much awe as relief, because I didn't expect to wake up at all. My momentary joy at waking is tempered by the knowledge that my time is almost up. At some point I need to move past the stage of depression and into acceptance that my life is ending, because it's obviously coming sooner rather than later.

"Greetings, Pareena Singh."

The unfamiliar voice and formal greeting make me sigh. Great, another doctor. I open my eyes to see who I get to deal with now. Then I frown, because I must be dreaming. Not only am I no longer in my hospital room and the man in front of me looks *wrong* somehow, like he's CGI and not a real person, but I'm seeing everything through heavy eyelashes. That's happened in my dreams sometimes, where I think my hair has returned. I reach up and, sure enough, there's thick, soft hair covering my entire head.

Tears spark in my eyes as I pull it forward to see the thick, glossy strands. They feel so real. *Look* so real. This is probably the most vivid dream I've ever had. Hm. I wonder if I'm in a coma. Do people in comas dream? Technically I have my doctorate, but becoming a psychologist didn't make me an expert on people in comas.

"Pareena Singh, why are you leaking?"

"Leaking?" I ask, looking up at the not-man. He gestures at my face, his movement awkward, as if he's not used to using his hand. I reach up to touch my cheeks and feel the wetness of tears as they overflow from my eyes. I hadn't even realized I was crying. "These are tears. I'm just... sad. I miss my hair so much and this feels so real."

"It is real," he says seriously. And then he starts telling me the most fantastical things I've ever heard. His name is Frllil and he's a Jabol Luminary, in charge of finding females for an alien race—and, of course, human females are the only compatible beings.

The last trilogy I read, the Tsenturion Masters trilogy, is, according to him, based on reality and I've been selected as a Tsenturion Tribute. I've been cured of my cancer and my body has been not only restored to prime health, but actually enhanced so that I will never have to worry about cancer—or any other illnesses—ever again, and my life expectancy has been expanded exponentially. That I will be trained, 'primed,' and then presented to my new master.

For a coma dream, it's pretty detailed. I haven't ever really thought of myself as the imaginative sort, but being trapped in a hospital room with no visitors for weeks on end has apparently sparked something in my brain. The desperation to get out of my situation, perhaps, or some kind of delusional wish fulfillment.

To be truthful, I'm not really into self-examination right now.

Yes, I know that some part of my brain has conjured this outlandish scenario, that I'm pretty much out of my gourd. But I can't stop touching my hair.

Is this real? Or has this been happening inside my head?

Of course it is happening inside your head, Harry, but why on earth should that mean it is not real?

For a crazy old man, sometimes Dumbledore did make sense. Does it matter that this isn't real? It feels real. My hair, which my fingers are continuously running through, feels real. The lack of pain feels real. Why not enjoy this dream while I can? Eventually, I will wake up and be thrust back into the awful reality of my current existence... or maybe I'll never wake up at all. Neither option is appealing. Even my subconscious thinks so, or else I wouldn't be dreaming about alien abduction.

For the first time in my life, I decide to follow the advice I gave so many of my patients and just go with the flow, for as long as it lasts.

"Okay," I say. "I'm a Tribute... so now what?"

Frllil is watching me with an air of anxious wariness, and I'm kind of getting used to his odd appearance, but it's still creepy when he smiles widely. It's so close to approximating a real, human smile, but the fact that it's so close somehow makes it more unsettling rather than less. It's the Uncanny Valley effect, but knowing that doesn't make it less strange.

"I must say, you're taking this a lot better than the last Tribute," he says, sounding very relieved.

Other Tributes—very interesting. Although, I suppose it only makes sense that my brain has included other humans in this dream. I'm very tired of being alone, after all. My subconscious apparently doesn't want me alone in any manner, even in a dream. I'm not sad about it.

"Is there any way to escape?" I ask, because it seems like he expects me to.

Frllil shakes his head. His expression doesn't change—he isn't sorry. If anything, he looks pleased. "There is no way for you to access the wormhole you came through, and a return trip would be inadvisable, even with the improvements I've made to your physical form."

I shrug. "Then resistance is futile. So, what comes next?"

"Now we begin your training."

Bogdan

BLACK SPACE STRETCHES BEFORE ME. I grip the sides of the command chair, willing my expression blank. But nothing hides my mood. My suit is as dark as the empty quadrant.

"Scan complete," Science officer Kalexston reports. "No signs of the enemy."

I glare at him for announcing the obvious. He ducks his head to study his screens. "Shall I scan again?"

"No. Officer Zakhar, take us on a patrol pass."

"Yes, Commander," Zakhar snaps to attention.

I am failing everyone counting on me.

Again.

The feeling is far too familiar, but it never becomes easier to bear.

High Commander Gavrill, the leader of our entire fleet—which makes him the leader of our entire race, since we are all that is left of it—put his faith in me to lead our warriors in his stead while he is distracted by his Tribute. I also failed at convincing him and the others that we aren't ready for Tributes. In my defense, I had not really thought the Jabol would be able to procure acceptable substitutes for Tsenturion females.

But they found a planet, currently accessible only through an unstable wormhole, on which there are many suitable females.

The thought strikes fear in my heart, although it is unlikely that the Vgotha would be able to mount an attack on that planet. While they know about the High Commander's Tribute, they do not know the location of the wormhole or the planet. Even we do not know it, only the Jabol involved in procuring them do. It is safer that way.

The bridge door slides open and a tall warrior marches towards me. I rise.

"Arkdhem, reporting for duty," the third in command salutes with a fist to his chest. He is a hand taller than me, but I am broader, with more muscle. Sometimes he wears extra battle spurs about his shoulders to make him seem bigger, but I know his true size.

"Commander," I glance at my screen. "You are not due for duty until later."

"I volunteered for a double shift." Most see Arkdhem as a pleasant, jovial sort. I know better. There's a reason he has risen so high in the ranks.

"Where is High Commander Gavrill?" I question, even though I can guess.

"With his Tribute. He and Dawn are celebrating ten semicycles since her abduction and return."

In the corner of my eye, Kalexston's suit lightens to a happy blush. A color that should never reveal itself on a warrior. "Has it been ten already?" he exclaims. "Truly a cause for celebration."

"Will they accept gifts?" Zakhar asks. His suit is light red. Another idiot.

"I don't know, but a visit would not be amiss. Perhaps at mealtime," Arkdhem says. The rest of the bridge breaks out in exclamations of intent to visit the Tribute and express their congratulations.

My fists clench at my sides. Fools, all of them.

"Perhaps if you have so much time to waste, you all should pull double duties," I bark, and the discussion quiets to a murmur. Arkdhem raises a brow at me. He knows better than to smile. I would beat his face off.

My fellow warriors are excited by the news of Tributes. They want more of them to come *now*, before we've even eradicated the Vgotha threat. Fortunately, the procurement process is both long and difficult. Made even more so by the High Commander's Tribute, Dawn. She insisted the protocol for selecting the tributes be adjusted, so that the women of Earth are given as much of a choice as can be provided to them. A choice which she feels was denied to her, although she is happy enough under the circumstances.

All the while, we are not given a choice about whether or not we even want Tributes on the ship with us. The Jabol provided Tribute Dawn to the High Commander on their timeline, not ours. Already she's proven to be a liability. We had one of the Vgotha ships within our sights when she was kidnapped. She managed to escape in one of their small pods, but then insisted it be released back into space so we could follow it. She said the pod—and the Vgotha ship she'd been taken to—were actually sentient, and allowed her to escape.

The pod disappeared, leaving us none-the-wiser about where the Vgotha have vanished to this time or why their 'sentient' ship might have assisted her.

The High Commander was too relieved to have her back and fully bonded to him to be able to focus on the Vgotha's disappearance. That duty has fallen to me, as his second-in-command, and I am *failing.*

I do not understand how they could have disappeared so completely.

We've been hunting the Vgotha for tsencycles and what Tribute Dawn described is technology like they've never had before. Where did it come from? When did they upgrade their ships? Who would have helped them?

So many questions and more. Over a thousand Tsenturion warriors depending on me. The High Commander relying on me.

When I reach my quarters, my suit retracts automatically. I rub my head, wishing I could remain on duty forever, and never sleep. Never remove my helmet.

There are times when I find myself wishing I had resigned my commission earlier. That I hadn't taken that last trip. Because then I would have been on Tsentur when the Vgotha destroyed it. I have no death wish, but the burden of living has become endless and with the addition of Tribute Dawn we have both hope for the future and an even higher burden.

She is another innocent life, another responsibility to bear. Adding more Tributes to our population will only increase the onus of keeping our small fleet safe from attack. Before, if the Vgotha had killed us, our mission of vengeance would have ceased, but we are all willing volunteers to the cause. We are all Tsenturion warriors, ready to lay down our lives in battle. The Tributes will be neither.

I march to my private console and scroll to a view of the solar system nearby, directing the unit to scan it for Vgotha signatures. A small gesture but at least it's something. I cannot sit in my quarters and do nothing.

I do not like to think about what would have happened if Tribute Dawn had not escaped from the Vgotha's clutches. The pain the High Commander would have felt... I know it too well. It is not a pain I would wish upon anyone. The only one who has a semblance of understanding is Medik, but his grief is so far beyond my own that I cannot fathom how he has remained sane. In some ways, he has taken all the remaining warriors under his wing and become our communal mentor, a replacement for our lost parents, but I have not been able to agree with him when it comes to the Tributes.

He sees them as our future's hope, but the truth is, they are just another thing we could lose.

2

———————

P^{areena}

I HATE FRLLIL.

I hate my training.

I definitely hate my 'Bride Trainer.'

I hate my brain.

If this is some kind of subconscious attempt to prepare myself for death... well, it's almost working. Because after days of training, which apparently means a *lot* of sexual arousal but no actual culmination, I am ready to do something drastic. Unfortunately, being a Tribute also means that I no longer have any control over my own body. It was far more fun reading about it than it is experiencing it, even in a dream. Whenever Frllil's not looking, I claw at the Bride Trainer he's put on me.

The Bride Trainer is a belt that goes around my waist and down between my legs, covering my pussy completely and splitting my buttocks like a thong. It's surprisingly comfortable when it's not driving me mad. When I stroke it, it feels like regular cloth but trying to break through it... well, I might as well be trying to tear apart steel. It's pliable, fitting to my shape exactly. Too exactly. I can't even wedge a finger between the thing and my pussy.

Frllil says its nanotechnology. The damn thing even cleans itself and me, after opening *just* enough for me to go to the bathroom but not enough for me to ever touch myself.

Supposedly my Tsenturion warrior will be able to control it with his mind, which is when it will finally be removed so that he can claim me. Which sounds hot, in theory, but it's not in reality. Well, in my dream-reality. Mostly it's so frustrating that I'm beginning to feel murderous.

It's *my* dream, I should be able to get it off and play with myself if I want to. The sexual frustration feels very real.

The fact that I haven't been successful makes me wonder if this is maybe an internal metaphor for my cancer. Just another instance in which I have a complete lack of control over a situation's outcome.

How very frustrating.

According to Frllil, this is exactly what being 'primed' is supposed to do. I'm plenty primed. I'm so primed that I couldn't possibly *get* more primed. I'm ready to climb the walls I'm so primed.

Frllil promises that I'll be able to climax when I'm finally given to my Tsenturion Master.

Bogdan.

A large part of my 'training' involves staring at photos of the alien male while being aroused by the vibrations through my training belt. Alien, but attractive. I'm pretty sure I'd be aroused even without the belt. Square shoulders, square jaw, he looks like a battering ram come to life. Alien, but attractive. Golden skin. Actual metallic golden skin. Not much of it is visible underneath the armor that covers his entire body though.

The armor changes color according to their mood, supposedly, but in every vid and photo Frllil has shown me of Bogdan, his armor remains resolutely black. I do catch flashes of color from the others around him, although I never see their faces. They're unimportant apparently; it is only Bogdan who matters, Bogdan who is going to be my world.

Right now, as long as I get off, that doesn't sound like too bad of a deal. Lurking in the back of my mind is the fear that I'll never get off again, that at some point this dream will end when I die... perhaps when I'm taken off of life support. I have such a weird imagination. I've accepted the fact that yes, I *am* dying, or already have. This is one long hallucination of the book I was reading. Pure deathbed fantasy. How do I know? I have eyebrows again and they look amazing.

But did I have to imagine so much orgasm denial?

Then again, I can't deny that it's working. Staring at the hot alien my mind has conjured up is a welcome distraction from my reality.

Who can worry about death when a vibrator is tormenting them while they're staring at what looks like six and a half, maybe seven, feet of pure muscle?

No wonder the Jabols hired the Tsenturions to be their muscle. The Tsenturions are so buff, when the time came for evolution to hand out muscle to the Jabols there was none left. Frllil is just an amorphous blob that can form into any shape at will. While he tries to hold his humanoid shape, he often 'ripples' in a way that makes my stomach churn. He changes more rapidly when he's excited.

Why my subconscious has conjured up such a strange being, I'm not sure but there must be some reason for it.

"Pareena, you will pay attention," Frllil chirps. He points at yet another vid of Bogdan. My pussy clenches and I want to scream because I already know it's going nowhere.

"Dr. Singh," I mutter, frustrated beyond belief with both him and the training.

The Jabol quivers around the edges of his form. "Explain."

"My name is Pareena Singh, and when I earned my PhD, 'doctor' became my title. You're pissing me off, so you don't get to use my first name anymore." Normally I'm not such a hard ass but my pussy is throbbing, and I want to cum!

Frllil gives a little trill. He's such a pill. He needs to chill.

Great, now I'm rhyming. I recognize the distraction technique and wish it worked a little better.

"I am using your first name to engender goodwill. I was instructed to do this by one of your species."

"The state I'm in, you're not engendering anything. And what do you mean, 'one of my species?'"

"Another hu-man," Frllil's pronunciation of the word is still odd, no matter how I've tried to help him. "Dawn Cahill. She was the first Tribute, you are the second. She instructed me in the proper way to address Tributes. After a certain period of time, we have become familiar and it is correct to use only your first name."

Well that explains why he finally stopped calling me 'Pareena Singh', but it doesn't help my frustration in any way. He's sexually torturing me, and I'm not even attracted to him.

I narrow my eyes at him, because I think he actually sounds a little petulant. Frllil is so often completely unemotional, but apparently the name thing is important to him in some way.

"Yeah? Well I'm going to start calling you He-Who-Must-Not-Be-Named if you don't help me out." The noise he makes is definitely unhappy and I hide my smile. "But you can use my first name if you get this thing off me." I rap my Trainer hard, but I can't even feel it through the tech.

"Your Trainer can only be removed by your Tsenturion Master," Frllil sounds both reproachful and frustrated at repeating himself again. Well, join the club. "I have explained this."

"Pretty sure I'm going to die first," I mutter. Because I'm well past 'primed' and yet there's no sexy alien in sight.

"You are not dying, Pareena. Your system was in a state of shut down when you first came through the *direth* wormhole, but your health functions have been restored." As usual, Frllil takes my statement completely at its word.

"I know, I know," I rub my face, feeling my eyebrows and then run my hands back up through my hair, luxuriating in the silky strands sliding through my fingers. While I want to scream at him, there's no point. This is all a coma dream, right? So I'd just be yelling at myself.

And I already know from my days of training that Frllil is easily confused by my emotions. He's pure logic. Thanks, whatever part of my brain conjured him up. "I'm just really, really, really ready to meet Bogdan."

Meeting Bogdan, aka, getting my orgasm.

"Your Master," Frllil reminds me sternly.

"My Master." I sigh but try to be agreeable. I'm no stranger to BDSM. I visited a munch or two and went to a few parties as a submissive. I'm not surprised by this aspect of my dream.

Orgasm control and denial can be a big part of BDSM. I didn't think it was one of my fantasies, but it must be for my brain to have dug it up. The only other option is that all of this is real, which, of course, is impossible.

Therefore, some part of me must have been interested in it. A really, really stupid part of me that didn't think through how awful being teased and denied an orgasm for days would be.

Or maybe I've already died and gone to hell.

My hand drifts upwards to my hair, stroking the long strands. My hair has become a comfort object. And I can't imagine that I would have my hair in hell. No, if anything, the return of my hair confirms that this is a formulation from my imagination.

Bogdan

I AM NOT surprised when my presence is requested on the bridge even though I am off duty. It is a normal enough occurrence.

I *am* surprised when I walk through the door to find the High Commander there, an actual smile on his face, and his Tribute by his side, on her collar and leash. The long dress she is clothed in would not be out of place on a Tsenturion bride. To our collective surprise, somehow the pair fully bonded in the manner of our people and her dress shows off the mating mark she now bears.

I thought for sure they would not be leaving the High Commander's quarters during this time of rest they are taking. If it weren't for the gold color of the High Commander's armor and his expression, I would be alarmed, assuming his unexpected presence indicated another unexpected Vgotha encounter.

That cannot be the case, though, and I do not know what else could have lured him and Tribute Dawn from his chambers.

"Commander." I come to a halt in front of him, my fist clenched in salute.

Something about the way Tribute Dawn is beaming at me makes me uneasy. While we have reached an understanding in interacting with each other, I have never seen her look so happy to see me. It is unsettling.

The other warriors on the bridge are staring with curiosity and it is obvious they have no knowledge of why the High Commander is present either. Which does not reassure me.

"Bogdan." He greets me with a nod, his suit turning brighter gold with a quick streak of something else through it. Ever since his mating with Tribute Dawn, his control over his emotional indicators has been affected. Or perhaps he just no longer cares. "I am pleased to inform you that your Tribute has been selected and her training is almost complete."

"*What*?!" I'm not the only one to practically shout the word, across the room, Arkdhem is now on his feet, his suit flashing red and orange with rioting emotions, the dominant one being envy, before settling to black. My own suit barely flickers, but I feel the emotions sticking in my chest, behind the wall of ice where I keep them. When the High Commander claimed Tribute Dawn, he'd said I would be next, but I had dismissed his words as a mere threat or perhaps even a jest. The Jabol chose the matches, not him.

"And she's the perfect candidate!" Dawn says clapping her hands happily while I stare at her. She has been my only ally against the procurement of more Tributes for some time, even though she's been helping Medik, the fleet's doctor, refine the selection program. I always assumed she was undermining it, as she was so outspoken against taking more human women from their home planet. To see her celebration of this shocking news feels like a betrayal. "Not only did she have almost no emotional attachments to Earth, but she was dying. We saved her life by taking her!"

This time my suit does flicker, too quickly for anyone to see the color, which is well enough. I cannot identify the emotion that stabbed through me so quickly and viscerally. But I am not unaffected at hearing that the woman would have died without the intervention of the Jabol.

Still... why must she be *my* Tribute?

"Why him?" Arkdhem nearly shouts the question. Although his armor is now a controlled black, his fists are clenched by his sides, and I do not think I imagine the frustration seething in his eyes. He is one of the biggest supporters of the program. "He doesn't even want a Tribute! He is not fit for one. Why not one of us?" He gestures to the rest of the bridge, but it is clear he really means himself.

I draw myself up. While I might not desire a Tribute, I will not let Arkdhem impugn my worthiness either. I have my pride.

"A Tribute for you?" I ask. My disdain does not need to be broadcast by my armor, as it is clear in my voice. "As what, a reward for allowing the High Commander's Tribute be captured?"

Red streaks through the black of his armor, shaded with the bright yellow of his shame. He takes a step toward me, the promise of violence in his eyes. If he wishes to fight, I will not deny him. In fact, I find myself eager to take out my own frustration on him.

"Bogdan! Arkdhem!" The Commander barks out our names and Arkdhem comes to a halt, still glaring at me. I turn back to the Commander and Tribute Dawn, ignoring the other warrior. My move can be construed one of two ways—either that I trust him not to attack when the Commander is watching, or that I do not consider him a threat, and therefore do not care that my back is to him. I don't care which way he takes it, but I hope it's the second.

Tribute Dawn gives Arkdhem a sympathetic look before focusing on me. The expression on her face is far less friendly now. This does not bother me as I do not wish to be friends. I wish to be left alone.

I stare at High Commander Gavrill rather than meet her gaze, knowing that I am not as immune to her pout as I wish. However, I will never reveal my weakness, and that is the difference between Arkdhem and me.

"The Jabol matched Tribute Pareena Singh with Bogdan," the Commander says, sweeping his gaze around the bridge as if daring anyone to contradict him. "It is a near perfect personality match, according to them." His eyes meet mine. Any hope that the Tribute might be bestowed upon a different warrior dies with his words. "You will prepare for your Tribute and fulfill your duty. Her file has been sent to you. I recommend that you read the provided manuals."

Because he knows that I am one of the few Tsenturions who hasn't touched the manuals. When the Commander and Tribute Dawn had bonded in the Tsenturion manner and it was announced that more Tributes were to come, I was the only one not to request the manuals.

I can feel the weighty stares of the rest of the crew, feel their collective wish that they were the ones receiving a Tribute. Arkdhem's envy I do not mind, but I do not want the others to think I am wasting a gift many of them long for. I know how to do my duty.

I will not allow her to distract me from the rest of my duties. I will learn from the manuals and I will train her as quickly and efficiently as possible so that she is well behaved and out of the way until the Vgotha threat is taken care of. And perhaps when the Vgotha are gone, I will no longer ache with loss and I will be able to set down this heavy burden of justice, and truly bond with my Tribute.

Until then, at least I will receive some enjoyment from watching Arkdhem writhe with jealousy.

"Of course, High Commander," I say formally, with another salute.

3

———————

B ogdan

ACCEPTING the congratulations of my fellow warriors, all of whom now look at me with the hope that they will one day be in my position, rankles. I leave the bridge with as much dignity as I can and return to my quarters.

While part of me wants to dwell and seethe, I do not have much time. As with Tribute Dawn, the Jabol did not inform us of my Tribute until she was nearly ready for me. Like us, they do not accept failure lightly, so they do not announce they have something until they are sure that they do. Which means Frllil is very certain that Tribute Pareena is ready.

Ready for me.

Something tightens my throat, an emotion I'm not willing to acknowledge, much less put a name to.

I will not be weak.

I will not fail.

Accessing her file, I push away everything that threatens my composure and make myself focus on my new assignment. That's all she is. I read about her life, finding myself strangely fascinated. She is a strong female. I cannot regret that her life is saved by becoming a Tribute. Perhaps her strength is why the Jabol decided we are a near perfect match. I am strong for my kin and she has been strong for hers as well as for herself.

She will need such strength.

I am relieved as I read through the file. Nothing about Pareena reminds me of *her*.

There is still time before my sleep cycle, so I begin to read the courtship manuals. High Commander Gavrill claimed that human courtship rituals are not so different from our own, but I will be thoroughly versed by the time my Tribute arrives. If they are similar enough, then she should be no trouble, but where they differ, I already know I will rely more on Tsenturion rituals.

She is to be a Tsenturion tribute, after all; her old life will be over and gone.

We will have that in common, at least.

"How are you, Bogdan? Are you prepared for the arrival of your Tribute?" The sneering question comes from Arkdhem a few daycycles later when we are at a meal, his tone implying that I am neglecting my duty. I glare at him. The only joy I have is knowing he wants a Tribute beyond anything, and he must wait. As I study him, his suit darkens slightly, a sign of the envy he was attempting to keep hidden.

Foolish male.

The lack of control over his emotions proves he is not ready for one. While he might want one more than I, I doubt his ability to master a Tribute. Especially having witnessed how he lets Tribute Dawn do what she pleases when he is her escort.

"I have nothing to prepare. My quarters are adequate. She is the one who must be prepared for me." The courtship manuals have reassured me of my role in the relationship. I will establish dominance and gain her submission and loyalty, and she will be the perfect Tribute, serving me in every way. The manuals describe how human females are capable of more emotional relationship and bonding, but I see no need to enter into a deep connection with my Tribute unless it is necessary for breeding. Even breeding feels a betrayal, but the chance to continue our race cannot be denied.

Arkdhem stares at me, anger flickering through his armor. For a moment, I tense, expecting a blow. He and I have fought before, but not recently. Arkdhem prefers to hide behind his jokes and smiles, while plotting his true intent. He is a smooth edge, while I am rough. No doubt a Tribute would prefer him to me, but it would likely be to her detriment.

"The Jabol are generous," I say. I do not need to taunt him outright. My words are enough to invoke his ire. "They have sent me copious footage of her training. I haven't had the time to view them yet, but perhaps you would review them and see for yourself how prepared she is for me?"

Arkdhem's suit darkens further. "Is that an order?"

I would not actually trust *any* warrior with intimate viewings of my future mate. Even as I think the words without inflection, pain flickers through me. I will not consider Tribute Pareena a mate, not a real one. Even so, she should not be subject to another male's gaze, especially of her special training to accept me as master. To share the recordings would be discourteous.

I ignore the part of me that feels possessiveness at the idea of Arkdhem viewing her training. I am merely possessive about her because it is my duty. It has nothing to do with her. I don't even know her.

Arkdhem meets my gaze with his own blank one. In the next moment, he smiles, and I realize I have been silent too long, withholding my answer. "It would be my pleasure to assist you with your Tribute in any way you wish. Is the footage stored on your personal console? I will access it, if you give me the code."

"No," I bite out. "That won't be necessary. No one need see the Tribute but me. I will do my duty by reviewing them myself."

Looking suspiciously like he wants to laugh, Arkdhem salutes me again and takes my spot on the bridge.

Drakk. I told myself I wouldn't care about my Tribute, but I have already broken this vow. If my suit turns any darker, it'll become a black hole.

MY MOOD DOES NOT CHANGE as I march to my quarters. On the lift from the bridge, Officer Borodem falls into step with me. As soon as the door closes, he turns. "If I may offer my congratulations, Commander, on procuring a Tribute—"

"You may not," I cut him off, as I have begun doing when congratulations are offered. The other warriors need to see a Tribute for what she is—not a prize or a reward, but another thing to protect, a living burden aboard our ship. "It is my duty."

"It is not merely a duty," the fool exclaims. Spines rise on my suit and he reconsiders. "Would that we all had such a duty." He moves away from me, finally recognizing my need for solitude.

I close my eyes and remind myself that most of my fellow warriors had no expectations for the last Mating Festival. They lost their families and friends in the Great Tragedy, as did we all, but they had not begun to make plans beyond the next mission.

My next mission had been to make a family. To be with *her*. And then it was all gone. *She* was gone, along with our plans, our future, our world. But I went on.

They know this, but they do not understand.

They do not realize what it feels like to have to replace the one I could not save.

Pareena

. . .

PRESENTATION DAY IS HERE. Finally. Frllil is more jiggly than normal. A sign of his nervousness? Why he should be nervous, I don't know. I'm the one having a coma dream which involves being thrust into the unknown. Despite all the training I've done, I feel completely unprepared.

That this entire sequence of events is a clear metaphor for death that my brain has conjured up does not escape me.

I'm gonna miss his weird face. Is it because I'm actually going to miss him or because I'm worried that the next step in this sequence of events is actually my death? Orgasm is known as the 'little death' after all. If I wasn't dying, I could have a field day writing a paper about all of this... if I could concentrate.

I'm a bit more distracted than usual. I had no idea I had so many fantasies about orgasm denial. I followed a few femdenial accounts on the Tumblr account I use for porn, but it wasn't my main kink. Nothing to warrant days of edging. I'm starting to think the Cruciatus Curse would be easier to bear.

I'm not quite ready to face Avada Kedavra yet though.

I really don't want to leave Frllil.

But what if I'm not about to die? What if I'm actually just continuing the dream, which was heavily affected by the books I was reading before I fell into this coma? In which case, what's about to happen might be really fantastic. I sincerely hope it's the latter. I want to see Bogdan and run my hands all over him and have fantastic sex and orgasms before I die.

Or maybe I'm already dead. Frllil was purgatory and now I'm headed to heaven.

I'm not Catholic, or Christian, or even Hindu like my parents, in fact I always considered myself an atheist, but the analogy is too on point to ignore.

Either way, it will all be over soon. I smooth the front of my gown nervously. This is the most attractive I've looked since I started chemo. My hair spills over my shoulders in shining waves, the nearly see-through dress clings to my curves, the dark red color setting off my coloring nicely. I feel pretty. Feminine. And I still get a thrill of happiness whenever I touch my hair.

"Now remember the process of the ceremony," Frllil flutters beside me, pushing me into the pod even as he tries to dish out last minute instructions. "Your role—"

"Is to leave the pod and walk down the row of warriors to my Master. Then Dumbledore places the Sorting Hat on my head, and I think *Ravenclaw* really hard—"

"What?" Frllil's platform zooms in front of me. His whole mass quivers in upset. Jabol, I've discovered, don't exactly have a sense of humor. And despite using books as a lure for women, they don't really understand fiction either. Trying to explain Harry Potter to him went over as well as him trying to explain how nanotechnology worked to me.

"Relax." I sigh. "It was a joke. I walk up to my Master and he'll begin the process of bonding our nanotech." Which Frllil hasn't really explained what that means other than we will 'touch' in a cere-monial manner and the bond will initiate.

"This is very important, Pareena Singh." Back to first and last names. I stifle a groan. "You must—"

"I know. I'm ready. I'll miss you, though," I say honestly. In a weird way, despite the training, we did bond. I'd say we're both Ravenclaws. We both want all the information and facts we can get our hands on. "You did a great job of easing the transition." I know that's the compliment he'll appreciate the most.

"Thank you, Tribute Pareena." Frllil puffs up happily. "It has been a pleasure to train you. I believe the process was much easier this time, in large part due to your attitude." This is not the first time he's referenced how difficult the previous Tribute was, and I can't help but be amused. Apparently, even in my head, I feel the need to excel in an imaginary comparison. Extending a tendril, Frllil waves as I step into the pod and lie down. The door swishes shut, cutting off the view of him on his platform.

I can feel the subtle hum of vibrations shift. The pod is moving. Supposedly it will only take minutes for me to reach my destination.

But minutes can feel like hours when you aren't sure what's going to happen next. Am I going to reach the next step I read about? Or is this my end?

I got this. I can do this.

Lots of positive self-talk. That was something I always advised my clients to use. Affirmations can be incredibly useful in developing a positive mental attitude.

Whatever happens next, I can handle it.

I almost start to believe it until the pod's vibrations change again. My jaw clenches shut in reaction as fear blooms in my chest. I'm here. Wherever here is. Before I can completely psych myself out, the pod opens to a large atrium. From the curved lines of the walls, I can only assume I'm in the belly of one of the big Tsenturion ships. Probably the Command Ship, a part of my brain supplies, since that's where Bogdan is supposed to be stationed.

Ranks of Tsenturions in full battle armor line my view, staring at me, waiting for me to make my next move. Right.

I can do this.

Pushing back my fear I step out of the pod and they snap to attention. Turning my head back and forth, I look over them. At the back of their ranks is a small raised platform with a gangplank leading up to it. It's exactly what Frllil described the ceremony would look like. Maybe that's the reason for the orgasm denial. If I wasn't desperate to climax, I'm not sure I'd have the courage to take that next step. Not with all these massive, intimidating males staring at me.

As if responding to my thoughts, the Bride Trainer whirs to life, like it's encouraging me to get moving. So, I take that first step. And then another.

The closer I get, the more my Bride Trainer vibrates. My body flushes, my knees trembling with need. I move faster, like an arrow seeking out my target.

There are five figures on the gangplank. Three are giant warriors in glittering armor. Frllil schooled me on the armor colors. Two of the warriors wear a neutral navy. The one in the middle is in shiny black. Could it be—

The Bride Trainer hits max power and I almost misstep. Fisting the folds of my dress, I force myself to walk slower, even though every nerve ending in my pussy is screaming at me to pick up the pace. Falling on my face wouldn't be a good first impression. Not that the Trainer is making it easy for me. I can feel the hot blush in my cheeks as the silky material of my dress rubs against my nipples and the heat between my legs becomes unbearable.

I stare up at my new master, his features much clearer now that I'm nearly to him.

Bogdan looks the same as he did in the training videos. Seven feet of pure muscle. Suit armor black as night. A lighter color flashes over the dark surface as I watch, too fast for me to register. Under his helmet, his jaw is set as he stares into the distance. Another alien warrior nudges him, and Bogdan glowers at the other warrior before transferring his foreboding gaze to me.

His expression is far from happy. In all the footage I watched of him, he is never smiling. I thought it was because he's an intense type of person, the type who becomes annoyed when you try to make small talk at work. He's been on duty for a millennia ever since his planet was destroyed. That's a ton of trauma right there. How do you deal with your entire species getting wiped out? Have these guys really dealt with their feelings about—

No. I mentally smack myself. Rule number one of sexual fantasies: do *not* psychoanalyze the imaginary aliens. Not what I'm here for. I'm here for an orgasm.

I'm too aroused to think clearly anyway. And I can't take my eyes off Bogdan. Master. My new Master. All of this is so formal. High protocol. I never got into the pomp and ceremony of BDSM before. Guess this is my chance to try it.

Thanks, brain.

I raise my chin and meet Bogdan's gaze. His face is blank. I'm almost to the gangplank, close enough to see when he looks me up and down. Nothing, not even a flicker of interest. Does he not like what he sees?

My hands automatically go to my hair, stroking a long strand that's settled over my shoulder for comfort. It's like a security blanket. *This isn't real. It's your fantasy. Of course, he likes what he sees, otherwise why would your subconscious have created him? You control this, if you want him to smile then make him smile!*

The warrior beside him nudges him again and he moves to the head of the gangplank, glowering in no particular direction.

And wow does he have a major glower, the kind that makes me want to drop to my knees to avoid it. All right then. I've fantasized about a strict dominant Master who will fulfill all my sexy fantasies, and my subconscious delivered. I can deal with this.

I hope he lets me orgasm soon. I mean, I hope I let me orgasm soon. This whole thing feels so real it's becoming more and more difficult to remember it's not, especially when things don't go to the way I want them to.

I climb the gangplank and stop in front of the giant warrior. With a smooth sweep of my arms, I spread my gown and dip my knees like I've practiced. It's not quite like a curtsy on Earth, at least not like one I've ever seen. My feet are together, and my knees bend forward. The Tsenturion version of a curtsy I suppose. Three, two, one, then I straighten but keep my gaze on the ground as the Bride Trainer's vibrations swell between my legs.

My part is done. I sway a little. *Just don't pass out.* I'm so close to orgasming I can almost taste it.

Bogdan hasn't moved, but I can feel his gaze on me. I lean towards him. My salvation. The Giver of Orgasms. At least, I really hope he is.

The tallest of the group steps forward and Bodgan salutes him.

"Commander Bogdan, as High Commander of the Tsenturion fleet, I present your Tribute."

I startle as the ranks behind me break out into a shouted chant. The huge room rings as over a thousand hands hit their armored chests in salute. The tall warrior—the High Commander—nods and steps back, reaching down to draw a small figure forward with a flutter of colorful robes.

There's a human on the deck with us. Blonde and draped in a flowy gown like mine, she's wearing a small smile. When I glance at her, she winks.

This must be Dawn, the first Tribute. Huh. She doesn't look like she could possibly have given Frllil as much trouble as he claimed. The attitude he described is not immediately obvious either. I smile back at her a little, feeling relieved not to be the only human and female. What must it have been like for her to be all alone?

She wasn't, remember? You're imagining yourself a human companion so that you won't be all alone.

I'm having so much trouble letting go and enjoying the fantasy that I can't help but wonder if part of me is worried that this is all real. Which sounds insane, but it's true.

Bogdan beckons me forward. His face is still blank, but his eyes burn, moving over my form, pausing on my lips, my breasts and further down before sweeping back up to my face. It really does feel so real. I try to relax into it.

Because this is it. The moment I've been waiting for.

My knees wobble, strangely weak. I studied the pictures of him, but I didn't expect the presence he'd have in the flesh. His face is as hard and chiseled as the armor he wears. His broad shoulders block out the sight of the ship. Up close, his armor is clearly molded to his skin. The amount of muscles clearly delineated on his body are inhuman. Obviously.

He reaches for me, something in his hand. Maybe some kind of tech to help with the nanotech bonding? Silently, I curse Frllil for not being more descriptive, but I step forward, ready to embrace him, when he lifts my hair. That feels nice. Then something clicks, a cool metal presses around my throat, and I freeze.

Did he just collar me?!

Frllil definitely didn't mention anything about that! Maybe I should have expected it because serious BDSM relationships often involve a collar, and I think I do remember something about it from the books I was reading, but I thought we'd at least get to know each other a little first. Not just wham, bam, collared ma'am.

The collar is smooth yet soft under my fingers. Not metal but not fabric either—or if it is, it's something I haven't encountered. I can't figure out how it latches, although my fingers frantically search for one.

Bogdan holds up the end of a long, glittering leash which now connects us and gives the lead a warning tug. "It is forbidden for anyone to touch your collar but me." I drop my hands but he's still glowering at me. He tugs the leash again, and the way it jerks on my throat makes me want to reach out and smack him. "The correct response is 'Yes, Master'."

I grind my teeth. *Do not curse at the giant alien.* If my subconscious was directing this scenario from my reading material, I definitely did not want to go there. "Yes, Master."

Despite my annoyance, my pussy throbs at the words. He turns back to the High Commander.

"The Tribute is acceptable." Without warning he's moving forward, past the warriors and human, tugging me in his wake. Wait a second... where's my ceremonial touch? Aren't we supposed to kiss, or hug, or at least hold hands or something? I feel bereft and more than a little lost at the suddenness of our departure. I wouldn't have thought being collared was going to be the outer limit of our interaction.

Dawn gives a little wave as we pass her by, and I see that she's also collared and on a leash. At least I'm not the only one. She looks happy though, even content, standing at the High Commander's side.

"Good luck," she mouths before Bogdan tugs the leash again and I hurry to keep up, almost stumbling through the door into the hallway and letting the low light swallow me.

Still no orgasm in sight. Drat.

4

———————

B ogdan

I MARCH down the hall to my quarters, leading my Tribute, doing my best to ignore her beauty and the way her tech already tugs at my consciousness. I am far too aware of the training belt around her waist and what it reveals about her state of arousal. Her nanotech responded to me as soon as I touched her, integrating with my own. It is not the full Tsenturion bond, but it feels so close to what I imagined the bond would feel like that I am disturbed.

Because of Tribute Dawn, I know the full bond is possible, but she and the High Commander did not immediately have such a strong connection. I am acutely aware of my own Tribute, which rouses both my temper and my protective instincts. Especially when she tries to dawdle in the hall, looking around rather than following me closely.

After a few tugs on the leash when she tries to slow, she seems to realize I will not be indulging her, and she matches my quick pace. Good. I knew from her file that she was intelligent.

Leaving the Ceremony so abruptly will cause questions, but I had no desire to examine my new Tribute in front of my Commander or the warriors. I have followed the bare minimum of protocol and everyone will have to be content with that. It is bad enough that she has been matched to me and that the tech bond is so strong so quickly. I do not trust myself to contain my emotions and therefore I need to sequester us.

The door to my quarters slides open and I march inside, relief washing over me now that we are in the safety of my own quarters, away from prying eyes.

"Stay," I order her. The beautiful female just stares at me silently and I turn away, needing a moment to myself, to adjust to my new reality.

My head throbs. I retract my helmet so I can rub my scalp, trying to soothe away some of the pain. Behind me, my Tribute sucks in a breath. I don't know why. I tell myself I don't care.

Pretending to ignore her, I drift to my console. The screen reflects her image, still watching me curiously from the center of the room.

She is even more attractive in the flesh than she was on the vids. Tawny skin, shining dark hair, big brown eyes. But much smaller than I expected. Somehow, she looked larger, more sturdy in the pics and vids. In the flesh it is clear she is fragile, delicate, and far too breakable, even with the changes the Jabol have made to her body. What were the Jabol thinking, abducting human women to be our mates? The top of her head does not even reach my shoulder and I must be three times her weight. I could crush her by lying atop her. How does the High Commander manage it?

"*Drakk*," I mutter the curse under my breath. Already I am over-whelmed by this new duty and I have barely begun.

"What's that, Master?" My Tribute's voice is low and sultry, tugging at my senses with feminine allure, yet her tone is hardly subservient. I know from the manuals from her world that I must begin as I mean to go on.

I turn and fix her with a foreboding glare. "I did not give you permission to speak."

She raises her chin, dark eyes flashing with emotion that I can feel a small spark of. She is annoyed by my response, and strangely unafraid. Small as she is, she is full of fire. The hard look in her eyes says she is strong... but her skin is so soft and fragile. She is an interesting dichotomy and I feel a reluctant admiration for her already.

From death she was rescued through the wormhole and delivered to the Jabol for training, and now she is here as my Tribute, yet she stands tall and proud. Still, her fire must be tempered. For one so small, she is foolish to think she can stand against me, even were I not a warrior.

Perhaps her intelligence was overstated.

Crossing the room, I loom over her. She doesn't shrink away. Either she is very brave or very foolhardy. I cannot help but feel some admiration for her courage, regardless, but I also know I must take control of her.

I take hold of her nape, gently but firmly, feeling the coolness of the collar against the warmth of her skin. She gasps at my touch, her lips parting, a reaction I approve of. Her nipples bead at the front of her filmy dress and I can almost feel her arousal. Or perhaps I can actually feel it, through the nanotech.

She is well primed.

A thousand tsencycles and I am mated. Just not to the one I should have been, because that is how long she has been gone. Loss stabs my chest, thwarting my own arousal.

No, not mate. Tribute. She is human. A prize for my stellar service, and a vessel to continue our race. As lovely as she is, I will not forget my warrior responsibilities nor my mission to destroy our enemies. No matter how soft her skin or enticing her scent, I will not be distracted from my vengeance upon the Vgotha.

My Tribute is my duty, nothing more.

Perhaps one day... but certainly not now.

And it is my duty to train her properly.

"Remove this," I growl and pluck at her gown. I release her neck and she sways backwards, her breath coming faster. She blinks, but obeys without protest, her movements graceful and slow. Something about the look on her face is almost trance-like. I cannot tell what she is thinking, but the nanotech informs me that her arousal has increased.

My seela stir as her body is bared to me, my own arousal growing as she steps out of the gown and straightens. I clench my fists to keep my suit from lightening. Her hair falls about her narrow face, brushing the tops of her breasts, which are full, rounded, the perfect size to fit in my palms. Her nipples are upturned, begging me to stroke them.

She actually smiles at me, tilting her head to the side, her body shifting to an even more seductive stance. My seela react immediately and my cock pulses, thickening with interest.

"You prefer me naked?" She flutters her eyelashes at me, her voice sultry. I do not understand why she moves her eyes in such a manner, but I have to admit, there is something oddly appealing about it.

"Inside my quarters, yes."

"Our quarters," she corrects me, throwing me off balance.

"What?" I did not mean to ask the question, but she surprised me so much that I did so before I could stop myself. Asking a question is not weakness, I decide. I need to know how my Tribute thinks if I'm going to properly train her.

"Our quarters." Her smile widens, confusing me. "Because I live here now, correct?"

"I... that..." Technically she is correct, but she makes it sound as though we will be equals within these rooms, which is not at all correct. I cross my arms over my chest, giving her a hard look. "You will be staying here with me. These are *my* quarters and you are *my* Tribute."

I emphasize *my*. She belongs to me and she is staying in my quarters. Both are mine. I can tell I have not established proper dominance with my stumble over answering her question though, because her smile just widens. I will establish my mastery over her now and then there will be no more question in her mind about whose quarters these are or who she belongs to.

I issue a neural command and a platform rises from the floor at the foot of the bed. I stop it at the perfect height for her to kneel upon it with her upper body braced by the bed. "Get on all fours. I wish to inspect you."

My Tribute blinks. It is her turn to be thrown off balance, to my satisfaction. "Right now?"

"Are you disobeying me?" If she is, I will be happy to demonstrate the consequences of doing so. My lower body throbs at the thought. Sometimes, one can take pleasure in duty.

"No..."

"No?" I point at the platform. "Then obey."

"No, it's not..." The seductive stance she had adopted has fallen away and she looks uncomfortable. I find her no less attractive this way, in fact I rather enjoy seeing her look a little more unsure. "I just need to... powder my nose."

An errant lock of hair has fallen over her cheek. Moving closer to her, I brush it back, my fingers lingering on her soft skin as I frown. She sighs and leans into my touch and the tightness in my chest eases.

"Why do you wish to powder your nose?" I caress her cheek and then run my fingers over her nose, not understanding her request but not wishing to be cruel if it is something important. She closes her eyes and my tech tells me that her arousal is increasing, her pussy growing slick and ready for me. Her responsiveness makes me want to draw her into my arms and sink back onto the bed, to learn all the ways to make her sigh and moan. I could spend cycles with her, exploring her body.

I stiffen, uncomfortable with the direction of my thoughts.

But I am meant to train her, to master her, and ultimately to protect her. To do the first two, I must explore her form. Thoroughly. I relax. This is my duty. And I will be recalled to the bridge when it is time to return to my regular duties.

"I meant that I need to use the little Tribute's room," she explains, but I do not understand the explanation and I frown down at her in further confusion. She sighs. "The bathroom. I need to pee."

Ah. I do not understand why she did not just say so, but Tribute Dawn sometimes says strange things as well. Humans do not always speak the way Tsenturions do and it is another reminder of the differences between us.

I release her and step back. "Go then. You have five minicycles. Then you will return, and your inspection and training will commence."

With a shaky nod, no longer looking so sure of herself, she sways in the direction of the bathing room. The rounded curve of her bottom is very appealing, and I am looking forward to seeing the secondary entrance all the manuals make much of. I can feel it through the nanotech, but I want to see it before I do anything to it.

Pareena

Holy hell. What have I gotten myself into? This fantasy is out of control.

I thought I could keep it together right up until he wanted to inspect me. The thought of getting on all fours for him to look me over, touch me... for some reason I balked. Even though I'm desperate for an orgasm, this is all happening so fast.

It's not real.

But it feels so real. If it didn't, it would be so much easier to just let myself go. I stare at my reflection in the mirrored surface of the wall. This helps me remember that it's not real. Because if this were real, I'd see a body eaten away by cancer, with my ribs showing through, skin dulled, and hair gone. Instead, my hair falls around my full curves, my skin glows with health, and my eyes are bright with energy.

Exactly as I wish I was.

Which means I need to get back to my fantasy and enjoy myself. I could wake up at any moment and be thrust back to cruel reality... or I could never wake up at all and this dream could just abruptly end.

It does not do to dwell on dreams and forget to live.

Dumbledore almost had it right. When there is nothing left to life and you're given the opportunity to live in the Mirror of Erised, you don't say no. I'm going to grab onto this particular dream with both hands and savor the ride. *Carpe diem* and all that. It's definitely what I would counsel a patient to do.

The giant warrior is waiting for me when I return to the bedroom. His suit has retracted from his torso, leaving only the lower half of his body covered, and his golden skin glitters in the low light. His muscles are ridiculously huge. If I hugged him, I'd barely get my arms around the barrel of his chest. The expression on his face remains as foreboding as ever. Why I find that such a turn on, I have no idea, but my alien master is as stern as any of the doms in my fantasies. Maybe sterner.

My pussy pulses against the training belt. I can't wait for him to take it off and touch me. There's no sense in feeling shame or embarrassment about an inspection, because this isn't real, right?

Bogdan points to the platform a few feet off the ground.

"Up." His command is said in a voice so deep it sends tremors through me.

I make myself move forward, well aware of how naked and vulnerable I am. Not real. Happening in my head. *Just enjoy the fantasy, Pareena!*

Taking a deep breath, I place my knee on the platform and push up with my other foot. With my knees spread wide to help keep my balance, I bend forward and rest my elbows on the bed. It is soft, but doesn't have too much give, and my breasts sway beneath me, my hair falling like a curtain on either side of my body and providing me with a tiny bit of coverage.

My ass and pussy are completely displayed by the position though, and for the first time I'm grateful for the training belt. Imaginary alien sex fantasy or not, my emotions feel very real.

"I will inspect you now. If you disobey me at any point, I will punish you."

The temptation to disobey is strong... exactly what would punishment entail? But considering that everything feels so very real, maybe I don't really want to know what my brain would come up with.

"We will proceed according to manuals."

"Manuals?" I echo the word without thinking and then cringe. "Sorry, Master, I didn't mean to speak out of turn."

I feel a little silly saying it, calling him Master out loud in a manner that isn't joking, but it feels oddly right too. Probably because I had always wished I could find a Dom who would become my Master. So my brain provided. *Thanks, brain.*

"The courtship manuals, like the one you were reading before you chose to come here."

"You mean the book I was reading about Tsenturions?" Aka the whole reason my brain must have latched onto this particular fantasy for my dream.

"Those books were modeled after your courtship manuals, I am told." Fingers touch beneath my chin and lift my head up, directing my gaze to a small stack of books at his bedside. Yikes. I recognize those titles, those authors. *Zylonn's Human Bride* by Sue Lyndon. *His Human Slave* by Renee Rose. A Berserker book by Lee Savino.

"These are your manuals?" My voice goes a little high and my ass clenches automatically. I downloaded these after getting into the stories already on the e-reader I now know Frllil sent me. Books with lots of sexy discipline. Drat. Where are the slow burn romances when you need them?

"They were collected from Earth. The Jabol tell us they are very popular."

"Yeah... as entertainment, not instruction books."

Bogdan gives me a patronizing look. "The Jabol sent devices to monitor your responses as you studied the manuals. The stories primed you for your role as Tribute."

That made almost too much sense.

"That's a huge invasion of privacy," I mumble and duck my head.

Or at least it would be, if this wasn't in my head. If I wasn't imagining this, I would be livid. Even knowing it's not, I feel indignant at the idea of aliens studying my kinky preferences for their own sordid reasons.

Bogdan releases my chin, letting my head drop back down. "Your responses were why you were chosen as a Tribute. This is the life you sought. Now that you are here, you will submit to me in all things."

I squeeze my legs together to hide my wetness. Fine. I was chosen. My brain has pulled from all my favorite books to put together my fantasy.

"Okay." I lick my lips and turn my head to look up at him. "What's my safeword?"

He gets the same blank expression as he did when I told him I needed to powder my nose. Apparently, that's what he looks like when I confuse him.

"I do not understand. You are safe here with me. You may use words, unless I forbid your speech."

"I mean, a word I can say to make the play stop."

"This is not play." He fists a hand in my hair and tips my head back, much less gentle now, and my body responds immediately. A whimper falls from my lips and I am quivering all over at his touch. Yes, please, more hair-pulling. "You are not in control. You will submit to my desires. I am your Master."

I'm panting now, my arousal back up to a full ten. I've been a bit back and forth, but now I'm finding it easier to get into the right mindset to just enjoy myself. Guess my fantasies of no control are coming true. In the safest way possible, but hey, might as well enjoy it.

"Consensual non-con. Okay. I can be down for some edge play." As long as I get my orgasm.

Bogdan's face goes blank, his grip gentling, and he turns to look at the books again. "I will do more research."

He releases my hair, starting to step away, and I panic.

"No, please, Master," I blurt, afraid he's going to walk off and start reading, leaving me here to burn. "Please. I will be good. Use me as you wish." I flush at my wanton words but push back my embarrassment. Especially because it works. He looks down at me, contemplation in his dark eyes.

"You will obey my every command."

"Yes, Master," I agree breathlessly. Yes! Let's get this party started!

"I will inspect you. If you are a good, obedient girl, I may permit your climax."

I press my lips together. Yes please, that's what I'm talking about!

He digs his hands into my hair again, rubbing my head like he's petting a cat. I love it, though. I almost want him to stroke my hair forever, except my pussy is pulsing like a second heartbeat, trying to get his attention. *Me, me, me!*

Bogdan takes his sweet time sliding a hand down my back, over my shoulders to encircle my arms. His hands are so big he can easily shackle my wrists. He crouches to explore my chest and belly, tracing my breasts with a single finger. I close my eyes and moan at the teasing sensation. When he rises and cups my breasts in both hands I hum happily. My nipples press against his palms, his fingers deftly massaging my soft flesh and I feel like I am literally turning to putty in his hands.

When he moves away, I almost protest, except that I feel the Bride Trainer moving against my swollen pussy and I realize it's receding. Yes! Tracing his hands over my back, he slides them down my sides to my ass and I sense him crouching down behind me, his hands on my ass cheeks, holding them apart as he inspects my pussy. At this point, he could breathe on my clit and I'd cum. Shivers spread through my body, little champagne bubbles, like I'm a bottle, corked, shaken and ready to explode.

Gripping either butt cheek, he pushes them even further apart and I realize it's not just my pussy he's interested in. I feel him staring at my little hole. I squirm a little and he grips me tighter. I wait for him to touch or lick me or something, but there's just a light brush of his fingers over my crinkled hole and then he moves on and I moan with disappointment.

The light touches return. He leaves almost no part of me unhandled. Not even my ears or toes, which he spends some time inspecting. He touches me everywhere—except my pussy. Almost like he's avoiding the one part of me I want him to touch the most.

When he returns to my breasts, I almost scream with the building sexual frustration. His fingers brush my nipples and I arch my back, sighing with pleasure.

"You find this pleasing?" He asks, pinching each nub lightly and I hum.

"Yes. More please, Master. You can pinch harder." Please do.

"I wish to understand your responses."

"I respond to you."

He steps away, his fingers falling from my nipples and leaving me aching, throbbing, and starting to get a little worried that I am really never going to come.

"Did I do something wrong?"

"You have forgotten to call me Master. Again."

Oops. "Forgive me, Master."

"You will learn your place. Perhaps now is time to test your response to punishment." He turns and a panel of the wall beeps and slides aside. Behind it is a closet of some sort. It takes a moment for my eyes to adjust and I gasp at the assortment of punishment implements hanging in neat rows. Floggers, paddles, long and thin reeds that will leave painful lines on my skin, straps made out of an assortment of materials and in a variety of lengths. A sadist's dream. A sub's nightmare. A masochist's hidden fantasy.

"These are Enforcers. I trust I will not need them often. I was out of practice, but I have been re-training myself to wield them, in order to discipline my Tribute when necessary." The matter-of-fact way he announces this makes the words seem all the more sinister. It doesn't matter though, all of it turns me on even more. I'm torn now—do I want him to punish me or fuck me? "We will start with the least severe and move to the one designed to impart the most pain." Apparently, they are lined up by severity because he picks up a softer looking flogger first, then one with knots at the end, and keeps up picking out 'enforcers' until he reaches a thin whippy-looking cane.

"You're going to use all of those on me?" I squeak out the words, unsure if I'm more excited, turned on, or terrified. His gaze whips toward me and I gulp. Shoot, I forgot again. "Master?"

"Obviously you are in need of a reminder of your place. This will be a demonstration of what you can expect if you continue to forget it. You are my Tribute and you will call me Master and obey my orders. I will have your submission and claim you in the manner of both of our peoples." He pauses, as if waiting for me to answer. I'm too busy taking in the wall of pain and I'm not really sure there was a question in there until he speaks again. "Well, Tribute? What do you have to say?"

I lick my lips. What else can I say? "Yes, please, Master."

5

B ogdan

MY TRIBUTE STARES at the wall of my Enforcers, dark eyes wide and full of interest. Her tongue darts out. My *seela* quiver, the thin tendrils around my cock very interested in the female in front of me. The tightness of my armor is almost painful against my arousal. I can feel a longing to join with her, to sink into her with my cock so that my *seela* may latch onto her soft skin and begin the exchange of biological information. According to the manuals, humans do not have *seela*, they have something called 'pubic hair' instead, but the High Commander has told me that his Tribute enjoys the difference between us.

The manuals also indicated that human females sometimes enjoy pain, that they are aroused by their punishments. Although, the females also seem more reluctant to be disciplined in the manuals, whereas my Tribute is almost eager. Perhaps that is an effect of the priming. The nanotech tells me she is as painfully aroused as I am, perhaps more so.

First, I must punish her though, so that she will know her place. I will prove myself a good, if demanding, Master and she will acknowledge my dominance over her. Then and only then, will I give her the pleasure she craves.

With a thought, I send an order to the platform. It shifts, rising to display her hindquarters even more than before. The middle section morphs and curves under her to take her weight off her knees. She ends up tipped forward with her head down and the perfect globes of her rear on display.

"You are nicely primed for your Master." The glistening folds of her womanhood are a wondrous sight. I cannot help but reach forward to touch her, to put my fingertip to her wetness, just to feel it.

She strains back towards me. "Master, please—"

I move my hand away from her pussy and spank her right flank, hard enough to leave a dark print on her tanned skin. "No. You will accept your discipline and if you please me, you will climax. Not a microcycle before."

My words are stern, but I find myself restraining a smile at her breathy sigh and minute tremors in her shapely legs. Her eagerness pleases me, calling to instincts deep inside my psyche. I stroke and tease her nether parts a minicycle longer. More fluid leaks from her lovely folds. I find myself probing and peering into her juicy slit, my lips parted and tongue ready to taste her. But I pull back at the last moment.

In due time, I remind myself. Discipline first.

"With proper training, you will be the perfect Tribute. Ready and willing to serve my needs." I mutter to myself, but she murmurs back anyway.

"Yes, Master."

My cock stiffens at her soft, submissive tone, my prime seela arching above in readiness. My lesser seela waft around my shaft as if searching for my Tribute. The tiny suckers open and close against the inside of my armor. It is all I can do to keep the armor on my lower body up, to keep them from tasting and fastening onto my Tribute's skin, pulling her close and holding her still for my cock's invasion. The thought makes me lightheaded.

I have chosen my Enforcers but find myself reluctant to start with anything but my bare hand on her warm flesh. My Tribute's skin is so soft. She was made to be touched, and I am happy to oblige. No more than is my duty, but it is my duty.

"We start with manual correction. This will not always be punishment. At times I will order you to present for inspection. I might spank you then, to remind you of your place."

I let my hand crash down on her curvy cheeks, admiring how they bounce and quiver with each light impact. I angle my hand to catch the underside of her bottom, fascinated by the way her flesh moves beneath my hand.

~

Pareena

BOGDAN IS HOLDING nothing back and it hurts so good. I can't remember the last time I was spanked for the sheer pleasure of it, and that is what this feels like. It doesn't feel like a punishment at all— yet. His hand is hard enough that it could certainly get there. But right now, with my arousal at an all-time high and endorphins running through my brain, I'm starting to think I might orgasm just from the spanking.

Cool air wafts over my pussy but does nothing to dampen the heat of my body. If the platform beneath me had not changed to fit along my stomach, I would be trying to sneak a hand down between my legs to touch my throbbing clit.

Instead, all I can do is lay there, ass in the air, moaning as he spanks me, lecturing me all the while.

"You must always submit to me." His voice is deep, commanding, the cadence almost hypnotic, like he's trying to use his hand to imprint his words into my flesh.

Smack!

"Whether it is pleasure or pain—"

Smack!

"I will give you what you need."

Smack!

I cry out as he punctuates his declaration with a flurry of sharply stinging swats, my pussy clenching in reaction. The spanking burns, but the heat is transforming inside me into something more erotic, more pleasant. Especially when he pauses and his hand squeezes each cheek in succession, as if testing how well-punished they are.

"Please, Master..." I manage to gasp out the words, wagging my hips up and down. Suddenly he stops spanking me and I feel two fingers slide into my dripping wet pussy. He has very big fingers, but I am so well-lubricated that he easily penetrates me, pumping them back and forth.

I quiver, gasping, and the pure bliss of having him inside of me is so intoxicating that I actually experience a small orgasm. The hot rush of pleasure does not satisfy the gaping need inside of me, but it smooths the edges of it, makes it bearable, as my pussy spasms around him. Utter gratitude fills me.

I can orgasm!

"More, my Tribute," he commands, his fingers moving again, rubbing over my g-spot and then I feel him touching my clit. "Climax for me." There had been a part of me that was so scared I would never actually get to come, but now I can feel it, inexorable and inevitable, ready to overwhelm me.

The platform under my body is the only thing holding me up as la petite morte engulfs me. It's weeks of waiting, culminating in the most intense orgasm of my life. If this is true death, I am no longer afraid. I am drowning in sensation, in ecstasy, in uninhibited rapture.

Truthfully, I'm almost surprised when the crescendo of my pleasure recedes and I am left panting and spent. My body throbs, from the more painful ache in my spanked cheeks to the satisfied pulsing in my clit. Bogdan's fingers slide out of me and the next thing I know they are in front of my lips.

I'm so shocked, so thrown off balance, by my continued existence and how real the aftermath of my spanking and orgasm feel, how real the scent of my pussy on his fingers smell, that I jerk away rather than opening my mouth. Before I can say anything, Bogdan has already moved his fingers away and is back behind me.

"Perhaps it is time to move on to the real discipline," he says.

"But—" I start to protest and then gasp as his wet fingers push into my asshole. I'm not a virgin there, but it's been a long, long time since that area has been touched by anyone other than a nurse. The burning stretch hurts and feels good all at the same time. My fists clench the sheets and I groan, my muscles trying to clamp down around him.

Bogdan

PENETRATING her secondary entrance seems to have the exact response the manuals indicated it would. I can feel her submitting to me, her body working to accept the abrupt invasion of my fingers and allowing me to do with her small hole whatever I please. The hot, dry channel intrigues me greatly and my cock throbs, my seela straining eagerly toward her. I ignore my own impulses though.

This is about my duty, not my body's sexual needs.

Pulling my fingers from her tight hole, rather than continue to test my willpower, I select an Enforcer. It's a small one, made of organic material much like the wood of her former planet. An oval shape not much larger than her hand. I'll pepper her bottom with rounded marks, layering sting over sting. A flick of my wrist is all I need for a warning. Nothing that will leave a mark for longer than a day or so. I tested the Enforcers on my own flesh first to prepare for my Tribute.

She's breathing easily, her body limp on the platform I've molded to my purposes, satisfied from the orgasms. I wish for a moment she was draped over my lap, bottom upturned over my knee, hair hanging to the floor.

My seela strain under my armor, reaching for her bare skin. Next time. Next time she will be over my lap when I discipline her.

The thought makes me pause, because why should I desire such an intimate change?

But part of my duty is to discipline my tribute as I see fit. If she is over my lap, flesh pressed to mine, I will better determine her responses. The fact that I will enjoy her writhing is not a consideration, I reassure myself.

"I will discipline you now." Her breathing becomes more rapid as I touch the hard surface of my chosen Enforcer to her rear.

I tap the Enforcer over her quivering buttocks, lightly at first and then harder. Her skin is darker than Tribute Dawn's and does not show the same pink, but I can still see the color changing. Her legs kick up helplessly and I pop the implement against the wet skin between her thighs.

With a yelp, she reaches back to try and protect her pussy. I grab her wrist and pull it to the side.

"If you cannot keep your hands down, I will restrain you."

"No, please, Master. I'll be good."

I keep hold of her wrists as I finish with a flurry of sharp smacks that leave her writhing and panting, a sob dragging from her throat, but she does not try to escape my hold. Only when she keeps her word to not fight do I let her go.

I am not done, though. This first discipline must be thorough and set the stage for what she can expect in the future. That each solid thud against her chastised flesh sends a hot gush of arousal through me has nothing to do with it. I select another Enforcer, modeled much like the previous one, but with a larger head, square-shaped. I angle it to catch the crease where her buttocks meet her thighs.

Pareena

I AM ON FIRE.

No matter how I try to convince myself that I'm not really feeling this pain, my brain doesn't cooperate. Each hard smack of the wood against my already burning bottom makes me jerk and flail, tears sliding down my cheeks at the blooming pain. Not just at the pain though.

At the release.

At the sheer joy of feeling something.

At the conflicting mix of sensations that sink into my skin, the utter ecstasy of feeling so alive, and the submissive rush that always accompanies a spanking for me. Or, that always used to. I still feel it though. The heady submission, the growing ache, each hard swat sending me higher and higher.

The hard wood smacks against my sit-spots, hurting me perfectly, deliciously, and sending more tears spilling down my cheeks. I am throbbing, burning, stinging all over. Not just on the surface of my skin, but deeper. I crave Bogdan's touch and he does not disappoint.

The spanking pauses and his fingers dip into my pussy. I can feel the excessive wetness from my previous orgasm as he rubs his fingers through my lips, exploring my sensitive slit.

"You are doing well." The praise is sincere, if a bit formal.

"Thank you, Master." I feel dreamy, but also a little hollow. As much as I enjoy his hand now curving over my bottom, the masochistic side of me craves more. I want the pain, the endorphins. I want to fly.

"As you have been so good, I will allow you to choose the next Enforcer."

It takes a moment for his words to penetrate the erotic haze that the spanking has sent me into. As soon as they do, I feel my anticipation surge and my bottom throbs. Nothing too harsh, not after the spanking he's already meted out but... "The belt, please."

I can hear the begging in my voice as I turn to look longingly at one of the implements he'd left hanging on the wall.

"This?" He leaves my side, walking over to touch the long, hanging strip of leather. At least, that's what it looks like to me. The *kurdzu* hide?"

"Yes, I love the belt." I almost sigh with happiness as he picks it up.

～

Bogdan

I PAUSE on my way back to her, thinking over her words. When I reach her again, I caress her right bottom cheek and then squeeze the soft flesh. The chastised skin is warm to touch. "You have been disciplined before."

"A few times. At a club. And a party." Her words are slightly slurred from the pleasure. So, she has been courted before. But either her previous master abandoned her when she sickened, in which case he was no master at all, or...

"Have you ever belonged to a master?" I squeeze her bottom more firmly and she croons happily as I dig my fingers in. The nanotech tells me that she does feel the pain, but she also feels pleasure along with it. Some part of her enjoys the punishment. Just as the manuals indicated. Truly, they are far more helpful than I could have believed.

"No. But I obviously fantasized about it." She lets out a little laugh, as if she just told a joke. Before I can ask what she means by that, she adds, "The belt was my favorite. Leather feels yummy."

Now it is my turn to chuckle. I do not know what 'yummy' means, but it's clear she means it as a positive thing. "I wonder if you will be able to say the same when I am through."

Unbelievably, she smiles at me through her hair, tilts forward on the modified bench and offers her already darkened bottom. "Do your worst."

I can't stop the swell of pride under my breastplate. My Tribute is strong and courageous. I unwind the strip of hide and crack it beside her head before doubling it over in my hand to give me more control over the long length.

"Breathe," I remind her when I notice she's gone still. From fear? From expectation?

Perhaps this discipline is not as effective as it should be, considering how she seems to be enjoying some of it. But I do know that she feels the effects, thanks to the nanotech. It also just seems to arouse her. In that way, she is very like a Tsenturion female.

The reminder nearly causes me to drop the kurdzu strap.

I shake myself, focusing on the here and now, because even if she is not a Tsenturion female, even if she is not my chosen bride, she is my Tribute and she deserves my full attention when I am disciplining her. When she wiggles her reddened bottom, it is easier to focus on her.

I lay the belt across her rear, admiring the pink edged mark that appears on the sultry curve of her bottom. She cries out but manages to hold her position, her bottom bobbing up and down, the welted stripe standing out against even the rest of her punished flesh.

"More, please," she begs.

I step back and paint thick lines on her backside, enjoying the loud crack of the Enforcer. As I work her over, my own body heats with exertion. My seela are practically screaming, dying for release from the hard shell of my armor. Judging by the slickness between her legs, she is enjoying the discipline, too. Her pleading words fall sloppily from her lips.

With a thought, I could remove my coverings and alter the platform I created to be at the perfect height for my cock. She's so wet, I would slide right inside, my prime seela flowing over the marks on her bottom, soothing and stroking. My lesser seela would suction onto her sensitive labia, delighting in the copious moisture, fastening onto the pinkish skin and splaying her for my invasion. Her inner walls would feel so good kissing along my cock. So soft.

I pause to regain control over myself, panting with the need riding me. But... I can't. I loosen my armor around my shaft and seela, relieving some of the pressure. I have no plans to use her body for my own satisfaction. Not yet. I have seen the change wrought upon the High Commander. How he lost himself in Tribute Dawn after her arrival and how he seems to have forgotten our duty to our lost, our vengeance.

The same will not happen to me.

What is it about these Tributes that they rouse such strong feelings?

Gripping her silky dark hair, I ease her head back and study her face. Her lips are pink and plump, slightly parted. I lean down to nuzzle my nose against her cheek, drinking in her scent, trying to determine what is so appealing about her. A sweet aroma, like the harvest flowers of my home planet. Her delicate jaw fits easily in my hand. Her cheek curves and she angles her head to place a small kiss in the center of my palm before she leans into my touch. I freeze at the freely given affection.

After a minicycle, she blinks and lets her head roll to look up at me. "Did I do something wrong? Master?"

A fist squeezes my insides. I barely find my voice. "No. You are ... perfect."

6

P areena

I LOVE this part after a good scene, my body warm and head high on the endorphins singing through me. The moment after the last strike and before my top opens his pants and rewards me with his dick. My thoughts blur, turning the strong figure of my dominant into an all-powerful god, my submissive posture into one of abject worship. I feel small and safe, tucked into my defined role. At the same time, the chemicals in my bloodstream have me flying, spread over the galaxy in tiny, glittering particles.

Bogdan looms over me, breathing hard. I don't know much about Tsenturion anatomy—yet—but there's a package in his pants I bet is for me.

He smells so good. Maybe it's just the nanites talking, but his scent fills my lungs like I need it, not oxygen, to breathe. If this is what it's like to be fully primed and bonded, it's awesome and scary at once. To need someone so much my skin is screaming for him. My mouth is watering and body aches with a craving to be touched. I'm a Bogdan addict and I need my fix.

"You did well," he tells me. "We will continue your discipline another time. It is not necessary for you to feel all the Enforcers now. In time, you will submit to all of them."

Facing the wall of implements, hearing my Tsenturion master promise to bring me to heel, My pussy throbs at the thought.

"Right now, I will test your response to pleasure."

Yes, please.

The platform rises under my bottom, tipping my front forward even more. I'm splayed embarrassingly, my well-marked hindquarters throbbing, face height for the tall warrior.

What is he—?

Two of his large fingers slide into my heated slit.

"Ooooh," my moan escapes. I wanted his cock but I'm in no position to complain, not tipped forward and strapped down like this.

"So responsive," he murmurs, sounding thoughtful. I strain back as much as I can towards his fingers. I just need a little more stimulation to tip over into orgasm...

He pulls out his finger and smacks my ass with a wet sound. Before I protest, his fingers return to my pussy.

"I wonder," he pulls my left butt cheek aside, opening me to his gaze. I imagine him taking in every inch of me, from my plump pussy to the brown whorl of my anus, and blush so hard my face is as red as my bottom. He probes deeper and my legs quiver. "Is all this lubrication from the pain?"

He swats my ass again, awakening the dulled sting of my punished hindquarters. My pussy juices in response.

"Or is it because you are trained to respond to me?" Large hands grip my bottom, massaging away the sting until the pain is a pleasant hum far away, adding depth to my rising desire. I'm dripping now, inner thighs coated in wetness. I've never been so ready for cock in my life.

"Both, Master," I answer his musings even though I can barely talk. Enough with the philosophizing. Let's get to the good part.

But his fingers explore my ass, brushing the sensitive crinkle. I clench my bottom and he smacks me in unspoken command to relax. When I do, he rubs his thumb over my asshole while his other hand returns to my pussy. It's embarrassing how much I like a finger in my ass. I'm not opposed to ass play but haven't had a dom I trusted enough to progress to this point.

"You are making more lubrication," he remarks, sounding both clinical and intrigued. For some reason that just makes me even hornier. "You enjoy this." It's not a question and he continues to probe my tight hole. "Perhaps some experiments are in order."

Is he going to focus all his attention to my ass? I love the thought of being anal trained, but right now my clit is feeling pretty neglected.

"Please, Master." I'm not above begging.

It's the right thing to say, because his left-hand drops and he returns his full attention to stroking and stimulating my clit and labia. He twists a finger inside me, and another, and when he adds a third, I'm undone. I'm so full, so hot, so *needy* that I almost joyously fall into the pleasure.

My climax slams into me, pleasure and pain and need colliding in my core, grains of gunpowder that had been waiting for a spark. I cry out, mouth open, convulsing on his thick digits which thrust deeper into my pussy. He keeps twisting them, stimulating me further, and my orgasm loops back around, curling through me, one climax turning into two, two turning into four, until I can't even count them anymore.

At some point he moves around to my front, bending to watch my expressions. All the blood has rushed to my face and I'm light-headed. He does something and the platform straightens out, so I'm lying on my front, arms at my side, cheek pressed to the smooth surface. My hair is stuck to my sweaty skin.

Bogdan dips so he's right in my face. The angles and planes of his face are too blunt to be pretty, but the effect is overwhelmingly masculine. I wonder what he'd do if I called him 'hot.' "What does my Tribute say after I've given her pleasure?"

"Thank you, Master." I sigh, and when he offers his wet fingers to my mouth, I clean them without protest.

~

Bogdan

MY COCK THROBS insistently as my Tribute licks her essence off my fingers. I command the platform to release her and I catch her before she rolls. Her weight is negligible, but she makes a soft and sweet-smelling armful as I carry her to my bed. I pause to order my resting place to grow larger and form a supply of thick blankets. I always sleep on a spare pallet, bare of comfort. Even when I sleep I will be ready to go on alert and race to duty if our ship is attacked. But such an uncomfortable resting place will not do for my Tribute.

She sighs when I place her on the newly formed plush surface. I brush her hair back from her face—the better to monitor her expressions—and rest a hand on her head. She stills under my touch. Her eyelids fall. Her chest rises and falls peacefully. Pleasure and pain wrung her out in their grip and now she eases into sleep, certain of my protection. I straighten proudly.

And she is the perfect Tribute. I did not overstate my approval. Not only is she sweet and obedient but she responds to discipline beautifully. I wonder if the High Commander's Tribute is the same. But Dawn always seems reluctant to conform to our laws. Not so with my Tribute. She is superior in every way. I would never shame the High Commander by telling him so, though.

I touch her face, admiring the soft curve of her cheek. She turns her head in her sleep, mouth open as if ready to accept anything I would feed her.

I force myself to step back. There will be time to explore all of her responses. For now, she must rest.

Guilt stirs in my chest as I look at her, a female in my bed, the soft emotions she stirs in me, the desire I feel... now that she sleeps and I am more clearheaded, it feels like a betrayal.

My com chirps, distracting me, and relief rushes through me. Immediately, I march to the screen in the corner of my quarters. First, I order the message alerts to mute themselves within the cabin. No need to disturb my sleeping Tribute, unless there is an emergency.

A few taps of my screen show our ship is cruising beside an asteroid belt. Scans show no sign of life, but the Vgotha have hidden in such areas before. I check the time. Third watch. Most days, I would be on duty at this demicycle. The High Commander took me off duty for the next semicycle, allowing plenty of time for me to train my Tribute. But she is sleeping. A quick scan of her vitals tells me she is entering a state of deep rest that she will not exit for some time, if undisturbed. There is time for me to report to the bridge.

The more I ponder it, the better my plan sounds. I will not have to see her, in the place where I always pictured another, and I will show my fellow warriors that it is possible to prioritize our duty over our Tributes.

I tell myself that leaving my rooms does not feel like a retreat.

"Commander Bogdan." Kalexston's suit flashes with surprise when I enter the bridge. I am not surprised to see him in charge over my usual watch in my absence, as he is technically in command beneath me when I am there. "What are you doing here?"

"It is my watch, correct?" I ignore the assembled warriors and head to the com as if everything is normal and this demicycle is like any other. As if I did not, a few demicycles earlier, receive a Tribute.

The warriors stare at me. In awe, no doubt of how I balance my duty with the responsibility of my Tribute.

"What are the results of the scans of the asteroid belt?" I ask, eyes on the rock-studded space on screen.

"We haven't done anything more than a preliminary one," Kalexston says, but his tone is strange, like he doesn't understand why I am asking. I turn to look at him impatiently.

"Well? What are you waiting for?"

Kalexston exchanges a glance with Miths and I can see the uncertainty in both of their stances. The operations officer clears his throat. "Commander, you are not on duty."

"I am present, so I am on duty."

"I mean... you were relieved of duty so you might tend to your Tribute."

"As I am here, you will assume my Tribute is well tended. Kalexston," I snap, and the warrior straightens to attention. "The scans. Now."

A few minicycles pass with the quiet hum of the energy scans. An asteroid belt on the edge of the galaxy is not something we'd submit to deep level scans, but the Vgotha are out there. We must be vigilant.

A soft hiss behind me warns me the transport has arrived. The warriors on deck rise and salute whoever entered the bridge. I turn more slowly and offer my salute.

"Bogdan," the High Commander presses his fist against his chest in acknowledgement. He doesn't look surprised to see me. That combined with his sudden presence means someone reported my insistence to take command. I resist the urge to look around, to see which warrior betrayed me. "You look well. How is your Tribute?"

"She is sleeping." The listening officers almost sigh, relaxing slightly as if they were worried about my Tribute. I suppress a glower. They should not worry about her. She is my concern. And she is fine.

"Good." The High Commander's suit is a neutral silvery grey, his expression blank. But something lurks in the corner of his mouth—a smile? "I require a meeting. Private quarters."

"With all due respect, we can discuss my duty here, so I do not abandon my post." I have the feeling that if I allow him to lead me from the bridge, I will not be returning this watch.

The High Commander is really smiling now, his amusement clear. "But you are not on duty. The post is not yours. Kalexston—" He motions, and the science officer steps up, ready to take my place.

"But my Tribute sleeps and I am willing to serve my watch." I almost feel as though I am begging, although of course I do not let any of that enter my voice or show on my armor.

"You were relieved of the responsibilities of command for the next semicycle. You have a new Tribute. You belong by her side." The High Commander's smile has dipped now, and he appears more stern than amused.

"She is resting. I have no reason to miss my watch. I do my duty."

"You have a Tribute. Your first duty is to her."

I can't hide the flicker of annoyance that streaks through my suit. "With all due respect, my first duty is to my command."

"No, it is to your Tribute. The entire race rests on your bonding with her."

Color flickers through my suit. Kalexston and Miths stare as if they'd never seen my suit respond to my emotions before. Maybe they haven't.

I clench my fists. My Tribute will not make me weak.

"Come." The High Commander turns, obviously expecting me to follow him. "Let us speak privately in my welcoming chamber."

"Is that an order?"

The High Commander's suit darkens slightly. He is losing his patience with me. "Yes."

He marches off the bridge. After a glare at the watching warriors, all of them since I do not know which individual reported my presence, I follow him. Murmurs start up as soon as I step off the bridge and I restrain myself from returning and challenging them all to a fight for daring to whisper about me and my Tribute.

To my surprise and displeasure, the Commander doesn't lead me to his ready room, an office close to the bridge, but boards the transport as if to return to his private quarters. I bite back my protest and follow him.

As soon as we step into his private chambers, the High Commander retracts his helmet and armor. I stand stiffly at attention, choosing to remain armored, although I retract my helmet. To remain fully armored would be tantamount to disrespect.

"Make yourself comfortable. I'm going to check on Dawn." He disappears from the welcoming chamber to the inner one reserved for sleeping. I turn away but can still hear the soft, feminine murmur of Tribute Dawn's voice and the High Commander's answering rumble.

When the High Commander returns, he commands the door behind him to close.

"Dawn will not be joining us. She's also resting." The High Commander's voice and demeanor changes when he refers to his Tribute. I have never mentioned it but am inwardly determined to never allow my Tribute to affect me so.

"I thought I told you to make yourself comfortable." The Commander shoots a wry look my way.

I straighten further. "I am comfortable."

"Relax, Bogdan, it wasn't an order." He crosses to the replicator and orders a beverage. "Would you like something?"

"No, thank you." I relax, as ordered, although I do keep my armor on.

Although he is the High Commander, in a personal setting, Gavrill is also my friend. As warriors, we keep to our strict hierarchy when on duty, but in a more personal setting we are able to speak as equals. Although, truthfully, I am often given more leeway even on duty, because of our personal relationship.

Gavrill takes a long drink, studying me.

"Bogdan, when the Jabol told us that Tribute Pareena was a near perfect match to you, Medik and I discussed whether or not we should heed their recommendation. We knew you would be reluctant. But we also knew your responsibility and commitment to a Tribute would be second to none, if you could overcome your reticence. Most of our warriors want a Tribute but wanting is not enough. Tributes need a strong, caring protector, one who treats them as the gift they are."

I hold back a smile. That is more in line with my thoughts. "You do me honor, High Commander. Of course, I will fulfill my role and prove a worthy choice."

He gives me a look and I realize he wasn't finished. "Tributes also need a warrior who will try to understand them and treat them as the individual they are, not just as a vessel for bearing our seed. I wonder if we should've given the Tribute to another. Arkdhem perhaps."

What? No! I nearly jerk to my feet; my armor flashing streaks of red and yellow as I lose control over my emotions. The image of the Tribute tangled in blankets on my sleeping platform flashes through my head. From the top of her dark head to the tips of her toes: she is mine. He gave her to me. He cannot take her away from me now.

When I open my mouth to protest, I notice Gavrill is smirking at me. "I see you are already possessive of Tribute Pareena. This is a good sign." He swirls the liquid in his cup, looking pleased and smug.

"I fail to understand why you are playing games, Commander," I grit out the words, using his title almost as an insult to show my displeasure with the direction of his conversation.

"No game. I needed to know if you will care for Tribute Pareena. She is precious."

"I understand. The Tributes are our only hope for the continuation of our race. She herself is a good choice. She is strong, brave, and well-behaved. I see her for what she is." I had already noted the differences between her and Dawn. There is no need to reveal to him that I feel I have the superior Tribute. He might take it as an insult. "Already she has submitted to my dominance. I will continue to train her."

The Commander's tone is gentle. "And you will bond with her? You are not fighting it?"

I come to my feet and turn away before I can stop myself, pacing to the wall, pretending to study it. Bonding. The connection with a mate so deep, two become one. We would share one another's sensations, thoughts, even feelings.

I run a hand down my armored chest. To have another being sensing every mood? Experiencing feedback from my emotions? At one point in my life, I was prepared for such a thing. It was all I wanted. Now...

"A bond is not necessary. The Jabol gave us Tribute Dawn without knowing if it was even possible."

"Medik thinks it is. He has been studying our biology and it has changed after Dawn and I fully bonded. Not to mention the mating marks." He pauses as if considering what to say next. "That's another reason we chose you. You were at the end of your tour and ready to attend the Mating Festival. You had gone through training for the transition. Like Medik, you would have been the first to return planet side." He doesn't continue to explain what went wrong. He doesn't have to.

When our ships returned to our home planet Tsentur, we found nothing but an asteroid field. We'd already known something was wrong when no one answered our coms, but we hadn't expected the entire planet to be gone. As the shock of what happened settled in, the High Commander ordered all members of the crew to battle stations. We all kept busy, under orders to hide and remain alert as we scanned for evidence of what happened. There was nothing we could do but search for the enemy who'd caused the destruction.

The Commander himself had remained on the bridge for over a semi-cycle, retreating to his away room for the barest amount of time to rest. The rest of us ate and slept as little as possible before returning to our posts. The few who broke down were given sick leave, sent to the medical bay and sedated. But many of us, me included, remained on duty as long as we could, so when we returned to our bunks, we fell asleep immediately, too exhausted to dream.

Our military training saved us. There was no time for me to sit in my quarters and grieve. We had an enemy to find and punish.

We've been hunting ever since.

And until now, I hadn't had to dwell on what I'd lost.

The air in the Commander's quarters is thin. Or my suit is too tight. I find I can barely breathe, and I flex my fingers, which have gone strangely numb. Yes, I was to attend the Mating Festival. Everyone knew that.

But I do not speak out of turn. I had told no one that I had already chosen my mate. That I was not looking for one, but that I would be presenting myself to a female for courtship. That she had already told me, before that last trip, that she would wait for me. I had wanted to be sure of her, to have the official acceptance of my interest, before I spoke of her to anyone.

"That was a long time ago." My voice is raw. Strangled by the past, by a memory of a sweet voice and warm smile. A female who was as delicate as she was beautiful, as kind as she was shy, and as enamored with me as I had been with her. I would have done anything for her... and instead, I did nothing. I was not there.

I failed her.

"Bogdan." Gavrill's deep voice breaks through the blackness that has engulfed me.

I turn. My reflection in the mirrored section behind him shows my armor has grown into full battle mode, without my conscious intent, complete with vicious spikes along my shoulders. As if I faced the enemy in these quarters, not my own Commander.

His voice is gentle. "You are my most trusted officer. Number two in the entire Tsenturion fleet. You always do your duty."

"Yes."

"Then I trust you in this. Get to know Pareena. Bond with her. Through the Tribute program we have a chance to reclaim some of what we had."

Never. I want to howl. We will never have another Mating Festival. There will never be a time when young warriors and their brides meet under the blooming night flowers and dance until dawn. And I will never see... *her*... again. This time I am prepared for the pain and I do not lose myself in the memories.

Gavrill claps a hand on my shoulder, avoiding the armored spines. "It's not easy. I know what you lost."

"I did not have a mate." Only a promise. Sometimes, in my dreams, I smell the night flowers.

"But you were closer to getting one than all of us." He regards me solemnly, even though he does not know how very close I was. "And now you have Pareena, the second Tribute of all time. Your loyalty and sense of duty has earned this reward."

"Reward?" I want to smash my fist into his unprotected face. "Would you give one to Medik? Who was mated for twenty deca-cycles and lost his whole family?" Tsenturions mate for life. To replace a mate is to spit upon the bonding ceremony. Many of us suspect that if we had not needed him so much, Medik would have followed his mate and family into death.

"No," the Commander has the good sense to drop his hand. He stays close and does not shift into a defensive stance. He is taller than me, though not as tall as Arkdhem. But I am broader. We would be evenly matched in a fight. "I would not dishonor him that way. But you were never mated. It is this loss that plagues you."

"We all lost." I know he is correct. I never mated. I owe her nothing... except justice. Vengeance. The eradication of those who took her life like she was nothing, like none of us were.

"Other's pain does not detract from your own. Forgive me, old friend. I knew you were grieving but didn't know how much. You feel things more deeply than most. *The prettiest castle has the highest walls,*" he quotes an old Tsenturion sage, his eyes sympathetic. Although I have never mentioned her to him, he now sees something that he had not before. Perhaps his bond with Tribute Dawn has made him more sensitive to such things.

The mirror beyond us reflects our contrasting forms. Me in full armor and the High Commander's armor in its resting state. I give the silent order to my suit to retract a little. The spikes slide away and the helmet recedes into my neck.

"I am not pretty," I mutter. "I am a warrior."

"Indeed." Gavrill puts his hand on my shoulder. "And I trust you will do your duty, whatever it may be."

Yes. I will do my duty to my Tribute. I will still avenge our people... and her. Somehow, I will find a way to do both. But my resolve is not reflected back at me; instead I see a hollowness when I look at myself. I am not the only one, either.

"Courage, Bogdan. You are the finest warrior in the fleet. You will not fail in this. Now. Return to your Tribute. Fetch her some food along the way. If she is resting, she will surely wake in need of nourishment. You do not want her to become hangry."

What the drakk is 'hangry'?

7

P areena

I wake up at a noise, aching and yet deliciously satisfied. The soft bedding beneath me feels almost like a cozy little cocoon. So much better than a hospital bed. It might even be better than my bed at home. *Thanks brain!*

Pushing up on one elbow, I turn toward the noise that woke me and blink when I see Bogdan standing in the middle of the room with a tray.

"Master?" I blink, just to see if he disappears, but no... my alien fantasy dream continues. "I fell asleep." Does one sleep in dreams? Apparently, I do. Perhaps there are levels to a coma and sometimes I slip into a deeper one.

I watch as he sets the tray down. Nothing on it looks even remotely familiar but some of it smells appealing and my stomach grumbles.

"You needed rest." He comes toward me, looking at me strangely.

There is something almost wary about his demeanor, which I do not understand at all.

Sitting down on the bed, he looks me over, studying me. The sheets have pooled around my hips, leaving my upper body completely naked. The training belt is back around my lower body, I can feel its snug grip against my hips and pussy, but I don't feel any need to try and cover myself.

Almost tentatively, he reaches out and traces a finger down the center of my nose and then over my cheekbones, like he's trying to map my features. Arousal stirs at his touch, innocent though it is.

My hand creeps over to touch his thigh and my eyes drop down. Pretty sure I just saw something move there, his bulge beginning to grow. Oh yes. Alien fantasy is back online and raring to go.

"Do you need me, Master?" I ask, my voice sultry.

His answers shocks me.

"No."

My mouth drops open, my hand freezing. Wait, what? That's definitely never happened in my fantasies before.

"You must eat." He stands, holding out his hand as if to help me up from the bed. "And then I will bathe you."

As if on cue, my stomach grumbles.

Well, okay. I *feel* hungry. Although I know the hospital is taking care of my physical needs, I wouldn't mind actually eating something. Especially if I'm able to taste it. Frllil never fed me anything except 'nutrient water,' which he said took care of all my needs. I figured that was my brain's interpretation of an IV or maybe a feeding tube.

But hey, the sex feels real and pretty amazing, maybe the food will taste real too. I'm willing to try.

"These are the things Tribute Dawn seems to like the most," Bogdan says as he leads me over to the table. Wow. Seriously, it all looks super alien. Sitting next to me, Bogdan picks up an orange-y cube that doesn't actually look like food to me and brings it to my lips. "Here. Try this. It is a fruit that she eats almost every meal."

I mean, my brain made it up, how bad can it be?

I open my lips and allow him to feed me.

To my shock, it's good. Fruity, almost like a citrus taste but not like any citrus I've ever eaten. It's like if a lemon was combined with a peach and had the texture of Jello. While I became really tired of Jello in the hospital, the flavor more than makes up for it.

I can taste again.

Looking up at him, I lick my lips. "Yummy. What else?"

Bogdan

Your Tribute is a gift.

I cannot bond with her. I do not want to, and I know that will be enough to keep the bond from forming. It does not appear where it is not welcome. But I can train her to be in tune with me. I can come to know her and become in tune with her.

Perhaps it will be sufficient. The Jabol certainly thought it would be, when they sent Tribute Dawn to us. We should not have to bond to be fully biologically compatible.

The High Commander and Medik will have to accept that as the best I can do. Tribute Pareena and I will not bond but she will still bear my young. If I claim her in this way, they will not reassign her to another warrior. Like Arkdhem.

Having the facsimile of a bond is not a hardship. I do not mind feeling her joy as she tastes the food I have brought. It seems she likes similar things to Tribute Dawn. Her teeth nipping at the tips of my fingers is both pleasant and arousing. At some point I will have to actually join with her. I do not think that will be a hardship either, yet...

Somehow, I do not feel ready.

The High Commander will not try to take her from me so soon after our discussion though. He does not know what I do or do not do in my own rooms. No one need know that I have not claimed her body yet.

It feels like another betrayal to *her* to even contemplate doing so, but I know I must. If I do not, eventually the High Commander may feel that he has erred in giving her to me and he might try to take her away. To give her to another.

Possessive anger, erupts inside of me. I am being forced along a path that I did not wish to take, far faster than I would go by my own choice.

"Master?" The soft question is accompanied by a hand upon my arm. "I'm finished eating. Are—are you alright?"

I realize I do not know how long I have been sitting there, not feeding my Tribute, while she took care of herself. I inwardly curse myself for not paying attention. I must do my duty.

"Come. I must bathe you." I scoop her up. She yelps in surprise, but grabs hold of my shoulders, pressing her soft body into mine. She has no fear of me, despite my abrupt actions, which I admire.

At my unspoken command, water pours into the massive bathing tank. Colorful soaps add a sweet, floral scent to the water. When I set my Tribute down onto the first ledge, she hisses as the shallow water laps at her waist.

"Are you hurt?" The Jabol chose a race that would match our anatomy, but perhaps immersion in water isn't something she's used to? There were bathing scenes in the manuals though. Hygiene seems important to their courtship rituals, I thought.

"No. Only sore. The water feels good." She scoots down to a lower ledge, immersing herself further. "This tub is huge." She giggles, the happy sound echoing off the hard surface of the bathing chamber. "All I need is some bubbles and I'd be set."

I do not understand what she means by bubbles, but seeing her cavorting in the tub, water sliding over and off of her skin, I feel my arousal rising again. With a mental command, my armor recedes, leaving me with nothing covered but my groin. Allowing my cock and *seela* loose now is too much temptation to bear.

"Come here," I order, and she scoots toward me with a smile. I stroke water droplets off her face when she reaches me, cupping her cheeks with my hands. "Present for inspection."

With my help, she gets on all fours on the highest ledge, where the water is shallow. I run a hand down the curve of her back and note her response. We are both humming in pleasure.

I enjoy touching my Tribute. From the way her breath stutters as my large hands coast over her back and backside, she enjoys my touch too. I reach under her to rub soap into her gently swaying breasts and she closes her eyes. With her head tipped back, I can watch every nuance of her blissful expression.

"You don't have to wash me, Master." Her voice is a low purr.

"You are my Tribute. It is my duty." I gather more soap onto the washing cloth and swirl it over her collarbone. My hand is so large it can cover most of her chest. I could break her, snap her bones easily, and I remind myself to be gentle.

I position her before me, having her tilt her head back to wash her hair. I am thorough, massaging her scalp as she sways on her feet, totally relaxed. I have to pick her up to return her to the top step.

Rinsing my fingers, I touch her face again, tracing the fine features. "You are so small."

"You are very large." Her mouth tips up and I can't help rubbing my finger over the pad of her lower lip. Soft as a petal.

Boldly, she rises to face me, water streaming off her flawless skin. Her hand stretches towards my bicep, the curve of my muscle uncovered by armor. She hesitates.

"You may touch me," I allow softly. My skin prickles and I swallow to hide my need.

Pareena

I KNEEL in between Bogdan's massive thighs, in a tub that makes me think of when Harry uses the Prefect's bathroom in the fourth book, and I run my fingers over his gold skin. His shiny hide is smooth, hairless, almost poreless. Tougher than my skin, but not as tough as the armor that seems to be a part of him. The black material is the skimpiest I've seen so far. Bogdan's version of letting down his guard, perhaps? His groin and upper thighs are still covered, his muscles bulging as if they'll burst at any moment.

There's an interesting bulge at his crotch. Large enough to make my mouth dry. What does alien peen look like? The books I read on Earth only seemed to have one consistent rule about the alien heroes: Always upgrade the dick.

What's hiding under that suit? Some sort of Bad Dragon worthy dong? Is he hiding it until I'm so consumed with lust when he whips it out, I won't run screaming?

Which brings me to another realization: somehow in the middle of all the orgasms, I kind of missed that he never actually had sex with me.

"What do you want me to do?" I meet his gaze, flirtatiously smiling up at him. Not sure why I'm so eager to take our physical relationship to the next level, when obviously I don't need sex for orgasms, but I am. My eagerness might have something to do with his Mr. Universe level muscles. Or the strong-jawed beauty of his face. He hasn't smiled or shown any pleasant expression, but the longing I feel restrained under his iron self-control is a turn on. He wants me. He just doesn't want to show it.

It's my damn coma dream, I should be able to get a smile out of him if I want it. And I should be able to get laid. *Come on, subconscious. Get with the program.*

He shifts on the edge of the tub and strokes my wet hair back from my face. Catches my chin in strong fingers, holding my face immobile, and looks deep in my eyes. Searching for something? I stare back at him, waiting.

Finally, he lets go. "You will bathe me."

Holy hell. Yes. I grab the washcloth he used on me and dip it into the bowl of soap-like substance. He slides fully into the water with me, so I can easily wash his torso. I enjoy touching his muscles, even though it doesn't really seem like his gleaming skin needs actual washing.

My brow furrows in confusion when I start to move the cloth lower, nearly reaching where his armor *still* covers him, and he catches my arms, stopping me.

"What about—"

"Enough. I will finish bathing you."

Dammit. I was just getting to the good part!

He turns me around and positions me as he wants. I'm bent forward so my arms prop on the top of the tub, I'm sticking my butt right at him. I know what's coming.

He nudges my feet apart and I obey, quivering. *Touch me!*

He spends countless seconds running his hands up and down my legs, pressing on my back to make my bottom arch up further, combing my wet hair to the side.

Come on, come on. Finally, he stands behind me, parting my inner thighs until I'm on display the way he wants, my bottom cheeks parted and nether parts flashing him. He rubs soap into my still sore bum with a touch as light as butterfly wings. His fingers drift over my pussy.

Yes, yes, yes...! I resist the urge to writhe. I don't move, don't breathe, wanting him to give me more.

"So small." He penetrates me with a finger and my body clamps on it. *More, more, more!*

To my dismay he rinses me and moves on. He dips the washcloth between my cheeks, then loses it to spread soap directly on my anus. The little hole tingles, but I don't protest. I want to see where this is going.

"And tight," he pushes a finger into my bottom, and I give a frustrated hum when it slides back out almost immediately. Then he starts squeezing my battered cheeks—a sensation that's uncomfortable in the most delicious way—and parting them, angling them so he can examine the small pucker. He sticks his face close and I can feel his hot breath against my sensitive skin. Nerve endings I didn't know I had come to life.

"All done," he mutters, abruptly getting out of the water and leaving me there, confused. I watch him, unsure of what to do, holding my vulnerable and erotically charged position, really confused about why we're not having sex. Picking up a large sheet of fabric that looks like a towel, he rubs himself down and then turns back to me. "Come here, my Tribute."

Wet towel, ick. But when he wraps me in it, it doesn't feel wet and the fabric soaks up every drop of water. He rubs another over my head and my hair is mostly dry by the time he's done.

"Go to the foot of the bed and wait, hands on your head," he orders, and I obey, though I'm getting tired of these inspections. He leaves for a moment and returns with a jar of goopy cream. Dipping his fingers into the stuff, he rubs it in, and it disappears into my skin, leaving a silky sheen. I suck in my stomach as his hand glides over my chest. Typically male, he's extra thorough around my nipples, spending triple the time around my breasts as anywhere else. When his hands swoop lower, he pushes my legs apart further and kneels. I can't hide my excited quiver as he dips his head to inspect my pussy.

～

Bogdan

THE NEED TO touch my Tribute is strong.

It is my duty, and I must learn her responses, her alien body, but deep down I also know that I am enjoying myself. I can feel my body urging me to bury myself inside of her, to fill her with my seed, to complete the bond. And when I am touching her, when I am distracted by her sweet scent and soft skin, the guilt stays away. It will rise again when we are done, but for now I am unburdened.

She moans as I stroke the soft petals of her body, wetness coating my fingertips. The tantalizing scent of her draws me inward, pulling me closer. My tongue flicks out.

The manuals said pleasure with mouths and tongues was possible and her moan, as my tongue slides up her center, confirms it. She tastes even better than she smells and I realize my chest is vibrating too. I am moaning, sinking my tongue into her and lapping at her essence like I am starving. Indeed, it almost feels as though this manner of touch is far more intimate than using my fingers.

I groan, my *seela* writhing in almost desperation to get at her and suckle at the soft folds of flesh protecting her channel. Her *pussy,* as the manuals called it. The word is soft, just like her.

Ignoring my thrashing cock, I feast on her, my fingers digging into her soft flesh, my only focus on exploring her with my tongue. When I move my mouth up to her second opening, licking at the crinkled hole, she gasps and tries to jerk away.

I slap the rounded curve of her bottom. "Hold still, my Tribute."

"Sorry... I just... wasn't expecting that." Her voice is breathy. Soft. Full of desire. She arches her back, offering her body up to me, her Master.

I drag my tongue over her sensitive crease again, pressing harder against the small opening, and she wriggles and gasps but doesn't move away. The whimpering is very pleasing to hear.

"Please..." She begs me sweetly. "Please, Master, fuck me."

She wants me to mount her. To fill her and seed her. To bond with her. Of course, she does, she is a Tribute. That is her purpose. But I feel my resentment stir anyway, even though I know she is only following her instincts.

Everything about my Tribute tempts me... she does not just tempt me to ignore my duty, she threatens the memory of *her.* With my Tribute's scent now imprinted on my brain, I realize that I can no longer remember *her* scent. Could I before my Tribute's arrival? I am not sure. I did not try to forget *her,* exactly, but I did not try to cling to the memories either. They were too painful.

Now it feels as though my Tribute's presence has begun to erase *hers* in the only place she still exists... my memory.

Everything inside of me rebels. Even my unruly *seela* quiet as I finally realize exactly what effect having a Tribute is having on me— it is everything I feared. My chest clenches and I pull away from her.

"Master?" She begins to lift her head. In a moment she will turn and look at me and I cannot have that. I do not want her to look at me. I do not want to see her liquid brown eyes, full of desire and temptation.

A mere thought makes the nanotech from the Bride Trainer flow over her skin, from her hips to all her most sensitive parts. I make them buzz, catching my breath as she cries out and drops her head again.

"Do not tell your Master what to do, Tribute," I say harshly, thickening the parts of the belt inside of her and she moans in response.

Relief eases my tension. I do not need to touch her to pleasure her. I will distract her with her training. She will climax and then she should need to sleep again. When she wakes, I will feed her and then train her until she needs to rest again. That is what the High Commander ordered, is it not?

And during this time, I will find a way to both do my duty to my Tribute and to preserve my memories of *her*... of my Harai.

Pareena

FREAKING BELT...

The Bride trainer is doing things for Bogdan that Frllil had *never* made it do. Things I'd never even guessed it *could* do.

The buzzing tech isn't just covering my pussy and ass, it's pushing inside of them, stretching me and filling me far more than his fingers had. Not only that, but some of it is sliding up my stomach and moving to my breasts. It tickles the sensitive underside of the hanging globes before seeking out my nipples.

Who needs nipple clamps when you have kinky alien technology?

I cry out as the pinch reaches the point of pain, making pleasure throb through me, and the belt begins to buzz and hum inside of me. My ass feels almost uncomfortably full, my pussy doesn't have a millimeter of nerves that isn't being stimulated, and now my nipples are pulsing in time with my swollen clit.

Collapsing, it feels like all the strength is being sucked out of my muscles. My orgasm wraps around me like a giant cocoon of ecstasy, smothering me in erotic bliss.

8

P areena

I WAKE in a tangle of blankets, my legs spread far apart so that nothing touches the swollen, over sensitized flesh between them. Even with the Bride Trainer covering my pussy, I don't want to close my legs.

No one ever told me how painful multiple orgasms could eventually become. Begging hadn't stopped Bogdan. He'd kept playing with the belt, finding new horrifically deliciously creative ways to stimulate my body until I'd been mumbling and insensible.

I turned my head, which is about the only part of my body I feel strong enough to move right now. I scowl. He's gone. Again. No big alien hottie lying next to me.

And he *still* hasn't actually done the deed.

As soon as my pussy recovers and I have the chance, I am going to jump him. Although, with Bogdan I might need a sneak attack approach. *Surprise! I tripped and fell onto your dick!* He might be mad at first, for taking control away from him... He seems very big on control.

Wait, I'm the one in control... this is my fantasy. Right? I keep forgetting because... well, because I don't feel very in control.

My stomach roars like a dragon. I'm starving again. It feels so nice to be hungry. Food would be even nicer, but I need Bogdan for that. At least, I think. All this advanced alien technology, surely there's a fridge somewhere. Or a minibar.

Sitting up, I see the filmy gown I'd worn earlier still pooled on the floor. I put it back on and move to the door.

The lights are on low throughout the chambers. Tsenturion officers must rate extra nice quarters. Bogdan has a large living space in addition to a large sleeping and separate bathing chamber.

He's kneeling in front of a wall section that has one of those removable panels. Their version of a closet? A small box, intricately carved out of something like mahogany wood, lies open before him. I can't see what's inside, but whatever it is, Bogdan stares at it like any moment it'll jump at him like a snake. In the quiet the only sound is his harsh breathing.

My stomach chooses this moment to gurgle.

Bogdan slams down the lid and rises, spinning around. *Yeesh, he's fast.* Gotta be those warrior reflexes. I back up when I catch the expression on his face, my heart tripping. Even in the picture Frllil had shown me, he'd never looked like this... like he was ready to attack. Behind him, the panel closes with an audible click.

"What are you doing?" His voice is harsh. His helmet appears between one second and the next, obscuring his face and the glittering anger in his eyes. The scary spines that pop out from the shoulders of his Batman-like suit make me want to run. Which is a bad idea. For the first time I feel a little uneasy and unsure of my safety.

Then I remember that's silly... this is all happening in my head. It's not like he can actually hurt me. Except... everything feels so real. If he did try to really hurt me, would I feel that the same way I do the spankings and the orgasms? Would my own brain do that to me?

"I..." I swallow audibly. "I woke up and w-was hungry." He is silent and I draw myself up, feeling very strange. I don't understand what his problem is, and I don't understand why my brain has created a problem, or a secret, or whatever. I should treat this like it's real, though right? Like everything else. "I didn't mean to intrude or spy on you or whatever." I flap my hand at the closet-thing behind him. "If it's personal—"

Without a word, Bogdan spins on his heel and leaves. Not just the room—his entire quarters. He heads to the main doors without pausing. They slide open just in time from him lumber through. The last I see of his giant form is him striding down the empty hall. The doors slide shut.

Well, crap. Now what?

$\sim$

Bogdan

LOOKING at the few keepsakes I have left from Harai has thrown me off balance. This is why I rarely acknowledge their existence. Normally they stay tucked away in my keeping place and just knowing they are there, safe, is enough. Now my Tribute knows they are there as well.

She would not touch them, would she?

My forward momentum grinds to a halt. Spinning, I move over to one of the wall consoles and use it to pull up a visual of the interior of my cabin. She is there, not looking at the keeping place, just pacing back and forth before she moves to sit down, looking thoughtful. Perhaps waiting for me to return with food?

I should get food.

I meant to go and retrieve a meal for her, before she could wake up, but I must have been lost in my memories for longer than I realized. The carefully pressed night flower Harai gave me on our last visit, to symbolize our promises to each other, to find each other at the Mating Festival upon my return. The small *suuki* rock, which the superstitious believe keep the owner safe from harm that she gave me the first time we parted. The lock of her hair tied with a ribbon. It is even softer than my Tribute's skin, but touching it gives me no pleasure.

"Bogdan? Where is Pareena?" Tribute Dawn's question makes me jump. I was so preoccupied I did not even notice her presence.

She is staring at me, her brow furrowed and confusion in her blue eyes. The pale strands of her hair are pulled back in what she calls a 'ponytail,' leaving her face and neck exposed. Beside her, Arkdhem, who is often her companion when the High Commander is on duty, is also staring at me but his expression is blank.

"I... she is back in my room. I needed... a respite. I am unaccustomed to sharing close quarters for long periods of time."

"Oh, well that makes sense," Tribute Dawn says, smiling at me. "It's definitely a bit of an adjustment. Of course, it's an adjustment for her, too. I was hoping to meet her, but Gavrill told me not to bother you two these first few days. But since you're out here without her..." Her voice trails off and she looks at me hopefully.

The idea of sending Tribute Dawn to entertain my Tribute is appealing, especially because the High Commander will not be able to chide me when I've made his Tribute happy. It will give me time to recover my equilibrium and ensure that my Tribute is not left alone for too long. Arkdhem's presence is decidedly less welcome, but at least there will be a guard.

Despite my insults to him, I know full well that he would be willing to lay down his life for both Tributes. He is not the fighter that I am, but he is highly ranked for a reason.

"If you would like to visit my Tribute, I have no objection."

Tribute Dawn sighs. "*Pareena*, Bogdan, her name is *Pareena*."

"I know that." I frown at her. I do not understand why she thinks I have forgotten my Tribute's name already.

"So why don't you use her name?"

It is not the first time Tribute Dawn has said something incomprehensible to me. From the exasperation on her face, this means something to her.

"She is my Tribute." Why would I use her name? Her name means nothing to me. That she is my Tribute means everything.

"Right. Never mind." Tribute Dawn shakes her head. "Okay, well, I'm going to go visit *Pareena*."

"Thank you for taking the time to visit my Tribute." I try to smile at her. Not just because she is being kind, but because I don't want Arkdhem to know how much it chafes to send him to look after my Tribute, even indirectly.

As I walk on, Tribute Dawn mutters something under her breath. It sounds oddly like 'hopeless.'

∾

Pareena

I COULD REALLY USE A THERAPIST RIGHT NOW.

The irony is not lost on me. But truthfully, a lot of psychologists and therapists see one themselves. I did both before and after I became sick. We know and value the importance of mental health. Despite the fact that I know this is all in my head—at least, I think I know that, I'm starting to question whether or not I *really* know since I keep forgetting—I could really use someone to talk to.

I feel an emptiness in my chest that makes me ache and... I swear it's not just coming from me. Is it possible to feel someone else's emotions?

Except that Bogdan isn't someone else, he's a figment of my coma dream. A really, really, strong figment of subconscious imagination who sometimes acts like my greatest fantasy come to life and sometimes acts completely different from what I want.

There's a teeny, tiny part of me that almost wonders if maybe I'm not in a coma and this is actually all real. That's why I need a therapist. I think I might have delusional disorder, because this bizarre delusion is starting to seem more like reality. I know I'm not schizophrenic, or at least I wasn't, but is it possible something has happened to my brain chemistry while I've been comatose?

Or maybe I feel this way because to my brain, it feels like I've been on this alien fantasy ride for weeks now. Living in it. Immersed in it. And it doesn't change. The only time it changes is when I 'fall asleep' and then 'dream.' Except obviously that must just be me going deeper into my coma. Or my subconscious resting from weaving this elaborate new life.

My thoughts are going around and around, trying to remember everything I can from my old life and the details of delusional disorder, as well as everything I know about nearing death awareness and near-death experiences. Hallucinations are common.

But do they always go on this long?

There's not really anyone who can tell me that. And until, and unless, I wake up, there's no way to know how long I've actually been experiencing this. It reminds me of the old stories of the Fae, where people would be kidnapped or accidentally stumble into a faerie mound and time warped. They could spend a thousand years there, only to return and find that mere minutes had passed—or the reverse.

The knock on the door is a welcome distraction. I jump to my feet and then realize I have no idea how to open it. Bogdan just walked over to it, so I do the same, but nothing happens.

"Hello?" I call out.

"Hi!" The cheerily feminine, slightly muffled greeting nearly makes me tear up. It's Dawn. Just hearing her makes me realize exactly how much I've craved friendly female companionship over the past weeks. Frllil hadn't exactly been the kind of being I could gossip or talk with and Bogdan definitely wasn't.

This also seems like proof that this is all my subconsciousness' doing. I wished for someone to talk to and *poof!* Here she is. Sure, she's not a therapist, but hey, I can't have everything. Although, the fact that I can't actually get to her is a point against my proof...

"I'm sorry, but I can't seem to open the door," I call back apologetically. "Is there a button or something?"

The door slides open and I jump back, startled. Dawn beams at me, a looming Tsenturion warrior standing just behind her. She's very California girl from head to toe, other than the long gown she's wearing and the collar around her throat. Actually, in some places in California, the collar wouldn't be at all unusual. Long blonde hair pulled back in a ponytail, blue eyes, and a bit of tan on her skin, which is impressive considering that she's on a spaceship.

Except that I'm imagining her, so I guess she can have a tan if I want. Trying to remember that this isn't real is starting to confuse me. Maybe I should just take Dumbledore's advice. I smile back at her. I'm just going to go with the flow and pretend it's all real so my brain can stop running around in circles about it.

It's real to me.

"Hi, I'm Pareena." I hold out my hand.

Dawn launches herself at me and I find myself laughing as she hugs me tightly. I hug her back and marvel at how good it feels to just hug someone. I can't remember the last time I did that either.

"Oh... I should have asked if you're a hugger," she says, almost directly in my ear, although she doesn't let go of me either. "Sorry... I just... I really needed this."

I laugh and both of our arms tighten before we break and step away. There are slight tears in her eyes.

"You have *no idea* how good it feels to not be the only human on board," she says, grinning broadly. "Especially when I'm outnumbered by mountains of testosterone." She gestures behind her. "This is Arkdhem. He's my... well, I guess he's my bodyguard but he's also my friend."

"Hello, Tribute Pareena." Arkdhem smiles at me and steps forward, offering his hand. "It is nice to meet you." I take it and he pumps it up and down three times in very controlled movements. From the proud expression on Dawn's face as she watches the interaction, I'm guessing she taught him how to shake hands. It is pretty cute how he makes it somehow overly formal.

"Nice to meet you too. Um... I guess, do you two want to sit down?" I gesture toward the couch thing.

"I will, but Arkdhem is going to go get us some food," Dawn says, smiling brilliantly at him. "Right?"

"Nothing with meat, please," I say automatically. It hadn't even occurred to me earlier when Bogdan had brought me food. Of course, since it's my brain creating the menu, that makes sense.

"That's right, you're a vegetarian?" Dawn asks, still beaming at me. Arkdhem doesn't say anything, just tilts his head and listens to our conversation. "Are you Hindu? Is that why?"

"I'm more spiritual than religious, but yes, my parents were vegetarians and so I was raised that way. I did try some meat when I was a rebellious teenager, but I never actually liked any of it and eating something I didn't like for the sake of rebellion didn't appeal to me, so I just went back to being a vegetarian." I smile at the memory. My parents hadn't known about my illicit meat intake, but that hadn't been the point. It was better they hadn't known. If they had and disapproved, I probably would have felt compelled to keep eating it.

Dawn claps her hands excitedly. "Oh, I'm so excited! Maybe we can do yoga together?" The expression on my face must have communicated my complete disinterest in the practice.

"I'm more of a runner," I said. At least, I had been, before the cancer. I liked movement. Going places. Staying in one place and breathing in different poses had been about as appealing as eating a meal of meat. Meditation is good for the soul, but I tended to find my meditative state on park pathways with my feet pounding against the earth and the sounds of nature all around me.

"Oh..." Dawn looks a little crestfallen. "I used to teach yoga... if you'd be interested in learning." She glances at Arkdhem. "And maybe we can figure out a path through one of the cargo bays or something." She looks back at me. "Unless you do sprints?"

Arkdhem looks confused. "Running? From what? There is no need to run from anything here. I will protect you."

Oh geez. Dawn covers her mouth as she begins to giggle helplessly, and she shrugs at me.

"Um, running for fun and exercise," I try to explain. "Just... just to run." Arkdhem looks more confused. My stomach chooses that moment to let out an embarrassingly large growl.

"Okay, I'll try to explain later," Dawn says, patting his arm. "Go get us some food for now?"

"Yes, Dawn." He smiles down at her, bringing his fist up to his chest, before exiting back out the door.

Then Dawn's stance changes entirely, to one of uncertainty, and she takes a deep breath as she meets my gaze.

"Okay, so now that we're alone, I have a confession to make," she says, the words coming out in a rush. "And if you hate me afterwards I totally understand although I hope you won't because you seem really nice and we're both stuck here and it would really suck if the only other human in this part of the galaxy hates my guts, but I don't want to start off a friendship with a lie. It's my fault you're here."

9

P areena

I BLINK, trying to process Dawn's confession. Her fault that I'm here?

Here where? Stuck in my head? Is this some kind of manifestation of whatever part of my body is responsible for my cancer? Or possibly a manifestation of my id, confessing that it's sent me into a coma dream of my deepest sexual fantasy?

"I don't understand."

She takes another deep breath, visibly steeling herself. Every line of her body reveals how anxious she is, and I have to stifle my urge to immediately reassure her that everything is fine when I'm not sure what she's talking about.

"I was the first Tribute. I meant to fight, to escape, but... well, it's not exactly easy," she says, hunching in on herself a little. I can practically see the guilt weighing her down. "I've been here for weeks and I still don't see a way, or I would totally help you."

"It's okay," I say soothingly, automatically shifting to the tone I'd always used with distressed clients. In the back of my mind, a part of me wonders exactly how Dawn's confession fits into this dream. Maybe some portion of me feels guilty over not accepting the reality of my impending death? "We can't always escape the situations we find ourselves in. Sometimes all we can do is make the best of where we are, and there's nothing wrong with that. You're one human, on a ship filled with warriors, alien technology, and no help. No sane person would expect you to be able to escape from that."

Because winning the fight against overwhelming odds doesn't always work. Not everyone could be David and Goliath. Sometimes, you were Braveheart or Boadicea and that is just part of life.

Dawn fidgets in her seat, wringing her hands in front of her. "But... when I realized I couldn't escape, and I couldn't keep them from abducting more women, I helped them choose *you*. You fit all the parameters, you were dying, we could save you... I was so excited because I wouldn't be alone anymore and even though the Jabol matched you with Bogdan, I thought, 'hey that has to be better than dying, right?'"

I sit up a little straighter, frowning at this insult to Bogdan. "What's wrong with Bogdan?"

Hearing my indignation, her eyes widen, and she holds up her hands in front of her in a placating manner. "Nothing!" Then she shakes her head. "No, that's not true, we're going for honesty here." She looks at me curiously. "He didn't exactly want a Tribute. In fact he's been the most outspoken against it. Actually, he's been the *only* warrior against it. Some of them don't seem interested in having a Tribute, but he's the only one who actively tried to stop the program. And... okay, I'm just going to say it—he's kind of a dick."

Maybe, but he is *my* dick, and so I can't help but feel a little pang in my chest when she says he didn't want a Tribute. That explains a lot, actually.

Except... wait, it only explains it if this is real. Why would my ideal fantasy be a hot alien who doesn't actually want me?

"Oh God, I'm sorry, I'm making things worse, aren't I?" Dawn asks, looking miserable. "Look, maybe we should talk about something else. Bogdan is a hardass but he's come around. I haven't heard him say a single thing against the program in days. I mean, not that I talk to him that much but—never mind. Still not helping. Want to talk about Earth? I miss being on a planet so bad, traveling in space seems really cool but I miss weather, and animals, and television. They've got a decent selection of spanking books here, but that's about it, and I try not to encourage Gavrill to pay too much attention to those because then he gets ideas that I don't need him to have. The hot sex makes up for a lot, but I still just miss *home*, you know?"

I blink. Most humans don't refer to anything other than intercourse as sex anymore. If they mean oral, they say so. "Hot sex? Like, actual penis in vagina sex?"

She gives me a strange look. "Well, yeah."

"Bogdan hasn't actually had sex with me," I admit, a pit opening up in the center of my stomach. I put my hand over it. He didn't actually want a Tribute... if we don't have sex, will we bond the way we're supposed to? Is this his way of keeping me at arm's length?

Dawn gapes at me. "Then what have you two been doing in here?"

"Pretty much everything else. He uses his hands, his mouth, the training belt... but I haven't even seen his dick," I confess. Normally I wouldn't be this open with a stranger, but this is different. If this is real, Dawn is the only other human around, and if it's all in my head, then she's just part of my subconscious.

"Oooo, they're so weird! They kinda look like a cobra snake, and they have tentacles instead of pubic hair, and the tentacles have little suckers on the end that feel *amazing*." Dawn looks thrilled at being able to impart this knowledge and I can't help but feel envious at the way her eyes go glassy at some memory.

Except that it's not really her memory, right? So it has to just be a manifestation of what I want sex with Bogdan to be like.

So maybe some part of my brain just wants me to have to work for it?

Who knew coma dreams could be so complicated?

Bogdan

WITH TRIBUTE DAWN on her way to entertain my Tribute, I find myself walking to the training arena. It is constantly filled with warriors, working to keep their skills sharp, so I know it will be easy to find a sparring partner. Working off the excess energy that my Tribute has left me with sounds appealing. Not nearly as appealing as working off the energy with her and actually finding a release... but since I can't bring myself to do that yet, I might as well do this.

A good sparring session should help clear my mind as well. I must refocus myself on my duties, my people, my vengeance. Then I can return to my Tribute with a clear mind. Perhaps that will help me control myself with her. At least long enough to reconcile my duty with my memories of Harai.

Entering the training arena, I immediately head to the sparring mats. This is one of the biggest rooms on the ship and, other than the dining hall, often the fullest. Today is no exception. I am aware of my fellow warriors pausing to look at me. I do not need to hear their whispered words to guess that they are wondering why I am here rather than with my Tribute.

As soon as I reach the sparring mats, Jakar and Volim, who have just finished a bout, approach me, curiosity in their eyes although it is not reflected in their armor. They have superb control over their emotions.

"Commander." They both salute.

"I did not expect to see you here," Jakar says, giving me the option of explaining my presence or of shrugging his comment away. Those warriors within hearing distance all pause, waiting to see if I will answer. While Volim is not interested in a Tribute, Jakar is and I cannot help but think that perhaps he is hoping I might not keep Tribute Pareena. I have been vocal in my protests against the program, even if I agreed to do my duty once she was assigned to me.

The idea of her being reassigned to someone else, even an honorable warrior like Jakar, sends a flash of jealous heat through me. He would be a better choice than Arkdhem, but yet... I cannot bear the thought of it. She is mine. My body feels it even as my mind and heart struggle.

"Tribute Dawn wanted to meet her," I say by way of explanation. It is close enough to the truth and it appeases all the listening ears. I see several nods out of the corner of my eye. Jakar and Volim chuckle and nod their heads in understanding as well, before moving off.

Since her arrival, Tribute Dawn has disrupted the natural order of things on the ship more and more every day. There is a reason Tsenturion Warriors did not take mates until they were ready to cease their military duties. Our lives are split into parts—childhood, service, and then mating and family. Trying to combine our service with mates and family is not only unwise, it is against the manner of our people, but the High Commander has spoken, and I seem to be the only one truly against the Tributes program.

Although, my feelings on that are now mixed too.

How could they not be when my Tribute was saved from death by the program? The idea of a universe without my Tribute in it is too uncomfortable to contemplate. I grit my teeth, eyes moving around the mats until I see Polixan looking back at me. He jerks his chin up at me and I move to his mat, my armor sliding down to the short pants.

Tsenturions do not fight in armor unless they mean to kill.

Pareena

AS DAWN TELLS me the details of the Tributes Program, half-reluctant and half-anxious for my approval, Arkdhem returns with our food. The tray contains a lot of the same things that Bogdan brought me before, but some new things to try as well. All of it is delicious.

"So, you convinced them to only take women who are about to

die, but you still feel guilty?" I ask, prompting her to talk more about the emotions I see playing across her face.

"I can definitely tell you used to be a shrink," she says with a strained laugh. She sighs. "Yes, I still feel guilty. I mean, technically we give them a choice with the survey, but who would actually believe that they're risking alien abduction? Did you?"

"Well, no..." I admit, thinking back to it. I'd thought it was a distraction, that answering might lead to something else which would entertain me and keep me from thinking about how weak and ill I felt and my impending death. Then I'd fallen asleep into this coma dream. Or I'd actually been abducted by aliens. Was it weird that I was starting to think the latter might actually be a real possibility?

Yeah, super weird.

That's how detached from reality I've become.

Maybe I shouldn't have taken Dumbledore's words so seriously.

"I did the best I could." Dawn sighs and looks at me with miserable eyes. "Do you forgive me?"

"Of course!" I say it immediately, firmly. I'm not surprised she asked. Dawn is wallowing in guilt over my presence, especially because having another human on board ship makes her so very happy.

"See, I said you were worried for nothing," Arkdhem chimes in, smiling at Dawn and nudging her with his elbow. There is something brotherly about his manner with her, which makes me smile. He is much more relaxed than Bogdan. He turns to look at me. "She has been fretting for days now, vacillating back and forth between being very excited and very anxious about your arrival. It has been most unpleasant." The last part is said in a teasing manner, which makes me laugh as Dawn groans and rolls her eyes.

"He's not wrong," she admits, sighing and setting down her empty plate. She looks around the room. "So... I kind of thought Bogdan would be back by now, if I'm being honest. I'd say we should give you a tour of the ship, but I don't want him to come back to an empty room. Find out where he is?" I blink before realizing she's asking Arkdhem, not me, to locate Bogdan.

Tilting his head as if listening to something we can't hear, Arkdhem nods his head after a few moments. "He is sparring with Polixan in the training arena. Would you like to go meet him there?"

"Yes!" Dawn's eyes light up. She grins widely at me. "Trust me, you're going to want to see this."

"Okay." I have to admit, I'm very curious now just because of her reaction. And it would be nice to see more of the ship and the Tsenturion warriors. Maybe I can see or find something that will help me determine whether this is a coma dream or reality.

Maybe it doesn't really make too much of a difference in the end, as long as it feels real, but I still want to know.

∾

Bogdan

As Polixan and I hit and kick at each other, I can hear the warriors around us talking. Their words flow over me, but I will contemplate them later. The Vgotha are eluding us again. We have picked up another trail, but it is leading in a direction that no one expected. Everyone is worried because the Vgotha have been acting out of character for weeks now. Even before Tribute Dawn joined us. She insists that the Vgotha leader wants to meet with the High Commander, but no one believed her.

Now, after weeks without action, the warriors are starting to wonder if there was some truth to her words. We have never gone this long without a battle and it has everyone on edge. That my Tribute has joined us, a second representation of the hope for our future, a few of them are starting to wonder if perhaps we should try to speak with them. I shake my head, but the words do not impact my emotions. I am too focused on keeping Polixan outside of my guard. I will contemplate their words later.

But then I almost fall over when I feel my Tribute's presence impinge on my consciousness, allowing Polixan to get in a harder blow to my shoulder than he should have been able to land. For a moment, I think I must be imagining things, because I shouldn't be able to actually *feel* her without the bond, which we do not have. Then I realize it must be her nanotech, alerting me, and I have just confused it with thinking I can feel *her*.

A murmur sweeps across the arena and Polixan steps backs, turning to see what everyone is looking at. Swallowing a grimace, I turn as well.

Possessiveness sweeps through me when I see my Tribute making her way across the arena, Tribute Dawn at her side and Arkdhem walking just behind them. He is watching over them as if they both belong to him. It does not bother the High Commander that Arkdhem treats Tribute Dawn so familiarly, but I feel my ire rise at seeing him do the same with *my* Tribute. He reeks of desperation and I curse myself for leaving my Tribute in his care. I should have heeded my instinct not to trust him.

What did they talk about? Did he say anything to her about me? Would he try to turn her against me?

There are a multitude of eyes now on my Tribute, admiring her, and she is looking back at them. Not just looking, *admiring*.

Pushing down a snarl, I stalk toward them. Seeing me coming, my Tribute's dark eyes open wide and her gaze travels over my body, her tongue flicking out across her lower lip. I can feel her arousal surge and I send a quick order to the training belt. It begins a low hum against her flesh, and she gasps.

As I come closer, Tribute Dawn frowns, sidling next to my Tribute. "What's wrong, Bogdan?"

"You should not be here," I growl, glowering at Arkdhem and addressing him rather than Tribute Dawn. "You did not ask my leave to remove my Tribute from my quarters."

Arkdhem just stares back at me insolently as Tribute Dawn's mouth drops open in indignation. "She's an adult, meathead!" Tribute Dawn says. "She doesn't need to ask permission to go anywhere!"

"She does, and *he* needs my leave to escort her," I respond, still glaring at Arkdhem. On Tsentur, no unmated male would escort another male's mate unless they were family, or her mate had agreed to it. I had allowed him to accompany Tribute Dawn to my room, because the High Commander had set him as her guard, but that assent did not extend to *leaving* my room with him.

"It's fine, Dawn." My Tribute steps around Tribute Dawn, her eyes on me. The focus of her gaze soothes something inside of me, something that riled when I saw her looking at the other warriors. "I should have realized that I would need to ask my Master for permission to leave the room." There is a small smile on her face, but I do not think she is being insincere.

"But—" Tribute Dawn begins to protest and my Tribute glances over her shoulder at her.

"The courtship manuals, remember?" My Tribute says to her. Tribute Dawn sighs and shakes her head. The High Commander is far too lenient with her. I am proud that my Tribute already knows her place better than Tribute Dawn ever has.

Holding out my hand, I stand stock still as my Tribute comes over to me. When she places her fingers in mine, I am relieved that my armor is mostly retracted. I do not know that I could have hidden the flash of pleasure that surges through me at her touch.

"Come," I say, pulling her against me. I give Arkdhem a dark look before turning my full attention to my Tribute. "We will go back to my room now."

"Yes, Master," she says cheerfully.

The emotion that rises in my chest, warming me throughout, is not entirely welcome.

10

———————

P areena

WITH ONE HAND on the back of my neck, Bogdan leads me back to our room. His room? I'm not really sure. He keeps saying 'his' room. Part of me wonders if that's another way to reject my presence in his life. The unwanted Tribute that he was forced to accept... but for someone who doesn't want a Tribute, he's awfully possessive.

I have to admit, that little show of jealousy in the training arena cheered me right up.

He must feel *something* for me, or he wouldn't have cared that Arkdhem was walking around the ship with Dawn and me. Or that I'd been ogling the other warriors in the training arena. Not that he needs to worry on that front. I might enjoy the scenery, but I don't want any of them. No, for some reason I want the grumpy, brooding warrior who supposedly didn't want a Tribute at all.

"So what now?" I ask, after the silent walk back to his room. I didn't want to ask in the halls, in case I didn't like the answer, but a girl can only take so much quiet.

"You left the room without permission," he says, his tone dark as he steers me toward the bed. "You've earned a punishment."

"You didn't tell me I couldn't," I point out, although I know that I probably could have figured out that he'd like a heads up. I've barely known him for twenty-four hours, but I already know that Bogdan might be the biggest control freak I've ever met. Or imagined. Whatever. Like it matters at this point.

He frowns and I swear I can feel his disappointment. Was he looking for an excuse to spank me? Hmm. Maybe I shouldn't have pointed out the flaw in his logic. According to what Dawn was able to tell me before Arkdhem returned, Tsenturion warriors were big into spankings and then sex. Or at least, her Tsenturion warrior is.

"You are correct, the fault was mine. From now on, do not leave the room without me or my permission. And you will not speak with other warriors."

"What if they speak to me first?" I ask. Not that any of them had. They'd all stopped to look at Dawn and me when we'd entered the training arena, and we'd passed quite a few in the hallways who had all bowed their heads to us before looking away, but not one had tried to speak with us. Well, except Arkdhem, but after Bogdan's little speech in the training arena, I got the feeling that he was an exception due to his position as Dawn's bodyguard. Or escort or whatever he was.

"They should not speak to you. You are mine." He pulls me to him, pressing my body against his, and I can feel my pulse begin to race again. There is no way I should be horny again already, and yet I am. One hand pets my hair, tugging it slightly so that I turn my head up towards him, while the other strokes the small of my back. "Medik and the High Commander are exceptions."

Okay, well that makes sense.

"What about Arkdhem?"

His hand fists in my hair, and my eyes widen as he pulls my head back more, baring my throat to him. It is an extremely dominant and seriously sexy move. If I had on panties instead of this stupid training belt, they'd probably hit the floor. What? I like a little bit of caveman in my men apparently. Even if he's not actually a human.

"What about him?" Bogdan growls the question—and is that my imagination or did I see a flash of red streak through his armor?

"He seems nice," I say cautiously. I don't want to prod his jealousy needlessly, but I don't want to lie either. "And if he's with Dawn all the time, I'm probably going to see him again. Am I supposed to ignore him? That seems rather rude."

Bogdan

NICE? He is a dung-eating *slythin*, a belly crawling reptile that lived in the wetlands of our home planet. That is perhaps an exaggeration, but in this moment, hearing my Tribute compliment him, that is the first thing that flashes through my mind. He wants my Tribute. I am sure of it. He wanted Tribute Dawn too but would never disrespect the High Commander by overstepping his bounds.

The way he took my Tribute from my room after I allowed him to accompany Tribute Dawn for a visit, it is clear I will not be afforded that same respect. I trust the other warrior to have my back in battle, but obviously I cannot trust him with my Tribute.

"Stay away from him."

She makes a huffing noise with her breath, putting her hands on her hips as she pulls away from me, as much as she can while her hair is in my grip. Something about the stance seems fairly aggressive and I cannot decide whether to smile at her spirit or punish her for being disrespectful to her Master. Since we are alone and there is no one to see her, I decide not to punish her. But I do not smile either. I don't want to reward bad behavior.

"He came with Dawn. She said he goes everywhere with her when Gavrill is unavailable. So am I not supposed to see her either?"

That would be unfair to her, I admit. But he would help himself to my Tribute if he could and that is unacceptable.

"I will speak to him." I grind out. My Tribute should not be deprived of another Tribute's company just because Arkdhem does not know how to behave himself. I force myself to loosen my grip on her hair, letting my hand drop. Rather than stepping away, as I assume she would, she leans in toward me.

"You seem mad," she murmurs, running a finger down my arm, following one of the red streaks. My body tightens immediately, shifting from frustration and anger to arousal without a single stop in between. The energy I'd hoped to burn off with sparring is back as if it never left.

"Come. We have been apart for some time. I wish to inspect you." That is not what I really wish to do, but it is the closest I can come to it. For now.

"Is it really necessary?" She sighs but complies when I pull her toward the bed and point to the floor where I wish her to stand. She makes no protest when I unhook her gown and let it fall into a filmy pile at her feet. The beauty of her body is now exposed for my pleasure. The training belt slides away from her intimate areas, turning into a belt in truth. She should always be naked in this room.

When I run my hands up and down her sides, her eyes half close. I stroke her up and down, over and over, tugging her close so I can trace the line of her neck and jaw, even her ears.

"Mmmm," she hums when I rub the small flange between my fingers. Her expression is dreamy. I have never been so fascinated with an ear before, but suddenly I must taste it. I tilt her head close and run my tongue along the edge. She shivers when I probe into the delicate channel and catch the soft lobe between my teeth, tasting it. Her legs shift and I draw her back to the bed, sitting down and pulling her into my lap. To my delight she sinks against me, curling up as if I am a particularly comfortable chair. The position puts her most enticing parts within reach.

Soon. Not yet. I turn her head and nibble at her other ear. She sighs and wriggles on my lap, stimulating my cock delightfully and making my *seela* strain toward her.

My arousal is matched by her own. Her nipples are tight beads, her breath coming in pants. I am sure that if I dip my fingers between her legs, they will come away wet with her arousal.

I dip my head to whisper to her. "Are you primed for me, my Tribute?"

"Always, Master." Her mouth is half open. I rub my thumb against the pad of her lip, and she tilts her head, drawing it into her mouth and giving it a good hard suck. My seela almost burst from my armor.

"I wish to see you climax," I tell her, and she wriggles again on my lap, setting space between us.

"I wish to see *you* climax," she responds. Her hand reaches between my thighs and strokes the bulge there. The touch is shocking, both because it is unexpected and because no one else has touched me there in so long. The need to be buried inside of her rises up inside of me, pushing at me, but I push back. I am the master of my emotions and actions, just as I am the master of her. I will not be manipulated by either.

I catch her hand and draw it up behind her back, forcing her breasts up and out. "Do not touch me without permission."

"Why?" Her breathy voice teases me. "What will happen?" She writhes in my grip, her intent obviously not to get free but to shake her breasts under my nose. Another attempt at manipulation. I cannot touch her there or she will think she has won. A pity, as I would have enjoyed playing with the soft mounds.

"I will punish you."

She squeals as I tip her over my lap. Yes, this is much more pleasing. I can watch her cheeks grow pink as she shifts on her belly, stimulating my cock, and she will know she is not in charge. I palm her backside, feeling her bottom wriggle as she kicks and squirms, trying to get free.

"This is what happens to naughty Tributes." I crack my palm on her bare bottom over and over, enjoying her shrieks. Finding pleasure in the way she writhes against me. Her bottom must be more resilient than Tribute Dawn's, considering the amount of punishment she can take. She's not distressed by the discipline, although indignant, and when I check her for arousal, she is perfectly primed, dripping wet with sweet passion for me. "What's this? Do you enjoy your discipline?"

She moans as I dip my fingers in and lifts her hips, trying to direct my fingers toward her pleasure nub. Of course, I will not allow her such a treat when she is being disciplined.

"You know I do." Her voice is sassy, and I immediately move my fingers away from her wetness. My Tribute moans in disappointment and then shrieks as I begin to spank her again, much harder this time.

SMACK!

SMACK!

SMACK!

"Is that how you address your master?"

"No! Sorry! Master, please."

She shudders and begs when I dip my fingers into her slick channel and gather the juices. I stroke the furrows of her sex, avoiding touching the fleshy protrusion that is the hot button to her pleasure. The manuals spoke of the clitoris as being impossible for most male humans to find but I locate Pareena's easily every time. Another reason Tsenturions are superior to other males. The ones that do find the clitoris don't understand the fleshy nub is only a small part of pleasure-receptor filled tissue.

Not every female will enjoy direct touch on the small, sensitive bud. Pareena seems to prefer indirect stimulus. She jumps when I apply too much pressure, but purrs when I stroke beside it. It is best if I do not get too close right away, but spend time teasing her until she is primed and beyond begging.

I do this now, alternating with sharp smacks to her bottom. This isn't a true punishment, only a reminder of who's in charge. Judging by the way she's now pushing up to meet my palm, she's enjoying it more than she lets on. I apply a round of swats to the top and bottom quadrants of each cheek and plunge two fingers into her tight channel. She throws her head back with a throaty moan.

"Do not climax without permission," I advise her. "You will not like the consequences."

"Will you belt me, Master?" She wriggles her bottom. Cheeky Tribute. I lift her and position her on the bed, her legs hanging over the side and hips propped on a pillow. When I return with the strip of *kurdzu* hide she calls a belt, I present it to her lips.

"Kiss it. And when I'm done you will thank me." I run a hand down her taut back to calm her. She is not afraid, but excited. Her juices are running down her leg.

"Count," I order and snap the belt against her warmed backside.

"One," she cries, her legs straining for the floor. I steady her with a hand on her lower back and lay careful stripes on her bottom and thighs.

~

Pareena

I MIGHT REGRET THIS TOMORROW...

The pain is delicious, but deep down I know I am overdoing it. I just don't care. The tears sliding down my face feel freeing. The arousal curling in my core is turning me into a horny, spanking-crazed slut. In the best possible way, of course.

Every crack of the belt across my ass makes me scream, and yet as soon as the burning sting fades from the initial impact, I crave another. I moan when he pauses, stroking his fingers through my arousal again, circling my clit and teasing me with a touch that is too soft to bring me satisfaction.

"Please, Master," I beg.

But his hand lifts again and my head drops down in disappointment.

Then he slaps my pussy.

I cry out as the tips of his fingers snap against my clit and the surrounding area, the exquisite agony making my toes curl. He does it again and again, as if he knows exactly what the stinging slaps are doing to me. My orgasm swells, close to bursting, but not quite making it.

"Please, please, please," I beg, chanting the word over and over again. Then his fingers press down over my mound, rubbing the whole area and my entire body jerks.

"Come for me, my Tribute."

The order, his deep growling voice, set me off and I scream with release as he moves his fingers in a circular motion. Ecstasy pounds through my body, taking every ounce of pain and twisting it, turning it into spectacular pleasure.

My arms collapse, leaving my upper body resting against the bed, quivering from the intense orgasm. Bogdan's fingers make one last swirl around my throbbing clit and then move away. I swear I can feel him staring at my pussy, like he wants nothing more than to thrust inside me, but something is holding him back.

Should I say something?

Do something?

Torn with indecision, I bite down on my lower lip and wait.

It doesn't matter that I just had an orgasm—I still want him. I almost feel like I *need* him inside of me, like there's a gaping emptiness that won't go away until he fills me.

"What do you say?" he asks finally.

"Thank you, Master."

I hold my position. Waiting. Hoping.

Finally, I turn my head to look at him over my shoulder. I was right. He is staring right at my upturned ass, but he's not moving. The expression on his face is conflicted, but full of desire. Then he notices that I'm looking back at him and his gaze lifts to meet mine.

"What is it, my Tribute?"

"Do you want me to really thank you?" Before he can stop me, I flip around, so that I'm kneeling facing him rather than looking away from him. His eyes lock onto my breasts and I put my hands on his thighs. The alien cock that Dawn described is right in front of my face, just his armor between us, and I swear I can see it move. "Let me pleasure you, Master."

"No." He steps back, turning away, and I let my hands drop, trying not to cry as the feeling of rejection wells up inside of me. Turning away, he moves to hang the belt back up on his Wall of Pain.

What am I doing wrong? Why doesn't he want me? I gather my courage. We can't keep going on like this.

"Master, I have a question." I'm pretty sure I see his shoulders tense at the question, but I persevere anyway. "Why haven't we had sex yet?"

Rather than answering me, Bogdan turns back around and walks past me, heading for the door while gesturing for me to get into the bed. "You should rest."

I scramble up to follow, ignoring his hand gesture. It's not like he gave me an order or anything. "Did I do something wrong?"

Black slides up around his body, his armor going back into place as if it can shield him from me. Hurt wells up in my chest. Dammit.

I catch up to him before he reaches the door to leave our quarters.

"Where are you going? Master?"

"You do not have permission to leave the room. I will be back soon."

The door opens and he whisks away, leaving me standing there feeling utterly rejected. I dig my nails into the palms of my hands, determined not to cry. Taking a few deep breaths, I push down the ache in my chest.

Talk about *wham, bam, thank you, alien.*

I guess I'm not getting an answer right now. Why doesn't he want to have sex with me? Dawn was surprised by it. We didn't talk about it with Arkdhem there, but maybe I should have... no. That would be a bad idea. Something about Arkdhem definitely rubs him the wrong way. I don't need to put more obstacles between us.

I'd think that maybe something is wrong with his equipment, but when I touched him earlier, he was hard and there seemed to be extra movement as well. I'm not sure what a cock surrounded by tiny tentacles is supposed to feel like, but it seemed to fit Dawn's description.

I pivot in a slow circle and go to pick up my gown. I would kill for jeans and a t-shirt right now, but regardless, I'm not just going to stand around here naked. I feel vulnerable enough already. My alien fantasy is starting to feel a lot more complicated than I ever expected. Another point to it being reality? I still can't quite swallow that though.

I wonder how much time I have before Bogdan returns. I suppose I could just walk out without him, but without Dawn I'll have no idea where I'm going. Plus, I doubt making him angry is going to help. I nibble on my thumbnail, a nervous habit that I've never quite managed to grow out of.

This isn't at all ethical but... I want to know what's going on and he's not talking. Dawn doesn't know. And this probably isn't even real, right? It's not really snooping if I'm imagining all of this.

And if I'm not?

I shake my head. My mind is made up. Hey, even Hermione knew that you have to break the rules sometimes.

I'll start with the secret panel on the wall where he hid that box. I was going to try and respect his privacy, but he's not talking and I'm getting pissed. And hurt. Besides, if he comes back and what's the worst he can do—punish me?

11

B ogdan

I MARCH DOWN THE HALL, acknowledging passing warriors' salutes and scowling when they congratulate me on my Tribute. I do not wish to think about my Tribute when my cock and *seela* are bellowing for relief. My jaw clenches and I rub my chest. I feel a kind of pain there, but it is a strange pain, as if it is not my own.

I do not like thinking about the look on my Tribute's face when I left the room.

Part of me wishes the Vgotha would appear, simply so I could justifiably stay away from her. Just for a little bit. Also, surely a fight with the enemy would take the edge off my constant state of arousal, where sparring did not.

Why haven't we had sex yet?

I do not have an answer that would satisfy the High Commander, so I do not think it would satisfy her either. I am unable to even explain it to myself.

I would not be betraying a mate. I have no formal allegiance to Harai, who is long gone and was far too kind to deny me happiness in the future. And yet every time I begin to get caught up in the moment, something holds me back.

It feels wrong to me, to have Tributes when we have not yet defeated our enemy, yet I seem to be the only one who thinks so.

My Tribute intrigues and challenges me at every turn and I enjoy her spirit as much as her body... but to bond with her... to breed with her...

Are we to create a new generation of Tsenturions when we cannot even guarantee their safety against the Vgotha threat? I shake my head, shoving away the panic and crushing guilt that threatens my composure. The decision has already been made, no matter that I disagree with it.

I will do my duty.

Somehow.

The scent of food and echoing loud voices signal an end to my walk. I stride into the mess hall to find more edible vegetation for my Tribute.

When I enter the cafeteria, several warriors hail me, acknowledging my presence. I nod but quickly look away from them to be sure none approach. It works; I have several moments of solitude to review the food lists and find ones I think my Tribute will enjoy.

In the end, the only Tsenturion other than High Commander Gavrill who would dare interrupt me when I obviously wish to be left alone steps up to my side. Medik is older, wiser, and not a warrior. He is an anomaly, a man who finished his service, mated, fathered children, but then came with us when our Medik was injured on duty. He was supposed to serve one mission and then return home... but there was no home to return to. During the mission, he'd preferred to go by his title, but after the Great Devastation, he'd given up his name entirely, demanding to be known only by his title, as his mate had been the last to speak his name and he did not want that taken away from him.

His loss was greater than any of ours individually, yet somehow, he has more hope than I do.

"Greetings, Bogdan. How goes the bonding of Tribute Pareena?"

"My Tribute's training is going well enough." I respond, my voice even. I specifically don't mention bonding. There has been no bonding yet. A feeling of guilt suffuses me, because there are many warriors who would love to bond with a Tribute, and yet I am fighting the bond with mine. However, the idea of bonding with her also fills me with guilt. There is no winning this scenario.

Medik just smiles.

"Is your Tribute unsatisfactory?" he asks.

"My Tribute is perfect." I snap the words out defensively before I realize it was probably his intention to goad me.

Medik cocks his head, a twinkle in his eye. Not a very soldier-ly gesture, but he has always been more expressive than the rest of us. "Perfectly suited to the Tribute program or perfect for you?"

"Is there a difference?"

Rather than answering, he just chuckles and continues on as if I had answered him. "I had hoped the altered questionnaire would yield good results. Dawn's input was invaluable. Has Pareena shared anything about her past life with you?"

If he were anyone else, his familiar use of my Tribute's name would rankle, but since it is Medik, I let it pass.

"The subject has not come up." Was that not what her file was for? What more do I need to know?

"Hmmm," Medik sips his drink, studying me. "It might be good to discuss life events before her arrival. Hers and yours."

I come close to blurting out how she found me looking over the contents of the betrothal box. Which is odd. I have never felt the need to share my personal experiences before. At times Medik has asked questions about my mental and emotional state, but I assured him my mental faculties would not interfere with my warrior duties. As long as my physical health is in peak condition, I have no need to review my memories.

"What purpose would it serve?" I scowl, as if displeased by the idea, but truthfully, I am curious. After all, he is the only male other than the High Commander who has ever been mated. In many ways, he has served as a paternal guide to all of the warriors in our fleet. We all lost our fathers and mothers to the Great Tragedy, and he stepped into the breach.

Medik is used to my severe expressions and, as usual, ignores this one. "She will surely wish to know more about the warrior she's been given to. I understand you are, ah, busy getting to know her in other ways," Medik's cup barely hides his smile, "but when you rest you might talk to her about each other."

"Perhaps I shall," I murmur. Now that he has suggested it, I cannot help but wonder if there are things the file did not reveal to me. Besides, knowing more about my Tribute can only be a good thing. The more I know, the easier I can train her to bend to my will.

"Excellent," Medik exclaims. "I wish you all success. Let me know if I can assist you."

I could protest that I have no need for his help. My Tribute will respond to my questions in a satisfying manner because she is obedient and acknowledges me as her Master, but I have another issue to tend to.

Before he can turn away, I catch his arm.

"There is a matter you can help with."

"Oh? Not a medical issue, I hope?"

"Of a sort. My Tribute does not eat the flesh of animals. I was able to provide a meal for her earlier, but I do not know if it was adequate for her needs on a continuing basis. What plant-based dishes provide the most nutrients for her system?"

Several minicycles later, I enter my quarters laden with two large platters of nutritional plant-based dishes. Medik was happy to help me select them.

I frown when I do not immediately see my Tribute and set down the platters. I feel strangely uneasy and sad. Am I feeling what she is feeling? Where is she?

"Pareena?" To call her 'my Tribute' when I am addressing her feels too strange and I remember how Dawn insisted I use my Tribute's first name, seeming to think I had an objection to it. I like my Tribute's first name. It rolls off the tongue in a pleasing manner.

A choked cry, on the other side of the bed, makes me rush forward. My Tribute is kneeling again, by the wall. When she looks up at me, tears are streaming down her face. The source of the uneasy sadness is clear. Somehow, I know what she is feeling. But I cannot focus on that revelation now, not when I can see her distress.

"What is wrong? Are you hurt?" I crouch and run my hands over her clothed body.

"I'm fine," she sniffles. "I'm fine." She catches my hand and presses it to her chest. "Oh, Bogdan, I'm so sorry."

"You are unhurt? Then why are you crying?"

She shakes her head, unable to answer. I gather her into my arms and hold my Tribute as she weeps. My insides feel as if they have been scrambled. I wish to fight but there are no threats in the room. What could have disturbed her?

My eyes fall on the open panel that usually hides the compartment where I keep my memory box. She's taken out the gifts from Harai, as well as the only items I have left from my parents and ancestors. I have not looked at the vid pics of my sisters and younger brother in decacycles, and seeing their faces now sends a pang of grief through me.

~

Pareena

As sad as I was feeling before, just looking at the pictures of children and realizing they must have all been killed when Tsentur was destroyed, is nothing to how I feel, watching as pure grief etches itself across Bogdan's face.

"I'm sorry," I whisper, leaning into him, holding onto him. I'm terrified he'll pull away from me, but if anything, he seems to sag against me. The anger he felt when I saw him looking through this box the last time is nowhere to be seen, and somehow that makes me feel even worse. "I went snooping."

"It… it is understandable." His words are stilted. Tight. I cannot tell if he actually means them or not. "You wish to know more about me."

I thought I felt his grief, but now I just feel a kind of emptiness, as if all emotions have shut down.

"You're not mad?" I ask, tentatively.

"No."

I hold my breath, but it doesn't seem like he's going to say anything more without prompting. "Who are they?"

We both look at the pictures simultaneously. I can guess who they are, but I think it will probably do him some good to talk about it. Maybe that's the shrink in me, but I've never seen anyone more bottled up than Bogdan is.

"My sisters. My brother. My family."

I swear I can feel the sadness coming back to fill the emptiness, as though just saying their relation to him has somehow breached the barrier against his emotions.

We are both silent again for a long moment. Sometimes silence is all that is needed to get someone to open up.

"Do you wish for me to tell you what happened?" His voice is reluctant, but that's not entirely unexpected. Still, I almost sigh in relief that he's making the offer. I wasn't completely sure he would, which *should* have been fine but… it's easier to maintain a professional distance when I don't have a personal stake.

"Would you?" I ask softly.

To my surprise, Bogdan leans back against the wall, pulling me onto his lap. I snuggle in, pressing myself against his body and doing my best to serve as a comfort during what I know will be a difficult talk for him. Frllil told me about the Great Tragedy. But it's different hearing about an event from someone who wasn't affected by it versus someone whose life was radically changed by it.

I can feel the rumble of his voice through his chest as he begins to speak.

"It was planting time. Night blossoms signal the time for the Mating Festival. Our fleet was late returning to Tsentur, which had never happened before in living memory..." His voice trails off, as if the pain is too much to bear and instinctively, I lean into him. I can already feel the tears gathering at the backs of my eyes again. Clearing his throat, his arms tighten around me. "I was to leave my duties as a soldier and return to the planet, where I would rejoin my family and travel to the Festival."

He falls silent again. Lost in the memories perhaps.

"Were you going to find a mate?" I ask gently.

"I had already found one."

The answer surprises me and I am glad he has me wrapped tightly in his arms, because I'm not sure I could have contained my shock. That was the last thing I'd expected, especially because I was told that Tsenturions could only bond with a mate once. But, of course, he didn't get a chance to bond with her.

My heart aches and a fresh wave of tears spills from my eyes. It's so incredibly tragic and yet I feel anger rising too. Not at Bogdan, but at the Vgotha. The unnecessary loss is so devastating, so infuriating, that even I feel it. Bogdan shouldn't be here. He should be happily mated, possibly with children. No wonder he didn't want a Tribute. It wasn't personal to me at all.

"Did you love her?" I keep my voice soft, calm. My therapy voice. Although the way my fingers stroke over his chest, trying to soothe him, isn't at all professional. I can't seem to make myself stop though.

"I did." The pain and sadness in his voice make me want to hug him for the rest of his life. "We had not bonded, but I was looking forward to our life together."

I choke a little, and then I realize that I'm crying a lot harder than I thought I was. My chest heaves, but I don't seem to be able to make myself stop.

"Hush." Now Bogdan is the one comforting me. Holding me

tightly, he begins to rock me slightly. "Do not distress yourself. It was a long time ago."

"It's so sad. You all lost so much." And no matter how long ago it was, I can tell it still affects him. It still affects all of them. How could it not?

12

B ogdan

I TRY to thumb away my Tribute's tears, but there are too many of them.

"It was a long time ago," I repeat the only thing I can think of to say, to try and comfort her.

"It still hurts," she whispers.

I cradle her head to my chest and let her cry, because she speaks the truth. *It still hurts.* No matter how long it has been, it still hurts. I rest my cheek against my Tribute's head. She fits into my arms perfectly, her slight weight replacing the heavy feelings I've carried for many cycles. The burden is still there, but fractured, like a stone broken into many pieces. Smaller pieces more easily dealt with. *It still hurts.* But perhaps not as much.

I have never cried before, yet my Tribute is weeping far too vigorously for just discovering my betrothal box. Could she be sensing my grief?

Whatever it is, I feel calmer when her sobs quiet. I pull the box closer and sift through the contents to find the ones not related to Harai.

I lift out a small jeweled dagger. "This was my grandmother's. She carried it always, until I came of age and she gave it to me." I thumb the pommel where a stone is missing. "She let me play with it when I was young, but I dropped it and broke the main setting. So, she took the jewel and added it to our family crest." I pick up the brooch she'd made from it. The black stone glitters in the bronze setting.

"This looks like onyx." My Tribute tentatively lifts her hand and I let her take it from me. She turns it over, inspecting it. Her eyes and nose are puffy and slightly discolored, but she seems to have calmed as well. She holds it up to my chest and giggles. "You should wear it. It matches your suit."

Because both are black. A small smile of amusement curves my lips.

"What about this, Master?" she asks, emboldened by my sharing. She reaches past me and touches the golden lock of hair, although she does not pick it up.

I remain silent for a long moment, staring at Harai's hair, feeling the ache... feeling the guilt of having my Tribute in my lap as I look at my intended mate's last gift. The High Commander has bonded with his Tribute, but I have not bonded with mine. Part of me still feels that the very presence of non-Tsenturion mates makes a mockery out of what had been a sacred bond on our planet. Yet, I still want my Tribute now that I have her.

"Was it hers?" she asks gently. I nod and a muscle in my jaw clenches. I am unable to speak, too overcome with conflicting emotions. My Tribute sets the brooches and dagger back in the box and twists around to cup my face. "It's okay, Master. I know you don't want a mate. I'm not trying to replace your lost love."

I blink. How did she know my thoughts?

"It was wrong of me to pry," she says, her fingers softly stroking my cheeks. I can feel the sadness in her, but also a kind of calm that creeps over me like a comforting balm. She is no innocent. She too has known grief and loss.

"Why did you?" I ask, curious. Medik did tell me to ask her more questions. I would not have thought that sharing more of myself with my Tribute would make me feel better, but it did.

"I wanted to know more about you. I want to be closer to you."

I frown, my arms tightening around her. "You are already close to me." I shift my legs underneath her for emphasis.

Surprisingly, her dark eyes twinkle with humor in response, her mood lightening. "*Closer* than that. I'm here for you, Master, Bogdan, however you want me. I understand if you want to wait."

She bites her lip and drops her eyes. My cock stirs.

Oh.

The urge to claim her wells up inside of me, stronger than ever now that she's told me that she understands... that she will wait. I don't know why, but somehow that one sentence breaks through the resistance that I have been feeling. I never fully understood my resistance either, so perhaps it is not surprising that I don't fully understand why her offer has affected it.

"I do not wish to wait," I say, abruptly standing with her in my arms. She grabs onto me, holding tightly and blinking in surprise as I carry her to the bed.

Her slight weight reminds me to be gentle. I lay her on the bed and pull off her gown, exposing her smooth skin to my touch. My cock is achingly hard, my *seela* unruly and writhing with the need to connect to her. *Yes.*

The Vgotha threat still exists, but we will eradicate it. My Tribute will just give me another reason to fight.

She can be distracting, but I have already proven, both to myself and to the other warriors, that I can attend both my Tribute and my duties.

The loss of Harai still hurts, but she is gone, and she would want me to be happy. My Tribute makes me... well, not happy exactly, but even before the Great Tragedy I was not a cheerful Tsenturion. But she makes me less unhappy. She soothes the sharp edges of pain and anger inside of me, even if she does not eradicate them entirely.

Rest peacefully, Harai.

The thought slides through my mind like a benediction, a release from a long sentence of grief and fury. Those emotions are not gone, but there are other emotions now too.

Curiosity. Affection. Admiration. Desire. My Tribute has awoken a side of me that I thought had died with Tsentur. It has been an uncomfortable and sometimes painful awakening, but now I don't want to hold back from her any longer. She is not the mate I intended to have, but she is my Tribute and she will be my mate.

I rear up over her, drinking in the sight of her lithe form sprawled on my bed. Her hair flows around her shoulders like a black river. Her gaze is lazy, eyes hooded, as she studies me as I am studying her.

Suddenly I wonder what she thinks of me. Does she long for my touch as I long for hers?

Her tongue darts out and swipes over her lips, and I have my answer. I command my armor to retract. Her eyes widen with anticipation and then widen even more when her gaze comes to my cock. The way her lips pop open in surprise, I know that she is impressed. My *seela* strain towards her body.

∼

Pareena

Dawn had not been exaggerating about the alien peen. If anything, she understated it.

It really does remind me of a cobra, rising up from a nest of tentacles, all of which are trying to reach me. There is one longer tentacle above all the others and my pussy clenches when I realize it's at the *exact* right spot to be able to stimulate my clit. I sit up, reaching towards them, the same way they're reaching toward me, and then I hesitate.

"Can I touch them, Master?" I ask, looking up at him.

The way he's looking at me is very human. All prideful male, pleased with my reaction to his cock.

"Gently." He threads a hand into my hair, and my mouth waters. Something about having a man's hand in my hair, his cock in my face, just always makes me want to suck it. Apparently, it doesn't matter that the cock itself is a little weird looking.

I don't go right for the gold though when I touch him, instead I stroke the longest tentacle of the moving nest while the smaller ones brush over the back of my hand as soon as it's close enough.

"They're soft." It's a really weird sensation—this whole thing is weird—but I'm surprisingly okay with all of it. "Almost velvety."

"I am not soft," Bogdan says, sounding insulted.

"Just the skin is," I reassure him. Apparently, males have some similarities no matter what part of the universe they come from. "I can feel that you're very hard." I wrap my fingers around the shaft of his cock, just under the flaring head, and he groans, his hips thrusting forward eagerly.

Considering how many times he's gotten me off without getting himself off, it's a testament to his willpower that he doesn't do more than that. I can't help but wonder what it would take to break that steely self-control. His cock flexes in my hand. Not the same way a human's penis would. Human genitalia is more rigid and it might pulse or throb, but it wouldn't actually *bend.* The hooded head flares, its edges moving up and down and reminding me of the way a stingray looks when it swims.

Holy shit.

The possibilities boggle the mind. And then add in the tentacles...

I giggle when the little strands pull at my skin, trying to wrap around my fingers. This is seriously the whole package. And I feel a little pang of disappointment that it's really unlikely Bogdan would get the joke if I tried to make it.

I move my fingers over the shaft, pulling them out of reach of the tentacles and then sliding back down. He groans again, his hand tightening in my hair, but that is his only reaction.

I can't help it. I have a Ravenclaw's curiosity and I have to know.

Dipping my head, I swipe my tongue over the broad, slowly undulating head of his cock. His skin is more textured than a human's and I wonder how it will feel when it's sliding inside of me. Right now, though, my focus is on what I'm doing to *him*. Bogdan's body goes rigid as my tongue explores his cock.

"What are you doing?" He sounds like he is choking on the words.

I look up at him and the expression on his face... shock, desire, curiosity. It's the most open I've ever seen him. I grin slyly up at him. "Didn't the manuals cover blow jobs? Oral sex?"

"Yes..." His voice trails off slightly and I suddenly realize that he might not have completely understood what the books were talking about if the Tsenturions don't have a frame of reference for it.

This should be fun.

~

Bogdan

MY TRIBUTE'S tongue flicks out again, running along the rippling ridge of my cock. Shivers run through me, but I am otherwise frozen, watching her taste my sensitive flesh. It is strange but extremely pleasurable as her small tongue explores me.

She works her way down to my cock and envelops the tip in wet heat. The sensation is enough to nearly unman me and my knees lock in place, body arching, sending my cock deep into her mouth. Instead of drawing back, she hums, sending tiny vibrations through my synapses. The pleasure is overwhelming. Seeing her dark eyes, watching her face, as she swallows me is the most shocking and erotic experience of my life.

As she moves inward, my lesser seela suction onto her face and pull her close. I can feel her arousal more strongly than ever, feel her pleasure in serving me. She is enjoying this. Not in the same way I am, but, nonetheless. I do understand, because I enjoyed tasting her, but I had not expected her to enjoy the same. The manuals had indicated that not all human females want to perform the oral sex.

My Tribute must be a superior human female, which does not surprise me.

My prime seela strokes her face. She closes her eyes, breathing through her nose as she sheaths my cock in her throat. My fingers are still fisted in her hair, but instead of pulling her off, I allow her to work up and down on my cock until stars fill my vision. My arousal tightens like a fist. If she continues, I will not be able to claim her.

She slides her mouth off, drawing in a deep breath. My *seela* release their hold, leaving small marks across her cheeks. Marks that arouse me even more, because of what they mean. Before she can plunge down again, I tug her away.

"Not that way." The urge to claim her, to sink into her and release my seed is too strong. I will not be able to hold back if she uses her mouth for the oral sex again.

"Did you like it?" she asks, breathless, her eyes bright as if I have been pleasuring her, not the other way around.

I trace my finger over one of the circular marks on her cheek. "I liked it very much, but I want to claim you now."

"Are you sure?" she asks, and I can see a spark of fear in her eyes, feel it in the nanotech. "Because if you start and then change your mind, I think I might actually cry again. And I really don't want to cry again today."

"I will not change my mind," I assure her. "You are my Tribute. It is time and I have waited long enough to fully claim you."

Too long, I am sure the High Commander would say. The other warriors would agree. But it is the right time for me, for us.

Pressing her back onto the bed, I move atop my Tribute, ready to truly make her *mine*.

～

Pareena

. . .

BOGDAN'S LIPS MEET MINE, taking my mouth before I can respond. His tongue slides against mine and I feel movement against my inner thighs, making me shudder in erotic anticipation. Were those the tentacles?

Yes, yes, yes, yes, yes please!

My arms move, sliding over his hard muscles, tentatively at first, because he hasn't really allowed me to touch him like this before, and then more... and more... I am greedy, exploring his body with my fingertips and he groans, rocking against me.

Oh my...

Those are *definitely* the tentacles, moving against the sensitive skin of my inner thighs, working their way to my pussy. The Bride Trainer retracts, leaving my sex open and exposed. A kind of fearful, excited anticipation fills me. What is this going to feel like?

Something moves against my pussy and then I feel it, pushing into me. The flared head is thick and strangely shaped, but I am soaking wet and it manages to push inside of me. I cry out against Bogdan's lips, my nails digging into his shoulders. It only takes him a moment to take my wrists and pin my hands down above my head, leaving me totally helpless beneath him, as he slowly impales me on his alien cock.

It *moves* inside of me, pressing against my quivering muscles in strange ways, all while his tongue strokes the inside of my mouth.

Talk about an alien invasion, I think, and then have to wonder if I'm a little hysterical.

It feels so incredibly good that I can barely stand it.

Something pulls at my labia, and I realize that the tentacles have gotten in on the act. The sensation is tingling pleasure, like bubbles traveling over my skin, and then it deepens even more, as if he's literally sucking on my pussy while he fucks me. When the super long one moves over my swollen clit, my whole body jerks in reaction.

His lips leave mine, and then Bogdan is staring down at me, watching my reaction as our groins press together. His strange cock is fully buried inside of me and his tentacles are stroking and sucking me and I can actually feel my toes curling.

"Oh... oh fuck... Please..." I beg, my need, my pleasure already rising higher and faster than I can handle. "It's like a tongue, licking... oh please... please don't stop..."

The *prime seela* that Dawn had told me about suctions onto my clit, tugging on the sensitive nub, and I scream as ecstasy surges, releasing the tension that had coiled almost too quickly and too powerfully inside of me. I writhe underneath him, my entire body quaking with the hot bliss... and then he rolls over so that I am sitting on top of him and it feels like he is even deeper inside of me.

Bogdan

I PROP up my Tribute as her body rocks in orgasm. As much as I long to unleash the full power of my desire upon her, I am too worried that doing so will hurt her. My control is close to snapping as it is. Having her on top of me will help keep me from causing her any harm.

She cants forward, clasping her hands behind my neck now that I have returned control of her arms to her. My whole torso is rigid, muscles bunching in an attempt to control my impulse to flip her on her back and pound out my need between her accommodating thighs. She shifts up and down, back and forth, wriggling as if it will help her accommodate the thick intruder.

"You're so big," she gasps.

"You're so small," I correct her. She whimpers and I hold her close. "Just wait." Her body is opening like a flower, coating my cock in her cream and allowing it to slide inside.

"No, I need you." she strains to seat herself, but I don't let her go. For a moment she struggles in my hold, pushing at my chest and grunting with exertion. I swallow my amusement. Her dark eyes flash defiance and it makes me want to laugh.

"Kiss me," I whisper, to distract her. Immediately she leans forward, obeying her Master's command. My lips claim hers, my tongue thrusting into her mouth. She moans as she moves, rising up high enough that it stretches the *seela* suctioned to her skin, before sliding back down my cock. Her head falls back, ending the kiss.

"Oh yes..." She shudders, arching, and I curve one arm around her back to stabilize her while my other hand seeks out her breast.

"Good girl," I say, repeating the accolade I saw most often in the manuals. I am immediately rewarded when her pussy clamps down around my cock in reaction. The hot, wet pulse of her body around mine is celestial.

"More," she demands, breathing fast and struggling to move. "Harder."

For the first time in what feels like forever, my face creases into a smile. "Patience, little one."

"*Now*," she half-orders, half-begs. My Tribute is bossy and it's adorable. Instead of anger that she dare to command me, as she has clearly forgotten herself in her need for my cock, I am amused and gratified by her overwhelming desire.

"Fuck me, Bogdan, please," she begs, resting her forehead on my chin, her pussy fluttering around my cock. Rather than chastising her, I decide whenever I am inside her, she will call me by name instead of Master. I like the way she says it.

Reaching down, I trace the plump petals spread around my hard shaft, displacing lesser seela as I measure how much more of me she needs to take. My hand comes away coated with her wetness. My prime seela is nestled beside the fleshy ridge of her most sensitive spot. It undulates gently, stimulating her constantly. No wonder she is mad with need.

"As you wish," I murmur, loosening my grip so that she can rise halfway up my cock. Gravity and my *seela* tug her down, impaling her again and making both of us groan. Tremors of pleasure ripple through her.

"I've never been so full." She is panting for breath. "Harder please, Master, fuck me."

"Bogdan," I correct her.

"Bogdan," she repeats immediately, her sultry voice turning my name into a sigh of pleasure. "Please, fuck me. I need you."

I need you.

Her words spark something inside of me, and my self-control slides away like a Vgotha ship on the run. My muscles bunch and roll as I rock into her, forcing her to ride my body like a boat bobbing on a wave. Her small body is suspended over mine, held up by my hand in her hair and my cock impaling her. Once I am sure she is fully seated again, I snap my hips and make her bounce.

A keening cry escapes her, and a flush creeps up her chest. She is climaxing. Again. What little control I had left is gone. I flip her onto her back. She is soft and wet now, her pussy adjusted to my cock. There should be no danger of harming her.

I grasp her hips and pound her, my lesser *seela* slackening and tightening to allow my movement, my prime *seela* wagging wildly against her clitoris. Her orgasm is non-stop, constant waves of wild sensation breaking in her body. I feel the feedback in the back of my mind, her pleasure and satisfaction a constant presence as my own climax grows to epic proportions, ready to crash into us both. Her mouth is slack, her eyes practically rolling back in her head, but her nails claw my back as if to urge me on.

My cock stiffens, hardening to its full length, my *seela* pulling at her flesh and initiating the exchange of bio information. Rapture erupts, carrying my seed with it into her body, leaving us shuddering together in mutual bliss.

13

———————

P areena

A SOFT TOUCH on my folds makes me whimper.

"Easy," Bogdan soothes, rubbing cream into my sore pussy. The ache diminishes almost immediately, and I sigh in relief. When I'd told him "harder," he'd definitely ended up taking me at my word. I wonder if this is how Lois Lane feels after she gets it on with Superman.

When he's finished, he looks at me, studying my expression. Giving him a lazy smile, I reach out and trace his hard features. He smiled earlier, I'm almost sure of it. I didn't realize it at the time, I was too desperate to be fucked, but the memory floats back to me as I lie in a post-coital haze. I never thought I'd see the big, surly alien let down his guard, but here he is, fussing over me, wiping off my sweaty limbs with a soft cloth and inspecting the puffy redness of my labia.

"That's normal," I tell him. At least, I'm assuming it's normal.

There's usually post-coital soreness after any vigorous sex, much less vigorous alien sex with a strangely shaped cock. "I'm fine."

"You are so tight," he muses, looking back down at my pussy contemplatively. "I will have the Bride Trainer prepare you before your next claiming."

I whimper at the thought of being filled, of going about my day constantly fucked by the Bride Trainer in preparation for my Master's cock. It sounds both torturous and unbearably arousing... actually, wait, I've done it before with Frllil and it was both of those things. But it seems like it would be even more so when Bogdan is the one giving the orders to the Bride Trainer instead of Frllil.

"I'm fine," I say hastily, half-hoping that he'll believe me, half-hoping he won't. He frowns at my dissent. "You're big, but I'm made to stretch."

He still frowns, but sits down on the bed beside me, tracing his hand over my hip as I roll onto my side to face him. I can't help but wonder how he's feeling, now that we've finally had sex. Am I the only reason for his frown or is he thinking about the Tsenturion woman he'd planned to mate?

Does he feel like he betrayed her?

It doesn't take my degree to know that he's suffering from a large amount of survivor's guilt. If I'd taken the time to think, I would have tried to talk to him about that before we became more physically involved... but thinking has not exactly been high on my priorities when it comes to Bogdan.

Wait, does this mean that I accept everything I'm experiencing is actually real and not just a really strong manifestation of my imagination?

And now my head hurts.

Bogdan distracts me by stroking his finger over my cheek, making a small circle.

"I like these," he says, sounding smug. All of my other thoughts go flying out the window.

"You like what?" I ask, confused. Breasts, ass, pussy, even thighs and lips... but my cheeks?

"My seela marks," he says. I can feel a little thrill of possession run through me, but I'm pretty sure it's not me that's feeling it. I think it's *him*. But more importantly—

"What *seela* marks?!" I sit straight up.

Amused, Bogdan brings me to the bathroom where I stare at the mirror in there. Reflective surface. Whatever. I run my fingers over the marks on my cheeks as they burn red hot with a blush.

"Oh my... everyone's going to know what I did!" Don't get me wrong, I love giving head. It's an act of service that speaks to my submissive soul, but I've never had it advertised on my face that I'd recently indulged.

Standing behind me, Bogdan puts his hands on my hips, pulling me back against him. I swear I can see the glimmer of a smile in his eyes. Males. Doesn't matter the species, they're all alike in some ways.

"I like it." Yeah, he definitely sounds smug. Turning my face to his with a finger he lays his lips against the marks. For such a big, brooding, mean-looking warrior, he's a remarkably gentle kisser. Sighing, I give in and feel myself slumping against him as the humor of the situation gets to me.

After all, who is going to judge me? I don't think the other warriors are going to. They're more likely to high-five Bogdan, or whatever the Tsenturion equivalent would be. Dawn? My impression of her is that she'll want to compare notes.

Turning to face him, I twine my arms around his neck and meet his mouth aggressively. For some time, I teach him the different ways to kiss—the fervent pull of lips and sly trespassing tongue, little nibbles on the edge of his lips and finally, the slow sucks that sends waves of heat through my body.

I end up facing the mirror, my hooded gaze taking in the sight of my brown limbs sprawled against his thickly muscled body. His large hand covers my breast, swallowing it up entirely. My black hair flows over his glittering skin in shocking contrast. Onyx and copper and gold. We look good together.

I think. I can't help but wonder if he thinks so too.

I'd wanted him to open up to me, but now I can't help but think of that memory box as being Pandora's Box. There's hope, yes, but it's also opened up a lot of other emotions. Not just emotions. Insecurities. I pull my lips away from his.

"Master..." My voice trails off, because I'm not sure how to handle this. He's not a client. It would be so much easier to ask if he was, but my emotions are involved too. Which, that's a revelation I'm also going to have to absorb, because I'm starting to believe all of this is real and not just a coma dream and the ramifications of that are something I'm not quite willing to face yet.

"Bogdan. When we are alone, you will call me Bogdan," he orders, and I pull away in surprise.

"Really?"

He stops trying to kiss me and frowns. "You do not wish to?"

"No, I'm... I'd love to call you by your first name. I'm just wondering—"

An alarm sounds in the room and I shriek, practically trying to climb Bogdan's muscled torso. His arms tighten around me, both reassuring me and holding me in place. The lights dim in the room for a moment, and through the door I can see his console flashing a red light.

"What is that?" I squawk, a little embarrassed by my reaction, but still freaked out. In my defense, nothing like that has happened since I've come onboard the ship. I didn't even know it was a possibility.

"It's all right," he soothes, running a hand down my naked back. "It's just an emergency summons to the bridge. Be quiet for a moment."

I almost bristle and demand to know more, but from the way he cocks his head I realize that he's hearing something I can't. Someone on the bridge, I'm assuming. *Just an emergency summons to the bridge.* I almost want to kick him. What *kind* of emergency? Are we under attack? Has there been a hull breach?

Because if this is all real, like I'm starting to believe it is, and the aliens saved me from death and I'm about to lose out on a fantastic life with a sexy alien who wants to dominate and spank me, I'm going to be really ticked.

His armor rolls over him, hiding the glittering skin under the dark panels and he steps away from me. Yeah, that's not reassuring. I almost whimper at the loss of his warm body against mine. I felt *safe* in his arms, dammit. Logically, I know I'm no less safe now that he's not holding me, but that doesn't change how I feel.

"I must go," he says, his voice deep and full of an emotion so deep it feels wrong to just call it 'anger.' That is what centuries of grieving, of loss without justice, of a burning need for vengeance sounds like. There is nothing in my education, nothing in my experience, to help prepare me for dealing with someone in that position. "There are Vgotha sighted within range of our ships, which means we are within their range as well. You must stay here."

"But—" I stop, because I can't think of a good reason to argue. He can't stay here with me, when he could be somewhere else doing something useful, and I definitely wouldn't be useful. I'd be nothing but a distraction. The truth chafes, but I'm honest enough to know it's true.

"Stay here," he repeats, striding to the door.

I hurry after him. "But what if you are gone for a while? Where is Dawn, can I go be with her?"

"Dawn will most likely be confined to quarters for her safety. You will remain here until I return or suffer the consequences."

I halt, even as a quiver runs through me at the thought of *consequences*.

Bogdan sees the shiver and stops as the door slides open. To my surprise, his expression softens, and he cups my chin. The almost gentle expression on his face is at odds with the foreboding black of his armor. "Please, my Pareena. Remain here where you are safe."

His plea twists my heart. Talk about unfair. But I summon my courage. I can do this. I can sit and wait for him until he returns to me.

"Of course, Master. Bogdan." I lean into his palm as he caresses my cheek.

Then he is gone, and the door is sliding shut, leaving me alone.

~

Bogdan

THE HALLS ARE BUSIER than normal with warriors scurrying to their posts, heeding the warning of the flashing lights. There is an almost constant update of information in my earpiece, but I won't be able to sort out what is important until I arrive on the bridge.

I enter the bridge with officers Kalexston and Zakhar. They salute the High Commander standing at the helm and take their places at their respective consoles. I march to Gavrill's side and salute.

"Bogdan." He acknowledges me with a nod. The tension threaded through his posture is reflected in his armor. "Apologies for interrupting your leave."

"No need," I respond. I will always do my duty. "Is this the same ship we picked up on scans earlier?"

The ship's signature flickers on the screen for a moment, making everyone on the bridge tense. We have followed a ship like that before, through a nebula, eventually abandoning it to retrieve Tribute Dawn. The next time we saw the Vgotha, they were boarding our ship and we still do not know how they camouflaged their ship signature.

The urge to run back to my rooms and check that my Tribute is still there and safe rises up, surprising me with its strength.

The signature on the scan solidifies rather than disappears and there is an audible sigh of relief throughout the room. These new tricks of the Vgotha are troublesome. Not just in what they can do, but how they are affecting the warriors' morale. Having Tribute Dawn snatched off of our ship, even without loss of life on our side, did not bolster anyone's confidence.

Late at night the warriors still discuss where the Vgotha ship's seemingly new technology has come from. Did they always have it? Did they purchase it from somewhere? What can it do?

The one chance we had to take apart one of their pods was lost when we attempted to follow it back to its ship instead. Like the ships themselves, it disappeared from our screens.

Which means it's very likely that we are walking into another trap.

But the Vgotha must expect us to suspect... so what is their current plan? The ramifications of all the variables are why I am glad I am not the High Commander. There was a time when I thought I could see things more clearly but looking back I know I would have acted too quickly and too rashly.

Now, with more to lose, I am more cautious.

"We are not sure," the High Commander starts to say, before he is cut off by Kalexston's excited voice.

"High Commander! We believe the Vgotha's current trajectory is going to take them to a planet!"

Everyone on the bridge goes still.

Never before have the Vgotha gone to a planet before.

Again, questions arise. Is this their home planet? A base? Or another trap? Perhaps, as the Vgotha leader claimed to Tribute Dawn when he captured her, they are hoping for a meeting on the planet's surface?

So many unknowns and all our warriors and two Tribute's lives riding on the answer. I scowl at the screens and then look at the High Commander. His jaw clenches and I do not need to ask to know he is thinking of his Tribute, back in his room.

"It might be a trap," he says in a low voice echoing my own concerns.

"That is the most likely scenario," I agree, my voice also low. The bridge is still alive with noise, the warriors scanning for other ships all around us, still following the original ship we sighted, and plotting course alternatives. Before my Tribute I would not have cared, I would have demanded we rush to it and destroy the ship.

Now I worry about the consequences of such a rash act.

"Dawn wants me to try to meet with them. To see what they have to say." The High Commander's voice betrays nothing of his emotions, but I know he would not speak of such a thing unless he were willing to consider it.

I want to scream my rage that he would even think of it, and yet there is now a part of me that understands. We have new hope. We have our Tributes. Do we want to risk them on continuing a war that the Vgotha seem to have tired of? They have been running for so long. Yet can that truly be enough punishment for their crime?

I do not know.

But I do know that I do not want any harm to befall my Tribute.

Yet, I cannot bring myself to speak, to condone such an outrageous suggestion. It betrays everything I believe in.

The High Commander looks away and shakes his head. When he speaks, his voice is raised so that everyone on the bridge can hear.

"We will follow them," he announces. "Track their course. Keep alert. All warriors on duty should remain battle ready. Be wary of surprises, scan all surrounding space as we pursue them."

The bridge swarms with activity.

More quietly, so only I can hear, the High Commander finishes his thought. "I will decide what to do when we know if we can even catch them."

14

———

P areena

I DON'T KNOW how much time passes after Bogdan leaves before I become bored. I nap for a bit, and then pop up and tidy the room. After some hesitation, I pack away the box of memorabilia back into the closet, because looking at it brings up too many uncomfortable questions, for both myself and him. The next time I get a chance to ask him directly to share his past, I'll do that. It's messy to play therapist to a sexual partner, but I can't help my training. And Bogdan is obviously still hurting.

Which makes me wonder—what sort of grieving process do the Tsenturions have?

The door chimes, interrupting my musing. A portion of it shimmers to show the visitor right outside.

"Dawn?" I jump up and go to the door, trying to remember how to get it open. The Vgotha threat can't be that bad if she's out roaming.

Either that or she disobeyed her Master. I don't want her to get in trouble, but I really, really want to talk to someone who isn't a reticent alien warrior.

"Pareena?" comes Dawn's muffled voice. "Are you in there?"

"Yes! I don't know how to get the door open." I search the side for a panel.

"Override," Dawn tells the door and there's a beeping sound. "Tribute Dawn." The door rolls back smoothly, making me frown. I wonder if I could even get out of the room if I wanted to. She grins widely at me, looking triumphant. "I knew asking Gavrill for an override code would be good for something. Although, technically it's supposed to be for my safety."

"I'm so glad you're here," I launch myself at her. Normally I'm not a hugger but the sight of another Earth girl is such a relief. I'm so glad my subconscious conjured up a human companion, even if she isn't a Potterhead.

"I thought you might want company." She squeezes me back.

"Are you allowed to be here?" I have to ask, wondering why I was ordered to stay in my room while she's out wandering the halls. With an override, no less. "You won't get in trouble?"

She shrugs. "Gavrill was already on the bridge when the alert issued. He's ordered me to stay in my rooms during an alert in the past, but he won't mind me coming to visit you. As long as I stay out of any potential danger areas, it's fine."

I invite her to sit on the couch-like piece of furniture on one side of the room. It's built for Bogdan's proportions, so we look a little like kids sitting in our parent's fancy parlor, but at least there's a place to sit other than the bed. "So there's a Vgotha ship?"

"Probably." She doesn't sound as concerned as I would have expected. "For now. They tend to blip in and out of the scans. This isn't the first time one has been spotted and then disappeared, but Gavrill is doing a double shift and I wouldn't be surprised if he keeps everyone on the bridge that long."

Guess I won't be talking to Bogdan any time soon. Although maybe it's better if he doesn't come back and catch Dawn here. And it will give me some time to figure out how I feel about everything he shared with me and the fact that it finally led to sex.

A little lost in thought, I suddenly realize that Dawn is studying me closely, her eyes squinting in puzzlement.

"What is it? Do I have something in my teeth?" I place a hand over my mouth. I hadn't seen anything when I was in the bathroom, but I'd been a little distracted... Oh. I realize what she's looking at.

"Um, no, not your teeth..." Her eyes widen as she realizes what marks she's seeing. "Ohmigosh, Pareena. Are those *seela* marks?" She looks like she is trying not to laugh. I appreciate the effort, but I end up giggling anyway, blushing madly as I do, and then she's giggling and we both end up laughing.

"Is that what those tentacle sucker things are called?" I ask, trying to sound innocent. I feel almost like a teenager again, gossiping with a girlfriend about sex for the first time.

"Yes." We erupt into another spate of giggling and Dawn shakes her head at me, her eyes sparkling. "You wicked thing, you." She sits back with a knowing grin. "I hadn't even thought about that side effect... what was it like?"

"You mean you never..." I wave at my face, still blushing, but my embarrassment is fading. While Dawn is clearly curious, she's not at all judgmental.

"Only a little bit." She shrugs. "He's never let me do more than lick or suck it for a few minutes before he pulls me off. I don't really argue, especially since it feels so good um... elsewhere." Now it's her turn to blush, but I know exactly what she means.

"The... *ah*... tentacles were very nice," I comment primly. Dawn and I exchange looks and burst into giggles like schoolgirls.

"Look at us, using euphemisms like old Victorian women," she chortles.

"Tentacles are just a lot to get used to." I mime wriggling them at her with my fingers, but of course, fingers can't do them justice.

"They're called *seela*," Dawn reminds me. "And then there's the big one, the *prime seela*—"

"Oh, yes," I nod enthusiastically. "Um, that's my favorite."

"Mine too," she says, grinning widely at me. Her eyes get a little bit of a hazy look, like she's not really looking at me anymore. "And if he takes you from behind—"

"Oh, that's genius." My mind reels with possibilities. Bogdan taking me doggy style on the bed, the little suckers tugging on my labia and freshly spanked bottom, the *prime seela* teasing my asshole...

"Mmmhmmm." Dawn nods knowingly, making me blush further. There's a long pause while we're lost in our own daydreams. She reaches over and pats my hand, breaking the moment. "I'm so glad you're here. It's nice to talk about this stuff with someone."

Which reminds me of the burning question of the day: what can I do to help Bogdan?

"Dawn..." I hesitate, not wanting to bring the mood down so quickly, but she's my best source of information. Who knows how long we have before Bogdan comes back. Plus, if she gets into trouble for coming to my room, I might not get this chance again for a while. "Can I ask you something?"

She looks amused. "Sure, ask me anything. Since we started the conversation with the beneficial uses of tentacles during sex, I feel like there's not much that can top that."

"The ice is definitely broken," I agree, smiling a little at her levity. "But this is more serious. Has Gavrill ever..." *Wait, that might be too personal.* I change tack slightly. "Do you think the Tsenturions grieve?"

"What do you mean?" Her eyebrows flash surprise, but she settles back onto the couch as if preparing for a long session, her head already tilted in thought.

"It's just... with the loss of their home planet... there was a lot of personal loss, too. I'm wondering how the warriors handled it. I'm particularly worried about Bogdan."

"Because he's so broody?"

"Yes." I wince internally at talking about his private life without him, but I need perspective. "I think he has a hefty dose of survivor's guilt and possibly other trauma layered on top of that. I'm not sure though, since they're not human, but they do seem to feel things in a similar manner to us. You know them better, though, and I've only really spent time with Bogdan and a little bit with Arkdhem now. What do you think?"

"That makes sense to me." She nods, warming to the subject as she continues. "When you think about it, these guys had their entire species blown up thousands of years ago, but then they were off chasing the enemy and functioning in war mode. I don't think they've ever stopped to grieve. Aren't there five stages or something?"

"You're talking about the five stages of grief postulated by Elisabeth Kübler-Ross," I say, automatically shifting to a more lecturing mode. I'm too well acquainted with it on a personal level to be able to talk about it without either going into professional mode or breaking down as I think about how it personally affected me. "The theory is people move through different stages of grief. Denial, anger, bartering, depression, and acceptance. People can move back and forth through the stages, or even repeat them."

"Right. I saw the Simpsons episode," she jokes, and I laugh.

"Americans tend to think of it as fact, but there's a lack of peer reviewed research to support it and there are other models. Some research has been done that shows humans have natural psychological resilience." I shrug, pretending a nonchalance I don't entirely feel. "On the other hand, I went through most of the stages while I was dying." Dawn's expression turns both sympathetic and concerned, and I continue before she can ask any questions, because I don't really want to talk about that. Especially since I'm becoming more and more convinced that I'm not dreaming. "But that's humans. There's no way of knowing if an alien culture would process loss and bereavement in the same way."

"Maybe you could talk to some of them and find out?" Dawn suggests.

"Like a group session?" I'm joking, because so far, I haven't really been able to interact with any of the Tsenturion warriors other than

Bogdan, and to a much lesser degree Arkdhem, but Dawn nods. Hmm. I have to admit, I'm intrigued by the idea. I'd have to adapt my technique and think of it as information gathering versus treating patients, although I could end up doing both.

"Medik and Arkdhem would do it, for sure. Gavrill's been busy with the Vgotha hunting, but I bet there are a few other officers who'd volunteer. Let's do it." Her eyes light up with enthusiasm for the idea and she stands up, which is when I realize she means right now.

"Now?" My voice rises a little in a kind of panic. I don't want to disappoint my new, and only, friend, but I also don't want to disobey a direct order. My bottom tingles at the thought and I am suddenly very aware of the wall of pain, even though it's behind me and I can't see it. "Bogdan said to stay here."

While I'm enough of a masochist to enjoy some punishments, actually disappointing him or causing him any distress would be worse than anything he could dish out physically. If it wasn't an emergency situation, I might be more willing to be 'naughty.'

Seeing my reaction, Dawn pauses and then grins widely. "Maybe you can't leave, but did he say anything about entertaining visitors?"

My lips quirk in amusement. Dawn is definitely what the BDSM community would define as a brat. She's also very good at getting around orders that she doesn't want to follow. I bet she keeps Gavrill on his toes.

"No." I draw out the word, because he didn't. It probably hadn't occurred to him that he would need to. I already know him well enough to know that he probably won't like it. On the other hand, it's not something that will interrupt this emergency or disappoint him, even though I'm following the letter and not the spirit of his order. "He didn't say I couldn't. I'm okay with exploiting this loophole."

My bottom tingles again as I say this. Some sort of bratting sixth sense warning me that I'm not going to come out of this unscathed.

But who knows... he might not even find out. And I need something to *do*. Being his sex toy is fun, but if this is all real, that's not going to be a fulfilling life for me. From how possessive he seemed in the training area; this might be a case of 'better to ask forgiveness than permission.'

Plus, I don't want to disappoint Dawn.

Yes, I can be a little subby when it comes to my friendships as well. Recognizing the fact doesn't always help me avoid it.

"A woman after my own heart." Dawn is all smiles. Maybe the High Commander's more lenient with her? Or she just likes being naughty. Come to think of it, we never really talked about punishments, I just assumed. I'll have to ask her later. "I'll go gather who I can and be back soon. We should be done before the double shift ends."

"Sounds good." I glance around the room. We can't all sit on the couch. Bogdan seemed to be able to conjure up new furniture with his mind. "Maybe I can figure out how to make furniture…"

"I'll bring chairs," Dawn waves a hand and the door opens. She steps into the hall as I remember something.

"One more thing—" I race to her, stopping just inside the door.
"Yes?"

"Bring back cookies." I grin at her. "A proper group session should include snacks. And cookies make everything better."

Bogdan

THE PLANET LOOMS AHEAD, its curvature blocking out the sight of the Vgotha ship.

"Faster," the High Commander orders, his tone full of frustration. It is not the first time, but it is already too late.

I grit my teeth, slamming my fist against my thigh in anger. We are going to lose them again. When we passed by the planet, all signs of the Vgotha ship had disappeared. The screens were empty, there wasn't even a signature to follow anymore. It was like the Vgotha ship had never existed.

Except that we'd all seen it.

When I find out who they got this new tech from, I am going to hunt them down and kill them with my bare hands.

"Put us in orbit," the High Commander ordered, his voice tight.

There are a myriad of possibilities before us. The Vgotha ship could also be in orbit, using the planet to hide their presence, just far enough ahead of us that we cannot see them, and they do not appear on the scans. It could have disappeared, using that technology they seem to sometimes utilize and sometimes not. Or they could have gone down to the planet itself. There should be some sign though...

Or perhaps not. If they can disappear from our scans in open space, perhaps they have a way to land on a planet without leaving a trail. Since we have never encountered a Vgotha on a planet before, there is no way of knowing. This might not even be new technology.

I peruse the large display of the planet. With its sheltering atmosphere and large expanses of water, the planet looks much like Tsentur. I swallow a knot of pain and longing and turn to the scans. "They could be using their deploying cloaking technology."

"Or they disembarked planet side," the High Commander says. He studies the scans of the planet. "There are plenty of forests for their kind to hide in." The Jabol told us that the Vgotha are very fond of wilderness. They did not have large population centers as we did but preferred to be a part of nature. Even after so many cycles on a spaceship, they could be more adept in such surroundings than any of us.

"But which is the trap?" Kalexston murmurs. A wave of unease ripples through the bridge. No one is comfortable with the new Vgotha tactics, and this one is more confusing than the others.

"Speed up our orbit and scan the planet," the High Commander orders Zakhar before heading to his seat. "All warriors on duty to defense positions."

In the past, a mere sighting of the Vgotha would not mean such measures, but I understand and approve of the High Commander's increased sensitivity to the threat. The last time we intercepted the Vgotha, they infiltrated our defenses, managed to board the command ship, and captured Dawn. It was a cowardly tactic, but the Vgotha have no honor.

I will fight to the bitter end to ensure they do not threaten Pareena. The Vgotha might be good at hiding, but they can't run forever. We will catch them, avenge Tsentur, and secure a safe future for our Tributes. There is no other option.

15

P areena

ABOUT TEN MINUTES after she left, Dawn returns with three warriors, including Arkdhem, and each of them is carrying a chair. Arkdhem is glowering at her, making me worry because the last time I saw him he was nothing but patience and smiles, but she catches my expression and waves her hand.

"Don't worry about the grumpy cinnamon roll, he's just mad because I went out without him."

"I must protect you," Arkdhem says fiercely, with an urgency that reminds me very much of Bogdan. There is an undercurrent to his words that makes it seem as though there is more to what he is saying than mere words. Possibly part of Survivor's Guilt? That would make sense. "I cannot protect you if you wander about without informing me. Do you wish to be captured by the Vgotha *again*?"

Wait, what's this about Dawn being captured? That hadn't come up when we talked before and that seems like a pretty big thing! I look at Dawn, startled, but she isn't paying any attention to me. Instead, she sighs and puts her hand on Arkdhem's shoulder. "I told you I was sorry. I just wanted to get some one on one time with Pareena, human to human."

She smiles winningly at him and Arkdhem scowls, but now that I look more closely, I can see that he's more fearful than angry at her. The expression resembles that of a put-upon older brother, doing his best to look after an unruly sibling that he's been put in charge of. Since I know he's basically her bodyguard, that makes sense.

"Anyway, this is Borodem and this is Corin," Dawn says, smiling at them. They don't smile back exactly but they do look at her fondly. "They are off duty and willing to be part of our experiment."

"Anything for the Tributes," Borodem says seriously, bowing his head slightly. Corin nods, just as serious.

"If there is a battle, we will protect you with our lives."

They aren't as broody and closed off as Bogdan, but they aren't as open as Arkdhem either. On the other hand, Arkdhem is also nodding in agreement at Corin's comment, just as serious as the other two. Maybe being serious is just a Tsenturion trait, even if Arkdhem smiled more when it was just him, Dawn, and me.

"Come on in and sit down," I say, gesturing. As they move past me, I pull Dawn to my side and whisper. "Did you tell them what the 'experiment' is?"

"No," she admits, whispering back. "I wasn't sure they'd come if I did."

Great. Well this should be interesting.

I move over to the bed so the warriors can put down their chairs facing it, giving Dawn and me a comfortable and more informal place to sit. I don't want this to be a formal thing, since I'm going to be asking questions about emotional stuff.

"What would you like us to do?" Arkdhem asks as he sits down. His annoyance at Dawn seems to have dissipated entirely and he is smiling slightly at me, waiting to hear what he's been called there for. I can understand why he and Bogdan grate on each other—they are very different. While Bogdan broods and holds grudges, Arkdhem doesn't seem to let anything keep him down for long.

Before I can speak, Dawn plops down on the bed and smiles sunnily at him. "Well, Pareena and I were hoping you could tell us about Tsentur. We're trying to be the best Tributes we can be, but sometimes our mates aren't always big on talking, you know."

She winks and Arkdhem shakes his head, sighing with a kind of resignation. Both Borodem and Corin shift uncomfortably.

"What about Tsentur do you want to know?" Corin asks, his voice deep and slow.

"Bogdan told me about the Mating Festival," I say, because that's the main thing I know about and that will hopefully lead in the direction I'd like to go in. All three warriors flinch. It's a tiny movement, but when done in unison it's very noticeable. I hurry on. "Were any of you preparing for the festival as well? Or did you have more years to serve as warriors?"

It does not surprise me that Arkdhem is the first to answer. Both Borodem and Corin look like they're already regretting agreeing to be a part of this, but Arkdhem... there's something about him. I do believe he truly cares for Dawn in a brotherly fashion, but there's something more. Like he's also motivated by something else, as if he's trying to impress both Dawn and me. I'm absolutely willing to use that to my advantage right now though.

"I had more cycles aboard the fleet to serve," he says, before leaning forward and speaking much more earnestly than Bogdan ever has. Again, I am struck with the impression of a young man, eager to impress a woman. But is that actually how the mannerisms translate between species? That is the unknown. "Now, though, all of us have served well beyond that and are ready for mates of our own."

He smiles widely at me. Corin and Borodem both nod. They aren't as eager and earnest as Arkdhem, but the longing in their expressions echoes his, even without the smile. There is a desperation there that shouldn't surprise me, but for some reason I hadn't expected it. Perhaps because Bogdan has been so standoffish from the beginning.

It's possible these three are more representative of the rest of the warriors though, since Dawn told me Bogdan was the only one outspoken against the Tribute program. I really wish I had something to write down notes on, but I hadn't been expecting to do this today. I'll just have to make an effort to remember everything that I can and make notes later.

I turn my attention to Borodem, smiling as warmly as I can and hoping he'll be receptive even if he's not as eager to share as Arkdhem is. "And what about you?"

Bogdan

WHEN I AM DISMISSED from the bridge, I find myself hurrying back to my room, much more eager than I normally would be. In the past, it would not have been uncommon for me to continue to work long past my shift. Now, all I want is to return to my Tribute.

I step out of the lift, grateful the hall to the officer's quarters is empty. As I approach my room, I retract my helmet. I am tired. I want to return to my quarters, remove my armor and spend time with my Pareena. Seeing her will be a balm on an otherwise wasted cycle. We spent every moment scanning for the Vgotha and found nothing. It is possible they have left the quadrant. Either that or they are on the planet. The only thing we are sure of is that they are not in orbit around it.

A sobering thought.

The planet itself is highly interesting. Dense forests and no discernible civilization.

We have a sample from the escape pod that returned Dawn to us. It was organic based—similar to plant matter. Perhaps organic matter from a planet such as this. Of course, that type of ship will not be not easy to find on a lush tropical planet, such as the one we are currently orbiting. Even if this planet is not the source of their new technology, it makes a good hiding spot for them.

If they are there.

The uncertainty is maddening.

My steps quicken as I approach my room. Time with my Tribute will ease me. I sent word earlier to Medik, asking him to bring her a meal and tell her to rest. I am not so tired that I cannot make good use of my pleasure trophy before resting. She seemed to enjoy bathing me. Perhaps we will start with that...

My door slides open, but instead of the quiet of my quarters and the gentle presence of my lovely Tribute, I am greeted by a shocking sight: a group of Tsenturion warriors inside my room, seated in a circle, with my Tribute.

I halt abruptly. My first thought is that I have somehow lost my way and come to the wrong room, but no, a second inspection informs me I have entered my quarters. My quarters, which are full of other warriors and two Tributes. The Tributes are seated on my sleeping platform. Tribute Dawn sits cross legged with her head propped on her hands while my Pareena sits on the edge, leaning forward. The rest of the warriors are facing her. None of them seem to have even noticed my arrival.

The sound of a low keening, like the dying sounds of a *kurdzu,* the four-legged beast that we hunted on planet Tsentur, fills my ears. It's coming from one of the warriors.

"And how does that make you feel?" My Tribute leans forward and places her hand on the arm of the warrior closest to her. I cannot see his face. Across from him, another warrior sobs, his suit flashing with grief and pain. It takes me a moment to recognize Borodem, a normally stoic warrior.

Next to him, Corin hunches in his chair with a sorrowful expression, his armor dark grey with misery. Sitting slightly separated from them is Medik, a platter of food resting on a table in front of him, as he observes my Tribute. Apparently when he brought my Tribute her food, he did not leave.

I grit my teeth at the invasion of my quarters, the open grief on display grating at my already tired senses, and the closeness of other warriors to my Tribute.

"What is the meaning of this?" I half growl, half shout.

Dawn shoots up like a warrior caught sleeping on shift, eyes wide and startled, full of guilt and a touch of fear. As well she should be. When the High Commander discovers she has wandered from his quarters, she will not be able to sit easily for a cycle. Corin winces and puts a hand on Borodem's shoulder. Together they rise and salute me, Borodem choking back his grief. I look away from him, the display of such open emotion making me extremely uncomfortable.

My eyes fall on my Tribute and my entire body stiffens with fury when I see that the warrior she is talking to, the warrior whose hand she is holding, is Arkdhem's. Touching *any* other warrior would be bad enough. That it is him, after I specifically forbade her to go anywhere near him, is enough for my suit to flash with red threads of possessive fury.

I step toward them. *"Get away from my Tribute."*

To her credit, my Pareena does not flinch, although she does jolt, as if just now realizing that she's touching Arkdhem. Immediately her hand falls away from his. She straightens but remains seated, gazing at me steadily with her dark eyes. Arkdhem steps in front of her, as if shielding her from me, and I nearly launch myself at him. I would have, if not for Medik.

"Ah, Bogdan, is your shift over already? My, my, the cycles spin faster and faster the older I get." Medik rises and putters over to the food, beginning to clean it up. A defusing tactic, as it puts him directly between me and Arkdhem. Now I cannot attack him as I would like. I could still behead him in three moves.

"I will ask again," I bark. "What is the meaning of this?"

"We're having a group therapy session," My Tribute answers steadily. She has not looked away from me, not once, even though she is having to look at me over Arkdhem's shoulder. A feat that would be impossible were she not on my sleeping platform.

"What is that?" I demand to know. I ask the question of her, but it is Medik who answers. Corin and Borodem are wisely silent, obviously realizing how close I am to violence. Surprisingly, Arkdhem is too, but his gaze is insolent, and I think if Medik had not stepped between us, we might have fought right here and now.

"A kind of experiment," Medik says. He extends a plate of brown discs in my direction. They smell good, although I do not know what they are. "Cookie?"

"No," I snap out. I do not know what a cookie is, but I do not want it.

I want my room to be empty other than my Tribute and me, I want some rest, and I want to know what the Vgotha are doing. I do not have the patience for any of this.

"We can wrap up," Tribute Dawn says quickly. "I think we went long enough for the first time."

My Pareena nods, still watching me.

"Why were you touching him?" I grit out. Arkdhem smiles widely at me and I nearly snarl. *I will cut that smile off his face if he is not careful.*

"A normal human gesture, meant to comfort," she explains smoothly. Arkdhem meets my gaze, his smile turning to a smirk, his own suit shimmering smugly.

I will paint the walls with his blood.

My Tribute walks towards me, skirting around him, her eyes fixed on mine. They are soft, like her voice as she tries to soothe me. "I missed you. This was only meant to kill time until you were free. And, as Medik said, it's an experiment."

"An experiment?" I test the word.

"Yes. I was wondering whether Tsenturions had a grieving process. These warriors were kind enough to share."

I remember that we're not alone in the room, and glare at everyone.

"But we're done now," my Tribute soothes. "So maybe you don't need this?" She motions to my right arm and I realize my armor has produced a long, double-edged blade in anticipation for battle.

"Fine," I grunt and let it melt back into my suit before drawing my Pareena close. To my relief, she tucks herself against my side and wraps her arms around my waist. I meet Arkdhem's gaze. He's watching my Tribute closely. When he notices my challenging look, he tilts his head and raises his brows.

I will blood you, my look says.

You will try, he tells me with his hard gaze.

"Well, that was fun," Medik finishes fussing over the food. "But I better get back to the med bay." He hoists the half full platter. "My patients will enjoy these," he announces to no one.

"Our apologies for the intrusion," Corin says with a salute. "We meant only to indulge the Tributes' request."

I grunt and jerk my head toward the door in dismissal.

Corin and Borodem move past me. Their armor is still tinged with grief, but they bow their heads to my Tribute as they go, with something like affection in their expressions.

Medik thanks the Tributes and smiles at me as he leaves. I let him go even though I am angry he did not inform me of the meeting in my quarters as soon as he discovered it. There is no sense in trying to chastise him. As the elder on board, and the best physician despite training other warriors to one day take his place, Medik does as Medik pleases. Even the High Commander cannot gainsay him when he decides on something.

But I can still kill Arkdhem. It would be most satisfying. Then I would never have to see his stupid smirk again.

Pareena plasters a hand against my chest and I realize I'm growling.

"I guess I better go too," Tribute Dawn says cheerfully, sidling toward the door. "Gavrill will probably be wondering where I am."

Both Arkdhem and I look at her and then each other. He nods and I shake my head. Of course, he informed the High Commander where Dawn was. He is charged with her safety. Why she would think anything different is a mystery. Arkdhem might be a piece of *kurdzu* dung but he knows his duty.

That will not save him if he keeps behaving dishonorably with my Tribute. My gaze hardens again and his does as well, our brief moment of unity over as quickly as it began. The threat of violence hangs in the air again, and this time Medik is not there to relieve it.

But my Pareena slides her hand over my lower belly, squeezing me tighter. "I missed you," she says again, gazing up at me.

And I decide Arkdhem will live another cycle. If only to cover the bridge while I spend time with my Tribute. Something which I am very eager to do, although my plans for our activities have changed slightly due to her 'experiment.'

"Out," I order just as the doors to my quarters hiss open. The High Commander stands just outside.

~

PAREENA

The dark expression on the High Commander's face makes me cuddle up closer to Bogdan. I'm pretty sure I'm in trouble, but he's still less scary than the High Commander.

"You were supposed to remain in your quarters." The glower he levels at all of us becomes more intense when it finally lands on her.

Undeterred, Dawn runs to him, jumping up to fling her arms around him and kissing him on the mouth. The dark colors of his suit shift and it glitters, like stars on a clear night. The effect is beautiful. Even though he is clearly unhappy with her disobedience, he holds her against him and kisses her back.

Out of the corner of my eye, I see Arkdhem go very still, and I turn my head slightly to see what's wrong. His suit doesn't give me any clues, but I can see the longing, the envy, on his face, his expression momentarily unguarded.

As if sensing that my attention has strayed, Bogdan's fingers slide into my hair and he turns my head to face him. Arkdhem's expression becomes tinged with anger, but then I can't see him anymore because Bogdan is kissing me. Deeply. Possessively. I realize that he is claiming me in front of Arkdhem with the kiss.

Wanting to do my best to soothe the savage beast—and maybe get myself out of some of the trouble I'm in—I kiss him back just as passionately. I press myself against him, sinking into the kiss, wanting him to know there is no reason to be possessive. There is no reason to doubt that I want anyone but him.

I hear the door slide and I pull away, turning my head. I catch a glimpse of Arkdhem's back before the door closes again.

There is a part of me that feels a little guilty over the blatant display between Bogdan and me. From talking with the three Tsenturion warriors, I now know how much each of them long for a Tribute of their own, for a family. I also understand Dawn's mixed feelings on the subject. If this is real, then I won't be the last woman abducted from her home. On the other hand, if the women are dying like I was, and they are given a choice...

Yet, is it really an informed choice? I'm still questioning whether or not this is even real, because the whole idea is so fantastical. Who could really believe that they're signing up to be an alien's mate?

"Did your shift go well?" Dawn asks Gavrill, her voice innocent.

I lean into Bogdan as the alien leader growls under his breath. He still looks displeased with her.

"Did you find the Vgotha?" I ask, hoping to distract both of the warriors. If Gavrill punishes Dawn the way Bogdan punishes me, I have a feeling we're both going to be sore soon. Might as well try to put that moment off for as long as possible. Plus, I'm curious.

"We are still searching," Bogdan says, his voice tight. "They have disappeared again. Possibly on planet, possibly deeper into space."

"Do not worry," Gavrill says, almost right on top of Bogdan. His arms tighten around Dawn even as his expression darkens even more. "They will not take you again."

I feel Bogdan's arms pulling me in even closer to him, as if he can't bear the thought of me being taken. I'm not too fond of the idea either.

"I still want to know more about that," I say, feeling a little put out that I'm the only one who doesn't know what happened. The amount of things Dawn has left out of our conversations is a little shocking. Then again, I suppose it's not exactly easy to know what to prioritize when you've been abducted by aliens and a new friend shows up. We both put alien peen pretty high on the list, but I would think a kidnapping by and escape from the enemy should be up there too.

Dawn just rolls her eyes. "I'm not that worried," she says, shaking her head. "I told you, Tor wasn't that bad. Just super sexist and a little bit of a jerk." She looks at me. "Obviously I escaped. Their ship even helped me."

"It helped you?" How... Why... What? That made no sense to me.

"It was a trick," Bogdan says immediately, his voice tight with anger.

"Some trick, sending me back unharmed and without getting what they wanted," Dawn mutters, rolling her eyes at him. I immediately get the sense that this is an argument they've had more than once. As much as I want to soothe my warrior, I have to admit, I'm inclined to agree with Dawn. She tilts her head at Gavrill. "So, what's this about a planet?"

The two warriors exchange glances and then Gavrill nods. Letting Dawn slide down the front of his body, he ushers her over to a screen on the wall, Bogdan and I following.

Bogdan makes a gesture at the console, and a giant hologram of a planet appears. With all the blue and green and white wispy clouds, for a moment I think its Earth... but then I blink and realize that the land masses are wrong. But it's so close that it hurts.

"They approached this planet and then disappeared behind it," Gavrill says. "We are uncertain if they continued on, using the planet to mask their flight, or if they landed."

"Oh, how beautiful!" Dawn exclaims, the longing clear in her voice. I feel that same longing, deep in my bones. "Can we visit?"

Excitement threads through me at her question and I look up at Bogdan. The expression on his face is not encouraging.

16

———————

B^{ogdan}

Visit? Both Tributes on the same planet where Vgotha might be? The very thought makes me want to stab something. My chest tightens and I can feel something like a scream bubbling up inside of me.

"What? No!" The High Commander barks out the words, thankfully able to speak, unlike myself. "It is not safe."

"But if you scan the planet for Vgotha and they're not there... wouldn't it be safe for us to visit?" Tribute Dawn asks, pouting. I recognize the look she gives him. It is the one she often gets on her face right before he gives in to whatever insane idea she's come up with.

"We have more scans to run. Many more," I say quickly, before he can be swayed by her big, pleading eyes. I have to avoid my own Tribute's gaze as well.

Before, I had thought the High Commander had grown soft with how often he allows his Tribute to do as she pleases, but now I understand better. They are not Tsenturions, they have their own culture and way of doing things. Sometimes they must bow to our way but sometimes, every so often, we should bend to theirs as well. Because we want them to smile and be happy.

"Yes," agrees the Commander immediately. "And they will take a long time."

My Tribute reaches up to cup my face in her hands, so that I can no longer look away from her wide, dark, pleading eyes.

"Please?" she asks. The hopefulness in her voice, the longing, is almost more than I can bear.

As if sensing weakness, Tribute Dawn chimes in. "Please? If you don't find any Vgotha on it? Just for an hour, I miss being on a planet so much... please, Gavrill, I rarely ask for anything..."

The sincerity in her voice is too much for the High Commander to bear. I know it as soon as I hear her plea. She is also correct that she rarely asks for anything. Which is why she so often receives what-ever she asks for.

Drakk.

"Please, Master," my Tribute whispers, pressing herself against me. "I'll do anything you want."

I do my best to harden myself against her pleas. "You will do whatever I want anyway."

A little smile curves her lips. "That's true, but wouldn't you like to see what I could offer that you don't know to ask for?" She licks her lips, reminding me that she has already shown me something new. The little marks my *seela* left on her cheeks are already faded. The idea intrigues me.

But...

"I will not risk your safety for pleasure," I say roughly.

"But if the Vgotha aren't there, then we'll be safe," Tribute Dawn says, still pleading. "And we won't go without you. You're great warriors, strong enough to protect two tiny females."

The High Commander sighs. Even though he sees through his Tribute's tactics, he is not immune to them. "I will think on it." Then his gaze sharpens, and he picks his Tribute up, hefting her over his shoulder as she squeals. "Excuse me, Bogdan. Tribute Pareena. My Tribute and I need to have a discussion about obeying orders, which she has already delayed for long enough."

"Understood," I say, putting my hand on the back of my Tribute's neck. "I believe I will be having a similar discussion with my own Tribute right now."

~

Pareena

THE FIRM HOLD of Bogdan's fingers on my neck is somehow both comforting and threatening. Watching Gavrill cart Dawn off over his shoulder like a sack of potatoes, and her just hanging there rather than talking back, convinces me that she's probably about to get her butt blistered too. And that, like me, she doesn't want to make her punishment any worse than it's already going to be because she doesn't even put up a token protest.

Although she does raise her head and wave to me as they exit, a rueful, resigned, and yet somehow excited expression on her face.

I know exactly how she feels.

I *know* what's coming. I *know* I'm in trouble. I *know* the Wall of Pain is in my future. But I'm not scared. At least, that's not my only emotion. I am a little scared, a little anxious, but I'm also turned on. Bogdan's finger is stroking the pulse on my throat and my nipples harden as he turns to me, looming over me, looking down at me.

It's strange how he can make me feel so safe and at the same time, so vulnerable.

"What did I tell you about Arkdhem?" It sounds less like a question and more like a whispered threat, his lips close to my ear, his body moving to press into me from behind. Goosebumps crawl over my skin and my bottom tingles in anticipation of punishment.

"I—" Before I can say a second word, the Bride Trainer comes to life between my legs, humming against my clit and pushing against my anus. I groan as the nanotech pushes into me like a plug, thick and punishing with how fast it stretches the tight ring of my sphincter. My knees tremble and I cry out at the sudden invasion, the shocking fullness... all while my pussy throbs emptily.

Using his hold on my neck to spin me around, Bogdan puts his forehead against mine. His eyes seethe with emotion that he somehow manages to keep from showing in his armor. Possessive anger. Hot jealousy.

I shouldn't have tried to comfort Arkdhem physically.

It had just felt so natural in the moment. He'd been upset, talking about his longing for a Tribute, for a family, and I had responded in a wholly human, if not entirely professional way. In that moment, I hadn't been thinking about Bogdan's orders or who Arkdhem was, I'd just reacted.

"I'm sorry, Master," I say simply, rather than trying to make an excuse. "It will not happen again."

I messed up and I know it.

Something flashes in Bogdan's eyes.

"I am pleased to hear you understand your transgression, my Tribute." His voice remains hard, grating. "That will not be enough to save you from punishment though."

To be honest, I hadn't really expected it would be.

~

Bogdan

THE SUBMISSIVE ACCEPTANCE I see in my Tribute's expression startles me. Tribute Dawn fights against the High Commander's dominance constantly and part of me expects my Tribute to do so as well. But she not only understands what she did wrong, she is willing to accept my discipline.

"I accept my punishment, Master," she says, her pupils dilating, her voice calm. There is a sense of serenity to her, one that I am coming to recognize.

My Tribute enjoys my dominance over her. She wants to submit. Unlike Tribute Dawn, who would aggravate me to death with her constant rebellion, my Pareena enjoys being taken in hand. No wonder the Jabol felt we would be well matched. She is perfect for me, in every way.

The calm that washes over me matches hers, my anger sliding away. I understand that it is me she desires, me she wants to submit to, not Arkdhem. I will still punish her for disobeying an order, but I am no longer choking on possessive fury.

My cock aches, my *seela* beginning to writhe in anticipation. Dropping my gaze to her pouty lips, I decide to work off the edge of my lust before punishing her. It will leave me more clear-minded and keep me from rushing through the process just to relieve myself.

"On your knees, my Pareena," I order.

I feel the responding heat of her arousal just before she obeys, her nanotech informing me that her bottom has clenched around the belt invading her there. Yes, I will make that part of her discipline as well. I remember what the manuals said about 'naughty girl sex' and my Tribute has been very naughty indeed.

Reaching down, I knock the straps of her gown away from her shoulders, baring her beautiful breasts to me. Hefting one in my hand, I pinch the nipple tightly, making her moan as she stares up at me. The lust in her eyes is echoed in my body.

My armor retracts and my cock undulates before her, my *seela* reaching for her, eager to latch onto her skin and leave their marks. I will ensure that no warrior will be able to look at what is mine without seeing the clear signs of my possession of her.

"Take me in your mouth." I cannot disguise the eagerness in my voice for this strange, human custom.

The touch of her tongue on my cock is just as heavenly as before, the warm suction igniting a storm of pleasure inside of me. Seeing her on her knees before me, one hand on her breast, the other entwined in her hair, my cock sliding between her lips while my *seela* pull at her skin, is highly arousing. Because of her belt, I know that I am not the only one so affected.

Still, this is supposed to be punishment. I pinch her nipple harder, twisting it slightly, while directing the belt to slide up her front, taking the place of my fingers. She whimpers, first at my fingers, and then at the way I have the belt tighten around her budded nipples. Now both of my hands are free to play with her hair while I use the belt to torment her body.

Thickening the portion of the belt filling her ass, I groan at the sensation of her crying out around my cock, pushing it in deeper until I hit the back of her throat. She rocks slightly, her hands coming up to press against my thighs and steady herself, but she does not protest or try to pull away. If anything, she sucks me harder, intent on pleasing me. This is how a human Tribute apologizes to her Master.

My cock stiffens, my need pounding through me. There is no reason to withhold my ecstasy and I climax with a loud cry, my fingers curving over the back of her head as I force her mouth down on my length. She submits willingly, her tongue and throat muscles working to pull every drop of my seed from my body.

I shudder and relax, panting slightly from the exertion of passion. When I open my eyes and look down at her, her skin is flushed, her eyes glazed with her own pleasure, and her cheeks are again speckled with the dark marks of my *seela*.

"Good girl," I say, caressing her head. She beams up at me, although her expression falters at my next words. "Now go bend over the bed. I must decide what I am going to punish you with."

~

Pareena

WAITING for Bogdan to pick out an implement of torture is a torment in and of itself. As if my needy arousal wasn't punishment enough. Or the thick plug now shoved up my ass. Or the tight pinch on my nipples. I hadn't even known the belt could *do* that. The only difference between the belt and nipple clamps is that when I bend over the bed, my upper body resting on the mattress, the pressure does not increase the pinch.

I'm almost a little sad about that, because right now my needy pussy is throbbing so forcefully that any distraction from it seems welcome. How long I'll feel that way once my punishment actually gets started, I have no idea.

"I think you enjoyed the *kudzu* belt too much last time," Bogdan muses aloud, walking in front of the Wall of Pain and inspecting his options. I can see him out of the corner of my eye and my bottom immediately clenches at his words. Which makes me pant, because my muscles are already almost painfully stretched around the tech invading me.

Talk about an alien probe.

I giggle.

Bogdan whips around, his eyes narrowing at me and amusement flees.

"I'm sorry," I immediately say, babbling out the words. "I really am taking this seriously, I promise, I'm just nervous. Or something." Because sometimes my sense of humor has extremely unfortunate timing.

Looking away from me, he picks up not one but *two* implements of discipline. They look like a paddle and a cane.

Ouch.

Yup, all amusement successfully chased away, to be replaced by quickly growing anxiousness.

He puts the cane looking thing down on the bed in front of me. I can see that it's not made of wood, but I'm not exactly sure what material it's made out of. Something shiny.

"What did I tell you about Arkdhem?" Bogdan asks, his voice deep and growly. Even though I'm pretty sure I assuaged any insecurities he has about the other warrior, I can still hear the possessiveness in his tone.

"To stay away from him."

And instead, I'd forgotten to ask Dawn *not* to bring her bodyguard back with her and then I'd let him sit closest to me out of all of the warriors during the session, and *then* I'd touched him. All in Bogdan's room. After being given a direct order. While I've never been the type to let someone else dictate my relationships, Bogdan had literally only told me to stay away from *one* warrior. Not a friend, just an acquaintance. If nothing else, out of respect, I should have at least tried to adhere to his wishes.

I'd gotten so caught up in what I was doing. I was distracted by thinking that this all might actually be real. Trying to figure out how aliens would deal with grief, I had let it slip my mind.

Truthfully, I also hadn't realized how long we'd be there talking.

I'd thought I wouldn't get caught.

Maybe Dawn isn't the only one who is a bit of a brat.

But I don't have much more time to think about it, because there's a whooshing sound, followed by a loud *thwack!* and I cry out as both cheeks of my ass sting with sudden flames.

17

P areena

Whatever that paddle is made out of, it *hurts*.

I start to jerk upright, an instinctive reaction to the painful blow that just landed across my entire ass, but a strong hand immediately pushes me back down, right in between my shoulder blades, and I'm pinned to the bed.

THWACK!

"Ow! I'm sorry!"

THWACK!

"I'm sorry, Master!"

THWACK!

It doesn't matter what I say, Bogdan paddles my bottom with measured, implacable strokes that have tears already sliding down my cheeks. I writhe on the bed, thankful that my movements don't affect how tightly the belt pinches my nipples. Thankful that the paddle doesn't do anything to push the belt deeper into my ass.

I'd wanted a distraction from the aching need in my pussy, but I'd been wrong. I'd take the needy pussy throbbing back now, because the way my bottom is now painfully throbbing is so much worse. Then I feel the plug in my ass come to life.

Oh fuck.

It's vibrating. So close to where I need it to. Too far to give me any satisfaction.

THWACK!

The pleasurable vibrations do nothing to make the paddle less painful upon initial impact and I cry out. Warmth spreads through my lower body, the licking burn from the spanking but also the needy flare of my arousal coming back online as the belt hums away. My nipples prickle, the pinch loosening and then tightening again, rhythmically tugging, like the nanotech is sucking on them.

THWACK!

My body tightens, my bottom clenching. Moaning, I dig my fingers into the softness of the bed. It feels like every sensitive part of me is throbbing, aching from the stimulation. The sensations are piling up until I can't tell which are pleasure and which are pain and I can barely breathe from the assault on my senses.

Bogdan

MY PAREENA'S pussy is swollen and shiny with her arousal even as she cries out in pain from her punishment. The *bokarr* swings easily in my hand, its length crossing her entire bottom, nearly wide enough to cover her cheeks completely. Her training belt is a thin strand bisecting her now dark red mounds. It parts into two strands to frame her pussy while staying well away from the sensitive inner folds and swollen clit.

The nanotech filling her ass hums against her clenching muscles, readying her for the final part of her punishment.

Putting down the paddle, I rest one hand on a swollen cheek, feeling the heat flare from her chastised skin. Despite my recent orgasm, my cock is already swelling again, reacting to her cries and her arousal. I shift my stance slightly and several of my *seela* reach out to stroke her hot flesh, sending a shiver up her spine at the light touch. I find it most pleasing as well. My *seela* crave contact with her and my cock swells even more, ready to impale her.

But her punishment is not yet complete.

She tenses when I pick up the *talin*. It is long and mostly stiff with just a little bit of bend, perfect for raising painful welts. I will be very careful with it for this first punishment though. From the manuals, I know the humans have something similar, but I do not know *how* similar.

So, I will be gentle.

"Three strokes with the *talin*," I tell my Tribute, picking it up from the bed. I'd deliberately placed it where she would be able to see it while I'd spanked her with the *bokarr*. The manuals had indicated that such a tactic would increase her apprehension and regret for misbehaving. I can feel her anxiety spike when I pick it up, so it seems to be working. "Then we will have the naughty girl sex."

Pareena

THE NAUGHTY GIRL SEX.

If I'd had any doubts as to what he meant, the way the plug pulses inside of me, making it feel even thicker, makes it very clear. My pussy quivers in response. 'Naughty girl sex' makes me hot. Not that I'm going to admit that to Bogdan when he clearly thinks it's part of my punishment.

But first I have to get through the cane. Because that's what the *talin* is and I know it.

Bogdan's hand drifts down from my shoulder blades to just above my ass, which is already burning fiery hot from the paddle. My cheeks feel swollen, like the skin is stretched too tightly, and I know this is going to hurt.

Snap!

A thin line of fiery agony blazes across the center of my ass and I scream into the soft padding of the mattress.

Snap!

Snap!

Two more strokes pop against my ass, just as hard and just as fast. I sob out the strikes, gasping for air as the initial bite fades and mutes, turning into a pulsing—but ultimately bearable—pain.

Then something buzzes against my clit and I moan as my poor, confused body comes alight with erotic yearning. I feel a little bit like a yo-yo, bouncing back and forth between extremes.

"Good girl," Bogdan croons and I shiver as I feel the belt sliding away from my ass, leaving me emptier and needier than ever. The buzzing on my nipples and clit intensifies. It doesn't make the pain go away, but it does distract. Ameliorates. Makes it feel almost good.

Something hot and hard and slick presses against my anus. I whimper as it presses forward. The ways in which Tsenturion cocks differ from human cocks has never been so starkly apparent. The tip is thinner and more pointed than a human's, but it widens a lot faster, and now it's nosing its way into my tightest hole, making me feel ashamed and aroused at the same time.

Naughty girl sex.

Because *good* girls don't do anal.

Good girls don't like it when someone shoves a cock up their ass.

But *naughty girls* get it anyway.

And *really* naughty girls, like me, get off on it.

The stretch of my sphincter to accommodate Bogdan's broad head stings and burns in a completely different way from how the flesh of my bottom does. I moan, pressing my forehead against the mattress, panting for breath as he pushes deeper. I can feel all the strange bumps and ridges along the length of his cock rubbing against my sensitive nerves.

The fullness is as disconcerting as the way his cock moves inside of me. Then his *seela* writhe over the reddened, sensitized flesh of my bottom and I cry out at the touch. It hurts... it feels good... and he's still sliding deeper into my ass.

~

Bogdan

My Tribute's second entrance is even tighter, hotter, than her pussy. I can feel her muscles clenching around me, making my movements harder. Thankfully the oil I slicked over my cock before I began to push it inside of her helps, otherwise I think this might be a painful endeavor for both of us.

Although it is somewhat painful for her anyway. Even if I hadn't just reddened and striped her ass, it would be uncomfortable.

Yet, she is taking it, without protest, for me.

The power I have over her does not feel half as sweet as her willing submission to me. It flavors my physical pleasure and I can feel the connection between us growing. The more she takes for me, the more I give to her, the more I can *feel* her.

Feel her pain, her pleasure, the sheer joy she takes in doing something that gives me pleasure. I could never have imagined that taking a Tribute, taking a mate, could feel like *this*. Would never have thought that a punishment would lead to such closeness, such intimacy.

I thought she would make me weak, but instead she makes me feel stronger than ever.

Then my cock bottoms out in her clenching ass, the heat of her cheeks searing my groin and *seela*, and any introspective thoughts are lost in the pure pleasure of being buried so deeply inside of her alternate hole. I grip her hips, groaning and shuddering at the way her entrance grips the base of my cock, so tight that without the oils on my shaft, I do not think I would be able to move.

I hear her gasp when I begin to pull out, her muscles moving over my length, my cock undulating inside of her, stroking the sensitive walls of her channel. My *seela* slap at her already reddened skin, exploring the welts the *talin* left, and I can feel the way her pain and pleasure intermingle, almost as though the sensations are my own. The high it gives me is intense and I find my own muscles tensing as I thrust back into her and begin to ride her hard. The way her body contracts around me, squeezing me so tightly, is exquisite.

I understand why the manuals made such a big deal out of this act now. Tsenturions fuck to breed—and for pleasure, but we know that breeding is always a part of it. It would never occur to a Tsenturion female to use her mouth. Tsenturions do not have a second opening, as our digestive systems are different from a human. This second hole, right beside her first, to be used purely for her mate and master's pleasure... It fascinates me. My Pareena has already made good use of her mouth and now she has submitted this entrance to me as well.

Even though she has been naughty, I reward her for her submission now, increasing the pleasurable buzzing on her clit and moving some of the belt to cover and then slide into her pussy. To my surprise, I can feel the tech as it pushes into her, almost as though it's rubbing along the underside of my cock as well.

Groaning, I dig my fingers into her hips and pump harder, faster, increasing the vibrations of the tech filling her pussy at the same time. Both of us will be able to enjoy it and I smile at her gasping cry of shock and desire.

~

Pareena

OH FUCK, *oh fuck, oh fuck...*

It feels like my entire body is curling in, the way my toes curl during a really good kiss, because of the chaotic mix of agony and ecstasy rioting through me.

Not just me. Through Bogdan too. I can feel his rising rapture, the way his possessiveness has become joyful rather than angry, the hot bliss he feels as he thrusts into my ass.

The movements of his cock inside of me are driving me wild and every full thrust makes me burn with the stretch. His cock is widest at the base and so my muscles are not able to fully adjust, but are forced open again and again and again... The stinging slaps of his *seela* are like little pinpricks of pain, somehow making the pleasure feel even more pleasurable.

I've had anal sex before, but I never felt this overwhelmed... this submissive. Now I understand why some people say that sex can feel like being *claimed*. That's exactly how I feel right now. Like I will never be able to completely separate myself from him again. He's too deep inside of me, his emotions and pleasure too intricately intersected with mine now.

With my pussy being filled, the vibrations humming along my nerves, it's like every inch of me is being stimulated. I am so full, so needy, and so completely caught up in an erotic haze of lust and pain that I can barely see straight. Tears are still filling my eyes, not from the spanking or from disappointing Bogdan, but because I am so overwhelmed by the sensations that my body is overloading.

"Please," I beg. "Please, Bogdan... Master... please, I need to come..."

He groans and thrusts hard, making me whimper at the jolt of painful pleasure that stabs through me. I can feel his cock stiffening even more inside of me, the way it does when he's close to his own climax.

"Come for me," he orders, and the tech around my nipples and clit contract painfully, vibrating madly, as my pussy is filled and emptied, like a cock thrusting in there as well, rather than just filling it.

I scream at the double assault, my orgasm rolling over me like a tsunami. My entire body feels like it shatters apart in erotic euphoria. When his *seela* latch onto my punished skin, I no longer even have the air to breathe, much less cry out. I can feel his seed pumping into me, a wet wash of heat inside of me, as my body finally gives out and darkness spirals.

18

B^{ogdan}

CURLING around my Pareena's sleeping form, I trace my fingers down her soft skin. Her bottom is still darker than the rest of her skin, but the color is already more muted than it was earlier, and her sweet curves are snugged against my groin. My *seela* gently stroke the raised welts the *talin* imprinted on her skin. Those should remain longer than the color the *bokarr* left.

I was not easy on her, but it seems the pleasure affected her more deeply than the pain.

I am not sure that Naughty Girl Sex is as much a deterrent as the manuals suggested it would be. Perhaps that is my fault though. I wanted her to enjoy it. Besides, she had already been punished enough.

I am more in tune with her emotions than before. It did not escape my notice that she was more upset by disappointing me than she had been being punished by me. Not that she enjoyed the bokarr or the talin, at least, not on their own, but she felt the worst about how she made me feel.

And I am not immune to being touched by her concern.

I feel her stirring against me.

When I first realized she had fallen unconscious I had panicked, thinking I had overdone her discipline, but a quick communication with Medik had assuaged my fears. Despite being altered by the Jabol to be healthier, stronger, and longer lived, our Tributes are still prone to some human weakness. Apparently Tribute Dawn has suffered the same, on occasion, when over-whelmed.

I kiss the back of my Pareena's neck, caressing her stomach as she wakes. She makes a happy sound in the back of her throat and then winces as one of my *seela* slides along the welt across the center of her bottom. I can feel that she is still sore, but the pain is not great.

"Ouch..." she mutters before turning her head slightly to look at me over her shoulder. Her dark eyes meet mine, still sleepy.

"Have you learned your lesson, my Pareena?" I ask her, keeping my voice stern. She blushes at my words and then groans, moving her hand back to curve her fingers over her bottom, wincing at her own touch. Why she would want to cause herself further discomfort I do not know, but I do not stop her.

"Ten points to Slytherin," she says under her breath.

I frown. "What is Slytherin? What points?"

The look she bestows upon me now is almost sad. "We're going to have to get you all some more reading materials other than alien abduction romances. Although, since you don't have Urban Dictionary, that still won't explain everything."

Ah. She is trying to distract me. I narrow my eyes at her as I slide my hand over her bottom and cup it just hard enough to apply some real pressure on her welts and she gasps.

"Perhaps your punishment was not as effective as I'd hoped," I say thoughtfully, but there is no real menace in my tone. Although I do not understand everything she says, I realize that her attempts at distracting me are also a joke. I can feel her slight embarrassment at being asked to discuss her discipline. "Have you not learned your lesson?"

"No, no, I've learned it," she quickly reassures me, wriggling to turn over and face me, as if such an act will protect her tenderized bottom from my intentions. "I will talk to Dawn and tell her I can't interact like that with Arkdhem again."

My arms tighten around her, pulling her into me. My seela begin to explore the juncture of her thighs. Idly and without purpose, but she still sucks in a sharp breath as they stroke her swollen pussy lips.

"You will not touch him or any other warrior, either." I growl.

"I won't. I promise it didn't mean anything."

"It meant something to me."

She reaches up to cup my face, her dark eyes searching mine, for what I do not know. I can feel her soften in my arms, her expression becoming sympathetic.

"Hey, I'm yours, okay?" She snuggles into me, holding me so tightly that my seela barely have room to move. It feels strange but nice. I do not object. "I have no interest in Arkdhem. He's not even really interested in me. He just wants a Tribute. Any Tribute will do. But you... I know you see me."

Playing with her hair, I know she speaks the truth. I can feel it reverberating through my chest.

~

Pareena

WHO KNEW Bogdan would be such a cuddle bug?

I definitely need to introduce him to Harry Potter though. Maybe we can even get access to Urban Dictionary somehow, but if I have to explain that '10 points to Slytherin' means butt sex, then I will. Because I think if I have to be mated to someone for the rest of my unnaturally long life span, he should at least get my jokes. And for that, he needs to read Harry Potter.

Does this mean I'm accepting that I'm actually not about to die and that, instead, I'm going to have a really long life in space?

My mind shies away from thinking about that too hard. Because if it's real... I'm starting to realize that I almost don't want it to be. If this is real, I've gone from having nothing to lose to having everything to lose.

So instead of dwelling on it further, I do exactly what Bogdan just accused me of doing—I distract. I'm distracting myself though, not him.

"Are you really going to let us go down to the planet?"

"You heard the High Commander say he would try. If there are no Vgotha." He adds the second part hastily and with a little bit of relief.

Hmm. I get the feeling he doesn't actually want me on the planet, Vgotha or no Vgotha. My eyes narrow suspiciously. "Do you expect there to be?"

Rather than answer yes or no, he sidesteps the question again. This time he leans forward as he does so, to brush his lips over my shoulder—which also helpfully breaks our eye contact. Helpful for him that is.

"The scans will tell us more."

"I'd really like to go." My tone is wheedling, caught somewhere between whiny and pleading. "Get some fresh air... I was stuck in the hospital for so long..."

My chest tightens because I'm not one hundred percent sure that I'm not still there... or what it really means for me if I'm not.

I feel Bogdan still as he contemplates the implications of my words. He's a bit of a creampuff, my Bogdan, even though he doesn't look it. That hard, brooding exterior was protection for the sweet, fluffy middle that makes up his real self.

"As long as it's safe." There is a firmness to his voice, and I know there's no arguing with him. "Your safety means more than anything to me."

Okay, well I definitely can't really argue with that. I melt a little bit too. I know part of it is that he has a need to keep me safe as part of his survivor's guilt, but I can also feel that his need is personal to me.

Which is supposedly part of the bonding process... or I can feel it because I've made him up and he is me. Yeah, let's get back to that alien planet thing. Because real or not, there's no way I'm missing out on a chance to be outside again.

"But if the scans don't find evidence of any Vgotha... then it's safe, right?"

"We will run more scans to be sure. Many cycles' worth. And send advance scouts to make sure the scans don't miss anything."

My lips twitch and I raise my eyebrows at him. "And then you'll take me to the alien planet?"

"Maybe you should convince me," he suggests, a wicked glint in his eyes, and he pulls me on top of him, making me laugh.

My ass is still sore from last night, my nipples feel oversensitive, and my pussy... is absolutely ready to earn ten points for Gryffindor.

But, even though I'm a Ravenclaw, we're definitely never earning sex points for my house. Hm. Maybe I shouldn't try to access Urban Dictionary either. I don't want to give him ideas.

Bogdan

THE PLANET SCANS and advance scouts recover no sign of the Vgotha. I grind my teeth. While we are all uncertain of our scanners, the advance scout reports are more concrete. There was a small blip on the scans, on one small island, that we couldn't account for, but the scouts found nothing. Arkdhem led them and announced it as being completely clear, possibly the safest place on the planet to take the Tributes because they were able to explore every inch of it. No matter how I feel about him, I know he and his warriors were thorough.

Multiple sweeps were made.

The planet is clear.

Yet I feel a rising anxiety. Perhaps just because a planet is so out of my control.

"You know what this means." The High Commander rubs his forehead. "I don't like it."

We would only allow our Tributes in a safe area, well-guarded, but still... I don't like it either.

"We should scan again," I say. There is no logical reason for my uneasiness, but I find I cannot brush it away either.

"The results will be the same." The Commander blows out a breath. "Dawn has been hounding me, accusing me of breaking my promise. I will not have her think me dishonorable. Have Miths prepare a landing shuttle suitable for a crew and our Tributes."

"It is perfectly safe," Arkdhem speaks up, frowning fiercely at us. He does not like being questioned. To do so shows our doubt in him... but it is actually not doubt. Just fear.

Fear of what I cannot control.

I grind my teeth. The island is small, we have scanned it, explored it, and found nothing. But suddenly it seems like the most threatening thing in the galaxy. So much could go wrong. Colors flash across my armor before I can wrest it back to black.

Arkdhem narrows his eyes at me. I hope the flashes were too fast for him to interpret. I do not want him to ever see my fear. I stare back at him, my expression impassive. I will not let him see me uncomfortable either.

The Commander shakes his head. "Prepare the shuttle. Arkdhem, you are dismissed to rest for now. When the shuttle is ready, I want you back to guide us."

Pressing his fist to his chest, Arkdhem nods and leaves the bridge. My fists clench at my sides as I stare at the screen. The planet, which had seemed so beautiful, now looks like a threat.

I want to believe in the superiority of our warriors but faced with the possibility of harm coming to my Tribute, I cannot deny the emotion that the Vgotha so often make me feel. The emotion I have tried to run from since the day Tsentur was destroyed.

I am afraid.

Pareena

WHEN DAWN KNOCKS on the door, I'm reading one of my favorite 'manuals.' Calling them that makes me snicker to myself. I hurry over to open it, only to find that I'm still locked out. Note to self: I really need to get Bogdan to give me access to it. In my defense, I got a little distracted. Not just by the punishment and sex, but also by the lure of the planet we're currently orbiting. I want to go down so badly.

"Override," Dawn says, and the door opens to her beaming face. I'm so shocked by her outfit that I barely even notice Arkdhem standing behind her, as usual.

"Where did you get that?" I ask, pointing at her jeans and t-shirt, suddenly very aware of the very pretty, flowing, and nearly see through gown that I'm wearing. I have an entire closet full of these gowns in varying colors but nothing else—and until now, I hadn't seen Dawn in anything else either.

Dawn beams at me. "I had a feeling Bogdan hadn't given you anything but gowns. Neither did Gavrill, but he let me use the replicator and eventually we figured out how to make some Earth clothing. I thought you might want a different outfit for going down to the planet."

"Are we going down to the planet?" I ask, trying to suppress my excitement in case the answer is no. Bogdan has been on the bridge for hours now and I haven't heard from him.

"Yes," Arkdhem says from behind her, smiling widely at me. "I have just returned from leading a scouting mission. We have scanned and thoroughly explored the island on foot. There are no Vgotha. The High Commander has already ordered a shuttle to be made ready."

Squealing with joy, I bounce in excitement and the next thing I know, Dawn's arms are around me and we're squealing and bouncing together. Arkdhem is still smiling as he watches us, his head tilted almost as if he's confused—or at least amused—by our reactions.

"Okay, so come on," Dawn says, pulling away from the hug and grabbing my hand. "We need to get you properly outfitted. There's no way you can explore an alien planet in that."

"There is nothing wrong with the gowns," Arkdhem murmurs.

We both give him a look as Dawn drags me past him.

"You would think that," Dawn says. Typical male.

The door swishes shut behind me and my bottom tingles, reminding me of the punishment I received not that long ago.

"Wait—" I manage to grind us to a halt. "Bogdan told me not to leave the room, remember?" He hadn't reinforced that order when he left for the bridge, but I don't want to take my chances. Especially since I'd be leaving in Arkdhem's company, even if Dawn is with us too.

"Well, you can't wear that," she says, gesturing at my outfit. Turning to Arkdhem, she gestures imperiously. "Call Bogdan, we'll get permission for Pareena to leave the room."

Oh yeah, Arkdhem calling Bogdan to get permission to take me out and around the ship. Especially, since I've technically already left the room, even though it's only by a couple of steps. That should go over great. But I don't protest. I can't help it that Arkdhem is Dawn's constant companion. And she's right, if we're going off ship, I want something different to wear.

"Yes?" Bogdan's voice, much surlier than he ever uses with me, makes me jump about ten feet in the air. Then I realize that Arkdhem is holding up his arm—using his armor to communicate with Bogdan and allow us to hear him.

"Hey, Bogdan, it's Dawn," she chirps cheerfully. "I want to take Pareena to the replicator to get some clothes for going planet side. Can she leave her room, please?" The way she says 'please' is rather pointed, almost like she's warning him that he better answer yes. My lips twitch in amusement before I wonder if I should make sure he knows that Arkdhem is coming with us too.

Then again, he must know, right? Arkdhem is the one who contacted him and he's almost always at Dawn's side when the High Commander isn't. I found out during the group session that he wants to learn as much about human females as possible, so that he can be a good mate. It's a very sweet sentiment, and I have to admit, he's far more charming than Bogdan or Gavrill are. Hm. Maybe that's why Bogdan doesn't like him very much.

There is a long pause.

"Pareena?" Bogdan asks, jolting me with his use of my name without the word 'my' in front of it. I don't think he's ever just called me by name before. "You wish for a different garment?"

"Just for being on the planet," I say, resisting the urge to move closer to Arkdhem. Bogdan can hear me just fine from where I am. "I'd rather wear boots, pants, and a top that's not flowy. It will be easier to move in and if there's any vegetation that might irritate my skin, it will be better to be covered up." Because I don't have any interest in encountering the alien version of poison ivy. Especially since, because it's alien, it might be even worse than the Earth stuff. Who knows what's down there?

There is another long pause.

"Fine," Bogdan says gruffly. "Just to the replicator and back. The shuttle should be ready soon. Stay close to Dawn." I take that last sentence as a reminder to stay away from Arkdhem.

"Woo-hoo, let's go!" Dawn cheers and grabs me by the hand. This time I don't resist at all.

I get new clothes! Planet clothes! I can't wait.

19

P areena

"THAT. IS. AWESOME." Dawn stares enviously at my newly manufactured Ravenclaw shirt. I grin and drape it over my arm, along with the jeans that we made. I'll have to try them on when I get back to my room, but I can already tell the fabric should be stretchy enough to fit. We couldn't figure out how to get images from Earth—apparently, the Jabol only sent over the manuals and our files... go figure—but the shirt is blue and has my house motto on it. That's good enough for me. "I didn't even think about anything like that."

"What house are you?" I ask, curious now.

She hesitates. "I'm not sure. Um, definitely not Hufflepuff or I probably wouldn't have been picked up by the Jabol. My lack of close relationships was a big part of the reason they thought I was an ideal candidate."

"I think you're a great friend," I say immediately reaching out to take her hand. "Maybe you're Gryffindor? You seem pretty adventurous."

"That's true." She brightens. "And I always liked Hermione."

"What are you two talking about?" Arkdhem asks, sounding completely lost.

"Harry Potter," Dawn tells him. "It's a book series that a lot of people really love back on Earth."

"And you love this series?" he asks, looking back and forth between the two of us.

"Always," I say immediately.

Dawn laughs, getting the reference. "I liked it a lot, it was fun."

Arkdhem wrinkles his forehead thoughtfully. "So, I should read these books?" Dawn and I exchange an amused look. I'm pretty sure that if we told Arkdhem he should paint himself purple, because it would impress his Tribute, he would do it. He's very goal focused.

"Not everyone loves it, and not everyone loves it as much as I do," I admit. "If you want to make sure you connect with your Tribute, you should wait to find out what her interests are."

He nods thoughtfully, but honestly, I'm not really sure he gets it. The way he talks to Dawn and me, he's always looking for whatever will make his Tribute like him. There are definitely a few things the majority of women look for in a potential mate, but he doesn't seem to quite understand that a woman's choice is highly individual. That being said, the Jabol must be doing something right, because Dawn and Gavrill are a good match from everything I've seen, and I think the same is true for Bogdan and me.

"Excuse me, Tribute Dawn?" We all turn to see a warrior; one I don't recognize, which is no big surprise. He's looking at Dawn hopefully. "I know it is not class time, but would you have a minicycle to spare—we need some help." He gestures down the hall to a small area where there is a small group of warriors, all of them in what look like various yoga poses.

Dawn lights up. "Of course!" She glances at Arkdhem and me. "I'll be right back!"

Before I can protest—or even think about what I might say to keep her there—she's off with the warrior, leaving me there with Arkdhem. Crap. This is *not* my fault, dammit. But will Bogdan see it that way?

"Um, let's go watch," I say, trying not to show how anxious I am to get away from him, because that seems pretty rude, and it's not *his* fault that he makes Bogdan feel insecure.

"Pareena, wait," he says, and I jump when I feel his fingers close around my arm, pulling me back to face him. Instinctively, I try to jerk away, but his grip is too strong. Not that he's hurting me, he's very gentle, but I'm no match for his strength. A little trickle of fear slides through me before I push it away. No matter what, I do not believe that Arkdhem would harm me.

Even if he were the type, to do so with Dawn and a small cadre of other warriors so close by would be the height of stupidity.

"Please let go of me," I say, keeping my voice calm but firm.

To his credit, he immediately releases me, but the intense way he's looking at me still makes me feel anxious. That and the fact that I'm definitely not supposed to be spending time alone with him, but here we are. Maybe the fact that the others are nearby will be enough to counter Bogdan's possessiveness?

"Pareena, please listen. You were given to the wrong warrior. You were to be with me." He puts his hand on his chest, staring soulfully into my eyes.

"What?" I step back. Had there been some ambiguity about which warrior I was matched with? That would explain Bogdan's insecurity about Arkdhem.

"Bogdan didn't even want a Tribute," Arkdhem says quickly, scowling. "The Jabol matched you with him, but they did not understand what they were doing. He is incapable of love."

"That's not true," I snap, surprising us both with my vigor. Just because Bogdan hadn't wanted a Tribute doesn't mean that he's incapable of love. In fact, I think part of his problem is how deeply he loves, not the opposite. "Look, I know he's Mr. Grouchy, but he's a good mate. I think the Jabol knew exactly what they were doing when they matched me with him."

Because I'm not sure just anyone would be able to understand where Bogdan was coming from. Not just anyone would be as patient with him as I have been. Although some of that stems from thinking that none of this is real... but I'm starting to think that I was wrong about that. Hoping that I was, in fact. I want this to be real and I want everything being offered to me. I'm willing to fight for it.

Arkdhem's expression turns to one of pity, which makes me grind my teeth together. "He is not suitable," he insists. "You should have been assigned to me. I *want* a mate."

"That's not—you can't—" Gah! I don't even know where to begin. His retort feels so very *Arkdhem*. He wants a mate and so he thinks he should get one. That we might not actually be well matched doesn't even occur to him. Heck, he'd probably try to change himself to meet my needs, but that's not what I'd want. I need someone who knows who they are and is confident enough to stand up to me. Someone like Bogdan. But Arkdhem's desperation tugs at my heartstrings. "We'd make a terrible couple, Arkdhem. Even if I didn't have feelings for Bogdan, you and I wouldn't be good together."

"You and Bogdan aren't bonded yet, correct?" I hesitate and that gives him all the information he needs, turning his expression sympathetic. "I'm sorry."

Dang, he's good. Ready to play the sympathy card. Offer his shoulder to cry on. Was this his plan all along?

I take a deep, painful breath, ignoring the knives lining the inside of my chest. I can't sit here deliberating about the state of mine and Bogdan's relationship. Arkdhem has shown his cards and I've got to shut this down once and for all.

"That's between me and Bogdan. Regardless, I am not your Tribute. And... I love him." Which I probably should have told Bogdan first, but Arkdhem has rattled me a little. I don't know how long a bonding is supposed to take. Does it mean something that we aren't bonded yet? Arkdhem seems to think so. *Breathe in, breathe out. Don't panic. It might mean nothing.*

Arkdhem's mouth pinches. "You do not know your feelings."

Oh no he didn't. "Don't try to tell me how I feel," I snap, finally losing my temper a little. "Let's be honest here, Arkdhem, when it comes down to it, I don't think you actually want *me*. I think you want a Tribute, any Tribute, and since I'm here and you don't like Bogdan, you think I'll do. But to you, I could be any woman, who I am as an individual doesn't matter."

A shadow falls over the warrior's face and I take a step back, suddenly a little fearful. Suddenly, Arkdhem doesn't seem so harmless. There is a long pause as we stare at each other.

"Very well." Arkdhem says finally, his mouth twisted as if he's eaten something sour. "But you will regret it. In the end, *I* am a better match." He says it so fiercely that I know he truly believes it.

Spinning on his heel, he stalks off toward Dawn and the other warriors, looking so hurt that I feel a little bad. But I feel way worse because I accidentally disobeyed Bogdan. I didn't mean to, of course, but I know he won't be happy when he hears... if he hears...

Ugh. Did I invite any that? I review all my interactions with Arkdhem. If I had known Arkdhem felt this way, I would've kept my distance from the beginning, taken Bogdan's admonitions more seriously. I thought Bogdan was just being overprotective, but no, there was something there. Still, I don't think I did anything wrong, but I'm not sure whether or not Bogdan will agree with that assessment.

I should tell Bogdan what happened. But a little voice argues with me. What purpose would it serve? He already wants to pick a fight with Arkdhem. Maybe now Arkdhem will back off and Bogdan will sense that he has, and everyone will get along. A girl can hope, right?

Bogdan

MY TRIBUTE IS HIDING SOMETHING.

Her worry is strong enough for me to feel, tugging at my senses, and nearly impossible to ignore. Perhaps our descent to the planet? Or the planet itself? The shuttle is already descending, it is too late for her to stay on the Command Ship, but she does not have to leave the shuttle if she so desires.

I capture her hand and squeeze. "If you are too nervous, you may stay on the shuttle."

"Oh no," she says, her mood lightening as she shakes her head at me. "You aren't getting off that easy. I want to step onto an alien planet. It's not dangerous, right?"

"We will be fine," I assure her. "This planet it heavily forested, including the island we are landing on, but we found a safe grassy area and cleared the vicinity of any predators. We set up a large perimeter for you and Tribute Dawn to explore."

"That's good." Her brow wrinkles. "You didn't disturb the area too much, I hope."

"No. The section we chose isn't populated with the larger, more dangerous fauna of this planet. And to clear the section, we set up signals that transmit a high-pitched frequency. Annoying but not fatal. All the larger beasts left already."

"Gotcha," she murmurs, but seems distracted. She tries to look around me at the rest of the shuttle crew, strapped to the sides of the narrow shuttle. I stiffen. Who is she trying to see?

Across from us, Tribute Dawn is secured next to the High Commander. Her face is split by a large smile and she wriggles in her harness, practically bouncing. I cannot make out exactly what she is saying, but she is chattering to him excitedly. Compared to her, my Pareena is subdued, and her unhappy emotions gnaw at me.

"You need not worry," I try again. "It will be an easy trip. I will keep you safe."

"I'm not worried." But now she's chewing on her lip and glancing over her shoulder before turning back to the front and nervously fidgeting in her seat. I turn to see who she's looking at and I am fairly certain she looked at Arkdhem.

Is she trying to communicate with him?

I blank my expression and look down at my Tribute. I had given her permission to go with him and Dawn to the replicator this morning. I had misgivings about it, but the need for clothes suitable for exploring the planet seemed more important than my dislike of Arkdhem. Perhaps I was wrong to think so, although the clothing she is wearing does seem more comfortable for her. She particularly seems to like the top for some reason. I can feel a small spurt of pleasure from her every time she looks down at it.

"Is there something you wish to tell me?" I ask.

"No, everything's fine," she says quickly.

We are not fully bonded, but I am enough in tune with her emotions now to know that she is being untruthful. Scowling, suddenly just as anxious as she is, I feel a kind of rage slipping over me. My Tribute is lying to me and it has something to do with Arkdhem. I am sure of it.

My suit flashes streaks of yellow and red. Jealousy. Anger. On display for anyone looking at me. Fortunately, no one seems to be. They have not witnessed my loss of control.

"You will tell me." I say to her, before turning in my harness to study Arkdhem. We Tsenturions are all in full armor and his is neutral gray. His face is turned away, so I can only see the side of his helmet. If he has said something to my Pareena to turn her against me... I will challenge him, and not even the High Commander will be able to gainsay me.

"Commence landing sequence," Kalexston says. There's a slight bump as we enter the atmosphere.

"Does it have to do with Arkdhem?" I growl under my breath so only she can hear.

"Later," she whispers back. "I'll tell you later. Promise."

Somewhat mollified, I lean back and brace for landing.

20

———

P areena

"THE SKY IS BLUE." Dawn sounds disappointed and I have to laugh.

"We could see that much from space," I tease her, but I know what she means, she wanted something very alien.

Instead, we got a planet that is slightly off somehow.

The sky is blue, but it's not quite the right shade of blue. It's close, but just off enough that I'm conscious of it and it's messing with my head a little. Same thing with the foliage. I've never been that interested in plants, so a botanist might immediately notice a lot of non-Earth fauna, but for me, I just notice that the green is a little wrong. Too deep in some places, too oddly hued in others. A lot of the plants look kind of shiny.

Enough to make me feel uneasy, despite how good it feels to be standing on actual ground, with a breeze blowing through my hair, and the sun shining down on me. I tip my head back to feel the warmth on my face.

Of course, it might not be the colors that are making me feel strange. I wonder if I'm picking up on Bogdan's emotions. He knows something's wrong.

Frankly, I'm wondering why I thought I could hide from him. He's more and more in tune with me. Thankfully Gavrill sensed the tension as well and, as soon as we disembarked from the shuttle, sent Arkdhem on a mission with several other warriors, while he and Bogdan lead teams around the immediate perimeter of the field we landed in.

Following orders, Dawn and I are standing in the middle of the field, right next to the shuttle, where they deemed us 'safest'. The woods are dark enough that I can't see into them, but I know there are warriors in there too. I'm almost a little amused at how serious they are, when I know they've already scanned the planet to death and sent scouts to explore the island. I wonder if their paranoia is symptomatic of the decimation of their homeworld or if it's just part of being a warrior.

At the other end of the field is the beach and I want to go running over there so badly. What I wouldn't give to go swimming...

"The perimeter is secure," the High Commander announces, striding back toward us with several warriors behind him. Bogdan is returning from the other side and I smile at him, although I still feel a bit anxious. He knows something's up, but I still haven't figured out the best way to tell him about Arkdhem's approaching me. Or if I even should.

Thankfully, there's no sign of Arkdhem and the warriors he's leading at the moment. They're still patrolling, taking samples of the planet to study back on ship. I feel a bit better that this little trip isn't just a jaunt to placate Dawn and me. Although, if it was, I wouldn't protest.

It feels so good to be outside. Smelling Earth-like smells. Actual ground under my feet. And every time the wind blows through my hair, I smile. The first time, I teared up. I missed this.

Bogdan says something low to Gavrill before approaching me.

The expression on his face is stern, almost foreboding, and my anxiety spikes. Dammit.

"Come," he commands, holding out a hand. Guess it's our Come-to-Master talk.

"This place is nice," I mention half-heartedly as he pulls me to the edge of the field, nearly into the forest. There are big prehistoric-looking ferns and a canopy of trees with low hanging blue orbs—some sort of fruit, offering both shade a little bit of privacy. "Thanks for letting us come."

"Sit here, my Pareena," he orders, pointing to a rock that's just about the right size for a bench. I sigh and do as he says, feeling like a student called into the principal's office. Back in the middle of the field I can see Dawn and Gavrill talking, and she's pointing to the beach. Maybe she can convince him to let us go swimming. Standing in the field in the sun is nice, but the beach would be even better.

Reaching down, Bogdan raises my chin with a finger, grabbing my attention. So much for distracting myself. "You are keeping secrets from me, Pareena. And you lied to me. You are anxious and worried, and it has something to do with Arkdhem. I do not like it."

I flinch and then frown as what he says permeates.

"Wait, how do you know I'm anxious and worried? And how do you know that I lied?" That all seems very specific. True, but specific. How could he possibly be sure of that?

"I can feel you." He presses a hand to his chest. "Here. Everywhere. Can you not feel me?"

A strong sense of worry and affection surges through me. Not just mine, his. And if I'm accepting all of this as reality, and not just a coma dream, that means I'm not feeling his emotions because I made them up, it means...

"Is this the bond?" I ask, a little wondering, a lot hopeful. Because this is not the first time that I've thought I could feel what he's feeling, even though we don't have the mate mark yet. That's supposed to come later anyway though. The insecurity that Arkdhem had stirred in me earlier fades, especially as I can feel Bogdan's affection—directed at me—grow.

"I think so." He tucks a strand of hair behind my ear, his lips curving up into a smile as he gently teases me. "I have never been bonded until now."

My eyes fill with tears of happiness. Yeesh, so emotional. But maybe since I'm also feeling his emotions, maybe that explains it.

"Do I have the mark?" I look down at myself, but my t-shirt covers up pretty much everything.

"I do not think so, not yet," Bogdan says, to my disappointment. He smiles, obviously feeling it. "Do not worry, my Pareena, it will come." Wiping away my tears, he lifts me, positioning himself to sit on the rock and arranging me in his lap. He's so big I fit easily. We cuddle like that for a moment of peace and I can feel our combined happiness coursing through me. This close, focusing on them, it is easy to tell which are my emotions and which are his, even though they are so similar. "We will discuss the bonding later. Now you must tell me what is troubling you."

I turn so I am facing him and put my forehead against his. I know he can feel the consternation rising inside of me. "You have to promise not to hurt anyone."

"I would never hurt you," he frowns, and I stop his lips with a finger.

"Not just me. Anyone." I give him as stern a look as I can. His body stiffens. "I mean it."

"Tell me," he growls. I sigh, realizing I'm probably not going to get him to promise anything. But chances are, whatever he's thinking is way worse than what actually happened, so maybe by telling him the bare facts it'll actually calm him down.

"Right after I finished making my clothes, a warrior came to ask Dawn for some help with some kind of yoga session he and some of the other warriors were having, which unintentionally left me sort of alone with Arkdhem for a few minutes."

To my relief, I feel Bogdan relax slightly. "I will not blame you for that, my Pareena," he reassures me, and I feel his fingers reaching up to my hair, twining a long lock around them. "I gave you permission to leave my room with him. You were in a public corridor while

Dawn attended to the other warriors, you were not truly alone. Is that all?"

I tense and I feel him tense again. "Um, well, almost all. He took the opportunity of near-privacy to express his concern over our mating and put himself forward as an alternative. I made it clear that I am very happy with you and I would not be happy with him, and he backed off."

Unfortunately, this time Bogdan doesn't immediately relax the way I was hoping.

"I see," he says quietly, before I can reassure him that it's really not a big deal. "And why did you not share this with me immediately? Why did you try to hide it?"

"I didn't want you guys to fight." I give him a pleading look, but he doesn't reassure me.

Pulling me to him, he gives me a hard kiss before lifting me off his lap so he can rise up and take my hand. I trot along at his side as we move back into the clearing, toward Gavrill and Dawn.

"What are you going to do?" I ask, worriedly.

"What needs to be done," he answers vaguely, but as we enter the brightly lit meadow, his helmet covers his face, along with his full armor.

Yeah. That's... not reassuring.

Bogdan

ARKDHEM TRIED to steal my Pareena from me. I can tell there is more to what happened between them than what she is saying. Not that she is lying, exactly, but she is—what is the human saying?—putting the best spin on it. None of her words can hide his dishonor though.

He abused my trust of him, which was little enough to begin with. I should have known better. He should have known better. It is not unheard of for Tsenturions to compete for the affections of a shared interest, but we are no longer on Tsentur and Pareena was given to me. She is bonding with me. Even on Tsentur, his actions would be seen as underhanded, as he waited until she was in his care, and I was not present, to announce his intentions.

This insult cannot go unanswered.

Arkdhem is leading his patrol back onto the opposite side of the field and I growl as soon as I see him. My Pareena pulls on my hand, her footsteps slowing, but she is no match for my strength, much less my anger.

"Please don't make a scene," she begs. "It wasn't a big deal."

Perhaps not to her, but she does not understand our culture, our rules of courtship. Those rules are changing now that we have Tributes, but not so much that it is acceptable for Arkdhem try and sneakily steal her away from me, to attempt to undermine our bonding without publicly announcing his intentions. Even with my general lack of trust for the warrior, I would never have dreamed he'd stoop so low.

He catches my eye and straightens, staring me down. The warriors following him stumble to a halt, obviously confused about why he's come to such an abrupt stop.

"Bogdan, please," my Pareena whispers, tugging on me, but it is too late. I gently shake her off, pushing her behind me so I can storm forward, my armor sliding over my skin. I feel her hesitation and then her resolve as she begins to follow me.

"Bogdan?" The High Commander's voice cuts across the field, but I do not slow. Out of the corner of my eye, I see him and Tribute Dawn heading toward me. But I will not be stopped, and I pick up my pace.

"I challenge you," I shout, pointing at Arkdhem. All other movement in the field seems to still, the other warriors staring in shock. There has not been a challenge among our warriors since the Great Devastation. I can already see the disapproval on some of their faces, as our focus should be on fighting the Vgotha, not each other... but Arkdhem has gone too far. "You approached my Tribute and attempted to sway her interest to you, while pretending to be an honorable escort."

"What?" Tribute Dawn gasps behind me.

Arkdhem says nothing, glaring at me. His armor was already up but now a helmet forms around his head. The other warriors of his patrol are now looking at him in shock and a little consternation. Wondering at his actions. He seems surprised as well.

Did he think my Pareena would not tell me? Did he truly expect her to choose him, even in such a small manner as keeping a secret from me? Then again, had I not pressed, she might have done just that, but not because she has any desire for him. I can feel that she has nothing but platonic affection and a touch of exasperation for him. But he still tried for more.

Coming to a halt, just out of any weapons' reach, I snarl at him. "You have no honor."

The jab makes him jerk but he just glares harder. I can almost see his mind working, deciding whether or not to meet my challenge. I have been a warrior for longer and I hold my position as the High Commander's second for a reason. In a fair fight, it is highly unlikely that Arkdhem will triumph and we both know it.

Yet to forfeit a challenge before it has even begun is an admission of wrongdoing, and he clearly does not wish for that either.

"Is this true?" The High Commander comes up behind me, directing his question at Arkdhem.

Now Arkdhem does look a little ashamed, his gaze swerving away from the High Commander's for a moment before he defiantly lifts his chin and nods. "Bogdan did not even want a Tribute. He wanted to end the Tribute program and keep any of us from receiving Tributes. Tribute Pareena deserved to know she had an option, a warrior who does desire her and would treat her with the reverence and care she merits."

There is a murmur of understanding from our fellow warriors, more than one of them eyeing me because there is truth to his words. Despite the way in which he approached her, they understand why... and they agree.

"She is mine," I declare. What I am about to say next hurts my pride a bit, but it is necessary. "I was wrong about the Tributes." I do not enjoy admitting that I had erred, but it is the truth. I would rather my Pareena know that I have changed my mind than keep my pride.

"How convenient," Arkdhem sneers back. "Now that you have one, of course. Pareena should have been mine." The possessiveness in his voice, the way he casually uses her name, sets off rage I have never felt before.

With a war cry, I hurtle forward, my armor creating a long sword that swings easily in my hand, no longer caring about the rules of combat or challenges. I want his blood.

"No!" My Pareena cries from behind me. "Stop!" I hear the low rumble of the High Commander's voice, feel her frustration and upset when he catches her and pulls her back. "Make them stop!"

21

———————

P^{areena}

Damn, damn, damn! I'm too late.

Bristling with spines and spikes that make him look bigger than ever, Bogdan is flying through the air at Arkdhem, his weapon aimed for Arkdhem's neck and my breath catches in my throat in fear. I don't want either of them hurt.

Arkdhem crouches at the last moment, avoiding the swing of Bogdan's sword, and he lashes out with his own weapons—knives that scrape along Bogdan's armor with an ear-splitting shriek.

"Calm down," Gavrill murmurs in my ear, holding me securely in place with one arm around my shoulders. Dawn comes up beside me and takes my hand, squeezing it tightly as we watch Bogdan stagger back. My heart feels like it has jumped into my throat. This is exactly what I didn't want to have happen! "They would have to severely damage their armor to do any actual harm to the other."

That is not as reassuring as he obviously thinks it is. I wish I had my own armor that I could don, so I could rush in to stop this madness. Although, watching them, I realize that armor might not be enough. They rush each other, meeting with a bang that makes me wince. Bogdan is bigger but Arkdhem is quicker, and I'm smaller than both of them. I'd be no match for either of their bulk. One blow would throw me across the clearing.

On the other hand, with a Tribute between them, they'd stop fighting, wouldn't they? If only Gavrill would let me go...

Arkdhem lands another blow as he rushes past Bogdan, spinning on a dime to stab his blades at Bogdan's chest and making me shriek with horror. Bogdan staggers back an inch before shaking the impact off and turning, his blade parrying Arkdhem's next thrust with a hair-raising clang and following it with a rough slash across Arkdhem's chest. Both warriors separate unsteadily.

I realize all the Tsenturion warriors are gathering to watch now. They crowd the clearing, keeping a wide circle around Bogdan and Arkdhem. Most of them have all their armor on too, in case one of the fighters accidentally slams into them, but no one makes a move to stop the insanity.

"This is crazy," I mutter as the two grapple. I have to admit, I'm starting to feel a little less frantic now that I can see the others are not worried, and especially since I can tell neither warrior's armor is giving way to the damage. "They're just going to pummel each other until one falls down?"

"Until one of them tires or lands what would be a killing blow if not for their armor," Gavrill says nonchalantly. "So far, neither has done so."

"So this isn't to the death?" I ask, because it looks to me like they're trying to kill each other.

Arkdhem narrowly manages to deflect Bogdan's sword from slashing across his neck.

"No, we cannot afford to lose a single warrior," Gavrill reassures me. That's... kind of reassuring? I guess?

I duck my head, unable to watch anymore. A wrenching noise

makes me cry out as I imagine how much damage the spines and weapons could inflict. I didn't realize I was so squeamish.

It's because I really care about Bogdan. Arkdhem too, to a lesser extent. Coma dream or no, my emotions have become entirely wrapped up in the Tsenturions.

Is this a dream though? Two burly warriors beating on each other until one succumbs... this is not one of my fantasies. Another screech makes me jump and I let go of Dawn's hand to turn and face Gavrill, grabbing onto his arm.

"Do something," I implore him, begging.

"They must fight it out. I cannot intrude without insulting their honor."

"Honor, shmonor. This is nuts! I don't want them to fight over me!"

Gavrill doesn't answer me. He turns back to the fray and I stomp my foot in frustration. Dirt flies from the gouged earth. The sky is still blue and pretty but with a soundtrack of battle cries and roars. This outing is the opposite of relaxing.

"Forfeit," Bogdan shouts.

"Never," Arkdhem shoots back and falls into a battle crouch again. I'm pretty sure he means it. I don't even want him, dammit!

Screw this.

The High Commander's hold had relaxed to allow me to turn and face him and I take advantage of it. If no one else is going to stop this exercise in stupidity, then I will. Twisting, I slip out of his grip and rush forward.

"Pareena!" He roars my name as Dawn shrieks it. I ignore both of them, running as fast as I can to reach the fighting warriors.

"Pareena?" Bogdan turns, searching for me. But Arkdhem, seeing an opening, morphs a weapon like a club and leaps towards him.

"Look out!" I scream, utterly terrified, trying to run even faster. A millisecond before Arkdhem lands the blow, Bogdan whirls and blocks it with both weapons. With a cry, he surges up, shoving Arkdhem off balance. The smaller warrior slams to the ground, arms upraised to protect himself from Bogdan's blow.

The blow never comes. Bogdan has already turned his back and is stepping toward me, catching me in his arms.

"What happened?" he asks, morphing instantly from brutal warrior to concerned mate. "What are you doing?"

"Trying to stop this," I say, tears rushing to my eyes. "I don't want you to fight."

Sighing, Bogdan presses his forehead against mine. "You do not understand our ways. He should not have acted as he did."

"I agree with that, but I still don't want you two to fight," I insist, reaching up to hold onto his shoulders, peering at him from under my eyelashes with pleading eyes. "I don't like it. Are you hurt?"

"No. I'm fine." He lets me inspect his chest, which I know Arkdhem's knives scored, but there's no sign of it. Other than a few smudges on his armor—from dirt, there's not a tear or indication that the nanotech has been compromised—he's whole and fresh as if he never challenged Arkdhem.

"You scared me," I half growl.

With an amused smile, Bogdan cups my face, giving a pleased rumble when I press my cheek into his big hand. He doesn't seem angry that I interrupted his fight. He switched gears immediately to make sure I was fine.

"So that's it? You concede?" Arkdhem shouts in our direction. The warriors try to shush him, but Gavrill waves them back when he wrenches out of their hold.

"I concede nothing," Bogdan says, shifting us so he's facing his former opponent, still holding me in his arms. His body is rigid even though his voice is nonchalant. His hands hold me in such a way he could easily move me aside. His helmet reappears but covers only half his face. "You acted without honor when you approached my Tribute."

"She should have a choice," Arkdhem shoots back. "I would be a better Master!"

Oh, no, he didn't.

"Enough." I snap out the word, raising my hand before Bogdan can respond. "Stop this. I'm the Tribute in question and Arkdhem is right. I *should* have a choice. No more fighting, you can just ask *me* what I want, and *I'll* choose."

The entire field falls silent.

Gavrill gives a cough that sounds suspiciously like a laugh, but when I glance at him, his face is as serious as ever and his armor shows nothing but a neutral grey. "Very well. Pareena, as the Tribute in question, you have the right to decide the warrior you would like as your Tsenturion Master. We'll uphold your decision, whoever you choose."

I raise a brow at Arkdhem until he nods, although the movement is jerky. He already knows I'm not going to choose him, but since he's the one demanding I have a choice and I now have the High Commander's backing, it's not like he can do anything other than agree. I feel a little sorry for him, but he's the one who put himself in this position. I turn back to Bogdan and meet his gaze. He looks a little worried, as if he's not sure he'll be the winner in this contest.

Good. He deserves it after scaring me with that fight.

"All right then, I'll choose." I pause and draw out the moment. Everyone is silent, but I sense Bogdan's heartbeat. His face is blank but his suit ripples, betraying his trepidation. "When we met, I didn't like you very much," I tell him. "You were cold, abrupt and entirely too closed-off. But you also always took care of me. And even though you have the reputation of being the surliest Tsenturion, I know that you are capable of more feelings. You feel things deeper than most. That's why you blocked yourself off from the pain. And even though there are other warriors," I glance back at Arkdhem for just a moment, "who might have wanted a Tribute when Bogdan did not, I will never be satisfied with anyone else. Bogdan is mine. I'm in love with him. I choose him."

A ripple of approval goes through the watching warriors as Bogdan's love, his joy, surges through me. The black of his armor twinkles and my lips open in surprise as I realize it's no longer pure black but instead is decorated with what almost looks like stars in the night sky. Everything that makes up who he is—his grief, his pain, his surliness—is still there, but so is our love, our bond. It is beautiful.

Gavrill nods. At his side, Dawn claps her hands.

"Oh, yay." She grins, bouncing a little.

I tip my head forehead and press it against Bogdan's. "I choose you," I whisper. "Always."

In answer, Bogdan tilts his head and meets my lips. I can hear Arkdhem cursing, but I barely notice.

"So that was fun, can we go to the beach now?" Dawn asks.

Bogdan

"Absolutely not." The High Commander and I respond to Tribute Dawn's question at the same time, although I must pull my lips away from my Pareena's to do so. Tribute Dawn makes an aggravated sound in the back of her throat.

"Oh, come on! If there were Vgotha hiding out anywhere in the ocean they'd definitely have taken advantage of the fight to come out and ambush us. None of you were paying attention to anything other than Arkdhem and Bogdan!" She points back toward the water. "An entire platoon of Vgotha could have snuck up on you and none of you would have noticed."

The High Commander and I exchange glances and then he looks back at Arkdhem. I look at my Pareena instead and almost groan when she meets my gaze with hopeful brown eyes. Tribute Dawn is not the only Tribute who wants to go to the beach.

"Arkdhem, you will spread the scouts out through the woods nearest the beach," the High Commander orders, as confident as ever, although I can hear a touch of resignation in his tone. Tribute Dawn makes a joyful sound and throws her arms around him. A small smile touches his lips, echoed in my own expression as my Pareena's excitement rises inside of me.

"Yes, High Commander," Arkdhem says through gritted teeth. He makes an abrupt gesture, signaling to the other warriors to follow his lead. With that one order, the High Commander has reaffirmed Arkdhem's place in our hierarchy, despite my challenge. I cannot be upset though, for my Pareena has chosen me. Perhaps I should even thank Arkdhem, for now everyone knows it. His pride has taken a severe blow and the High Commander must think that is punishment enough.

As the warrior whom Pareena chose to be hers, it would be ungracious of me to insist on more.

"Very well," the High Commander says, taking Tribute Dawn's hand in his. "Let us go to this beach."

It is hard not to be infected by our Tribute's obvious joy, but both the High Commander and I remain on alert as we cross the field. Tribute Dawn was not incorrect in her assessment of the distraction the challenge between Arkdhem and myself provided, but that does not convince me that the water is safe. There is so much of it and the Vgotha are not the only threat. Who knows what lurks in the depths of the waves? There was too much water to fully scan but we know there are some very large creatures residing there, with no way of knowing how close they can come to shore or if they are a threat.

But we do not even make it to the water. The moment the High Commander steps onto the sand, there is a ripple in the air before us, making him shout and push Tribute Dawn behind him, shielding her with his body. I am already doing the same with my Pareena as the rippling intensifies, an image growing and sharpening in the air. Ridges rise on my armor and my helmet encases my head, my battle blade grows in my right hand, ready to defend my Tribute, my mate.

"What's happening?" Pareena tries to come around on my other side and I push her back. I feel her hands on the back of my waist and realize she is peeking around me. It is good enough. I remain focused on the figure as Gavrill issues an alert to the patrolling warriors: Warning, intruder, beach.

The figure solidifies, remaining slightly translucent in a way. A hologram. The ugly visage grins at us and behind us, Tribute Dawn gasps in recognition.

"Greetings, High Commander." Antlers grow from his head.

Otherwise, his anatomy is similar to a Tsenturion's, just covered in short grey-green fur. We have seen his face before, when he contacted the High Commander after kidnapping Tribute Dawn, demanding a meeting in exchange for her. It was an obvious trap and one we did not fall for.

"Tor." The High Commander's voice is a deep growl, full of rage.

"You can put down your weapons," Tor waves a hand at us, sounding amused. "This is only a projection. I thought perhaps you might listen better if you did not feel threatened."

"Vgotha scum." The High Commander is seething. "You dare face me after you used underhanded maneuvers to board our ship? Kidnap my Tribute? Hurt her?"

The Vgotha makes a face. "I did not mean to harm her. I did not realize how delicate human females are. Listen—"

The High Commander points his sword at the Vgotha leader. "No! I will not listen to any of your lies. We will not rest until the universe is safe from you."

"I do not wish to fight." The Vgotha actually seems frustrated. A weakness? I will have to think on it later. Right now, my focus is half on the hologram of Tor and half on scanning our surroundings. I relax minutely when Arkdhem and the other warriors come running out of the forest, heading straight for us.

"You speak as if I care what you wish."

The other warriors slow as they reach us, spreading out to surround the hologram. We need to get the Tributes back to the shuttle. But if the Vgotha can broadcast this message into our midst, what else can they do?

"We are not your enemy," Tor says. "The—"

"You weren't until you destroyed our home, our families, everything in our civilization." I snarl at him, my head jerking around, my rage swelling. "You failed though, you failed to kill us too, and we will eradicate you."

"That is what I am trying to tell you—"

"Enough!" The High Commander strides forward. Tribute Dawn tries to follow him, but Arkdhem fulfills his duties, hooking his arm around her waist and dragging her back as she curses him. At least he is good for something.

The High Commander slashes his weapon through the hologram, a vertical strike that splits the image in half and ends with a crackling screech of metal as the blade finds the source of the image. The last thing I see, before Tor's face blinks out, is murder in his eyes.

"Get the Tributes back to the ship," the High Commander roars, pointing his blade at the ocean. "Warriors, form ranks around them!"

Three Vgotha ships are rising from the water, coming just far enough forward that they are out of the range of our shuttle's weapons, and twin fears clash in my chest—mine and my Pareena's. Their doors open and Vgotha warriors jump from the openings, splashing into the shallows. With our bodies between them and the shuttle, trying to use any of our distance weapons would risk harming warriors—or worse, Tributes.

"Go!" I shove my Pareena at Kalexston, who is standing beside Arkdhem, both of their faces grim. Dawn is struggling against Arkdhem's hold, cursing at him, and he twists her around, flipping her over his shoulder.

"Bogdan, no!" My Tribute protests even as Kalexston picks her up and begins to run back the shuttle, mere steps behind Arkdhem. My heart aches at the mournful sound of her voice, but I will not fail her as I failed Harai... she will be safe, even if it is at the cost of my own life.

22

P areena

I'm going to kill Bogdan.

If he survives this, that is. I'm terrified that he won't. That neither of us will.

The warrior carrying me comes to an abrupt halt, his shoulder jerking against my stomach.

"Into the trees!" I hear Arkdhem shout. Immediately, the warrior under me changes course, heading for the forest. Lifting my head up so that I can see more than the ground, I immediately spot the Vgotha ship flying above us and I push down the scream that bubbles up in my throat. Is it going to beam us up? What will I do if it does?

A feeling of helplessness rises up inside of me, the same way I felt when the doctors told me the chemo wasn't working anymore.

Because I finally really truly believe, one hundred percent with no doubts, that this is all real. I feel it down to my bones. Bogdan is real. Our love is real. This second life, this second chance at *every-*

thing... it's real. And if I'm about to lose it just when I've fully accepted that I really have it, I'm seriously going to kill someone.

The forest swallows up the sounds of battle, the canopy hiding us from the Vgotha ship, but the warrior carrying me barely slows. I can hear Arkdhem ahead of us, crashing through the undergrowth and I groan as the 'ride' becomes even bumpier.

The breath *oofs* out of me as the warrior grinds to a halt again, his body tense beneath mine.

"Surrender, warriors. There is no need for battle. You are heavily outnumbered."

I immediately recognize the voice even though I've only heard it once before, since that one time was just a few minutes ago. My breath catches in my throat and I begin to struggle against the warrior holding me again. Dammit, I am not being taken prisoner while over some stranger's shoulder!

To my surprise, the warrior doesn't fight me. He sets me down, carefully, gently. Then I realize it's to protect me. He and Arkdhem have put Dawn and me down between them, both of them in position to shield us from the Vgotha who move out from between the trees. Four of them in total, including Tor, their leader.

"We will never surrender to you," Arkdhem says fiercely, the hate clear in his voice.

"Don't be foolish," Tor sneers back. "We won't hurt you unless we have—" Just like before, he doesn't manage to finish his sentence before the Tsenturion warrior who was carrying me springs forward with a battle cry.

Launching himself at the Vgotha standing directly in front of him, he grabs the other warrior and flings him at a second Vgotha.

"Run!" he shouts at Dawn and me, pointing at the opening between the Vgotha that he's just made.

Instinctively, we grab each other's hands as we follow his order. Panic is clawing its way up my throat and I am so, so glad I'm not wearing one of the Tsenturion gowns. A branch whips against my leg as I run, my fingers squeezing Dawn's so hard that it hurts.

I don't even know where we're running to.

But it doesn't matter.

Something catches me around my middle and the breath *oofs* out of me as it begins dragging me backwards. I claw at the restraining rope, before realizing it's actually some sort of vine. *What the—?* Beside me, Dawn screams as she fights the vine now dragging her along the ground.

The forest is alive.

I shriek, struggling, my fingers clawing uselessly at the thick vine and I can feel Bogdan's panic as he feels mine, right before the ground seems to rise up and swallow me whole.

~

Bogdan

SOMETHING IS WRONG. I can *feel* it, even through my concentration on the battlefield. Terror rising up inside of me, yet somehow apart from me... because it is not my emotion. It is my Pareena's. She is frightened and I... *I am not with her.*

I turn toward the field, my eyes seeking her, hoping she is finally safe... but the shuttle is still there and there is no sign of Arkdhem, Kalexston, or either Tribute. A Vgotha ship passes overhead, as though scanning the tree line, and narrowly avoiding a shot from our shuttle. A chill runs through me. Where are they? What has frightened her?

Something hits me from behind, taking advantage of my distraction, pulling my attention back to the battle. The Vgotha warriors are unexpectedly brutal fighters and my distraction could have easily ended in my death. The Jabol had told us they were cowards who would not engage us face to face, and until now that has proven true. Even when they kidnapped Tribute Dawn, right from our Command Ship, they did so sneakily. That is why they destroyed our whole planet in one blow, because they could not possibly win in a fair fight.

They have apparently honed their fighting skills since then, for they are formidable.

They are not as well armored as we, but their claws are even more vicious than our nanotech weapons and they fight like demons possessed. Where Arkdhem was unable to pierce my armor, the Vgotha weapons do not suffer the same flaw. My armor is some protection, but it is not complete. I snarl at the fiery pain that lashes across my back, turning and slashing blindly as the other warrior falls back.

Where is my Pareena?

The thought pounds through my head even as I face off against the Vgotha. I do not even wish to fight him. I do not care about killing these Vgotha nearly as much as I do about ensuring my Pareena's safety. But if I must kill them all to get back to her, then I will do so.

The Vgotha beast across from me snarls and launches himself at me. I slash at him and he actually manages to spin in midair, avoiding the blow. Quickly, I turn and lash out with my foot, kicking him just as he lands and sending him sprawling backward. His feet lift into the air and then swing, pulling his body back upright so that he lands facing me, eyes bright with furious intent.

Facing off with him, trying to ensure that no one else sneaks up on me... the Vgotha have shredded our lines and now it is an all-out brawl. The line across my back still stings. I can feel that my armor has closed around the breach his claws made but the injury remains. We lunge at each other again. I duck under his strike, managing to slash him across his side, but he catches me on his backswing, raking my thigh. Turning, I ignore the wounds as I face him again, gritting my teeth against the pain.

Before we can engage again, there is a loud blast of sound through the air, making all of the warriors—Tsenturion and Vgotha alike—jerk toward it in instinctive reaction. But when we turn back to fight, the Vgotha are running. At least two of them are carrying another Vgotha over their shoulder, although it is impossible to tell if they are dead or injured. My breath heaves out in a long sigh, confusion and dread rising inside of me.

Something is wrong.

"Come back here, cowards!" Someone yells, their voice full of anger.

But they are not cowards. I cannot think that anymore, not after fighting them. The Jabol described them as beasts, a label that rings true, but they are more than that. They have proven it today. I can tell that I am not the only injured Tsenturion warrior on the field, and I am certainly not among the worst of the wounded.

That sound we heard was a signal, a call to retreat because... because they've gotten what they came for? Horror at the realization fills me.

"Pareena!" Her name is a roar and I pelt toward the shuttle, my eyes scanning the field for my Tribute. Out of the corner of my eye, I can see the High Commander doing the same, yelling Dawn's name. I reach for her internally but... I cannot feel her. *"PAREENA!"*

23

———

P areena

"PAREENA? PAREENA!" The high-pitched way the nurse is saying my name sounds almost frantic.

I suck in a lungful of air—and moan. It hurts to breathe. The morphine must be wearing off again. I reach for the little button that they gave me to help control my drip.

"No—" I mumble to the nurse, trying to wave her away with my other hand. I'm too tired to deal with more tests. "Don' wanna—"

"Pareena, please, please wake up." Huh. The nurse sounds terrified. Weird.

"I'm awake," I tell her with a groan, forcing myself to focus. What has gone wrong that makes a nurse sound that scared?

My eyes pop open. I'm strapped down to a large table. An operating room? But this doesn't look like a hospital. Grey-green walls, hewn out of rock. A damp, earthy smell. What the hell?

I strain to raise my head. Across the room, Dawn is chained to a wall.

Dawn. Not a nurse. *Tribute. Tsenturion. Vgotha.*

Oh no.

"Pareena! You're awake." Dawn slumps in her chains. I feel a small trickle of relief that both of us are still clothed. That's hopefully a good sign, right? "Thank fuck, I was starting to get worried."

"Wha—" my mouth feels numb, full of cotton. "What happened?"

"The Vgotha got us," Dawn says grimly.

"But where are we?" I ask, becoming more and more alert as every second passes. Unfortunately, that also means the pain in my side is increasing. I grit my teeth against it, trying to focus on what's important. "Are we still on the planet? I thought it was safe here."

"I'm guessing we're really far underground. I doubt the Tsenturions had scans to go this deep. Or we're under bedrock maybe? Or even under the water. I have no idea."

"I feel like I'm high," I mutter, shaking my head, trying to shake off the wooziness that's lingering.

"The air is different down here—probably not the right mix of gases for a human," Dawn says, although her voice isn't certain. She's definitely more awake than I am though, so she's probably had more time to think about it.

"Excellent guess, little human." The deep, rumbling voice rolls through the room. I crane my neck as the giant from the clearing strides into the room, muscles rippling. He reminds me of an elk, graceful and powerful, but bipedal and with a humanoid face. There's a kind of wild beauty to him, but he's also terrifying. Especially when I'm chained up on a table and have no idea what he wants with us.

"Tor," Dawn practically growls his name, glaring at him. "Wasn't one kidnapping enough?" She strains, tugging at her bonds. I wish I could do the same, but just trying is enough to make me stop and pant with pain. *Ow.*

"Stop struggling," Tor orders, although he sounds more exasperated than anything else, like he can't believe she's even making the attempt. "There is no escape. Not this time." Turning his back on Dawn, he walks over to me, frowning.

"You are wounded," he says, and he almost sounds sorry about it. Now that he's looking, I can stretch out enough to see that there's blood soaking through my t-shirt, just underneath my right breast.

"Oh my God..." Panic squeezes at my chest. I'm hurt and at the mercy of the enemy. Even if he does seem like a strangely solicitous enemy.

"Do not worry, little female," Tor rumbles. I stare up at him, not sure how to interpret the caring concern that I swear I see in his eyes. "Something cut you deeply when you were being pulled here. It was unintentional. I will heal you." He reaches into his shirt and pulls out a strange looking device. I don't exactly have time to look at it closely before he's pulling up my shirt and pressing it against my skin. I don't even have time to protest, just cry out in surprise at the sudden cold then hot sensation.

"Leave her alone!" Dawn shouts. Pain lances through the spot where it touches me, and I gasp in agonized shock as the blackness roils again and I pass out.

Bogdan

THEY ARE GONE.

I sink to my knees when I see Arkdhem stumbling out of the woods, bleeding sluggishly from the shoulder he's clutching. The expression on his face is one of horrified despair and I know... I know. The warrior might be underhanded and dishonorable when it comes to trying to steal my Pareena from me, but he would never harm either Tribute. He would fight to the death for them, if need be.

For him to look like that...

I reach for my Pareena again, but I cannot feel her emotions. Our bond is too new, or perhaps the distance too great. I feel sure that she is alive, but I also fear that is only my great hope and not the reality.

Still, the Vgotha did not harm Tribute Dawn when they had her in their clutches before. Tor had taken her to demand a meeting with the High Commander. I can only hope this time will be the same. Shame rises in me as I remember counseling the High Commander to forget Tribute Dawn when she was taken, to let the Vgotha keep her, and request a replacement from the Jabol.

Now I understand.

My Pareena is not replaceable. It does not matter that we have not fully bonded yet. I do not want any Tribute but her.

"Arkdhem..." The High Commander's voice is hoarse. "Please, tell me the Tributes are hidden in the forest."

The warrior's shoulders hunch in. "I cannot, High Commander. The Vgotha found us before we could find a safe place to secure the Tributes... they outnumbered us... we made an opening and told the Tributes to run but they did not get far. There were vines that came up out of the ground, aiding the Vgotha... we tried to fight..." His voice breaks and he suddenly sounds very young. "Kalexston did not... he... he fought honorably until the end, but the Tributes were captured."

Kalexston is dead.

Guilt swamps me. He is dead because the Tributes had been the Vgotha's goal. If I had not given my Pareena into his keeping... I had been trying to protect her, but I had made the wrong choice. I should have been there, beside her, holding her. Then Kalexston might be alive and my Pareena might be safe.

The High Commander practically vibrates with tension. "Gather our dead and wounded," he orders finally. "We will run scans. Spread the fleet out around the planet—our scouts, everything. If a single ship lifts into the air that's not ours, I want to know. Do not leave them any space where they might launch unobserved."

It will stretch our warriors and our ships to their limits, but it makes sense. They are somewhere still here on the planet. We would not have been able to miss a ship taking them into space. They must have run into the forest, to wherever they were hiding before... it's highly possible they aren't on this island anymore, but they *must* be somewhere on the planet still.

A hand claps onto my shoulder and I realize I am standing there, staring upward into the sky, as if I will somehow be able to discern my Pareena's location from the angle of the sun. I turn my head to see the High Commander's—Gavrill's—eyes looking at me with grim sympathy.

"Hope is not yet lost, my friend," he says softly, his armor glimmering with repressed rage and distress, but his voice is calm. "We will regroup and then we *will* find our Tributes and take them back." I nod at the promise in his words, although I cannot unclench my jaw to answer. I am afraid that if I do, I will lose control of myself.

I move as if in a dream, following the High Commander back to the beach. Two warriors go with Arkdhem to the forest to collect Kalexston's body. Surprisingly, thankfully, there is only one other body to recover. Borodem will never get his Tribute. A deep sadness settles over me.

We have lost a few warriors over the tsencyles we've spent hunting the Vgotha, they are not the first... but they are the first since the Jabol finally delivered on their promise of Tributes. The first since we were given *hope*.

Grief is followed by anger, but there is also relief that our losses were not greater. They could have been. The Jabol descriptions of the Vgotha's hand-to-hand fighting capabilities were highly inaccurate. If we were not constantly training, despite the fact that this was the first time we'd met the Vgotha on an actual battleground, we would have been easily overrun. We will have to train harder than ever in case we ever face them off ship again. The knowledge is both humbling and disturbing.

First new technology on their ships that allow them to elude us and now this? The Vgotha threat is greater than ever.

And my Pareena is in their hands... The last time I felt this helpless was after the Great Tragedy. The only difference is now I also feel the most dangerous of emotions—hope.

24

_____

Pareena

WHEN I COME TO, the ache in my side is gone, replaced by an intense tingling. I gasp and automatically wince, expecting shooting pain from the movement but... nothing. I sigh in relief.

"Pareena?" Dawn calls out to me. I lift my head to look at her. It's all I can lift because even though Tor did something to heal the wound, I'm still tied down. At least I don't have to crane my neck as far. The table under my shoulders has elevated a little so I'm half sitting up, which also allows me to breathe a little better.

"Present," I return weakly, giving her a lopsided smile.

"Oh, thank goodness." Dawn sags back against the wall, her hair falling in her face. "He said you would be, but... I just didn't know whether or not to believe him. I don't think he would mean to hurt you, honestly, but I could always be wrong."

"I'm okay," I reassure her, although I'm not entirely sure that I am. Physically, I do seem to be fine now, but emotionally... mentally... My brain feels like utter chaos. "Except... this is all real, isn't it? It's not a dream?"

I'd pretty much come to accept that it wasn't, but now I'm almost hoping it is. Because I don't want this part to be real. I want to be able to click my heels together and magically be returned to Bogdan. But if this is real, then that's not going to happen. Accepting that I was abducted by aliens once? That was hard enough. Accepting that it's happened again and I'm never going to see the alien that I fell in love with again? That makes me want to start screaming and never stop.

Dawn's face softens as she looks at me. "No. It's not a dream."

"You know, when I first woke up with Frllil, I thought I was in a coma. That this all was the product of my imagination. I mean, that's a lot easier to believe than something like, I was abducted from Earth via an e-reader. My cancer is cured, and I have an alien master. And now, I've been abducted a second time, and I'm caught in an inter-species feud where both sides want to annihilate the other."

"That's some imagination. You know what they say, truth is stranger than fiction," Dawn tries to joke. Neither of us laughs and her expression turns sad. "This is all real, I'm afraid. I'm real. You're here. This," she waves a hand at the room, stretching as far as the chain allows, "is happening."

"Damn."

"Yeah."

"This happened to you before, right?" I need to keep moving forward. If I stop, I'll panic. I can't do that yet. When I'm back with Bogdan, I'll let myself freak out. "You never told me how you escaped. I think we should definitely go over that now."

"Last time I escaped because the ship helped me," Dawn says, shrugging one shoulder a little ruefully.

"What the what?" That entire sentence makes no sense.

"I know it sounds crazy, but that's what happened. I was crying in my cell and all I wanted was to get out... and then a door opened and I swear, the ship led me through itself to an escape pod and then the escape pod took me back to Gavrill." She sighs. "The Tsenturions wanted to experiment on it but I convinced them to let it go and try to follow it back to the Vgotha ships... it escaped, but I'm kinda glad it did."

"You're talking about it like it was alive." I'm fascinated by the idea.

"I think it might have been. Before Gavrill put it back into space to follow it, the Tsenturions discovered that it was made of living organic material. Like a really smart mushroom or something. I think it decided to help me."

"I guess that's why we're in a cave instead of on a ship," I reply, a little glumly, tugging at the bonds on my wrists. My head falls back as the stark reality of our situation is really driven home. Captured by Vgotha, who are obviously working to keep us from escaping the same way Dawn did the first time, and I no longer even have the faint hope of waking up in the hospital.

Part of me can't believe I convinced myself that this was all a dream. I've *never* had dreams that felt so real. I think deep down, I always knew it was happening, I just didn't want to admit it. Because being abducted by aliens to be a sex slave isn't something that's supposed to happen in real life. Considering the trauma of cancer and knowing I was dying, followed by the trauma of being abducted by aliens, believing everything was a dream was my brain's way of protecting myself.

Huh. I wonder if other Tributes will be more likely to handle being abducted the way Dawn did or the way I did. She wasn't already dealing with trauma at the time she was taken, unlike me. She told me she had lost her family members before abduction, but their deaths weren't recent. Maybe being in the midst of a first trauma when abducted led to dissociation.

"What are you thinking about?" Dawn interrupts.

"Oh... nothing important. Therapist thoughts." I make a face. I need to focus. Because this is real and if I ever want to see Bogdan again, we need to escape. I can't even feel his emotions right now but I'm sure he's furious and terrified... emotions that start to rise in myself when I realize I don't even know if he's alive. Swallowing back the fear, I shake my head. I have to operate under the assumption that he's alive and well or I'll completely break down. This is my second chance at life, dammit. I'm not going to let myself break down unless I know that something has happened to him. "What do you think the Vgotha want with us?"

"Before the attack, Tor said something about wanting to meet with the High Commander," she says slowly. "That's what he said he wanted last time too. I don't know why though. And I don't know why he thinks attacking them will help—"

"The Tsenturions attacked us," a deep voice interrupts. Tor strides back into the room, almost prowling, like some great beast out of a fairy tale. He swings his great antlered head my direction and I freeze like a rabbit sighting a predator, suddenly unsure of myself. "Tribute Pareena. I trust you are feeling better?"

"Oh yeah, I'm doing great," I try for sarcasm, but my voice comes out breathy and scared. I shrink back on the table as he looms over me.

"Leave her alone, asshole!" Dawn yells at him and out of the corner of my eye I can see her struggling again. Straightening, Tor makes a gesture, not unlike a Tsenturion ordering a door to open on their ship. Part of the wall seems to grow outward, a grey-green mask moving almost like nanotech to cover her mouth. Her eyes are huge and frantic as her cries grow muffled, but she's still breathing.

"What did you do to her?" My voice has gotten a little shriller. So much for sounding brave.

"Nothing that will harm her. Her shrieks have begun to hurt my ears." He grimaces slightly, shooting a look over his shoulder that would make most people quail in fear. Dawn glares back at him.

"Let her go," I demand, my own fear sliding away in defense of my friend. It doesn't hurt that so far, while he looks threatening, Tor hasn't actually done anything to hurt us. Heck, he healed my side. Then again, I wouldn't have been hurt if he hadn't had us kidnapped...

"Not unless she will keep silent and allow me to speak. I have waited a long time for this audience and time is of the essence."

"Destroying the entire Tsenturion planet wasn't a good way to get their attention." I scowl at him. "Maybe you should've just left a message at the beep."

With a grunt, he waves his hand at my table. Streams of grey-green table matter flow up my shoulder, starting to cover my mouth.

"Wait," I sputter. "I'll be quiet. Just... tell me what you want with us. Maybe I can help."

He pauses. Another flick of his wrist and the gag flows away and becomes part of the table again.

Alien tech is so cool. Super creepy, but cool.

"I have been trying to communicate with the High Commander for some time. A message could not be sent over normal channels. There was no way to ensure it would not be intercepted and corrupted."

"Well, kidnapping us is not going to create any good will between you," I point out, keeping my tone reasonable. I find myself falling into my therapy voice, pointing out the flaws in his logic. "They're probably pretty upset with you right now. On top of the whole geno-cide thing."

For a long moment, Tor stares at me and I shrink back, thinking that maybe I've gone too far... Then he turns away and with a wave of his hand, a portion of the wall smooths out. Images appear as if on a screen—the clearing where we were. There are Tsenturions in full armor patrolling the empty space. One runs out of the woods to the center where Arkdhem stands, clenching his fists over and over again —it looks like he's giving a report. They're searching for us.

I don't see Bogdan or Gavrill and my heart aches. My heart sends a plea out to the universe that they're both unharmed.

"They'll find us, you know," I tell Tor quietly. "They won't stop looking until they do."

He snorts. "They will not find you. They did not even know we were here on this planet or they would not have brought you here. But now I have the upper hand and the High Commander will listen to my demands." Tor's dark gaze turns to the screen. "Once he is desperate enough, he will do anything. Even talk with a Vgotha."

~

Bogdan

I TEAR A SAPLING UP by its roots and toss it aside. Beside me, the High Commander does the same. Behind us, Tsenturion warriors comb the undergrowth. I refused to leave the planet and almost as soon as he'd gone up to the Command Ship and ensured his orders to create a blockade around the planet were being followed, the High Commander returned.

Neither of us can sit by idly, waiting for news, when we could be looking for our Tributes. Even if I find nothing, I must try. All I am sure of is that my Pareena still lives. I cannot feel her emotions, but I feel sure of that.

The High Commander hefts another sapling and sends it crashing into the brush. "It's no use. We should burn this place to the ground."

"Once we are sure Dawn and Pareena are not here." We don't even know if they are still on this island, but I know neither of us will risk the fact that they might be. The only thing we can be sure of is that they are still on the planet.

The High Commander covers his face with a hand for a moment. When he drops it, his face is frozen like a mask, anguish writ in every line of his body.

"I cannot do it, Bogdan," he says quietly, so that no one will overhear. In that moment, he is not my High Commander, he is my friend, and he is in pain. "I cannot sacrifice her for our people, and I cannot sacrifice our people for her. I do not know what to do."

Clapping my hand on his shoulder, I bow my head forward until our foreheads touch in a show of shared grief.

"We do not know what Tor wishes," I say quietly. "But your Dawn was unharmed the last time he took her. No matter how the Vgotha feel about us, there is no reason to think they'd hurt the Tributes."

"We have hunted them for so long and now..." Gavrill sighs,

closing his eyes. "I don't know what to do. What concessions I might be willing to make." He looks at me, pain in his eyes. "Perhaps you were right, and the Tributes are a weakness we should not have indulged in until the Vgotha threat was eradicated."

"No," I say immediately, pulling back and shaking my head. "I was wrong, and you were right. Your Dawn, my Pareena... they are worth more than their ability to bear our children. They are the hope for our future, and they brighten our lives. I cannot imagine how hard is it to have your Dawn taken from you a second time, but you cannot give up." I grip his shoulders. "Your Tribute needs you, High Commander." Although he has been speaking to me as Gavrill, I deliberately use his title to push him back into his role.

It has the effect I hoped for and he straightens up, determination firming his jaw.

"The planet is blockaded," I say. "They are here. All we have to do is find them."

There is a subtle shift in the color of his armor—it is still the bluish gray of despair and mourning, but there is something new there too. Something more determined.

I would not have expected myself to be one for rousing speeches, but my Pareena has changed that about me. She has given me something I did not have before—a reason to live rather than a reason to die. Sending her off with another was foolish. I should have gone with her. If—*when*—I get her back, nothing will ever take her from my side again.

Grief for Kalexston, for Borodem rises again. They have already been taken back to the Command Ship where their bodies will be prepared for full funeral honors. Kalexston's death especially weighs on my conscience, but I will ensure he did not die in vain.

We will tear this planet apart looking, if we must. There is nothing in the universe that will keep me from my Pareena. And then the Vgotha will pay for their crimes.

Pareena

"WHAT IS IT YOU WANT?" I ask, a little worried by the almost manic gleam in his eyes.

"We Vogtha have been persecuted and hunted unjustly for too long. The age of hiding and cringing in shadows needs to end, we need peace." The way he says it is almost a threat and I can only imagine how he thinks peace will be obtained. To be fair, the Tsenturions seem to feel the same way about Vgotha, but...

"The Tsenturions hunt the Vgotha because you destroyed their planet and everyone on it. You're the aggressors. You struck first. You blew up Tsentur. Of course, they were going to come after you."

"That is what your warriors think, the lie they were told." His face twists in anger, making him appear truly frightening. I am glad that anger is not directed at me. "That is what I want to tell them. The truth behind our supposed attack on Tsentur."

I'm a therapist, I know better than anyone that there are multiple sides to any story. The Tsenturions seem sure... but so does Tor.

"What is the truth?" Because there are a lot of things that don't add up. I admit, I got a little frustrated when Gavrill wouldn't let Tor get a word in edgewise. He was a hologram, not even there in person, and Gavrill wouldn't let him finish a sentence. I'd wanted to know what he wanted, just from natural human curiosity.

"The Vgotha did not destroy Tsentur."

"Okay..." I draw out the word, tilting my head at him. "Do you have any proof of that?"

A grim smile curves his lips. "Not so long ago, we finally acquired some."

He waves his hand and the screen showing the Tsenturions searching for us changes. No more forest, I can now see a landing deck, much like the one where the presentation ceremony was conducted. Instead of Tsenturions, blob like creatures ride little platforms around. The creatures look like Frillil, when he wasn't trying to look humanoid.

"The Jabol," I say. "What does this have to do—"

"Watch," Tor commands, his voice deep and resonant in this underground cavern.

So I watch. The video speeds up, the Jabol racing around the platform, interacting with their computers. I don't know exactly what I'm seeing but the air feels heavy. Something bad is about to happen on screen, I can sense it.

Groups of Jabol cluster around a console in front of a large screen of their own, all of them practically vibrating with excitement. The screen in front of them shows a view of space... and then a giant planet floats into view.

"Planet Tsentur," Tor explains in a bleak voice just as the Jabol being to sway back and forth. Something on the bottom edge of the screen is beginning to glow, brighter and brighter, turning a threatening red.

And I can't breathe. Somehow, I know what's about to happen. I've seen Star Wars but... this isn't a movie. It's real. A large beam of energy shoots out from the Jabol's ship, straight at the planet. It ripples, flaring and pulsing, and that horrifying bright red light surrounds the planet.

A minute later—probably more, because the video is sped up—Tsentur explodes. They did it. The Jabol Death Star-ed Tsentur.

25

P areena

SEEING Tsentur explode has both Dawn and I nearly limp with horror. Knowing it happened was bad enough... watching it... I can only imagine the terror of the Tsenturion people when that terrible red glow surrounded their planet. They would have known something was wrong, that something was happening. I can only hope they didn't suffer when the final blow came.

"How?" I gasp out the word, tears surging in my eyes. "How come Gavrill and the others don't know this?"

"The Jabol were trusted merchants who commonly traded with the Tsenturions. A ship of theirs would have been welcomed into Tsenturion space," Tor says darkly, still staring at the screen. "When the High Commander's ship returned home, they were there to greet him and tell him about the horrible Vgotha who had destroyed Tsentur."

For a long moment the room is quiet, but I feel like I've just survived an earthquake. My whole world view is shaken, but at the same time, I can't make sense of it. Why would the Jabol do that?

"You could've doctored that footage," I say, but I'm not certain. Across the room, Dawn's eyes are wide, and tears roll down her cheeks as well. Both of us are affected, confused... I don't know who to believe. "Why would the Jabol even want to blow up the Tsenturions' planet? Like you said, they traded with them."

"The Jabol needed protectors. They faced a new threat, risen from the ranks of the species they kept as slaves."

"What threat?"

"The Vgotha." Tor's voice echoes in the chamber, filling the shocked silence. "Have the Tsenturions ever wondered where the Vgotha came from?"

"Um..." I look at Dawn, because she's known them for longer than I have. She shakes her head slightly, eyes wide over the gag, her expression just as troubled as mine.

"They treated us as beasts of labor, enslaved for centuries." Tor snarls, shaking his antlered head. "They do not see other species as being equal, do not consider us important. The Jabol are not fighters. They focused their technology on exploiting and experimenting on other species, but they did so subtly, knowing that war would thwart their efforts. They grew complacent, thinking the Vgotha were too stupid, too ignorant to even want to be free of their tyranny. But they were wrong. We revolted. Stole ships and escaped their tyranny, and then returned again and again to free more of our people. They needed strong protectors who would regard us as the enemy, without having to explain what they had done to us."

"So, they blew up Tsentur and framed you," I whisper. It could be a lie. A trick. A trap.

But I believe him.

Tor bows his head.

"Do you have proof? That you were enslaved?" I brace for more videos.

In answer, Tor lowers his head, turning so I can see the bare skin on the back of his neck, a worn patch where no fur grows. There, in faded ink, is a tattooed symbol of a circle with three wavy lines traveling horizontally across it. I still, my breath catching. I immediately recognize that symbol, I saw it all over Frllil's facility. I never asked what it meant, I just assumed it was a Jabol thing. Well, technically I guess it is.

"This marks me as property of the Jabol," Tor rumbles. "I've bore it since birth. The slavers took me from my mother and gave it to me before I was sent to the children pens and raised for a single fate: to work and die in the mines. The Jabols need supplies for all their tech."

"They didn't use robots?" I blurt. I can't get my mind around this.

"Why would they waste their great intellect on building and maintaining machines for such a low purpose when they had easily replaceable labor?" He sneers and I know he's not speaking his opinion but repeating something he must have heard once. "Every one of my race was captured and pressed into work. Indeed, I was sent to the most dangerous places, for as a child I was small and could fit into the narrow spaces where the Jabols found the best ore."

I stare into Tor's white eyes, feeling like I've been crushed under a boulder. My stomach roils and threatens to bubble over.

If this is true, then everything the Tsenturions believe about the Jabol and Vgotha is wrong. The race they've been hunting for years, in a misguided sense of punishment, is innocent. The real aggressors, the Jabol, control the narrative and rule the Tsenturions in their own way.

This is awful. I can't imagine someone like Frllil being so cruel... but then again, he's willing to capture human women, risk their lives by bringing them through a wormhole, to be the brides of aliens. And before Dawn got involved in the program, they didn't even ask for the negligible consent that I gave. So maybe I'm not the best judge of what Jabol ethics might lead Frllil to do... I don't like to think that he had anything to do with the destruction of Tsentur, because I *liked* him, but that doesn't mean I'm right.

Maybe the Jabol are a little like humans and there are some who are capable of committing terrible acts and some who are really good people. Or maybe they're *exactly* like humans and even the really 'nice' ones are capable of terrible things, especially when it comes to others that they think are different or less than them.

But none of that is what is most important.

"We have to tell them," I finally say. I still feel sick, but there's not time. "We have to tell the Tsenturions what really happened." The horrible image of Tsentur's broken pieces is still on screen.

"What do you think I've been trying to do?" Tor snarls. "The High Commander is unwilling to listen and now more of my Vgotha warriors have *died* because he is too much of a Jabol pawn to meet with me. I cannot send the message without risking the Jabol knowing about it. So now I have you and eventually he will have to agree to a meeting."

"Maybe but... that won't make him a better listener." I look up at Tor, meeting his gaze. "Let us go. *We* can take him the video and tell him everything you just told us. *We* can speak for you."

Tor's brow furrows, but I can tell he's thinking about it. He shakes his head. "I would rather speak for myself."

"You can't force someone to listen to you," I say in exasperation. "If you drag him, unwilling, to a meeting, he's not going to be in a listening frame of mind. Kidnapping us was an act of war, that makes you the bad guy in this scenario, even if you're trying to do the right thing in the long run. The Tsenturions lost everyone they loved long ago they're going to be too freaked out to listen to you if you're holding us over their heads the whole time."

At least Gavrill and Bogdan will be, since they're the most emotionally involved, but since they're also the top two ranking warriors in the fleet it doesn't really matter if someone else might be thinking more clearly. "But if you let us go back, it's a clear peace offering and it's exactly what they *won't* expect."

Dawn makes a muffled noise behind her gag, like she's trying to talk. Narrowing his eyes, Tor studies her.

"No screaming," he says, and she nods in agreement. With another wave of his hand, the gag recedes.

"I escaped last time, because your ship helped me," she says quickly, like she's afraid she won't be able to get the words out before he gags her again. "Gavrill and the warriors were already confused by that, confused by the fact that you didn't harm me at all, they *wondered why.* If *you* let us go, deliberately, that just makes everything you're saying more believable."

Tor begins to pace, obviously thinking about our words but unsure of changing his plan.

"Send Dawn back," I say suddenly. "I'll stay here."

"No," Dawn gasps, but I keep talking to Tor.

"I trust you. Someone has to start trusting around here. It may as well be me." And my negotiating skills might keep me alive even if this is a trick. I definitely get the impression that Tor likes me better than Dawn. "Maybe if I show some trust, you will too."

"You're a brave one," Tor rumbles, pausing beside me. He cocks his head as he looks down at me, studying my expression.

"Thank you?" It comes out as more of a question than anything else, because I'm not sure if that's really a good description for me right now. I don't feel particularly brave. Just out of options.

"I wouldn't mind a Tribute of my own." He caresses my cheek with a callused finger. Dawn chokes on a gasp.

Argh. Males. I very gently move my face away from his touch.

"I'm not interested in that sort of relationship," I say firmly. "I'm already in one and it's complicated enough."

A strange sound fills my ears, like rocks rolling into each other, and I realize he's chuckling.

"So brave. And honest. Very well. I will not claim a Tribute... yet."

"So, you agree? You'll let Dawn go?" I persist.

"No," Tor clicks a finger and both our bonds release. "I've decided. Both of you will go back."

"What's the catch?" Dawn rubs her wrists, scuttling past Tor to help me off the table.

"If I only send one of you back, it will still seem as though I am the 'bad guy,' yes?" He speaks the slang a little oddly, although he definitely gets the general idea. "So, I will be definitely not-the-bad-guy and I will send you both back. But if the Tsenturions do not listen to you, if they attack us again, we will not hold back this time. We have new ships, new weapons, and we will destroy them. I will not accept any further unnecessary losses of my people. After today, many are already unsure that we should forgive the Tsenturions for their ignorance."

"Fine." I'm not going to argue with him, I'm just going to have to hope that Gavrill will listen better to Dawn and me than he has to Tor himself. "Can you give us a copy of the video? We promise we will only show it to the high command, in a secure location." The Jabol definitely won't like the Tsenturions knowing they're really the enemy. We need to keep this a secret as long as possible. I can't keep it from Bogdan though. Thankfully, as Gavrill's second-in-command, he's part of the high command.

Dawn and I lean against each other, not so much because we can't hold ourselves up, as to just reassure ourselves that we're really okay. That we have support if we need it.

Tor motions and the wall ejects a tiny cylinder. When he hands it to me, my fingers curl around it, gripping it tightly. So much depends on this one little cylinder.

"Follow me." Tor leads us into a long corridor, the rough hewn walls glitter in the light he pulls from a pouch on his waist. The light is dimmer than I would like but it's just enough to see by. Dawn and I stumble along behind him, keeping our eyes to the ground so that we don't trip over anything.

I can't tell how long we walk or how many turns we take. I do know I couldn't easily find my way back through the caves, definitely not without getting lost. Every so often we hear voices, deep rumbling ones, and I know it must be more Vgotha. I guess Tor didn't have to check in with the others about his plan.

I have to admit, now that I'm here, I'm curious about the Vgotha and how their society is structured. Do they live the same way as they did before they were enslaved by the Jabol? How has their society changed since they escaped? More questions pop into my head—do they have mates? Children? A home?

I keep from asking any of my questions though, unsure of their welcome. I also am not sure I want to know all of the answers. It's too sad. Too infuriating. And I can only handle so much right now.

The corridor begins to get brighter, my leg muscles starting to burn with exertion, and I realize we're going uphill. As the opening appears in the distance, Tor comes to a halt, turning to look at Dawn and me. A little worm of fear wriggles through me; he's not going to change his mind about letting us go, is he?

"Many cycles passed before the Vgotha understood why we were being hunted," he says, his voice sad. "Many more before we discovered what really happened, and even more until we could prove it. During that time, we fought to defend ourselves. But we are tired of living in hiding. My hope is that you will be able to convince the Tsenturions to hear us out."

"We want to help," I say, speaking for both Dawn and I. She nods her head, surprisingly quiet. "Thank you for trusting us."

"If they do not believe the vid, if they do not believe you, tell the High Commander—we are no longer the easy prey they found us to be initially," Tor says, his eyes flashing even in the dark. I go very still, my breathing stuttering a little. The male is an apex predator and right now he is deadly serious. "Tell him, the Riknari gave us the vid. They gave us our new ships and tech. And if we do not prevail on our own, they *will* be back to help us."

"Who are the Riknari?" I ask, confused and a little scared. Something about the way Tor said their name made me think he was making a *really* dramatic statement.

"Just tell the High Commander." Tor nods and points to the long corridor. "Now go. Turn right when you get out of the cave."

Glancing at each other, Dawn and I instinctively reach out to grab each other's hands and we run the last long length of the corridor together, bursting out into the forest from a cave. Panting, I look over my shoulder to see that the blackness of the cave swallowed up any sign of Tor, if he is even still there watching us.

I look at Dawn. "So? What do you think?"

She chews on her lower lip. "I don't know. I mean... he *did* just let us go..."

"They did that with you before though, kind of," I point out.

"The *ship* did." She rubs one hand over her face. "But... I felt like he was telling the truth. Or at least, what he believes is the truth. Maybe he's right. Maybe this was all a frame job and the Jabol are the real bad guys."

Which is a really hard thing to swallow. Because that means *our* guys are also the bad guys in a way. Duped. Ignorant. But still fighting on the side of evil.

I reach for my usual standby of dealing with things I don't want to think about—distraction. Turning in a slow circle, all I can see are trees.

"So, I guess we go right?" Sadly, there's not a path or anything. That would be way too easy, I guess.

"Um... it does look a little less dense. And I guess if we're going to trust Tor, we might as well trust that he's not just sending us out here on the planet to die," she says. Good point. So, we start walking.

I am extra thankful that we got 'planet' clothes. I can't even imagine how much harder this would have been in a filmy Tsenturion gown. I'm not sure that Dawn is right about this direction being less dense, but it's definitely not more densely forested than any of the other directions.

I'm not sure it matters anyway.

"I think Tor definitely liked you better than me," Dawn says after a few long minutes of silence.

"Um..."

"He's kind of hot, right? In a weird, Dark Elf kind of way."

Huh. Now that she mentions it, he does kind of look like a Dark Elf. A little furrier than I pictured them, but close enough.

"Do you think he has a weird penis too?" she muses.

"It would be kind of disappointing if he didn't," I respond with a laugh.

I guess if we have to hike across a weird alien planet, looking for our alien mates, we might as well talk about weird alien peen.

Unfortunately, it's a hot weird alien planet and I'm sweaty and thirsty within twenty minutes... which is, thankfully, when we hear someone yelling our names.

26

———

B ogdan

"PAREENA!"

I can't believe my eyes.

The High Commander had set the ships to scanning the planet at regular intervals, but we hadn't actually expected it to pick up anything. Not after the first scan when we realized the Vgotha had managed to not only hide themselves, but to obscure the nanotech signals from the bride training belts.

At best, we thought we'd catch a ship as it lifted into the air.

Instead, suddenly, the bride trainers flashed their location on our scans. They were not on the island, which means all our searching there had been useless. Even knowing it could be a trap, Gavrill and I had immediately led a team to where their signatures had been picked up. The forest was too dense for a shuttle, but we landed as close as we could and he and I began running straight for their location, shouting their names.

If the Vgotha were there, we wanted them to know we were coming, in hopes of springing the trap. The other warriors hung back, waiting to see what happened.

"Bogdan!" My Pareena runs through the trees, joy on her face, streaking toward me. The relief that I feel upon seeing her is so over-powering that when she jumps forward and against me, wrapping her legs and arms around me, I fall to my knees. I can feel her again, feel her joy, her love, warming me from the inside out. The sparkles on my armor swirl and flash like tiny nebulas moving over me.

Close by, Gavrill and Tribute Dawn are having a similar reunion, his hands running over her as if he cannot believe that he's touching her again. I know how he feels.

"How did you get away from the Vgotha?" I ask, holding my Pareena so tightly that it is a wonder she can breathe. Pride surges through me. I already knew my Tribute was a wonder, but even I would not have expected such a wonder from her. Unless perhaps the ship somehow helped them again? I am rather skeptical of such an idea. I cannot imagine the Vgotha are so incompetent that they would fail to block an avenue that had already been utilized.

"Not now," Gavrill says, his voice snapping out as he becomes the High Commander again. "We're too vulnerable here on planet. We'll head straight back to the ship. Medik is waiting and you can tell us your story there." He turns to our other warriors. "Go back that way, find where the Vgotha are hiding and destroy them."

Strangely, I feel my Pareena tense, feel her uncertainty and... I am not certain what else, but I do not think it is good.

"Wait!" Tribute Dawn yells out and all of the warriors freeze. "Um, you should *all* come back with us, okay? You shouldn't go after the Vgotha until Pareena and I tell our story."

The High Commander gives her a long look, his face stony, but he nods before lifting her into his arms, refusing to let her walk. He looks at the warriors, who are waiting for his order. "Guard our retreat."

Since I am already holding my Pareena, I begin to move toward the ship as quickly as I can. The skin along the back of my neck prickles, as though there are watchers in the woods, but that is impossible. The scans did not see any Vgotha and there is no sign of them now. Perhaps they were pursuing the Tributes and fell back when they saw us? I tighten my grip on her, eyes scanning the trees for further threat.

"You're safe now," I kiss along her hairline, moving quickly through the forest. As soon as I get her back on the ship. "The Vgotha will never touch you again, I vow it."

For some reason, I swear I can feel her consternation increase. I tighten my grip on her, picking up my pace as the small clearing where we landed appears. I don't understand the emotions I am picking up from her and that causes me even more concern.

The shuttle door opens as we rush toward it, the warriors around us alert for another Vgotha attack. Medik is waiting inside with two warriors he's been training as his assistants. Transport platforms hover beside them. Gavrill and I both ignore the platforms, electing to carry our Tributes and set them on our laps for Medik to scan. Pareena leans against me, the side of her face nuzzling into my shoulder.

"No internal trauma," Medik announces. "And no external wounds as far as I can see." He frowns, pausing as he runs the scanner over my Pareena's stomach.

"What is it?" I snap out the question, too wound up to be polite.

"It looks as though…"

"I *was* hurt," she says, and my chest tightens. "The Vgotha healed me."

Emotions clash inside of me. She was hurt—fury and hate. She was healed—reluctant gratitude. I might not want to be grateful to the Vgotha for anything, I might not want to think one single good thing about them, but I cannot be angry that they spared my Pareena any pain. Even if they were the ones to cause it.

"We should get some armor," Tribute Dawn says. "Why don't our belts work as armor like your nanotech does?"

"Because they were made for Tributes, not warriors," the High Commander says.

"And so we don't need armor?"

The High Commander nods. "Exactly."

"Okay, but I keep ending up in situations where armor would be handy. I'm just saying."

I growl, not liking the reminder. Perhaps we *should* speak with the Jabol about adjusting the Bridal Trainers to also have protective functions. I do not like to think that it would ever be necessary, but I will choose my Pareena's safety over my own pride without hesitation.

"Okay so..." Tribute Dawn looks up at the High Commander. She seems paler than usual, although that is not entirely surprising. Both Tributes have been through an ordeal. "When we get back to the ship, we need to speak with you and Bogdan. Alone." She glances at Medik. "Medik too, would probably be a good idea."

I would rather take my Pareena back to my room to check her over thoroughly myself, but she's already nodding. I can feel how serious she is through our bond. As happy as she is to be reunited with me, there is something weighing heavily on her mind.

"Yes," she says quietly. "I think just the three of you to start."

Pareena

It ends up being four of them gathered in Gavrill and Dawn's room, because Arkdhem was waiting for us as soon as the shuttle docked. He apologized over and over to Dawn for allowing her to be taken, even though she told him it wasn't necessary. I was just relieved that the warrior who had been guarding me wasn't there doing the same. She ended up telling Arkdhem to come too. Possibly to reassure him that us being taken wasn't actually a bad thing.

I don't protest because Arkdhem *is* part of the high command, but I'm glad that it's just them. This is going to be hard enough and I think it's best the leaders decide how to present the information to the rest of the warriors. Dawn and I are really only observers to Tsenturion culture, I can't begin to predict how they will react.

Gavrill sits down in his chair, Dawn on his lap, and Bogdan does the same with me. Despite the seriousness of the situation, I can't help but be a little amused. Then again, it's not like I want to let him go either. I lean against him and I'm not sure whether it's to draw on his strength or because I'm preparing to comfort him.

"What is it you need to tell us?" Gavrill asks, his expression serious.

"A message from the Vgotha," Dawn says in a rush, speaking even faster when Gavrill's expression changes. I can feel Bogdan stiffen beneath me—and not in the fun way. Neither of them wants to listen, but unlike with Tor they aren't immediately interrupting her either. "They've been trying to meet with you because they didn't dare send a message that might get intercepted. They aren't the bad guys, they didn't destroy Tsentur, the Jabol did."

There is dead silence in the room. I can feel Bogdan's emotions—they go straight to denial and fury.

"Lies," Arkdhem snarls, getting to his feet and glaring at us. Beside him, Medik sits as if frozen, his expression completely blank. "The Vgotha are dishonorable cowards, they are scum, and the Jabol are our allies. Why would you believe such a thing?"

"Because they showed us this," I say quietly, pulling the small cylinder Tor gave me out of my pocket and holding it up. It's only as I do so that I realize, I have no way of knowing how to access the information on it. Fortunately, Medik suddenly begins to move again, and he reaches across the table, plucking it from my fingers. After a long moment of examining it, he twists, and a hologram leaps out of the end of it... I recognize the scene immediately, a smaller version of what Tor showed us.

"What is this?" Gavrill asks as the Jabol start to race around in the image.

"Just watch," Dawn murmurs, interlacing her small hand with his.

I sit rigid, studying the Tsenturion's faces. I can't guess what they're thinking, although I can feel Bogdan's growing confusion and anger, his utter grief and devastation when the planet finally explodes. Medik bows his head so that I can no longer see his face.

"That's what they wanted to show us," Dawn says as the three warriors stare stone faced at the hologram showing the rubble of their homeworld. "That and proof that the Vgotha were a slave race, imprisoned by the Jabol and treated cruelly. And when the Vgotha broke free, the Jabol were afraid of their vengeance. So, they destroyed Tsentur and framed the Vgotha."

Arkdhem snorts derisively, obviously not believing any of this.

"You think this is truth?" Gavrill asks, his tone neutral.

"I do," Dawn murmurs. "I know it's crazy, but...I don't think Tor is lying." She looks at me.

"I don't either," I say. "I can understand why you'd be reluctant to believe it—"

"I can't believe I'm hearing this. This proves nothing," Arkdhem interrupts, furious. He slams his fist down on the table in front of him. "We lost *two* warriors today to the Vgotha and you come in here with this... this fake vid, these Vgotha lies—"

"Lost?!" Dawn's horrified question cuts him off. "Who did we lose?"

"Kalexston, who gave his life trying to keep Tribute Pareena from being taken," Arkdhem glares at me as my heart sinks into my stomach. That must have been the warrior who had been guarding me. Dead? He was dead? "And Borodem who fought them and fell on the beach."

"Oh no..." I breathe out the words, tears springing to my eyes. I feel awful about Kalexston, but even worse about Borodem... he'd had so much hope for the future, for *his* future and now...

"That's not the Vgotha's fault," Dawn insists, although there are tears now running down her face. "*They* didn't attack first. *They* didn't lie to you. *They* have just been trying to meet with you and *you* didn't listen!" Realizing what she's saying, how it sounds like she's actually blaming her mate, she claps her hands over her mouth and stares at Gavrill in horror and apology.

"It all comes back to the Jabol," I say quickly. "If they destroyed

Tsentur and lied to you from the beginning—"

"*If*," Arkdhem mutters, his faith still clearly rooted in the Jabol.

"Then it's completely understandable why you'd react the way you did today. But they lost warriors today too and Tor still wants to end the fighting... he let us go because he wanted to get this message to you so badly."

"The Vgotha are known for their tricks," Gavrill says, his voice still neutral.

"Known by who?" I ask gently, since Dawn still has her hands over her mouth, and someone has to ask. "The Jabol?"

Silence falls again. A muscle in Gavrill's jaw clenches. Bogdan's emotions roil so violently I can't tell what he's thinking, what he believes.

Slowly, Medik gets to feet. "I... If you will excuse me..."

"Yes, of course," Gavrill says immediately, his voice softening. "We will speak later."

Nodding, seemingly dazed, Medik practically stumbles from the room and I bite down on my lower lip. Maybe Bogdan will allow me to seek him out later. He's obviously in a bit of shock and even though it's not really my fault, I can't help but feel a little responsible.

"We cannot trust a vid from the Vgotha," Gavrill says finally, his voice gentle because he can tell he's disappointing Dawn. "They have every reason to lie."

"So do the Jabol if the Vgotha are telling the truth!" she retorts.

"It is very convenient that they suddenly have this vid now," Arkdhem says with a sneer. He is the most outwardly opposed to believing the Vgotha, but Bogdan has been so quiet, I can't tell if he agrees with Arkdhem or not.

"They said they got it—and their new tech and ships—from someone called the Riknari," I say, remembering that we were supposed to tell them that. I didn't actually expect much of a reaction, but both Arkdhem and Gavrill stare at me, completely thunderstruck, and I can feel the deep shock that ripples through Bogdan. Tor had been right—it does mean something to them. Something big. "Um... so, uh, what does that mean exactly?"

27

———

B ogdan

Our Tributes have delivered shock upon shock in a short period of time. Finding them running through the forest had been a joyful one. The vid they'd shown us was a confusing one, because watching it I could feel nothing but pain, but I also do not know if it can be believed.

The Riknari... That is the biggest shock of all.

"They're a... legend," I say slowly. I look at the High Commander and then at Arkdhem. The latter shakes his head, not believing that the Vgotha have the Riknari on their side any more than he believes in what the vid showed us. Me? I do not know what to believe. But the Riknari... it would explain so much. Why the Vgotha tactics changed. How their ships managed to hide from our scanners. Why their ship returned Tribute Dawn after she was captured.

"They're a... a fairy tale," Arkdhem snaps and I frown at him, not understanding what he means, but both Tributes immediately nod. "They do not actually exist."

"Then how do you explain the new Vgotha ships?" I am not convinced the Vgotha's story, that the vid, is real, but... I cannot deny that it might be possible. That very possibility, knowing that we might have been working for those who slaughtered our people all these decacycles, makes me want to rage and weep at the same time.

"But what *are* they?" Tribute Dawn asks.

"They are the Great Defenders," the High Commander says. "It is said that they fight throughout the universe on the side of those who have been wronged. They cannot be bribed, cannot be deterred... they are an extremely advanced race of beings with highly advanced technology. Not much is known about them, but sometimes when a great injustice has been done or an oppressed people are fighting against tyranny, they appear to help. Sometimes with goods or weapons, sometimes medicines, and very occasionally they will aid in battle."

"Why wouldn't they have contacted you directly after the Great Devastation?" Pareena asks, sounding fascinated.

"Besides the fact that they do not exist?" Arkdhem mutters.

"We did not go seeking their help," Gavrill says. His armor flickers, too quickly for me to catch the emotion. I am sure he is as conflicted as I. Arkdhem is the only one who appears sure that this is a Vgotha trick. "It is a large universe. They cannot be everywhere. We lost our people... horribly... but we immediately had allies, tech, everything we needed to seek our justice."

Except that if the Jabol were truly the ones to destroy Tsentur, then it was not justice. And our warriors and ships, enhanced with Jabol nanotech, had been hunting innocents. The exact type of situation in which the Riknari might appear to help.

My chest clenches at the thought.

"You'll need to do more research," Tribute Dawn says quietly. "We need to at least look into what the Vgotha are claiming. And you can't hunt the Vgotha until you know the truth... and we have to stop the Tribute program until we know."

"What?" Arkdhem barks, anger flashing over his suit.

"Please, Gavrill," Tribute Dawn begs. "Any more Vgotha deaths *will* be on our heads. Even if you're not sure, you can't claim ignorance anymore if it does turn out to be true."

"Tor lost warriors as well, but he still is trying to do the right thing," my Pareena says softly. I can feel her sadness, her belief in Tor. I do not *want* to believe, but I am not unaffected by her emotions. "He said that he is not willing to lose anymore. He said that if you attack again, he will no longer hold back."

"And he has Riknari weapons," the High Commander murmurs thoughtfully. His shoulders sag with a sigh. Before battling the Vgotha warriors on the beach, we may not have been concerned, but they proved the reputation of their cowardliness wrong. They did not harm the Tributes. They *chose* to send the Tributes back. Either it is a very good trap... or it is the truth. Finally, the High Commander shakes his head. "I must think more on this."

"You are going to treat this... this deceit as *truth*?" Arkdhem slams his fist on the table again in his frustration. I cannot fault him for his reaction. Without my Pareena's sincerity, her belief, tempering my responses, I might very well have agreed with him.

"The Tributes are correct, we must investigate," the High Commander says. Relief blows through me—a little of mine and much more from my Tribute. "In the meantime, we cannot let the Jabol know we... are questioning their version of events or that we have been in contact with the Vgotha."

"So what if we find the Vgotha? Will we just let them go?"

"I see no other alternative."

Dawn and I visibly relax.

"This is madness. You're endangering the whole fleet—your Tributes! The whole tribute *program*." Arkdhem's armor flashes his anger, his despair.

I tighten my arms around my Pareena.

It is true—if the Jabol are the perpetrators of the Great Devastation, if they were willing to destroy our entire planet and manipulate us into being their weapon, then we must do everything in our power to destroy *them*. We will need to focus all of the energy we've been using to hunt Vgotha and turn it on them instead. But we are intertwined with them... our alliance, our technology, and our Tributes.

Without the Tributes we have no hope for the future. The two we've received are not enough. But we cannot ignore what the Jabol have done either, if the vid is true. The ramifications of these revelations go far deeper than just a change of alliance.

"If this information is correct, we have been dishonored," the High Commander snaps back at Arkdhem. "If it is true, then the real killers of our people have gone unpunished and they have used *us* as their hunting animals. I will not have us further dishonored."

"Or it's a trick and the Vgotha are waiting to crush us!" Arkdhem growls the words, his suit flickering so quickly through colors that I can tell he has lost control over his emotions. "Are we just to stand idly by if they attack us?"

"No." The High Commander gives him a hard look. "But we will not attack first again either. Not until we have had time to look into the vid and their claims. If they attack first then we will annihilate them... but for now, we will pull back from the planet and figure out our next step. Until we have decided how to investigate, none of this will be discussed outside of this room, with anyone. That is an order."

The colors on Arkdhem's armor swirl and then mute to a neutral gray. He nods his head, but his expression is stony. "Yes, High Commander."

"Yes, High Commander," I echo. "If that is all for now, I would like to retire with my Tribute."

"Permission granted," the High Commander says. "I will give the order that we are to move back from the planet for now. Arkdhem, you will take command on the bridge and oversee our... regrouping. The scout ships will need refueling by now."

Regrouping sounds better than a retreat, but we all know what it really is. Still, keeping the planet under blockade for long term, especially now that we have our Tributes back, is inadvisable. The warriors will grow weary and the smaller ships will run low on fuel.

We will pull back and then... see what the Vgotha do as we decide what *we* will do.

It is not a bad plan. The lack of action chafes, but I would rather see to my Pareena than anything else right now.

"Yes, High Commander," Arkdhem and I say in unison.

As I carry my Pareena to our quarters I cannot keep my mind on my duty. The Vgotha. The Riknari. The Jabol. Those are the beings I should be thinking about. Instead, all of my focus is on my Tribute. The feel of her back in my arms. The softness of her hair against my neck. The press of her curves against my body.

The door slides shut behind us and I carry her over to the bed, setting her down on the edge. "Strip," I order her, but the command is almost gentle. "I want to inspect you."

To my surprise, my Pareena shakes her head. "I don't want to do that," she says, reaching up to tug at my armor. "Make love to me, Bogdan."

"What?" I understand the terminology from the manuals, but I am unsure of how to proceed. "But—"

"Right now." Her hands start to roam over my chest, up to my neck, and her head tilts back as if asking for a kiss. "Please, I need to feel you."

Something pulses inside of me. I can feel her desire, her need. I have heard of the mating fever as it takes soldiers after a death-defying fight. I did not realize it would be the same for Tributes. Kneeling in front of her, we are on an equal level, and I pull her into me. Her legs part for my body, but it is my stomach that presses against her core, not my cock.

"You have been through so much, my Pareena," I whisper in the small shell of her ear, nuzzling it. "I want to inspect you and then you should rest."

"I don't want to rest," she says stubbornly. "I thought my second chance at life was over. I thought I'd never see you again. I want to feel you, inside of me."

I clasp the back of her neck and press my forehead against hers. It stills her for a moment, her anxious need softening as I touch her. Everything in me hums in pleasure at the softness of her skin, the lustrous umber of her eyes. I could live forever like this, pressed close to my Pareena as she rests in the circle of my arms. "Did you mean what you said? When you proclaimed your choice before all the Tsenturions?"

"When I chose you?" Surprise flashes over her face and her forehead creases. An off-key twang jars the smooth melody unraveling inside me. "I told everyone I loved you. Did you think I was lying?"

I can feel her temper rise, but I am honest.

"I hoped I would be your choice, that you felt the same for me as I do for you, but when the High Commander gave you leave to choose, I was not sure what you would do."

"Well you should have had more faith in me. Sometimes, Bogdan, you can be a complete ass," she huffs. Although I know I should punish her for speaking to me in such a disrespectful manner, I cannot help but laugh. I enjoy her fieriness and I can tell she means it almost affectionately. "But no, I wasn't lying. I don't ever want to lose you. I'll be honest, when I first woke up and saw Frllil, I thought I was dreaming. In fact, I thought I was having a coma dream for a really long time, but I wanted it to be real. I thought that my mind made all of this up because it was so close to my sexual fantasies. *You're* my every fantasy, Bogdan."

She burrows closer, and I understand her desire for me to penetrate her. We both wish to be joined as closely as possible.

"This is real. And you are mine." I shift so she straddles my great body, her hair flowing around her face. "You belong to me forever." I snap my hips upward, making her bounce. Her pupils dilate, her large, dark eyes growing larger and darker. "My mate. And I won't allow you to forget it. I will show you how very real I am."

In a rapid fighting move, I flip her over, so I am seated, and she is over my lap face down. She makes a muffled sound as I peel her 'jeans' away from her bottom, almost tearing the fabric when I can't remove it fast enough. It is not nearly as convenient as a Tsenturion gown and I make a note that she should only be allowed to wear these 'jeans' on special occasions.

"Since you do not feel you need rest, I will make love to you as you wish... but first you must be taught proper respect. You should not call your Master an ass."

I am not at all surprised by the lack of regret I feel from her.

"Well then don't doubt my feelings for you," she mutters.

SMACK!

The satisfaction I feel from having my Tribute across my thighs, her soft bottom quivering from a hard slap, is immense. It soothes the anxiety that built up inside of me when I was searching for her, making me feel more connected to her than ever.

"I will not doubt your feelings again, and you will learn not to insult me," I say calmly. Immediately, I feel a hint of mischief trickle through her and I shake my head, although I do not bother to hide my smile since she cannot see my expression.

"I'm sorry for calling you an ass, Master," she says, but I can both hear and feel her insincerity. This spanking is not truly about addressing her behavior, though, and we both know it. Still, some of the formalities must be observed.

"You will be once I am done disciplining yours," I tell her and raise my hand again.

28

P areena

I SQUEAL as Bogdan's hand comes down again and again on my ass. I could tell he wasn't truly upset with me, and considering I'd just been abducted and recovered from the Vgotha I'd kind of thought he'd go a little easier on me, but that is not the case.

Smack! Smack!

"Ow, Master, please!" I try to twist away from his hand. The spanking hovers between punishment and pleasure and I'd really prefer the latter. Instead of indulging me though, Bogdan just takes a firmer grip on my body, tipping me forward even more on his lap so that my fingers press against the floor to help keep me from feeling completely off balance.

Every stinging swat makes my pussy clench and I cry out as my desire surges. I can already feel tears gathering in the backs of my eyes. Not because the spanking hurts so much but because I'm so relieved to be back over my Master's lap, to feel his discipline... and hopefully I'll be feeling his cock very soon, too.

My legs kick out, but they're tangled in the jeans and my movement is restricted. I moan as Bogdan's hand pauses for a moment, caressing the warmed cheeks of my ass before seeking out my pussy. I can feel the nanotech from the bride trainer creeping over the front of my mound and sliding over my clit. I moan when the vibrations hit, just enough to tease me, not enough to get me off. His fingers push into my pussy, but only for a moment, just long enough to coat the digits in my wetness before he's pressing them against my ass.

The tight ring of my anus stretches, and I whimper, wriggling on his lap as he slowly sinks his fingers into the narrow space.

"I wasn't that naughty!" I protest, although my objection is admittedly half-hearted at best.

Bogdan chuckles and I can feel his amusement. "No, but you did call me an ass... I think you meant it as a hint for what you wanted."

"I definitely did not," I retort, although my toes curl as he pumps his fingers harder, stretching the small hole. The slight burn has me panting with desire. I want him inside of me so badly, but for some reason I can't turn off the sass.

"Oh, well then." He slides his fingers out of my ass, leaving me aching and hot all over, the teasing vibrations on my clit feeling so much worse now. Dammit!

~

Bogdan

I CAN FEEL my Pareena's rising frustration and I chuckle. I will not torment her for very long, though. I am too relieved to have her safely back in my arms. Even though she does not see the need for rest, I am determined she will get some. If I have to fuck her into submission to ensure that she rests afterward, then so be it.

SMACK!

I begin to spank her bottom again and she wails. Not because of the pain, as I am not spanking her nearly as hard as I could be, but because she is flush with passion and aching to be filled.

SMACK!

SMACK!

My cock rocks against her side as she writhes on my lap, my *seela* straining against the inside of my armor.

Shifting the aim of my hand, I land the next swat directly on the pouting lips of her pussy and my Pareena cries out in pain and pleasure. Ordering the nanotech away from her swollen clit and back to the belt around her hips, I aim the next swat carefully and the tips of my fingers snap against that tender bud. I can feel the aching need, the ecstatic agony, the blow produces, and I do it again.

And again.

She sobs, bucking her hips upwards, on the verge of orgasm...

Rather than giving her the final swat that she needs, I lift her up off my lap.

"Wait! No!" she cries out, scrabbling uselessly and trying to keep her position so that I will keep spanking her sweet pussy. "I was almost there!"

"I know," I chuckle, tossing her onto my sleeping platform on her back. "There are more punishments than just spankings, my Pareena."

"Stupid manuals," she mutters, making me shake my head. I am amused that she believes I would be helpless to punish her without the manuals. But perhaps I should read more of them, as they do have such interesting ideas.

I pull her *jeans* from her body so that I may spread her legs and lift the hem of her shirt up above her breasts. The rounded curves with their brown peaks are too tempting to resist and I lower mouth to the luscious bounty.

Pareena

. . .

Being edged as a punishment sucks.

On the other hand, I'm pretty sure Bogdan isn't going to keep punishing me much longer. His hot mouth closes around my nipple and I moan, arching my back and wrapping my legs and arms around him. Well, trying to. He holds himself apart from me, keeping our bodies from touching the way I want them to, *need* them to, and it's driving me wild.

The sensitized skin of my bottom rubs against the sheets beneath me, my clit throbbing between my legs after being spanked, and the hot suckling of my nipple creates a maelstrom within me, pulling me into its grip. When Bogdan plucks my hands from his shoulders, pinning arms down beside my head, I feel my entire body spasm in reaction to being rendered so completely helpless beneath him. His big body is between my legs, keeping me from being able to press my thighs together and rub, and I can feel the tickling sensation of the very tips of his *seela* questing over the tender skin of my inner thighs.

"Please, Bogdan," I beg, writhing as he switches his attentions to my other nipple, leaving the first one tightly budded, wet and throbbing in the cool air. "I need you inside of me, I need you to fuck me... claim me..."

He groans around my breast and I feel his weight come down on me more, the flexible head of his cock parting my pussy and teasing the lips with its waving motions. Then his mouth moves away from my nipple and covers my lips, keeping me from being able to say anything. I open my mouth, taking him inside me the only way I can right now, sucking on his tongue and trying to rub my pussy against the tip of his cock.

I can feel his own desire, barely held back by his self-control, his determination to torment me, and I let my own emotions go completely. If I can feel him, then he can feel me, and I wallow in the passion that was threatening to overwhelm me, letting it swamp me completely.

It works.

He groans and then his cock is pushing inside of me, stretching me open so wonderfully as he thrusts forward. My pussy shudders around the bumps and curves of his shaft, my clit practically pulsing with joy when his *prime seela* slides around it. I cannot use my arms, but my legs wrap around his hips, pulling him into me until he is completely buried in my aching pussy.

I moan against his lips as he recedes, and then cry out again when I feel the nanotech from my belt trickling down the crease of my bottom and sliding into my ass, quickly thickening and stretching the tiny hole. The sudden double penetration is shockingly erotic. I am so completely full of him, our passion twisting around each other... It's like we've completely opened ourselves to each other, to our love. I no longer have any doubts that he's real and he no longer is trying to hold back from me.

That's when it happens.

The hot pleasure is interrupted by a sudden stabbing pain on my arm.

"Ow!" I tear my lips away from Bogdan, my head jerking around to see the problem. My arm throbs but the skin is unbroken. A jewel-like shape of thin golden lines appears, pulsing lightly. "What the—"

"My Pareena," Bogdan murmurs, his tone almost savagely possessive. Startled, I look up at him and see him staring at his own arm where a similar image glows. I thought I was in tune with his emotions before, but now I can feel *everything* rushing through me—wonder, ecstasy, heart-bursting happiness.

And love. So much love. His eyes are shining as he meets my gaze, a smile unlike any other spreading across his lips.

"These are our bond marks," he says reverently.

"I can feel you," I whisper. "It feels..." My voice trails off as I try to find the right words.

"Like coming home. You are my home, Pareena."

For a being who has lost his home and spent centuries without, that means *everything*. Tears spark in my eyes, choking me and I can't speak, so instead I arch my back and lift my head, pushing up to meet his lips in another passionate kiss. The mark on my arm tingles and suddenly he's thrusting into me in a frenzy.

His seela latch onto my pussy and I scream against his lips, my orgasm exploding in a fit of ecstasy that consumes me heart, body, and soul.

Bogdan

My Pareena.

Completely mine now. By choice and by the mark. I cannot decide which gives me more satisfaction. Curled up with her in my arms, our bodies sated from pleasure, I feel... at rest. Peaceful in a way that I had never expected to feel again. I mourn the loss of Harai and the life that might have been, but I think she would be happy to see me where I am now.

I am happy to be where I am now. I wish it had not come at such a cost... but I cannot change what happened to my people. All I can do is try and work to better their future.

"Bogdan?" My Pareena's fingers stroke down the center of my chest, as though she is petting me. "Are you serious about considering evidence of the Vgotha's innocence?"

I wonder if the bond allows her to follow my thoughts as well as my emotions or if the Vgotha are just at the forefront of her mind as well. "I do not know if I can fully forgive them. They have fought with us many times. And the losses of Kalexston and Borodem are fresh in all our minds."

"Mine too," she says quietly, shifting slightly in my arms so that she can look into my eyes. I see the sadness there, feel it in my heart. "But... Tor lost warriors as well. And poor choices were made by both sides that led to those losses." A small smile curves her face, although there is not much humor in it. "Neither Tsenturions nor Vgotha seem to be very good at talking."

"Then it is a very good thing that we have you and Dawn now." I brush her hair back from her face. "You are both very good at talking."

"I have a *degree* in talking," my Pareena says, and this time her eyes sparkle with real amusement. "I just... you're going to consider what the Vgotha have said, right?"

"For you, my Pareena, I will consider anything. For you have proven anything is possible." It will not be easy, and I do not know how the rest of the warriors will feel, but for her I will try.

She leans in for a kiss, but before our lips meet, a chime from the bridge com interrupts. I still, fully alert.

"Bogdan, you're needed on the bridge." Medik's voice harsher than usual. Something is wrong.

"What is it?" I rise to my feet, shifting seamlessly into warrior mode, protectiveness surging through me.

"Vgotha ships are departing the planet."

29

———

P areena

THE VGOTHA ARE LEAVING the planet? Although, it makes sense. If they stay there, even hidden from the Tsenturion scans, they are vulnerable because the Tsenturions—and therefore the Jabol—know exactly where they are.

"Drakk," Bogdan races to the door and I scramble to follow, snatching up a gown that's laying on the couch as I go. It'll be faster to put on than the jeans and t-shirt. As the doors open, Bogdan realizes I'm right behind him and he turns to face me, pointing his finger back toward the bed. "Stay here, you need to rest."

"No." My voice wobbles but I take the opportunity to tug my dress on over my head before putting my hands on my hips. "If they're attacking, I want to know. I *need* to know. I feel responsible." If he locks me in, I'll figure out a way to override the door and deal with the punishment later. "Please, Bogdan, I need this."

He hesitates for only a moment. "Very well," he says finally. "But you stay at my side and follow orders at all times. You must be silent while we are on the bridge."

"I understand," I nod vigorously. Hand in hand, we race to the bridge, passing warriors on the way who are all scrambling to reach their stations. I only hope we're not too late.

As soon as the turbo lift opens onto the bridge, Bogdan practically leaps out. The Vgotha ships on are the screens and Arkdhem is barking orders to aim weapons at them. Medik stands off to the side, his expression blank, and I can't help but wonder if Arkdhem even knows that Medik called Bogdan. My heart jumps into my throat... is Arkdhem about to start a new battle?!

I hover at the back of the room, next to the lift, not wanting to distract any of them—and definitely not wanting to get in Bogdan's way.

"Hold fire," Bogdan orders, overtop of Arkdhem. The Vgotha fleet is rising from the planet on the screen and I realize it's not a scan—we can actually see them. Arkdhem turns to glare at Bogdan, his armor streaking red with anger.

"I am not attacking," he snaps, bristling. "I am preparing us in case *they* attack."

"They are flying away from us," Bogdan says harshly, and I can feel his mistrust of Arkdhem's motives. He looks around at the other warriors on the Bridge. "We will not fire on the Vgotha unless they fire on us first."

"But Commander..." I recognize Corin, who looks distraught at Bogdan's orders. I bite my lip. He and Borodem were good friends, I can only imagine how he's feeling right now. Bogdan was right. This is not going to be easy. Even though the Jabol are ultimately the ones at fault, it is the Vgotha who have directly caused their losses. That the Tsenturions have caused the Vgotha loss as well may or may not matter to a grief-stricken warrior.

"What?" All the officers besides Bogdan look shocked.

"You heard me," Bogdan folds his arms over his chest, glowering harder than ever. *Glower Maxima!* It's almost as good as a Harry Potter spell. The officers all put their heads down and avoid his gaze. Even

Corin bows his head and turns away, although I can see the muscle in his jaw clenching with anger.

The lift slides open beside me again and the High Commander strides on deck, Dawn following him a few steps behind, the same way I had done with Bogdan. She's pale and looks relieved to see me, sidling over to stand beside me. We grip hands, the same way we did in the forest, looking to each other for support while surrounded by warriors whom we know will disagree with what we think should happen.

"Report," Gavrill demands in a sharp voice.

"High Commander, the Vgotha ships are retreating from the planet," Arkdhem replies, standing at attention. "When they were visible on screen, I prepared us for battle, in case they engaged. Bogdan arrived on the bridge shortly before you and countermanded an order I hadn't yet given." He glares at Bogdan, but it's not as impressive as Bogdan's glower. I don't think anyone can glower as well as my mate.

I know that's a weird thing to be proud of, but it kind of reminds me of Alan Rickman's best Snape glare and, well... it's hot.

"Please, High Commander... Why aren't we attacking?" Corin asks, although his question is closer to a demand. He flings his arm at the screen, pointing. "They're *right there.*"

Gavrill hesitates for a long moment and the warriors stare at him, obviously picking up on the fact that something has changed. Several of them glance at Bogdan and then Arkdhem, confusion and worry creasing their brows. I know that Gavrill didn't want to tell everyone the message Tor sent Dawn and I back with, but I'm a little worried that if he doesn't say *something*, this may end up as a mutiny situation.

"It is possible..." He says the words slowly, almost quietly, and then clears his throat to speak a little louder. "It is possible the Vgotha were not responsible for the destruction of Tsentur. You all know our Tributes returned to us unexpectedly. The Vgotha let them go, sending a message for me with them."

"It's a trick!" Corin snaps out immediately and I don't miss the fact that Arkdhem immediately nods in agreement.

"It may be," Gavrill says seriously. "But until we know, we are *not* going to engage with the Vgotha. The High Command is still reviewing the message the Tributes brought us and we will decide on our next course of action soon."

"We can't just... let them go!" Corin fumes. "They killed Borodem today. Kalexston." A murmur of agreement, soft but noticeable, travels around the bridge. Dawn and I both tense. I'd known that this wouldn't be easy news for the Tsenturions to digest, but seeing it play out in front of me really drives that home.

"And we killed some of theirs. If what the Vgotha say is true, all of those deaths lie at the hands of those who made it appear that the Vgotha were the ones who destroyed Tsentur." Gavrill is very careful to talk around exactly *who* the Vgotha have accused of doing so, and I can't blame him.

The officers on the bridge are already on edge. Accusing the Jabol... it could push them over it, whether or not they believe it's even possible. I bite my lip to keep from speaking. It is part of my personality to want to keep the peace, but I don't know if I could say anything that would help right now. As if sensing my thoughts—and he very well might be—Bogdan glances at me and gives me a subtle shake of his head.

"I will not have it!" Corin shouts, slamming his fist down. "We cannot disregard the deaths of our warriors—"

"Stand down, officer," Gavrill says sharply. The very air in the room is thick with tension and I feel like I can barely breathe. On screen, the Vgotha fleet suddenly disappears, streaking away from both the planet and the Tsenturions, and Dawn and I both let out relieved sighs. Unfortunately, that draws all eyes to us, and we immediately stiffen again.

Not all of those gazes are friendly anymore.

"You're making a mistake," Corin says acidly, turning his hostile gaze back to Gavrill. "You've become soft. The Tributes have made you emotional. Weak. They have been easily tricked with Vgotha lies, but you should be better than that."

"Officer," Medik puts his hand on Corin's shoulder in an attempt to console him, coming up to him from behind, but Corin whirls, shoving the older man away in anger. Taken unaware, Medik goes flying and falls against a console. Dawn and I cry out. Several officers rush to help the fallen older warrior. I can see the expression of regret that immediately crosses Corin's face when he realizes what he's done.

"Warrior Corin!" Gavrill's voice roars out. "You will stand down and present yourself to the brig for disciplinary matters."

Still rigid with anger, Corin flexes his fists and then nods his head. He walks briskly to the lift, and both Dawn and I shrink back as he approaches, afraid of the fury-fueled grief roiling over his armor. He doesn't even look at us as he passes. Our movement takes us closer to Medik and Dawn pulls me along with her, obviously concerned.

"Are you all right?" She asks, as Arkdhem helps the older warrior to his feet.

"I'm fine," Medik reassures her, although he doesn't have his usual air of quiet confidence about him. "He tried to pull his force at the last moment. He just caught me off balance."

Gavrill begins speaking again, addressing all of the warriors on the bridge, and we fall quiet. "We are reviewing evidence and will provide a debrief soon. For now, you will not speak of any of this outside of this room."

I wonder how many times he'll have to say that before this is all over.

There are some hard decisions to be made soon. I'm glad I don't have to make them.

Nodding at Arkdhem, Gavrill turns to collect Dawn, silently passing command of the bridge back to his third.

"Warriors, stand down," Arkdhem says. There is bitterness in his tone. Whether it's because he realizes Medik didn't trust him and called Gavrill and Bogdan to the bridge, or because he wanted to attack the Vgotha and was thwarted, I do not know.

~

Bogdan

I PUT my hand on the back of my Pareena's neck. She is staring at Arkdhem again, but now I can feel all of her emotions and I do not worry over why. She is suspicious of him and somewhat concerned, none of which sparks even the slightest hint of jealousy or possessiveness.

Of course, the mate mark on her arm does not hurt.

Guiding her away from the bridge and into the lift, I stroke her mate mark with my free hand, just as Tribute Dawn looks over at us and the doors close.

"Oh my... you have your mate mark!" Tribute Dawn squeals in delight. I feel my Pareena's surge of answering happiness. Then Tribute Dawn's eyes move to me and they widen. "And your suit has changed!"

Indeed, it has. I am surprised she has not noticed before now, but it is not a very showy change. My armor's default color is still the endless black of space, but with the glitter of a swirling nebula now in its depths.

"It sparkles," Pareena announces proudly.

What? "No—"

"It totally does!" Tribute Dawn gushes.

"I am a warrior." I glower at both of them, which for some reason makes my Pareena feel both happy and proud. I had thought the same on the bridge, but I do not understand the reaction. I glower harder. "I do not sparkle."

"If you say so." Tribute Dawn turns away but she's grinning. So is the High Commander.

"It's a little sparkly," Pareena murmurs. I give her a look. *Behave.* She shivers happily as she feels the erotic threat emanating from me.

"Congratulations," the High Commander says, his fingers seeking out his Tribute's mate mark to stroke. The two of them exchange a look and Tribute Dawn smiles, her hand moving overtop her stomach.

"We have some news of our own." Tribute Dawn blurts out. "Gavrill wanted to keep it a secret but I have to tell somebody and you two should definitely know." The High Commander beams rather than chiding her for disobeying his wishes and a suspicion rises inside me. My Pareena is much quicker to leap to a conclusion.

"What? No!" Pareena gasps.

"Yes!" Dawn squeals. "I'm pregnant!"

Gavrill clears his throat. "We do need to keep this between us and Medik for a time." A wrinkle grows between his brows, probably because he cannot help but think of the other things that we must keep between us for now, but when he looks at his Tribute his expression softens.

"Is everything all right?" Pareena asks. "Everything's... normal?"

"So far tests are all good. I'm healthy," Tribute Dawn assures her. "Medik realized it when he scanned us after we returned and told us privately."

It was probably a good thing she did not know before the Vgotha captured her. I cannot imagine how much worse the High Commander's reaction would have been if he'd known his Tribute was breeding when she was taken. My Pareena leans in to hug her friend tightly in congratulations. I look at Tribute Dawn's stomach, but so far, I cannot see any difference.

She carries the hope of our race in her womb... and the proof of the Tribute's compatibility only makes the situation with the Jabol more fraught, but still, I feel joy at the news.

"So, what now?" Dawn asks, snuggling into her mate. "Are you going to tell the warriors about the Jabol?"

"I will have to eventually," he says, exchanging a worried look with me. As Corin and Arkdhem have shown us, not all of them will take it well. "First, I must tell them that the Vgotha may not be the enemy we thought. I will tell them about the Riknari. The fleet retreating rather than attacking will help. That they attacked in order to take you captive and killed two of our warriors..." He sighs. "It will take some time. But in the meantime, we can search for answers. We cannot allow the Jabol to know our plans, so we will have to pretend to continue hunting Vgotha, but really, we will be hunting for proof. I want to try to contact the Riknari myself, if it is possible, to see what they say."

The doors to the lift open, effectively ending the conversation. We cannot talk about any of this in the halls of the ship. Not yet.

"Are you okay with this?" Pareena whispers to me as I lead her back to our room. "It's a lot to take in."

She is right. And in times past, I would have raged louder than Arkdhem.

So much has changed. But the biggest changes are inside of me.

I do not want to lay down my weapons before I have avenged my family and my people, but my first duty is to my Tribute.

"Whatever the future holds, I will rise to greet it. As long as I have you, my Pareena," I whisper back. I feel her love wrap around me.

Despite the many unknowns in our lives right now, I feel a happiness that I had never hoped for. We have more challenges to face, but nothing feels insurmountable with my Pareena by my side.

EPILOGUE

Marta
In the fading light of evening, I am dragged back to consciousness with a pained groan. My forehead pulses with agony, stabbing splinters radiating through my whole body.

What happened?

A cough clutches my chest and I whine and sputter trying to breathe, the renewed pain threatening to pull me under again. At least the ringing in my ears has stopped.

Ringing from the explosion. A fucking bomb??? Fucking cartel.

Miraculously, other than a sharp knock when everything fell, my head is clear of the wreckage. My right arm flops when I try to move it to wipe dust from my face, but after a long moment I manage to get it working. My left arm throbs painfully but won't move and after an initial attempt, I don't try again. The right is enough. Grit scratches my cheek but I scrub my eyes clear enough to open them. It's just light enough that I can assess the damage... and I almost wish I couldn't.

My legs and torso are hidden, trapped under rubble of the building that practically came down around me. I can't feel them, but going by the weight they're under, I'm thankful that they're numb.

That or I'm going to start feeling them any minute and it's going to be awful. This is definitely the worst situation I've ever found myself in.

I try to take a deep breath and fire flashes along my side. *Internal organ damage? Highly possible.* My right hand explores my head. *Mild contusions, probable concussion.* My left arm can't move at all. *Broken... possible shoulder dislocation.*

Situation: desperate.

Think, Marta.

My cell phone is in my pocket. It's basically a satellite phone. With the places I go, it's best to always be connected to some form of communication. I force my arm to go fishing until darkness invades the edges of my vision. When I draw my hand up, it's bright red. More liquid leaks out onto the dusty rubble beside me. A small pool, dark and growing.

That's a lot of blood. Too much blood.

I'm so fucked.

A strange sort of resigned sadness trickles over me and I sigh, leaning my head back and resting for a moment. The sky beyond the squat buildings of the Barrio is so pretty. Pale pink tinged with gold.

There are shouts in the distance, honking cars. But the cartel owns this part of town. If they blow one of their own buildings, no one will come to investigate.

"Be safe," My mother had pled with me before she died. *"That job is going to get you killed."*

She feared for me as she'd feared for my father, another fallen soldier in the fight for truth.

Sorry Mama... you were right. Again.

No one is coming to help.

No one even knew I was here, chasing a whisper of a lead about an American billionaire making bank—and not just through his pharmaceutical companies but from other drugs as well. Last time I checked in with my managing editor, I was in Mexico City. She doesn't expect me to check in for another day. There's no way I'm going to live that long.

My breath claws through my middle. I could try again to dig out my cell phone, but I have even less energy than I did before. Judging from the amount of blood leaking onto the ground, I don't have much longer.

I definitely hadn't wanted everything to end this way... on the brink of exposing corruption without managing to file my final story. I'd wanted my life to matter. If I'd at least managed to find the proof I was looking for and send the story to my editor before I died, I would have thought this sucked but... at least it would have been worthwhile. Instead, I'm going to die a failure.

And in so much fucking pain.

I force myself to relax on my uncomfortable, rubble-strewn bed, and let my breathing slow. The sun is almost gone now, gilding the horizon with fire. *My last sunset.* So beautiful. I close my eyes. I feel like it's just for a moment, but when I open them again it's full dark and something shimmers in the corner of my vision. My brain feels muzzy. Did I lose consciousness again? The minutes slipping away with my life blood...

I crane my head to distract myself, trying to see what is glowing, and a bright rectangle greets me, shining in the rubble.

My e-reader.

Huh.

I reach out and my hand falls on the smooth surface. I scrape my knuckles against the rocks but when I draw the device to me, it's unharmed. The screen has not a single crack. Unbelievable. And it's on... I guess somehow the explosion hit the power button and it didn't automatically turn off. So I must not have been unconscious for as long as it feels like.

I wipe my bloody fingers on the inside of my collar to clean them as best I can before clearing the screen of dust. I never knew who sent the mysterious device. I assumed it was a co-worker's idea of a joke, loading up a next generation reader with tons of naughty erotic stories, but when I asked around, no one confessed.

I am so glad it is here now. The home screen glows to greet me like an old friend. It has no data and can't connect to Wi-Fi—no calling for help—but its familiar presence soothes me.

At least I can die doing my favorite thing—reading. The pain I'm in is debilitating, but hopefully this will help distract me from... everything.

Before following a man that I am pretty sure runs the local section of the cartel, I'd just finished reading a hot alien abduction story. It opens right to the end of the last book in the Trilogy, but instead of the last page of the book, the e-reader screen flashes with a question I'd never seen before.

Are you Marta Flores Romero?

My lips move with the question. Huh. Weird. I should not be connected to Wi-Fi but... hey, if someone is asking, I'll answer. Maybe they can send help? The hope that rises in me is almost shocking.

Yes, I press the blinking answer.

Do you want to die today?

Holy hell.

No, I press the button. I really, really don't want to die. Duh. My lips move, forming words that I don't have the energy to actually speak. *Help me.*

Tears begin to slide down my face, blurring the screen's instructions.

<Swipe right for abduction>

I try to move my finger, but I can't. The pain is gone, the numbness spread from my lower half to my shoulders, creeping up my neck.

Marta Flores Romero, the device beeps. *<Swipe right for abduction>* The button flashes. I can't move.

Subject's vitals are failing. Initiating emergency sequence.

A pulse of light rolls over me and the pile of rubble, expanding like a sunrise.

And everything goes dark.

～

Arkdhem

Silently seething, I can only watch as the shuttle carrying the

High Commander, Bogdan, both Tributes, and a small team of warriors descends back to the planet. The warriors the High Commander had instructed to find the place where the Vgotha had been hiding had been unsuccessful. The Tributes have convinced him to take them back down again to see if they can find the cave they'd been held in.

We *could* be pursuing the Vgotha fleet, but instead I am stuck on the bridge, useless, while the High Commander and Bogdan risk their Tributes yet again. We are fairly certain the Vgotha have fled the planet entirely, but there is no way to be sure. Not only that, but we don't know all the dangers that the planet offers. And the Vgotha could have left traps.

All points which I made when the High Commander informed me of his plans, and which were dismissed.

Just as I was dismissed.

Twice now, I've had the responsibility of protecting the High Commander's Tribute, and twice now I have failed. Which was why I've been left behind this time. The High Commander said it was because someone must stay in overall command of the ship, since he planned to be on-planet for as many cycles as it took to find the Vgotha's planet side base of operations, but I know it is because the High Commander has lost faith in me.

In fact, it now seems as though the High Commander has more faith in the Vgotha than he does in me, his third in command. The entire reason he wants to find their base of operations is to see if they left anything that will help prove they are innocent of destroying Tsentur. Something I find very difficult to believe.

If they are innocent, why hadn't they tried to meet with the High Commander before?

If the Jabol are guilty, why are they trying to perpetuate the Tsenturion race by providing us with Tributes?

I find it very convenient that the Vgotha are suddenly claiming innocence and providing dubious 'proof' against the Jabol. It could be completely fake. It is suspicious that right when the Jabol have finally found compatible mates for the Tsenturions the Vgotha found evidence that they were set up. If the Vgotha's goal is the complete destruction of the Tsenturions, then of course they would want to interfere with our matings. If they succeed in doing so, then they can just keep running, secure in the knowledge that we will eventually die out, because we cannot breed.

The High Commander acknowledged all the points I made, all the questions I asked, and then decided to go planet side without me anyway. He was far more swayed by Tribute Dawn's belief that we have all been duped. I don't blame her. We have become close and I understand she holds some resentment toward the Jabol for abducting her from her former home and life, even though she is happy now. She hadn't liked the Tribute program to begin with. But, in this, she is wrong and she is leading the High Commander astray.

The warriors look at her and Pareena and see our futures... all of which was provided by the Jabol. Everything the Vgotha claim would shatter that... it would destroy us a second time, in a blow possibly even more devastating than the first because it would be the eradication of hope.

I cannot accept that.

And I am not the only one.

Corin had not been present on the bridge when the High Commander had ordered the warriors not to speak of the Vgotha's claim. He ran into more than one warrior and told them what he knew, on his way to be disciplined after attacking Medik. Word spread quickly, and the warriors are torn on whether or not to believe the Vgotha. Most of them feel as Corin and I do—the Vgotha cannot not be trusted.

Many of them are unhappy to be in orbit above the planet, rather than pursuing the Vgotha fleet. I heard the mutterings when the High Commander opted not to follow the Vgotha fleet and investigate the planet instead. I obey my orders, though, and have not told anyone that the Vgotha have accused the Jabol of being the real attackers. The entire fleet would have likely torn itself apart at the news, which also would have served Vgotha purposes.

By their accusations, they have set us up perfectly to destroy ourselves. Thankfully, Dawn and Pareena decided to share the message the Vgotha gave them with the high command only. The Vgotha had likely been counting on them blurting out the lies in front of multiple warriors.

Halfway through my shift, during which nothing happens because the Vgotha have fled and we are still just circling this *drakk* planet, the bridge com chimes with an incoming transmission from the shuttle. I nod at Jakar, who opens the channel. The High Commander's face appears on the main bridge screen.

"Commander Arkdhem, we have located the Vgotha's den, with the help of our Tributes. The location is secure and there are vestiges of their technology that were left behind. Their base was very large, and it will take us time to search through it."

"Yes, High Commander," I respond dutifully. "Will the Tributes be returning to the Command ship?"

The High Commander's armor flickers and he shakes his head, his expression changing slightly, to one I recognize. Dawn has talked him into something. It is an expression I've worn often enough as well. Although, I do not fight against indulging her the way the High Commander sometimes does. If—*when*—I receive a Tribute of my own, I will happily indulge her every whim as long as it does not affect her safety.

In my opinion, the High Commander indulges too many of the wrong whims of his Tribute, but it is not my place to ever express such an opinion.

"Dawn and Tribute Pareena will be staying planet-side with us," the High Commander says, sounding slightly pained. "They are the only ones who have personal experience with the Vgotha technology. They also wish to observe the Earth custom of a 'honeymoon' and spend some time off ship with their mates."

From my conversations with Dawn, I know what a honeymoon is, and I nod my understanding. This is likely as close as she thought she could get to the Earth custom. I would not allow it of my own Tribute, at least, I would have found her a much safer location. One that hadn't recently served as a Vgotha stronghold and didn't have the risk of being riddled with Vgotha traps. I've already made my opinion clear to the High Commander and repeating myself in front of other warriors will only be to my detriment.

"Deep in the caves our tech can only communicate short-range and it does not seem to reach beyond the cave system, so you will be the acting High Commander while I am on planet," he finishes with a nod.

"Thank you, High Commander," I reply, keeping my expression solemn. It is an empty gesture of faith, as he has already privately given me orders.

Keep the fleet orbiting around the planet. Watch out for incoming Vgotha or Jabol ships. Do not engage unless you are attacked first. I will return once we have thoroughly investigated their base here.

I am just here to keep the chain of command, not actually use it.

At the end of my shift I return to my room and throw myself on the bed mat. The empty bed mat that I long to share with a Tribute. I thought perhaps Pareena... but she was too enthralled with Bogdan, even though he did not deserve her. Had not even wanted her. Hadn't wanted anyone else to have one either. But now he has her... and the Vgotha's claims threaten the ability of the rest of us to even hope for a Tribute. My fists clench in anger.

But there is nothing I can do.

My door chimes. Someone is there.

Forcing myself to my feet, I answer it, and am surprised to see Medik standing there, his expression agonizingly conflicted. I cannot recall the last time I saw him so agitated.

"What is wrong?" I ask immediately, my armor spreading over my skin in reaction. I know we are not under attack, because the bridge would have informed me, but something is clearly wrong.

Medik looks over his shoulder, stepping into my room and I step back, surprised by the furtiveness of his actions. But when he speaks, I understand.

"Frllil has contacted me. Another Tribute is ready for pickup." And he does not know what to do. How to respond. So, he has come to me, the figurehead acting High Commander while the real High

Commander and his second-in-command are planet side, cavorting with *their* Tributes. I know that description is not entirely fair, but I also know that there will be plenty of time when they are *not* working and investigating. Dawn was very clear on the purpose of a honeymoon.

Drakk.

"What should we do? We can't leave her there with them... if they... if..." Medik's voice trails off and I realize that he also thinks the Vgotha's lies might be valid.

I have no fear of the Jabol. I do not believe they are anything more than our allies, but I grab onto his excuse for breaking the High Commander's orders.

"Of course, we cannot," I say immediately. It is true enough, after all. Surely if the High Commander were here, he would agree. If the Jabol are everything the Vgotha claim, we cannot leave an innocent human female in their grasp. That I do not believe the Vgotha lies makes no difference. My actions will be the same. "I will send a War Ship to collect her. The rest of the fleet and the Command Ship will remain here, in orbit, as the High Commander ordered."

Medik relaxes. "Good, good." He smiles at me and I realize he truly was worried. It is amazing how the lies of our enemies can undermine even the most secure of alliances. "And congratulations, Commander. I did not want to tell you, in case it would have affected your decision, but Frllil said this Tribute is matched to you."

To me.

My tribute.

My armor flashes bright gold and Medik's smile broadens. I can see the relief in his expression. Clapping me on the shoulder, he nods and then exits my room, leaving me standing there with my universe turned upside down for the second time in my life.

Immediately, I spring into action, calling into the bridge and ordering a War Ship fueled and prepared to retrieve the Tribute —*my* Tribute—from Frllil's waystation. A War Ship that I will be on. The High Commander will understand my absence, when he is informed of it, given such momentous tidings, and my presence is unnecessary anyway.

It won't be long now. Anticipation rushes through me as I hurry through the corridors. Soon, I will possess her. My Tribute. My Future. My Mate.

She is waiting for me.

I am coming, my heart.

THANK you for reading Alien Tribute! We're grateful to all who read Alien Captive, demanded Bogdan & Pareena's book and waited patiently—or not so patiently—until we wrote it. Now you have to wait for Arkdhem & Marta's book. (*evil cackle*)

Thank you also to Miranda and Jane for editing and proofreading, and our lovely beta readers—Katherine, Nick, Karen, Marie, Annie, Marta, and Jessica. We couldn't do this without you!!!!

-- Golden Angel & Lee

ALIEN ABDUCTION

ALIEN ABDUCTION

This Tsenturion warrior has waited a thousand years for a mate, and nothing will stop him from claiming me.

I was dying, but now I'm fine. My e-reader sucked me through to another universe, where I'm healed and being trained as an alien bride. Don't get me wrong, I'm grateful for the new chance at life, but I'm not sure I want to be mated to a hulking, brooding, bossy alien.

Though he's kinda hard to resist...

Relationship status between me and my giant alien abductor: it's **complicated.**

Alien Abduction is a hot alien warrior romance, starring one stubborn human and the Tsenturion warrior strong enough to master her.

Disclaimer: the authors are not responsible for any actual alien abductions that may result should you purchase this book. ;)

1

———————

M*arta*
I'm alive.
I shouldn't be.

The last thing I remember is my e-reader blinking at me, and half my body being buried under a pile of rubble after a bomb went off. I'd been bleeding out. I'd been dying but now I'm alive. Unless... am I supposed to be heading toward the bright light?

I blink but the light above me remains the same. It appears to be mechanical and not the bright light of heaven drawing me in.

"Hello, Marta Flores Romero, please do not panic." The deep voice from off to the side startles me, but I don't panic. Mostly. My brain immediately starts going to work, picking up clues. Male voice, deep, and with an almost pleading note to it.

"Uh, okay. Panicking isn't really my thing anyway." I start to try to sit up and my heart flutters when I realize I'm tied down. Okay, the whole 'don't panic' thing makes a lot more sense now. I bite my lip.

I will *not* panic. I'm not dead, but there are also things worse than death. All the reasons why I might be tied down to whatever I'm lying on flit through my head, and none of them are good.

"I am pleased to hear that. Please remain calm, and I will remove the restraints."

Okay, that's marginally reassuring. I try to look towards the voice—even my head is strapped down to the table—and I can see some movement in the darker area of the room, but I can't see who the voice belongs to.

"Is there a reason for the restraints?" *Keep it conversational. Don't show panic if he doesn't want you to panic. You can do this.*

"Previous representatives of your species have proven difficult when making the transition from Earth to here."

That's ominous. What does he mean, *representatives of my species?*

"Where is 'here' exactly? And who are you?" I squint at the darker section of the room, trying to see if the speaker is hiding there.

The straps slide away from my wrists, ankles, torso, and head all at once, freeing me entirely. I lift my head, staring down at myself for a moment, before sitting straight up. It's only then that I realize I'm uninjured. Completely. The lower half of my body, which had been crushed, is in perfect condition.

I can see that because I'm naked except for a pair of black panties that fit me perfectly. Smooth, unblemished, bronze skin, and not a single injury that would account for all the blood loss.

I stare at myself in shock before remembering and jerking my head around to find the source of the voice. I was right—he was hiding out in the shadows, but it's not a 'he', it's an 'it.' Literally an 'it.'

A large blob of Jello wobbles forward into the light. It's tall enough to come up to my shoulder, but that's exactly what it looks like, Jello. Or maybe tapioca pudding, because of the color. I don't feel remotely hungry looking at it though. There's something a little nauseating about watching it move.

Panic bubbles up in the back of my throat, even though I said it wouldn't.

This is the freakiest thing that's ever happened to me, and I haven't exactly lived a quiet life.

It's not like I can control my emotions, but I can control how much I let them show. The good news is that I'm used to crazy situations. And I have an amazing poker face. I push the panic away, knowing that it won't help me right now. And I promised I wouldn't.

Besides, there's no reason to panic just because I woke up naked and healed in a strange place with a moving blob of Jello. Yup. No reason at all. Waking up with the cartel would be far worse, right?

"My name is Frllil. I am a Jabols Luminary. You are located in my ex-planetary lab on the third moon of the eighth planet in the Jabolian system." The voice is definitely coming from the blob. I stare at it. How is it talking? There's no opening that looks like a mouth, nothing that would indicate it has vocal chords, but there's no doubt it's speaking to me.

There's also no doubt what it is.

"You're an alien."

"That is the word you would use to describe me, yes."

My brain is finally catching up, and is suddenly going a million miles a minute. *Holy shit, aliens! Aliens are real! This is the story of a lifetime!* Except... except I'm in his lab, located on the third moon of the eighth planet in the Jabolian system, which means absolutely nothing to me, but I sincerely doubt it's anywhere near Earth. The urge to call my boss subsides.

"And why am I here?" The question pops out of my mouth. In every sci-fi book I've ever read, there are only three options for what the aliens want: to conquer Earth, to experiment on humans, or to mate with us. I've read a lot about that last option, but I am having trouble believing that I'm genetically compatible with extra shiny tapioca pudding.

"You are here to undergo the training necessary to become the Tribute to a Tsenturion warrior." Something about the words triggers a memory in the back of my brain. Didn't I read some books about Tsenturions?

Hm. Maybe this is a hallucination... but I've had hallucinations before. The most vivid ones were during a spirit quest with a tribe I was writing a story about, and even then I knew that they weren't real. This—despite everything—feels real.

"Yeah, I'm gonna need a little more than that, because none of those words made sense together." I cross my arms over my chest and glare at Frllil, hoping I look threatening. Can Jello be threatened? I mean, seriously, what am I going to do if he doesn't answer me? I'm not even sure he has bones, though there have got to be some kind of internal organs, right?

Thankfully, he starts talking. I can't tell if he's intimidated or not, but I'm guessing 'not.'

It turns out the little bit I remember from the Tsenturion books was right—there's another alien species (not Frllil's) and they need compatible mates. And humans are a match. Even though I should probably be freaking out, I mostly feel excited. The panic has receded, and the astounding nature of my current position is really hitting home.

This is... this is incredible. I am talking to an actual alien. How many humans can say they've done that?

Well, now that I know aliens are real, maybe a few more than I would think, because who knows how many true stories have been dismissed as lies, but still. *They're real! They exist!* And they saved my life. At least, Frllil did. And I am very happy to be alive.

Frllil explains to me about the Tsenturion Warriors and *why* they need human females. I hear about the loss of their entire planet at the hands of another group of aliens called the Vgotha and how they became allies with Frllil's race, the Jabols. The Jabols were also persecuted by the Vgotha until they made contact with the Tsenturions. Now the two work together, combining the Jabols' technology and the Tsenturions' military expertise, to remove the threat to the universe.

All my journalist instincts are tingling by the time he's done talking. Not that anyone back on Earth would care about something that's going on light years away, but man... what a story. And it's kinda nice to know that it's not just Earth that has all sorts of violent and fucked up situations going on.

Not that I'd wish harm to others, but somehow I always imagined other aliens looking at us from afar, seeing all our wars and bigotry and the disdainful way some people are treated, and thinking, 'Nope.

Not gonna touch that.' To know they have their own problems is somehow comforting. Like, maybe I've been abducted and moved halfway across the universe, but how fucked up people can be to each other... well, that's something I'm familiar with, and apparently it transcends species.

Sad, but familiar. That's a good description.

"Okay, so, you're going to train me to be a good little alien bride, and... what do I get out of this, again?" I eye Frllil a little dubiously. Granted, he's got me dressed for the part, but he seems to be missing some of the necessary equipment. He's a blobby little thing, and not at all arousing to look at.

"You get to live," Frllil replies, and his words hit me like a punch to the gut. "I saved your life. You would be dead right now if not for me."

Oh, okay. It's a debt, he's not actually threatening my life. I think.

"So, you're saying I owe you?" I ask, just to confirm. Debt is something I'm familiar with, and I do have my own sense of honor. On the other hand, giving up the entire rest of my life—an especially long life, according to Frllil, since my biology has been changed to match a Tsenturion's—seems a little demanding.

"If that inspires your cooperation." Since he doesn't have a face, it's kind of hard to pinpoint exactly how he feels about it.

"What happens if I don't cooperate?" I ask. Rather than getting a verbal answer, after a moment, something hits me right in my clit.

I don't mean that metaphorically. It's like a zap of electricity right on the most sensitive part of my body and makes me double over and gasp for breath, both hands over the panties. Except... they aren't panties. I can't shift them away from my body at all. I can't even feel my clit, and my clit can't feel my fingers. The panic that had receded is starting to come back, because holy fuck, that hurt like nothing I've ever experienced before.

Who electrocutes someone in the clit?!

And then the not-panties start to hum. The vibration is soothing for a moment and then it begins to grow. I moan, my thighs trembling, both of my hands pressed over the front of the panties—but I have no control.

The acute pain has morphed into hot pleasure as all my most sensitive bits tingle and buzz. I press my hands against the not-panties, trying to find the edges, to pull them away as the sensory overload begins to swamp me, but there's not even the tiniest gap for my fingers to slip under.

"Stop it... I get it..." I gasp out the words as the vibrations climb higher. My nipples perk up, swollen and aching as the rest of my body careens towards orgasm. But I don't want to come in front of Frllil. I don't want to be that vulnerable in front of him. I don't want to be vulnerable at all—no matter what, I've always had control of my body and my reactions, but now he's controlling me, and it's terrifying.

To my shock and relief, the vibration stops. I'm only relieved for a moment, though, and then I feel like whimpering, because even though the vibration stopped, I am so close to orgasm that the need to finish the job is so strong, it's painful. My fingers are still pressing down on the not-panties, right over my clit, trying to rub... but I can't feel it at all.

I bite back a curse. My entire body is throbbing painfully.

"Good." Frllil sounds pleased, the fucker. "We will begin with your priming now."

My priming?

The vibration begins again, much lower than before, a tease that will not bring me the orgasm my body now craves.

"Come over here," Frllil says, blopping along towards one of the walls, which suddenly turns into a screen. I manage to scramble off the table and follow him, biting my lip against the low hum that flutters against my pussy, continuing to tease me. On the screen, an incredible hunk of muscle and sex appeal appears.

He has golden skin that actually shimmers, a humanoid body and facial features, and muscles upon muscles upon muscles. My jaw drops. Even without the weird panties, I feel like my clit might be humming after seeing this guy.

"This is Commander Arkdhem, third-in-command of the remaining Tsenturions. You are his Tribute. The High Commander and Commander Bogdan, the second-in-command, have already received their Tributes: Dawn Cahill, and Dr. Pareena Singh."

My jaw drops. Other human women?

Actually, that's encouraging. It must have been scary as hell being the first person to be taken by these aliens. Knowing that two others have come before me and lived to tell the tale is reassuring.

As he wraps up his explanation of how I'll be mated to Commander Arkdhem and that it's Frllil's job to 'prime' me for that mating, the pile of Jello focuses back on me. How I can tell he's doing so when he's a blob, I don't know, don't ask me to explain, but I can feel it.

"You are certainly the calmest and most agreeable of the Tributes so far," he says, sounding pleased.

Is it weird to feel good about that? I've always had a bit of a competitive streak. I'm the best at being calm after being abducted by aliens? Cool. Though it does make me wonder what their reactions were. Screaming? Fighting? Maybe he didn't save their lives. It tends to put things into perspective.

Still, these not-panties are now driving me a little crazy and I'm feeling a lot less agreeable, but I can fake it for a while longer. At least until I've had more time to figure out my situation, and whether or not there's anything I can actually do about it. Right now, I'm completely at Frllil's mercy, and I know it.

"I'm here now. Like you said, you saved my life. I didn't want to die and now that I'm here, well, might as well make the most of the situation. Besides, I've read a lot of books about sexy aliens, and had a lot of fantasies about it. Now I'm supposed to argue when one of my fantasies is coming to life?" I sound more agreeable than I'm actually feeling, but there's a lot of truth to what I'm saying too.

And the more the vibrations hum against my needy pussy, the more I'm interested in having that particular fantasy fulfilled.

Maybe I should be freaking out more, but all my life, I've rolled with the punches. Why stop now?

"That is exactly why we provided that book," Frllil says, sounding even more pleased. "The purpose was to identify females who would be agreeable to being part of the Tribute Program."

Oh. *Oh.* So it was my reading habits that got me into this. That... actually makes a lot of sense.

"Cool, tell me more," I say, doing my best to ignore the way my pussy is humming. I squirm, trying to find a way to relieve some of the pressure—or add some—but apparently, these are magic panties, and I can't quite figure out how to make them work for me. The best I'm going to be able to do is try and distract myself.

If I learn more about Frllil and his tech, maybe I can find a way to make the panties less frustrating—or even get them off of myself.

BY DAY Three of being cooped up with Frllil, I'm ready to scream from sexual frustration. Being 'primed' is bullshit. Especially for this long. The vibrating panties—aka 'Bride Trainer'—are a torture device, I'm convinced of it.

Not that I'll ever admit to a weakness, so I do my best to ignore it and instead try to distract myself by asking Frllil a million questions about his work, his tech, the Jabol culture, Dawn and Pareena... the stuff that won't turn me on the way just thinking about a Tsenturion warrior now does.

Yeah, not going to think about Arkdhem. Because being primed means being constantly aroused with no completion. It's orgasm torture of the highest form, and it sucks *burro* balls.

Still, my priming seems a lot easier than what Dawn Cahill went through. Reading the files on her training as the first Tribute, I am very glad that the training process changed after her. Thanks to her. Whatever. Getting stuck with needles full of an aphrodisiac sounds awful. The nanotech belt is bad enough—and at least it has some upsides, like being self-cleaning and taking care of my 'waste.'

I'm spending my days with Frllil, who is trying to make me focus on what a good little Tsenturion mate is supposed to do—be ready and willing to have sex, as far as I can tell—while I attempt to distract him with all my questions. He seems to find my thirst for knowledge commendable. Since he can't spend all his time with me, he gives me access to the archives and, once he's shown me how to use the Jabolian equivalent of a computer, I spend my free time searching through them and trying to ignore the state of my needy vagina. And, honestly, other than the incessant sexual arousal, it's not a bad way to spend my time.

I'm learning about real life freaking aliens! God, if I ever get back to Earth, I'm so writing a book. It will probably have to be fiction, unless I can bring some proof with me, but who cares? It'd be one hell of a book, and hopefully informative for any other poor woman who gets sucked through her e-reader to be a Tribute.

My chances of getting back to Earth seem pretty slim, but hey, a girl can dream.

There's a lot of information about the Tsenturions—their customs, and how they lived before their planet was destroyed by the Vgotha. Their alliance with the Jabol. Jabolian culture—which seems to be mostly focused on the gathering of scientific data and research, as well as making a study of other alien species. I look, but there's very little about the Vgotha. The number of unknowns make them seem even more threatening.

There's a lot about Earth, though, and the other two human females who came here before me. Dawn Cahill and Dr. Pareena Singh. There are pictures too, which are reassuring. Both of them are beautiful, but within the normal range. They aren't supermodels or anything, which means that Arkdhem shouldn't be disappointed with me.

And why do you care if he's disappointed with you?

Shut it, I tell the little voice in my head. Sometimes my competitive streak can take over and I know it, but I don't need to compete with these women for looks. Also, I'm being brainwashed by Frllil into caring.

But I can't even be mad at Frllil. He's just doing his job, and he's not doing me any harm, other than not letting me orgasm. Otherwise, he's a very lenient alien abductor.

And I can't forget that I could be dead right now. *Should* be dead. I was dying, and I wasn't going to be able to do any more good or help inspire any more changes until he saved me. No, I'm not going to be able to make my mark on my world anymore, but maybe I can make my mark on their world, the Tsenturion's world. And as more than a breeder, that is absolutely something I'm determined to do.

Frllil says Arkdhem is the third in command of the remaining Tsenturions, so he's highly placed in their society. I can see where Dawn, the High Commander's Tribute, has already changed the Tribute Program. Unlike me, she wasn't dying when she was sucked through her e-reader. She'd had a life, she'd had a future, and so she fought to change things for the Tributes who came after her.

I can do that too.

Maybe I was thinking too small when I wanted to change the world. Now, I have a chance to change the universe.

2

———

rkdhem

The closer the ship gets to Frllil's lab, the farther I am from the Tsenturion fleet and my duty. A small thread of guilt over disobeying the High Commander's orders has sunk into my very bones, but I do not let it distract me from my self-assigned mission.

Not only is the Tribute *my* Tribute, but if, as the High Commander believes, the Jabol are the ones who destroyed our planet and not the Vgotha, then she is in danger. Still, I know there will be a price to pay upon my return. I could have contacted the High Commander and interrupted his honeymoon, or even waited for him and Dawn, his Tribute, to return. But I did neither because I did not trust that he would agree to retrieve her.

Not with the anger that he has towards the Jabol right now, after uncovering their supposed perfidy.

I am still unsure whether I believe the Vgotha's account, or the vid they showed us of the Jabol destroying Tsentur, but either way, I cannot leave a Tribute—*my* Tribute, my heart—in their hands. I will take whatever punishment the High Commander deems necessary when I return, as long as she is safe. Whether or not the Jabol are our true enemy is irrelevant when it comes to her.

"Commander Arkdhem, we are approaching," Vardill says, looking up from his screen. Sitting in the Command Chair in the center of the bridge, I nod, unable to keep my armor from flashing gold and announcing my happiness, or the smile from curving my lips. I do not care about the show of emotion, though—what warrior would not feel the same when confronted with the imminent joining with his mate? Certainly, none of the other warriors seem surprised. They look at me with a mixture of hope and envy, each one wishing to be the next to receive their own Tribute.

"Open a channel to Frllil to announce our arrival." My heart races in my chest, my hands gripping the ends of the arm rests more tightly. Soon, I will be able to touch her. Hold her. Worship her.

My Tribute.

～

Marta

If I'd thought the not-panties—I still refuse to call them a Bride Trainer so they're vibrating not-panties as far as I'm concerned—were annoying on a low hum, they are so, so much worse on their current setting. My pussy lips buzz, but no matter how I shift, I can't get the humming vibrations to touch my needy, swollen clit.

I just want to get off!

"Their ship has arrived," Frllil says, sounding a little anxious as he escorts me to the pod I'll be taking to the claiming ceremony. "Are you ready?"

"Ready." I smile at him, ignoring my frustration with both him and the panties. One thing I've learned about Frllil and the Jabolian society as I've been here is that they're very duty-conscious. He's doing the job that he was assigned to do, and even though it's sexual torture for me, it's not personal on his part.

I can see why that pissed off the previous Tributes—especially Dawn Cahill, apparently—but I try to be nice to Frllil anyway. We've formed a sort of friendship, the kind that I haven't had in years, thanks to my work. Maybe it's from proximity to each other, but I truly believe he's at least a little fond of me, and as for me... well, it's hard to admit but I'm actually kind of attached to the blobby guy.

My dad had always taught me not to get involved in situations as a journalist. We're supposed to be the outside observer, watching but not part of it, but that hasn't been possible here. Besides, new planet, new rules. My mom would be happy that I made a friend, even if it is a blobby alien who's training me to become the breeding mate for a different alien.

Hmm. On second thought, she might not be so happy about that part, but she'd be happy about the friend thing.

"Are you going to walk me down the aisle?" I ask, teasing. A little pang hits my heart. I'd never expected to get married back on Earth. I'd always been more married to my job, but when I was a little girl, I'd always assumed my dad would fulfill that duty. A wave of grief and longing passes over me. I miss him so much... but I push the emotion aside. I barely cried when my dad and mom died, I'm not going to break down now. It won't be helpful to my current situation.

If Frllil had eyes, I bet he'd have blinked. Instead, he pauses a moment, as if considering my request.

"I may accompany you, if you wish. It would be highly irregular, but there is no protocol against it." He still sounds hesitant, though, and I shake my head.

"It's okay, Frllil. I was just trying to lighten the mood." I've done most things in my life on my own, why would this be any different? Besides, Dawn and Pareena both went to their Claiming ceremonies alone. I can, too. "I'm a big girl, I'll be fine."

It's not like it's going to be that hard. I arrive, walk down the aisle past the rows of Tsenturion warriors, and meet Arkdhem for the first time. My big alien hottie. He'll look me over and give me some kind of ceremonial first touch, and then he'll take me back to his quarters to claim me.

My body hums in anticipation, ready to reach some kind of climax. Anything to make this incessant ache between my legs cease.

At this point, I'd probably be ready to mate with Frllil if that was my only option, just to make the hot need go away for a little while. The fact that the only being who is supposed to get me off is a super hot, big, golden alien with muscles upon muscles is not the worst thing in the universe.

Fulfill my physical needs now. Figure out the rest later. It's basically how I've lived most of my life, even if I've never done anything quite like this.

Don't forget, the big guy really only wants you for breeding.

Yeah, yeah. That's a problem for future Marta, and only if I get pregnant. According to Frllil's notes, the Tsenturions have not reported anything about the other two Tributes conceiving yet—and Dawn was mated to the High Commander months ago—so I'm not super worried. I should have time to figure things out.

And until then, no-holds-barred kinky sex with Arkdhem sounds great. After a thousand years without sex, he's probably got a lot of energy to work off, and I am here and ready to help.

I'm certainly dressed for it, in a filmy, light purple gown that barely covers anything. My nipples are clearly visible through the material. It looks really nice against my golden brown skin and dark hair and I have to admit, I feel stunning.

"Here we are." Frllil comes to a stop outside a small oval pod. It looks big enough to hold me and maybe two other people. Good thing I'm not claustrophobic, and that the ride is short. He turns towards me. At least, that's how I interpret his movements. Since he doesn't have eyes or a face or anything, it's kind of hard to tell. "Good luck, Marta Romero Flores." He pauses, hesitating for a moment. "It has been a pleasure coming to know you."

"You too, Frllil. I'm gonna miss you." I sigh. "I have so many more questions I could ask."

There's an odd pause and then part of his blobby self extends, turning into a hand. Automatically, I reach out my hand as well, and he drops a small round object into it.

"This is a special comm unit. Put it in your ear. If you have questions or you need to contact me, press your ear closed for three of your seconds and, when I am able, I will contact you."

"In my ear?" I ask a little dubiously.

"You will not be able to feel it. And when I contact you, it will be as if I am speaking in your ear. I will be able to hear anything you say."

Okay, sure, why not. I reach up and drop it into my ear. It's the oddest sensation, as if it's rolling around and then suddenly it comes to a stop. Nothing. I poke my finger in my ear, trying to feel it, but instead of a ball, there's now a very smooth patch just inside. Nanotech is freaking amazing. This is way better than the not-panties.

"Good. It is secure," Frllil says. "Time for you to go."

"Thank you, Frllil."

I step into the pod. Time to go meet my mate and my destiny.

I would be lying if I said I'm not hoping to also get the orgasm I'm craving. Because I'm pretty sure I'm going to go insane soon if I don't. And it's going to be hard to figure out how to make my mark on the universe if I'm distracted by my body's craving for sex.

Arkdhem

The pod containing my Tribute comes to a rest at the end of the aisle, opposite the platform I'm standing on. The ranks of warriors between it and me somehow seem far too many, when a few moments before, I had worried about there being far fewer than there were for Dawn or Pareena.

It does not matter the size of the audience. What matters is her.

The door to the pod slides open, and there she is.

Despite the distance between us, I can see how beautiful she is. Her lush curves strain the filmy gown she is wearing, and I can imagine how full and soft she will feel in my hands. The Bride Trainer is visible beneath the lavender fabric and it swirls around her legs as she walks towards me.

Her hair blows around her shoulders, the sun glinting off it, and my *seela* begin to move as my cock perks up with interest. I know from Dawn and Pareena that human males do not have *seela*. The two Tributes call them 'pube tentacles,' but neither of them seem to have any complaints. Hopefully my Tribute will not, either.

As I stare at Marta, drinking in the sight of her, I can already imagine peeling her gown off her. Knowing that everyone can see her beautiful body so clearly through the filmy gown makes me want to growl with possessiveness, but I hold my position.

The rows of warriors stare at her with both hope and reverence. Another Tribute. Another symbol of hope for our future. Marta makes three, and I am very aware how lucky I am to have her. I would never deny my fellow warriors the sight of her, no matter how it stirs my possessiveness, because I know they are not really thinking about her.

No, they are thinking about the day when they may receive a Tribute.

I can only hope that they do. If what the Vgotha say about the Jabol is true... but my mind rejects those thoughts. I need to focus on the present and the female coming toward me, not on the possible issues of the future.

Her gaze meets mine, her large, dark eyes fringed with long lashes, her pouty lips slightly parted. I can see the glazed look on her face, so similar to Dawn and Pareena's when they arrived, announcing her arousal. Plump nipples press against the shimmering fabric she wears, begging for my touch.

I grit my teeth, forcing myself to remain stoic, which is not at all easy for me. My armor is bright gold—so bright, it is practically glowing—and it is all I can do to keep myself from running down to meet her.

She reaches the ramp and walks up, her gaze locked with mine. Her breasts heave with every breath she takes, and her tongue darts out to wet her lips. I nearly groan as my cock springs fully to life despite my best efforts to remain stoic, my armor flashing brighter with my own arousal. My *seela* writhe with need, aching to latch on to her.

She is supposed to stop at the top of the ramp, she is supposed to wait for me to come to her, but instead she suddenly lunges towards me. I automatically reach out to catch her as she leaps upon me, wrapping her legs around me, and I find myself holding an armful of female flesh for the first time in my life.

Damn panties—or maybe it's his armor, but I can't feel anything on the spot right where I need it. The vibrations had gotten more powerful as I walked towards Arkdhem, the sexy gold alien who is supposed to finally give me some relief, and I couldn't contain myself. So I jumped on him and tried to rub my pussy against him, but the vibrations immediately ceased, denying me my orgasm, and I can't feel anything through the stupid panties.

Behind me, the ranks break out into a shouted chant, and Arkdhem laughs, his hands curving around my butt. I can feel his calluses against my skin, but—again—nothing where the panties cover me.

"My Tribute is eager," he says, chuckling and squeezing my bottom. Holy hell, that feels good. I whimper a little. I know I was supposed to wait, but fuck that. I'm a 'go-getter,' and the closer I got to him, the less I cared about what I was supposed to do.

"You have no idea," I tell him. Yeah, yeah, Frllil told me there was all this pomp and ceremony and I'm totally ruining it, but I can't bring myself to care right now. This big alien is hard and hot between my legs right now and I want to be able to *feel* him, dammit! I could scream with the sexual frustration running through me, except that it wouldn't provide any relief.

He turns to the big alien next to him, who is also as sexy and yet somehow, I don't find him as appealing as the one holding me— which is a little weird, because why should I have a preference? But maybe that's part of the conditioning Frllil did with me. Pretty much my entire 'priming' was done with me staring at pictures of Arkdhem. That's got to have some kind of effect on my psyche.

I'll worry about that later, when I've finally gotten to experience some alien peen and I'm not so damn horny.

"I will take my Tribute to my quarters to complete our joining," he says to Sexy Alien #2. "You will helm the bridge. Set a course back to the fleet."

Hands still on my ass, he turns and carries me into the ship.

Fuck yes, finally!

Peeking over his shoulder, I can see the rows of warriors breaking rank, some of them shaking their heads, as Arkdhem carries me into the ship. Oops. Oh well. He doesn't seem to mind, and that's the important thing.

3

M*arta*

Being carried to Arkdhem's rooms is another exercise in frustration. I still can't feel him through my panties, but my nipples are stiff and rubbing against his armor. The fabric over them is textured, and they're becoming so sensitive that the constant motion and rubbing is almost painfully stimulating.

I whimper, squirming against him.

"Are you well, my heart?" Arkdhem asks as I wriggle.

"These panties are driving me nuts," I wail. Pride? Who needs pride? I don't. At least, not right now. I need to climax, and sacrifices must be made. Pride can take a hike if it'll get me off. "I can't feel anything through them."

"Soon." His deep, sexy whisper in my ear makes my heart do a funny pitter-patter, flip-flop. "My nanotech is already bonding with yours. Can you feel this?"

Mother fucker...

The spot right over my clit begins to hum harder than the rest of my panties and I shriek, rocking my hips against him and panting as the sensation swirls through me. So close, I'm so, so close—and then it fades away again.

"Fuck!"

He chuckles again and I would slap him, but then he says something that makes me feel a lot better.

"We are here." A door swooshes open behind me and I can feel his sudden rush before I'm unceremoniously dumped onto a bed.

The gown's skirt slides around my legs, and I stare up at him as he reaches down to pull it off of me. It's more of a tunic with some rope to hold it in place than a dress, and easily slides off when he tugs at the knots holding it around my waist.

I look at his armor a little dubiously, because that looks like a lot of work to take off and I'm not sure I can wait that long, and then suddenly it melts into his skin. Holy golden humanoid, he's even more beautiful in person than he was in the pictures. I want to touch every inch of his muscled body... and maybe lick it too... except then my gaze falls to his crotch, and I can't help the small shriek that falls from my lips.

He's so humanoid in every way that, even though part of my brain was hoping for some freaky alien peen, I don't think I truly believed it would be all that different from a human male's. Boy, was I wrong.

Yeah, there's a shaft and a head, but the head doesn't look anything like a mushroom. It's got a blunt point and then flares out, almost like the shape of a stingray, and the 'wings' even flap gently up and down. I gulp, trying to imagine what that will feel like inside of me.

The rest of his shaft is thick and ridged, growing wider towards the base, and at the base where his cock meets his body is where the really freaky stuff is.

Tentacles. Lots of tiny tentacles with one particularly long tentacle right above his cock. I've never been much into hentai but I'm suddenly wishing I'd watched a little bit more to help prepare me for this. Where do they all go? Do they go anywhere, or do they stay on the outside?

I shiver. *Two women have been through this before you, and they're okay. You can do this!*

But are they okay? I haven't actually met them yet, so how do I really know that? At some point, I need to contact Frllil and tell him that he really needs to add Alien Sex 101 to the priming curriculum because Tsenturion anatomy was not covered in the course material.

"You are well primed for me. Do not worry. I will make you feel very good." Arkdhem grips his shaft and pumps it. The little tentacles wave wildly in response. I can't take my eyes off of them. With his other hand, he cups his fingers around the writhing tentacles, clearly catching on to my interest. "These are my *seela*. They will help make you feel good too."

The panties hum to life again and I fall back against the bed. *Fuck*! My hips lift upwards, leaving me gasping. I press my hands against my pussy, but I still can't feel the pressure thanks to the damn panties. The freakiness of Arkdhem's alien peen suddenly means a lot less in the face of my overwhelming need.

Arkdhem

I can feel Marta's need thrumming through me, thanks to the nanotech. Already, we are bonding. I love seeing her squirming and writhing for me. From the way her eyes grew big, I could see that she was surprised by my *seela*, but Dawn and Pareena's discussions had prepared me for that. I am looking forward to showing her how good they can make her feel.

Kneeling on the bed, I push her legs apart, but I keep the Bride Trainer over her pussy for now, continuing to stimulate her while I run my hands up and down her limbs. Her skin is so soft. She moans, reaching down and pressing her hands over her pussy. Such a needy sound. Such a sweet, desperate female.

Leaning down, I press my lips against the skin on her pillowy thigh, just beneath the Bride Trainer, and she nearly levitates off the bed.

"Holy shit, Arkdhem!"

I like to hear my name on her lips. Turning my head, I do it again to her other leg.

"Please... just fuck me... Enough teasing, I'm dying up here!"

"No, you are not. I will not let you die. But I will pleasure you and make this special. The manuals indicated that the first joining between a male and female is very important to humans."

"Manuals?" She sounds confused, and the glazed look in her eyes makes me wonder if she's understanding everything I'm saying.

I nod at the stack of books on the table next to my bed. I have studied them every night, ever since the Tribute Program began, for when I received my own Tribute. I also added a few new ones after Frllil sent me the reading list from her 'e-reader.' Marta's eyes widen.

"Oh, my god... You have Sara Fields... and Cari Silverwood... and —is that the *Claimed Brides* anthology?" It's hard to tell exactly how she feels about the stack, but I am rather proud of them. I have read all of them cover to cover.

"Yes. I have an extensive collection of manuals from your world." The best collection of any of the Tsenturions, in fact. Even before I met her, I was dedicated to ensuring my Tribute has the best of everything, and now that I have her, I am glad I am so well prepared.

Marta whimpers. "Those aren't... they aren't..."

"Pareena and Dawn have explained that they are fiction. I understand that every female's needs are different. I look forward to ascertaining yours." I smile at her, moving up along her body to press my lips to her soft stomach. She moans as my hands slide up her sides to her breasts, cupping them.

Soft. She is so soft and squeezable. I want to touch every inch of her. To memorize every spot that arouses her. I lick and suck, tasting her, teasing her. My hands roam over her body. She is so sweet, so responsive, and everything the manuals claimed she would be. My cock is throbbing and my *seela* are reaching for her as I slowly make my way up her body, settling my knees between her thighs and spreading her legs wide. Responding to my desires, the Bride Trainer retracts, turning into a belt around her curvy hips, revealing her to me fully.

Her dark pink pussy gleams with wetness, displaying her arousal, and I want to crow with triumph. Finally. Everything I ever wanted, everything I have worked for all these long tsencycles, is here as my reward.

My sweet Tribute. My Marta.

<u>MARTA</u>

Arkdhem is absolutely wicked with his tongue and hands, and if I didn't believe in aliens, the only other explanation my brain might be able to come up with is that I've died and gone to heaven. But I do believe in aliens, and right now this one is doing absolutely sinful things to my body. He's exploring every inch of me, touching me, tasting me, and by the time he's spreading my thighs and lining up his cock with my pussy, the tiny tentacles—his *seela*—don't seem like such a big deal. Weird alien peen is kind of to be expected, anyway.

The longest one at the top taps against my clit as he begins to push inside me and I gasp at the sensation, my hands fisting in the sheets. Kneeling between my legs, he looks down and watches his cock as it presses into me, opening me up, and I can't reach him at all. My hands clench around the sheets beneath me, needing something to grip as hot pleasure rushes along my veins. I whimper, my head thrashing back and forth as the strangely shaped tip stretches me open in a completely different way than a human cock would.

I can actually feel it moving inside me, the sides gently flapping and stroking against the walls of my pussy. Arkdhem groans, shuddering, and pushes deeper. The bumps and ridges along his cock are the most delicious friction as he starts moving, thrusting a little deeper with each stroke, filling me a little more. His cock seems to swell inside me. He rocks his hips slightly and lights burst behind my eyes, an odd keening noise escaping from my lips.

I feel so full, so hot. My body is on fire for him.

Then the little suckers fasten onto my labia and inner thighs, tightening and pulling me closer until Arkdhem and I are joined by multiple tentacles. The sensation is intensely pleasurable and I cry out, gasping in shock. They're like nothing I've ever felt before.

Arkdhem reverses his glide, pulling out so only the wedge head of his cock rests in my pussy. The little tentacles pop off and wave like sea anemones in the ocean current, as if desperate to reattach themselves. Arkdhem slides back and sheathes himself fully inside me. Everything inside me clenches. My orgasm blooms slowly, a satisfying warmth in my belly.

Yes. This is what I need.

"More... fuck me, Arkdhem... I need more..."

Arkdhem moves in a sensual rhythm, his cock curving deep inside me, slowly picking up his pace. Each time he bottoms out, the wavy ridge of the biggest *seela* catches the edge of my clit, tickling it. I rock to greet it eagerly, rubbing myself against his body and the long tentacle. As if sensing my desire, it somehow latches on to my clit, producing a sucking sensation, as if a tiny mouth has begun suckling my most sensitive organ.

White hot ecstasy blasts through me so hard and fast that my eyes roll back into my head and I scream as my entire body tenses. I feel like I'm about to levitate, the intense pleasure rocking through me, leaving me panting.

The suckling sensation immediately stops and my watery muscles go lax, leaving me whimpering.

Arkdhem has stilled, concern on his face. "Marta? Are you all right?"

"Yes. Oh, god, don't stop. Please don't stop." It doesn't matter that I just had a massive orgasm, my body wants more of him. Craves more. The burning sensation hasn't quite stopped, like an itch that needs to be scratched, and I need him to keep fucking me. I need to feel him come in me.

Is this something the priming has done to me? Because I've never felt like this before. Or maybe it's the 'bond' Frllil talked about, that I didn't put a lot of stock in. Now I wish I'd paid a bit more attention, but I figured he'd been talking about an emotional bond. Not a physical one.

Taking me at my word, Arkdhem starts to thrust again. Tears of pure happiness leak down my cheeks as a wave of ecstasy makes my pussy clench. Now that he's reassured I'm well, it's like a dam has broken, and he's fucking me harder and harder into the mattress. The *seela* reattaches itself to my clit and starts suckling and I scream and writhe in glorious, filthy rapture.

I'm coming and coming again, the golden ripples of pleasure rolling, cresting, breaking over me. I've barely come up for air when another climax pulls me under. I scream. I sob. I writhe in abject pleasure as my alien lover fucks me senseless. Arkdhem groans, gripping my bottom and rocking with greater urgency. The tentacles pop on and off depending on his proximity, doing their best to seal us together.

Arkdhem's powerful body moves over me. His cock probes deeper with each thrust. I wrap my legs around his hips, dig my fingernails into his golden skin to pull him closer, and hang on for the ride. Sweat slicks my body. Arkdhem's jaw is tensed and his eyes glitter as he palms my ass and hitches me closer. The broad head of his cock bumps a spot deep inside me and I explode again with a shout. My insides quake. Only his body pressing me into the bed holds me together.

"Yes..." The huge Tsenturion slides almost all the way out and slams back inside, bumping the spot again. I can barely hear him over my own gasping cries. "Come for me again, my sweet Tribute. My heart."

~

Arkdhem

My TRIBUTE's inner muscles pulse against my cock as I slide in deep. Her climax is almost continuous now. Her knees grip me. My *seela* suction tight to her smooth skin, hard enough to leave red marks. I want to mark her. To paint my name on her skin with my cum and leave it there for her to wear. When the time came to wipe it off, I'd immediately mark her again.

I've never had such possessive thoughts, but now that I've had them, they won't stop coming.

If Marta ever has to leave the room, I want her swathed in robes with a sign hanging from a chain around her neck reading 'Arkdhem's Tribute.' Or maybe I'll just keep her in my room forever, tied up and waiting for me, the ship systems monitoring her vital signs so I can return to her side at a moment's notice. Or keep her caged near the bed, just outside of my work zone so I can keep an eye on her.

Yes, that's preferable. We never have to leave the room again.

I want to bury myself inside her and stay here, always.

And with that thought, I come deep inside my tribute for the very first time. She cries out as my seed floods her, her body arching, and I lean forward, pressing my forehead against hers. She reaches up and wraps her arms around me, her lips meeting mine in a desperate kiss.

My cock pulses inside her as I delve my tongue into her mouth, our bodies pressed so tightly together, it feels as though we are one.

And, in some way, we are. Our nanotech is now fully bonded. I can feel her body around me, against me, feel her heart beating rapidly in her chest against mine. She is now my everything, and I vow we will never be separated again.

4

M*arta*

My eyes are half-closed and I'm lying on the bed, blissed out on pleasure. Arkdhem glides out of me slowly and I shudder with after-shocks. My pussy feels empty without him, but it also feels sore as hell. He gave me more orgasms than I could count, and I'm torn between wanting more, and wanting to sleep for a week.

Arkdhem leans over me, his large form casting a shadow over my face. My eyes are a little unfocused. I blink. I may have fallen asleep for a moment, overcome with the afterglow. And now, long fingers are stroking my cheeks, smoothing my eyebrows.

Arkdhem traces down my nose and his thumb rubs my lips. I smile so he knows I'm awake but he doesn't stop exploring my skin with long, soothing strokes. His fingers follow the curve of my neck and shoulder, then dip down between my breasts.

He's exploring me, but without the urgency he had before. It feels both odd and nice, and as soon as I can get up the energy, I want to return the favor.

He touches one nipple and toys with the rising flesh. It crinkles at his touch and that seems to fascinate him. I shudder a little at the newly rising pleasure trickling through me. Arkdhem circles a finger around the flat brown areola before returning to my nipple, and I moan. He runs his knuckles under my breast and caresses every inch of my flesh. It's a long while before he moves on, and even though I've been thoroughly sexed up, my body's already stirring again.

Though, I guess it's not that surprising. I spent days being primed. It's probably going to take a full-on sex marathon to sate me.

His fingers drift lower down, poking and exploring my belly button. Now my hips are shifting as he moves lower yet. I want to jump him again.

"Have you ever seen a human woman before?" I ask. My voice is husky, strained. Maybe I was screaming a little loudly, there at the end.

His hands still but he doesn't take them away. "I have."

Oh, right, duh. He met the other Tributes. But did he see them naked? Did they let him touch him like this?

A shot of jealousy makes me push up to my elbows and ask, "Like this?"

"No, my heart. Never like this." He's almost smiling, as if he knows I'm jealous and he likes it. His answer reassures me and I settle back onto the bed. He resumes stroking down my sides. I want to arch against him like a cat. Who knew that I like to be petted? "I have seen other Tributes, yes. But none naked." His voice deepens. "And none so lovely as you."

I'm stretching and preening like a pampered pet, and now I want to purr.

His fingers have found the soft skin of my inner thighs. He laves my legs with long strokes. I stretch my thighs wide, letting my labia open like a flower. Here's hoping he'll take the hint and touch me where I'm aching. But nope, he ignores my throbbing sex. He spends a minute running his fingers over my upper thighs and contrasting that with the silky skin in between, as if fascinated by the difference. Then he grips my calves. His massaging fingers release all the tension in my body. He grasps my foot, and his thumbs run up my arch. He discovers how ticklish I am, and also the groaning noises I make when he rubs the tension out of a particular spot. I feel totally pampered and boneless, and also incredibly turned on.

But instead taking advantage of this, he rises off the bed. *Meu deus*, that is a beautiful body. Tall, broad shouldered, golden with all sorts of muscles that a human man doesn't even have. All in the glittering gold of his skin. The weird cock that is already erect again, despite the fact that he pulled away.

"Are you hungry, my Tribute?"

Sure I am... for him. My stomach gives a little grumble.

Right. Sex burns calories. And epic sex burns a lot more. And that was epic, even if it was vanilla. Although, the tentacles were an unexpected bonus.

"A little," I admit, even though I'm pretty sure it's going to delay my turn for sexploration. Food is fuel, after all, and I don't want to pass out from hunger before I get the chance to do so from pleasure.

He nods absently and starts walking away, still gazing at my prone form lounging on the bed as if he can't tear his eyes away. He goes to the wall and says something. I'm too distracted by his tight, gold, naked buns to see what's happening, and the next thing I know, he's carrying a tray full of dishes back to the bed. Whatever's on the tray smells amazing even if the food looks strange. From here, it looks like lots of bright blue and purple foods—a clash of colors I've never seen in food before. One dish holds mounds of what looks like ice cream but it smells meaty. My mouth waters.

Arkdhem sets the tray on the bed. "The replicator can make food from your planet, but I thought you could try some of my favorites as well. At least one of the other Tributes likes each of them, so I know they are compatible with humans."

"You thought right," I say, because my favorite thing to do in a new country is go to an outdoor market or grocery store and be dazzled by the unfamiliar foods and packaging. I'm also touched by his thoughtfulness that he's offering foods he knows that one other human likes. I'll probably try everything eventually, because that's how I am, but starting with things I'll hopefully enjoy sounds good.

My stomach is asking for food, *now,* so I reach for what looks familiar—a plate of square brown cookies in the corner. British type tea biscuits. I could eat the whole plate, and maybe I will. I just burned a thousand calories, right?

Before my fingers touch the biscuits, Arkdhem gently catches my wrist and guides my hand away. He holds the first bite of something to my mouth: a purple fruit that has a knobby surface.

I close my eyes as I part my lips, feeling the brush of his fingers against them as he puts the piece in my mouth. The purple fruit has a knobby surface and citrusy flavor like an orange, and the texture of avocado. It's surprisingly good.

"So these are your quarters?" I ask after I swallow. If he's not sexing me up, I want to know more about where I am. I am a question machine, and if he's going to be my mate, he's going to have to get used to that.

"Yes." He offers up another bite to eat and I give up trying to figure out why something that looks like ice cream smells meaty. I close my eyes again and just let the flavors burst on my tongue. It tastes like steak but the texture is more pasty, kind of like a paté.

"So, you've never had a Tribute?" I know the answer, having reviewed the files, but I want him to keep talking. I want to know more about him, specifically, and I'm hoping to get more than a one-word answer. He's going to need to get used to being peppered with questions and giving more satisfactory answers. I require it of the people close to me. It's probably why my boyfriends didn't last very long—that and my work schedule, and general lack of interest in keeping a relationship.

"No." He takes a moment to stroke my lips, even though I'm not a messy eater and I don't think I've spilled anything. The gesture feels incredibly intimate and he stares into my eyes, making it even more so. "You are my first. My only."

My stomach is getting full. I don't even know what I've eaten. I keep expecting him to explain what these foods are but he seems to be preoccupied with just watching me. He hasn't even eaten, himself. When he's picking up another bite, I snatch a tea biscuit and offer it to his mouth. "You must be hungry."

He smiles a little and lets me feed him. His features are mostly humanoid. I can't get over the strange golden skin. I end up stroking his face and now I understand why he took so long to explore me. His skin is silky smooth to my touch, warm, and the more I touch him, the more I want to.

"Where is your suit?" I ask, tracing the edge of his jaw. Before my question is over, his armor is rising from his skin, forming right under my fingertips into the lower half of a helmet. Almost like a medieval knight's armor, but with the ability to shape itself.

"This is the suit," he says. "It responds to my mental commands."

I run my hands down his shoulders. His armor is still rising, growing wicked-looking spines that curve from his back. I would hate to fight someone wearing this. I guess that's the point. My not-panties aren't nearly as cool, although it's nice to know they can be a belt instead of underwear.

Arkdhem is a warrior. From what I've read, the Tsenturions are a military culture. I filed that away as useful information and intellectually, I understood, but it's another thing to lie in bed with my new lover and see it first hand. It reminds me of the great loss he and his people have endured and my stomach twists with sympathy for them. I can't even imagine the kind of rage and grief he's felt... and yet here he is with me, seeming perfectly happy.

It places an unexpected burden on my shoulders. The idea of being a Tribute, a female to fuck, was easy in some ways. Emotional stuff... not so much. I'm not a touchy-feely person, at all. I didn't expect to feel emotions for him, especially not so soon after meeting him, but it's hard not to when I think about what he endured.

So I do what I do best: I distract myself and keep touching him, focusing on the armor and his skin, and how the two are both the same and different. On a scientific level, it's fascinating.

Arkdhem seems content to let me explore him as he explored me earlier, so I don't stop.

"My skin and my suit are bonded. The nanites make it one and the same."

"Incredible." So are all these epic muscles of his chest and shoulders and arms. He's leaner than some of the images of the Tsenturions I've seen, but just as built. He has the tight muscles of a marathon runner, or a mountain climber.

And he's mine, all mine.

I spread my hands over his pectoral muscles—or what would be called his pectoral muscles if he were a human man. If I could, I would purr with satisfaction. Without thinking, I move into his lap so I'm on my knees straddling him, my thighs spread wide. I'm definitely not having any issues with my emotions now—I've only got one emotion going on, and it's desire. My core touches his muscled midriff. His large hands come to support my back and the armor flashes gold before melting into his skin as if it was never there at all.

"So... you've never shared your quarters with anyone?" I venture, curious, as I run my hands over his newly smoothed shoulders. Frllil's files were full of information, but they didn't contain anything. Humans are the first species found that are genetically compatible with Tsenturions, supposedly, but there was no indication of whether or not they've ever found another sexually compatible species.

"Not since becoming an officer. I've been here alone." There's a sadness in his eyes that tugs at me, reaching out to those messy emotions I'm trying to ignore. I should move on from the topic, but I'm too surprised to change the subject.

"All this time? You've never... been with anyone?" He's had duties and held a military office. But if what he's telling me is right, he hasn't had sex for a thousand years. And he still took the time to go down on me before sexing me up. Impressive.

"Yes," he replies. "I've waited for you, my Marta."

Holy shit, not only did I fuck an alien, I popped his cherry! Also —*holy crap!* If he was that good at sex the first time, I can only imagine what he'll be like when he's had some practice. Though, as he said, he did have the 'manuals', aka the sex books. Back on Earth, women wish men would read romance and take some notes. Here, I have an alien who has been using them as instruction manuals, and I am not complaining.

I rock a little bit against him. Ooh, that feels nice. I can rub my clit right against the edges of his muscles.

His cheeks widen with his smile. He knows what I'm doing but he seems willing to allow it. His hands reaffirm their grip on my ass as he dips his head close. "You were worth the wait."

We're chest to chest, sitting as intimately as a couple can. I've just met him, but this feels right. My desire ramps up even as I continue to question him. "So you spent all those years on duty or here, no breaks?"

"It was easier to lose myself in work than do anything else. For all of us. I was hardly the only one."

Right, the destruction of his people. I stop rocking against him. "I'm sorry for your loss."

"Thank you," he says. "It was a long time ago." The grief flickering in his eyes belies his statement. He reminds me of some of the soldiers I met back on Earth, those who would joke about their experiences with hollow eyes and voices. Then he blinks, and the emotion is gone, hidden away, the same way as the veterans I'd met. His hands glide up my back, still exploring. He adds, in a wondering tone, as if he can't believe his luck, "For so long, we've had nothing but vengeance, justice, to drive us, but then Frllil told us he'd found a compatible species. Now we have hope again, a future we can build towards. And now I have you."

The way he looks at me... as if I'm some kind of reward that's worth having been alone for so long. My heart aches.

"So you really have been around for a thousand years?" The mind boggles. I can't imagine. I'm in my thirties and I feel old beyond my years sometimes, with everything I've done and seen, but that's nothing compared to him.

"Oh yes, the nanites remove any sign of aging. And now you will live as long as I do."

"Seems like a long time." I frown. I've forgotten to keep rubbing against him. Now I want to research... But I also want more sex. Decisions, decisions. But my first instinct has always been to follow the story. "What—"

"Patience, my heart," Arkdhem interrupts me, smiling. The heat in his eyes tells me exactly what he is thinking, and I can feel his *seela* beginning to writhe against my thighs again. It's an odd sensation, but arousing as well, especially because I know exactly how they feel now. "There is plenty of time for questions. But right now, I have another pressing need."

One of his hands comes between us and his fingers strum my lower folds, seeking out my clit. I whimper a little, squirming on top of him.

"But... I want to know..." My voice is a little bit breathless. Conflicted. Because I don't know what I want more—him, or answers.

Smack!

His palm lightly cracks on my right buttock. I straighten and stiffen, then melt. The heat from the sting is delicious. Nothing like a little bit of punishment to get my head in the right space for intimacy. Amazing that this alien light years away from my home planet gets that better than any guy I've ever dated.

My hips tilt forward again so I can rub myself against him exactly how I want. He smacks his left hand against my left buttock.

Yes! Spank me, golden alien daddy!

He grips the back of my neck, arching me backwards. I quiver in his hold. He's totally in control, and my body revels in it. Being dominated like this has always been the only way to get my brain to turn off during sex. "There will be time for you to learn all you wish to know. For now, I am going to fuck you again. The manuals say that to complete your claiming in the manner of your people, I must earn your submission."

Oh, well, damn. That sounds hot. And fascinating. Also possibly painful. All the filthy hot books I read start running through my head, with all the sinfully sexy scenes. I might be in trouble here, but my nipples are already perked up and I'm wet all over again, and not just from his seed.

He keeps spanking me lightly, his left hand still gripping my hair and tugging my head back so my face is turned upwards. He seems to be studying all my expressions, the way I jolt when his hand smacks down particularly hard, the way I quiver when his fingers massage my bottom.

His fingers explore the crack of my ass, and I stiffen. I've never done anal play with another guy, though I've read about it and I've wanted to. I've done some explorations on my own, but they were more uncomfortable than anything else. Definitely nothing like how my books made it sound. But Arkdhem's long index finger is like magic, sliding into my ass, slick and hard, and making me feel so hot and full. The sensation is both strange and good. I shudder, letting my head fall back as I moan.

He goes back to smacking my ass again. A low burn develops in my sit-spots. The heat warms my whole core, and my hips rock faster.

I'm close to orgasm when he tugs my hair, turning me and pulling me over his lap. I land on my belly over his hard thighs, with my bottom pointing upward and my face almost to the bed.

Once I'm in position, he splays a hand between my shoulder blades, keeping me down. His other hand is free to toy with my upturned buttocks and the seam beneath my cheeks. I wriggle, trying to get my clit the stimulation it needs so I can come, and he smacks my bottom harder.

"Be still, my sweet Tribute," he orders, and my belly clenches at the commanding tone.

He explores my lower lips. Finding the wetness of my pussy, he chuckles to himself. He can tell that I'm loving this.

I can't keep my hips from twitching as his fingers dance over my folds. He's got me pinned, and damn if I don't find that hot. I try to get my hands free and he catches them too, pinning my wrists in the small of my back.

And then his finger goes back to probing my bottom. He circles my bottom hole and I tighten my buttocks automatically to keep him out. Another chuckle above my head, and he goes back to spanking me in an even pattern. Left, right, left, right. A few slaps to my upper thighs, and the lower curve of my bottom. Lightly at first, awakening warmth in my cheeks. Once I've relaxed, he increases the intensity. The stinging slaps spark more heat in my rear, but with the endorphins washing through me, I'm floating. I'm so high, I barely notice when he stops.

He shifts me off his lap and onto a pillow. I'm still belly down, with my throbbing bottom propped high. Perfect for spanking—or doggy style.

And, yep, after a few more playful smacks to my heated flesh, he's parting my legs and gliding into me from behind. My sex is sopping, and yields to his hard girth. There's a delicious stretch and then he's bottomed out in my pussy, his taut groin pressed against my burning buttocks. I groan into the rumpled bedding.

He winds his fingers into my hair again and tugs my head back. To relieve the pressure, my back arches, and I push my chest off the bed. He reaches a hand around to my front and delves between my legs to find my clit.

"Come for me, my Tribute." His clever fingers catch the sweet spot to the left of my clit. My climax muscles are already quivering.

I'm going to be so sore tomorrow.

But I don't care.

I come hard, screaming his name.

5

rkdhem

Having a Tribute is so much more than I imagined.

For so long, jealousy and envy consumed me when I looked at Dawn and Pareena, especially Pareena. I did not think that Bogden was worthy of her. I hated him for receiving a Tribute before me. But now, I understand.

Pareena was never meant to be mine, because the universe was bringing Marta to me. I had become impatient, thinking any Tribute would do, but now I know, no one but Marta would complete me.

Lying on my side, I lean on my elbow, looking down at her and memorizing every feature on her beautiful face. Her tanned skin, a beautiful bronze color somewhere between Dawn and Pareena's shades, the slope of her nose, the long, black eyelashes that brush against her cheeks. She sighs softly in her sleep and turns her face towards me. After I claimed her several more times and thoroughly pleasured her, we ate another round of food supplied by the replicator and she fell asleep almost immediately afterwards, satisfied in every way.

I reach out to run my fingers through her hair. It is curlier than either Pareena or Dawn's and multi-hued, with both darker undertones and lighter strands that almost match her skin, as if she combined both of their hair colors. I am fascinated. Human females come in such a wide variety of shapes and colors. Tsenturions are all gold, without any of the differences, with similar body types.

My comm unit chimes, and I growl under my breath at the interruption. *Drakk.* I do not need to answer to know why they are calling. We are a single ship, and I need to be on the bridge for my shift. I did not want to ask my fellow warriors to take over my duties so that I can indulge myself with my Tribute, now I am wishing I had.

But duty calls.

I push to my feet as Marta moves beside me, suddenly stirring now that I am getting up, and blinking sleepily at me.

"Where are you going?"

"I have a shift on the bridge. I will be back. Stay here. Rest." I lean down and press my lips to her forehead. My armor slides over my body, covering me. I send a signal to the nanotech, and her Bride Trainer grows from her belt to cover her again.

"But—"

I give her a stern look.

"You will need rest. I will have food sent to you. When I return, I will take you on a tour of the ship."

Turning on my heel, I leave the room quickly. Not because I want to, but because it is so hard to, and the more I look at her and her adorable pout, the less I want to leave. My body aches to return to her the moment I begin walking down the hall, despite being physically sated. It is as though I cannot get enough of her.

Is this how it always was between mates? I do not know. I do not remember. It has been so long since we lost the rest of our people, and I was not ready for a mate when the last festival was held. Perhaps I should ask someone... but does it really matter?

That is the past. Marta is my present, and my future.

~

*M*ARTA

As the door slides shut behind Arkdhem, I groan. There is no way I'm staying here like a good little girl and waiting for him to come show me around. I can make my own way around, thank you very much. And I am way too curious to stay cramped up in here all day, not knowing when he'll be back. There's nothing to do in here.

Arkdhem is happy to have a Tribute and to get laid—can't blame him there—but either he clearly knows nothing about humans, or the previous two Tributes were utterly lacking in curiosity.

I groan as I roll over and get to my feet.

I'm sore in places I've never been sore before. That alien cock hit all sorts of spots that no man ever touched, and the *seela*... Looking down, I giggle as I see all the red hickey spots he left on my thighs, and I know there are more under the panties. Tentacle hickeys. They look ridiculous, and yet I like seeing them too. Which strikes me as a little odd.

Back on Earth, I never let a man mark me. But then, human men didn't have tentacle pubes to help pleasure me. And it always felt like men wanted to leave hickeys to mark me as a possession. No one is going to see these.

I make a face at the panties. Those, I could have done without. But they're not as bad now that I've gotten my big O several times over. Actually, my vagina could probably use some armor right now, to help protect it.

First things first. I inspect the room. There's nowhere to keep clothes—which makes sense when I remember that Arkdhem literally wears his in his skin. There's the pile of books, of course, but nothing else I can see for entertainment. The bathroom is nice, with a large tub and shower area.

But there's nothing that makes me want to stay in here longer than I have to. Looking around, I see there are no clothes for me either—other than the robe I arrived in, which Arkdhem had tossed on the floor. The ceremonial gown might not be much, but it's what I have. I've gone undercover wearing less in the past. Shrugging it back on, I head for the door. Unlike for Arkdhem, it doesn't immediately slide open when I approach.

"Open." The door remains firmly shut.

No wonder Arkdhem thought he could leave me cooped up in here. I scowl. Kick the door. Hmph.

A memory stirs in my consciousness. When I was with Frllil, on one of the days I was exploring, I followed him into a room that was kind of like a library, with a lot of shelves, and he either didn't realize or forgot, and accidentally locked me in there. Once he realized what had happened, he taught me the override command, which was supposed to be used in such situations. He'd said it worked in almost all Jabol locations.

This was a Tsenturion ship, but an awful lot of it looked exactly like Frllil's setup so maybe they used the same technology...

"Bllilligillar." The door swooshes open. "Ha!" I pump my fist in the air. That's Marta: 1, Bossy Alien: 0.

Stepping out into the hall, I look around. It's empty, no sign of other Tsenturion warriors anywhere around. Lots of grey walls. No decoration. But it is a military ship, so that's not exactly surprising. It's also not particularly interesting.

Are you sure you want to do this? The cautious side of my brain rears its head at the most inopportune times. *Arkdhem is not going to be happy, and you know what happens in those books you read when the alien isn't happy.*

Oooh, spankings. I've always wanted to be spanked. And the little slaps he gave me during the last round of hide-the-weird-alien-peen sparked my curiosity. Of course, it'll probably hurt too. But, even though I haven't known him very long, I can't imagine Arkdhem actually harming me.

Is it weird to trust an alien I've never seen until he became my mate? Absolutely. Yet, I can't shake the conviction that I'm safe with him. Maybe it's a side effect of the nanotech. Frllil did say there would be some.

Wandering down the corridor, I don't bother trying any of the doors. I'm assuming that the Tsenturions don't all bunk in the same hall, which means these should all be bedrooms. I don't want to disturb anyone at rest, and I definitely don't want to be stopped to answer questions.

When I get to the first crossroads, I do a quick eeny-meeny-minie-moe, and end up taking a right hand turn. This corridor looks exactly the same as the previous corridor. I wonder if I'm still walking past bedrooms.

About halfway down the hall, I come to a grinding halt as the right hand side of the corridor opens up into a kind of sitting area. But it's not just any sitting area. There are a few couches and benches, yes, but the main point of it is the huge window that looks out into space.

I gasp, slowly walking towards the big, open blackness. Seeing how far it goes outside the window is giving me a weird kind of vertigo, but it's like I'm hypnotized by the sight. I can't look away, and I need to get closer.

A foot away from the glass, I come to a halt and reach out a shaking hand. Being able to see my reflection is the only reason it doesn't look like I'm reaching out into the blackness of space itself. I can see stars off in the distance, so far away, and I suddenly feel very, very small and insignificant.

But it's so beautiful.

~

Arkdhem

Everything is going smoothly for the trip back to the fleet. Too smoothly.

I know eventually I will have to face the High Commander again, and that he will not be happy. While I remain ready to face whatever repercussions my actions have wrought against me, I am aware of every passing microcycle of our return trip, because each microcycle brings me closer to the end of this easy bonding time with Marta.

When the return trip ends, I will be subject to disciplinary measures, and I do not know how much time any punishment will allow me to have with my Tribute.

I almost wish for some kind of interruption, some sort of small delay, to give me more uninterrupted time with her.

Sensing my distraction, Argan turns to me.

"Commander, if you like, I can maintain the course and alert you only if an issue arises."

Having already not done my duty once—leaving the fleet to retrieve my Tribute rather than following through with the orders the High Commander gave me—I am loath to leave my command post but... the trip is going smoothly. And I do not want to waste one precious microcycle with Marta.

Finally I nod, albeit a bit reluctantly. "Thank you, Argan."

"Of course." He grins, fist to his chest in salute. "We all need to make accommodations for the reception of a new Tribute."

That is true. I remember that the High Commander himself left Bogdan and me in charge of the fleet after Dawn joined us. Feeling a little better, I salute Argan back, and leave the bridge.

My feet move much faster returning to my quarters than they did leaving, my heart lightening with every step I take. 'Eager' does not begin to describe how I feel. I want nothing more than to spend all of my time with Marta, until our inevitable return to the fleet.

As soon as I reach the door, it registers my nanotech, and slides open to admit me.

"I am back!" I stride into the room with a wide grin on my face. But there is no answer. And there is no Marta sprawled out on the bed where I left her. My heart begins to pound rapidly. The door to the bathing room is open, and she is not there either. I rush through the room anyway, as if there is somewhere she could be hiding from me, and then back out into the hall, looking back and forth frantically.

Where the drakk is she?

~

MARTA

"Marta!" My name is roared so loudly that, even far down the hall, I jump and whirl around.

I'm not sure what's behind the door that I'm currently trying to get into, but the fact that it's locked and also resists the override command that Frllil taught me has my curiosity burning. I can hear the upset in Arkdhem's voice, though, as he yells my name again.

My butt is already tingling, as if in either anticipation or warning, because yup, my big sexy has discovered my absence, and he's pissed.

"I'm here!" I yell back, hoping that maybe if I act like everything is fine, I'll mend some of the damage. Also, I know from my books that trying to hide or escape the consequences will probably result in a heavier punishment than facing up to it.

"Marta?" Arkdhem rounds the corner and sees me standing at the end of the hall. His suit is flashing red and yellow, and the bright colors are only partially soothed when he lays eyes on me. The yellow dwindles, leaving mostly red. "What are you doing outside the armory?"

"Is that what this is?" Damn. Now I really wish I'd been able to get in. Not that I think I would need a weapon to protect myself from Arkdhem, but I also don't like the idea of being completely defenseless... plus, I bet they have some cool stuff in there.

Arkdhem comes to a halt in front of me, crossing his arms over his chest. I don't need the brightly flashing red armor to tell me that he is one pissed-off mate—I can see it all over his face. Shit. Putting my hands behind me, I bat my eyelashes innocently as he stares down at me.

I'm not scared, exactly, but I'm starting to think that maybe the impetuous decision to wander about the ship on my own wasn't that smart. To be fair, I'd expected him to be gone a *lot* longer. And I hadn't actually agreed to his command that I stay put.

"How did you get out of the room?" His voice is low and tight, like he's holding back from yelling at me again through sheer willpower.

"I walked through the door." It's the truth. I've been in court enough to know never to give more information than is asked for. Keep it simple, honest, and—above all—don't volunteer anything.

Arkdhem narrows his eyes at me. "The door was locked."

"Was it? Then how did I get out?" I bat my eyelashes again. Yeah, it's cliché, but hey, it worked more than once on Earth, so why not now? Might as well try. I arch my back, pushing my breasts up as well. His gaze drops to them and he silently stares at my boobs for a long moment.

Hooray for boobies! Weapons of mass distraction all over the universe.

Unfortunately, it doesn't take very long for him to remember that he's mad, though at least he does seem a little less mad than he was a second ago.

He scowls at me and holds up his arm. A little video appears above his wrist and it takes me a moment to realize that it's basically a door cam, showing me coming up to the door. Dammit.

"Bllilligillar." My voice sounds odd and tinny, but it's clear. "Ha!" Video me pumps my fist in the air. I sigh. I just had to celebrate, didn't I?

"Sorry?" I say, wrinkling my nose and trying to look as sweet and innocent as possible.

It doesn't work.

Arkdhem literally tosses me over his shoulder like I weigh nothing and swings around, heading down the hall, carrying me like a sack of potatoes.

"Hey! Arkdhem! I really am sorry!"

Smack!

The swat to my ass is nothing like the playful ones he gave me before, and I gasp at the painful sting.

"You certainly will be," he says darkly. My sweet cinnamon roll has a stern side, and I've awoken the beast.

"I already am! I promise, I won't do it again." I'm babbling. I never babble. On the other hand, I've never been tossed over someone's shoulder and spanked before either.

~

Arkdhem

My Marta is a strong-willed female, I can tell. I like her that way, but certain orders are for her safety. While I trust my fellow warriors with my life, it's a whole other thing to trust them with my mate. I do not want to break her will, at all, but she does need to bend, at least until she learns our customs and rules. I shake my head at all the trouble she could have gotten into on her own.

She gasps and wriggles on my shoulder as the Bride Trainer pushes relentlessly into her bottom hole and begins to pulse. The manual put particular emphasis on how important that hole is to putting a female into the proper submissive mindset. I had not been particularly interested in it, because it is not necessary for breeding, but now I realize ignoring it may have been a mistake—one I will not make again.

"Arkdhem, please!"

Already I can tell it is working. She sounds much less defiant and sassy than she did when I first confronted her. And when she lied to me.

The door to our chambers slides open again and I carry my squirming mate inside and over to the bed. Putting her on her feet, I quickly strip her dress back off while she stares up at me pleadingly.

She might protest, but I can feel her arousal through the beginnings of our bond. The hard buds of her nipples are standing at attention again, begging to be pinched and sucked. Despite my anger and disappointment, my cock surges to life, my *seela* begin to writhe. I am not sure there is anything she can do that will quench my desire for her.

That will not save her from a deserved punishment. The manuals were very clear, and I witnessed how well the tactics worked with Dawn and Pareena; it is best to start as I mean to go on. That means I cannot give her leniency for a first offense, doing so would only encourage her to offend again.

"Turn around and bend over." I cross my arms over my chest, my gaze stern. My armor is no longer flashing red, but the neutral black still flickers with it.

Marta's mouth opens and closes, as if she was about to protest and then thought the better of it. Good. Ducking her head, she turns around and bends over the bed. The sight of her obedience, as well as her beautiful bottom pointing at me, sets my pulse racing. She is perfection.

"Good girl." I send an order to her nanotech and the Bride Trainer recedes into her belt, except for a thin line that travels down the crease of her bottom and into it, where her small hole is stretched around its insertion. "Now you will stay there and think about what you've done wrong while I make a call."

It is only the work of a few moments to contact the bridge and tell them to update the overrides. It is something we probably should have done anyway, now that we know the Jabol are possible enemies. We are in ships they provided for us, and we have never changed the override commands, because we trusted them.

I make a mental note to tell Gavrill to change the rest of the fleet's as well.

Then I turn my attention back to Marta, studying her in silence from behind. My mate is beginning to squirm again.

6

———

M*arta*

Waiting is awful.

Some things, I am very patient about. Waiting for the perfect lead to follow. Tracking a tiny thread of information. Letting silence hang in the air while I wait for someone to confess their secrets to me.

But waiting for a spanking? Nope. I just want to get it started. Waiting for it to happen is awful. And I know that's exactly why he's making me wait. The big jerk. Some cinnamon roll he's turning out to be.

And yet, this bossy side of his is turning me on. Even without the panties humming against my pussy, I know I'd be squirming. It makes no sense. I've never liked being bossed around. Then again, I've never had a guy try to do it in the bedroom. They always assumed that because I was so independent outside of it, I wouldn't want to be submissive inside of it, and I had felt too ashamed to ask.

It really is like one of my books come to life, and my pussy is aching. Even the thick probe that's filled my ass is turning me on. I've never done anything anal before, and it hurts and feels good all at the same time—and he's not wrong about it making me feel more submissive too. It's hard to feel large and in charge with something rammed up my butt.

It's been quiet back there for a minute.

Is he looking at me?

Is he ignoring me?

I peek over my shoulder, and then whip my head back around.

He was totally looking at me.

My pussy gets wetter. Hotter.

Knowing that he's staring at me from behind, waiting for him to come spank me... Yes, the waiting is awful but it's also hot as hell.

The room is so quiet that I can hear him as he moves up behind me, placing his hand on the cheek of my ass. My muscles clench around the nanotech plug, making the stretched entrance ache.

"Do you understand why you're being punished, my heart?" His voice is firm, but gentle, his hand caressing the spot where I know he's going to spank me first. My heart races, my pulse pounding so loud, I can actually hear it.

"Because I left the room after you told me not to." I mean to sound defiant, but somehow my voice comes out small.

"And because you lied to me about it."

Oh. Right.

His hand lifts and comes crashing down on my ass. This is no playful swat. It stings and burns and I shriek, jerking upright. I don't make it very far before there's a hand between my shoulder blades, shoving me back down into place.

My pussy quivers.

I am so fucked.

~

Arkdhem

The thick fall of Marta's dark brown hair spills over her shoulder. Her bare bottom is a work of art. The Bride Trainer frames her rear cheeks, flowing over her hips like a harness that holds the plug in her bottom. Lower down, the chastity belt-like piece has opened to give me access to her plump lower lips. The dark curls framing her pouting labia are already slick, and the honeyed scent of her arousal fills the air.

I thoroughly researched the manuals in preparation to receive my Tribute, but the reality is better. I send a command to the Bride Trainer to widen the plug inside her, and a little gasp greets me as it stretches her from the inside out.

I rub her upturned bottom, stroking the silky skin almost reverently. Her plump curves make me ache to claim her. The only thing better will be the sight of her punished bottom glowing red.

I set my left hand in the small of her back to steady her. My first slap makes her gasp. I admire the slight jiggle, and the faint mark of my handprint.

This will be a much harder spanking than the one earlier. She enjoyed that spanking. She will not enjoy this one—at least, not during her punishment. I may allow her to come once she has been thoroughly subjugated. While I enjoy my Marta's fiery intelligence and curious spirit, when it counts, I mean for her to give me her submission and her surrender. With training, she will be the perfect Tribute.

I smack her left cheek and then her right. I divide her bottom into several quadrants and make sure I pepper each evenly. Her upper thighs and sit-spots get their own share of attention, and soon her entire backside is painted pink. She's wriggling and moaning. My cock is painfully hard.

I flip her onto her back, and her eyes widen in surprise. As pleasant as it is to watch her bottom turn bright pink, then maroon, I wish to see her face. I hold up her legs and continue punishing her. Each swat makes her jolt, causing her breasts to bounce. It gives me an idea.

I give another command to the Bride Trainer. It streams up her front to circle her breasts, framing them.

It's an erotic sight. Marta's red bottom wriggles but cannot escape the black plug wedged between her bright red cheeks. On her upper torso, the Trainer acts like a harness, surrounding her breasts, revealing more than it conceals.

Perhaps when we are in my quarters, I will keep my Tribute naked but for the Bride Trainer. Every morning, I can design the Trainer into a new formation that plugs her ass or even her mouth, and frames her breasts and punished bottom. My cock hardens at the thought.

For now, I command the Bride Trainer to attend to my Tribute's breasts. Thin tendrils stream from the main part of the harness to encircle her nipples. The tendrils tighten, pinching them. Marta writhes, her hands flying to cover her breasts.

"Hands above your head," I order. Instead of restraining her, I wish to train her to present herself willingly for punishment. I remember a phrase in one of my favorite manuals by Tymber Dalton. Or was it Maren Smith? "You are bound by my will," I intone.

Her chest heaves, her pupils darkening. Slowly, she obeys, stretching her arms up over her head. The movement causes her back to arch slightly, which pushes up her breasts.

"Good girl," I praise her, and reward her with another round of spanking. She still twitches and winces as I punish a particularly sore spot of her rear, but other than biting her lip against her adorable gasps and squeaks, she behaves.

I send the instructions to the plug in her bottom. It widens slightly and she moans, pink cresting on her cheeks. Her bottom has heated to a fever burn. I can sense it through the bond, and although her rear throbs painfully, it has awakened arousal in her lower half.

I could so easily push apart her legs and sheath myself inside her, and soon, I will. But first...

"Well done." I let her legs down. She shrieks as her sore flesh touches the bed. Before she can roll away, I reach forward to wind a hand in her hair and guide her to her knees in front of me. She looks up at me almost gratefully. It will be a while before she sits comfortably. Her cheeks are flushed, and while there's no sign of tears, her eyes are half closed, almost sleepy with surrender.

I keep hold of her thick brown hair and step closer. "Now it is time for you to thank me for your punishment."

My suit separates, revealing my erect member. Her dark brown eyes widen as my *seela* burst forth, stretching and straining towards her face.

~

<u>MARTA</u>

ARKDHEM'S COCK bobs in front of my face, its flared head moving in its alien manner. This penis is porn-sized, but that doesn't take into account the extra appendages—namely the large flange of his prime *seela* that's waving in front of me, almost brushing my forehead. Then there are the tiny tentacles, their suckers end-upturned, as if seeking my face. Sure enough, as he steps closer and I prepare myself to take him in my mouth—exactly the way the heroines in the naughty books I read thank their Doms for punishment—the *seela* latch on to my face and pull me forward. I keep my mouth open, and his length glides over my tongue. His salty meatiness fills my mouth. He groans, and I moan around him.

He cradles my head, studying how I take his cock. He threads his fingers into my hair and my scalp registers a bit of tension followed by a sharp tug. But the slight pain of hair pulling only sends a flash of pleasure to my pussy. I don't know how my wires got crossed—pain is pleasure, and pleasure is so intense that it hurts—but they did, and it works.

I raise my hands to steady myself, but remember him ordering me to be bound by his will. The phrase was hot enough to make me come, so I box my arms behind my back like a good little sub.

"Good girl," he murmurs, and I melt into a puddle. I open my mouth wider and accept him, stroking my tongue along his length, closing my eyes as his prime *seela* brushes my forehead. The tentacles on my face suck harder. As I bob my head up and down his length, the *seela* pop on and off. I'm going to have hickeys after this, all over my face, but I'm not mad about it.

Arkdhem guides my head for the first few times I take his length deep, but mostly lets me control the pace. But he's still in control. I kneel before him, the plug filling my ass. The Bride Trainer harness around my chest tightens, pinching my nipples. My pussy is dripping on the floor.

He steadies my head again. On instinct, I take a deep breath, and let him plunge my head down on his cock. He curls over me, grunting as he makes me swallow his sword. When he pulls out again, I'm gasping, tears running down my face. He thumbs them away reverently.

Then he thrusts deep into my mouth again. I relax my jaw and let him dominate me. The *seela* whip about my face, brushing my jaw and suctioning on, helping me hold position. Arkdhem's hips surge forward until his prime *seela* covers my eyes. He judders uncontrollably until, with a grunt, he empties himself down my throat. He immediately pulls out with a gasp, catching my chin to make sure I'm okay.

"Good girl," he murmurs, wiping away my tears. He seems almost fascinated by them, secret sadist that he is.

I lick my lips and look up at him. My ass is burning, my pussy is throbbing, and my clit wants attention, but satisfaction at pleasing him spreads through me in a warm glow.

He lifts me and positions me on my hands and knees on the bed. I settle in, expecting him to remove the plug and reward me. But he presses into my pussy. I gasp as both the plug and his cock fill me. The *seela* are active again, the long flange of the prime *seela* brushing my burning ass cheeks, and the smaller tentacles suctioning onto my chastised bottom.

Arkdhem seats himself fully in my pussy. His groin rubs the heated skin of my backside, making me groan. At the same time, little shivers of pleasure run through me at the full feeling. The Bride Trainer bits on my chest clamp tighter onto my nipples, but the pinching pain is lost in the overwhelming storm of sensation.

Arkdhem winds a large hand in my hair, tugging my head back. "Do not come," he orders, even as he starts thrusting hard enough to make my breasts bounce in the Bride Trainer harness. His groin slaps my ass, igniting the sting of the spanking all over again. I grip the bed blanket and grit my teeth, trying to hold off my orgasm. Arkdhem's hips slow their rhythm, and it's almost worse, because every time he bottoms out in my pussy, he grinds against my clit.

"Arkdhem," I gasp, and he pauses. I pant, so grateful that he's let my orgasm subside.

The butt plug filling my ass shifts, and I realize Arkdhem's tugging on it, pulling it out slightly and pushing it back in. He's essentially fucking me in the ass with the plug.

Arkdhem resumes fucking me slowly. His cock drags over my G-spot and I drop my front to the bed, too weak to hold myself up anymore. My orgasm is rising, a bright blaze in my mind. It's so close, a huge tide I can't possibly hold back.

"Arkdhem, please," I beg.

"Call me 'Master,'" he orders, and when I do, he bucks his hips and orders, "Come."

And I do, sobbing happily into the bed, practically insensate.

When I come back to my senses, I think I might have fallen asleep again for a bit. I feel groggy. Befuddled.

Thank God for alien nanotech, because I'm pretty sure my pussy should be raw and chafed at this point. Unfortunately, the nanotech doesn't seem to be doing anything for the state of my ass.

Ouch.

Reaching back, I touch my hot cheeks and let out a hiss of breath. Spankings really hurt a lot more than I thought they would.

"I hope you learned your lesson," Arkdhem says sleepily, pulling me into his side and sliding his hand down to cup my buttock. The nanotech panties recede for his hand, so he can palm the full red mound, and I hiss again, squirming against him as the stinging pain flares.

"Yes, I did," I say. I learned that I'd better not get caught, because spankings aren't nearly as fun as my imagination had made them out to be. At least, disciplinary spankings aren't. I'd much rather have fun spankings. Though, the rest of it was fun... but sitting on my sore butt later won't be.

So, yeah. No more tempting spankings just for the sake of getting spanked.

"Would you like to have your tour of the ship now?" Arkdhem chuckles when I immediately sit upright, and then let out another little whimper as my weight presses my butt into the bed. *Ow, ow, ow.*

"Yes, I would," I say primly, pretending to be unaffected by both the renewed throbbing in my cheeks, and his amusement.

7

____

M^{arta} Redressed in my gown, I accompany Arkdhem out the door and back into the hallway. As before, this corridor is empty.

"These are the sleeping quarters," he says, confirming my earlier guess. Nice to know I haven't lost it just because my brains have been fucked out.

As we walk through the corridors, headed who-knows-where, with my arm wrapped around his, Arkdhem starts to question me.

"What did you do on Earth?"

"You mean my job? That's what I spent most of my time doing." Because of its nature, I hadn't had much time for hobbies other than reading. My e-reader had been easy to take along with me wherever I went, and when I didn't have that, I could always access the app on my phone. I make a mental note to check out that pile of books that Arkdhem has, eventually.

"Yes. Dawn was a yoga instructor, and Pareena was a psychologist. What did you do?"

I remember that from the files that Frllil had on them. "I was an investigative journalist. I followed leads for stories, and reported on them." A sudden question pops into my head. Arkdhem brings up Dawn and Pareena a lot, and I kinda figured it was because they were the only two humans to join the Tsenturions so far, but now I realize he talks about them in a very familiar way. "Do you spend a lot of time with Dawn and Pareena?"

"Yes. I became their friend. And I was Dawn's guard when she first arrived." He smiles fondly, and I feel a little trickle of jealousy. "You will meet them when we return to the fleet." His smile flickers a little. Does he not want me to meet them? How close were they?

I don't get a chance to ask any of those questions, though, because I can hear many voices for the first time since we began walking through the ship.

"This is where we eat," Arkdhem says, leading me forward. The doors are open to a large room where many Tsenturion warriors are gathered, all of them seated, and eating. The food smells different, but that doesn't faze me. Everything I ate earlier was delicious and, as much as I traveled on Earth, discovering new foods was always something I enjoyed.

Though, I would also kill for some pizza right now.

"Do you want to go in?" he asks.

"I'm still full from earlier." I shake my head. Honestly, I probably could eat a little, but there's something intimidating about walking into a room full of warriors. Probably the fact that my butt is still sore and stinging slightly underneath my dress. I don't want them all to watch me try to sit down for the first time after my spanking.

And maybe I'm still feeling a little vulnerable because of that spanking.

Though, if anyone asked me, I would go to my grave denying it.

Satisfied with my answer, Arkdhem leads me on.

"Tell me more about being an investigative journalist. What is it?"

I laugh and explain as he continues to lead me down the corridor, telling him some of the stories that I uncovered, the prizes I won. A feeling of pride fills me as I remember how much I managed to do, but also sadness, because that's over. But, I remind myself, it could have been over because I died. Instead, I'm getting a new chance to make a difference somewhere else.

I just have to figure out how.

"This is our training area," Arkdhem says, and I pause in my stories to look into it. There are some half-naked Tsenturion warriors wrestling on a mat in the middle, and others doing what look like training exercises around the edges of the room. Damn. Maybe I don't need books for entertainment, I can just come here and watch this.

Not that I want any of them other than Arkdhem, but that is a lot of eye candy to enjoy.

"I do not understand," Arkdhem says after a long minute.

"What?" I tear my gaze away from the sexy display of alien flesh. If these guys could get to Earth, they'd have no shortage of volunteers to be Tribute. Ha!

"I do not understand. You regularly put yourself in danger so you could tell others the terrible things that some people were doing?"

That's actually a pretty good summation of my job; he understands it fine. "Yup."

"But why? Why put yourself in danger? You were not a soldier."

Oh, okay. Cultural differences. I can handle that. I had to navigate that all the time for my job, especially being a woman. Not to mention all the people back at home who didn't understand either, because they were worried about me, like my mother.

"Because I made a difference. My articles uncovered secrets, showing the true side of powerful people who needed to be brought down. Because of my articles, there have been companies who changed their policies to treat their workers better. Some, who were polluting the areas around them and making people sick, have had to pay to make them better, and some of them have gone out of business since then. Governments have changed their laws. I wasn't just uncovering the truth, I was making a difference and bringing about change to the world—good changes that helped people." My sadness over no longer having that rises again, but I push it down.

There's nothing I can do about it. Someone else will have to help them now. Hopefully, I'll be remembered for the good I did before I disappeared. I look up and realize that Arkdhem is staring at me.

"What?"

"You are even more amazing than I knew."

I can't tell him what those words meant to me—not that I'm given the time. His mouth descends on mine, kissing me almost desperately, and the next thing I know, I'm swung up into his arms. He's carrying me against his chest like we're on the cover of a romance novel, and rushing me back to his quarters while I giggle madly.

It's amazing my vagina hasn't caught fire from all the friction yet, but it hasn't.

The doors to Arkdhem's quarters glide open and the next thing I know, I'm bouncing onto our big bed. I yelp as my chastened cheeks touch the blanket. I'm still sore from the spanking.

I flip over to my hands and knees and start to crawl up the bed but my big gold mate grasps my ankles and pulls me back down. There's a flutter in my pussy at the sight of him towering over me in his full armor. His gaze is hot and intent on mine as he drags me down the bed and parts my legs. I try to plant my feet into the mattress to push my hips up and get the pressure off my poor bottom, but he maneuvers me onto my back and down to the edge of bed where he's kneeling. His palms cup my rear cheeks, and he squeezes. I whimper but can't deny how the sting awakens my arousal. My pussy is already slick, ready for him. He wedges himself between my knees and tosses up the filmy garments that he dresses me in to wear out of the room. Something rips and he grunts, almost growling as he tears the rest of it out of the way.

I'm flat on my back, abs tightening as I fold in half to watch him take control. My legs are spread wide around his lean bulk. The Bride Trainer flows away to reveal my pussy to him. His nostrils flare as he inhales my scent. I squirm, but his left hand comes to my inner thigh, holding me open. With his right, he spreads my labia with two fingers and leans in as if studying my open sex. I'm dripping.

"Master," I whisper, my voice gone husky. He hasn't specifically instructed me to call him 'Master' every time we're in the bedroom, but it's hot, and he definitely likes it. And when he's happy, he's more inclined to make me happy, right?

"Lie back," he orders.

I obey, raising my hands over my head in the way I know will please him. The move pushes up my breasts. My nipples are still sore from their earlier treatment, pink and puffy.

"Good girl," he purrs. His thumb strokes up my labia.

The Bride Trainer probes my ass lightly, and then more intently until it stretches my private hole. I moan. Arkdhem taps the hard plug.

"Soon, I will take you here," he promises. I reach down automatically to cover my ass, and he smacks my pussy.

My legs snap closed but the bulk of his shoulders is in the way.

"No, no," he says with a wicked smile. He really is a secret sadist. "Hold your legs open," he commands.

I fist my hands at my sides and force myself to relax as he palms my pussy, grinding the heel of his hand against my clit. His hand rises and falls, spanking me once, but not too hard. A forceful heavy petting.

I keep my legs open, my eyes wide on his.

"Good girl." His hand falls again, this time, giving me a harder slap. My legs quiver and I arch my back, gritting my teeth. I register the force of the smack, but the sensation is confused by the stimulation on my clit. "My obedient Tribute." He thrusts two fingers into my pussy. "It is time for more training."

Arkdhem

After only two tsencycles, I am impressed by how well my Marta has accepted her training. She has learned to hold herself open to me, her hands bound by my will.

Even now, she lies with her arms stretched overhead, open to me. Her nipples are red and puffy from the pinching of the Bride Trainer. The sight makes me want to lower my head and lap at the tortured buds to soothe them, giving her relief from the torment caused. I can't bring myself to regret causing her a small bit of distress. Her pussy grows so wet when I dole out small doses of pain, the bitter bite tempering the endless sweetness of our interludes. She responds so well to the precise pain and I live for her reactions: the widening of her eyes, the pink flush to her golden skin, the way she bites her plump lip or opens her mouth to release husky, full-throated cries.

This session will not be easy for her. I intend to test the limits of her body in the most delicious way. A body like hers was made to be worshipped and I intend to do just that, but push her to the limit of both pleasurable pain and painful pleasure that she can endure.

Luckily, I studied the manuals often, and know them well. My extensive knowledge will allow me to create an experience neither of us will forget.

To start, I order the Bride Trainer to form a thin thread between her nipples. I visualize the item I read about in the manuals until the nanotech creates what I want: a delicate chain connecting the pincher-like sections that claim her nipples. Once it's formed, I give it a light tug. Her body shudders with the new, shocking sensation, her back arching beautifully to take the pressure off her punished tender buds.

"Keep your arms above your head, bound by my will. And open your mouth," I order her gently, and place the chain between her teeth. If she jerks her chin up, it will pinch her buds even more, forcing her to be complicit in her own torture.

With her nipples taken care of, I lower myself down to study her pussy. The pink lips are plump and slick under the dark down. Her little pleasure bud is starting to peek out from under its fleshy hood. I thumb the apex of her folds, not quite touching her clitoris. She shudders again, this time enjoying my ministrations. But her movement jerks the chain leading to her nipples, and her sigh turns to a distressed squeak.

I cannot suppress my wicked smile.

❦

Marta

It's the smile that clues me in. If I had any doubts, that deliciously evil smirk wipes them away. Arkdhem's a fucking sadist. My poor pinched nipples are evidence of that.

I'd be more upset if he wasn't everything I've fantasized about: a cuddly and attentive daddy-ish dom who pampers me in and out of the bedroom, but turns up the strict when it's time for punishment. Or, in this case, funishment. Even with my bottom freshly spanked, my body is hot and eager for anything else Strict Alien Daddy wants to dish out.

I stare down my body at Arkdhem, still keeping my arms up. He touches my pussy lightly, and I tense to keep from moving too much and causing extra strain on my nipples. My body is already warming, my pussy dripping in anticipation of both erotic pain and pleasure.

The next thing I feel is the plug forming in my ass, sliding deep and growing thicker until it stretches my ass to the point where it's all I can think of. The temperature in the room has gone up ten degrees. I squirm slightly, then whimper as I remember what movement does to my nipples. Fuck.

Still grinning, Arkdhem spears my pussy with a long finger, turning it and stroking the inside of my wall, finding my G-spot. After a few moments of him massaging my inner tissue, waves of pleasure begin to ebb through my core. The sensation ripples out from the source in my belly.

He lays his mouth over my vulva and probes my entrance with his tongue, at the same time keeping up that steady, deep massage with his hooked finger.

I'm moaning around the chain in my mouth. The sensation in my pussy grows sharper and my head goes back automatically. The movement sends a fresh burst of pain up from my clamped nipples. I moan again, this time in protest.

Arkdhem chuckles and clamps down on my legs when I try to close them.

"This is part of your training," he says. "You're being so good, but a few more sessions, and you will be perfect. Keep the chain in your mouth," he orders. "And do not come without permission. I will only give it to you if you beg, but if you lose the chain from your mouth, you'll be punished."

Not fair! I grimace at him. He's going to do his best to make me come, and if I come without asking permission, I'll be in trouble. But if I open my mouth to beg, I'll lose the chain. He's diabolical.

"For punishment, I will spank your pussy," he continues.

At that, my body clenches, sending a fresh wave of heat through me. Apparently, I find the thought of a pussy spanking super hot.

"So what will it be, my Marta? Will you be a good girl? Or will you defy one or both of my orders?" His thumb finds my clit as his inserted index finger rubs my G-spot. Meanwhile, the plug in my bottom swells, filling me to the point where my pussy spasms with need. My spanked bottom throbs in counterpoint, and I whimper.

"Do you need me to tie you down?" he asks, sounding almost solicitous. As if he'd tie me down for my benefit.

"Nnnnh," I answer. I will keep my arms up myself. He trusts me to remain bound by his will, and for some reason, I don't want to disappoint him.

"What's that?" He cocks his ear closer.

Bastard. I grit my teeth and shake my head in a tight movement, so as not to pull my nipples.

Arkdhem's eyes gleam as he lowers his head to lick my clit again. It's all I can do to keep my arms stretched above my head. Between the pressure inside my pussy and the wet tongue on my outer folds, my orgasm is rising. Even the rough heat in my bottom adds to the intensity. I shake my head as if I can deny it, and the movement pulls on my nipples. The sharp tug short-circuits my synapses, tripping another swell of arousal. I grit my teeth and fight it, which only makes it grow.

Arkdhem pauses mid-lick. "Are you a good girl?"

I nod, ignoring the way this movement makes my breasts bounce with the clamp. I whine around the chain of my mouth, pouting down at Arkdhem.

It does no good. "Do not come until I say so," the big golden bastard reminds me. His tongue flicks my clit, and his finger twists deep in my pussy. I feel the entire galaxy rotate. In all my wildest fantasies imagining a heroine sexually tormented by a big alien, I'd never imagined this.

I make a strained noise that would be a 'please' if I were not so obedient in keeping the chain between my teeth.

This time, it works. Arkdhem rises, and removes his finger from my pussy. My orgasm still hovers close, but it's nowhere as imminent as it would be if he kept licking and probing me.

"Good girl. You've done so well." He plucks the chain from my lips. I'm relieved until I realize he's ordered the Bride Trainer to create another chain, this one forming a clamp he hovers right over my clit.

"No," I gasp. Too late. He attaches the clamp right to my clit. The pinch makes my toes scrunch. My poor, swollen clit pulses.

"Breathe," he advises me.

"You breathe," I snap back. "I can't believe you—"

He holds something to my mouth, and presses it between my lips mid rant. It's nanotech similar to the Bride Trainer, and it fills my mouth and flows around my head, forming a sort of gag.

"Asshole!" I mutter, but luckily the word is muffled.

"Shhh." Arkdhem taps the font of the gag, looking pleased. I glare back at him. I'm filled in every hole. My nipples throb in their clamps. My belly is still tensed against the pinch on my clit, but the sensation isn't so bad. The sting competes with the stretched feeling of my full ass and the slight burn of my spanked bottom. If I had to rank the discomfort, in first place would be the inside and outside of my ass, then my pinched clit, and finally, my nipples. And then the gag, although it's more annoying than anything. It's preventing me from cussing Arkdhem out, which might prevent me from getting punished. So that's good, I guess.

"Beautiful," he breathes right on my pussy. "I should dress you up in this every day. You will wear the chain, the clamps, and the gag. Oh, and your plug. Nothing else."

I grumble behind the gag, even though the thought of that is sorta hot. All the sensations are mixing in my body, overflowing. Arkdhem strokes my pussy again, close to my clit, and the discomfort I tallied earlier disappears, swallowed up with the screaming need to come.

"I'd like to try something." He stands and goes to the wall. His body blocks the replicator, but I can tell he's creating something. Now what?

He comes back with a long, narrow, cane-like stick that ends with a tea bag shaped flap at the end. A replicated version of a riding crop.

"I have heard about this." He whips it through the air, and tests the leather flap on his leg.

He's gloriously naked now. With the riding crop, he looks like the alien version of a sadistic lord in an erotic Victorian novel. I had a rare precious few kinky historical books on my e-reader. Now, it seems, I will live one of the scenes.

Arkdhem taps the end of the crop on my breast, using it to prod my clamped nipple and nudge my clit. I can't tell whether the sensation is agony or ecstasy, but it doesn't matter—by some strange alchemy, it adds to my building orgasm.

Automatically, I bring my hands down to shield myself, and Arkdhem tuts. "Naughty girl. Hold position."

I obey. I bite down on the gag, trying to keep control of the coiling tension in my core.

"I should punish you for that," he says in an offhand manner. So arrogant. Just like a Victorian lord. "I wonder... can you keep your arms up when I do this?" He touches the crop to his lips. I tense. The crop falls right onto my pussy.

WHAP!

I seize up but don't move my hands. The jolt makes me jerk, and my breasts bounce.

"Well done," Arkdhem says thoughtfully. "Two more."

WHAP! WHAP! He doesn't give me time to brace. But it's nice to get them over with.

"Very good," he purrs. "You deserve to be rewarded."

He gives a regal nod, and nanotech streams from somewhere and bind my ankles and my wrists. Probably not a good sign.

Once I'm fully tied down and helpless, Arkdhem checks the bindings, and paces to the end of the bed. I get the feeling he's fulfilling a particular fantasy.

"So lovely." He prods my pussy with his crop. He leans back as if waiting to enjoy the show.

At some silent order, the clamps on my nipples and clit open and fall away.

"Nnnn!" I shriek behind the gag. It's too late. The blood rushes into my tender buds and it's no use, the orgasm I've been holding back is now a tsunami of sensation. It sweeps over me, making me shake. My ass clenches around the plug with each breath-stealing wave, but my pussy aches to be filled. It's too much sensation, and not enough.

It wrecks me. If I wasn't bound, I'd roll into a ball. Tears leak from the corners of my eyes. I'm gasping around the gag—and suddenly, it's melted away. I let out a final, keening cry. Arkdhem's eyes slit. He's watching me like a connoisseur who's just been presented with the masterpiece of his life.

Fucking sadist.

And I realize what I've done.

"I didn't tell you to come," he says, and taps the crop against his palm. He kneels between my legs and brings his hand down on my pussy. Hard.

SMACK!

I jerk in my bounds, and howl. My poor pussy is going to be as pink as my ass.

The crop nudges my labia, stoking the fire that's starting to flicker to life.

WHAP! The next blow is from the crop, and it jolts my clit. Unbelievably, a fizz of sensation shoots through me. It's almost like a mini orgasm. Warmth is growing in my belly—the firestorm growing.

Arkdhem grins as if he knows what's putting the disbelieving look on my face. He alternates spanking my pussy with the crop and his left hand until I'm panting.

Then he taps the crop over and over on my labia, while thrusting a finger inside to find my G-spot again.

"Master!"

"Beg," he orders, and I do, in a rush of words, "Please. Please, I'll do anything, just let me come—"

He tosses aside the crop and goes to his knees. His mouth seals on my punished pussy. His tongue plunges into my entrance. Lips, tongue, fingers, it's all too much. Another finger fills me, and he stops tonguing me long enough to command, "Come."

His mouth fastens over my clit, and sucks. I come so hard, white stars burst behind my eyelids. I arch off the bed, straining in my bonds. My feet scrabble against the sheets. I ride the tight crest of the orgasm, and crash into another one.

And then he's stretched over me, gliding into my sopping pussy with one hard thrust. He fills me perfectly. With the stretch and burn inside and outside my ass, it's almost too much.

"Come," he orders. "Again." And I do. My pussy milks his cock and he speeds the rhythm of his hips, an intense look on his face. His thrusts rock my body. I'm stretched between the restraints, fully open to him and unable to resist the relentless pounding. The glide and burn is just what my next orgasm needs to start building.

"It's too much," I moan. "I can't—"

"You can. It is my will. Come for me, my heart. Let me feel your pussy squeezing my cock."

I scream and sob as another orgasm is wrung from my body, leaving me exhausted and completely satisfied.

Damn. I want to hunt down whoever gave Arkdhem the bride manuals. Best and worst present ever.

8

M*arta*

In the following days, Arkdhem and I act like newlyweds on a honeymoon. In this case, the groom being a seven-foot alien warrior with armor that can change color and retract at a thought. Arkdhem shows me around the ship, and I meet several more of the officers. I'm really eager to meet the other two Tributes, but until we rendezvous with their ship, I settle into enjoying my new existence as a Tsenturion mate. When Arkdhem is on duty, I hang out with Medik, or simply stay in my quarters and sleep. I'm usually wrung out from the white hot sessions and sexual appetite of my Tsenturion warrior. Of course, Arkdhem wants to mate as much as possible—he hasn't gotten any in a thousand years. And I'm all too happy to accommodate him.

"Let's talk about the Tribute Program." We're in the bath, soaking after another marathon sex session where he tied me to a specially designed piece of furniture and used the Bride Trainer to edge me for what felt like hours. He finally forced me to come over and over with a plug in my ass. I fell asleep and woke up sticky—hence the bath.

"What do you want to know?" he asks.

"So we're just supposed to repopulate the entire Tsenturion race?"

He grins. "Do you have an objection to that?" His hand moves to casually cup my breast. His palm rubs my tender nipple, and even though he just made me come so many times I begged him to stop, pressure builds in my pussy at his touch.

"No." In this moment, I do not have an objection to it at all. His smirk turns smug, because he knows it. "Who came up with the plan? The Jabol, or Medik?"

"The Jabol approached us with the plan. And the High Commander approved."

He shifts slightly, removing his hand from my breast. He tenses up when he talks about High Commander Gavrill, and I'm not sure why.

"Hey." I scoot closer to him. "Is something going on between you and the High Commander?"

"What?" He regards me with a look of surprise.

"You tend to look uncomfortable when you talk about him."

"Before I left to retrieve you, we had a... misunderstanding. But it will soon be resolved."

"Misunderstanding? Does it involve me?"

"You are entirely too intelligent, my Marta."

Which isn't an answer. I press myself to his side, and he puts an arm around me.

There must be a healing serum in this water, because my sore ass and pussy already feel better. A few more minutes, and I'll be ready to jump Arkdhem again.

But first: answers.

I touch his knee, admiring how the water droplets make the golden surface gleam. "I can tell you're upset about something you're keeping from me. You can't hide your emotions from me—I'm a pro at it, and I can spot it when someone else is doing it."

"You do not hide from me."

"You're the only one," I insist. "I've opened up more to you than to anybody."

"Marta." He closes his hand around my wrist. I let myself be drawn into his lap, straddling him. It feels so good to be close to him, to have his naked skin gliding over mine. I've never felt so safe with anybody in my life.

"You can share with me," I say, leaning back to look him in the eye. "I've shared with you." And I have. Over the past few days—or daycycles as they're called on the ship—I've shared everything about my life. It's amazing that I feel so comfortable opening up to someone I've just met. But maybe that's a side effect of almost dying.

I told him about all my work and my past life, the dangerous situations I've been in. How I felt like I had to risk my life over and over, otherwise I'd be letting my father's legacy down, but at the same bearing the guilt of making my mother worry all the time.

I've bared myself emotionally and felt more naked with Arkdhem than with anyone else. But he accepted it all. I will do the same for him.

"In all my years as a soldier, I've obeyed my High Commander's every order—but one. But one act of disobedience is enough to mar my record. I hope, in time, I will be able to make amends."

What order did you disobey? It's on the tip of my tongue to ask, but he squeezes my bottom—which still has some soreness—and says, "You were asking about the Tribute Program." He's changing the subject, but I let him because I want to hear more. I make a mental note to ask him more about Commander Gavrill later.

"The Commander didn't tell the whole crew about the Tribute Program at first. We did not have much hope of finding compatible mates. The Jabol believe humans and Tsenturions share a common ancestor. But we didn't know whether the tests they ran at a distance were accurate until we acquired the first Tribute."

"But now you know we're compatible?"

"Yes," he says simply. Which doesn't do the subject justice. There are a lot of things to consider—human-alien compatibility, how the pregnancy will go, and also, just how many babies are we three Tributes supposed to have? There's more to this story.

But when I think of Arkdhem, alone and waiting for me all these years, my heart squeezes. I do want kids with him someday. Making them will certainly be fun.

"What do the other Tributes think of all this?"

He pauses before answering, his face thoughtful. He takes my questions seriously, which I appreciate. And he never seems to get tired of them, unlike my ex-boyfriends, who seemed intimidated by someone who was always probing for the truth that lay beneath the surface.

"There was an adjustment period," he says carefully. "For both of them. But now, they truly have come to care for their mates." He looks almost pained when he says it, and I can't stop myself from touching his jaw.

"I'm sure it was easy if their mates are as wonderful as you."

"Thank you, my Marta," he says. The tender look in his eye makes my chest ache in the best way. Sometimes I sense him watching me with almost reverence. I don't have to look at him to know he's thinking of me.

It's amazing to feel so connected to someone so soon—and also a little freaky. I need to talk to someone about this--someone like me.

"I can't wait to meet Dawn and Pareena," I say. "When are we meeting up with them?"

The tension returns to Arkdhem's shoulders as he replies, "Soon." His suit/skin color has dulled slightly. He doesn't want to speak about this anymore. It's amazing how quickly I've picked up the minute changes in his expression and armor color, and can read his emotions that way.

"Okay," I say, so he'll relax. "No more questions." He wants to enjoy this moment, and honestly, so do I.

I trace the smooth edge of his shoulder. I'm not sure whether the hardened flesh is muscle or nanotech, or some combination of both. It's fascinating, and I make a note to go ask Rhodian more about the bio-nanotech. I wish I'd asked Frllil more about it, but I didn't realize exactly what it was until I saw it in person.

"My curious mate." Arkdhem cups my chin and nuzzles my cheek. I shift on his lap. In the water, his *seela* suction onto my hip, pulling me closer. In a few minutes, I'll be straddling him and riding him to another climax. But for now, it's nice to just cuddle. And explore.

Arkdhem's large hands slide around to cup my backside, steadying me as I mold my palms to his shoulders. His skin is back to a pale gold, darkening to a richer bronze lower down. Glimmers of color play over his skin under my fingers, like he's responding to my touch.

"What is it like?" I murmur.

"What is what like?" he asks, a slight uptilt to his lips telling me he's amused that I couldn't keep my promise not to ask questions for more than a minute.

I chase a bead of water down the smooth plane of his pectoral muscle with my forefinger.

"To have people know what you're feeling." The bead of water disappears into a smooth groove between his pecs. I spread my palm over his chest, and a flush follows my hand: purple tinged with pink and a little gold, like a sunset. Talk about wearing your emotions on your sleeve.

"There are some among us who choose to hide their emotions," Arkdhem sounds amused. "I have always found it better to be honest."

"Do you?" I slide my hand lower and Arkdhem's abs flex, turning to steel. "Are you ever tempted to lie? To pretend you're feeling one way when really you're feeling another," I clarify.

He captures my hands, and holds them between us. "Is that what you do? Hide your emotions so you do not feel them?"

"No." I press our joined hands to my collarbone. "I feel my emotions. They're a deep, knotted mass in my middle." And they'll never be unwound.

He kisses my knuckles. "Perhaps I can help with that."

"I doubt it," I answer, my breaths coming quicker as his *seela* latch on to my inner thighs, positioning me more firmly over his cock. "But you can try."

Arkdhem cups the back of my head, cradling me close for his kiss.

The *seela* are more insistent, tugging my hips down and suctioning over my labia until I gasp.

Arkdhem lifts me and the *seela* pop off in quick succession, sending tremors through my body. My mate rotates me so I'm bent over the side of the bath, with my elbows resting on the wide brim. Instead of tile, the bath is made of the same protean matter as the bedroom furniture. It feels softer, more like rubber, supporting my middle.

Arkdhem's hand threads into my hair and tugs my head back gently. My back arches, and I blink up at him from my contorted position. He runs his hand over my bottom and teases my labia with his fingers. I catch my breath, quivering in his hold. A few more strokes in the right spot, and I could come...

Smack! His palm cracks onto my wet skin. The water makes the sound echo louder than usual. He claps his hand on my opposite cheek. A few more hard smacks, then he swirls his fingers between my lower lips, stroking me lazily.

"You do not have permission to come," he informs me.

"But..." I whine, just like the bratty heroine I've always suspected it'd be fun to be.

Smack! "No. Behave."

A few more cracks to my bottom make me roll my lips between my teeth.

Stern bathtub Daddy for the win!

He takes his time teasing my clit and the sensitive pucker between my bottom cheeks, then sets about turning my rear pink. The water on my skin makes the spanking sting more, somehow. Why is that? Is it a physics thing? I could research it later—but then Arkdhem delivers a flurry of smacks that send every thought out of my head. My bottom is burning, sharing its heat with my pussy. I shift on my knees and Arkdhem tips me forward, so I'm even more helpless, bent over the bath with my rear in the air.

I'm gritting my teeth and trying not to cry out—no idea why it's a goal of mine not to make a sound, it just is—when the thought comes: *He's trying to make me cry.*

A little sound escapes me then. Not a sob, not really, but a little mew of protest? Surrender? My heart's melting a little, knowing that Arkdhem cares so much about my feelings, he's trying to give me an outlet. All the pain and tension and teasing my clit is meant to culminate in a catharsis of some sort.

I heave a sighing breath, and Arkdhem rubs my bottom. "That's it." He gives me a few hard swats that reverberate through me, shaking something loose in my insides.

A rush of emotion, not quite sadness but overwhelming in the same way, washes through me. The knot in my chest loosens, leaving me feeling lighter.

I realize Arkdhem has stopped spanking me. He lifts me back into his lap and cradles me in the water, letting me lean on one hip so I don't have to sit on my sore backside. The water is warm, and it feels good to curl up against my big strong mate.

"Do you feel better, my heart?"

"A little." I turn my lips down in a pout. "I didn't cry."

"That's all right." He hoists me closer. "Maybe next time."

"Maybe," I murmur. I'm sore and horny and a little bit sniffly, but mostly loving how close I feel to him. I stroke his sculpted bicep with my thumb. The water droplets glide across his golden skin, making it glitter. Under my hip, his cock is growing hard. I grin to myself. Now we get to the good part.

A flicker in the corner of my eye makes me turn. Someone's in the room with us. Where there once was empty air, there is now a nine-foot tall golden warrior standing in front of the bath, dressed in full Tsenturion armor.

My scream echoes around the bathing room.

The plates of the helmet retract, revealing the Tsenturion's face. He does not look happy.

"Arkdhem," the intruder growls.

I scramble to my feet before I realize the image before us is a little grainy and translucent. There's no one here—the figure in front of us is actually a projection.

Arkdhem rises in a rush of water. His large hand cups me protectively and he moves me behind him, inserting himself between me and the projection so he's blocking my view of the intruder with his impressive backside. Water streams down his back, sluicing in rivulets down the grooves of his muscles.

"High Commander. A minicycle, please. My mate and I require privacy."

I peek around Arkdhem's hip. So this is Dawn's mate, High Commander Gavrill. He looks twice as intimidating as he does in the Archives. His armor glitters with red on black so bright, it's enough to hurt my eyes. Between the face plates of his helmet, the High Commander's eyes are black.

This is not good.

"You have one hundred microcycles," the High Commander growls. "I will meet you in your quarters." The image flickers, and blinks away.

9

———

A *rkdhem*

I CLOSE MY EYES, a kind of grief and regret passing over me, even though I cannot truly feel either. Not when it comes to my Marta, my Tribute, my heart. I do not regret going to get her. I would make the same choice over and over again.

But the High Commander has been my mentor, the male I wanted to most impress, for so long that I cannot help but wish there had been another way. I knew I was going to disappoint him and had accepted it, but facing the reality of his censure hits me harder than I thought it would.

My chest aches, and my jaw clenches, along with my fists. It's a physical pain, one that I wish I could have avoided.

Hopefully he will understand when I am given time to speak with him directly. After all, he has his own Tribute. His Dawn. He knows the pull our mates have for us.

"What the hell was that about?" Marta's voice is shriller than before, and I open my eyes to see her standing with her arms crossed over her chest, staring at me with consternation and worry. I want to reassure her, but I am unsure how to.

"Marta, I must go. Remain here. I will dress and deal with this." I will explain myself to the High Commander and then return to explain myself to her. It is not that I meant to keep secrets from her, exactly, but though I would make the same choice, I am not proud of disobeying my commander, either.

"No." She jumps to her feet. "I want to go with you."

The earnestness in her expression, her immediate bravery, pierces my heart. Cupping her face in my hands, I lean in, stroking her cheeks gently.

"Please, my heart. Let me face this. It is me he is angry at, not you, and I would not have you bear the weight of his wrath for me."

"I don't understand..." Her eyes move to stare beyond me at the space where the projection invaded our privacy. Where the image of the High Commander had stood, interrupting our intimacy and casting judgment upon us. Something almost angry stirs in my breast, but I know I am the one in the wrong. No matter my feelings on the subject, I was given an order, and I disobeyed it.

I will accept my due punishment.

"What's going on?" Marta's eyes beg me for an explanation and I groan. There is no time, and yet I cannot leave her like this. But I have to.

"Marta... I have not been entirely honest with you." My jaw clenches at the words. "The High Commander has reason to be angry with me."

"Wha—"

"Stay here, and I will return to explain everything." I press a kiss to her forehead, still holding her face in my hands, before releasing her.

"No, wait—"

I can hear her call after me as I stride away, my armor plating my body as I move into the main room, the door to the bathing room sliding shut between us. The color of my armor is a dull grey, so different from the glittering gold that matches my skin that I have worn for so many days now. I flex my hands as I walk into my room, forcing my chin up as though I have nothing to be ashamed of.

False bravado, but right now, it is all I have to cling to.

I sincerely doubt my Tribute will be overly long in joining us, and I hope to get as much of my dressing down over with as possible before she does.

Thankfully, the High Commander's projection is already there, waiting for me. Odd to be thankful for that, since the very sight of him sends a small quiver through me. I feel like a young child, facing his disappointed father after disobeying him. It is not a comfortable feeling.

His eyes flash at me, jaw clenching as I stand in front of the projection and salute him. The High Commander wastes no time in chastising me.

"You were given orders to remain planet side and take control of the fleet in my absence. You abandoned your post and ended up light cycles away, on the edge of Jabolian territory. Explain yourself," he demands. Every word feels weighty with his tightly leashed anger, and it is all I can do to keep my own composure.

"I received word from the Jabol that my Tribute was ready." I stand straight at attention, looking him in the eyes, despite my impulse to drop my gaze. "So I went to retrieve her. You did tell me the next Tribute would be mine."

The High Commander's suit darkens to an inky indigo, flashing with streaks of red, indicating the depth of his anger.

"I did not tell you to disregard your duties." He snarls the words. "You didn't even send word. We could have been trapped on that planet. We could have needed your help and you would have been gone. You deserted your post when you should have waited—or, at the very least, *contacted me* so I could make the decision. You were *not authorized to do so.*"

Marta

I scramble out of the bath, feet sliding on the tiles. I'm butt naked and, unlike Arkdhem, I can't just mentally signal my skin to grow some wicked cool Tsenturion armor. Too bad. It would be nice to be able to think a thought and be dressed that quickly.

By the time I've located a suitable robe that's not completely see through, Arkdhem is out in the office like area of his quarters. The projection of the Commander seems even bigger out here, dominating the spacious room. Is it life sized? If so, the Tsenturion Commander is huge.

The High Commander's projection crosses his arms over his armored chest. He's even wearing his helmet—and a few wicked looking spines protruding from it make him seem even bigger.

"You were out of communication range, and I did not want to disturb you on your honeymoon," Arkdhem replies smoothly. His armor is fully plated but without any the threatening protrusions the High Commander is displaying. There is something about his stance that hovers between defiant and conciliatory, like a teenager trying to convince his parent not to ground him after sneaking out of the house. I should know, I've looked the same way plenty of times. "I believed time was of the essence, so I did not follow protocol. You are the one who believes the Jabol are not to be trusted. Rather than leave her in the hands of a potential hostile force, I placed Corin in command, and went to retrieve her."

Wait, what? Hostile force? The Jabol aren't to be trusted? Surely not. Frllil is one of the least hostile and unthreatening creatures I've ever met. Well, other than having the ability to snatch human women from Earth and then train them to be alien brides.

Hm.

Okay, they might have a point, when it comes to Earth women, but how the heck are the Jabol potentially hostile to the Tsenturions? That goes against everything I learned in Frllil's archives.

"We don't know if the Tribute was under threat," the High Commander grinds out.

"We didn't know if she wasn't," Arkdhem replies. "Especially if the Jabol discovered that we have had contact with the Vgotha."

What... they what?! The species who destroyed theirs?

My head is spinning this way and that, as new information collides with my desire to know what the hell is going on with my personal life. I've never had my personal life interfere with a story lead before, since I never had a personal life worth anything to me. It's both startling and unnerving for me to realize that I'm as invested in Arkdhem personally as I am in knowing what the hell is going on.

The commander grunts in begrudging concession. The spines on his helmet lower a few inches, and his face plate retracts fully.

"Arkdhem." The commander's voice is low and tired. He sounds like he's talking to a friend. "You should have followed protocol and told me. We were in communication range thirty five point nine percent of the time."

"I couldn't risk my Tribute," Arkdhem says, a tinge of sadness in his voice. For the first time, he looks away, casting his eyes downward, and my heart goes out to him. He looks so sad and I realize that this is more than a soldier being chastened by his commander... I might have been pretty on the mark with my comparison of him as a teenager to his dad. He cares about what the High Commander thinks of him, as more than just his superior officer. "If it were Dawn, you would have done the same." There is a pleading note to his voice.

Dawn is High Commander Gavrill's Tribute. It's a good argument, but the male shakes his head regretfully. His shoulders roll, and then the commander's mask is back in place. The dynamic between them has shifted again, from personal to professional, and fear strikes through me.

This is a military society, after all, and it sounds like Arkdhem disobeyed orders. What kind of punishment do they have for that? What are they going to do to him?

"You will face disciplinary actions for your desertion of duties." If there is a note of regret in the High Commander's voice, it's hard to hear. I bite my lip, watching the scene play out before me, not sure if it will help or hurt if I speak up.

Arkdhem brings his fist to his chest in a formal looking salute, bowing his head. "I expected nothing less."

"We could have been attacked and you left us helpless. We could have had need of all our forces, and you not only abandoned your post, you took others with you, none of them aware that they were aiding you in your desertion. You used their ignorance for your personal benefit. I cannot let these actions pass without punitive measures. The crew will need to be informed of the private orders I gave you, and the reason for your discipline explained."

"I will accept my punishment," Arkdhem says. His eyes remain on the projection of the High Commander but his hand extends to me. I shoot from my spying spot, holding my robe closed with one hand so I don't flash everyone, and take his hand with my other. Arkdhem folds me into his large body, my back to his front. His palm splays over my chest, pinning me against him and helping keep my robe closed. "Marta is worth it. She's worth everything. The Tributes are our future, but Marta is even more to me than that."

There's a long pause. The High Commander is so still, he may as well have turned to stone. Then his gaze flickers to the right and down. For a second his face softens, transforming so completely, my heart stutters.

Then his gaze returns to Arkdhem and turns black once more. "Do not attempt to run. We will lock on to your location and we will be there in microcycles."

This time, the projection doesn't fade, but merely blinks away.

I clutch at Arkdhem's arm around my chest, needing his closeness while I marshal my thoughts. I shimmy to face him and hook my arms around his shoulders.

"Disobeyed only one order, huh," I say to break the ice. "You might as well tell me everything. I'm going to find it out anyway, and I'd rather hear it from you."

"Very well." Arkdhem sighs. "I shall."

Two minutes later, he has moved us to sit on the bed. He insisted I change into a new outfit, a long tunic over flowy pants. The fabric covers me a lot better than the robe or any of the flimsy dresses I've worn before, so I'm not complaining. After the way the High Commander saw everything, I wish I had some armor of my own. I mean, I was already wishing for armor, but that really solidified my desire.

In short sentences, Arkdhem explains what he has done: how the High Commander privately commanded him to keep orbit around the planet where he and Dawn were honeymooning, and how Arkdhem decided to deliberately disobey his directive. It might seem like such a small thing, after a lifetime of good service, but I spent a lot of time around the military when I was chasing stories on Earth, and even more time around cartels where disobedience didn't mean punishment or dishonorable discharge, it meant death.

"So you were supposed to stay at your post and you left?" I clarify, rubbing my forehead. There has to be a way out of this for him, but that is so cut and dry when it comes to the military types that I'm not sure what I can come up with.

"You were too important. I could not leave you in the hands of the Jabol. Even if—" he breaks off what he's saying and shakes his head. "That is not important."

"It seems important to the High Commander."

A flash of navy in Arkdhem's suit catches me by surprise.

"Gavrill already has his Tribute," Arkdhem growls. "What right does he have to deny me mine?"

Whoa, that's a lot of bitterness. I want to probe deeper, but I sit quietly, waiting for him to keep explaining.

He blows out a breath. "And now I'll be called to atone for my crimes. But it is worth it. He kneels before me and clasps my hands. "Anything is worth it for you."

"How will you atone?" What I'm really asking is how bad the punishment will be. It didn't seem like the High Commander was going to be calling for his death or anything, but I have no idea what kind of 'disciplinary actions' an alien race might deem justifiable.

"I'll be judged by the High Commander and a panel of my peers, who will decide my punishment."

"Not the fun type of punishment, I'm guessing."

His lips jerk into a tiny smile at my attempt at a joke. "No, my heart." There's a thud in the corridor, and his body tenses. "They are coming."

I grab his hand as he stands. We'll face this together. No matter what.

The rhythmic thuds grow louder until the sound stops outside the door.

Without Arkdhem's permission, the door glides open and a bunch of warriors march in, each in full armor. At the front of the squad is the High Commander. Like the rest of his soldiers, his helmet covers his face.

I knew this was going to happen, and it's still hella intimidating. Arkdhem squeezes my hand. Gavrill's helmet swivels down as he notes our hands are joined. "Release the Tribute."

I grab Arkdhem's wrist with my free hand before anyone can say anything else. "No," I say. My voice quivers a little, so I firm my abs and project properly. I try to slide in front of Arkdhem, to shield him with my body, but he maneuvers me back so that he's shielding me instead. That still doesn't stop me. "I'd like to know what's going on." I say it firmly, hoping that the whole Tribute thing means I get some leeway, and that I'm not about to face my own punishment for disobeying the High Commander.

"This warrior has committed treason and abandoned his post. He will now be disciplined by the High Command."

To my shock, Gavrill sinks to one knee so he's closer to eye level with me. "He will not be harmed, Marta Flores Romero; simply held for his crimes. If you will come with us, we will make sure you have not suffered any mistreatment." His helmet retracts a little, letting me see his eyes, which have lightened to a deep navy. Looking at me, his expression seems almost... kind.

So the High Command thinks Arkdhem abused me as well as disobeyed orders.

"I'm fine. I prefer to stay with Arkdhem."

"Babe, I've got this." A human slips in from the hall and pokes her head out from behind the warriors. She's pale and slender, her long brown hair pulled back into a sleek ponytail.

She's half the size of the warriors, but they all step aside for her, giving her a clear path to the High Commander.

Gavrill rises and takes her hand much like Arkdhem took mine. Large armored warriors and small humans—we're mirror images of each other.

This must be Dawn, Gavrill's mate. When she tilts her head to study me, a jolt runs through me. It's been a while since I've seen a human being, and although Dawn looks tiny compared to the warriors, she's actually a few inches taller than me.

"Hi," she says in her American twang. "I'm Dawn. Pleased to meet you." Her mouth twists. "I wish it was under better circumstances."

Better how? Better as in: 'we haven't just been abducted by aliens,' or, 'your mate isn't accused of treason and they're not going to separate him from you.'

"Sure," I say.

"If it's all right, we would like to talk to you separately," Dawn continues while her mate and the other hulking warriors stand quietly. It's kind of adorable how they're letting her take charge. I'd be amused if the moment wasn't so tense. "Look, I understand that you may not trust us yet. In which case, I'm asking Gavrill—I mean, the High Commander—if there's a way you can talk to us privately and still see Arkdhem. And he can somehow see you?"

She cranes her head up towards her mate. The soft expression is back on Gavrill's face.

"That will be difficult," he murmurs, "because I do not wish to put you and her anywhere near the brig. And that is where Arkdhem belongs."

"What if we use my tablet? Set it up so Marta can have a video link to Arkdhem?"

"That can be arranged." The High Commander touches Dawn's cheek and strokes it gently. "Thank you, my Dawn." She flushes a little, and nods. That doesn't seem scripted.

Dawn looks at me. "Marta?"

I hesitate because video can be doctored. Who knows what sort of high tech these aliens have? But Dawn is making an effort.

"Okay," I say. "I'll accept that." I turn to Arkdhem.

"Go with the Commander's Tribute," he orders softly, and touches my cheek in a similar move to Gavrill's, and I flush just like Dawn did. Damn, I do feel something deep in my chest. Real human emotions.

I swallow. "Will you be all right?"

"As long as I am reunited with you."

"You will reunite us?" I ask the High Commander.

Gavrill nods slowly. "If that is what you wish."

Squeezing Arkdhem's hand one last time, I walk slowly to stand by Dawn.

"This way." She whirls, and I follow her from the room, looking back as the contingent of guards close around my mate.

10

M*arta*

As I step out of the room alongside Dawn, I get my first really good look at her and manage to hold back a gasp when I see her rounded belly. Holy shit, she's pregnant! That wasn't in Frllil's files!

I can't help but wonder if he knows, and I have to squash the urge to call him on his comm-unit... especially after what Arkdhem said about not knowing if the Jabol are trustworthy. I don't know what's going on yet, so I shouldn't make any hasty moves, like make someone else's pregnancy announcement for them. That's a messed-up move back on Earth all on its own; out here, where entire species are at risk, it seems like it would be even worse.

"Are they going to hurt him?" I ask Dawn, instead of commenting on her stomach. Also messed up back on Earth is assuming a woman is pregnant. She looks like she is, but for all I know, she's gained a bunch of weight in just one area of her body that happens to be her stomach, thanks to alien cuisine. So I do not comment on the pregnancy until she tells me something herself.

I don't know if I can trust her answer, but I can't think of anything else to say to him.

"No. But they will discipline him." She gives me a sympathetic grimace when I glance back over my shoulder. I can't see Arkdhem, but I can see the group of Tsenturion warriors walking away from us, going in the opposite direction down the hall, and I know he's at the center of it. "I don't know what that means though. Gavrill has yet to explain, especially since I'm pissed as hell that he's going to punish Arkdhem in the first place." She makes a face. "I think what he did makes perfect sense. Gavrill's just got a stick up his ass sometimes."

Yeah, from what I know about Dawn, she would not be on board with the whole military view of things. Despite everything, I can't help but smile. Gavrill must have his hands full dealing with her.

"So, uh... did you have a good honeymoon?" I ask, since it appears that we've got quite a bit more corridor to go. I wouldn't think that I would be able to tell the difference between space ships, but at a certain point, I realize that we've left the ship I was on and are now walking down the corridors of a different one. The High Commander and his warriors must have boarded our ship.

"Yes." She tosses her ponytail over her shoulder, smiling wryly. "At least, up until the end. It was a bit of a surprise when Gavrill tried to comm Arkdhem and got Corin instead. We cut our honeymoon short." She's still talking about Arkdhem's insubordination. "How are you doing? That might be kind of a silly question, considering, but..."

"Oh, I'm fine." I wave a hand. The sooner I convince everyone of that, the sooner I can be reunited with Arkdhem. I hope. The worried look she shoots me makes me think I have a lot of work left to do.

"Here." She gestures to the right of the curving hall. A door glides open as she approaches. "We can talk more privately in here." She sweeps her hand out, indicating that I should enter first. Inside is a simple, white-walled room that would look intimidating without the decor. A white, human-sized round table surrounded by chic salmon pink chairs, and a matching painting on one of the walls, makes the place look a little less like an interrogation room.

There's someone inside already waiting for us, seated at the table with her hands around what looks like a tea cup. A human. It only takes me a moment to recognize Pareena from the pictures Frllil had in his files, though she looks very different from the professional headshots he'd gathered from Earth.

Seeing her sitting there makes me think of her profession—she's a psychologist. Doctor Pareena Singh. Suddenly, the room seems a little more like the interrogation room I first likened it to. I press my lips together and turn to Dawn.

"Where is Arkdhem?"

"Probably already in the brig. Speaking of which—" She waves a hand at someone down the hall and when I look, there's a warrior walking up to us with a solemn expression on his face. Even though I know that's the usual expression for all of the warriors, my stomach still clenches a bit with worry.

Does he know who I am? Does he know what's happening with Arkdhem? Is that why he looks like that?

"Tribute Dawn," the Tsenturion says gruffly, not looking at me, and hands my guide what looks like a tablet. "They've set up the video feed."

"Thank you," Dawn says, handing the thing off to me as the warrior bows and walks away.

Hesitantly, I touch the screen and the tablet lights up. Unlike anything I had at home, there's no screen filled with options.

Instead, the display shows an image of Arkdhem standing in a three-sided room. His armor covers his body and his hands are fisted at his sides. He's standing rigid like he's up against a wall. The air in front of him ripples a little—it's a see-through pane made of something like liquid glass. There's room enough for him to walk back and forth and there's even a bench for sitting, but instead, he stands there, motionless, staring at nothing.

I want to hug him so badly.

"What happens now?" I can't take my eyes off my mate.

"There, he'll wait for sentencing. But first, the High Commander will want to talk to you. Now, get inside, Pareena's been dying to meet you." She gently turns me by the shoulders and pushes me into the room. I don't bother resisting. My brain feels frozen and I don't know what to do, so I let her guide me. For now.

"Hi," I say as I walk in, my gaze meeting Pareena's. She smiles at me warmly, but it doesn't reassure me. I'm not sure anything could right now.

"Hi Marta. I'm Pareena, and I'm also the ship's counselor. How are you doing?" It's the same question Dawn asked me, but coming from a psychologist, it feels a lot more loaded. She gets to her feet and holds out her hand for me to shake. It's harder to take my own hand off of the tablet than I would have expected, but I make myself do so.

"Um. Fine? I mean, other than being separated from my mate and not knowing what his punishment is going to be. That sucks a lot." I glance down at the unchanging image of Arkdhem.

"I can only imagine," Pareena says sympathetically. "If it helps, Dawn and I are totally on your side. Arkdhem is our friend, and we want to help. Is it okay if I ask you some questions?"

"Sure." What else am I going to do? And, even though I don't know her or Dawn yet, the fact that both of them say they want to help is my only hope. They're mated to the High Commander and the second-in-command of the fleet. If anyone can help me, it'll be them.

"Anyone want tea?" Pareena asks as Dawn and I settle into our chairs.

"Oooh, I do." Dawn jumps back up immediately, but Pareena touches her arm.

"You sit. Take a rest."

"I'm fine," Dawn says but relaxes back in her chair, stretching out her legs and rubbing her convex stomach. "Do we have any cookies?"

"Of course." In the corner, Pareena types into the replicator and returns with a tray set with teacups, a steaming tea pot, and a platter of cookies. She serves the tea and pushes the cookies right in front of Dawn. "These are as close to my favorite tea biscuits as I can make them."

"Thank you." Dawn takes two and shoves them into her mouth. I can't help but smile. Being around two other humans feels both odd and nice after so long with Frllil and then Arkdhem. I'm still eager to see Arkdhem again, but it's nice to see my own species again and be around familiar mannerisms. I grab a cookie of my own, though I nibble at it, rather than scarfing it down the way Dawn did.

"Now," Pareena turns her serene smile on me, "we can talk properly. We don't know anything about what's going to happen with Arkdhem unfortunately, but do you have any other questions?"

Oh boy, do I ever.

∽

Arkdhem

I STAND IN THE BRIG, right up against the transparent wall. Beyond my prison, two guards stand at attention near the door. Soon, the High Commander will walk through and interrogate me further.

Every microcycle feels like an hour. They have fixed a tablet across from me. Every so often, it blinks on for a few microcycles to give me a few precious moments of Marta's face. She's sitting at a white table, eating and speaking with the other Tributes. There's no sound, just the images—and too soon, it blinks away. I don't dare look elsewhere, in case I miss that precious glimpse.

To stand here and watch my Tribute for only a few moments at a time is torture, although the High Commander did not mean it as such. I know he meant it as reassurance, to be able to see and know my Tribute is well. But any microcycle away from Marta is painful. My nose touches the fluid border between myself and the rest of the room.

The screen blinks on. There are Dawn and Pareena at a table on either side of my Tribute. Marta has a blank expression on her face but her eyebrows rise a little bit. Dawn is waving her hands as she speaks, almost knocking her beverage over. Pareena nods at whatever Dawn is saying, but keeps checking Marta's expression.

My Tribute is the most beautiful of them all.

When my screen blinks off, I am gripped with the pain of losing sight of her again. The worry over what will happen to her.

Wondering why it is taking so long for my fellow warriors to come for me.

Logically, I know I have not been waiting long, but my patience is already wearing thin. Whatever discipline awaits me, I would rather get it over with.

Color crawls over my suit until it looks like it's broken. My emotions run one into the other. One of my shoulders is red, the other orange. The bright colors deepen to purple and blue. My lower half is black. The darkness is at my midriff, and it's rising, along with my frustration and grief.

It is not as though I wanted to betray my people. But I do not know where I would have made a different choice. For all the High Commander says I should have come to him, he has his own Tribute to protect. How could I trust that he would put her in danger in order to retrieve mine?

And he does believe the Jabol are dangerous.

He was willing to not only listen to the Vgotha, but he believes their tale that the Jabol enslaved them and destroyed Tsentur in order to secure our services as warriors when the Vgotha rebelled. Me? I am not so sure. The Vgotha are a worthy foe in battle. The Jabol? Not so much. I do not see how they could have done all of that. I do not think they could have fooled us for so long.

But I know the High Commander was taken in by their story.

I left the majority of the fleet to guard him and his Tribute while I retrieved mine. I deserted my post but... it is a new world. We are no longer purely military. Before Tsentur was destroyed, warriors would retire to become civilians before taking a mate. That is no longer the way things are done. Changes should be—need to be—made in order to accommodate our new circumstances.

Surely the High Commander and the others will see that.

The door glides open. I jerk my head up. I'm ready to face my high commander. But it is not the High Commander who drives into the room, but a warrior clad in black armor.

Bodgan.

My lip lifts in a familiar snarl. Out of everyone on the ship, it had to be him. We have never gotten along. He did not even want a Tribute, and yet he received Pareena anyway. I was so sure he could not deserve her, could not treat her appropriately, that I attempted to battle him for her.

Now, I am glad I lost, because otherwise I would not have my Marta, but I still do not think he deserves her.

He gestures to the two guards to leave, and they do. He approaches the open side of the brig and stops in front of the invisible current keeping me in.

"Hello, Arkdhem."

~

MARTA

"AND THEN THERE IT WAS! And I was like, 'Oh my god, those are tentacles!'" Dawn's arms flail and she opens her mouth in a mock scream. Pareena's giggling into her tea cup, and even I can't help but chuckle. Dawn is so funny and animated.

Pareena is more collected but she has some funny stories too. Apparently she'd thought her whole abduction and mating was a super sexy dream she was having. Which… I can't blame her, especially since she'd been in the hospital dying when she was taken.

We're on our third pot of tea, and the cookie plate holds only crumbs. We've talked about *everything*. I now know more about their mates' sexual prowess than I ever wanted to about anyone else. But it's informative.

What's weird is I'm oversharing as much as they are.

"The *seela* did throw me off at first," I say. My cheeks are hot with a blush, but I can't stop the words from spilling from my mouth. I can't remember having a gossip session like this since high school, but there's something therapeutic about it, and not just because Pareena is an actual psych. I used to chat with my editor about leads over drinks, but that probably didn't count as girl talk. My editor and

I weren't close friends. Friends wasn't something I really excelled at, but Pareena and Dawn kinda feel like what I remember friends being like. "But now I like them. I'm not sure I could go back to regular peen. Not sure what that says about me."

"Once you go tentacles, there's no going back," Dawn quips.

"So glad I'm not alone." I swivel in my chair to Pareena. "How's the psychological evaluation going? Did I get an A?"

"You did fine," Pareena assures me, laughing. She's not like any psych counselor I've ever met, and I had to go to a few back on Earth after some particularly harrowing assignments—at my editor's insistence. I wish Pareena had been one of them. She's incredibly easy to talk to.

Dawn cackles. "Don't tell me she's normal."

"No more abnormal than the rest of us." Pareena rests her chin on her hands, still smiling. "But the really important thing is how you feel about Arkdhem."

I swallow hard. Feelings? Yeah, talking about sex I can do, but talking about my feelings? Suddenly, Pareena reminds me a lot more of the therapists I saw back home. I roll my eyes. "Does it matter? The sex is great. That's more than I had back on Earth."

"Do you feel like you have a connection to Arkdhem?" Pareena presses, the therapist side of her coming through a little more strongly now. But I have a lot of practice at avoidance.

"When his little *seela* suckers latch on to my pussy, I do," I say as crudely as possible. Pareena narrows her eyes at me, studying me like a bug under a microscope, and I get the feeling that she sees right through me. Which is not comfortable. I shift in my seat, avoiding meeting her gaze.

"Damn right." Dawn tilts her head. "Gavrill is coming." She sounds breathless.

A few seconds pass, and the door doesn't glide open. I can't tell how she knows her mate is on his way—if he even is. There's only one explanation, but it's one that Frllil had discounted in his notes: the full bonding of a Tsenturion male to his mate.

"Can you sense him?" Holy shit. They're hiding a lot from Frllil.

Dawn's pregnancy. The full bond. And I've been so busy talking about hot alien sex that questioning them about the Jabol and Vgotha completely slipped my mind, which isn't like me at all.

Then again, it's not like I have a story deadline. Maybe that's why I'm so easily distracted.

"Yes," Pareena answers, because Dawn's mouth is still full of cookie, though she's nodding. "We can sense our mates. There's a sort of bond."

"Really?" For some reason, I don't want to tell them about the research I did on the Tsenturions and them. It seems a little bit like an invasion of privacy, for one, and for two, I want them to trust me. I can't decide what to tell Frllil myself until I have more information.

"Yes." Pareena leans over the table towards me. "Do you feel anything like that with Arkdhem?"

"No, but I'm not really a touchy feely sort of person. I prefer to look at things logically." The words trip off my tongue by rote. The same answer I gave over and over again to my therapists back home.

"So how do you feel about Arkdhem?" Dawn asks, getting up and moving towards the door, like she's getting ready to jump on whatever comes through it. She's that sure that her mate is on her way. It's both startling and worrying.

"I like him," I say, fiddling with my hair. "I mean, the sex alone—"

"Is it just the sex?" Pareena probes. "Or is there more?"

"I don't... I don't want him to be hurt. I'm worried about him with this whole discipline thing."

Under the table, I clutch the tablet. Last time I checked it, Arkdhem was standing in the brig, staring out of the glass like he was hoping I'd appear before him. I know what he was hoping for because I was hoping for the same thing. But acknowledging it to myself was hard enough; sharing it felt impossible.

"I want to be with him," I say, after staring at the tablet in silence for several moments. That is the best I can do.

"That can be arranged," Pareena says. "We just want to make sure—"

The door glides open, and the High Commander strides in.

11

M*arta*

The High Commander looks as intimidating as I remember, and I shrink back into my seat a little. Dawn, on the other hand, jumps right on him. He easily catches her, holding her against him and giving her a thorough kiss before letting her slide down his body.

Seeing them together messes with my brain a little. I want to dislike him for interrupting me and Arkdhem and then separating us, but seeing how gentle and caring he is with Dawn makes it kind of hard. I, of all people, know that people are more than one thing. They can be both kind and cruel, depending on the circumstances and how they view the person in front of them, but it's never been personal the way it is right now.

"Tributes," he greets us as he puts Dawn back on her feet. She leans into him happily, his arm wrapped firmly around her. I push my chair back to stand, and he signals me to stay seated. "Please, sit."

As he moves towards the table, my eyes fall to the tablet in my lap. It looks like Arkdhem is talking to someone. A warrior in dark armor.

I trace Arkdhem's face on the screen with my finger. There's an ache deep in my gut. I miss him way more than is logical, and I can't help but wonder if the bond Pareena was talking about is part of it. If she and Dawn bonded with their mates, maybe Arkdhem and I really are bonded too.

Does that mean some of what I feel is him missing me?

"Babe, this table is designed for humans. Human women." Amusement laces Dawn's voice as the High Commander pulls out a chair and moves to sit down in it. I'm pretty sure I hear Pareena snicker, but it's too quiet for me to be completely sure.

"I will manage," Gavrill assures her. When he sits, it is kind of comical. I wait for the chair to creak and fall apart under his bulk but it doesn't. His knees poke up over the table. Like an adult sitting at a kiddie table. At any other time, I would have laughed, but I'm too nervous right now.

"Tribute Marta Flores Romero," he greets me. The formal greeting reminds me of Frllil.

"Please, call me Marta." It's a little hypocritical, since I'm having trouble thinking of him as anything other than 'High Commander' despite knowing his name, but being called by my full name like that is unsettling. I finally broke Frllil of the habit, I don't want to start all over again.

The High Commander glances at Dawn, as if asking permission, and she nods.

"Marta," he says my name carefully as if testing it out. "Do you understand the charges against Arkdhem?"

"Yes."

"And has Tribute Pareena explained the bonding?"

"I understand that I'm bonded in the way of your people to Arkdhem," I say slowly. What can I say to help Arkdhem? Not that I want him to avoid punishment. I just want him to be okay. "Or, if I'm not totally yet, I will be soon. Because the Jabol made sure I was compatible with him. Right?"

"That is correct." A new voice at the door makes me jump. I hadn't even noticed it opening, which doesn't say much for my survival skills. It's like I've forgotten everything I knew. Arkdhem fucked it all right out of my head. I need to get my shit together because all my instincts seem to have deserted me. The male standing there is different. Older. Softer in demeanor somehow, and he's not wearing armor like the rest of the warriors. "May I enter?" he asks, and Gavrill waves him inside.

"Marta, this is Medik, the Tsenturion's physician," Dawn introduces us.

"Hello," I say, and this time, I do get to my feet to shake his hand. He smiles in a friendly manner as he does it, completely comfortable with the human gesture, which makes me feel more comfortable with him immediately.

"Hello," Pareena greets Medik. Both she and Dawn are all smiles, looking at him like he's their golden alien grandpa.

"Dawn, Pareena. Marta," he greets us all and turns to me. "I have looked over your scans and report from Frllil, and assured Gavrill that you are in perfect health. Moreover you do not seem to have been mistreated." It doesn't escape my notice that he says the High Commander's name in a very familiar manner, and not at all like a subordinate.

"That is good," says the High Commander, turning to me, his expression softening. "But you should not have been put through this ordeal."

"I'm fine." If the High Commander were human, he might hear some of the warning and impatience in my voice. Apparently, Dawn hasn't taught him about the word 'fine' though, since he seems unperturbed, while Dawn and Pareena exchange a worried glance.

"I am glad you were unharmed. Of all our protocols, the most important is the safety of our Tributes." He says the words with grave seriousness. What an interesting way to put it. Dawn rolls her eyes. Pareena looks like she wants to say something, but I beat her to it.

"I'm glad you have such strident protocols in place," I say with a straight face. Not sarcastic at all, nope, not me.

The High Commander seems to think I'm sincere. "Our protocols have kept us from devolving into chaos. That is why there are such strict consequences for those who break them."

I stiffen. Meaning: Arkdhem is in big trouble.

Gavrill continues, "Now, there is the matter of your bond. Medik has assured me we can break the nanotech. It will be difficult, but—"

"Whoa, hold on," I say, holding up my hand. I don't care if he is the High Commander and leader of an entire fleet, I'm going to interrupt his ass and find out what the fuck is going on. Break the nanotech? Surely it can't be that easy. Pareena and Dawn seem to think that being able to feel Arkdhem's emotions would be important. "If I feel what Arkdhem is feeling, does that mean we're bonded?"

"Yes." Pareena looks a little relieved. She shoots a glare at the High Commander, and Dawn has gone stiff beside him, looking upset. Not that he seems to notice. "Yes, that would be the bonding."

"It can still be severed," the High Commander says, his voice somewhere between firm and gentle. "We have not attempted it with a Tsenturion-human mating yet, of course, but for Tsenturions paired with an unsuitable mate—"

"Hold up." I raise my hand again. "You want to break us apart?" Both Pareena and Dawn are looking more and more upset, but that's nothing compared to how I'm feeling. I might not want to admit aloud how much Arkdhem already means to me, but I'll be damned if I let them take him away from me.

"Yes," the High Commander says. "Immediately, if you want."

I drop my hand and clutch the tablet in my lap, staring at him. "Why would I want that?"

"Once we break the bond, you will no longer be Arkdhem's mate." He says the words like that makes everything clear, and I suddenly feel very sorry for Dawn if this is an example of his listening comprehension skills. Has he not heard one thing I've said since he barged into mine and Arkdhem's lives? Beside him, Dawn is starting to wriggle, a dark look on her face. Pareena now has her arms crossed over her chest, and she's glaring at the High Commander.

They hadn't been lying about being on my side, and that gives me even more courage to defy the leader of an entirely alien species.

"I don't want a new mate." I say the words clearly. Succinctly.

"I know this isn't an ideal situation." His tone gentles a little, not that I care. "You have already bonded, but our protocols require—"

"Why can't I just remain bonded to Arkdhem?" I interrupt him again. I don't care about their protocols.

Gavrill's suit darkens to a blue that's almost black. His voice is stern when he says, "Arkdhem's crimes cannot be rewarded."

"She's not a reward, she's a person." Dawn looks like fire's about to shoot out of her eyes as she jerks away from her mate. I silently cheer her on as she slaps her hand down on the table. "Unless you think *I'm* a reward for good behavior? In which case, maybe we should break our bond, because I don't think forcing a woman to break her bond because *you* don't like it is good behavior."

The High Commander's suit flashes pure white. He reaches for his mate, but Dawn slaps his hand away, still glaring.

"High Commander, I thought we were past this," Pareena says in a quiet tone that holds as much anger as Dawn's outburst. "Tributes have their own emotions and desires, which are valid and must be treated as such, unless you want us to feel like objects and as though we aren't valued."

"Yeah, what they said," I add, crossing my arms over my chest and enjoying the panic rising in Gavrill's face as he faces a united front of furious human women. I don't even need to argue my point, Dawn and Pareena are doing it for me.

The Tsenturions want human Tributes? They're going to have to learn how to deal with us.

~

Arkdhem

"Bogdan," I say warily.

Bogdan's suit is glossy black as usual, but there's no sign of the bright gleaming stars that appeared after he bonded with Pareena.

His helmet fully covers his face, and a forest of spines protrude from his armor. He looks ready to fight.

I'm standing right up against the shimmering barrier of the brig that's keeping me prisoner. As Bogdan comes to face me, my own armor starts to respond to his warlike stance. The nanotech bulks up, adding protective mass to my legs and torso. My helmet extends to cover my skull and jaw, but I don't allow it to shield my face.

"How was your honeymoon?" I ask in a bland tone.

"Terrible," he growls. "Thanks to you."

"So that's why you're in a bad mood." I tap my helmet. "Oh, no, wait, I forgot who I was talking to. You're always in a bad mood."

Bodgan continues like I haven't spoken. "Instead of a nice relaxing vacation with my Tribute, I ended up learning of your betrayal, and racing to hunt you down."

Racing? I'm flattered. But instead of goading him further, I try to reason with him. "It couldn't be helped. My mate was potentially in danger."

Bogdan scoffs. "A convenient excuse, but you and I both know you don't believe what the Vgotha have told us about the Jabol. The High Commander might believe your lies but I know the truth." He points a finger at my face, close enough to the barrier to make it ripple in warning. "You would have acted against orders and gone to pick up your Tribute whether or not she was in danger."

"It's true," I say. Why deny it? I think that the High Commander and Bogdan have been duped by the Vgotha. Dawn has resentment against the Jabol, and the Vgotha's story fed into that. But I also know that Bogdan now believes the Jabol to be our true enemies. "Would you not do the same for Pareena if she were in Jabol hands?"

"Do not speak her name!" Bogdan's roar reverberates around the brig.

So he's still touchy because I tried to seduce his Tribute. And I can't help twist the knife. "Perhaps that is why you didn't have a good honeymoon. Your Tribute senses that you do not truly care for her." Red streaks ripple through Bogdan's armor, but I continue. I don't have anything better to do, and my own anger and frustration have built and built and built while I've been waiting for whatever will happen next. Bogdan has always made a convenient outlet for such emotions, and I still do not think he deserves Pareena. "If you were truly worthy of her, you wouldn't have resisted bonding with her for so long."

"Be silent," he roars. His suit flashes red with anger, the color streaking through the deep black. "The only reason you're still standing is because the High Commander would not allow me to beam into your private quarters and challenge you directly. But now the High Commander isn't here." A weapon forms in Bogdan's hand, and he points it straight at my face.

Automatically, my helmet forms to fully shield my face. The spines have grown on my armor so that I am a mirror image to Bogdan, a Tsenturion in full battle array.

"You threaten an unarmed soldier?" I raise my empty hands. As long as I'm in the brig, my nanotech is blocked from forming a weapon, and he knows it. He also can't attack me. The barrier would block his thrusts; it's solid on both sides. "How honorable. How brave."

Bogdan absorbs the blade back into his armor. "I don't need a weapon to destroy you. Face me, if you dare." He hits the panel on the side of my confinement.

And the barrier between us disappears.

∼

MARTA

"HIGH COMMANDER, if I may, these are excellent points," Medik says in his grandfatherly tone. Gavrill looks at the Medik with an *'E tu, Brutus?'* expression. He looks like he's in pain.

"Arkdhem has proved himself unworthy of a Tribute. Not that Tributes are objects." The High Commander turns to Dawn pleadingly, reaching out to her. "Dawn, I did not mean that you are an object or a reward. I understand that Tributes are people who should not be given out like trophies for good service."

"Do you?" Dawn huffs. "Because it sounds like you're trying to recall Marta like she's a toy Arkdhem can no longer play with."

"My love, no." The High Commander succeeds in capturing Dawn's hand. She begrudgingly lets him, her face averted. He's winning her back over. I bite my lip because I don't really want to break up their relationship too, any more than I want my own broken. "Tributes are a gift. But not because they are objects. Because your love is the most important thing, and shouldn't be squandered on the unworthy."

"You don't have to be worthy to receive unconditional love, that's the point," Dawn says, shaking her head. "You don't get to choose who the Tributes love."

"I will forever be grateful that you have given me yours." Gavrill kisses Dawn's knuckles. The moment is so tender, I avert my eyes. This smacks of an old argument.

"What Dawn is trying to say is that if you truly believe Tributes are equal to Tsenturions, you must afford them the same agency as you do yourself," Pareena is in counselor mode. "If there is to be any unbonding, it must be Marta's choice."

Still holding Dawn's hand, the High Commander shakes his head. There is now real pain on his face. If it wasn't my own future he was pained over, I might feel sorry for him. As it is, I'm okay with watching him wriggle like a worm on a hook for a while longer.

"I cannot allow a warrior who's abandoned his post to retain his Tribute. The punishment must fit the crime."

"With all due respect," Medik adds, "we are no longer simply a military society. Tsenturions and Tributes now form a civilian society, as well, at the same time as we are at war. We must forge a new path for our protocols and customs. By our old ways, as a warrior, Arkdhem would have never mated while performing his duties. Trying to assign old protocols to our current situation, while not acknowledging the changes happening, will only lead to more inconsistencies and issues."

"Hear hear," I murmur as the High Commander groans. Dawn pats his shoulder sympathetically, but there's a smug expression on her face. I only know that if they try to take me from Arkdhem, I won't let it happen without a fight. "If you try to mate me with someone new, I'll bite his dick and his fucking *seela* off."

Ignoring the High Commander's horrified look, I glance back down at my tablet to check on Arkdhem, and gasp loudly.

"What is it?" Pareena asks.

"Arkdhem's gone." I hold up the tablet, shock and worry pounding through me. The space where he'd been confined is now empty. What happened to him? Where did he go? I try to reach for him through the bond, but all I feel is anger, which I'm pretty sure is my own, considering the current topic of discussion.

Before I can completely freak out, Gavrill takes the tablet from me and taps the screen, changing the angle of the cameras.

Arkdhem appears again—and he's grappling with the huge warrior in black armor. *Who is that?*

"Dammit, Bodgan," Pareena snaps, shocking us all. "Not again." She shoves out of her seat, and rushes from the room.

12

———

M<u>*arta*</u>

SNATCHING the tablet from the High Commander's hands, I bolt after Pareena, my heart pounding in my chest. Arkdhem is fighting! And not only that, he's fighting Pareena's mate! What the hell is going on?

But deep in my heart, I know... Pareena's mate is likely as pissed as the High Commander, but that doesn't mean it's okay to hurt my mate, dammit! Stupid Neanderthal warrior mentality.

"Tributes," the High Command roars after us, his chair scraping the floor as he rises. "I command you to halt! If two warriors are fighting, you cannot engage—"

"Oh, leave them alone," Dawn snaps. "We are NOT done talking about this—" Her voice is cut off as the door slides shut. *You tell it to him, Dawn!* Maybe she'll pound the message into Gavrill's thick head. In the meantime, I hope Arkdhem's all right. If he kills Pareena's mate...

I follow Pareena through the twisting halls of the Tsenturion ship, moving as fast as I can to keep up with her.

"I can't believe this. I thought he was over it..." Pareena mutters, before her voice goes quiet enough that I can't hear what she's saying anymore.

I want to ask her what's going on but she dashes around a corner at full speed, and I skid a little as I try to follow.

I can tell we're getting close to where Arkdhem is because battle cries are ringing out, echoing down the hallway. Ahead, several Tsenturion soldiers are peering through a door.

"Why are you just standing there?" Pareena shouts at them. She hustles forward at double time and whisks around them before they realize she's there.

"Wait!" One of the waiting soldiers notices her but it's too late—I've already dashed past him and the other three Tsenturions to enter the room as well. They were too distracted by Pareena to notice me until it was too late.

Just inside the door, Pareena stops short, and I crash into her. I don't blame her for stopping. The entire brig has turned into a battle scene.

Arkdhem and another warrior in black armor with fearsome spikes protruding from his helmet and back are going at it. The black-armored warrior is bigger and bulkier, but Arkdhem is taller and leaner, and that makes him more agile. The two of them are slugging it out with their fists, the snarls and roars terrifying to hear.

"Stop," Pareena yells at the same time as I shout Arkdhem's name. Neither of the warriors hears us. Pareena turns to one of the waiting Tsenturions, putting her hands on her hips. "Weren't your orders to guard the prisoner?"

"Yes?" one of the soldiers replies, and winces as Bogdan slams Arkdhem into the wall, shaking the entire room. I wince as well, watching them with my heart in my throat, but I know better than to step in. I don't want to give Bogdan ammunition against Arkdhem. He probably wouldn't hurt a Tribute on purpose, but I am Arkdhem's tribute, so maybe he wouldn't care. "But Commander Bogdan gave us orders—"

"So? You were supposed to be guarding Arkdhem *from* him. When your commander gives you a stupid order, don't indulge his idiocy!" Pareena yells at them. They all look at each other, unsure what to do.

"Oh my god," I mutter.

"Don't just stand there!" Pareena waves her arms at the guards. "Do something!"

The four soldiers look at each other as if waiting for the others to go first.

"Ah, well, Commander Bogdan told us to stay back and not interfere. We weren't actually told we were guarding Arkdhem from the commander, and we can't disobey a direct order—"

Pareena draws herself up to her full height, which is about half the size of the shortest Tsenturion, her eyes flashing. "*High* Commander Gavrill is on his way," she announces. "What will he say when he finds that you have allowed this fight to go on?"

The four warriors sigh. One by one, they shrug and their armor grows bulkier, their helmets forming to cover their faces.

"Stand back, Tributes," one of them orders, and the four of them wade into the fray.

"Well done," I whisper to Pareena.

"Thanks. Mentioning the High Commander usually works," she whispers back, rubbing her face with her hand. "We really do need to establish some new protocols though. The way the warriors follow orders can be good in some situations, but obviously it's not going to work all the time."

"I think they're more afraid of you than the High Commander," I murmur. We share a brief smile, but then turn back to the fight, biting our lips.

The brig guards trudge over to the fighting warriors.

One of them raises his hand. "By order of the High Commander, we command you to stop—"

Before he can finish, Bogdan's fist smashes the warrior in the chest, sending him flying into the wall.

Pareena and I wince in unison.

Arkdhem kicks a guard down, and leaps over him to tackle the third. Bogdan jumps on the fourth. Both Arkdhem and Bogdan's arms rise and fall in synchronized punches. Guards One and Three fall to the ground. Great. Apparently, *now* they're going to get along and fight alongside each other instead of fighting each other.

Ugh. Men.

But it is a really impressive display of martial prowess. Pareena and I are suddenly getting a first-hand exhibition of why Bogdan and Arkdhem are the second- and third-in-command of the Tsenturions. When they were fighting each other, they'd been evenly matched—but fighting against two to one odds with other warriors?

Not a problem.

And it's not that the guards aren't highly skilled and vicious fighters themselves. They are, and I can tell, their movements happening in a blur, determination on their faces.

It's just that Arkdhem and Bogdan are that much better.

The second guard tries a sneak attack on Arkdhem from behind, lunging forward to wrap his arms around Arkdhem's shoulders. Without even pausing, Arkdhem snaps forward, using the guard's momentum to whirl and knock out Guard One, who had just staggered to his feet, with a roundhouse kick.

"Holy shit! KO!" I shout. Then I catch Pareena's eye and grimace, falling back. "Sorry. Got caught up in the excitement." Is it my fault I had a thing for watching MMA and cage fights back home, and I forgot for a moment that there were serious stakes here?

She shakes her head and grumbles something about an overdose of testosterone being contagious around here. I bite my lip.

Guard Four has somehow grown what looks like a mace out of his armor. Pareena gasps as he swings it towards her mate's face. But spikes grow out of Bogdan's gauntlets, and *he catches the mace in his hands.* He doesn't even pause, pulling the guard towards him as he jerks his own knee up. The guard is bent over double when Bogdan slams him into the wall, and he topples down.

"Good job, babe!" Pareena cries, clapping her hands.

It's my turn to raise a brow in her direction. She covers her flushed cheeks and mumbles, "I guess it's easier to get carried away than I realized."

The brig guards are officially out of the fight. Three of them lie motionless by the wall. The other is groaning, his helmet half hanging off of his head.

But that means Arkdhem and Bogdan are free to attack each other again. And they waste no time trying to kick each other's ass.

Arkdhem leaps past Bogdan, smashing his helmet. One of Bogdan's spikes falls off.

But Bogdan turns and throws the mace at Arkdhem, catching my mate off guard.

Arkdhem staggers. Bogdan bellows in triumph, and gives chase.

"What do we do?" I cry.

Pareena shrugs helplessly, turning her attention back to her mate, fear and worry clear in her expression.

Now the two alien warriors have lost their weapons and are grappling with each other. Bogdan punches Arkdhem's shoulder. Arkdhem shudders, his suit blackening with the blow, but remains upright to retaliate with an elbow to Bogdan's face.

Pareena and I are both holding our breath. At some point, we started holding hands.

I turn back to the fight. The force of the blows have torn some of the armor. There are small and large pieces of it littered around the room. A bigger piece—a breast or backplate—lies in the middle, threatening to trip someone. I didn't realize the nanotech could come off that way.

Sections of Bogdan's and Arkdhem's armor have turned gray. Most of the spikes have broken off. It doesn't look good.

"They're going to fight until one surrenders." Or worse—someone gets fatally injured or dies.

I don't want that to happen to either of our mates.

After a few tense moments of grappling, Arkdhem slides out from Bogdan's grip and throws a punch that sends the larger warrior crashing down to the floor. On the way, Bogdan's leg flies out and manages to trip Arkdhem. The larger warrior finds his feet quickly while Arkdhem is still rolling away. In a lightning fast move, Bodgan is on him, fist rising high in the air. He's going to bash Arkdhem's skull in.

I don't even think. With a sharp cry—"No!"—I throw myself between Bogdan and Arkdhem, covering Arkdhem's head with my body.

"Marta!" Pareena's cry follows me. Bogdan cries out as well, I can hear the horror in his voice, but I can also feel his movement.

They're so fast, by the time I had thrown myself between them, his fist was already falling.

I'm braced, waiting for the inevitable pain, for my possible death. I have no armor. No protection. I've only known Arkdhem for a week. But it's in that moment that I also know, I've somehow fallen in love with him, and I would be willing to die for him. I have no regrets.

There's an explosion of sound next to my head, the screech of metal against metal, and I lift my head in a daze. Somehow, Bogdan managed to redirect his fist and it's slammed into the floor beside my shoulder, rather than actually hitting me.

The big male jerks back, up onto his feet, leaving me lying across Arkdhem's head. He stares at me and the indent he left in the ship's floor, as if realizing how close he came to killing me. I stare back at him, my heart pounding so fast that my chest feels tight, like it's closing in around itself, and I can barely breathe.

Pareena careens past us, slamming into her mate's chest, and wrapping her arms around him. The only way he and Arkdhem could get to each other now would be through the two of us.

"Enough," she tells him firmly.

Strong hands pick me up as Arkdhem pulls me off of his head, giving himself enough room to sit up. His golden face seems a little paler than normal, but otherwise unharmed as the nanotech peels back, exposing his skin.

"Are you okay?" I ask him, cupping his cheeks.

"Yes, my Marta." He stares at me like he's drinking me in with his eyes, trying to memorize every tiny millimeter of my face. Like he's afraid I'm going to be taken away from him again. I throw my arms around him, clinging to him. Fuck that. If they try to separate us again, they're going to have to deal with a hella pissed off Brazilian, and there's no way they're ready for that.

"What were you thinking?" Bogdan roars at Pareena.

"I was trying to knock some sense into you," she shouts right back. There's no sign of calm counselor Pareena. She pushes her long black hair out of her face, demon flames dancing in her eyes. "And I can ask you the same question. What were *you* thinking, attacking a fellow Tsenturion?" She pounds her tiny fist against his huge shoulder.

Before Bogdan can answer, the High Commander strides into the room, obviously seething. I don't need to see the colors of his armor to know that he's on the last leg of his patience.

Dawn's right behind him. She see us, gasps, and starts forward but he catches her and cradles her in front of him, his hands on her rounded belly.

Arkdhem scrambles to his feet, lifting me with him. We face the High Commander and Dawn in much the same position—me in front of Arkdhem with my back to his front and his arms around me. Beside us, Bogdan gently turns Pareena to mirror us, but not before she punches her mate's arm once more. I cross my arms over my chest and glare right back at the High Commander.

The brig guards have made it over to the door, and are helping each other up.

"I ordered you to watch the prisoner," the High Commander snaps at them. "What happened?"

The brig guards look at each other and then at Bogdan, silent and unsure of themselves.

"High Commander... Commander Bogdan ordered us to stand back and allow him to talk to Commander Ark—I mean, the prisoner." Guard One looks pained at having to narc on Bogdan, but he's also not going to lie to the High Commander. More cracks in their current protocols showing through. I can't help but feel a little smug. I'm going to shove all these cracks in the High Commander's face until he caves and gives me what I want—my mate.

"I goaded Bogdan to challenge and attack me," Arkdhem says smoothly.

"He is a traitor to our kind," Bogdan mutters.

The High Commander puts up one hand to stop them, glaring. "Enough. Report to the med bay," he orders the guards. They salute stiffly, and stagger off.

"And you two. What am I going to do with you? I should throw you *both* in the brig." The High Commander glares at them. "Bad enough that you have to go at each other, but you injured more warriors in your feud now! And endangered your Tributes!"

~

Arkdhem

STIFFENING, I hold more tightly to Marta than before. I had not known she was in danger. I wouldn't have expected her to be anywhere near me when Bogdan and I were fighting.

When she'd thrown herself atop me, in between Bogdan and myself, my entire world had come to a horrifying halt. I still couldn't believe she'd interfered in a Tsenturion duel and come out unharmed. For that, I owed Bogdan thanks for his superior self-control. She should have been killed, and I know it.

The need for gratitude rankles.

"Perhaps we should have a cooling down period," Pareena suggests in her more normal, calm voice. She squirms in Bogdan's arms as he fusses with her hair, already looking calmer now that she is with him.

"Maybe Arkdhem could just be confined to his quarters until the trial," Dawn suggests with a glance at me and Marta. I appreciate the gesture, but I already know that will not be granted. The Tributes have a great amount of sway in what happens to them. Not so much in what happens outside of their sphere.

But the High Commander shocks me.

"Very well," he says, though he does not look happy about it. Both Bogdan and I stare at him in shock. "Arkdhem, until the trial, you are to remain in your quarters, including for mealtimes. Your Tribute may come and go as she pleases."

I gape at him as Bogdan makes a disbelieving noise.

"You're just going to reward him with a vacation for committing treason?" He sounds enraged. I can't blame him. I expected to remain here for the rest of my time until my trial. And then to suffer far worse afterwards.

"Being stripped of command isn't a reward, just as being confined to quarters isn't a vacation," Gavrill growls back.

That is true. Knowing I am being stripped of my command is shameful. Everyone will know, and they will know why. But the why —Marta—makes it worth it.

"What about his Tribute?" Bogdan waves a hand towards us before securing it right back around his own Tribute. I snarl at him.

"Marta," my Tribute snaps, and I tighten my arms around her. I do not want Bogdan's attention drawn to her, but that does not stop her. "My name is Marta."

"Marta," the High Commander emphasizes her name, "will decide where she wishes to be."

There's something in the tone of his voice, in his expression, and I narrow my eyes at him, glancing at Dawn and Pareena. Both of them look pleased, and Dawn actually pats his arm.

Ah, the Tributes at work again. They have changed us so much, from Dawn's arrival, and then more changes wrought after Pareena's. But I have no complaints.

"I want to stay with Arkdhem," Marta says.

Happiness surges through me so strongly that I could explode with it. It's easy to ignore the sound Bogdan makes. My Tribute, my

Marta, just chose to stay with me. There is no better feeling in all the universe.

The High Commander nods. He doesn't look particularly happy either, but he does not tell Marta she cannot or that she should not. Yes, I certainly detect the deft hands of our Tributes in the High Commander's change of heart.

"Very well. At any point, if you wish to leave, you have only to comm the bridge."

"I can do that," Marta says. She rubs her forehead and I sense relief coursing through her. I cuddle her closer.

"Bogdan, you clearly incited this incident," the High Commander continues. "For that, I am going to transfer your command from the bridge—for the next two cycles—to overseeing the waste compaction on level eighteen."

Trash duty. Another time I would have enjoyed his punishment far more, but being entirely stripped of my rank is far worse.

"But—" Bogdan protests.

"Argue with me, and I'll add another few semicycles of assisting Medik in the med bay. You can clean and sanitize all the fluid sample containers."

"So I get trash duty, and he gets a free vacation with his Tribute," Bogdan grumbles.

"Yes," the High Commander replies seriously. "And it's your fault. If you hadn't attacked him, he would still be residing in the brig."

This time, I do have to bite back my smile. I am free, and it is Bogdan's fault.

"Don't forget, he's been stripped of his command," Gavrill adds. "Your trash duty is temporary. His punishment might be permanent."

Bogdan shuts up, and lets Pareena lead him away.

But Gavrill's grim pronouncement has wiped my good humor away. Is that a hint at what's to come? A permanent demotion? Will I be cast down to the bottom ranks of warriors, to work myself back up again?

There is no shame at being in the bottom rank, but there is in losing rank. It is a grave dishonor.

Marta makes a noise of concern, and I push my regrets away. Whatever shame I must bear, whatever punishment I must endure, she is worth it. I said it before, and I meant it.

"We will escort you to your quarters," the High Commander says, and I nod. Gesturing, he steps aside and I reluctantly let go of Marta so she can move. She immediately grabs onto my hand—which pleases me—and the four of us walk down the hall.

13

———

M *arta*

"Do you need medical attention?" the High Commander asks, eying Arkdhem as he and Dawn escort us through the hallway. Dawn seems mollified when it comes to the High Commander, but I'm not feeling quite so generous.

While I'm getting some of what I want, it's hard to forget that he's still going to be the one in charge of disciplining my mate. I'll trust that he'll let us remain together after Arkdhem's trial is over. Until then, I remain wary.

"No." Arkdhem shrugs his shoulder and winces. The nanotech there is still grey. He and Bogdan really beat the hell out of each other. I want to smack him and hug him at the same time. "I have a basic armor repair kit in my quarters. And a rest cycle will fix most of the damage."

For a moment, I think the High Commander is going to say something, but instead he sighs. I sneak a glance at him and there's a faraway expression in his eyes, like he's thinking.

We walk in silence the rest of the way, which is a little uncomfortable, but I don't feel up to breaking it. When we've reached Arkdhem's quarters, the High Commander blocks the door to face us.

"I have not forgiven you for what you've done," he says to Arkdhem. "By leaving your command when we were planet side, you left us exposed. All turned out well, but that does not negate the risk or the choice you made by not contacting me. The chain of command exists for a reason, and that does not change even though we now have Tributes."

Dawn looks troubled, maybe because it's impossible to argue that point. She bites her lip, and I look down. My mind races, but I can't come up with a good point against what the High Commander said, other than I'm glad Arkdhem came for me. But would I have still been glad if it *had* meant harm to others?

No. No, I would not have been.

"I understand," Arkdhem says quietly. "I cannot apologize for retrieving my Marta, but I wish I had contacted you before leaving." That's the first time he's said so, but I think he means it. Seeing the High Commander's reactions, maybe Arkdhem now realizes the High Commander wouldn't have left him hanging.

The High Commander nods, his expression grave.

"You will suffer the consequences. The Council will meet in three daycycles. Until then, you remain here with your Tribute." Stepping aside, he gestures. Dawn is clinging to his arm and she gives me a look as Arkdhem opens the doors to his quarters and we step inside, as if to say that she'll do what she can.

I hope she can do a lot, because the High Commander's final words to us don't do much for my confidence.

"She is the only reason I haven't forcibly broken your bond. She spoke up for you. You owe her a debt."

I'm holding my breath. My body's shaking with the aftermath of everything. The thought of our bond breaking makes my legs wobble like I might collapse.

I didn't even know I had a bond, but I don't want to lose it.

What if the Council decides to split us up anyway? How much power does the High Commander have?

My fear must show on my face because Dawn gives me a quiet thumbs up. But she drops her hand before her mate turns to her.

And with that, the doors to Arkdhem's quarters glide shut.

The second the door slides shut, Arkdhem swings me towards him and brings his mouth to mine. He cradles the back of my head gently but his lips are not so gentle on mine, his tongue thrusting, plundering. I lean back and hug my arms around his neck, pulling him towards me.

He lifts me up without taking his mouth from mine, and walks to the bed. I end up on his lap. We make out like high schoolers at a drive-in theater.

Then he's grabbing the back of my neck and turning me, guiding me belly down over his lap.

"What's going on? I squeak. I wriggle but get nowhere. Arkdhem's pulling up my robe thingy and no sooner than my upturned bottom is bare is his hand crashing down.

Crack!

"If you ever put yourself in danger like that again..." The fear in his tone alarms me more than anything.

"I won't. I promise." I kick. "I'm sorry... I wouldn't have done it. I thought you were going to die!"

He wrenches me upwards and fastens his mouth to mine again, kissing me like it's the last thing he'll do. I hold onto his shoulders and accept his kiss, hoping to calm his fears.

He pulls back, his chest heaving. His eyes close a moment. "When I saw the weapon leave Bogdan's hands, and I was across the room and I could do nothing to help you..."

"I didn't know what else to do. It was not my finest moment. I won't do it again." I place my hands on either side of his face until he looks at me. "But how can you ask me to remain on the sidelines when your life is threatened?"

"I do not deserve you," he breathes.

I surge up in his arms to meet his mouth, and for a long while we swap bites and licks and half kisses, drinking of each other until I'm drunk on him and woozy.

When he finally fists his fingers in my hair and draws back my head, the slight bite of pain is delicious and brings me back.

"You put your life in danger," he growls, his hand tightening in my hair, enough to sting. It's also hot as hell, and a little scary because my butt is suddenly tingling, as if in warning of what's to come. Naughty girls get punished.

My half closed eyes fly open.

"Never come between two fighting warriors," he says, giving me a little shake.

"It was dumb, I know," I confess, which isn't going to help my case any.

Arkdhem's eyes slit, but his grip loosens on my hair. "My heart almost left my body." His hands slide to cup my face. "You are my heart, Marta. You must take greater care." His thumb rubs my bottom lip. "It gives me no pleasure to tell you, you have earned a punishment."

I almost snort. He's not displeased about having to punish me. His cock is rock hard under my butt.

I'm tempted to echo what he's been telling Gavrill and say something like 'I accept the consequences,' but school my face into a serious mask.

He feathers another kiss on my lips before lifting me up and undressing me slowly. The garments slip away easily. Maybe that's what's up with these Tribute robe things—they're designed to be removed quickly.

When the fabric is pooled at my feet, he orders me to go to the bed. "All fours, now."

Heart pounding, I do what he commands. My pussy is already wet. It seems to be excited at the thought of punishment, knowing how that's been twined with erotic pleasure in the past.

As if sensing the turn of my thoughts, Arkdhem adds, "You are not to come."

Damn, of course not. This is punishment.

I peek behind me. Arkdhem's gone to the replicator and gotten a cane. He snaps it against his leg. It whistles through the air and leaves a long gray line on his armor.

I suck in a breath. That's going to hurt.

I quickly turn back before he notices me peeking. If he does catch me, he doesn't say anything. He returns to my side and sets a hand in my back.

"Three with the cane," he says simply. I try not to whimper.

The strikes come quick as lightning.

Slash! Slash! Two horizontal burning lines cross my backside. The third and final one is angled across the other two.

Backside smarting, I wait to see what else will happen. Three cane strikes, harsh as they are, can't be the whole of my punishment.

I don't have long to wait. The Bride Trainer starts stretching and filling my ass, as per usual. This time, the plug grows to a greater thickness. It's uncomfortable as hell, but my pussy is still dripping.

Arkdhem strokes my bottom. The plug fills me to the point where I want to moan. If Arkdhem pulled it out after a few minutes, my asshole would be gaping. Does that mean he's finally going to...

"Naughty tributes get their asses fucked," he says. "And they don't get to come."

I shiver. My nipples are hard points. This is going to be a really enjoyable punishment—for him. Suddenly, there's a little extra burn inside my stretched rear.

"While I'm waiting for you to be ready, I think I'll warm your bottom, inside and out."

The plug is really burning now, and I'm squirming. What has he done?

"I believe the manuals call this 'figging.' It's an ancient technique usually involving ginger." Arkdhem rubs my bottom, the soothing touch counterpoint to the teeth-gritting sting within. "I was able to replicate it quite nicely."

"It hurts," I whine.

"It's supposed to." He checks my pussy, his long finger gliding and hooking around to massage the inner wall until a lovely warmth spreads through me. "And yet... you're wet." I can hear his smirk.

Damn him. He knows how much I respond to these punishments.

The burn in my bottom is getting worse.

Arkdhem has me kneel up and box my arms behind my back so he can play with my breasts, caressing them, pinching my nipples, watching my expression carefully.

I'm almost grateful when he plucks at my nipples because the sensation dulls the sting in my backside a little.

"Shall I do something to help with the pain?" he asks.

I narrow my eyes at him. It sounds like a trick question. "Whatever you like, Master," I answer carefully.

He grins and tips me over his lap, propping my ass high in the air. Now his big palm is swatting my already cane-striped ass. He'll turn it pink between the red lines.

He smacks each cheek, dividing it into four quadrants again—six including my sit-spots. He peppers each quadrant. The sharp sensation of his palm distracts a little from the cruel bite of the ginger-like plug, but when he stops, my bottom is throbbing—inside and out.

"Ow, ow, ow," I chant. Did I ever wonder what figging would feel like? I wish I could go back in time and delete that particular fantasy. This sucks.

The skin around the plug feels seared. The plug is still growing, stretching me even wider.

Suddenly, Arkdhem spanks the plug.

I gasp but my pussy juices further. He spanks it again and then suddenly the plug begins to vibrate.

"Oh no..." I writhe on his hard lap.

"Yes." His fingers rub my pussy folds, collecting moisture. He presents his fingers to my lips, making me taste my own juices.

Then he eases me off his lap and down to my knees before him. He pulls my head up to face the broad head of his cock. The *seela* suckers latch on to my face.

I'll definitely have face hickies after this. And if any of the Tributes see me, they'll know exactly what happened. Heat floods my face at the thought.

Arkdhem makes me suck him, holding my hair and guiding my head. The cane gives me a warning tap from time to time, threatening to swat my ass when I don't follow instructions quite right. I bob my head vigorously, trying to win his favor as my ass burns. Arkdhem grunts above me, his cock seeming to swell in my mouth. I redouble my efforts. Maybe if I please him enough, he'll let me have a turn... which I need desperately. Even though my ass is on fire, I have never been so turned on.

But he pulls out of my mouth suddenly. The *seela* come off my cheeks with little pops. He tugs my hair, moving me into a new position. I rise off my knees and scramble to follow his lead. I end up on the bed, propped on my hands and knees. The cane taps the insides of my thighs, forcing me to spread them wide.

Arkdhem places the cane in my line of sight, and presses on my back until my face is planted into the bed, cheek to the coverlet. My ass is high in the air. Presented to him.

My thighs quiver with the strain of keeping my legs so wide, but my nipples are hardened points pressing into the bed. Arkdhem cups my ass and all my attention goes to the mass of sensation in my bottom.

The Bride Trainer melts away, leaving my ass gaping wide, but empty. The burn is gone and I melt in relief, but then the broad head of Arkdhem's cock breaches my entrance. It stings, burns, aches...

He moves slowly, letting me feel every inch of his cock as it pushes into my ass. I moan, shuddering, clenching. Would a human cock feel different? I'll never know. The sensations are odd, but I don't know if it's only because he's an alien, or because he's in my ass.

It hurts, and yet it feels good. It stings, and yet it throbs. I pant for breath as he fills me, feeling as though there's not enough room in my body for all the air I need. I can't draw a deep breath, not while he's still sliding into me, invading my most intimate space and claiming me completely.

I whimper as he bottoms out, his *seela* stroking the curves of my ass. I feel his cock flexing inside me, the strange head moving and massaging my inner walls. It's depraved torment, the kind that messes with my head as much as my body.

I've never let a man take me like this. Never would have, back on Earth. I wasn't saving it, exactly, I just never thought I'd want anyone to do this to me. Not that Arkdhem asked. And that makes me even hotter, even though back on Earth I'd cut off a man's balls for the presumption.

But he's not a man. He's Arkdhem. My warrior. My mate. My everything, whether I ever admit it aloud or not.

"You will not come," he orders, but then he drops his hand, reaching around my hip to massage my pussy.

Not fair!

Pleasure sparks through me. I grit my teeth and try to focus on the burning stretch in my ass.

"Arkdhem—" I gasp. "Master, please."

He smacks my labia lightly. "No."

The sharp swat makes me grit my teeth but at least it made my orgasm fade. Except, it didn't, not really. The mess of sensations—the stretch, the burn, the fullness, the slight cramping in response to Arkdhem's huge rod filling my back channel, the tension in my back and the delicate little nibbles of the *seela* on my chastised bottom—it all swirls into a whirlpool of overwhelming feeling. And even though most of those sensations should not be pleasurable, they add to the growing pressure of my orgasm.

"Master," I half-whine, half-beg.

"This is punishment, my heart." But he takes his hand away and grips the front of my thigh, pulling me more fully against him. "Now, attend to my pleasure."

His arrogant order sends shivers of delight through me. But I'm not sure how I can do anything, stretched and stuffed and half mindless from fighting my climax.

I can only grip the sheets and hold on as his thrusts rock me forward into the bed.

~

Arkdhem

MY TRIBUTE'S ass is impossibly tight and burning hot. I'm fighting my own climax as I glide in and out of her tight channel. Her flesh is rosy from my palm. Her bottom clenches on my cock, the ring of muscle tightening around my member. My *seela* aid my thrusts, suctioning greedily to her chastised flesh.

Through the bond, Marta's emotions wash through me. She's overwhelmed by sensation, vacillating between the forces of pleasurable pain and painful pleasure.

Moving harder, faster, I let my emotions take the reins of my movements, pounding into Marta's rear entrance with all my frustration, all my fear.

The manuals referred to this joining as 'naughty girl sex,' and I completely understand as I fill her forbidden hole. The taboo adds to the excitement, and I can feel it in the fluttering of her pulse and her emotions.

To take her in this manner does not provide pure pleasure. There is pain as well, despite the care I took in breaching her, and yet she bears it for me. For my pleasure.

I have never experienced the like. It's not just her willing submission, it's what she's willing to do for me. How far she's willing to go. For me. Singly. For so long, the Tsenturion race has been about what is good for the whole of us, but she saw me. Arkdhem.

She chose me.

Insisted on staying with me.

Let me claim her, fully, in the manner of her people, enduring pain for me, giving her pleasure over to me.

I grip her hips harder, pounding into her from behind. With each thrust, my *seela* pop off and fasten back on, and she cries out as they ignite more sparks of pain from my spanked behind. I can feel the heat emanating from the welts through the sensitive organs, and they stroke along her raised flesh, my fascination echoed by my body's response.

"Oh god," Marta gasps, writhing and bucking beneath me. I can feel her muscles clenching around me, increasing my own pleasure. I can hear the confusion in her voice, feel it in my core, as she is caught between pain and pleasure. "Please, Master. I'm going to come."

"Naughty Tribute," I murmur, watching my *seela* stroke along her bottom, my fingers digging into her hips as pleasure wracks me as well. "Very well. If you can come while I fuck your ass, you may."

I will not deny her ecstasy if she manages it. She has earned it.

I thrust hard, pounding into her from behind, reveling in the way she cries out, her scream rising higher and higher until she goes wild beneath me. I bury myself inside her, groaning with my own climax as she squeezes my cock, milking my orgasm from me in long, rapturous spurts. I can feel her coming around me, as lost to the pleasure as I am, my own echoing back at her and sending both of us careening through sheer sexual bliss as the connection between us enhances every bit of our mutual pleasure.

When she goes limp beneath me, I panic for a moment before realizing she is merely unconscious. Blissed out. Such things were spoken of in the manuals.

It is with smug satisfaction that I clean her and myself up. When I curl my body around hers, I feel her stirring again, and she moans a little.

Kissing the top of her head, I pull her in closer to me.

"Holy fuck... I am wrecked..."

I don't understand what she is saying, but 'wrecked' does not usually mean anything good.

"You are perfect," I respond, stroking my fingers through her hair.

"Right back at ya." She yawns. Her tone is flippant, but I can feel the depth of her emotion radiating through the bond, because my own matches hers, and the two amplify each other.

Still, I keep things light, sensing her desire for levity after such an intimate experience.

"Whenever you disobey me, you will get the naughty girl sex," I tell her, still stroking her hair. She wriggles against me, making a small humming noise. Still, she should know there are real consequences. "You are never to put yourself in danger again. I will not be so gentle for a second infraction."

"I won't," she mumbles, half asleep and fading fast.

My arms tighten around her, my voice lowering to a whisper. I'm not even sure she can hear me, but in some ways, that makes the words easier to say.

"I cannot live without you. You are my heart."

14

M*arta*

When sleep peels away slowly, the first thing I feel is my sore bottom. It feels hot as a dying sun. No wonder I ended up sleeping on my stomach. I touch my cheeks, half expecting raised marks from the *seela* suckers. My skin is smooth, but my lips are tender and puffy from the plundering kisses.

I roll to my side, stretching from the awkward position. A shadow falls over me—it's Arkdhem, holding a glass of water.

"I thought you might be thirsty," he murmurs. I reach for the glass greedily. The movement tips me to my back and I yelp. Planting my feet on the bed, I raise my hips up so my poor throbbing bottom is elevated.

"Let me help you." Arkdhem sounds faintly amused. He shifts me into his lap, letting me lean against him so my weight is centered on my hip. I gulp the entire glass in one go as he holds me. He strokes back my sleep-tousled hair and, when I'm done drinking, moves onto tracing my eyebrows and my kiss-swollen lips. I close my eyes and let him retrace the marks he's left on my body.

I want to wake up slowly, savor this moment. It so easily could have been different.

"We came close to being separated, didn't we?" I ask.

"Yes, my heart." He runs a finger down the line of my jaw, pausing to press on a few tender spots. Maybe I do have some face hickeys.

I catch his fingers and meet his gaze. "I won't let it happen. I'll fight for you."

He squeezes my hand. "I don't deserve you."

"Perhaps not." I shift on his lap, wincing when my bottom comes in contact with his hard thighs. But I want this conversation to happen face to face. "I want to be with you, Arkdhem. I know we've just met, but this..." I lick my lips, searching for words. It's time to be honest. To dissolve any boundaries between us. I've never lowered my walls for someone like this. It's scary, but exhilarating. "They asked me if we had a bond. I said yes."

Arkdhem turns his head and kisses my fingers. "I feel it too," he murmurs.

"For this to work, we need to be honest. I don't want anything between us."

"I understand."

"So why did you do it? Why did you disobey orders if you knew the consequences? Help me understand." The questions that have been bubbling in my mind are coming up to the surface again, but more than that, I want to help him form his defense for the trial. There has to be something we can use to gain him leniency.

His eyes unfocus, like he's seeing something I cannot.

"The Jabol are our allies... but recently, the High Commander was given cause to mistrust them. The Vgotha, whom we blamed for the destruction of Tsentur, used Pareena and Dawn to gain an audience with the High Commander."

My lips press shut from asking questions. There's something in his voice, or maybe it's the bond that I feel, that makes me think he doesn't really want to talk about this. That he's not sure he believes it.

I don't want to distract him or pull him off topic. I'm also having trouble reconciling Frllil and the Jabol with the picture I was getting from the other Tsenturions.

"They claimed that long ago, the Vgotha were captives of the Jabol. Forced to work in the mines and do physical labor to support the Jabol society."

"They were slaves," I say flatly when he pauses. Thankfully, that's all he needs to prod him back into talking.

"Yes. And then their leader Tor found a way to free them. The Vgotha claim they simply wanted freedom and a place to live in peace. But the Jabol wanted to keep them enslaved. Many Vgotha were killed, and they retaliated... and then the Jabol decided they needed help. Firepower. Warriors. The Jabol say that the Vgotha destroyed our planet, and we trusted them. They had been longtime traders with us. We had never heard of the Vgotha before, but after meeting them in battle multiple times, it was easy to believe what the Jabol said of them."

He rubs his chin and I bite my lip, sensing he's going to say more. Waiting for it.

"The Vgotha showed us a vid of the Jabol destroying our planet. Some kind of weapons that rained down destruction on our people. The only reason our fleet survived was because our ships were in deep space on an exploratory mission. When we returned, there was nothing left of our home but rubble. The planet and everyone on it was gone."

I'd read about some of it in Frllil's files, blaming the destruction on the Vgotha, but that didn't have the same kind of emotional impact as talking to someone who was actually affected by it. Who had returned to his planet to find it gone. His family and friends, gone. The only ones left being those who were with him.

"That's awful," I whisper. *Fuck Frllil, too, if he knew about all this and didn't tell me. But would he have? He seemed so dedicated to the program, to continuing the Tsenturions' race... is that motivated by guilt, though?* "I'm so, so sorry."

"It was a long time ago, my heart."

A long time ago, but I can feel the echo of my own sadness inside me, a deep, empty ache that throbs and pulses like a physical node in the center of my chest. He's not over it. How could he be?

"So that's why you didn't want to leave me with the Jabol." I press my fingers to my chest where I can feel his pain, thinking fast.

All the conversations I've heard finally make more sense. I can tell Arkdhem is torn about whether or not to believe the Vgotha's version of events, but the High Commander and Bogdan apparently find them credible.

Because Pareena and Dawn were the ones to facilitate the communication?

I really need to talk to the other Tributes about this as soon as I get the chance.

"Is there any way the Vgotha's vid could have been faked?"

Would all this advanced alien tech make that easier, or more difficult? It's impossible for me to know.

"Perhaps. It would be difficult, but..." Arkdhem shrugs, appearing troubled. "The Vgotha say they received the vid from the Riknari."

"Who are they?" I was starting to feel a little exasperated, not to mention frustrated. No one had mentioned a fourth group!

Arkdhem

Blinking, I refocus on my mate, whose impatience is making itself known to me. I give myself a little shake, the corners of my lips curving upwards.

"You have fitted yourself so well into my life already, sometimes I forget that you have not always been here. I apologize. I do not mean to leave you in ignorance." The temper that was flashing in her eyes softens, and I pull her to me, giving her temple a kiss. "The Riknari are known throughout the universe for their dedication to both justice and peace. They help those who are unable to help themselves—such as, if the Vgotha were enslaved by the Jabol, the Riknari would want to help them."

Falling silent, I again ponder whether or not I truly believe the Vgotha were given their tech by the Riknari. If it is true...

"Have the Riknari ever been wrong?" Marta's face has that blank expression I have come to recognize from when she is processing information. It is another question that I did not expect, because none of us would ever think to ask such a thing.

"Not that I know of." I shake my head. "It's said they have an all-seeing oracle, who is able to see every side of a situation and come to a fair and just conclusion. I have never heard of an instance of the Riknari taking a side that was undeserving or which abused their trust."

Though, now, I do have to wonder. Could the Vgotha have fooled the Riknari somehow?

There are certain certainties that I have taken for granted for so long, it never occurred to me to question them. I know the High Commander puts great stock in the Vgotha's claim that the Riknari gifted them with the technology to defeat their oppressors.

But it also brings up the question: if the Riknari were aware of the situation with the Vgotha and the Jabol, if they knew about us and had the tape of Tsentur's destruction, why would they not have championed our cause? Offered their help to us?

I know the High Commander's point of view, which is that the Riknari are a small race and they could not be everywhere at once, but it still doesn't sit well with me. Why the Vgotha and not us? If they helped the Vgotha at all.

Marta's fingers caress my arm, settling some of the tension that has begun to grow in my body.

"And someone saying the 'oracle said' is enough proof for your High Commander?"

I do not blame her for the dubious quality to her question. It would not be enough for me, and I do not think it would be for the High Commander, not when coming from a source we have no reason to trust.

"No, the Vgotha said the Riknari provided the vid of Tsentur's destruction from the Jabol's own records."

I shake my head, as if doing so could clear away some of the images that flit through my mind. I will never forget watching that vid for as long as I live.

∼

Arkdhem's mood has gone dark, not that I can blame him.

But... the Jabol's own records? The same ones Frllil gave me access to?

There's a spark in the back of my head, a blinking light in the darkness. The barest hint of a fairy light, tugging me onward. I used to feel this way when I stumbled onto something good—key information, a witness, or whistleblower willing to talk. My editor said I had a 'nose' for a good story. And now my writerly senses are tingling.

I keep real quiet. That's the first journalistic lesson I learned: once you're with a source, listening is ninety-nine percent of the job.

"And even though you weren't sure about the Jabol's guilt, you defied his orders and came for me anyway."

The monumental decision that changed his life, and not for the better. But he did it for me. If he hadn't, and the High Commander had decided against retrieving me, what would my fate have been? I shiver, because although I like to think that Frllil would have sent me back to Earth, I also don't know if it would have been possible. Were any of the enhancements he'd given me reversible? Would he have cared? Or would I have been written off as a regrettably failed experiment?

"I couldn't leave you with the Jabol for one microcycle longer than necessary. If there was a slight chance the Jabol had done this heinous thing, I didn't want you in their clutches. They might easily find out that the Tsenturions learned the truth, and hold you for ransom. Or... worse."

I bite my lip because Arkdhem's thoughts so closely align with mine. And he was assuming that the Tsenturions would have wanted me, would have cared what happened to me. I'm not so sure that's true.

Not fun to think about. I almost make a face. I'm glad Arkdhem didn't leave me there for long. I'm glad he's my mate. I squeeze his hand, and he returns the pressure.

There's a long silence. Arkdhem seems lost in thought. So I ask the question I know the tribunal will ask.

"Why did you go without notifying the High Commander?"

"Because I didn't want to risk him telling me not to go." His brows form a surly line. "I broke the chain of command for you, Marta. And I'd do it again."

"Well, that's a lot." I joke, blinking a few times because my eyes are stinging. Not that I'm getting emotional or anything. There's a feeling in my chest, like some tightness has eased. My brain wants me to say something meaningful back to him—I feel like I should, but I have no idea what. I'm not good at this at all. I give him a subdued smile. "Thank you for telling me."

"Do you have any questions?"

"Not at this moment." I rub my face briskly, wiping away any trace of tears that might have leaked out. "I think I need to process everything, and then I'll have questions."

"I understand." He leans forward to kiss me softly on the forehead. "I must go to work now."

"I thought you weren't allowed to leave your quarters."

"I will work at my private station here. I must finish handing over my command."

My insides twist. This has to really suck for him, losing everything he's worked for. If it does, he hides it well. But then, he would, wouldn't he? He's the type who wouldn't want to make me feel bad. He might spank like a sadist, but deep down, he's a bit of a cinnamon roll.

But, of course, because I'm me, I have to keep pushing.

"How do you feel about that?"

He touches my hair. "You are worth any price."

More tightness in me unravels. I believe him. He's waited a long time for a mate. Maybe he won't blame and resent me, after all.

"I think I'm going to rest a little bit more." I shift onto the bed, and wince as my tender backside touches the sheets.

He looks smug. "When I return, I will bathe you. It will help you heal."

I nod and curl up on the bed. I close my eyes and wait until he's left the room. I might have told him a little lie. I do want to rest, but I also want to talk to Frllil.

I still have the comm that will supposedly let me reach him, though I haven't tried to use it yet. With Arkdhem in the other room with the door shut, he shouldn't hear me.

For this story, I want to go straight to the source.

15

M *arta*

I HUNCH down close to the bed until my mouth is only inches away from the pillow, which will hopefully muffle the sound.

I press my finger to my ear, hoping that it works as easily as Frllil said it would. I don't hear anything.

"Frllil," I whisper, trying to activate the comm in my ear. Does it need more than me pressing it? Silently, I curse myself for not asking more questions, but it's not like there had been time to.

When his voice comes on, it is a little crackly with static, but clear enough for me to easily make out his words. "Marta Romero Flores. I am here."

Despite all that Arkdhem's told me, I feel some relief when I hear Frllil's voice. He might be part of an alien species full of criminal masterminds, but I felt like we were friends. Ish. I think. Ugh, I hate having to second guess my gut—I've relied on my instincts for so long, it feels wrong to have to do so.

"I have some questions," I say and hesitate. I don't want to tell him everything Arkdhem told me, but on the other hand, I don't want anyone else caught up in this crazy mess. "Are there any more Tributes coming in?"

"I have not yet located the next match, no."

My gut says to trust Frllil. My brain is screaming against it. But if I'm going to, then now is the time. He doesn't have a new Tribute, so I don't have to worry about anything bad happening to another human woman if the Vgotha are telling the truth. And the priority is finding out who we can trust.

On the other hand, if it turns out I shouldn't trust Frllil, I don't want him to know that the Tsenturions and Vgotha are in contact with each other. Thankfully, there's a good reason why the Tsenturions might be questioning the Jabol that has nothing to do with the Vgotha.

"Have you heard of the Riknari?"

"Yes. What is the problem, Marta Romero Flores?" There's a touch of impatience in his voice, which prods at my temper. "I do not have time for these odd questions. I have my duties to fulfill."

Yeah, that's what worries me. I've met a lot of people willing to do monstrous things in the name of 'duty.' It's not hard to believe that there might be aliens willing to do the same. My own emotions are harder for me to control than usual. Because of Arkdhem's influence on me? Because of the bond?

I don't know, but I know it's partly my temper rising that prompts me to be blunter than usual.

"The Riknari have contacted the Tsenturions and told them the Jabol have a weapon that destroyed their planet."

"That would be unthinkable," Frllil says immediately, not a hint of hesitation in his answer. "We are a peaceful race, dedicated to research."

How unthinkable is it really, though?

Because, the more I think about it, the more sense it makes. If they're such a peaceful race, having a warrior race at their beck and call would be good, right?

"The Riknari say the Vgotha were enslaved by the Jabol."

"They were not enslaved. We are technologically superior. We traded their services for our technology." He sounds like a small child, reciting a history lesson. But I'm from Earth and I know all too well how some people like to rewrite history, especially when it covers topics that make them or their ancestors look bad.

"What happened when they didn't want to make that trade anymore?" I ask.

"I... well, they left, of course. And then attacked us because they were angry that we did not want to give them our technology for free." He's so matter-of-fact about it, as if he's never questioned what he's been told once in his life.

"Have you ever looked into that?"

"What? No. Of course not. There is no reason to. The Illumination Guides would not lie to us. That would be unthinkable."

This is like dealing with a child. Maybe he's right to have blind faith in these leaders, but I've only ever seen blind faith go wrong. Maybe the aliens are more like humans than I thought, even the ones like the Jabol, who look and seem nothing like us.

Or maybe that's just my human cynicism. All I know is, I'm not willing to take Frllil's blind faith to my own heart. I have always questioned everything, and I'm much more into the Riknari way of trying to see things from all sides so I have all the information before I start making judgment calls. It's clear Frllil hasn't considered the Vgotha side of things at all, or questioned anything he's been told. Which I don't understand at all, but that's how it's sounding to me.

I blow out a breath, pressing my forehead against the pillow and closing my eyes. "Frllil, is it possible your Illumination Guides, if they had such a weapon, would annihilate the Tsenturion planet without telling the general populace?"

"Without a public debate? They are our guides, they do not make decisions for all of us without informing everyone. It would be unthinkable." He pauses as he says that word again, like he's realizing how many things he's saying are 'unthinkable,' and is finally thinking about them. I bite my lip to keep quiet and let him work through whatever he needs to mentally. When he speaks again, his voice is much more subdued. "They would not but... if they did then the record would be in the Archives. Everything must be Archived."

"Is there any chance I can look?"

"It is raw data. You cannot assimilate it. There is so much information in the Archives that we Jabol rarely attempt to assimilate all of it, we focus on our own areas of research." There's something in his voice now, like he's realizing that maybe he's taken a lot on faith without actually researching it. He sounds almost distracted. "I could look, though. If what you say is true..." His voice trails off. He still doesn't believe it. Doesn't want to believe it. I don't blame him. Sometimes ignorance truly is bliss, at least for the ignorant, especially when it allows them to ignore the harm they've done to others. He adds in a softer voice, "The Tsenturions might want revenge."

"We need to know the truth, Frllil," I say, coaxing him. "If you think you can do it without getting into trouble... Please. You must see how important this is."

If it's true, it means that not only have the Tsenturions been lied to, but it sounds like a large portion of the Jabol have, as well, about a lot of things.

"I will scour the Archives," Frllil says finally. "I will comm you once I know the truth. You will see. They could not have done this. It is unthinkable." His voice sounds like he's determined to prove me wrong, and I hope he's right. I really do.

"Thank you, my friend."

"Yes, Marta. I am your friend, and you are mine."

With that, the comm goes silent.

I drop onto my side, curl up, and close my eyes. I can rest now. Soon, I'll know the truth and I can share it with Arkdhem. It feels like a good thing.

Hours later, I am awoken when Arkdhem comes and carries me to the bath. I want to tell him about my research with Frllil, but bite my lip. Later. When I have answers.

The hot water makes me hiss. Arkdhem studies all my bruises.

"I should not have waited so long to apply the healing cream," he says, examining a particularly angry looking welt.

"It was meant to be punishment." I shrug. "I kind of like them." I go to straddle his lap and grit my teeth when the movement awakens new soreness. The soothing bath is helping, but not much.

He grimaces, shaking his head. "This is too much. I will take you to Medik."

"Oh my god." I cover my face with my hands. Medik is going to see evidence of our sexual perversion. Of course, he probably knows all about it; he probably was the one who gave the manuals to Arkdhem in the first place. "I'm seriously okay, I would tell you if I wasn't."

And to be honest, I'm going to be kind of pissed if I lose my bruises. They feel like badges of honor, not something that needs medical attention. My sadist cinnamon roll doesn't seem to know which of his instincts to lead with.

"Come, my Tribute." Arkdhem scoops me out of the water. He wraps a towel around me but I'm still damp when he starts out the door.

"I can walk," I protest, clutching the towel over my breasts. "They're just bruises!

Arkdhem

SHAKING MY HEAD, I put Marta down on the bed as a chime at the door sounds. Marta jumps, apparently not having realized that I've already summoned Medik, that I did so when I was still looking her over.

"Enter."

"You could've let me get dressed," Marta grumbles, tightening the towel around herself. I give her a look of amusement as Medik enters. There is no reason to be shy in front of him.

"My Tribute may have suffered harm," I explain, getting up and gesturing to her. With a stubborn expression on her face, Marta wrinkles her nose at me, displeased.

"Not from the fight, I hope," Medik says, hurrying over, concern on his face. "If so then you should have commed me a lot sooner."

"No, no, it's not from the fight," I say, and Marta groans, covering her face, which is suddenly very red.

"Arkdhem, go stand over there." She points to the corner. Her cheeks are darkening with color, more than I have seen in all the time we've had together, and I find it both fascinating and incomprehensible. I do not understand why she is changing colors now.

"Why?"

"Because this is embarrassing enough without you hovering over me." She presses her hands against her face. "Oh my god, just go, please. I can't remember the last time I had anyone join me at a doctor's appointment, especially when I don't actually need an examination."

"If you wish, you may keep the towel covering any part you do not wish me to see," Medik says to her seriously. I frown. He needs to see the bruises to ensure I did not do too much damage in my zeal for punishment.

Despite Marta's insistence that she is fine, I want his medical opinion.

"Thank you, I will." Marta looks at me again and for the first time I see that she truly is uncomfortable and does not wish my presence so close to her. "Please go stand in the corner?"

When she uses that pleading note, I cannot deny her.

Sighing inwardly, I go to the corner where she indicated, glancing over my shoulder as Medik bends over her.

"Marta, do you have any particularly bad aches or sore spots?" Medik asks.

I bite my tongue, because he's asking her, not me, but it's difficult.

"Not really. I really am fine."

"How about you let me look at the worst of it, just to soothe Arkdhem's nerves?"

I scowl into the corner, but I don't protest. Whatever will prompt her to let him examine her.

"Oh, fine," she mutters, and I hear the rustling of fabric.

I glance over my shoulder to see what she's showing him—the towel that's wrapped around her has been lifted to show an ample curve of buttock. The dark coloring of bruises over her skin makes me wince. She isn't as pale as Dawn, but that portion of her skin is lighter than the rest, and the bruises stand out more clearly.

There is a part of me that loves seeing my marks on her. That part makes me very uncomfortable. I do not want to harm her, after all, even for punishment.

"See? It's not that bad." Marta's voice is indignant at having to suffer through Medik's examination, and my lips quirk. She is a fiery spirit, my Marta.

Medik lifts his head and his eyes meet mine, amusement dancing in them. One of his hands rests on Marta's hip, fingertips on the nanotech belt.

"Arkdhem, she truly is fine. Certainly, you have not—"

Mid-sentence, Medik flickers. Not just him, Marta too.

What the frakk?

I'm already in motion, but it's too late. They flicker again, looks of surprise on their face, and then they both disappear.

"Marta! Medik! Marta!" I run forward, throwing myself at the bed where my Tribute rested only a moment before. The impression of her body is still there, on the sheets, but she is gone, and my hands fall through the space where she'd rested only moments before.

Sheer panic guts me.

What just happened?

How?

Why?

I howl with all the savage terror coursing through me, my armor shooting to pure black, flashing with jagged edges of sickening reds and yellows.

The door opens behind me, but I cannot look, do not hear the shouts of the warriors tumbling into the room to find me throwing the bedding around, as if I might find her somehow hidden beneath it. My chest is too tight around my rapidly beating heart as one thought pounds through my head, over and over again.

She's gone, she's gone, she's gone.

16

———

M^{arta}

I DON'T REMEMBER what the sensation of going through the wormhole while I was dying, but I imagine it is something like this. I feel like I'm being squeezed, suffocated, and pulled apart all at once. Like my body is being stretched in every direction, so completely that my molecules are about to go careening into different directions as I explode, only to suddenly be compressed again, into too small a space.

When it abruptly ends, I vomit—right down onto the gleaming floor in front of me. How I immediately know it's different from a Tsenturion floor, I have no idea, but I do.

Jabol. That looks like the floor from Frllil's lab.

Horror jabs through me as the obvious conclusion lurches through my mind, despite how splintered and disjointed my thoughts are.

Dumbass, dumbass, dumbass.

"What is the meaning of this?" Medik's voice is loud. So loud. I wince as I raise my head. He's pushing himself up to his feet, swaying on them, but he manages to move in front of me, like he's trying to protect me.

On the other side of him, I can see Jabol. Four of them. Is one of them Frllil? I have no idea. They all look exactly alike. Even more so than the Tsenturion warriors, who at least have defining features. How do you tell one blob of Jello apart from another?

Easy answer—you don't.

I can't tell if one of them is Frllil.

"Who is that? How did he come with her? Is that her mate?" One of the Jabol quivers. Can a blob quiver with indignation? I moan slightly, trying to push myself up the same way Medik has, not wanting to be on the ground in front of hostile aliens, clutching the towel to my breasts.

"No, that is the Tsenturion Medik." One of the other blobs bobbles forward and somehow, now that he's spoken, I recognize Frllil. The dirty little traitor. I glare at him, but he doesn't seem to notice me. "He was touching her nanotech when she was transported."

My brain feels like it's working in a haze of fog, but I get what he's saying—the nanotech is how they were able to teleport me. That's scary as hell. Does that mean Pareena and Dawn are vulnerable too?

"He is unnecessary," the first Jabol says. "Eliminate him."

A blast of light shoots from one of the other Jabol and hits Medik squire in the chest and I scream as Medik falls in front of me, dropping to my knees, no longer caring about the towel. There is a large hole burned into his armor, which seems like it's trying to rapidly repair itself.

"No," I whisper, my shock and horror freezing me in place, hands hovering over the gaping wound. Something stings my eyes, and it's not until I feel the wetness on my cheeks that I realize I'm crying. "No, Medik... no..."

He smiles, and for a moment I think he's going to be okay, despite everything.

"Sala..." He breathes the word out like it's a benediction, his eyes closing.

I wait, and wait, and wait, but his eyes don't open again, and his chest is still. He's gone. He's truly, actually gone, cut down in front of me without an ounce of compassion or care for him as a person. They fucking Cedric Diggory-ed him.

"No." I whimper the word, tears sliding down my cheeks unchecked.

The sound comes roaring back into my ears and I can hear Frllil yelling. But it's too late. It's far too late.

"You said you wanted her for questioning! No one was supposed to be hurt! This is unthinkable!"

Oh Frllil. You poor, deluded asshole. I close my eyes, choking on the sob that's trying to work its way out of my throat. It doesn't take a genius to figure out what happened.

He went to his Illumination Guides and either asked the wrong questions, or told them enough that they became suspicious. Wanted to talk to me. And he'd been wrong about them. So, so wrong.

I would feel sorry for him if he wasn't so damn stupid. He's gotten Medik killed. Anger sweeps through me. Rage. All accompanied by a helplessness that makes me want to scream.

"He was unnecessary. Stand back, Frllil. You have clearly been diverted from your path by interaction with these lower forms. We will guide you back to the One True Path, as we are meant to do."

Frllil bristles, or as close as he can to such a thing.

"There is no One True Path! What are you talking about?"

"Silence, Frllil." The first Jabol's edges roll in a way that nauseates me and seems vaguely threatening somehow. I press my lips together, leaning against Medik's body, still trying to figure out what to do. If there is anything I can do. "We are the Guides. We have found the One True Path. We will show you the way."

What was vaguely threatening now comes out as outright intimidation.

Frllil quivers, falling back silently.

There will be no help from him. I am all alone.

~

Arkdhem

Marta is gone.

I rock back and forth on my bed, the gaping hole in the center of my chest unbearable. It is like losing Tsentur all over again, but far worse... any hope for the future that I'd had left is gone—ripped from me, and I don't know by whom, or how to get her back.

The only thing that keeps me from throwing myself out the airlock is the tiny bit of the bond that still tethers us together. I can feel her. Or I am fooling myself. But I am almost sure I can feel her. And as long as she is alive, I might be able to get her back.

And if I don't, then I will hunt down whoever has taken her to the ends of the universe and take my revenge, no matter what the High Commander has to say about it.

"It must be the Vgotha again!" Corin growls the words, one of his arms around me in support.

"No way," Dawn protests from her spot beside the High Commander. "They wouldn't. Besides, how would they have? When they took me, and when they took me and Pareena, there were battles. Not people disappearing without a trace. That's something the Jabol do."

"My Tribute is right." The High Commander's voice is hard and full of determination. "The Vgotha, for all their tactics and technology, have never been able to transport anyone in such a manner. The Jabol, on the other hand..."

"That is not proof," Corin argues, his arm tight around my shoulders, as though he is determined to hold me together by sheer force of will. He is a good friend, but I am hardly in a mindset to truly appreciate it. "The Vgotha's tech has been growing, we may not have seen everything they are capable of. Every time we turn around, they have something new."

"He's not wrong," Bogdan points out. For once, the second's presence doesn't grate on me. I don't care about him.

I only care about Marta.

The bed beneath me shifts slightly, and I lift my head to see Pareena taking a seat next to me. She is close, though not touching, her dark eyes full of sympathy that hurts to see because it means there is reason for it. Because Marta is gone.

"Can you feel her, Arkdhem? Through the bond?"

"Only enough to know she is alive." My voice is hoarse from screaming, the words rasping out of me from a pained throat. And yet nothing hurts as badly as the emptiness of my arms. "For now."

"Hey now, no defeatist attitude." Dawn approaches me from the front. Unlike Pareena, she has no hesitation in crouching down in front of me and putting her hand on my knee. But then, Gavrill and I have a very different relationship than Bogdan and I. The warmth of her hand does nothing to alleviate the coldness gripping me from the inside out. "If she's alive, we can get her back."

"Can we?" The bitter words fall from my lips. "Can you guarantee that? Because I know—all we Tsenturions know—there are some things we cannot change. Some things we can never recover."

Silence falls as the mass grief of the warriors fills the room, the thread that has always connected us since the destruction of Tsentur, no matter our differing views on anything else. No matter how Bogdan and I disagree, no matter how we fight, there has always been that common connection between us, between all of us. It is something Dawn and Pareena cannot truly grasp, and I am glad of it for their sake.

There is a long moment and then Dawn gathers herself, shaking her head.

"Look, I can't know what you went through, but I know if I were Marta, I would be pissed as hell that you'd given up on me before all hope was lost. Yeah?"

My mate is fiery. A fighter. A survivor.

All she has already lived through has proven that.

Dawn has a point.

I gather myself, looking up at Gavrill, asking him as a fellow Tsenturion and not as one of his warriors. "Permission to leave my quarters." The gravel in my voice adds to the hollowness of my tone. "We need to find who took my Marta."

"Permission granted. Let's go to the bridge."

~

MARTA

HUDDLED AGAINST MEDIK'S BODY, I have to push back against my grief. I cling to him, unwilling to move away until I absolutely have to, trying to get my brain working again and looking around the space where I've landed. There has to be something I can do. Something I can use.

I remember accepting my death when I was trapped beneath rubble on earth and bleeding out. This isn't the case now. I can still move. I'm surrounded by crazy ass tech. There has to be something I can do, even if it's taking these fuckers down with me.

My death will *not* be meaningless.

The room is circular, and there's a slight humming vibration beneath my legs, indicating that we're on a ship. There are no windows, but there are a lot of screens in the room around us, all showing different diagrams and things that I can't read.

Frllil is moving steadily away from the rest of the Jabol, shrinking back into a corner. I resist the urge to scream at him to do something. I already trusted him once. I won't make that mistake again.

The other three Jabol are arguing in the center of the room, one of them pushing at a console and clearly becoming increasingly frustrated.

"Why isn't it working?" he trills, turning his focus to Frllil, who shrinks back again.

"The nanotech was always meant to bond the Tribute to the Warrior," he squeaks. "In doing so, it seems to have undergone enough changes at a metaphysical level that it no longer responds to our initial tech. The only reason it was possible with Marta is because she is the newest of the Tributes, and the tech has only changed a little since she was delivered to the Tsenturions."

Is it my imagination, or does he glance at me after he speaks? Either way, I do feel a little better knowing these assholes can't get their hands on Dawn and Pareena. Not for lack of trying.

The three immediately fall to arguing about how they might be able to recover Dawn and Pareena. It's clear they mean to use the Tributes to force the Tsenturions to do their bidding. What's worse, I'm pretty sure it will work. That must be why they were in such a hurry to match the highest ranking officers to Tributes—it wasn't just an acknowledgement of their rank, it was a backup plan.

I'm seething, scanning my eyes across everything, looking for something I can use... we're definitely on a bridge of some kind, but none of the tech looks like anything the Tsenturions have. It's a lot more like what Frllil had, but all the stuff he wouldn't let me touch— that I actually couldn't touch because it was meant to be used by blobs of Jello, and not bipedals.

Though it feels wrong, I even force myself to look down and subtly scan Medik's body, in hopes that he has something I can use... some kind of weapon, some remnant of his armor.

All the while, the Jabol's argument is getting louder. For a group on the 'One True Path' they don't seem like they have one mindset.

I am sorry, Marta.

The voice sounds like it's inside my head, not in my ear, and I jerk upright.

The Jabol aren't looking at me or Frllil, and he's off to the side. Something is tossed to me, and I automatically reach up to catch it. It looks like a small stick.

"What was that?" one of the Jabol asks, his body quivering. How much did he see? I can't tell, and I squeeze the thing against me, huddling closer to Medik.

I am sorry, Marta. You must tell them to fire immediately. When you get back. Tell them, fire immediately. It is important.

"What was that?" the Jabol demands, one of them moving closer to Frllil, the other towards me.

Fire immediately. *It's important.*

And then the world goes black again.

Arkdhem

WE'RE WATCHING the recording of Marta disappearing from my quarters all over again, my jaw clenched against the unruly emotions rushing through me, when something begins to flicker in the center of the bridge. Several warriors shout, their armor coming up. Alarms ring in our ears.

"Stop!" I roar. I recognize the look. The flickers.

In the center of the waving air, two forms appear: Marta on her knees, Medik on his back.

"Fire immediately..." Her voice is a whisper as I reach her, pulling her into my arms, almost unable to believe she's really there.

"What?"

"Fire immediately!"

Her voice coincides with another shout.

"High Commander! A Jabol ship just appeared on our screens! It is armed!"

"Fire immediately!" Gavrill's command repeats Marta's words, and then she shakes herself, her face and expression clearing, as if coming out of a daze.

"Wait!" she cries out. "Frllil is still on there!"

But it's too late.

Fiery explosions appear on the screens and I pull her into my arms, pressing her face into my chest so she can't see the Jabol's ship exploding... and it's only when Dawn screams that I look down and realize everything we have lost.

Medik has not moved, not because he is dazed or injured... there is a single wound gaping open in his chest that his nanotech has not even tried to repair because no repair is possible. There is no point.

Medik is dead.

I hold Marta tighter to me, this new loss pulsing through me and doubling the anguish between us. It does not erase my joy at having her back in my arms, but it exists alongside it... one hole has been closed, and another has opened.

"No! Medik! *No!*" Gavrill falls to his knees beside Medik's body, his voice broken because he already knows the truth.

All around the bridge, warriors are falling to their knees as a grief that we thought was buried tsencycles ago is reawakened, the bridge awash with armor in flickering blues and greys, reflecting our mourning. Dawn wraps her arms around Gavrill from behind, tears streaming down her face. I rock Marta against me as she sobs, my own tears joining hers.

The man who served as father to all the warriors since Tsentur was destroyed, is gone.

17

———————

M*arta*

I WAS WRONG ABOUT FRLLIL. He wasn't a worthless coward. He saved me, and sacrificed himself. And the guilt of knowing that my thoughts about him before his death were so insulting is eating me as much as the guilt of being so useless in the face of danger. I should have saved myself. I should have saved him, and Medik, and... instead, I was the ultimate damsel in distress, saved by outside forces.

Once I handed the little stick thing over to the High Commander, I curled up onto Arkdhem's lap and did my best to shut out the world —like the useless human being I was. Arkdhem carried me back to his rooms and I fell asleep, unable to face reality for a moment longer.

As I came awake, there was a murmur across the room.

I open my eyes to see Arkdhem standing in front of his vid screen, the High Commander on the other screen, both of them talking softly to each other. Does this mean Arkdhem is still going to be undergoing trial?

Tears well in my eyes. I seriously will fall apart if I have to take one more hit.

You think you haven't already fallen apart?

Ignoring the mean little voice in my head, I push up to a sitting position. Seeing the movement out of the corner of his eye, Arkdhem immediately glances over to me and then says something to the High Commander before turning off the screen. As he approaches the bed, I curl up into a little ball, and his expression turns sympathetic.

I can feel his grief in my center, a pulsing ball of unhappiness that is even greater than my own.

"Medik... Frllil..."

"They're both gone." Arkdhem sits on the edge of the bed, his own loss heavy in his eyes, and I scoot closer to him.

"Frllil was one of the good ones," I say, leaning into him. Arkdhem immediately pulls me onto his lap. My muscles respond the way they always do, relaxing into him, even though I don't deserve the comfort. "It's not fair."

"It is not fair, but this is war," Arkdhem says.

"Will you declare war on the entire Jabol race?"

"Frllil sent a data pack over with you. Only a small portion of the Jabol were responsible, but they were allowed to continue with their 'research' by the leaders. The general populace had no knowledge of what was going on. But examples must be made. Gavrill has sent Tsenturion ships to the Jabolian system."

I clutch his hand. "They're not going to..."

Arkdhem shakes his head.

"We will not destroy their entire system or any of their planets. But we will take out the military outposts we had created for them, and the weapons stores they had acquired for us. We'll also disseminate the data Frllil provided so the Jabol know what was sanctioned without their knowledge and be given the truth of their leaders, and then we will leave. What happens next will be up to them, and whether or not they believe us." He pauses for a moment. "The leaders of those who believed in the 'One True Path' were all killed onboard Frllil's ship. I don't know how he managed to get all that information to you, but he did."

"What about the Vgotha?"

"The Vgotha have a choice. They can seek revenge against their former enslavers. But after all this time, they might just want peace."

"I hope so. I don't think the entire race is evil. Frllil wasn't."

"Frllil was very brave. We are still working on decoding all the information he had on the device you gave us."

"What do you think is on it?" I ask, and then immediately feel guilty again for that little bit of curiosity. People—well, aliens, but still people to me—are dead, and I want to know what data one of them left behind.

A sick feeling surges through my stomach.

"I don't know, but I'm looking forward to finding out." His hands sweep over my hair and I wonder how much of my own feelings he can sense. Not much, I hope. "Frllil will not have died in vain. We will decode and use all of the data he's sent us. Already, he has saved both the Tsenturions and the Jabol. If not for the bravery he showed and the information he sent, I think the High Commander would have shown far less mercy to the Jabol population."

Well, that's something at least. Innocents won't die because of a message that I passed along.

I cling to that bit of knowledge as Arkdhem continues to cuddle me.

"Medik's funeral is in a cycle; do you want to go?" he asks softly, his voice gentle, as if he's telling me I don't have to if I don't want to.

And I don't want to, but I think I need to.

"Yes," I whisper. But I don't move. I let him hold me in the dim lighting of the room, letting his presence and his comfort keep the rest of the world away for just a little while longer.

~

MARTA

. . .

As I stand beside Arkdhem in a sea of Tsenturion warriors, the air of sadness is palpable. Their communal grief chokes me, amplifying my guilt. I should have done something to try to save Medik. Anything. He wasn't even supposed to be there—only I was.

Gavrill leads the funeral proceedings from a raised platform in the middle of the crowd. Dawn is by his side with a bowl of flowers in her hands. Pareena stands across from Dawn, holding another, identical bowl. Bogdan looms behind her. The room is full of dark grey armor, tinged with blue. It is a beautiful color, but sad, and my eyes tear up at the very sight of it.

"At all our previous funerals, Medik was up there with them," Arkdhem murmurs, his voice tight. "He served as father to all of us, after we lost ours, and now we serve as his sons, in place of those he lost."

My throat and face are tight as a slow procession of warriors carries a pall bearing Medik's body up to the raised platform. I swallow and clear my throat several times, but the knot isn't dissipating.

"To all those gathered, we remember the fallen," Gavrill intones. "We honor our dead. The many we have lost. Remember them well."

I jump as everyone around me responds, "We will remember."

Arkdhem's hand is on my shoulder. I raise mine and squeeze it tight. Now that funerals are so rare, each one is a reminder of the destruction of their planet. It's a chance to reflect on that huge loss.

How did the warriors grieve the genocide of their race? Did Medik hold a ceremony like this? Or did the warriors simply pick up and move on, numbing themselves with duty, trying to forget?

They couldn't focus on their duties, though. They were warriors who had made it their life's mission to protect the weak. And they could not protect what was most sacred to them.

No wonder the Jabol's manipulation worked. The High Commander must have jumped on the chance to give his warriors a new purpose. And now they've fulfilled one purpose—justice against those who destroyed Tsentur—but lost the other. There will be no more Tributes without the Jabol.

Medik was an integral part of the Tribute Program, as well.

Both died together.

Arkdhem touches my shoulder. "It is time." He hands me a tray with a medical scanner, and a few other tools Medik used.

Dawn and Pareena have each done their part of the ceremony. Pareena sprinkled water over Medik's still form in a symbolic cleansing. And Dawn surrounded Medik's body with flowers.

Now it's my turn. I climb the stairs and lay the tray of Medik's tools at his feet.

"We remember the fallen's chosen duty," Gavrill says to the crowd. "How he served us all."

"We remember," the crowd responds.

I bite my lip. Dammit. I blink a bunch of times, moving blindly back to where Arkdhem waits. He folds his arms around me and I snuggle against him, wanting to hide.

He ducks his head close. "You did well."

I shake my head a little.

"What is it?" he asks.

"I can't stop thinking like a reporter. It's easier when I can be a watcher. Removed from all this." I wave a hand, feeling lame. "Just a reporter." I'd still had occasional survivor's guilt, but it hadn't been like this.

Arkdhem takes my hand in both of his. "You are not only a reporter, my Marta," he says simply. "You never were. And now you are my mate. We are bonded and our grief, as well as our joys, are shared."

Dammit, I don't want to cry. I grit my teeth and nod, and focus on the proceedings. Arkdhem keeps watching me closely, though.

Gavrill and the women have left the platform. It rises up over us all, folding over Medik's body. Turning into a small space craft.

The small funeral craft rises and hovers in the air before gently moving towards the end of the hull. The air shimmers briefly as an airlock activates, sealing us off from the funeral craft.

The Tsenturions turn as one. The small ship bearing Medik's body is still drifting towards the back of the hull. Then the doors open and the ship exits the hull. My ears pop, and I cling to Arkdhem to steady myself. The seal keeps us all from being sucked out of space, but we can still watch the funeral craft drift into the emptiness beyond.

"It's like a Viking funeral," I murmur.

"What is that, my Marta?" Arkdhem leans down.

"A Viking funeral. Um... The Vikings were another warrior culture back on Earth," I explain. "At least, we think that's what they were... They didn't really write anything down." I'm babbling. "Anyway, I should shut up and just watch."

In the space beyond, the rest of the Tsenturion fleet has lined up to make a corridor of ships. Medik's funeral craft floats between them, heading to the stars beyond. Like a Viking funeral, but in space.

As the funeral craft reaches the end of the corridor, streams of light shoot out of the nearest Tsenturion spaceships and lock onto the small craft. A bright flare from the explosion, and the tiny ship bearing Medik's body is gone, destroyed by the weapons. There's nothing left but space dust. I gasp, a tremor running through me.

"He's with his mate and family now," Arkdhem murmurs.

"*Meu deus.*" I turn away, a hand over my mouth. Arkdhem cradles me against his body. I'm glad we're not up in the front but in the back because a shocking wave of *something* washes over me. My face feels tight. I gulp for air, but my lungs feel too small. I'm about to be sick. What is happening? Is this grief?

Arkdhem softly strokes my back.

"I don't cry about things," I say through stiff lips. "This isn't me. But..." Ugh, my words are stuck in my throat. I'm about to vomit... or something. I clutch my chest and bend double.

And then the words burst out. "*It's my fault!*"

I claw at Arkdhem. *Get me out.*

He scoops me up and carries me to the back of the hall. My face flames, but the warriors simply part to make way, and no one stares at me.

Arkdhem sets me down in a quiet corner where everyone's backs are to us. I'm shaking. Something weird has happened to my body—my insides are like knives, cutting me.

Arkdhem cups my face and leans down so he's all I see. "Tell me."

"It's my fault," I choke out. "It's my fault he's dead."

"No, my Marta. It was the Jabol's fault. Not Frllil's," he amends because he knows that I don't like lumping Frllil in with his evil supervisors, "but Frllil's superiors. They and they alone are to blame for the deaths."

"But if I hadn't..." I trace my actions back through everything. If I hadn't sent Arkdhem away... If I hadn't been embarrassed at my appointment with Medik...

"Perhaps it is my fault, then," Arkdhem says as if reading the line of my thoughts. "I brought Medik to you. When Frllil's superiors tried to retrieve you, anyone touching you would have gone. It is my fault that I was not holding you at that moment. If I had also been taken, I could have slashed through any enemies." He looks like he wants to fight someone, right now.

I tremble a little, my face feels stiff. "You don't know if that would have happened. They could have killed you. Medik was hardly weak. The Jabol had a weapon prepared that decimated his armor." Now I really am going to be sick. If I had lost Arkdhem...

"And they could have killed you," he counters.

"But if I hadn't been asking questions and gotten Frllil to dig for more information in the Archives..."

"Then things might have happened another way—a worse way. The Jabol committed atrocities. We were always going to come to war, and all involved would be at risk." He pauses. "Unless you wish that the Tsenturions never found out the truth—"

"No, no." My stomach has calmed down. Under Arkdhem's comforting touch, I relax a little.

He lets me stand frozen for a minute, then asks gently, "Have you thought through all the possibilities sufficiently? Can you lay to rest this blame? Does blaming yourself honor Medik or Frllil's death?"

"No," I admit.

He touches my cheek, right under my eye. His finger comes away wet.

"I don't cry," I parrot. "I don't cry at things like this."

Arkdhem wraps his powerful arms around me. I let him cuddle me to his chest. "Perhaps this time, you do."

*M*ARTA

A NEW PLATFORM has risen up to replace the one that left, and Pareena climbs the stairs to address the crowd.

"And now I'd like to welcome anyone who wishes to come up, one by one, and share a story about Medik. If you want to. You can say what he meant to you. Let's lift up his memory and remember him as he'd want us to. Then we can grieve and live our lives—which he'd want us to do."

As soon as she steps away, Bogdan climbs up the stairs. He looks as surly and fierce as ever, but when his gaze touches on his mate, it softens.

"I will start," he says in a begrudging way that makes me think that Pareena put him up to this. "Medik... when I received my Tribute, I did not know how to bond with her. I did not know what to do with her. Through my grief for my lost family and through my rebirth as my Tribute's mate, he counseled me. He stood in my father's shoes and guided me, the way a father would." Another pause with even more glowering, as if he resented having to share his emotions. "That is my memory of Medik."

Yeah, Pareena definitely put him up to this. But it works. There now a line of Tsenturions forming at the stairs.

"Thank you for sharing," Pareena murmurs, and motions for the next warrior to ascend the platform.

I hug Arkdhem's waist. The giant wave of grief has passed, and I don't feel like crying anymore. Down in the crowd, I can see Dawn leaning against her mate. She's broken down into full-on waterworks, but she gets a pass because she's pregnant. Not like me, who broke down even though I don't really have a right to.

Pareena's cheeks are wet but she's in her element, helping others process their emotions, helping them through their grief. Unlike me, she's useful, and the warriors respond to her, letting her comfort them.

A memory pings at me as I listen to the stories the warriors tell of Medik. The last thing Medik said to me. I'd almost forgotten, with everything that happened immediately afterwards.

"Arkdhem... What is Sala?"

"Sala? Sala was Medik's mate's name."

And just like that, I choke on tears again.

18

———

M*arta*

The memorial service has just ended when Arkdhem bends down to whisper in my ear, "Marta, will you come with me? There's something you should see."

"Now?" All I want to do is go back to our rooms and lie in bed. Not move. Not think. Maybe sleep some more. Unconsciousness is bliss.

"Yes."

But he wouldn't ask if it weren't really important. I duck my head and let him pull me down the hallway.

"The communication officers contacted me just before the service. They've broken through the encoding in Frllil's device," Arkdhem tells me.

"What? Why didn't you say?" I quicken my steps, pushing aside my melancholy. My curiosity has always been my driving force, and I feel an overwhelming need to know what was on that device. Arkdhem picks up the pace, and by the time we reach the communications deck, we're jogging. Of course, I'm out of breath, and he's not.

We enter a small, darkened antechamber, and cross immediately to a door. Arkdhem lays his hand on the side of the wall to request entry.

The lights dim even further, and Arkdhem squeezes my hand.

"Why is it dark?" I ask in a hushed tone.

"It's part of the decryption. Apparently, the information is light sensitive."

A second later, a whooshing sound signals that the door in front of us has glided open. The room beyond is much larger, and lit with a 3D model that's glowing, suspended in the middle of the room. Arkdhem ushers me in and the door closes behind us, keeping in the darkness. There are two Tsenturions to the left of us, but my eyes are fixed on the model of a galaxy in front of us. The spiral pattern hangs in the air, rotating slowly. The center is bright yellow, but the tendrils are pale white. Almost a milky color...

Is that what I think it is?

"What have you found?" Arkdhem asks. His hands come to my shoulders, steadying me. I put a hand over his large one.

"It took a day-cyle to realize dark-light would help us decrypt the code," one of the communications officer says almost apologetically. "But from there, it was easy. The data contains one thing: a map to a particular star system."

"Oh my god..." I breathe out the words, and immediately bite my lip. It's too soon to tell, isn't it? The Milky Way can't be entirely unique in its appearance, in the whole universe.

As the Tsenturion speaks, the image before us rotates and then starts to get larger, as if someone clicked a button to make us zoom in.

"Which star system?" Arkdhem asks as the galaxy spirals grow bigger and then disappear on the periphery of the image.

"It's not one that our systems recognize. It's incredibly far away. The map centers on a particular star—you can see it here." A point in the image grows bigger, becoming a familiar-looking glowing orb circled by a few multicolored dots. "It has nine planets... well, eight planets? It's kind of hard to tell with that last one."

I gasp. "*Meu deus!*"

It is! That's it!

"Marta? What is it?" Arkdhem steadies me as I point.

"That's our system! That's Earth!" The image of my home planet is suspended in front of us. It looks familiar: two icy points at either end, and blue and brown continents in between. There's Ecuador, in the middle.

I stare at my home planet, and there's an ache deep inside me.

"How far away?" Arkdhem asks, seeming to realize that I've been struck speechless.

The IT Tsenturion clears his throat. "Far. It would take us at least two tsencycles to reach it. But the data contains clear instructions on how to navigate the wormhole. Once we reach the galaxy, we can find Earth."

I put a hand to my lips, a gesture my mother did often when she was surprised. "I can't believe it. We can go back! Dawn, Pareena, and I—we—can all go home!"

Arkdhem squeezes my shoulders as he asks the IT guy, "Rodion, do the instructions include temporal coordinates as well?"

Rodion babbles something I don't understand about wormholes and coordinates.

"What does that mean?" I turn to Arkdhem.

I can't see his face in the darkness, but he sounds very grave as he says, "It means you can return home, and only a few years will have passed on Earth. Without temporal coordinates, we would return to your planet centuries later."

My mouth falls open. "Right. Wormholes."

I'm no physicist, but faster than light travel would have some effect on time, wouldn't it?

Arkdhem's large hand passes over my hair. "A way back to your planet. Frllil left you this for a reason."

"His final gift." My eyes sting. I'm glad it's dark in here.

"We're done decrypting the data, if you wish to turn on the lights," Rodion says.

"Um, yeah." I dash my fingers over my face. I seem to be suffering from an excess of emotion. Again. My body is hot and cold all over.

Must. Not. Cry.

Maybe I'm just overwhelmed. I never thought I would be able to go back home. When the lights come back up, I whirl to Arkdhem and grab him. "Isn't this amazing?" I gush. "We can go back home!"

We can tell our friends and family that we didn't die. Introduce the Tsenturions to human women, the human way instead of through abduction. Use their technology to save our planet. Use our women to save their race. So much good could come from this. For the first time since Medik was killed in front of me, I feel joy. Hope.

God, we really could change worlds. Universes.

"Yes," he replies softly. His face is strangely blank, his eyes hollow.

"I can't believe it," I repeat. I want to run around the ship, shouting for joy. "This is going to be so great."

And yet, there's still a hollow ache at the center of my chest, but I push it aside. It's only natural that some grief should linger, despite this momentous news.

For some reason, it doesn't occur to me that it might be Arkdhem's ache I'm feeling.

More and more, all the implications are coming together in my head, little connections on how beneficial this will be to both races. But we'll have to present it in the right way. And that will be my job. I'm going to be the one to break the story, and introduce the Tsenturions to the humans.

~

Arkdhem

MY TRIBUTE IS SO happy as we return to my quarters. The bond between us bubbles over with her excitement. Her cheeks are a shining pink. She's muttering to herself now.

"I could break the news through the BBC, or maybe the New York Times. They snubbed me for my last article, though. So maybe I'll choose the LA Times instead. Or the Washington Post. Just to stick it to them, the snooty bastards. This will have to be done carefully, though…" She whirls to me and takes in my subdued expression. "Oh Arkdhem… Is it wrong of me to be so excited? This is the scoop of a lifetime!"

She's practically crowing, and I understand. It is the same way I felt when I was made second-in-command. I can tell how much it means to her.

"Not at all," I answer. Her happiness should be my own, but the taste is bittersweet.

I want her to return to Earth and further her career. I do. But I do not want to be left behind. What will Dawn and Pareena think? Will they be caught up in her excitement, and determined to leave their lives as Tributes as well?

If so, the High Commander and Bogdan are not going to be happy with me.

Although, Dawn and Pareena have been Tributes far longer than Marta has. Their bonds with their mates are deeper. Perhaps they will not have the same impulse to leave so quickly as Marta does.

I rub at my chest, where the ache inside is increasing.

I was so afraid that the High Commander would take her away from me, but it turns out it was not him and my upcoming trial that I had to fear… it is Marta's home planet. And how can I compete with that? If given the opportunity, of course I would want to see Tsentur again.

But you would want her to go with you, wouldn't you?

Yes, of course, but it is different for her. She did not choose to be part of the Tribute Program, not truly. And even if she had, she had no way of truly understanding what she was signing up for.

Flopping down on her back on the bed, she stares up at the ceiling. Despite how energized she was a moment ago, that does not stop the melancholy from creeping back in. I know that only too well.

Duty only takes one so far.

Eventually, you have to stop and feel again.

"I can't believe I thought Frllil was a coward," she whispers, her voice choking up a little.

Getting onto the bed with her, I pull her into my arms, offering her my comfort. I will hold her for as long as I can, until I have to let her go.

~

*M*ARTA

"A*LL RIGHT*, Arkdhem. Tell us why we are gathered here," the High Commander says. We're all sitting around a circular table—we three human women and our mates, plus the Tsenturion Rodion, who was one of the IT specialists who cracked Frllil's encryption.

It's only been a few hours since the memorial service ended. Dawn and Pareena are still red-eyed from crying, and my own eyes still feel scratchy. Arkdhem insisted on the meeting, telling everyone it was important.

Bogdan has his arms folded over his chest. He's glowering at Arkdhem.

My mate is unfazed. "My Marta has something to announce." He touches my arm.

"Well, Rodion and I," I pipe up. "He's the one who figured out the encryption."

"What encryption?" Dawn looks puzzled.

"There was more information encoded on the disc Frllil gave to Marta," the High Commander interjects. "More than the information about the Jabol and that One True Path nonsense. Although, I did not know it had been decoded." He raises his eyebrows at Rodion, who shrugs.

"We wanted to be able to give you a full report, and we had to test some of the information. Arkdhem and Marta were essential to us figuring out there was anything worthwhile on it."

"It was his last gift to us." Suddenly, there's a knot in my throat. I swallow around it a few times. Stupid emotion, making me choke up.

There's a sheen to Dawn and Pareena's eyes. It makes me feel a little better.

"Are you saying this message came from the enemy?" Bogdan growls.

"Frllil wasn't the enemy," I blurt, ready to argue. I'm not the only one ready to defend Frllil's memory.

"Don't call him that!" Dawn slams the table. "He was our friend!" Her face screws up, and she looks like she's about to weep. The High Commander puts an arm around her.

"We understand. He is not the enemy," he says soothingly.

Bodgan opens his mouth, probably to argue. We all glare at him.

"Bogdan," Pareena murmurs, and lays a hand on her mate's arm and he concedes defeat.

"Very well. The Jabol Frllil who is not our enemy," he grumbles.

"If your concern is safety, I had the contents thoroughly scanned to be sure there was no weapon," Arkdhem says. "The message was simply information. Rodion can explain the security protocols."

"Yes, allow me to explain." Rodion launches into a bunch of technical jargon as if he's been waiting for his moment. The High Commander looks vaguely interested but he keeps glancing down at his mate. Dawn looks tired, poor thing, and I'm sure Rodion's droning voice isn't helping.

Pareena nods like she's listening but her eyes are starting to glaze over. So are mine.

"Perhaps we can save the full explanation for later," Arkdhem cuts into Rodion's rambling. "Let Marta tell you the important details."

I squeeze my mate's hand gratefully. The smile he showers on me is almost... sad. It makes me pause.

Lately, my mate has been quiet. At his end of our bond, there's a flicker of something like... loneliness? Even despair. I'm going to have to figure out what's going on there. But first, I'm excited to share this news.

"Marta?" Arkdhem prompts.

"Um, yes. The point is, Frllil left us a message. Rodion and his team worked on decrypting it."

"We weren't sure what we had found, though, until Arkdhem

brought Marta to us," Rodion continues, giving me a wide smile. Our lack of interest in the technical details doesn't seem to have fazed him at all. "To us, it was just a random map and coordinates."

"What map and coordinates?" Pareena asks, sitting up straight.

Rodion activates a display in the center of us, but it's not the same as before. He's been hard at work the past few hours, and he's apparently recalibrated it so he can show us the map in the light. The galaxy, as I saw it before, appears, and then there's a zooming feature that makes me feel a little motion sick before Earth blinks into view.

Dawn gasps, covering her belly with her hand. "Is that what I think it is?"

Pareena looks blank. Next to her, Bogdan is frowning, but as far as I can tell, he has resting dick face.

"It's Earth," I confirm. "And there are coordinates. That's what the map is. It gives us a way back. We can go home." I throw my hands up in the air, beaming. If I had confetti, I'd be tossing it.

Silence.

I glance around at the faces, but no one seems excited. What the fuck?

Then Dawn bursts into tears. Loudly, noisily.

"Give us a moment," Gavrill says, and scoops her up and exits the room.

Pareena doesn't seem surprised by the outburst. At all. "Let's take a break," she announces, and turns to her mate.

I'm already rising out of my chair. Arkdhem follows me to the corner of the room, where I punch the replicator buttons to order a cup of *cafezinho*—or a beverage as close to sweet black coffee as the replicator can make.

"That is not the response I was expecting," I grumble. "I thought they'd all be happy about it."

"Give them time," Arkdhem replies softly. He sounds so sad, I whirl around.

"Arkdhem, what is wrong? What aren't you telling me?"

"Nothing is wrong," he says stiffly. "I am happy that you can return to Earth."

A whisper of loneliness echoes in our bond. *Don't leave me.*

And it all becomes clear. He thinks I want to return to Earth alone.

"Oh, no." I take his hand. "You misunderstand. I don't want to leave you."

"No?"

"Of course not. Why would you think that? You're my mate." I take a deep breath. Emotions aren't my favorite thing, but I need to convince him. Show him that he matters to me. I could have died without him ever knowing how I felt about him, and I wasn't okay with that. "You're the other half of my heart. Anything we do, we do together."

19

———————

M*arta*

BY THE TIME Gavrill and Dawn return, I've made a bunch of cookies and tea for everyone and set it out. Rodion sits down and awkwardly takes a cup, holding it in his hands rather than trying to drink from it, like he's not quite sure what he's supposed to do with it.

Mentally, I put human mannerism and etiquette classes for the warriors on my to-do list.

"Sorry about that," Dawn says, cradling a cup of tea. She smiles a little weakly. "I'm just emotional."

"Understandable," Pareena says. "It's a lot to take in." She's sitting directly on Bogdan's lap, calmly dunking a cookie into her tea. "Especially after coming to terms with the thought of living with the Tsenturions for the rest of your life. The chance to go home is almost overwhelming."

"Sorry, guys," I say. "I should've broken it to you more gently. I thought it was good news."

"It is good news," Pareena says. "There are things I miss about Earth. It would be good to see my family and friends again. To let them know I didn't die."

"But what about our mates?" Dawn blurts. Gavrill covers her hand with his own.

"If you wish to go home, I will not stop you," he says.

She shakes her head, more tears in her eyes. "There's no way I'm leaving you. I made our choice long ago."

"*Meu deus*," I burst out. "What do you mean, go back without our Tsenturion mates? Why does everyone keep thinking that's what I meant? We can use the Tsenturion ships to get there. We can all go back—all of us. We can teach the Tsenturions how to date. They can help us save our planet, and the people on it. Better the lives of everyone."

And I can be the reporter who breaks the news, convinces everyone that the aliens aren't there to invade us, and that we should all get along. I have a feeling there will be quite a few alien romance readers who are completely on board with getting to date a six-and-a-half-foot tall gold aliens with tentacle pubes and giant alien penises. Tsenturions are going to go from no hope for their species to too many applicants.

"What about the temporal capabilities?" the High Commander asks, looking at Rodion.

"The temporal capabilities are fine," Rodion jumps in, nodding his head so vigorously that his teacup shakes, spilling some liquid over the sides. Quickly, he puts it down on the table in front of him. "It will take a few human years, but we can get there."

"We need to be careful," Pareena warns thoughtfully. "Humans aren't known for being tolerant of something new. Aliens—real aliens... well, not everyone will be welcoming. Some people can't even handle differences between them and other people, much less an entirely different species."

"Most people will be on board once we show them how the Tsenturion tech can eradicate disease and increase their technology," I argue. "Trust me, I know exactly how to spin this. That was—is—my job."

"It won't be easy." The High Commander looks thoughtful, turning his attention to me. "We will need a good liaison between the Tsenturions and the human media."

Pareena chuckles. "I would say that Marta is more than up to the job. Not to mention, she wants it. And she's right about being able to present the story in the right way. That's going to be incredibly important."

"And I can interview you as a source," I tell her. "Your credentials are pretty great. You can help explain all this to people in terms they can understand." I give up on playing cool and rub my hands together. "Am I wrong to be excited?"

"No, no," Dawn says, even as her tears are shining on her cheeks. "This is the scoop of a lifetime."

The table erupts in separate conversations. The High Commander questions Rodion, while Arkdhem and Bogdan listen and interject from time to time, while simultaneously listening in on Pareena and Dawn reminiscing about what they'd like to see when they get back. Pareena wants to see her family. Dawn wants to see her grandmother's house. Me? I want to see my editor. Yeah, I've got some issues.

Pareena gets up to make more cookies, and I follow her.

"What are your thoughts on continuing the Bride program?" I ask. "With a few modifications. Make it more like a dating app." I hold up my hands to do fake quotes. "'Swipe right for abduction.'"

"There would have to be several modifications," Pareena says.

"You could put it together," I suggest. "You've been doing enough studies on the Tsenturion males... they're going to need help adapting to human customs. Um, and we may need to get them some new manuals."

Pareena laughs, but her eyes have lit up from within at the thought of this new challenge. I know exactly how she feels.

"Yes... hm... there are quite a few ways I've thought of that would be a good way of helping warriors and Tributes understand each other. I wasn't sure how willing the warriors would be while they had Tributes coming to them one at a time, but on Earth, they'll be on our home turf... hm..." Pareena wanders back towards the table, already deep in thought, and I laugh, returning to Arkdhem's lap and listening to my friends talk about what they remember from Earth.

I don't have any family or friends for Arkdhem to meet, but there are some things I want to show him... and I definitely want to be there for his first experience of moqueca and other Brazilian dishes. There are some things the replicator has *not* been able to duplicate.

"WELL, THAT TURNED OUT GREAT." I'm still bubbly when we reach our quarters.

"I am glad." Arkdhem still sounds tired.

"Hey." I poke him. "You thought I was going to leave you? I would never leave you."

He sits on the bed and I climb onto his lap, straddling him. His large hands cup my backside. My skin hums with the contact—the nanotech waking up.

"I know that now," he says. His hands move up and down, stroking my butt and my back. I rock slightly, ready to be turned on, but not quite yet. I want to enjoy our closeness.

"What did Gavrill want to talk to you about?" The High Commander had pulled Arkdhem aside while Pareena and I were discussing alien dating apps.

"The Council met to make a decision, deciding that the trial was unnecessary. It seems I will be relieved of command permanently."

I stiffen. "What?"

Arkdhem continues as if he hasn't just dropped a bomb into the conversation. "I will have plenty of time to support your career." He smiles, though I can see he is conflicted about what he's saying. "I will be the Tsenturion half of the liaison between your people and mine. It is an important job."

"But you won't be a warrior anymore."

"No."

I reach through the bond, trying to gauge how he feels. Sadness. Resignation. But also a kind of determination.

"I'm sorry."

"I'm not," he says softly, stroking my hair back. "I would not change anything that has happened to me, because it brought me to you. This is how Tsenturion life was always supposed to be... the time to be a warrior ends, and the time to have a family begins."

Awww.

"Well, I guess we'll have more time to be together then." I rock forward and rub a little against his cock. A bolt of heat shoots through me, reverberating between us as passion floods the bond. "And make plans for when we get to Earth. Humans aren't exactly known for their calmness in the face of something new. We will have to craft an excellent media campaign to present to world leaders and the news outlets."

"You are the perfect human for the job," he says. "I have the utmost faith in you, my heart."

I hum, rocking a bit faster. Arkdhem's armor has melted away, and his *seela* have somehow ripped apart my garments so they can suction onto my sex. One of them fastens on my clit and pulls in a strong, sucking motion. I moan, melting towards him. Stars burst behind my eyes as my clit is stimulated relentlessly, leaving me shuddering atop him.

"Oh, Arkdhem, that is good," I gasp.

"Call me Master," he orders, and when I do, he lifts me a little and reseats me onto his cock, stroking into me with a body-shuddering thrust. The Bride Trainer is at work, sliding up my stomach to pinch my nipples, and swelling to fill my ass. Ecstasy floods the bond between us. Mine. His.

The connection is so intense, I'm crying. And laughing. I am caught between joy and despair, craving the intimacy between us. Needing it to push back the darkness inside of me.

The *seela* suction onto my legs and pop off as Arkdhem lifts me off his cock, helping him reposition me on his lap.

"No, don't stop. I'm okay." I gulp.

"Do not lie to me." He catches my chin. "Marta. Tell me what you need. Anything, and I will do it."

I swallow.

"I still feel guilty about Frllil. And Medik. I feel guilty that I'm excited about returning to Earth when they're gone… that I get to do things I always wanted to do while they don't." It's survivor's guilt and I know it, but putting a name to it doesn't make the emotions any easier.

"If it had been you, would you want them to stop their lives and doing what they wanted?"

I wrinkle my nose at him. "No, of course not. And I know they wouldn't expect it of me… I just keep feeling like there was something more I should have done."

Arkdhem's eyebrows rise. "More? More than surviving what should have killed you? Not just now, but multiple times?"

"I didn't survive on my own, though, only because Frllil saved me. Both times. I was useless," I say quietly. I never thought of myself as the damsel in distress, but that's what I'd been. I'd been at the mercy of the universe, and it had chosen to save me, for some reason, but things could have been so different. I'd had no agency, no say, and if it wasn't for Frllil, I wouldn't be here right now.

"You were not useless." Arkdhem sighs in exasperation, shaking his head. "At all times in battle, I must rely on my warrior companions to watch my back. I have been saved by those around me more times than I can count, and I have saved them as well. Does that mean that we are all useless?"

"No, of course not, but that's different. You're relying on each other. No one was relying on me."

"No?" He cocks his head at me, hands sliding up and down my sides. It's not quite an erotic touch, but it's not exactly soothing either.

"Frllil was relying on you to pass on his message, both the verbal one and the disk. Without you, his plan would have failed. The Jabol responsible for Tsentur's destruction would have escaped. We might have wreaked our revenge on perfectly innocent Jabol."

"All I did was blurt out a message that got him killed because I was too freaked out to think through what I was saying," I grumble. And then I squeak because suddenly I'm being flipped over. No longer straddling Arkdhem's lap, I find myself over it, butt up in the air, and his big, alien hand caressing my buttocks instead of my side.

Uh oh.

~

Arkdhem

Now that I understand what is plaguing my Tribute, I know what I must do. There is a part of me that hesitates as well, because I had worried about punishing her too harshly before, and that worry led to further events... but I know Medik would happily have given his life to save hers. He would not regret that he ended up on the Jabol ship, and that his death was what spurred Frllil to truly see his superiors for what they were. In some ways, it might have even been a relief to finally be able to lay down his duty and join his family. He had served far beyond what he was supposed to and I would not tarnish either those long years or his final sacrifice by seeing them for anything less than what they were.

He would not want Marta wracked with guilt, or me.

He would want us to have the long years of happiness that Tsenturions used to have.

And I am now the first Tsenturion to retire to civilian life in tsencycles. I will not waste that, and we will live every day in Medik and Frllil's honor, with gratitude for the sacrifices they made for our futures.

"You conveyed the message Frllil asked you to. You did exactly what you were supposed to do."

There's a moment of silence, and I know she doesn't agree with me.

Smack!

My hand tingles where I swatted her.

"Ouch! I didn't say anything!"

"That's right, you didn't. Did you or did you not do what Frllil asked of you?"

"I did." She sighs. Wriggles. "I should have done more, though."

"Says who? Other than you? You were in hostile territory, naked, and weaponless, not to mention disoriented. Medik was unable to defend himself. He may have no longer been a warrior, but he had been, once. He was armored. What do you think you could have done that he couldn't?"

This time, as she thinks over what I've said, I spank her again—much more lightly than before, but still hard enough to sting, and make her wiggle.

"Okay, okay! You have a point!" The words come grudgingly.

"Good girl." Despite everything, I can feel the way she softens against me at the accolade. She is a good girl. "But I am still going to turn your bottom red, and you can think back to this moment every time you start blaming yourself for situations outside of your control. The only person who thinks you should have been able to do more is you, and it is unacceptable that you don't see how much you did do under the circumstances."

20

M *arta*

What did I do?

And would I have expected Dawn or Pareena to have done the same in my position?

Medik hadn't been able to defend himself. Do I really think I could have saved him when he, a full Tsenturion warrior in battle armor, hadn't been able to?

Talk about hubris.

And Frllil... I could never have done what he did. I didn't know how to use Jabol tech in the same way he did. I'm not even sure I had the right parts to do so. I could have never taken down their shields and exposed them to the Tsenturions' scanners. Even if I had, the Tsenturions would have never fired on the Jabol without a reason to do so.

I had given them that reason. They had listened to me because I was a Tribute.

Every time Arkdhem's hand comes down on my bottom, the message is reinforced.

I did everything I could, and I did what I was needed to do.

Smack!

Wriggling, I squirm on Arkdhem's lap, whimpering as he continues to land hard swats on my cheeks. I can feel the heat growing in my bottom, which clenches around the nanotech plug filling me, increasing my erotic discomfort.

And my pussy is so very, very wet—a fact Arkdhem discovers when he reaches around to check. His fingers stroke my sensitive folds, and he chuckles over my head. Pleasure flows through me, turning even my burning bottom into a delicious inferno. I hold my breath, hoping he'll continue to fondle me.

No such luck. He returns to spanking me, but the pain/pleasure switches in my brain have gotten mixed up again. Every stern swat sends heat blooming through my core. My clit pulses. Instead of squirming away, I'm lifting my bottom to meet his swats.

"Have you learned your lesson?"

"Yes, Master," I murmur. My voice comes from far away. I'm floating a little. But then the plug in my bottom starts to grow... and vibrate.

"I think you are enjoying this too much." The plug starts to push in and out of my ass—Arkdhem must be using it to fuck me. "Perhaps I should find a new way to punish you."

At this moment, with my bottom and core a mass of sensation ready to boil over, more punishment sounds *great.*

"Yes, please, Master," I moan. Then I'm lifted and laid back on the bed, my hair spilling around my face. I hiss and try to plant my heels in the mattress, pushing my hips up to keep my poor tortured bottom from touching the blanket.

"Spread your legs." Arkdhem swats the inside of my thighs lightly, and rearranges me with my knees bent and thighs stretched wide. He looms over me, naked and gorgeous. My pussy pulses, needing to be filled—jealous of the thick, hard length in my ass.

Arkdhem's cock protrudes between his legs, his *seela* stretching as if desperate to latch on to me. This delay is as uncomfortable for him as it is for me.

"Keep your legs apart," he orders. "Bound by my will."

I stretch my arms over my head, offering myself up to him. Complete surrender. He pauses, taking in my naked display. My chest is taut, my legs quivering from the strain of spreading my knees wide. My pussy is open to him.

His eyes hood, and then he murmurs my reward. "You are perfect for me."

His large hands come to rest on my inner thighs, spreading them a little further. Then... "Hold still." And he slaps my pussy.

My body jolts, my thighs jerk, but I keep them spread apart. A small smile touches Arkdhem's lips.

Sadist!

"Good girl," he croons. And he smacks my pussy again. This time, the slap barely registers. Heat detonates between my legs and rushes up my front. My lip quivers.

"Master!" I'm teetering on the edge...

And he knows it. "Come." He pats my pussy over and over, light strikes that grow in intensity until the final, hard *Pop!* Pleasure bursts from my clit.

I convulse, sparks flying through my body, sizzling up from the backs of my legs and burning through my torso. My mouth falls open as I cry out.

Arkdhem's weight comes onto me. He pins my wrists and settles his hips on mine, grounding me even as he strokes inside my body. I convulse again. His cock fills me, pushing against the plug that's heated and *vibrating* in my back channel. I'm completely stuffed. My mouth hangs open as if I can gulp extra air, make extra space in my body. But there's no room in my body but for him.

A storm of my cries fill my own ears as Arkdhem pounds me into the bed.

The *seela* suction onto my punished pussy lips. One finds my clit and sucks so hard, I soar to another planet. Planet Pleasure.

When I return to consciousness, Arkdhem is still inside me, but he's stilled. His heavy body rests on mine in delicious weight. His lips brush my face. "Marta. My beautiful one. My mate."

Slowly, I raise my chin and meet his kiss, sipping on his lips. The Bride Trainer has shrunk in my bottom, lessening the feeling of fullness. Still inside me, Arkdhem rolls so I'm draped on top of him, a boneless blanket. Flutters fill my body as I readjust to his still hard cock spearing my pussy. Soon, he'll be up for Round Two, but in the meantime, he's giving me a reprieve. And he's adorable, gazing up at me like I'm the sun he orbits. My cinnamon roll. My secret sadist.

"Thank you for spanking it better," I whisper.

"Anytime." His palm squeezes my heated rear, massaging roughly. I whimper and wriggle closer. It hurts so good. "Kiss me, my heart."

I slant my head and obey, only to break away and breathe against his lips, "I love you."

"And I you," he murmurs. "No matter what the future brings, I will gladly face it. As long as I'm with you."

EPILOGUE

M*arta*

Several lightyears and a space/time continuum later...

I did get the scoop of a lifetime. The news in every country and every language was that aliens are real, and we can meet with them. They are here to help.

Dawn and Pareena both gave birth to the first Tsenturion/human babies on the trip here. Stella and Aadhya—two little girl warriors who already know how to fully form their Tsenturion armor. Gavrill and Bodgan are torn between pride and worry, both hovering, and egging their little warriors on.

I've been busy writing articles and introducing the Tsenturions to all the world leaders. The alien technology and the medical knowledge that Medik left behind has cured most all human diseases, and went a long way to building goodwill between our species.

Arkdhem was relieved of his Tsenturion officer duty permanently, but serves as my bodyguard. We're both human/alien media liaisons. Ambassadors of peace.

And we're expecting our first little one in six months.

The entire Tsenturion race fleet has been able to enter into a human/Tsenturion dating program. There are many men and women who have always dreamed of being mated to an alien, and this is their chance.

The Vgotha also decided to travel to Earth with us, and several of their warriors have entered the dating program. Some of them are fearsome, with wings and tails—but apparently, there are plenty of humans who include 'sexy wings' and 'naughty tail' on their list of dating preferences.

Tor was the first of his people to visit Earth. He fell in love with a second grade school teacher in Jamaica, and they've settled together quite nicely after a few false starts. They live on his ship for half the year, and spend the other half in a Vgotha-sized house near her mother. Tor's favorite food is now curried goat pasties.

Also, the Jabol have elected new leadership. Better leadership. Best of all, they sent a small gift to us. Apparently, before the explosion, Frllil was able to upload his consciousness to a storage facility on a far off moon. The Jabol found it, and sent it to us. Rodion figured out how to download Frllil's consciousness into a robot designed to Frllil's own specifications. He looks exactly like Chris Hemsworth. He hopes to soon enter the Tsenturion Brides program to find his own mate.

So, we all have our happy endings. And with Tsenturion Brides program, everyone else can have theirs too.

We invite you now to enter the Tsenturion Brides program.

Based on Medik and Frllil's ingenious system, we've created a series of books for all those who want to have a Tsenturion master. Your responses to this text have been recorded.

Rest assured that all potential Tsenturions Masters have thoroughly read the interspecies relationship manuals, including [Alien Captive], [Alien Tribute] and [Alien Abduction]. They are well practiced in the art of bride training. 😈

Our system has a 100% efficacy rate. Satisfaction guaranteed.

Click here to be added to the waiting list to be matched with an alien mate: https://www.subscribepage.com/tsenturionbridesprogram

EXCERPT: BRUTAL MATE

Khan

Spaceports always have a potent stench—the result of so many species crammed into a small space. I hold my breath against the stale reek of recycled air as I navigate the dark corridors on my way from my ship to the dark cantina. Only after I've settled at a table do I adjust my hood and take a careful inhale. The jumble of scents isn't always unpleasant. There are just so many smells all at once. No wonder my fellow Alphas prefer our home planet to space travel.

Today, the air is flavored with a thick musk from the Ogsul, the reptilian species running the auction. There are a million of them slinking around this spaceport. There's a hint of sulfur from a Buruwr, a giant, gelatinous creature sitting in its own trail of slime right in front of the auction stage. But underneath the overwhelming cacophony of smells, there's a delicate scent. Fragrant. Floral. Slightly musky.

The cantina is full of alien creatures, but no sign of what could produce such an amazing aroma. The perfume is growing stronger, like someone filled the room with a bouquet of blooms. But it's not a flower; it's a female. There are rumors of a special female to be found on the spaceport. That's why I'm here.

The stool creaks under me as I shift my weight. A few creatures glance my way and snap their gazes from mine. No one wants to catch the attention of an Ulfarri Alpha.

I rap the dinky table and, after a minute, a reluctant Ogsul trudges across the room with a drink for me.

"Brutal One." The Ogsul bows and leaves the smoking vat of my preferred fermented drink on the table beside me. I sniff but don't touch the oily liquid.

"Wait," I growl. A tremble runs up from his scaled tail to his hairy shoulders, but the Ogsul stops. "Tell me about the auction."

A pause. I don't have to negotiate or threaten. As an Alpha, my reputation precedes me. They call us the Brutal Ones for a reason.

"Sorry," the Ogsul says. "I get my chief." And he scurries away.

I settle back on the stool. The honey scent is growing heavier, sweeter. My canines ache, and my own rich scent is growing stronger in response.

Maybe the rumors are true. Maybe my travels across the galaxies have finally met with success. Maybe the time has come for me to find what I've been searching for all my life, what any Alpha would kill for: an Omega.

"Brutal One." Another Ogsul, this one taller with bulging eyes, appears at my table. He doesn't tremble but stands rigid, several lengths away. I beckon, and he takes a small step closer.

Close enough. I lean forward, keeping my face in shadow and my voice low. "Do you have the female?"

The thick black hair on his arms rises. "We have many females. For auction." His stumpy arm motions to the stage.

"But the…" If I say the word *Omega*, it's as good as shouting. "I heard you have something I want," I murmur.

Ahead and to my right, the giant, slug-like Buruwr quivers, more bitter-smelling goo leaking from it onto the floor. Creatures across the universe will pay to plant their seed in the Omega's fragrant, sacred womb. If the Buruwr wins the bid, it will take what is mine.

It will not win. I slide my hand down to stroke the hidden curve of my scimitar.

"There are tales that you have found what I am seeking. I am here, and I am willing to pay."

The creature's throat vibrates, a bitter scent pouring off his shaggy and scaly hide. But when I set a bag of coins on the table, his eyes bulge bigger.

"Yes," the Ogsul says, bobbing his head. "An Omega."

"You have one?" I forget myself and growl. The Ogsul leaps backwards a length faster than such a bulky creature should move. I curl my fist around my scimitar handle. "Where is the Omega? Tell me, now." I've searched long and far for a female to adequately replace the Omegas of my kind. So far, no luck.

"We prepare her. Auction."

"Is she Ulfarri?"

"No, Brutal One."

Damn. Probably some cow-titted creature. But a womb is a womb. And I want heirs.

"We have serum," he squeaks. "There is a creature we found that can take the Omega serum."

Interesting. I must learn more about this serum. But first... "Describe this creature."

"It called *Hoo-man*." The Ogsul pulls out a holopad, and shows me a shadowy image. Not much to be seen but a small, frightened face surrounded by a mass of golden hair, peering out between the bars of a cage. Pale skin peeks out between shredded clothing.

"Frail," I sneer. "That will not satisfy me." I don't know this for sure. I won't know until I'm in a room with her. And if she is an Omega...

"It sentient," the Ogsul tells me. He takes a step forward, apparently overcoming his fear in his eagerness to make a sale. "Pretty. It won't disappoint."

"Fine." I feign boredom. "Show me."

The Ogsul's throat works up and down before he answers. "Auction soon."

I growl again, and the low murmur in the cantina is sucked away. "I do not wish to attend an auction," I say into the silence.

"Many creatures here to see the Hoo-man."

Hoo-man. I curl my tongue around the foreign word. This is another dead end. "Very well." I wave a hand, and the Ogsul bows and keeps bowing as he backs away. Like I've granted him a favor. Which I have. Maybe I won't kill anyone today.

My throat vibrates with a low growl. My hand tightens on the handle of my blade. I pride myself on my control, but there's one situation where even an Alpha struggles to keep control: the rut. When we're in heat, when we scent a sweet little Omega in the vicinity, even the most powerful Alphas are mindless.

And I'm as powerful as they come. I've fucked females of every size, shape, and species, and enjoyed most, but there's one type which has eluded me until now.

The sacred Omega.

My fated mate. The one female I was born to fuck.

Could this Hoo-man really be an Omega?

I lick my lips. The perfumed scent is thicker now. Still delicate and sweet, but growing in intensity. Is this the Hoo-man? My cock is awake, throbbing in my breeches.

The cantina is near packed now. Creatures stand between the tables, facing the stage. They've come to gawk over the pretty slaves of all different species, fitted with translation chips which will allow them to understand and speak any of the known languages, regardless of their own origin.

The Ogsul are a strange lot, but they do hold a good auction. I heard rumors they had a serum that could produce Omegas, but only now has that been verified. The last of the Omegas disappeared on Ulfaria a generation ago. If I can find one... I can breed her.

The Hoo-man was a pale, frail looking thing in the picture, but if she produces such perfume, I will buy her. And if anyone tries to bid higher, I will show them why my species, the Ulfarri, are called the Brutal Ones.

Perhaps this night will be more promising than I thought.

Getting to my feet, I take to the shadows, leaning back against the wall, crossing my arms. I'm tall enough to see easily over the heads of the other assembled males in the room. A wide variety of species have come to purchase a female, judging by the stinking males crowding this cantina. The small, cruel Rheeza, with their horned skulls and pointed noses. The docile, almost painfully shy Alags, with their four arms and purple skin. In the corner hunches a rare Haggat. So pale as to almost be translucent, his blazing third eye flicks back and forth over the assembled crowd of males, all of whom are apparently desperate for an Omega female.

They're all weaklings compared to me. Compared to the Alpha. I already pity the females they'll purchase. The one I choose—should I find the Hoo-man worthy—should be grateful she's escaped a much worse fate.

There's a screech, then a crackle, and then one of the Ogsul plods onto the stage. He's holding a microphone and looking enormously pleased with himself.

"Gentlemen, thank you for traveling such long way," he begins in his thick, guttural language. He seems to have a much broader vocabulary than most of the Ogsul I've met before. "As always, we have a fine array of females for you to choose from, so please be generous in your bids." He hesitates, then hums and leans forward. "I'm especially pleased to be able to tell you that we have one of the rarest kinds of females on offer for you tonight." He pauses for effect again before continuing. "An Omega."

There's a hum of excitement traveling around the room, and I know that every other male is thinking the same thing I am:

That Omega will be mine.

The noxious stench in the room thickens as the dozens of males lean forward, eager to get a glimpse of the first female slave for sale. I duck my head further in my hood to gain a little reprieve from the blend of sweat and testosterone. No trace of the sweet floral scent from earlier, the perfect honey scent like light on my tongue. Curse my sensitive sense of smell. I should have brought a breathing mask. Thank Ulf I'm not in rut, else I'd be gagging by now.

"First female on offer is number 327, a shy little Tyreen!"

There's a deep rumble of lowered voices as the obviously petrified slave is shoved unceremoniously onstage. She has thick black hair falling in waves down to her knees, her dress is torn, and all six of her nipples are clearly visible through the sheer fabric. I can almost sense her trembling from my position at the back of the room. Leaning forward, I inhale deeply, concentrating in order to separate her scent from the other smells in the room. There's definitely an underlying trace of sweetness, but it doesn't stir me. I lean back and fold my arms once more.

A female with six breasts and pale lilac skin will always garner attention from some males, and there are a flurry of bids being roared from one end of the room to the other. At length, the Tyreen is sold to a great beast of a Dajok, who has difficulty hiding his smug grin as he strides toward the stage to claim his new slave.

One after another, females of all kinds are led onto the wooden platform, all of them in various states of undress. Some look petrified, others look mutinous. But they're all sold, regardless. There is no escape. That is the way of the universe.

I fondle the handle of my scimitar. It's been ages, and there's still no sign of the promised Hoo-man. The stench of so many species crammed into a small space is thick enough to cut. I still have plenty of competition. Only the wealthiest and most powerful would stand a chance at winning her, so the males of lesser species are contenting themselves with the other goods on offer. Most of them have already collected their new purchases and left, so I have a clear overview of the males I must beat in order to make the rare jewel mine.

"And now, saving the best for last, I'm proud to present the promised Omega! A Hoo-man!" the Ogsul host announces.

As the evening's highlight is propelled onstage, the remaining males lean forward as one, myself included.

So, this is a Hoo-man. She's smaller than I anticipated—a lot smaller. Pale pink skin, two arms, two legs, two breasts. But the cloud of tousled hair around her head is a glittering gold, her eyes are huge and innocent and, when her rich, honeyed perfume hits my nostrils, I bite back a roar as the rut grips me with no warning; no preamble.

Suddenly, my cock is rock solid and pounding, my skin prickles, and my pulse is thudding in my ears.

I'm no longer able to form a coherent thought. My entire being screams just one thing:

She will be mine.

READ BRUTAL MATE NOW!

Check out all Lee's sci fi Omegaverse romance (co-written with Tabitha Black)

Brutal Mate
Brutal Claim
Brutal Capture
Brutal Beast
Brutal Demon

ALSO BY LEE SAVINO

Want more sci fi romance? Check out the Planet of Kings series written with Tabitha Black. Start with Brutal Mate.

Sci fi romance

Planet of Kings with Tabitha Black
Brutal Mate
Brutal Claim
Brutal Capture
Brutal Beast
Brutal Demon

Tsenturion Warriors with Golden Angel
Alien Captive
Alien Tribute
Alien Abduction

Dragons in Exile with Lili Zander
Draekon Mate
Draekon Fire
Draekon Heart
Draekon Abduction
Draekon Destiny
Daughter of Draekons
Draekon Fever
Draekon Rogue

Draekon Holiday

Draekon Rebel Force with Lili Zander
Draekon Warrior
Draekon Conqueror
Draekon Pirate
Draekon Warlord
Draekon Guardian

~

Dark Mafia Romance

Mafia Brides
Revenge is Sweet
Vengeance is Mine

A Dark Mafia Romance trilogy with Stasia Black
Innocence
Awakening
Queen of the Underworld

Beauty and the Rose trilogy with Stasia Black
Beauty's Beast
Beauty & the Thorns
Beauty & the Rose

~

Contemporary Romance

Royally Bad
Royally Fake Fiancé

Beauty & The Lumberjacks

Her Marine Daddy
Her Dueling Daddies

Paranormal romance

Berserker Saga
Sold to the Berserkers
Mated to the Berserkers
Bred by the Berserkers (FREE novella only available at
www.leesavino.com)
Taken by the Berserkers
Given to the Berserkers
Claimed by the Berserkers
Rescued by the Berserker
Captured by the Berserkers
Kidnapped by the Berserkers
Bonded to the Berserkers
Berserker Babies
Night of the Berserkers
Owned by the Berserkers
Tamed by the Berserkers
Mastered by the Berserkers
Surrendered to the Berserkers

Berserker Warriors
Aegir
Siebold with Ines Johnson

Bad Boy Alphas with Renee Rose
Alpha's Temptation
Alpha's Danger
Alpha's Prize
Alpha's Challenge

Alpha's Obsession
Alpha's Desire
Alpha's War
Alpha's Mission
Alpha's Bane
Alpha's Secret
Alpha's Prey
Alpha's Sun

Shifter Ops with Renee Rose
Alpha's Moon
Alpha's Vow
Alpha's Revenge
Alpha's Fire
Alpha's Rescue
Alpha's Command

Midnight Doms with Renee Rose
Alpha's Blood
His Captive Mortal
The Virgin and the Vampire
(All Souls' Night anthology exclusive)

Cowboy Romance

Wild Whip Ranch with Tristan River
Cowboy's Babygirl
Taming His Wild Girl

ABOUT LEE SAVINO

Lee Savino is a USA today bestselling author of smexy romance. Smexy, as in "smart and sexy." Find her in the Goddess Group on facebook and download a free book at www.leesavino.com!

Find her at:
www.leesavino.com

EXCERPT: MATED ON HADES

"Welcome to your new home for the next four twenty-cycles," he said, stepping aside so she could enter the cabin behind him, his tone dryly sarcastic. "As you can see, you would have been better off with my parents."

Rather than telling him that the room was about the size of her entire living space back on Earth—and unlike her home there, this room wasn't crammed with equipment—Jules just looked around as she walked past him. Sparsely furnished, the massive bed on the far wall dominated the whole area. It was even bigger than the bed in her room at Tobik and Sirilla's, and she'd thought *that* was huge.

Turning around, she enjoyed the disgruntled look on Tarrik's face as he set her bag down next to the open closet door. Since his clothing seemed to consist mostly of pants and a kind of tunic vest that she'd seen on a lot of winged Hadesians, there was plenty of space for her meager belongings.

"This looks great," she said. "As long as you keep to your side of the bed."

Now his expression was almost infuriated. "Of course I will. I'm not the one who can't keep her hands to herself."

"Excuse me?" Jules' hands slammed onto her hips as she glared back at him. "Since when have I not kept my hands to myself?"

"Uh, that would be last night when you kissed me."

She gaped. "You kissed me!"

"I sure as hell did not," he snapped back. "I'm not even attracted to you."

"Is that why your cock was digging a hole in my stomach last night when *you kissed me*?"

"Look, just stay on whichever side of the bed you pick, keep your hands to yourself, and this trip will be over before you know it."

Jules was still sputtering and trying to find a good retort as he swept out of the room. *Jerk!* She couldn't believe she'd let him have the last word.

"Stupid butt monkey," she muttered, flopping back onto the bed just to see how it felt. It was ridiculously comfortable of course. Which only made her more irritated with him for some reason, even though he had nothing to do with it.

He'd definitely kissed her first.

At the very least, they'd kissed each other.

Her lips pursed as a wicked idea occurred to her. It would be playing with fire a little bit... but on the other hand, he definitely deserved it. And it would be even more amusing than keeping his ship grounded until her say so.

Just as that thought flickered through her mind, she felt the reverberations of the ship as it began to blast off. Excitement surged. She, Jules, who had never even thought she would see planet other than Earth, was now on her second spaceship this week and off to see a whole *bunch* of planets.

While part of her couldn't help but wonder what was happening back on Earth, if anyone was helping those in need, another part of her was thrilled to be on an adventure. New places, new beings, new things to see and do... If this was how traveling made Tarrik feel, no wonder he didn't want to give it up.

As soon as she thought it, she scowled. She didn't want to feel sympathy for him dammit.

Pushing any thoughts of the alien male aside, Jules made herself get up from the bed and start unpacking. The sooner she was done, the sooner she could explore the ship.

THE SYSTEMS WERE RUNNING PERFECTLY, the entire crew was happy, and Tarrik was feeling a lot better than he'd expected. The only thing that would make this trip better was if Juliette wasn't on board.

Not that she was in the way. No, she was entirely helpful, going out of her way to make herself useful.

Tarrik told himself he wasn't jealous over the way she and Mrik had obviously bonded. They definitely weren't behaving as though they were sexually attracted to each other—Tarrik knew that Mrik would never move on Tarrik's female regardless—but he still got a gnawing feeling in his stomach when he saw them laughing together. It might be more envy than jealousy though... she definitely didn't smile at him that way or laugh with him...

Not that he'd given her any reason to.

Because I don't want to, he reminded himself for the umpteenth time. The problem was that saying it wasn't making it true.

She was beautiful when she smiled. Engaging when she laughed. The rest of the crew definitely liked her, she'd already made fast friends with his maintenance engineers, Lessys and Sasslys, who were both Vloss and mated to each other. When they asked if Juliette had ever seen anything like them before, she said they looked like miniature Godzillas, without the back plates. The whole crew found this hysterical when Myrik looked up what she was speaking of.

So he wasn't in the best mood by bedtime.

His mood got a hell of a lot worse when he laid down and Juliette announced she was going to take a shower.

"Great," he said. And then nearly choked when she started undressing right in the middle of the bedroom. She pulled her shirt over her head, revealing tanned skin, soft mounds of her breasts filling out her feminine support, a gently rounded stomach that he suddenly ached to draw his tongue over... When she began tugging down her pants, he finally managed to find his voice again even if it did sound like he was being strangled when he spoke. "What the gark are you doing?"

Juliette glanced at him and he bit back a groan as her pants slid to the ground, revealing muscled legs and tight-fitting panties. The white underwear wasn't the sexiest he'd ever seen, it was more utilitarian than anything else, and yet he found he couldn't look away. The temperature in the room seemed to have risen by a few degrees and his tail was lashing back and forth furiously as his cock started to swell.

"I'm taking a shower," she said, blinking at him like he'd said something incomprehensible.

"The shower is in there." Pointing to the facilities, he shifted slightly to hopefully cover up his growing erection.

"Why do you care?" she asked, pulling off her support garment. Tarrik almost whimpered as her rounded, full breasts were revealed, perfectly sized to fit in his palm, with tightly ruched brown nipples just begging for attention. His erection swelled to fullness and his tail had taken on a mind of its own—any attempt to control it was useless. "You're not attracted to me, remember?"

Turning, she bent at the waist to pull her undergarments down, giving him a glorious view of her ass before she sauntered into the bathroom.

Closing his eyes didn't help in the least. The image of her naked body was burned into his retinas. Gark it, he didn't even *want* to forget.

When he heard the water turn on, he did groan, because now all he could think about was the hot water sluicing over her body, caressing her skin the way he wanted to.

Garking...

Laying back in the bed, Tarrik jerked off the tunic he was going to sleep in out of respect for her. Immediately he fisted his hand around his shaft and groaned as he began to pump, closing his eyes and picturing her rounded bottom and the little smirk on her lips... the way the water would slide over her breasts and stomach and down between her legs... he hadn't gotten nearly as close a look of *that* as he'd wanted to.

He'd seen images of nude human females though, and his feverish brain extrapolated for him.

Wet flesh, ripe and ready for him.

He pumped his cock harder, faster as he imagined her bent over for him, the way she had taken off her underwear, his hand slapping against her ass as he pounded into her from behind, his tail twining around her breasts...

He wanted her *bad.*

Pleasure surged and his *jimen* spurted, sticky and hot onto his stomach, leaving him only slightly less wound up.

WAS HE... WAS HE MASTURBATING? JULES' paused as she washed her hair, her body flushing as she heard another low masculine groan, just barely audible to her. Yeah, so much for not being attracted to her.

Of course, she was very much in the same boat. Just stripping down in front of him had given her a little thrill. She'd never known she had a little bit of exhibitionist in her, but she'd definitely gotten turned on feeling his eyes sliding over her naked skin with every article of clothing she'd peeled off. It had made her feel freaking sexy.

Knowing he was out there jerking off after the little show she'd put on...

Well that just made her feel even sexier.

It didn't help that she hadn't gotten laid in... geez, it had been months since her last encounter with the male kind. So she also had a lot of pent-up sexual energy to work off.

Her hands moved over her body, slick and soapy, touching her hard nipples and massaging her breasts before moving down her stomach. Leaning back against the cool wall, she kept one hand on her breast while the other slipped between her pussy lips. Biting her lip to keep her own moans quiet, she closed her eyes and pictured him coming into the bathroom, watching her touch herself...

Then he wouldn't be able to stay back. He'd step in, crowding her in the shower, his body hot and hard against hers as he lifted her up, and she'd wrap her legs around his waist as she slid down his body and right onto his hard cock.

Shuddering, Jules managed to keep her noises to heavy breathing as she rubbed out a hard, fast orgasm that took the edge off but didn't completely satisfy her. She didn't want to take too long in the shower though; she definitely didn't want him to think she was in here getting off to him... the same way she was pretty sure he was getting off to her.

Stepping out of the shower, Jules quickly dried off and went into the main cabin. The lights were already dim and Tarrik was on his side of the bed, the sheets pulled up to his waist and he'd built a wall of cushions down the center of the bed. His muscled chest and arms were clearly visible—he'd taken off his tunic and it lay in a crumpled heap on the floor. Had he been wearing anything else? Or was he naked under the sheet?

Don't think about that!

In the dark, her body thrumming with sexual frustration, Jules was no closer to sleep than she had been when the lights had been turned on. Despite the wall of cushions between them, she was far, far too aware of the insanely sexy alien on the bed with her, less than a foot of distance separating them. How much body heat did a Hadesian emanate? Because she swore she could feel him.

Then she really did feel something, touching her ankle between the sheets, and she shrieked, kicking.

"Sorry, sorry!" Tarrik's deep voice actually sounded sincere. "That was my tail, sorry."

Jules' heart pounded so hard it felt like it was going to go right out of her chest as her fear of the unknown settled.

"Well get your tail under control," she hissed at him, pulling her legs up slightly, closer to her body and telling herself that she definitely was not going to think about the possibilities of a tail that had a mind of its own.

"It's not exactly easy," he hissed back. "I can *smell* your arousal. So don't bother lying and telling me that you aren't."

Heat flushed her cheeks and she was very glad the room was dark enough that he wouldn't be able to see her blush. "That's just a physical response—and you were the one who started jerking off while I was in the shower!"

"You stripped down in front of me!"

"*You* said you weren't attracted to me!"

"I lied, alright?!" There was a strange ominous red glow in the darkness and suddenly cushions went flying. Tarrik loomed over her, wings spread slightly in his agitation. Holy fracking radiation. He freaking glowed in the dark. "I'm attracted to you, okay? That doesn't mean I want to mate you."

"I don't want to mate you either, you overgrown ignoramus."

"But you want to *fuck* me, right?" From the way he said 'fuck', she could tell he'd looked up the human word at some point but that it wasn't terminology he was used to. The glow of his skin brightened a little more, illuminating her body as he taunted her, his own sexual frustration clear on his face. It was eerie and sexy all at the same time and this time when his tail curled around her ankle, the heat of his flesh warming her skin, she didn't jump or kick.

"Oh shut up and do something useful with your mouth," she snarled back, reaching up to grab his face and pull his lips down to meet hers.

～

Mated on Hades

THE CELESTIAL MATES agency always knows what - or who - you need.

. . .

TARRIK WOULD DO anything to avoid breaking his mother's heart, so he begrudgingly signs up for Celestial Mates and agrees to come home and settle down once the agency finds his match. There's just one catch: he's not ready to give up his free and easy life traveling the galaxy. And he's doing exactly as his mother asked, so what will it hurt if he makes himself as unappealing as possible on his mate application?

JULIETTE IS a woman on the run. Her attitude, and more importantly her hacking skills, have pissed off all the wrong people. Now the target of a contract hit, she's decided the solution to her problems is to leave the planet as fast as she can. The Celestial Mates program is exactly what she needs. By the time her "mate" realizes she's impossible to live with, hopefully it will be safe for her to return to earth. She wasn't counting on a seriously hot alien who looked like the devil and could do the most sinful things with his tail...

THE SPARKS FLY at first meeting when their chemistry ignites. But they can barely stand to be in the same room with each other.

THEY SHOULDN'T WORK AT ALL.

BUT CELESTIAL MATES **always knows best.**

ALSO BY GOLDEN ANGEL

Free stories on her website

Stronghold Doms and Venus Rising (Contemporary Bdsm)

Bridal Discipline and the Domestic Discipline Quartet (Victorian Domestic Discipline- this is Lee Savino's favorite!!!!! :)

Big Bad Bunnies (paranormal romance)

Dark erotic romance under the pen name Sinistre Ange

Standalone novels - including a sci fi romance involving an alien who has a naughty tail...

ABOUT GOLDEN ANGEL

Angel is an international best-selling BDSM and interracial romance author and self-described bibliophile with a "kinky" bent who loves to write stories for the characters in her head. If she didn't get them out, she's pretty sure she'd go just a little crazy.

She is happily married, old enough to know better but still too young to care, and a big fan of happily-ever-afters, strong heroes and heroines, and sizzling chemistry.

She believes the world is a better place when there's a little magic in it.

Sign up for the Angel Legion newsletter here - https://mailchi.mp/9eb82a414844/angelnewsletter - and grab several FREE sexy stories immediately in a welcome message!

Read on for an excerpt from her alien romance, Mated on Hades...

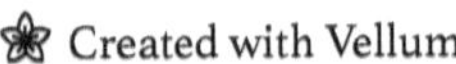 Created with Vellum